The Chloe Chronicles

A Novel

Chris Bournéa

All World Books
Multicultural Fiction

Cover Model: Veronica Astudillo-Seitz

Library of Congress Cataloging-in-Publication Data is available upon request.

ISBN: 978-0-615-41599-4

10 9 8 7 6 5 4 3 2 1

For my mother, Shelly, who has always nurtured, supported and encouraged me...

PROLOGUE

Chloe took a deep breath as the glass elevator reached the skyscraper's top floor. Heights weren't her forte.

Stepping off the elevator, she realized how glad she was to be off that death machine. She had almost gotten sick to her stomach as the elevator lurched past floor after floor. She had to force herself not to turn around and stare down at the dizzying view.

Waiting for her at the entrance to the penthouse suite was Bill Sykes, the building manager. She greeted him, shaking his hand.

"This is it," said Sykes, flicking on a series of light switches. He filled her in on the building's history and offered to give her a guided tour.

"Would you mind if I took a look around on my own?"

"Sure. I'll be downstairs in the lobby if you need me," said Sykes, tossing her a ring of keys and hopping on the elevator.

Chloe collected herself and made her way around the site that was to house her new entertainment corporation, CYB Enterprises Inc.

The Wellington Tower – one of the tallest skyscrapers not only in Manhattan, but in the entire world – was built in the 1930s by the Wellington Corporation, as Sykes had related. Hugo Wellington, the president and CEO of the international conglomerate, was an eccentric business tycoon who became a billionaire several times over with only a ninth grade education. A staunch supporter of the arts, Wellington had envisioned the building to be a breeding ground for creativity. The Wellington Tower was now home to some of the most powerful titans in the entertainment industry.

Several prestigious firms had offices in the recently renovated, state-of-the-art facility. Publications such as *Newsline*, the weekly periodical that was a rival to *Time*; *Famous and Fascinating*, the monthly magazine that chronicled the lavish lifestyles of celebrities; and the tabloid *Fact or Fiction?* were housed in the Wellington Tower. Music giant DMR Records, graphic design and marketing agency IDG Media and various television and film production companies also had offices there. A major cable network operated studios in the building from which live news updates were broadcast and talk shows were taped.

Chloe felt as though she were entering another dimension as she peeked in the rooms that composed Wellington's penthouse suite, some of which were vacant, some filled with ancient-looking furniture, still in the same positions in which they were left years ago. The suite had been sealed since Hugo Wellington's death in the late 2000s, and everything was covered with a thin layer of dust. This little self-guided tour was wreaking havoc on her sinuses.

Chloe decided to keep most of the art deco architecture intact. She liked the walls of glass bricks and the framed, vintage posters from the Ziegfeld *Follies*. All that was missing was a few contemporary flourishes that reflected her individual tastes. She jotted design ideas on a notepad as she walked down a long, dark hallway, stopping at a vault-like metal door at the end. She fiddled with the zillions of keys on the huge ring Sykes had given her until she found the right one.

"*Voilà*. Open, Sesame!" she declared, turning the key.

She entered the suite that had served as Wellington's private apartment. It had been his home away from home, a place where he slept after working long hours executing finely-crafted business deals and where he entertained foreign clients.

Butterflies began fluttering in Chloe's stomach. Wellington had allowed no one inside his sanctum except his closest advisors, friends and business associates. The tycoon's fortress in the sky had been the subject of more speculation than Willie Wonka's chocolate factory or the Wizard of Oz's chamber in the Emerald City. Everyone was dying to know what Wellington had in there. Rumors abounded that the recluse kept everything from torture devices he used on disloyal employees who leaked his business secrets to sex toys he used on the many mistresses he kept outside of his fifty-year marriage to wife Winona.

There were also rumors that Wellington's ghost haunted the apartment, where he composed his will, took his last gasping breaths and made his dying wishes. Though he had lived to a ripe old age, outlasting most of his contemporaries and bitterest rivals, he apparently had unfinished business. Supposedly, his soul patrolled the rooms and scared outsiders away. There were reports of strange disappearances – building maintenance staff falling to their deaths out of the floor-to-ceiling windows, potential occupants vanishing into thin air, never to be heard from again. Chills danced up Chloe's spine as she pressed on.

Behind yet another door was the sumptuous bedroom. A four-poster bed sat atop a tiered platform. Chloe stepped onto the platform and lay down on the notorious bed where Wellington, a strikingly handsome man in his day, allegedly conducted affairs with screen goddesses, seduced unsuspecting young secretaries and accommodated female heads of state from around the world. Chloe looked up and smiled at herself. There was a mirror on the ceiling.

The bed creaked as Chloe sat up. She giggled, imagining the previous occupant's bawdy adventures in that very spot.

Connected to the bedroom was a spa-like bathroom. Everything was made of black marble, except for the solid-gold fixtures. The room, equipped with a shower, hot tub, massage table and built-in television, was fit for a king – or queen. A row of huge dressing-room bulbs on either side of the mirror above the sink illuminated the room. Chloe checked her appearance. She had to look her best, for someone special was to meet her here any moment.

She added a touch of mascara to bring out her burgundy-brown eyes, brushed on a hint of rouge to accentuate her *café au lait* complexion and flipped her long, silky, jet-black tresses over her shoulders.

"*Magnifique*," Chloe declared, brushing a speck of lint off her pale gray, pinstriped power suit.

The bathroom led directly to Wellington's office. Chloe removed the dust sheet off the leather chair and sat down. She felt comfortable sitting in the place where Wellington had wheeled and "dealed" with the movers and shakers of the world. He had made investment deals with Arabian shieks and discussed global affairs with presidents and prime ministers while sitting in this very seat.

Chloe familiarized herself with Wellington's gold-plated pen set and blotter. She envisioned her own name on Wellington's gilded nameplate: *Chloe Y. Bareaux, President and CEO*. On this same desk she would soon be signing her own deals to option the movie rights of bestselling novels and bring the tales of up-and-coming writers to the big and little screens. She would, of course, star in and executive-produce the projects. This space would be the perfect headquarters for her burgeoning empire.

She swiveled in the chair to face an immense wall made entirely of tinted glass. She could see out but no one could see in. It was true, people did look like ants from these heights. She gazed out at the Manhattan skyline, reflecting on how far she'd come.

PART I

PART I

Chloe elbowed her way through the rush-hour crowd and emerged from the frenetic underground Métro station. She fell in step with her best friend, Gigi, as they made their way past the Arc de Triomphe and down the avenue des Champs-Elysées, one of Paris' most famous and busiest thoroughfares. They held hands and swung them in the girlish habit that, as teenagers, they had not yet outgrown.

"Hey, Gi'," Chloe said, stopping to examine a movie poster. "Why don't you finish window shopping and I'll catch up with you."

Chloe stared into the beautiful face of her favorite French actress, Valérie Bourdain, who was locked in a romance-novel embrace with her handsome leading man on the poster for a film called *L'Affaire Scandaleuse (The Scandalous Affair)*. Chloe renewed her vow that one day her own face would adorn movie posters.

"Hey, Chlo', come check this out."

Chloe looked up to see Gigi standing a few feet away in front of a window of a prestigious art gallery called La Galerie Nouveau, which showcased the work of emerging artists. She shifted her bookbag and scurried to catch up with her friend.

She caught sight of her reflection next to Gigi's in the gallery window. Though they had been raised like sisters and were both the products of interracial unions, their side-by-side reflection illustrated the contrasts in their appearances. Gigi was not only shorter and bustier than Chloe, but several shades lighter. Gigi's thicket of reddish-brown ringlets was already beginning to frizz up in the unseasonably warm, early-spring day.

"What do you think of this Théo Landry? He's a new artist people are buzzing about." Gigi motioned toward the gallery window, where the vibrant canvas clashed with her black eyes.

Chloe wrinkled her nose at the mention of the obscure abstract artist. Gigi had been drawing since before she could write and was as knowledgeable about art as Chloe was about the movies.

"What's it supposed to be?" Chloe said, cocking her head, wondering if the painting was supposed to be viewed sideways.

Gigi pointed toward a squiggly design in the center of the painting. "It reminds me a little of Basquiat."

Chloe made no attempt to hide her ignorance. "Who's that? Another dead French guy?"

Gigi laughed and tossed her curls. "He was a black American – Haitian, I think. We just studied his work in my art class."

Chloe giggled at the way Gigi pronounced "art," with the *r* stressed at the back of her throat. Her thick French accent sometimes made it difficult to understand her. They attended a bilingual school, but Chloe's mother was American and only occasionally lapsed into French or the Creole patois of her native New Orleans. Maxine Bareaux had always stressed the importance of learning "the King's English," and as a result, Chloe had no accent and was sometimes mistaken for an American tourist on these after-school shopping trips with Gigi.

"It's amazing what people will pay for those paintings," Chloe took Gigi's arm and led her away from the gallery. "You could do better than that with your eyes closed."

"One day I'm going to have my own show at La Galerie Nouveau," Gigi said with a backwards glance at the gallery window as they came to a stop at an intersection. Turning back to Chloe, she added, "When I'm a famous artist, I'll design the posters for your movies when you're a star. Deal?" She held up her pinky finger.

Chloe held up hers and interlocked it with Gigi's – the gesture they'd used since childhood to seal a pact. "Deal."

The girls' afternoon jaunt eventually led them to Trocadéro, a touristy area with terraced gardens near the Eiffel Tower that was always humming with mimes, sketch artists and street performers. Chloe and Gigi pushed their way into a crowd of onlookers watching breakdancers perform. The girls clapped and snapped their fingers to the beat as the young ambassadors of Paris' underground hip-hop culture moved in robotic spurts and spun on their heads.

Chloe swayed to the rhythm, losing herself in the music and ignoring the flashes from the tourists' cameras. She looked up and noticed a man angling his lens at her.

"What's that guy doing?" Chloe said to Gigi, pointing out the handsome young, dark-haired man who continued to click photos as he came closer.

"He's kind of cute," Gigi said, fluffing her curls and raising the skirt of her school uniform, which was already above the regulation knee-length.

The man slung his camera around his neck and offered his hand. "Hi," he said in English. "I'm Grant, Grant Herschel. I'm an American."

Chloe just looked at the man, clutching her bookbag like a shield, but Gigi stepped forward and shook his hand as if they were old friends.

"An American, huh?" Gigi said in a flirtatious tone. "We could show you around."

Chloe marveled at Gigi's brazenness. Chloe had seen this transformation when Gigi had a crush on some boy at school – a different one every week, it seemed. Chloe had never even kissed a boy yet, but Gigi seemed to crave attention not only from their pimply-faced classmates at the Lycée, but from any member of the opposite sex who happened to cross her path.

"How old are you girls?" the man said, running his hand through his thick, jet hair in a nervous gesture that seemed to indicate his discomfort with Gigi's forwardness.

Chloe remained silent, adhering to her mother's admonition never to talk to strangers – especially strange men asking personal questions and snapping photos. But Gigi continued her coquettish behavior.

"We're eighteen," Gigi said.

Chloe elbowed her. Not only was Gigi's statement untrue – they were just finishing up their freshman year at the Lycée and neither would turn fifteen until summer – but Chloe had sense enough to know that they shouldn't be leading this stranger to believe they were of legal age and eligible for whatever he had mind. The man scratched the stubble on his chin and looked the girls over. "Eighteen? You look kind of young."

"You look pretty young yourself," Gigi replied, also giving him the once-over.

"I'm an exchange student majoring in photography and I'm working on an assignment to find candid shots of passersby in public places." He punctuated the statement by holding up his camera. "I was so taken with you two I couldn't resist."

He smiled at Chloe, but she said nothing and stared into his striking blue-green eyes, trying to discern if he was telling the truth or concocting some story to gain their trust.

The man continued to direct his attention at Chloe. "Do you mind if I ask your name, Mademoiselle?"

Gigi stepped closer to the man. "I'm Gigi, and this is Chloe."

Chloe elbowed her again. She had no business telling this stranger their real names.

"Have you ever thought about modeling?" The man was still looking at Chloe.

"I've done a little bit here and there," Gigi said, lying again in a transparent attempt to impress the man. "We were backup dancers in one of Prince's videos."

"Oh, really?" the man said, stepping past Gigi and approaching Chloe. "I hope you don't mind me saying this, but you have a great look, very exotic but still girl-next-door. You're still growing, I take it, but you have good height and good posture. While I'm in Paris, I'm apprenticing with Lucien Girard, and I'm learning how to spot potential."

Chloe brightened at the mention of the noted Parisian fashion photographer, whose name was credited in French *Vogue*, *Seventeen* and many of the other European and American magazines she and Gigi thumbed through at newsstands.

Chloe looked with renewed interest at the young man with the camera. It was hard to believe someone thought she had the potential to be a model. She towered over the boys at the Lycée and was always a wallflower at school dances. She felt gawky, all arms and legs, unlike the petite yet already-curvy Gigi.

The man fished a scrap of paper and pen from the pocket of his jeans jacket. "M'sieu Girard is doing a shoot for *Vogue* in New York this summer and he's looking for models to take with him," he said, scrawling a number and address on the paper.

Chloe took a step backward, keeping her distance. For all she knew, he could be some pervert who told this tale to all the young girls he molested in the park.

As the man related the details of the summer excursion to New York, she struggled to keep her emotions in check but screamed with excitement on the inside. She had always wanted to visit the fast-moving American metropolis she had seen as a backdrop in so many movies. And to have the opportunity to visit the place where she was born was especially exciting.

The man held out the paper. "I'd like to bring you in and do some test shots," he said to Chloe. "If they turn out well, I'll show them to M'sieu Girard and he might be able to use you. Give me a call and we'll set something up."

Gigi intercepted the paper. "We'll do that," she said, smiling and stashing the paper in her bosom.

Chloe nodded at the man, grabbed Gigi's arm and pulled her away. Chloe turned to look back at him, and he held up his camera and once again snapped her photo.

2

The subway car screeched to a halt and Chloe hopped off as soon as the doors parted, tugging on Gigi's hand and nearly dragging her friend up the stairs of the Métro station.

"What's the rush?" Gigi said, lagging behind Chloe as they reached the street.

"Hurry up." Chloe pushed past a courier, nearly knocking the oversize package out of his arms in her haste. "This modeling opportunity is the most exciting thing that's ever happened to me and I can't wait to tell Mother about it."

"You didn't think that guy was serious, did you? Saying he's a photographer who can get you into modeling is probably just one of his pickup lines."

Chloe looked askance at her friend. "You sure seemed taken with him."

Gigi grinned. "Just a little harmless flirting. I have to have my fun."

Chloe shook her head at Gigi's shamelessness and pulled her along past the chic boutiques that lined avenue Montaigne, the city's nexus for art, music, theater and fashion. The names of Christian Dior, Louis Vuitton, Chanel and other top designers beckoned from awnings. The girls weaved past model-thin women in the latest fashions, their manicured hands clutching the leashes of impeccably groomed pooches that served as living accessories.

Chloe and Gigi stopped before a window display with an ultra-modern living room scene, a mannequin in a custom-made evening gown reclining on an elaborately upholstered *chaise longue*. Above the storefront, the words "Chez Maxine" flowed in lavender neon script.

Chloe swung open the shop's glass door, still holding Gigi's hand. "You better vouch for me if Mother asks if this guy's legit.'"

"Have I ever let you down?" Gigi said, following Chloe into the shop.

Inside, staffers scurried around the small yet meticulously organized design studio. In one corner, a young black woman with neat dreadlocks crouched over a drafting table, adding flourishes to a sketch of a wedding dress. In another corner, a white girl with spiky, multi-colored hair conferred with an Asian guy in a baggy athletic suit who resembled the breakdancers Chloe and Gigi had seen earlier. The odd pair was as mismatched as the different fabric swatches they compared against a pair of curtains hanging from a window mockup.

Chloe spotted her mother consulting with another female staffer, who was fitting a dress pattern on a tailor's mannequin. Chloe was a carbon copy of the well-kept Maxine, who had given birth to Chloe when she was barely out of her teens. Even at the end of a long workday, Maxine was the picture of simple elegance in a white blouse with an oversize collar, a charcoal gray pencil skirt and black open-toed heels. Her stylish pixie cut brought to mind Halle Berry, one of Chloe's favorite American actresses. Like Halle, Maxine had a body that sent men's tongues wagging. Maxine, who had been a dancer in her younger days, kept herself in tiptop shape and, at thirty-five, was frequently mistaken for Chloe's older sister.

"Hi, Mother," Chloe said, kissing Maxine on the cheek.

"Oh, hi, *ma chérie*. What brings you girls here?"

Gigi plopped on a desk. "Chloe wants to ask you something."

Maxine shooed Gigi off the desk. "Girl, you better watch where you're putting that fast tail of yours." She swatted Gigi on the behind, then hugged her.

"I'm always saying the same thing, but of course she never listens to me," said Simone, Gigi's mother, approaching in a slinky dress that revealed curves identical to her daughter's. She cradled an account ledger in one hand and tossed her long, flaming red hair with the other.

"Oh, honestly, Simone," Gigi said, flipping her hair in an unconscious pantomime of her mother. "You always have to make everything about you."

Chloe had witnessed the tension between Gigi and her mother being played out with increasing frequency since the girls hit puberty. Gigi's new practice of calling her mother by her first name – something Maxine would never allow – was a declaration of independence.

Gigi couldn't grow up fast enough, while Chloe clung to the last remnants of girlhood. And Simone, a single mom the same age as Maxine, unwittingly contributed to her daughter's disdain for authority. Whereas Maxine was quick to correct people who mistook her for Chloe's sister and assert her parental role, Simone seemed to relish the attention when the same thing happened with her and Gigi. Of course, people usually guessed Simone to be Gigi's half-sister since Simone was white and even paler than her mixed-race child.

"You may think you're grown, Miss Thang," Simone said, her French accent the only thing keeping her from sounding like a sassy black woman from one of Chloe's favorite American sitcoms, "but you're not too big to give your mother a hug."

Gigi wriggled from her mother's embrace and straddled a chair. "Please don't refer to yourself in the second person."

Simone sneered at her daughter. "Don't correct me. And don't sit like that in a skirt. It's not ladylike."

Gigi cracked her gum and ignored her mother. Simone clucked her disapproval and turned her attention to Chloe, kissing her on either cheek, European-style. "To what do we owe this surprise visit?"

Chloe signaled to Maxine, who was examining the dress pattern again. "Mother, do you have a minute? I need to discuss something with you."

"Can't it wait, dearest?" Maxine said, pinching the fabric in various places. "I'm trying to get a million things wrapped up before we close for the day."

"But there's something I need to –"

Chloe stopped short when she saw Maxine was no longer listening.

"I like the cut, Céline," Maxine said to the young dressmaker, "but it needs to be taken in more at the waist."

The Asian guy came over, and Chloe saw him glance at Gigi, who was all too happy to oblige him by sitting up and poking out her ample chest.

"Sorry to interrupt, Madame Bareaux," the guy said timidly to Maxine, like a schoolboy asking his teacher for a hall pass, "but Lydie and I are trying to decide which fabric to use with those curtains for the Fitzroy project and we could use your input."

Maxine threw up her hands. "God, is this day ever going to end?"

"I keep telling you life would be easier if we specialized in one thing – interior design *or* dressmaking," Simone called as Maxine followed the guy to the window mockup. Simone turned to Chloe. "But of course, that would be *so* unlike your multitalented, multi-tasking mother who thinks she's Superwoman."

Chloe smiled, understanding that Simone knew Maxine better than anyone. Gigi's mother had handled the books for Chez Maxine since the business was a one-woman operation, with Maxine using the sewing and embroidery skills passed down by Chloe's grandmother, Mama Louise. Chloe and Maxine still lived atop the business in a converted loft that had once been a sewing factory.

While Simone answered the constantly-ringing phones and Gigi busied herself doodling on a sketchpad, Chloe traipsed to Maxine's side and tried once again to get her attention.

"There's this opportunity I found out about today for a summer job," Chloe said, trying to describe the young photographer's offer in a non-threatening way.

"That's good, *ma chérie*," Maxine said, not looking up from the curtains she was inspecting. "I think it would be good for you to get some practical work experience."

"Actually, the job is in –"

"Damn it!" Maxine hiked up her skirt and crouched to the floor, inspecting the hem of the curtains. "This line is uneven. This order is going to have to be completely redone."

Chloe caught Simone's eye across the room and they shared a chuckle over Maxine's perfectionism. Maxine was always checking and rechecking the minutest of details. As she was fond of saying, she refused to give a client shoddy work and prided herself on her reputation since the business bore her name.

"We'll get to it right away, Madame Bareaux," the young man said, springing to remove the offending curtains from their rod.

Maxine rose to her feet. "See to it that you do."

Chloe followed Maxine back to the other side of the room. "Like I was saying, the job is in –"

"No, this is not quite what I meant, Céline," Maxine said, fussing with the pattern the dressmaker had hemmed with safety pins.

Chloe opened her mouth to speak again, but was interrupted by Simone this time.

"When you get a chance, Max, I need you to sign off on the invoices for the Lefevre account."

13

"Do me a favor, Mo'," Maxine said, her voice muffled by pins she'd stuck in her mouth. "Stash them in my briefcase and I'll look over them tonight after dinner."

Chloe was used to her mother bringing work home. Whenever Chloe complained that her mother was always preoccupied with work, Maxine explained that she sacrificed to give Chloe the comfort and security she never had.

"This still isn't right. Come here, *ma chérie.*" Maxine tugged on Chloe's wrist and pulled her in front of the mannequin.

While Maxine wrapped a tape measure around her adolescent frame, Chloe flashbacked to childhood memories of her mother making her clothes and dolls by hand. Though she'd never tell Gigi or any of their classmates, she still slept with Mr. Buttons, the teddy bear who got his name because Maxine had made his eyes by sewing on buttons.

At her mother's direction, Chloe held out her arms and allowed Céline to fit the dress pattern on her like a live mannequin. Chloe glanced at Gigi, who was humming while she etched a photograph-quality replica of a jar of pencils sitting on a nearby desk. Chloe smiled, thinking of the fun she and Gigi had as little girls playing dress-up in Maxine's hand-sewn garments while their mothers tended to business.

"Now it's perfect," Maxine said, taking a pair of scissors and applying one last snip to the dress pattern. She patted Chloe on the cheek. "All we needed was a model."

"Speaking of which," Chloe said, seizing her chance, "the summer job I've been trying to tell you about is a modeling opportunity in New York."

Maxine threw down the scissors and turned to look at Chloe, finally giving her daughter her full attention. "*New York?*" Maxine stressed the words as if they were the name of some rare disease.

Chloe nodded and breathlessly recounted the encounter with the photographer earlier that afternoon. She held out her hand and turned to Gigi, who produced the slip of paper with the photographer's contact information.

"This guy could be some psycho," Maxine said, examining the paper.

"He seemed okay to me," Gigi said with a shrug, as if honoring her pledge to back Chloe up.

Maxine looked unconvinced. "Did you honestly think I'd let you go gallivanting off to New York with a total stranger?"

"You could go along and chaperone," Simone, the more liberal parent, spoke up. "I can run the office while you're gone."

"It could be fun, Mother," Chloe said, proceeding with caution. "Maybe on the way back, we could stop off in New Orleans and you could show me where you grew up."

Maxine's face contorted at the mention of her hometown, and Chloe immediately realized her tactical error. Maxine had shared precious little of her past and became mysteriously tight-lipped whenever the subject arose. All Chloe knew was that Maxine's heritage was a spicy gumbo of several different cultures. Maxine identified as a black woman but, growing up in the melting pot that was New Orleans, had French and Spanish as well as African-American blood coursing through her veins. Chloe longed to explore her roots, but Maxine's silence was an indication that she had no intention of satisfying Chloe's childlike curiosity.

"Will you at least take me to meet with the photographer," Chloe pressed, "so we can find out the details?"

Before Maxine could answer, Henri, her effeminate male administrative assistant who was perpetually clad in black, appeared.

"Comtesse de Prideux, the client from Zurich, is on Line One and wants to know when the drapery order is going to arrive," he said.

Maxine flashed a scolding glance to the design assistants who were scurrying to redo the curtains in the opposite corner. "I'll take the call in my office, Henri." She handed the paper with the photographer's contact info back to Chloe. "We'll talk about this later, *ma chérie*. Right now I have to take this call."

Chloe stuffed the paper in her pocket. She knew not to press the subject any further.

Chloe sprawled on her bed in the loft apartment above the design studio, straining to concentrate on her algebra homework. Her bedroom reflected her not-quite-complete transition from girlhood to adolescence. An oversize snapshot of Chloe and Gigi donning Mickey Mouse ears during a preteen excursion to Euro Disney was pinned above the bed, which was littered with school papers, teen magazines and inside-out T-shirts and jeans from a recent shopping trip with Gigi.

Chloe closed her algebra book. Trying to study was useless. All she could think about was the photographer's offer and the trip to the States. She scavenged through the papers scattered on the bed until she located the slip of paper with the photographer's number. She reclined against the headboard, studying the paper and clutching Mr. Buttons. Convincing her mother to meet with the photographer was going to require a tricky balance of patience and persistence.

Maxine had skipped dinner, remaining downstairs in her office to finish up paperwork. And when Chloe finally heard the front door to the upstairs loft open and close, she decided to give her mother time to unwind before bringing up the modeling opportunity again. As she had learned countless times when seeking her mother's permission, timing was everything.

Chloe busied herself studying again, and when she glanced at the clock on her nightstand, it read nine-fifteen. Nearly an hour had passed since Maxine had retreated to her bedroom and now was as good a time as any, Chloe figured.

She padded down the hallway, guided by the sliver of light coming from underneath Maxine's bedroom door.

"Mother?" she said, knocking lightly. When there was no answer, she let herself in.

Upon entering, Chloe found the room unoccupied and figured Maxine was taking a bath. She was turning to leave when she noticed a shoebox bulging with old photos on the edge of the bed. She sat down and rummaged through the photos.

She gazed longingly at a black-and-white photo of her long-deceased grandparents, Papa Frank and Mama Louise, onstage in a smoky nightclub in New Orleans' famed French Quarter. Papa Frank had died before Chloe was born, but Mama Louise had been a loving, consistent part of her childhood. Chloe loved to curl up in her *grand-mère's* lap and hear stories from the days of when she and Papa Frank eked out a living as musicians. In the photo, Papa Frank was blowing into a trumpet while Louise, looking like a silent-film star in one of her handmade beaded gowns, crooned into a microphone. The contrast in her grandparents' appearance explained the light brown complexion Chloe had inherited from Maxine. Papa Frank was a light-skinned Louisiana Creole with wavy hair, while Mama Louise was a dark brown woman whose people hailed from the French West Indies. Chloe recalled these scant details from her grandmother's stories.

Mama Louise had said she always regretted that Maxine was shuttled from relative to relative while she, Papa Frank and their band toured nightclubs around the world. They had even played Paris' heralded jazz venue, the New Morning Club, long before Chloe was born.

Beneath the photo of her grandparents was a snapshot of Maxine dressed like a Vegas showgirl in an elaborate headdress, sparkly, sheer bodysuit and tail of multi-colored feathers. She was holding a large feathered fan beneath her dark eyes, which were encircled with silver glitter, tiny rhinestones and heavy black mascara. Chloe recognized the scenery in the background as the Moulin Rouge, the famed nightclub where Maxine had danced when she first came to Paris in her late teens. Maxine never talked about her days as a dancer, and all Chloe knew about that chapter of her mother's life was that she had met Chloe's father at the club.

Chloe had no memory of her father, whom her mother never married, and photos of him were conspicuously absent from the shoebox. Chloe didn't even know her father's name. She only knew that Maxine's relationship with the white Frenchman was short and not sweet. Whenever Chloe would ask about her father, Maxine would abruptly reply, "You don't need to know anything about someone who contributed nothing to your life."

As a result of never knowing her father and having no living extended family on her mother's side, Chloe's identity was a question mark. A jigsaw puzzle with many important pieces missing.

She continued to sort through the photos, hoping to find clues to the past, when Maxine appeared in the doorway. Her mascara was smudged and Chloe could tell she had been crying.

"I was just going through some old things. When you mentioned the States this afternoon, I started reminiscing," Maxine said.

Chloe set the box aside. "Have you given anymore thought to the trip to New York this summer?" She paused, adding with caution, "And maybe New Orleans?"

Seeing the photos of her grandparents had fueled Chloe's desire to see the city that held so much history and heritage, especially for her family. She longed to walk the streets her mother walked as a child, see the famous jazz clubs where her grandparents performed and visit the ornate cemetery where the Bareaux ancestors were buried.

"I don't know," Maxine said, sitting next to Chloe on the bed. "We're so busy at work, and I haven't been back to the States in years."

Like a host of black American musicians, writers and nightclub performers who had come before her, Maxine was an expatriate and had found liberation in Paris from the limitations of race. From Chloe's fuzzy childhood memories, she knew that Mama Louise and Maxine had relocated to New York after Papa Frank died. Maxine had left for Paris shortly thereafter, right out of high school, and had briefly returned to New York to stay with Mama Louise when she discovered she was pregnant with Chloe. Since giving birth to Chloe in New York, Maxine had not been back to America and seemed intent on keeping Chloe in the insular world she had created in the City of Light.

"Can we at least meet with the photographer?" Chloe said, clinging to the hope that she could gently persuade her mother.

Maxine scooped the stray photos from the bed and returned them to the shoebox. "I'm exhausted and we both need to get to bed," she said, placing the lid on the box with a gesture of finality that signaled the discussion was closed as well. "I'll think about it. That's all I can promise."

3

At the sound of the afternoon school bell, students of various ages and nationalities spilled forth from the Lycée Américain. The bilingual private academy attracted the offspring of foreign diplomats, international business executives and artistic expatriates of all sorts, as well as the brightest Parisian students.

Chloe and Gigi descended the steps of the historic building in Paris' Latin Quarter, lugging their heavy books like mason's blocks.

"She didn't say yes and she didn't say no," Chloe said, issuing a full report as promised about the outcome of last night's talk with Maxine about the modeling opportunity. "She said she'd think about it."

"I hate that. At least if they say no, you know not to get your hopes up."

When Chloe and Gigi reached the bottom of the steps, they were met by a tall, sandy-haired boy whose athletic physique was apparent through his rumpled, light blue uniform shirt, crooked tie and wrinkled khakis. Chloe recognized him as Gaston Gervais, one of Gigi's interchangeable boyfriends.

"Let me get those," Gaston said, taking Gigi's books in his muscled forearms, the result of daily practice sessions with the lacrosse team.

"Oh, Gaston, you're so sweet," Gigi swooned in a damsel-in-distress tone that made Chloe want to vomit.

"What are you guys doing this weekend?" Gaston said.

"Why? What do you have in mind?" Gigi said.

"I was thinking maybe we could double-date."

Gaston was joined by a brown-eyed, olive-skinned boy with curly brown hair and an equally strapping build. Chloe's breath quickened at the sight of François Jamet, who sat behind her in algebra and whom she'd had a crush on since the beginning of the school year.

"Maybe we could catch a movie," François said, his voice somewhere between a manly murmur and teenage squeak.

"Why don't you let us get back to you on Friday?" Gigi said coyly, to Chloe's relief.

Maxine was adamant that she wouldn't let Chloe date until she was sixteen, which seemed light years away. Delaying Gaston and François' proposition until the end of the week would buy Chloe some time to wear Maxine down.

"Okay," François said, "but in the meantime, don't study too hard." He knocked Chloe's books from her hands and took off running.

"*Fils de pute!*" Gigi shouted, calling François a "son of a bitch." "Gaston, go beat him up."

Gigi took Gaston's elbow and led him in pursuit of François like a trained attack dog. Chloe gathered her books, not sure if she should interpret François' prank as an immature signal that he liked her or simply dismiss it as a boyish antic. If he wasn't tormenting her in class, tugging on her ponytail or trying to copy her pop-quiz answers, he acted like she didn't exist.

Chloe looked up to see Maxine standing at the curb next to an awaiting taxicab. The fact that Mother had never learned to drive and relied on cabs and chauffeurs was the only aspect of life in which she allowed someone else to steer.

"What are you *doing* here?" Chloe said, approaching her mother with a scowl. She was far past the age where she needed Mother to escort her home, and Maxine was usually so consumed with work that she only made appearances at the Lycée for parent-teacher conferences.

"I thought about that modeling offer you told me about and I made an appointment," Maxine said. She held open the door to the cab's passenger compartment. "Hop in."

Chloe's scowl quickly turned to a wide grin. Glancing over her shoulder, lest any of her friends see her, she pecked her mother on the cheek and followed her into the cab.

The taxicab pulled up to an address on the rue du Faubourg Saint-Honoré.

Chloe peered up at the modern skyscraper. "This isn't the address the photographer gave me."

"Come on, *ma chérie*," Maxine said, opening the door, "we don't want to be late."

Once inside the building, Maxine tugged at Chloe's uniform skirt and nagged her to stand up straight. When the elevator doors opened, Mother took her hand like a toddler and led her into the lobby.

"The Lillier Modeling Agency?" Chloe said, reading the sign behind the receptionist's desk when they stepped off the elevator. "This isn't Lucien Girard's studio. What's going on?"

Maxine left Chloe's question unanswered and gave their names to the receptionist, who informed them that Monique Lillier, the head of the agency, would see them right away. The stellar reputation Maxine had built in the fashion world apparently preceded her, allowing them not have to wait to see the *über*-agent who was famous throughout Europe for plucking young girls from obscurity and transforming them into stars.

The woman who greeted Chloe and Maxine was as tall and lean as the models she represented. Her shiny brown hair was coiffed in a pageboy and she was wearing a tweed blazer, billowy cream blouse, black slacks and stilettos – an outfit ripped from the pages of French *Vogue*.

"*Bonjour*, Madame Bareaux, thank you for meeting with me," Monique said, the gold bangles on her wrist jangling as she shook Maxine's hand. "And this must be Chloe."

Chloe attempted a smile as the woman's scrutinizing gaze passed over her frame. The woman led Chloe and Maxine to a spacious office overlooking the Elysée Palace and instructed them to have a seat across from her sleek Lucite desk. As was her custom, Maxine took control of the situation, and Chloe didn't have to do much talking except answering Monique's occasional query.

"My daughter is interested in modeling as a way to earn part-time income to save for college," Maxine told the agent, getting right to business. "If she were to sign with your agency, I wouldn't want any assignments to interfere with school."

Monique nodded deferentially. "Of course, Madame Bareaux." She once again looked at Chloe critically. "How tall are you, *cher*?"

"She's five-seven," Maxine blurted before Chloe could answer. "She's still growing, and I don't want anyone putting her on any crazy diets. Modeling isn't going to be her life; I want her to enjoy being a teenager."

If Maxine wanted her to enjoy herself, Chloe reasoned silently, she should have let her meet with the photographer she met in the park instead of bringing her here.

"And I don't want her doing any poses that are too provocative," Maxine added. "She's still a child."

Chloe grumbled at Mother's remark. When was Maxine going to start treating her like a young woman with a mind of her own?

"I'd like to see how you'd handle yourself on a runway," the agent said to Chloe. "Why don't you walk for me, *cher*?"

Chloe continued to sit with her arms crossed, peeved at her mother for duping her. Maxine nudged her, giving her a look that Chloe recognized as, "Don't embarrass me in front of a stranger." With a dramatic sigh, Chloe got up, clumped across the carpeted office, then pivoted and repeated the same motion in the opposite direction. She kept her attention focused on a spot on the wall throughout the entire exercise, looking like one of those pissed-off models she'd seen when thumbing through magazines during her after-school window shopping jaunts with Gigi.

"We're going to have to work on that walk," Monique said, making notes on a pad. "But you have good posture."

Maxine's nagging to make her sit up straight and not slouch at the dinner table paid off after all, Chloe reflected as she returned to her seat with an intentionally clumsy thud.

"We would love to represent your daughter, Madame Bareaux," the agent said to Maxine, as if Chloe weren't in the room. "Normally I would say her inexperience would count against her, but the Collections are coming up and all the designers are looking for fresh young faces. I should have no problem booking her."

Monique thumbed through a desk calendar and mentioned a date.

"That's perfect," said Maxine. "She'll be out on spring break."

Chloe glared at her mother. How could she do this? First she deceived her and now she was signing her up for some gig on her vacation without even consulting her. She could think of a thousand other more fun ways to spend her spring break than being stitched into ridiculous clothes and being forced to parade in front of Parisian high society.

Chloe deliberately slumped in her chair as Mother and Monique Lillier discussed the terms of the contract the agency was offering. She felt like a little kid, when she was running a fever and her mother would drag her to the pediatrician's office and discuss whatever remedy the doctor prescribed in grown-up language she couldn't understand.

Maxine reiterated that she reserved the right to refuse future assignments that would conflict with Chloe's studies. As she told the agent, she had no intention of letting her teenage daughter be swept away by the exploitative fashion world.

Chloe sulked in the taxicab on the way home. She couldn't find the proper words to convey the level of contempt she felt at the moment for her mother, so she pouted and stared out the window. If her mother was going to treat her like a child, she was going to act like one.

"I know you wanted to follow up with that photographer who approached you in the park, but it's just not safe," Maxine said, patting Chloe's knee, as if consoling a petulant grade-schooler. "Men like that prey on young girls. This way, you'll be with a reputable agency, professionals who know what they're doing."

While Maxine prattled on about the dangers waiting to devour naïve young girls, Chloe took out the slip of paper with the photographer's contact information and crumpled it in her fist. She would be forever left to wonder if the guy was actually who he claimed to be.

"And then she signed me up with this agency without even asking me," Chloe said to Gigi in exasperation.

The girls lay side by side on Gigi's þed. Gigi had the smaller bedroom of the Left Bank apartment she shared with Simone, and every corner bulged with art supplies. A canvas with a half-finished still life leaned against a paint-smudged desk that was cluttered with acrylic tubes and brushes. Etchings covered nearly every inch of wall space. The only sign that the room belonged to a teenage girl instead of a prolific adult artist was pinups of American pop stars above the bed.

"This Monique lady said she was going to put me in the spring fashion shows, but I'm not doing it." Chloe continued to vent to Gigi, who murmured an occasional sympathetic "mmm-hmm" while drawing on her ever-present sketchpad. "My mother can't force me."

Gigi sat up, beholding the sketch she was working on from afar and shuffling through her colored pencils, as if deciding which to use next. "I think you should do it."

Chloe adjusted the pillow under her chin and pivoted her head toward Gigi, not sure if she had heard her correctly. "What did you say?"

"I think you should go ahead and do the fashion show." Gigi selected a bright red pencil and began applying the bold color to the sketch.

"And give my mother the satisfaction of thinking she not only tricked me out of meeting with that photographer, but got me to sign with the agency *she* picked? Why in hell would I do that?"

"You could get discovered by some big-time movie director at the fashion show. A lot of Hollywood types go to those things. I've seen them on TV."

Chloe sat up, suddenly inspired. "You're right. I didn't think about that."

"And even if this doesn't turn out to be your big break into acting, I'm sure it pays way better than a regular after-school job. With the money you'll make from modeling and after I get good enough to sell a painting, we'll take that trip to New York together when we're eighteen." Gigi added one last dash of color to the sketch and held it up. She had drawn the two of them standing in front of the Statue of Liberty in matching "I Love New York" T-shirts, with a heart colored in bold red to symbolize the "Love" part.

Chloe took hold of the sketch. "Gigi, you're a genius," she said, turning down the corners of her mouth to show she was duly impressed.

"You'll go with this agency your mom picked out and make her think you're doing things her way, but you'll be saving your money so we can go to New York on our own one day." Gigi held up her pinky. "Deal?"

Chloe interlocked her pinky with Gigi's. "Deal."

Gigi took the sketchpad and tossed it aside. "Now. We have other things to talk about."

Gigi reached into her nightstand drawer and took out a Gauloise, the French cigarettes she had been pilfering from Simone's boudoir.

"Like what?"

Gigi lit the cigarette and took a puff. "Like hooking up with Gaston and François this weekend for that double date." She exhaled, cradling the cigarette between her index and middle fingers like an experienced smoker.

"Forget it," Chloe said, waving away Gigi's smoke rings. "I asked my mother about it when we got home from the modeling agency. I figured since she tricked me into signing with that Monique lady, she at least owed it to me to let me go out and have some fun this weekend. But she said no. She insists she's not going to let me date until I'm sixteen." She pulled her legs underneath her, sitting Indian-style on the bed. "I don't know what I'm going to tell François when I see him in class on Friday."

Gigi grinned. "Tell him you want him to come over and jump your bones."

"You're gross!"

Chloe grabbed a pillow and walloped Gigi, who immediately snuffed out her cigarette and responded in-kind. Soon, feathers were flying as the girls screamed and laughed with abandon.

The door flew open and Simone stood in the doorway. "What's going on in here?"

"How many times have I told you to knock, Simone?" Gigi spat out a feather, slyly positioned herself to hide the ashtray on the nightstand, and stared defiantly at her mother.

"Don't talk to me like that. You girls can have your fun, but I don't want you tearing up the place. Pascal and I are going out tonight and I don't want to come home to a big mess." Simone stepped further into the room, sniffing the air. "And why does it smell like smoke in here?"

Chloe and Gigi looked at each other. Chloe had warned Gigi that she was going to get caught lighting up sooner or later. Chloe could see the reels in Gigi's head turning, formulating some cover story about a science project for school that involved fire. But before Gigi could open her mouth to lie convincingly – one of her major skills in addition to artistic talent – a handsome young man appeared in the doorway and slid his arm around Simone's waist. He didn't look much older than Chloe and Gigi, which wasn't surprising. As Simone approached middle age, she seemed to be out to prove that younger men still found her desirable and, like her daughter, she changed boyfriends like a bored TV viewer surfing channels. Chloe often mused that Simone's surname was ironic, considering her predilection for young men who were not yet established. Simone's young lovers couldn't afford to buy her expensive baubles from the world-famous boutique founded by renowned French jeweler and watchmaker Louis Cartier, to whom Simone was not related.

"Are you ready, *bébé*?" the man cooed in Simone's ear. With his tousled dark hair, stubble and shabby-chic appearance, he had the look of the art students who hung around the Sorbonne's campus.

"Why don't you go wait in the car," she said, unwrapping herself from his clench. "I'll be down in a minute."

"Whatever you say, *bébé*." As the man turned to leave, his eyes locked on something in Gigi's direction. "Did you do that?" he said, inching forward.

"Did I do what?" Gigi said, looking at the man warily and leaning back on the nightstand to conceal the ashtray.

"This." He came so close to Gigi that Chloe thought her friend was busted for sure. But instead of reaching behind Gigi to reveal the ashtray, he crouched and picked up Gigi's sketch that had fallen to the floor during the pillow fight. "This really shows a lot of ability for someone your age." He motioned toward the sketches and paintings dotting the walls. "Did you do all these?"

"No, I hired someone to come in and do them with the pitiful allowance Simone gives me," Gigi replied tartly.

Simone scowled in response.

"These are really good. I'm a grad student at the Sorbonne," the man continued, confirming Chloe's impression. "If you want, I could show you some techniques that could help you get even better. If you're this good now, then you could –"

"Pascal, why don't you wait in the car? The girls need to get back to studying," Simone spoke up. She stood in the doorway with her hands on her hips, and it was obvious she didn't like the attention her boyfriend was giving her daughter.

Pascal nodded and set the sketch on the bed. As he left the room, Chloe noticed his eyes linger on Gigi's chest. Instead of shrinking from the attention, as Chloe would have done, Gigi stared back at him flirtatiously.

"You girls behave yourself," Simone said, stepping out of the room.

"You do the same, Mother Dear," Gigi sassed.

As soon as the door was closed, the girls broke out in unrestrained laughter.

4

Chloe sat in the dressing area at Le Salon des Miroirs, the venue where hot young designer Fabrice Morel's runway show was being staged. Stylists chased half-dressed models with hairbrushes, mascara wands and garment racks. The frenzied scene resembled how Chloe had envisioned what being backstage was like on the opening night of a highly anticipated new play.

"Camille, I can't get this hairpiece to stay in place. I need you!" a statuesque blonde shrieked from across the room at the woman who was styling Chloe.

"You'll have to finish up your makeup yourself, *cher*," said the stylist who was working on Chloe's makeup, setting down her eyeliner pencil amid the arsenal of cosmetic instruments that crowded the dressing-room table. "I have to go deal with Babette's latest crisis. This is her fifth hissy fit of the day, and the show hasn't even started yet!" The stylist shuffled away in a huff to attend to the hysterical model.

Chloe picked up the eyeliner pencil, her hand shaking as she darkened the dramatic circles under her eyes. Each time someone entered or exited through the curtain that separated the dressing area from the runway, she trembled all over as she caught sight of some high-powered fashion editor or some other member of Paris' haute-couture glitterati. She couldn't do this, she couldn't go out there and have all those people judging her.

"Girls, you need to hurry up," said a young man with a badge imprinted with the name "Gustave," who was directing the backstage action, passing by the makeup table Chloe was sharing with two other girls. "You go on in five."

One of the models looked askance at Chloe in the mirror. "They're getting younger every year," the leggy brunette said, slathering gloss on her pouty lips.

"Tell me about it. The Collections are becoming like one big adventure in babysitting," the other one, an exotic-looking black girl in a huge afro wig, said in an equally catty tone.

Chloe kept her focus on the mirror, trying not to let on how much the older models' comments had shaken her. She had been naïve to assume that the more experienced girls would mentor her and show her the survival techniques they'd picked up from years of traipsing the runways of Paris, Milan and Madrid. Instead, they seemed to view her as competition and were showing her no love. She did her best to ignore their barbs and imitate the expert way they applied makeup.

"Okay, girls, we need you to line up to get ready to go out," Gustave announced.

As the other models rose to take their places, Chloe took a moment to collect herself. "I can do this," she whispered to her reflection.

While the other girls had taped photos of rock-star boyfriends or beloved lapdogs to their mirrors, Chloe had pinned a photo of her favorite actress, Valérie Bourdain, to hers. The snapshot from *Paris Match* depicted Valérie Bourdain as the heroine in her latest movie, power and self-confidence radiating from every pore.

Drawing inspiration from her idol, Chloe decided she would get through this by pretending she was playing a role. In her mind, the chaotic dressing room became the backstage area at a theater where Chloe was to make her big debut. Those people out there were clapping for her, clamoring for her to come on and wow them with a mesmerizing performance.

Taking her place in line behind the other girls, Chloe psyched herself up. These worldly, twenty-something women who had graced dozens of runways and magazine covers around the world were merely supporting players in the production in which she was starring.

When Gustave parted the curtain leading to the runway, Chloe was nearly blinded by the spotlight that shone down on the T-shaped platform and deafened by the dance music that ejaculated like gunfire from enormous speakers on either side of the runway. She counted as the other girls strutted out before her, trying to remember her place. Gustave nudged her forward onto the platform and she froze, gawking at the people surrounding the runway. They were all as beautiful and well-dressed as the models.

For a moment, Chloe stood in place despite Gustave's prodding, and considered retreating behind the curtain and running out of the building. When she caught sight of Maxine, however, smiling at her with a "you can do it" expression from the right side of the runway, Chloe somehow marshaled the strength to propel herself down the platform. As much as she liked to think of herself as almost grown, her mother's presence brought her comfort.

Striding down the runway with the pissed-off model's stare she'd practiced, Chloe remembered she was an actress playing a role. She was someone else, and she allowed her imagination to transport her to a place where she didn't notice the mean glances as she passed the other models or the critical expressions of the fashion editors and photographers.

When she neared Maxine, who was sitting next to the agent Monique Lillier, both women beamed approval. The gesture further boosted Chloe's self-confidence, which was teetering as much as her balance on the stilt-like heels she was wearing.

Reaching the dressing area again, she didn't have time to evaluate her performance. A team of stylists pulled her out of the clingy gown she'd worn in the opening and shoehorned her into her next change. She was forced to overcome her modesty, her body parts exposed along with the other girls during each change. It was difficult not to compare her still-developing body to the older models, but some of them were so emaciated that they looked like they were arrested in puberty.

After her last romp down the runway in one of the designer's couture gowns, Chloe plopped down at the makeup table, happy to be done with her portion of the show, finally able take a breather. Her adrenaline was still pumping and she began taking deep breaths to try to come down from the exhilarating yet nerve-wracking experience of her first runway show.

Gustave passed through the dressing area again. "Is there a Corinne or a Clementine here?" he said, passing by Chloe's table.

"Uh, do you mean Chloe?" she said, timidly raising her hand like she would have done in class.

"*Oui.* You're Chloe? The designer wants to see you."

She didn't say anything at first, wondering if she had done something wrong and feeling like she was being summoned to see the headmaster in school.

"Is there a problem?" she asked, still anchored to her chair.

"Problem? No, mademoiselle, he wants to escort you down the runway for the finale."

Chloe gaped at Gustave, as if to say, "Are you for real?" Though a novice to the fashion scene, she knew accompanying the designer down the runway at the conclusion of a show was an honor reserved for only the most talented – and usually more famous and experienced – models.

"Are you sure he meant me?"

"*Oui, oui.* Come along." Gustave clapped his hands together, as if to hasten her. "Fabrice has to take his bow. You're wasting time."

Chloe glanced down the table at the other girls, giving them a "who knew?" shrug. They responded by directing icy stares at her, as if this slight was proof positive that Chloe was a newbie out to usurp their hard-earned status, like Anne Baxter undermining Bette Davis in *All About Eve*, one of Chloe's favorite classic films.

Before rising, Chloe turned to her photo of Valérie Bourdain, silently thanking her for the good luck and confidence boost.

"Ah, here's my muse," Fabien said in heavily-accented English when Chloe joined him behind the curtain to prepare to walk down the runway for the finale. In his funky blazer, Jim Morrison T-shirt, bleached-out jeans and spiky "faux-hawk," he looked more like the lead singer of a punk band than an up-and-coming designer.

"*Merci*," Chloe said, careful to lift the hem of her dress so as not to trip as she ascended the steps of the platform. "This is such an honor."

"The honor is all mine." He presented her with a bouquet of roses. "You're fresh and new, and so am I. We complement each other, no?"

She took his arm and let him lead her past the curtain, back onto the runway. She smiled, not letting on how achy her feet were from prancing in high heels for the past hour, while Fabrice waved to the applauding audience members.

Chloe drank in the applause, allowing her imagination to transport her again. Instead of a fledging model, she was an in-demand young actress who was taking a curtain call with the brilliant playwright who had supplied her with a complex and intriguing character to inhabit.

Reaching the end of the runway, Chloe once again caught sight of Maxine, who was clapping enthusiastically and looked as though she would burst with pride. Monique looked equally impressed at the fact that her newest find had performed much better than expected.

"Do you know how rare it is for a designer to choose an unknown model for the finale?" Chloe heard Monique say to Maxine. "Your daughter's a natural at this."

"I know," Maxine replied, adding in a wry tone, "that's what I'm afraid of."

Chloe and Gigi burst through the Lycée's double doors and galloped down the front stairs and into the brilliant afternoon sunshine.

"I'm glad I don't have to think about algebra again until next year. I'm going to scream if I have to look at another equation," Gigi proclaimed. "I'm pretty sure I flunked the final."

"Did you even read the study guide I made for you?"

Gigi's guilty expression answered Chloe's question. "You know art's the only subject I care about. You're the smart one."

Chloe waved off Gigi's comment. "You could get good grades, too, if you actually studied instead of sneaking out to see Gaston."

It was no wonder that Gigi barely passed to the tenth grade. Save art, boys were her only extracurricular activity.

"I *didn't* sneak out to see Gaston," Gigi insisted. She paused, then added with a grin, "I was with Erique last night."

The girls broke out in raucous laughter. Chloe's laughter soon faded when they reached the bottom of the stairs and she saw François and Gaston approaching. François had been ignoring her since she had to turn down the double date offer a few weeks ago because of her mother's rules. He didn't even look at her when she turned around to pass him handouts in class.

"What are you guys going to be doing this summer?" Gaston said.

"Just hanging out, sketching and painting and stuff," Gigi said. "But Chloe's going to be modeling."

Chloe shrunk at the mention of her new pastime. It was weird when kids at school came up to her in the hall and told her they'd seen pictures of her runway debut in the newspaper. She didn't like the attention. But she'd agreed to book a few assignments over the summer. She'd already opened a bank account in her own name – her first – to begin saving for that New York trip she and Gigi were going to take when they turned eighteen.

"We're going out tonight to celebrate the last day of school," Gaston said. "You wanna come with?"

"Sounds like fun," Gigi said.

Chloe glanced at François, but he was bouncing a lacrosse ball and not looking at her.

"Great. Why don't I pick you up around eight?" Gaston slung his arm around Gigi. "What about you, Chloe?"

François looked up, his eyes finally meeting hers. He seemed to be probing for an answer. She wanted nothing more than to say yes. She allowed herself to fantasize for a moment, dreaming of a summer of long, hot afternoons spent lying under a shade tree with François, gazing into his eyes and kissing him and letting his hands wander wherever...

"Chloe?" Gigi tapped her on the shoulder, shaking her out of her daze. "Are you up for the double date tonight or not?"

Chloe shot Gigi a dirty look. She knew Maxine wouldn't let up on her no-dating-until-sixteen dictum, even when school was out.

"I- I'm sorry." Chloe's expression pleaded with François to forgive her, but he'd gone back to bouncing his ball. "I can't."

Gaston shrugged. "Whatever. It's cool." He kissed Gigi, and Chloe felt a pang, marveling at how grownup they seemed. "Why don't I walk you home?"

Gigi clutched Gaston's hand, which was draped over her shoulder. "Chloe, you going to be okay taking the Métro by yourself?"

"Yeah, go ahead. I'll be fine."

Gigi and Gaston toddled off, entwined like vines on a trellis.

Chloe lingered at the bottom of the steps, not knowing what to say to François. She wanted to tell him that if it was up to her, she'd not only consent to the double date, but find some way that they could run away and be alone together.

"Hey, I saw your picture in the paper," he said after a moment, finally looking at her again.

"Yeah?" she said tentatively, not sure if he was going to follow up his statement with some adolescent wisecrack.

"Yeah. You looked really pretty."

She felt her cheeks growing hot. He had never complimented her before, and she didn't know how to respond.

"Maybe I'll see you around this summer," he added.

She managed a smile. "Yeah, maybe."

He stepped closer, and she reflexively shifted her books to the other side. She had spent the better part of the afternoon cleaning out her locker and she didn't want her books and papers tumbling to the ground if François decided to start acting like a jerk again and tried to knock them out of her hands.

Instead, he ran past her, joining a group of boys and began tossing the lacrosse ball back and forth.

5

Chloe and Gigi strolled hand in hand down the Champs-Elysées, browsing the shops that lined the avenue. Dusk was beginning to set on the City of Light, but the girls took pleasure in not having to rush home now that school was out for the summer.

"Hey, isn't this the movie you wanted to see?" Gigi stopped and pointed to a movie poster near the entrance of a theater.

Chloe recognized the poster she had seen earlier that spring advertising *L'Affaire Scandaleuse (The Scandalous Affair)*, the steamy new romance starring her idol, Valérie Bourdain.

"They won't let us into that movie, Gi'. We're not old enough."

"All we have to do is buy a ticket for something else and sneak in." Gigi punctuated the statement with an emphatic "*duh*," as if explaining something that should have been completely self-evident.

"Even if we could get in," Chloe reasoned, "when it lets out, it would be after curfew."

"You mean after *your* curfew."

"Exactly. I'm the one who has to go home and deal with Maxine Bareaux."

"Oh come on, Chlo'. Simone's out with her boyfriend and I don't feel like going home alone."

Chloe bit her lip, staring at the movie poster. "I'm sorry, Gi'. School's only been out for a week and if I break curfew now, Mother won't ever let me stay out late again and the rest of the summer'll be ruined."

Gigi took Chloe's arm. "Okay," she said in resignation. "Let's go."

The girls proceeded toward the closest Métro station, but Chloe stopped suddenly.

Gigi stared at her. "What's up?"

Chloe said nothing, her bottom lip trembling. She motioned toward the theater exit. An American romantic comedy that was also playing had let out, and François was among the moviegoers coming out of the theater. On his arm was a blond girl Chloe recognized from school. Chloe's heart ached like someone was stepping on it as she watched François laughing with the girl. He escorted her away from the theater and down the street, their hands in each other's back pockets.

"Forget him." Gigi rubbed Chloe's back. "Let's get out of here."

"No, wait."

Chloe had always been the good girl, always obeyed her mother and done what was expected of her. And what had it gotten her? If she was more like

Gigi, more defiant, she would have ignored her mother's unfair rules and went on that double date and *she* would be the one on François' arm.

"Let's go to the movies," Chloe said. "It'll take my mind off everything."

Gigi looked uncharacteristically cautious. "You sure? What about curfew?"

"I don't care anymore."

Chloe marched up to the box office and asked for two tickets to the tame American comedy. After the usher tore their tickets, Chloe and Gigi casually strolled to the theater where the sexier adult movie was playing and took seats near the back. Thankfully, the theater had already darkened. Chloe wanted to lose herself in the fantasy unfolding on the screen.

When Chloe's heroine appeared onscreen, she disappeared into the older, sophisticated woman's world. In spite of her pain, Chloe was overtaken by that magical something that always happened when she visited this sanctuary of flickering lights and shadows. Her troubles vanished and she became part of the story.

A couple sitting in the row in front of them made out during the love scenes, and Chloe couldn't help but picture François doing the same thing with that blond girl.

Chloe tugged on Gigi's sleeve, making her change seats, moving away from the groping couple and closer to the screen. Once settled again, Chloe stared up at her idol, magnified larger than life. She admired how Valérie Bourdain not only commanded the screen with her mesmerizing beauty, but the power she wielded over her leading man. Valérie wasn't some shy schoolgirl nursing a broken heart, she was a confident woman in full control. Chloe could only wish that she could one day possess such power.

Maxine paced, nearly wearing a hole in the living room floor. The glow from the streetlamps outside provided the only light. It was one o'clock in the morning and she was nearly frantic. Chloe was supposed to be home by eleven.

"Where is she?" Maxine questioned the universe, wringing her hands.

In an attempt to steady herself, Maxine sat down at her Louis XIV secretary desk, flicked on the lamp and began sorting through a stack of mail she'd been meaning to get to. A glossy brochure caught her eye and she held it under the lamp.

"Our Lady of Chastity," Maxine said, reading the name on the cover of the brochure that was stamped above a photo of a complex of ivy-covered, stone structures.

Maxine leafed through the brochure, which advertised an all-girls Catholic academy just outside London. With Chloe's top grades – the result of Maxine's

31

insistence that her daughter always do her best – solicitations from private schools, advertising scholarships and campus amenities, were not uncommon. College brochures were even starting to trickle in, despite the fact that Chloe's graduation was three years away.

Maxine took one last glance at the brochure and set it aside, busying herself paying bills. She jumped when, suddenly, the locks in the front door turned and Chloe entered.

Chloe turned on the lights and looked startled to see Maxine waiting up for her. "What are you still doing up?" Chloe asked, as if she'd gotten out of bed to get a glass of water and discovered Maxine fully awake.

"No, the question is, what are *you* doing coming in at this hour? You know your curfew is eleven. I was worried sick."

"Sorry." Chloe's tone was unbelievably nonchalant. "Gigi and I decided to catch a late movie. I lost track of time."

"You should have called."

"I thought you'd be asleep. I didn't want to wake you."

Maxine crossed her arms to keep from shaking her child. "What were you seeing that let out so late?"

"What is this, the Spanish Inquisition? Why are you making such a big deal out of this? It's summertime, Mother. Most of my friends get to stay out as late as they want."

Chloe's defiant tone took Maxine by surprise.

"We're not talking about your friends, we're talking about you, young lady. And you have a curfew of eleven o'clock, not one in the morning."

"Mother, I'm going to be fifteen in a month, for goodness sake. Stop treating me like a baby. Simone lets Gigi do whatever she wants."

"Yeah, and look how Gigi's turning out. That girl is already too fast for her own good, and I don't want you ending up like that."

"Just because you got knocked up with me when you were a teenager doesn't mean I'm stupid enough to do the same thing." Chloe stamped down the hallway and slammed the door to her room.

Maxine was so stung by her daughter's words that she had no reply. Chloe had tapped into one of Maxine's greatest fears – that her daughter would end up pregnant and unmarried, just like she did, and end up jeopardizing her future. Maxine had worked too hard and sacrificed too much to let that happen.

"You should have heard the things she said to me last night," Maxine said to Simone over lunch the next day at La Closerie des Lilas, the Montparnasse sidewalk cafe where Ernest Hemmingway had written *The Sun Also Rises*. "She tries to sneak in past curfew and then sasses *me*, as if I were the one doing something wrong because I tried to correct her. If I would have talked to my mother the way that girl talked to me last night, she would have knocked me into the middle of next week."

"You think you have it rough? Chloe's a good kid. Gigi's got me going prematurely gray. I found another gray hair this morning and I'm going to have to make an emergency appointment with my colorist." Simone chomped into her *baguette-jambon*, a ham sandwich on French bread. "I wish her father were around," she added wistfully.

Maxine listened with interest, surprised that Simone brought up Gigi's late father. She seldom referred to Maurice Townsend, the African-American jazz bassist who had died in a car accident while on tour in the States when Gigi was just three years old.

"We kept talking about getting married and giving Gigi his name, but it just never happened," Simone continued. "If only Maurice hadn't been drinking when he got behind the wheel of that beat-up old van he and the guys in the band used to tour in…" She trailed off, staring into space while she nibbled her sandwich. "Maybe if Gigi had a father figure, she wouldn't be so starved for male attention from the boys at school. *Sacré bleu!* I don't know what to do with your godchild!"

Maxine stabbed at her salad, ignoring an American couple at the next table who were attempting to order by translating with a French-English phrase book. "If I don't get Chloe under wraps right now, I can see her becoming more and more rebellious, especially if she keeps hanging around *that one* of yours, Miss 'I-Think-I'm-Grown.'"

"You know we can't break them apart, Max." Simone picked at her sandwich. "They're inseparable."

Maxine set her fork down, watching another American couple walking by with cameras strapped around their necks, turning a map this way and that, obviously trying to find their way to some landmark.

"I can't be around to watch Chloe every minute," Maxine said. "We're busier than ever, but she's too old for a nanny."

Simone nodded empathetically. "I know what you mean. I'm so afraid Gigi's going to get pregnant. I can't bear the thought of being a grandmother at my age." She sighed. "I wish I could put an iron chastity belt on her and lock her up until she's eighteen and out of my hair."

Maxine slapped the table, shaking the water glasses. "That's it! You've got it!"

Simone looked puzzled. "I've got what?"

"Chastity."

"No, honey, trust me, I lost that a long time ago," Simone said, plucking her napkin from her lap and daintily wiping her mouth, "way before I had

Gigi."

"I'm talking about the perfect solution to our problems, Mo'."

"We're not animals. We can't eat our young," Simone said, giggling.

"When you said, 'Chastity,' that made me think of this boarding school, Our Lady of Chastity. It's an all-girls college prep academy just outside of London. According to the brochure they sent, the school has an international reputation and has been known to turn out female doctors and lawyers and politicians."

Simone took another bite of her sandwich. "Sounds pretty good so far."

"And this is the best part: it's run by nuns. Strict nuns. Mean nuns. Nuns that don't take any foolishness."

"I think I'm starting to like this idea, Max. What are you suggesting?"

"That we send our rebellious teenage daughters to boot camp. That ought to shape them up."

Simone propped her elbow on Maxine's shoulder. "You know, since we have each other, sometimes being a single mom's not so bad."

Chloe stood with Maxine, Gigi and Simone in the busy terminal at Charles de Gaulle Airport.

"Mother, I don't want to go," Chloe said. She had just turned fifteen and her mother was sending her packing. She had been looking forward to her sophomore year at the Lycée, making new friends. Now that her mother was shipping her off to boarding school, any remote chance that François would ask her out again was gone.

"You'll be fine," Maxine said, straightening Chloe's collar. "But you make sure you call me every day."

Earlier in the summer, Maxine and Simone had escorted Chloe and Gigi to London by train and taken them on a tour of Our Lady of Chastity College Preparatory Academy for Young Ladies. The ancient halls were imposing, gloomy edifices that gave Chloe the creeps.

She had specifically told her mother that she had no intention of being locked away in that dungeon for the remainder of her high school years, that she would rather die. Maxine had ignored her wishes, just as Simone had ignored Gigi's protests.

"Why are you doing this to me, Simone?" Gigi said. "You're ruining my life."

"You're fifteen. You don't have a life."

"I have more of a life than you."

"That mouth of yours is precisely why I'm sending you to the nuns," Simone huffed. "Maybe they can do something with you, because I'm done trying."

The final boarding call for the next flight to London sounded over the intercom. Chloe couldn't believe that her first time on an airplane wasn't a trip to New York or some other exciting place, but to some stuffy boarding school.

"You two don't want to miss your flight," Maxine said. "You'd better be going now."

"Bye," Chloe said shortly, turning to walk away.

"Come back here," said Maxine, pulling her daughter close. She embraced Chloe for a long time, and finally let her go. "I love you, *ma chérie*."

"If you love me so much, why are sending me away?"

"Because I want the best for you."

"The same goes for you, Gigi," Simone said

"Yeah, yeah. Tell it to the pope." Gigi cracked her gum and stared at the ceiling.

"I'm going to miss you, you bad girl," Simone said, swatting Gigi on the behind.

"You're sending me halfway across the continent, and now you're going to get mushy? Save it." Gigi pushed Simone away.

"I love you, and I know you love me."

"Yeah, right. Let's get out of here, Chloe."

The girls picked up their carry-on bags and tromped to the boarding gate.

"Make sure you wear your sweater to class. London can get pretty chilly in fall. I don't want you catching cold," Maxine called. "Oh, and I packed Mr. Buttons."

"I swear, my mother must think I'm four years old," Chloe muttered to Gigi. Secretly, she was glad Maxine had packed her childhood teddy bear. At least she'd have something familiar to cling to.

Maxine and Simone waved at their daughters until they were out of sight. Chloe was so consumed in thought, wondering about how she was going to survive living away from home for the first time, that she didn't see the tears in her mother's eyes.

6

The Patron Saint of Dorm Assignments had been merciful and put Chloe and Gigi together. Thank God their names both started with letters at the beginning of the alphabet. Chloe was beyond relieved that she didn't have to put up with some strange girl and her strange habits all year long. She was already familiar with Gigi's annoying ways and knew how to deal with them.

Chloe was unpacking the large trunk that contained most of her personal items when Gigi entered their room. She had just come back from taking another tour of the grounds.

"Well, I have good news and bad news," said Gigi. "The bad news is I ran into the headmistress, Mother Superior, and she seems like a real tight-ass." She added with the devilish grin Chloe recognized so well, "The good news is there's an all-boys academy a couple of miles down the road called St. Thomas."

Chloe shook her head and laughed. Leave it to Gigi to find an oasis of testosterone in this virginal desert.

Maxine barely looked up from the paperwork splayed across her desk when Simone rapped on the open office door.

"I just finished the invoices for the Bergeron account, so I'm going to head home." Simone lingered in the doorway. "Unless there's something else you need."

Maxine adjusted her reading glasses, poring over the file. "No, hon', I'm fine. Thanks."

"Okay, then. I guess I'll go get ready for my date tonight."

Maxine looked up. "Pascal again?"

"Yeah. He's taking me to a rock concert. We'll probably end up at my place afterward. With Gigi off at boarding school, I have the apartment all to myself now and can bring dates home whenever I want."

"Not that anything ever stopped you before."

Simone sneered. "Very funny. So, what do you have lined up for the weekend?"

Maxine swiveled in her chair and retrieved a file from the cabinet behind her desk. "I'm so busy finalizing the details for this new account, I'm probably going to be here late tonight and I'll probably end up working tomorrow, too."

Simone approached the desk. "Max, you've always been a workaholic, but this is the third weekend in a row you've spent at the office. You need to get out."

"I appreciate your concern, but I'm fine. I've got everything covered."

Simone sat on the edge of Maxine's desk. "Why don't you just admit it?"

"Admit what?"

"You miss Chloe. It's okay. As much as I'm glad to have Gigi out of the country and at the mercy of the nuns who can keep her in line, I miss that little hellion, too. I don't like going home to an empty apartment, either. If I didn't have my male friends to keep me company, I'd go crazy from the loneliness and boredom."

Maxine opened the file and began scribbling notes. "Unlike you, Simone, I don't need constant male attention to make me feel good. I'm doing just fine on my own, thank you, and if I don't get this work done, no one else is going to do it."

Simone reached out and closed the file. "This work will still be here Monday morning. You can't keep doing this, Maxine – using work to fill the void. For the past fifteen years, you've made raising your daughter and running the business your whole life. And now that Chloe's not around, you don't know what to do with yourself."

Maxine reopened the file. "I have plenty to do."

"But nothing outside of work. I don't know about you, but I don't want to look up one day and find that life has passed me by. That's why I'm going to have as much fun as I can right now." Simone jabbed Maxine. "And you need to do the same. Why don't we go out tomorrow night?"

Maxine sighed. Simone was relentless. "I have no interest in going to bars."

"Who said anything about a bar? Hey, what about that fundraiser?"

Maxine trained her attention on the paperwork, making notes again. "What fundraiser?"

"I gave you the invitation, remember?" Simone shuffled papers around the desk until she located a card embossed with gold lettering. "This is it. It's a charity ball benefiting a local orphanage. It's at Jacques Chevalier's estate."

Maxine took the invitation from Simone and examined it. "Jacques Chevalier? Where have I heard that name before?"

"He's always in the society pages. He owns one of the biggest shipping companies in Europe and hosts a lot of fundraisers for children's charities. He's a widower, very eligible." The same gleam danced in Simone's green eyes that often sparkled in her daughter's when Gigi was up to no good. "We should go. You should wear that strapless Christian Lacroix and maybe you'll score. It's about time you got someone to clean out those cobwebs between your legs."

Maxine tsked. "And you wonder where Gigi gets her foul mouth."

Simone stood, smoothing her skirt. "I've got to go. Pascal's picking me up at seven."

"Now I can finally get some work done."

Simone hovered at the door. "Don't work too late." She pointed a scolding finger at Maxine. "And don't forget about tomorrow night."

"Get out of here, will you?"

After Maxine heard the front door to the studio open and close, she set aside the file she was working on and picked up the invitation to the charity ball. Maybe Simone was right. Maybe she did need to get out and circulate.

Chloe stood at attention in a row of her classmates in Our Lady of Chastity's gymnasium as the headmistress ticked off a seemingly infinite list of rules and regulations.

"There will be no speaking out in class unless you raise your hands, and no swearing. Taking the Lord's name in vain is grounds for suspension." Mother Superior, in her severe black habit and stuffy British accent, traversed the row of students like a drill sergeant scoping out new cadets.

Chloe glanced nervously down the row of girls, who were all clad just like she was in the school's prim navy-blue-and-green, plaid uniform skirts and heavily starched white blouses. Gigi hadn't yet arrived for orientation and Chloe was worried the headmistress was going to discover the unexcused absence at any moment. Chloe had tried to nudge Gigi awake when she left their dorm room, but Gigi just mumbled she'd get up in a few minutes and rolled over, pulling a pillow over her face.

"Skirts are never to rise above knee-length." Mother Superior stopped in front of a girl who had compensated for her anti-regulation uniform skirt by pulling her knee socks higher. A withering glance from the headmistress caused the girl's shoulders to slump.

The headmistress's probing gray-blue eyes scanned the students at her command as she paced to the front of the line, the soles of her patent leather shoes clapping against the gym floor and the crucifix dangling from her habit clanging against the clipboard she wielded like the archangel Gabriel's sword.

"Are there any questions?"

None of the girls made a sound. No one dare ask this all-knowing, all-seeing handmaiden of the Lord to repeat herself.

"Very well. I'll take attendance and then you may be excused to report to your classes."

Chloe held her breath as Mother Superior consulted her clipboard, calling off names beginning with the A's. Still no sign of Gigi. While the headmistress was scolding a classmate for her threadbare sweater and overall sloppy appearance, Gigi slinked in and squeezed next to Chloe.

Mother Superior stopped mid-sentence, swiveling to chastise Gigi with one of her withering glances. Chloe swore the old woman had eyes in the back of her head and a hotline to God.

"Miss Cartier?" Mother Superior pointed at a line on her clipboard with a razor-sharp nail. Gigi nodded, which produced a frown on Mother Superior's already-grim face. "The appropriate response is, 'Yes, ma'am.'"

Gigi said nothing, slouching in her slightly-out-of-line position, as if daring the headmistress to punish her lack of uniformity. Chloe stared at her friend in disbelief. Gigi's boldness knew no bounds.

Chloe watched as Mother Superior slowly walked to where Gigi stood, taking the new girl up on her challenge. Chloe braced herself for the torrent of harsh words that would undoubtedly besiege her friend, but Mother Superior remained surprisingly collected.

"Miss Cartier, tardiness is not acceptable. All students are to be up by seven a.m. for breakfast in the dining hall, followed by morning Mass." She calmly placed her hand on Gigi's back, correcting her pupil's slumping posture. "And you are to stand up straight and carry yourself like a lady." Mother Superior paused, adding, "Do I make myself clear?"

Gigi continued to stare at the headmistress in an astonishing act of insubordination, and for a moment Chloe feared the woman would lose her cool, haul off and slap Gigi across the face.

"Yes," Gigi said finally.

Mother Superior raised her eyebrows, prompting Gigi to add sullenly, "Yes, *ma'am*."

The headmistress lingered in front of Gigi for a moment, as if warning her that she had gotten off easy this time but should not expect such lenience in the future, then returned to taking attendance. Chloe breathed a sigh of relief.

Gigi leaned over and whispered in Chloe's ear. "Uptight as she is, I bet she could use a good screw."

Chloe bit the inside of her cheek to keep from laughing.

Maxine and Simone stood in the ballroom of a magnificent eighteenth century chateau among the crowd of well-heeled philanthropists who had gathered for the charity ball.

"I told you to wear the strapless Christian Lacroix," Simone said to Maxine, sipping Dom Perignon and surveying the crowd. "There's a lot of rich, powerful men here. You want to advertise the goods and let them know you're available."

Simone was doing just that in her low-cut black Chanel gown, while Maxine had opted for a modest off-white organza evening gown from her own collection.

Maxine was too busy studying the chateau's ornate architecture and antique furnishings to listen to Simone's ramblings. "Will you look at that crown molding? All the wood is original. This house could really be a showplace. It just needs a little updating. I can't stop thinking of what I could do with this place if I was given carte blanche."

Simone resumed her scolding tone. "Do you hear yourself? We're at one of the biggest social events in Paris and you can't stop talking about work. If I hadn't dragged you here, you'd probably still be chained to your desk. Haven't you noticed the men who keep looking our way?"

"I didn't come here to be picked up," Maxine said. "I let you talk me into this because it's for a good cause."

Maxine had already put in her bid for a Renoir print she could hang in her office. She had found several bargain-priced items in the silent auction, which was also serving as an estate sale for the late wife of the man who was hosting the event.

"Look at those shameless hussies," Simone said, gesturing toward the women who were in line to greet the debonair host. "I read in the society pages that Jacques' wife passed away not even six months ago, and these women are throwing themselves at him. They obviously can't wait to dig their claws into him and his fortune."

Maxine peered around the women who were angling for the host's attention, fluffing their hair and jutting out their bosoms. The fawning women blocked her view and she couldn't get a good look at Jacques Chevalier. Not that it mattered. Work demands were such that Maxine had no interest in adding her name to his long list of pursuers.

"*Pardon*, Mesdames."

A good-looking man approached Maxine and Simone and introduced himself as a live string ensemble began playing another number.

"Would you care to dance?" He directed his gaze at Maxine.

"Yes, she would." Maxine, anxious for a free moment without Simone's prodding, pushed her best friend toward the man.

Simone smiled at the man. "I'd love to dance. I'll join you in a second."

The man backed toward to the dance floor, beckoning for Simone to join him.

"Remember what I said," Simone said, setting her champagne glass on a nearby tray and fluffing Maxine's bosom like a throw pillow. "Show off the girls and work the room."

Maxine slapped Simone's hand away. "Leave me alone, will you?"

Just as Simone joined the handsome man on the dance floor, Maxine saw another man approaching. Spotting an open set of French doors, she escaped to the patio to get some fresh air.

Chloe and Gigi stood behind Our Lady's chapel, sneaking cigarettes before curfew, when they'd have to return to the dorm for lights out. When Chloe said she needed something stronger than caffeine and chocolate to ease the stress of adjusting to their new environment, Gigi offered to teach her how to inhale.

"I don't know about this," Chloe said, holding one of the Gauloise cigarettes Gigi had smuggled from Paris and coughing so hard she was sure she was going to upchuck a lung.

"Ah, you'll get the hang of it eventually," Gigi said, whacking Chloe on the back. "Hey, isn't that Sister Maureen?"

Chloe waved away the smoke cloud encircling her head and craned her neck around the life-size statue of the Virgin Mary they were standing beside to get a view of the beautiful young novice rushing in the back entrance of the library.

Chloe gave Gigi a puzzled look. "So? She runs the library."

"Yes, but it's after-hours. And look who's behind her."

Gigi pointed out Mr. Gottlieb, the only male lay teacher on campus, sprinting to catch up with Sister Maureen. When he finally caught up, he looked around as if afraid of being spied on and hurriedly followed her into the building.

"I bet you they're doing it," Gigi said, grinning as she expelled a puff of smoke.

"That's gross!" Chloe exclaimed. "First of all, she's a nun. Second of all, Gottlieb has got to be the most unattractive man in England!"

With his nonexistent biceps and toothpick legs, Gottlieb hardly had the body of a man that would cause a woman who was committed to God to renounce her vows. He was probably fifteen to twenty years older than the twenty-something nun and was losing his hair, trying in vain to camouflage it with a bad comb-over.

"Sister Maureen's not a real nun yet, she's just studying to be one," Gigi argued. "And besides, it doesn't matter what Gottlieb looks like, if he's good in bed, that's all that matters."

"I think I'm going to gag," Chloe said, hacking this time not so much from the cigarette smoke but from the visual of the pretty nun-in-training in an embrace with the loathsome biology teacher who was known among the student body as "Frogface." The nickname was mean but accurate commentary on the fact that he resembled the pitiful creatures whose dissection he oversaw.

"Didn't you see the way they were sneaking around? It's so obvious Gottlieb is slipping Sister Maureen his *Charles-le-Chauve*."

"It's not obvious to me."

"Any fool could see it," Gigi continued, taking another puff. "You don't know the first thing about sex."

Chloe shrugged, unable to counter that point. "Maybe. One thing I *do* know is that a woman who looks like Sister Maureen would never fall for a science nerd like Gottlieb."

"If he's good in the sack, he could have any woman he wanted, even Mother Superior," Gigi asserted. "It's probably been so long since *she's* had any, she's probably dying for some."

Chloe cradled her cigarette, flicking ashes to the ground. "Do you really think Gottlieb is good in bed?"

"We could find out."

"How?" Chloe took a drag on the cigarette.

"You could sleep with him."

Chloe nearly choked, coughing out smoke again. "No, *ma amie*, I'll leave that pleasure to you. You can have old Frogface all to yourself."

"Can you imagine Gottlieb in nothing but his boxer shorts and those stupid argyle socks?"

Chloe and Gigi cracked up at the notion, but their laughter was interrupted by the appearance of a nun at the edge of the cathedral.

"What are you girls doing back here?"

Chloe and Gigi quickly hid their cigarettes behind their backs and stared blankly at Sister Francesca, a stocky Italian nun who taught health and doubled as the gym instructor. Chloe almost didn't recognize the nun in her full-length habit. She was used to seeing Sister Francesca in her headdress, Our Lady of Chastity T-shirt and baggy shorts, her sagging breasts heaving under her crucifix and her pudgy knees knocking as she demonstrated volleyball serves.

"I asked you girls what you're doing," the sister said as she came closer.

"We were, uh…" Gigi looked up at the statue of the Virgin Mary. "Just praying. I just found out that my mother had… surgery and we were praying to the Madonna to speed her recovery."

Chloe stifled a giggle. Gigi's statement wasn't a total violation of one of the Ten Commandments; Simone probably was undergoing a collagen injection or some other youth-extending procedure somewhere in Paris at the moment.

Sister Francesca looked skeptical, and Chloe held her breath, swallowing smoke as the nun came closer. To her relief, the sister puckered her lips in a pitying expression, the fine hairs of her not-so-faint moustache crinkling. "*Poverina*. Come on. We'll pray together."

As the nun closed her eyes and dropped to her knees, the girls quietly stamped out their cigarettes. Muttering incantations in Latin, Sister Francesca pulled the girls into kneeling positions beside her under the statue's outstretched arms. Chloe glanced at Gigi, who was staring up through her steepled hands at the Virgin with a pained expression, as though she were praying for release from the nun's long-winded prayer

*****

42

Maxine ventured onto the patio overlooking a beautiful garden, the wind rippling through her gown as the setting sun streaked the sky with brilliant shades of orange and purple. The scent of gardenias, which were just starting to bloom, reminded her of New Orleans.

"What's a beautiful woman like you doing out here all by yourself?"

Maxine turned to see a handsome stranger standing in the shadows, his features swathed in cigar smoke.

"I just thought I'd get a breath of fresh air," she said, backing closer to the railing as he neared.

"I know what you mean," he said, standing next to her. "These functions with all of these pretentious people can be overwhelming."

Maxine nodded in agreement, the sounds of the revelers in the adjacent ballroom in the background. "This house is amazing. I've been marveling at it all evening."

"I'll have to pass your sentiments on to the owner," the man said.

"Oh, you know him?"

"Quite well."

From the man's precocious smile, it was obvious that he *was* the owner. Maxine had come face to face with the host and not even realized it.

"I'm Maxine Bareaux," she said, extending her hand. "It's a pleasure to meet you."

"Jacques Chevalier, and the pleasure is all mine," he said, kissing her hand.

Maxine wasn't sure if the shiver that went up her spine was from the chill in the evening air or contact with the handsome man. He had a distinguished air, with his wavy, salt-and-pepper hair and toned physique that was apparent through his well-fitted tuxedo. Maxine surmised that he was forty-something, at least ten years older than she, but it wasn't apparent except for a few lines around the eyes that gave his regal face character and contrasted with his boyish playfulness.

"'Maxine Bareaux,' that's a lovely name," he said in his sexy accent, looking at her with his light brown eyes, which glittered with flecks of green and gold in the twilight.

She fanned herself, starting to feel a little warm in spite of the chill in the air. "*Merci.*"

"It sounds French, but your accent is American?"

"Yes. Louisiana Creole. I'm originally from New Orleans."

"Ah, New Orleans," Jacques said, as if fondly recalling the name of a lover. "I used to go there often as a young man when I was in the navy. That city gave me many good times and a lot of great memories. It's such a vibrant city, with its jazz and great food and beautiful women." He looked at her pointedly.

Maxine turned away from the intensity of his gaze, looking out over the grounds. "Do you tend the garden yourself?"

"No, I leave that up to my groundskeeper, Bernard. That garden was Marguerite's pride and joy."

"Marguerite?" she said, turning to him.

"My wife. She passed away a few months ago. Ovarian cancer. By the time they found it, it had metastasized."

Maxine looked out at the garden again. "I'm sorry."

"Don't be. We had a full life together, even if it was too brief."

Maxine was quiet for a moment, not sure of what to say. "Your home is beautiful."

"*Merci*. It has a lot of history. It was once used as an underground stop by the French Resistance. When Marguerite and I found this place, we fell in love with it. Restoring it was supposed to be our big project together, but she passed away before we could finish."

Silence descended again, with Jacques puffing on his cigar.

"I helped renovate a chateau just like this in Chartres," Maxine said after a moment.

"Oh? You're in the design business?"

"Yes, interior design and dressmaking. I have a boutique, Chez Maxine."

"Really? You know, I'm tired of looking at drywall and plastic sheets and walking under scaffolding. I'd love to meet with you sometime and talk about finishing the restoration."

"I'll write my contact information in the guest register. Why don't you give me a call at the office some time?" She extended her hand in a business-like gesture.

He enveloped her hand in his. "I most certainly will. I look forward to the opportunity to speak with you again."

7

Returning to campus after a too-brief trip home during Christmas break, Chloe hurried to the school library, excited to begin the new semester and start her assignment as a library assistant. All new students were required to fill a campus position before the end of the school year. Gigi got stuck being an office helper, forced to spend countless hours making copies and stuffing envelopes under the headmistress' watchful eye.

While Gigi complained about her assignment, Chloe gladly signed up to be a library assistant. She didn't mind that it required manual labor, having to climb a wobbly ladder to re-shelve heavy volumes. Surveying the tall stacks of age-old classic tomes as she entered the library, she felt right at home. She'd always loved to read, and this was the perfect assignment.

"*Excusez-moi*," Chloe said, approaching the librarian, who was seated at a desk in the center of the room with her back turned. Used to speaking French during the holidays in Paris, Chloe quickly corrected herself. "Excuse me. I'm the new library assistant."

The librarian turned around, revealing herself as Sister Maureen. Chloe took a step backward, taken aback to see the young novice she and Gigi had spied earlier in the school year cavorting with Mr. Gottlieb. Even though Chloe had defended Sister Maureen against Gigi's absurd notion that the young nun and middle-aged science teacher were "doing it," Chloe still felt awkward in Sister Maureen's presence. It was as though Chloe knew a secret about her.

"You must be Chloe," Sister Maureen said with a smile, rising from the desk and extending her hand.

Chloe shook her hand, noticing that the young woman was even prettier up-close, even without a stitch of makeup. With wisps of curly brown hair peeking out from under her headdress and falling into her heavily lashed brown eyes, Sister Maureen had a girlish quality. Instead of the shapeless habits worn by the older nuns, the novice donned a blouse, sweater and skirt that revealed a shapely figure that was particularly impressive for someone who was taking a vow of chastity.

"Why don't you tell me a little about yourself, dear, while we get started shelving these books?" Sister Maureen said in a cheerful British accent, pushing an overflowing cart toward the stacks and motioning for Chloe to follow. "Are you from London?"

"No," Chloe said, sizing Sister Maureen up as they began placing books on shelves, trying to determine if she really was violating her vows with Gottlieb. "I grew up in Paris."

"Oh, how exciting. Are you French?"

Chloe remained quiet while placing a book on a shelf. She always squirmed when someone asked her to describe her mixed-up, complicated heritage. "Well, my father was French – uh, *is* French – and my mother is black and French Creole. She's from New Orleans, in the States."

"What a wonderful place, New Orleans." Sister Maureen leaned toward Chloe, lowering her voice as she handed her another book to file. "Don't tell any of the nuns this, but when I was in college at Cambridge, I went to Mardi Gras one year for spring break. Oh, what a time I had with my friends."

"Really?" Chloe said, intrigued that Sister Maureen had visited the city where Chloe's family was from. "That does sound like fun."

"Oh, it was. It's a great city. I take it you've been there with your mother?"

"Actually, I've always tried to get her to plan a trip, but she always says she's too busy or has some other excuse."

"Well, you know how we adults are – always so busy." Sister Maureen pushed the cart further down the aisle. "Speaking of which, I'm afraid we've got a lot of work on our hands today. One of the big, old libraries in London just updated its collection and donated dozens of discarded books. There's a lot of filing to do before you go on to the next class on your schedule."

Chloe liked how Sister Maureen pronounced the word "schedule" the British way, so that it sounded like "*shed*-jewel."

Time raced by as they worked together to empty the cart. As Sister Maureen handled each classic novel, she commented on how much she'd loved reading it.

"You must read this, dear," Sister Maureen said, holding up a weathered copy of Victor Hugo's *Les Miserables*. "I had a double major in literature and drama at Cambridge and I wrote my thesis on this. I saw the musical when it came to London and I think it would be a great show to stage here at Our Lady for the annual production with St. Thomas."

"If we did put on the show, I might want to try out," Chloe said tentatively. "I've always wanted to act." She had never revealed her dream to someone in a position of authority before, and she hoped Sister Maureen wouldn't dismiss her acting ambitions as silly.

"I'm not in charge of the theater department, of course. That's Sister Georgina's job. She's been here since the dawn of time and Jesus will probably return before she retires," Sister Maureen said with a chuckle. She added with a reassuring wink at Chloe, "But if the school ever did decide to put on *Les Miz*, I bet you'd be perfect to play the female lead, Cosette, since you're from Paris."

Sister Maureen handed the book to Chloe, smiling again, her eyes radiating warmth and sincerity. Chloe was already taking a liking to Sister Maureen and decided it was nobody's business if the novice was having a forbidden affair with Gottlieb.

When the bell rang, Chloe could hardly believe an entire class period had flown by. She could stay in the library all day talking about books and life in general with Sister Maureen. Unlike the stern Mother Superior and the other stuffy old nuns, the novice was forward-thinking and relatable.

"I'll give you a pass to get into your next class so you won't be written up for being tardy. That would be a terrible way to start off the new semester," Sister Maureen said, leading Chloe to her desk. "Who's the teacher?"

Realizing biology was her next class, Chloe shifted her weight from one foot to the other, hesitating to answer. "Mr. Gottlieb," she said slowly, studying Sister Maureen's face to gauge her reaction.

46

A glimmer of a smile passed across Sister Maureen's face, and Chloe tried to surmise if that meant the unattractive, older man was indeed the novice's lover.

"Poor Gottlieb," Sister Maureen said, scrawling her signature on the tardy excuse. "He's got his hands full, being the only math and science teacher on campus." She leaned toward Chloe and lowered her voice. "Just between you and me, it's because Bishop Griffin is under the mistaken impression that women aren't capable of teaching math and science. I consider myself a good Catholic, but the Church can be so antiquated and sexist. I think women should be allowed to be priests, and at the very least be able to teach math and science at an all-girls academy. You know, Sister Catherine has a doctorate in molecular chemistry and used to be a chemical engineer with an international research lab before she entered the order."

"You're kidding!"

A student browsing the stacks turned to look.

"Sshh," Sister Maureen chastened. "Sister Barbara is a mathematician," she continued in a more hushed tone, "and used to teach at Oxford before she came here."

"Gosh. I didn't realize the sisters had lives before they became nuns."

"There are a lot of things about this place that would surprise you."

Chloe stared at Sister Maureen, trying to decipher if the cryptic remark was some kind of veiled confession about the affair with Gottlieb.

As if interpreting her thoughts, Sister Maureen added, "You know, I minored in biology at Cambridge and I've been meeting with Gottlieb in the evenings after I close the library to help him prepare lesson plans. He's really overwhelmed and he insists that we meet in secret, because he's too proud to admit that he can't handle the workload."

Chloe giggled and quickly covered her mouth. She was so relieved to hear a plausible explanation about the clandestine meeting she and Gigi had witnessed that she couldn't control her laughter.

"What are you so tickled about?" Sister Maureen said with a friendly expression that begged Chloe to let her in on the joke.

Chloe paused, then decided she could open up to this young, progressive-minded woman who was not that much older than she. "I was hanging out behind the chapel after Mass with my best friend Gigi this one time and we saw you and Mr. Gottlieb going into the library, and Gigi assumed you two were…" She trailed off, straining for a tactful way to describe Gigi's theory that Mr. Gottlieb was "slipping Sister Maureen his *Charles-le-Chauve*."

To Chloe's relief, she didn't have to finish the sentence. Sister Maureen seemed to pick up on what Chloe was about to say and burst out laughing.

"That's the funniest thing I've heard all day!" Sister Maureen exclaimed, once again attracting the attention of the girl who was browsing the stacks. "Me and Gottlieb!"

Chloe shared Sister Maureen's laughter, and it was as though they were two peers dishing campus gossip rather than an interaction between an authority figure and a pupil.

When the second bell rang, announcing the beginning of the next period, Sister Maureen handed Chloe the tardy pass. "When you give this to Gottlieb," she said with a playful twinkle in her eye, "tell him I said hi."

Maxine made one last adjustment to the window treatment in the parlor of Jacques Chevalier's chateau and climbed down from the stepladder to survey her handiwork. This renovation had turned out even better than she expected and was set for completion ahead of schedule. The project had a much-needed creative outlet over the past several months that Chloe had been away at boarding school.

Maxine picked up her clipboard and turned to continue her walk-through of the refurbished wing, checking off items on a list. She was so absorbed in her work that she bumped into Jacques, whom she didn't notice standing in the doorway. She had grown fond of his now-familiar scent – a combination of his musky cologne and the Cuban cigars he was always puffing on.

"You're very efficient, Ma-*dam*."

"Thank you," she said, startled. "I pride myself on my work."

"As well you should. I'm delighted with the way everything has turned out."

"I'm so glad. There are just a few finishing touches to take care of and we'll be done. I've enjoyed working with you." She extended her hand.

In that Gallic way of his, Jacques cradled her hand and kissed it. In an effort to disguise the flash of arousal that swept through her, she withdrew her hand, cleared her throat and gestured toward a white sheet hanging above the fireplace.

"I added one minor detail I hope you'll like."

Jacques' eyes glimmered. "I can't wait."

Maxine climbed back on the stepladder and, with a flourish, removed the sheet, revealing an ornately carved wooden sign above the fireplace that read "Chateau de Chevalier" with elegant fleur-de-lis on either side.

"What a nice touch." Jacques shoved his hands in his pockets and rocked on his heels like a little boy admiring a shiny new bicycle in a store window.

"I thought the house needed personalizing," Maxine explained, "so I took the liberty."

Jacques offered a wan smile. "I'm glad you did."

For a moment, their eyes lingered.

"I was just doing one last walk-through," she said at last, breaking eye contact. "Would you like to join me?"

"*Oui*. My time is yours."

Maxine stepped down from the ladder and, in her high heels, missed a step and nearly fell. Jacques rushed forward and caught her, his strong arms cradling her back.

"*Merci*," she said softly, freeing herself from his grip, her cheeks flushing. She picked up her clipboard, trying to regain her composure. "Why don't you follow me?"

Maxine led Jacques on a tour of the refurbished wing, pointing out his specific design requests she had fulfilled – a Gothic sconce here, a plush throw rug there. She concluded the tour where it began, in the parlor where the new "Chateau de Chevalier" sign hung.

"You've done a fabulous job," Jacques said. "Marguerite and I bought this house, hoping to raise a big family here. I stopped working on the renovation when she got sick and didn't have the strength to finish…" He paused, looking down. His eyes met hers again and he added, "But now you've turned it into a home again."

She blinked back tears, touched by his sincerity. "I was just doing my job."

He took the clipboard from her, set it aside and took her hands. "I feel like I've gotten to know you these past few months. I think we've gone beyond a strictly business relationship. I feel something for you that I haven't felt since Marguerite, and I hope you feel it, too."

Maxine looked out the window, surveying the grounds and the garden where she and Jacques had had their first encounter at the charity ball. She had to admit that she, too, had feelings for him beyond the usual client relationship. He had stirred long-dormant emotions she hadn't experienced since Chloe's father, and it scared her.

"I'd like to keep seeing you after the renovation's done," he said. "How about lunch? I'd like to take you out to celebrate the renovation being done and treat you for all your hard work."

Maxine glanced up at the portrait of Jacques' late wife hanging above the sofa. The woman stared back at Maxine, a reminder that her spirit still permeated the house.

Averting her eyes from the portrait, Maxine picked up her clipboard again and began making notes. "Jacques, I'm sorry, but I make it a rule never to go out with clients."

He grinned, looking like a schoolboy again. "Well, technically, I'm not a client anymore since the remodeling project is coming to an end."

Maxine took a step backward, grappling for words. Finally, she broke into laughter, tossing her clipboard aside. "I guess I can't argue with that."

8

During biology class, Gigi passed Chloe a note:

Check out Gottlieb's crotch. He's got a serious hard-on. He's thinking about Sister Maureen.

Smooches, Gigi

Chloe laughed to herself. She couldn't wait until after class when she could tell Gigi that she had jumped to the wrong conclusion about Sister Maureen and Gottlieb, just as Chloe had argued. Chloe couldn't wait to rub in the fact that she was right, despite Gigi's condescending assertion that she didn't know the first thing about sex.

Chloe balled up the note, turned around and looked at Gigi, who sat directly behind her. Gigi crossed her eyes and stuck her tongue out. Chloe was able to stifle her laughter until Mr. Gottlieb turned from the blackboard and faced the class. When Chloe noticed the bulge in his crotch, she couldn't hold it back. She broke into uncontrollable laughter, causing everyone to turn around and look at her. She tried to stop laughing but couldn't. Each time she caught sight of the protruding erection in Frogface's pants, she was seized by another giggling fit.

"Chloe," Gottlieb said, "you're causing a disturbance. What's the reason for this outburst?"

"Nothing, sir," Chloe said, trying desperately to squelch her laughter.

"Be quiet."

"I'm sorry," Chloe said, chortling.

Gottlieb glanced at the balled-up note in her hand. "What's that you've got there, young lady?"

She abruptly stopped laughing. "Nothing," she said, trying to sound unconcerned, putting her hands, along with the crumpled note, in her lap.

"Let's see what you have in your hands, Miss Bareaux. Put your hands on top of your desk," Gottlieb ordered.

Chloe dropped the note in her lap as she folded her hands and put them on top of her desk. Gottlieb walked over to her lab table and stood over her.

"You know the proper way to sit. Cross your legs like a lady," he instructed.

As Chloe reluctantly crossed her legs, the note fell to the floor and rolled next to Gottlieb's feet.

"What's this?" he said, bending down and picking the crinkled ball off the floor.

"That's just a piece of scrap paper," Chloe lied, praying he wouldn't open up the note and read it.

"Scrap paper, huh?" he said, uncrumpling the page and examining it.

Chloe's heart stopped as Gottlieb read the note. His face turning bright red, he looked down at his crotch and ripped the note to shreds. Chloe almost lost it again. She knew Gigi was dying to laugh, too, but she was really good at staying cool under pressure. Chloe never knew anyone who could turn her emotions on and off the way her best friend could. Chloe envied her and wished she, too, had a tighter rein on her emotions, instead of being so sensitive.

"Chloe and Gigi," Gottlieb said, "go stand in the hall. I want to talk to you both after class."

"*Ooooh*," the other girls sighed dramatically.

"Silence!" Gottlieb shouted as Chloe and Gigi rose from their seats and made their way to the hall.

"We're in big trouble," Chloe said to Gigi once they were safely out of Gottlieb's earshot.

"Don't be silly," Gigi said confidently. "Gottlieb can't punish us for what was in the note."

"Says who?"

"Anyone with eyes could see that Frogface had it hard, and I was merely stating my opinion that he was thinking about Sister Maureen. Teachers are always telling us to express ourselves."

Chloe grimaced at Gigi's bravado. "I'm so embarrassed. I'll never be able to look that man in the face again."

"*He* should be embarrassed. I'm not."

"Nothing embarrasses you. I just hope he doesn't tell my mother about this. She'll kill me, and Simone's going to kill you."

"Don't worry. Gottlieb wouldn't dare tell anyone about what was in that note. You see he ripped it up. He knows he's busted. He doesn't want anyone to know he and Sister Maureen have a thing going on."

Chloe peered down the hall at Mother Superior's office, the light from the doorway streaming into the dark corridor like an ominous portal to the lair of the Angel of Judgment. "I hope we're not going to get suspended."

"Will you relax?"

When the bell rang, the other students poured out of the classroom, gaping at Chloe and Gigi like jury members who had rendered a guilty verdict to would-be felons. Chloe and Gigi remained in the hall until Gottlieb came to the door, still looking angry.

"I'd like to have a word with you ladies."

The girls followed him back into the classroom and stood in front of his desk.

"What was that note all about?" he asked, sitting down and drumming his fingers on the desk like a judge grilling the accused.

Neither of the girls responded.

"I asked you two a question. Would one of you like to answer me?"

Chloe and Gigi exchanged conspiratorial glances.

"I'm sorry about the note," Gigi spoke up, sounding dramatically sincere. "Chloe and I shouldn't have been goofing off in class. It's just that –"

"It's just that what?" Gottlieb interrupted, stroking his chin, as if trying to determine whether Gigi was going to reveal evidence of his alleged affair with Sister Maureen.

"Maybe I shouldn't say anything," Gigi said.

Chloe surmised from Gigi's coy tone that she was baiting the teacher and was about to deliver a load of bullshit that just might save their hides.

"What are you getting at, young lady?"

"Well," Gigi said slowly with a sideward glance that Chloe interpreted as a cue to keep her mouth shut and let Gigi talk them out of this mess, "Chloe and I overheard Sister Maureen telling another nun that she has a crush on you, being that you're an older, sophisticated man who's so knowledgeable and worldly and good at what he does."

"I see," Gottlieb said, his expression brightening as he continued stroking his chin.

Chloe stared in wide-eyed awe at Gigi, amazed at her friend's audacity and inventiveness.

"We just assumed the two of you were... you know, seeing each other," Gigi said, looking down at the floor like the naïve, innocent and contrite pupil she most certainly was not. "We were wrong for making assumptions. We deserve to be punished."

Chloe reached behind Gigi and pinched her on the back of her leg, cautioning her not to overdo it.

"Look, girls, I'll give you a break this time," Gottlieb said, standing as the bell announced the next class period. "You were just going off what you overheard an adult say. If I let you go, you must promise never to repeat what you heard Sister Maureen say."

"Oh, absolutely. Our lips are sealed. Right, Chloe?" Gigi looked at her, and Chloe noticed the familiar gleam in her eye.

"Right," Chloe replied, knowing her friend was going to get the rumor mill going about Gottlieb and Sister Maureen as soon as she stepped foot out of his classroom.

"You're both excused. You may go to your next class," Gottlieb said, as though he really were a judge letting two petty criminals go with a warning.

"Yes, sir," the girls said in unison. They gathered their books and left the room.

"You dirty little liar, you," Chloe said as they maneuvered through the crowded hallway. "Now Gottlieb is going to think Sister Maureen has the hots for him. I talked to her about it this morning and she laughed at the idea."

Chloe hoped Gigi's lie wouldn't prompt Gottlieb to make a move on Sister Maureen during one of their secret work sessions. Having gotten to know Sister Maureen a little, however, Chloe had the sense that the novice could handle herself – rebuffing Gottlieb's advances without hurting his feelings.

"Of course Sister Maureen is going to lie about having a thing for Gottlieb. She doesn't want anyone to know she wants to have one last bang before she commits herself all the way to God," Gigi reasoned. "And anyway, all that matters is that I saved our asses."

Chloe shook her head and laughed as they reached their next class.

"I've heard a lot of good things about this place," Maxine said when she and Jacques arrived at Alain's, the restaurant he'd suggested for their lunch appointment. She refused to refer to the outing as a "date."

"The food here is great. I'm friends with the chef," Jacques said, opening the door for Maxine and ushering her into the restaurant.

"Would you like your usual table, M'sieu Chevalier?" the maitre d' said as they entered.

"No. Something closer to the front this time. A man doesn't invite a lovely lady to lunch, only to hide her away in the back."

Jacques offered his arm to Maxine as the maitre d' led them to their table. She noted the inviting ambiance. Rather than one of Paris' trendy, touristy restaurants, the establishment – named after its well-known chef – was an intimate bistro tucked in an out-of-the-way corner of the Montmatre district. Diners chatted in undertones while a violinist played soft music.

"How about this?" the maitre d' said, approaching a table near the front window overlooking the quiet avenue outside.

"Maxine?" Jacques said, turning to her.

She liked how he sought her consent on the selection of the table, characteristic of the gentlemanly way he'd conducted himself throughout the renovation.

"This is a nice view," she said, nodding thanks to the maitre d' as he pulled out her chair.

"You look especially beautiful in this light," Jacques said once they were seated. He reached across the table, took her hand and kissed it.

She shuddered at the feel of his lips on her skin and immediately steered the conversation toward business matters. "I'll send my painter over to your house to do the touchups in the morning."

"Do you ever stop talking about work?" His eyes twinkled in the afternoon sun streaming in through the window.

Maxine shrugged. "It's my life," she admitted. "Especially since my daughter's away at boarding school."

"What's your daughter's name?"

"Chloe. She's a sophomore at Our Lady of Chastity in London." Maxine reached into her purse and produced a wallet-size snapshot.

Jacques tilted the photo toward the afternoon sunlight. "I see exceptional beauty runs in the family."

Maxine looked down modestly and took a long sip from her water glass. "*Merci*."

"I was an only child and always dreamed of a house full of children, which is why I was hosting the fundraiser for the orphanage the night we met. I guess you could say it's a cause close to my heart, since Marguerite and I were never able to have children of our own." He trailed off, staring past Maxine as if deep in thought.

The silence was broken when a stocky man with curly, brown hair and wearing a chef's uniform approached the table.

"M'sieu Chevalier, always good to see you. I see Eugène seated you at a different table. I hope it's to your liking." The man, his cheeks flushed as if he'd been laboring over a hot stove, jubilantly shook Jacques' hand. "I don't believe I've had the honor of meeting your beautiful companion."

The man turned to Maxine, and she recognized him as the proprietor of the restaurant. Known as the Parisian Emeril Lagasse, Alain Bisson was an international celebrity whose recipes graced best-selling cookbooks. His reservation-only establishment was frequented by movie stars and diplomats.

Jacques made the introduction and Alain kissed Maxine's hand in that gentlemanly yet flirtatious way that she recognized as the custom of Frenchmen. He gestured for the maitre d', who soon appeared at the table and presented Maxine with a long-stemmed red rose.

"Thank you, it's lovely," Maxine said, taking in the scent.

"Ah, but not as lovely as you, Madame." Alain punctuated the statement with a wink.

Jacques cleared his throat. "Don't you think it's time to for you to get back to work, M'sieu Bisson?" he said in a lighthearted tone.

The chef affected a wounded expression, like an innocent man accused of wrongdoing. "I'm just making my guests feel welcome."

Jacques lowered his menu and gave Maxine an amused look as if to say, "Yeah, right," as the chef ticked off the lunch specials.

"May I recommend the smoked quail with Ligonberry vinaigrette? *C'est magnifique.*" The chef rubbed his hands together, as if about to tackle a particularly succulent recipe.

Maxine closed her menu. "Sounds delicious."

"The lady has spoken," Alain declared, slapping his hands together. "I'll personally prepare your meal with tender loving care." He winked at Maxine once more before taking their menus and leaving the table.

"He's a character," Jacques said with a chuckle when the chef had returned to the kitchen.

Maxine nodded, smiling. "He's something else."

The chef must have made good on his promise, Maxine noted, because the quail was so tender it could be cut without a knife. Jacques selected a merlot, and while she normally didn't drink during business hours, such expertly-prepared French cuisine seemed to go naturally with wine.

The conversation was as stimulating as the meal, and she and Jacques shared more about their backgrounds over lunch. Maxine was impressed to hear that, like herself, Jacques was a self-made entrepreneur, having grown up poor in the small fishing village of Callelongue, on the outskirts of Marseilles.

"My father was a fisherman, so I guess the sea is in my blood," Jacques said, sawing a piece of meat. "I joined the navy right out of high school, which is where I got the idea to start the shipping business. After I got out of the service, I worked double shifts as a longshoreman to save money to get the business up and running."

Maxine sipped her wine. "Seems like your hard work has paid off."

"I didn't feel like I'd made it until I was able to retire my mother," he said. "When I was growing up, she cooked and cleaned for other families to help make ends meet. After my father passed away, I bought a little villa for *Maman* in St.-Tropez." He looked into Maxine's eyes. "It's a gorgeous area. I have a yacht and a little cabin down there. We should take a long weekend down there some time."

Maxine didn't immediately reply. She was enjoying his company, but she didn't want to move too fast.

She started to tell Jacques as much, but was interrupted when the restaurant's violinist approached the table. Jacques whispered something in the man's ear while slipping a bill in his hand.

"*Oui*, M'sieu." The violinist nodded at Jacques, smiled at Maxine and began playing "*La vie en rose.*"

Jacques extended his hand. "Would you like to dance?"

Maxine looked around, as if he were speaking to someone else. "Now? It's the middle of the day. I'm sorry, but I really don't dance, not anymore."

Jacques looked intrigued. "*Anymore?*"

"I used to be a dancer. But it was years ago, before my daughter was born."

Jacques raised an eyebrow. "Oh? It seems there are many things I have yet to discover about you, Mademoiselle Bareaux. Tell me more."

Maxine took another sip of wine. "I grew up idolizing amazing performers like Josephine Baker and Josephine Premice, and I knew they got their start dancing in Paris. I left home at eighteen to come to Paris and dance at the Moulin Rouge. It was a dream of mine, but I stopped dancing after I had Chloe. I try to stay in shape, but I haven't danced in years."

"Well I certainly can't let your talents go to waste."

Before she could protest further, Jacques led her to the restaurant's small dance floor. He pressed his body against hers and they rocked in time to the music. She took in his musky scent and allowed him to cradle her in his strong arms. She rationalized that she was burning off calories from the delicious, rich meal.

"I had a lot of fun," Maxine said when the waiter brought the check, which Jacques immediately seized.

"I'd like to see you again," he said, reaching across the table and taking her hand.

She resisted the urge to pull away, to retreat into the cocoon of nonstop work and solitude she'd built around herself.

A faint smile crossed her lips. "I'd like that."

9

Chloe stood next to the bleachers in Our Lady of Chastity's gym, watching her classmates dance with boys from St. Thomas in the center of the room where Sister Francesca normally demonstrated basketball free throws and volleyball serves. Chloe sipped her punch as a DJ spun the next tune, a frothy dance-pop number she'd seen performed by a teen singer on the British musical variety show *Top of the Pops.* It was strange seeing her peers out of uniform, as the spring mixer with St. Thomas was the only time students were allowed to wear street clothes.

"I haven't seen you dance one time tonight," Gigi said, sidling up to Chloe and handing her a napkin full of butter cookies that matched the small mountain in her own hand. "This mixer is the last chance we have to get to know the boys from St. Thomas before we head home for Easter break."

"I haven't seen you out on the floor, either," Chloe said, chomping into a cookie. "Every time a guy asks you to dance, you always say no."

"I'm saving myself for Jeremy."

"Who?" Chloe said, sensing Gigi was about to tell her all about her latest crush.

"Jeremy Dutton. He's only the cutest, most popular boy at St. Thomas," Gigi said, as if she were referring to a celebrity Chloe should have known about.

Gigi gestured across the room to a pack of boys who were clustered around a tall boy who commanded their attention like the head of a military unit. Chloe eyed the boy, whose cherub-like face was framed by Pre-Raphaelite blond curls. He had the athletic body of a rugby player, topped off by a noticeable bulge in his too-tight jeans.

"What's so hot about him?" Chloe said, unimpressed. Even from across the room, Chloe could tell the guy had a stuck-on-himself attitude.

"For one thing, his dad is Britain's ambassador to France," Gigi said, flashing Jeremy an adoring smile, "so he speaks French and we have a lot in common."

"How do you know that?" Chloe asked.

"Being an office helper has its perks," Gigi replied with an up-to-no-good smile. "When I delivered the flyers for the mixer to St. Thomas, I got to take a look around and check out the goods."

Chloe laughed. "Our moms pack us off to an all-girls boarding school, and you still find a way to scope out the opposite sex."

Gigi continued to smile flirtatiously at Jeremy and he seemed to catch sight of her, wrapping up some lame joke he was telling and ignoring the fawning laughter of the boys who surrounded him. He made eye contact with Gigi and began moving across the room toward where the girls stood, the pack of boys trailing him like ants following a leader hauling a giant breadcrumb.

"You wanna dance?" Jeremy said, not bothering to offer a greeting.

"Sure," Gigi replied in a seductive tone, her body language screaming, "I'm available."

"Here," Jeremy said, handing the cup of punch he was holding to one of the other boys, like a high-ranking general passing off an empty gun clip to a lackey.

"Will you hold this, *si'l vous plait*?" Gigi said, handing her cookies to Chloe and grinning in triumph.

As Gigi and Jeremy headed to the dance floor, the pack of boys dispersed, except for the one holding Jeremy's cup.

"Would you, uh, like to dance?" the boy stammered, throwing a shy glance in Chloe's direction.

"Uh, no thanks, not right now."

She felt sorry for the boy, watching him retreat to join the others. It was silly, Chloe knew, but she was still nursing her wounds from seeing François, the boy she liked at the Lycée, with another girl at the movies over the summer. She wasn't ready to deal with the opposite sex, even if it was just for a dance.

"You've been standing here all evening, dear. Don't you want to go out and dance with your friends?" Sister Maureen said, approaching Chloe.

"Oh, I'm fine," Chloe said, smiling at the librarian she'd come to know and like in the past few months.

"I guess dancing with the St. Thomas boys wouldn't be that much fun, anyway," Sister Maureen added, "with Mother Superior on patrol."

Chloe shared a laugh with Sister Maureen as they watched the headmistress traversing the dance floor, making sure boys and girls stayed an appropriate distance apart and chastising the random Our Lady student who was bold enough to wear a dress or skirt that was too tight or too short.

"It must be a drag being a chaperone and having to baby-sit all of us," Chloe said to Sister Maureen.

"It's not so bad. The music's pretty good. I made sure of that by getting Mother Superior's permission to hire a really good DJ."

Watching Sister Maureen snapping her fingers to upbeat tune that was playing, Chloe remembered that the novice was barely a decade older than the academy girls.

"You should get out there and dance," Chloe said as Sister Maureen swayed to the beat.

"Oh, no, that wouldn't be proper," Sister Maureen said, straightening up as Mother Superior shot the young nun one of her chastening looks. "Besides," Sister Maureen added with a wink at Chloe, "Mr. Gottlieb asked me to dance, but I didn't want to encourage him."

Chloe looked over at Gottlieb, who was standing by the punch bowl with his arms crossed, looking as out of place among these gyrating adolescents as a weed in a well-tended sunflower garden.

"Your friend, Gigi, certainly seems to be having a good time with that St. Thomas boy," Sister Maureen said, motioning toward the dance floor.

"Yeah," Chloe said, watching Gigi moving in time with Jeremy. Chloe noticed Jeremy kept looking down at Gigi's jiggling breasts as they danced.

When the tempo slowed down, Jeremy pulled Gigi close. There was something about the way he touched her, as if he were handling an object that belonged to him, that Chloe found unsettling. Gigi, however, was obviously enjoying clinging to Jeremy, until Mother Superior stalked over and pulled them apart, warning them that such contact was forbidden.

"That St. Thomas boy should have known better than to try to get away with dancing so close," Sister Maureen commented. "He could have gotten Gigi in big trouble with Mother Superior if they'd gotten any closer."

"Yeah," Chloe said, still watching Gigi and Jeremy warily, "but I guess she can handle herself."

Simone and Maxine stretched in front of the mirrored walls in a dance studio near the headquarters of Chez Maxine.

"I can't believe I let you talk me into taking this class," Simone said as women of different shapes and sizes filed in. "I thought you gave up dancing when you had Chloe."

The instructor, a tall brunette in a French braid and a pink and purple, striped leotard, took her place at the front of the class, turned on up-tempo music and began leading the class through warm-up exercises.

"Jacques has me dancing again," Maxine admitted, following the instructor's lead.

"You mean he has *us* dancing," Simone gasped, already struggling to keep up. Sweat beaded her forehead, dampening the ridiculous neon headband that matched her new gym outfit. "How many nights have you been out with him this week?"

Maxine suppressed a smile, bending at the waist and touching her toes. "A couple of times. He took me to the ballet last night."

Simone huffed as the instructor picked up the pace and demonstrated a high-stepping routine worthy of those Moulin Rouge girls with whom Maxine once shared a kick line. "It's getting pretty serious between you two. Have you told Chloe about the new man in your life?"

Maxine had been putting off telling her daughter about Jacques. For the longest time, it had been just the two of them and she didn't know how Chloe would react to having to share her mother with a strange man.

"I'm going to introduce her to Jacques when she and Gigi come home for Easter break next week." Maxine twirled, nearly knocking over the top-heavy, less-coordinated Simone.

Simone retreated to a corner and took a swig from her water bottle. "*Mon Dieu!* I'm out of breath already."

Maxine continued moving, not missing a step. "How many times have I told you to stop smoking those Gauloises? We're not as young as we used to be."

The instructor came over and prodded Simone to rejoin the class, as if chastising a preschooler who needed to be shown how to play nice with other children.

"I think Chloe will take to Jacques." Simone swung her arms and frenetically moved her feet, imitating Maxine and the women surrounding them. "I wish I could find someone nice like him."

"What about Pascal?"

"We're on again, off again. You're lucky to have someone stable and financially secure like Jacques. The girls need a father figure."

Maxine gave Simone a wary look. "Father figure? Who said anything about that? Jacques and I are taking it one step at a time. Let's not get ahead of ourselves."

Simone panted, trying to keep up with Maxine. "Yeah, that's easy for you to say."

Chloe lay surrounded by books and papers on the bed in Gigi's room in Paris, thumbing through a chemistry book.

"What the hell are you doing?" Gigi said from her position on the floor, doodling on her ever-present sketchpad.

"Studying." Chloe scribbled a particularly troubling formula in her notebook. "You know we have mid-terms when we get back to school next week."

Gigi put down her charcoal, reached up and closed Chloe's book. "It's spring break. We're supposed to be on vacation."

"Maybe if you studied more and partied less, you wouldn't have had to hide your last report card from Simone."

Gigi sat up. "Speaking of partying, we got invited to one this weekend."

Chloe opened her book again. "Really? Who's throwing it?" she said, not trying to disguise her lack of interest. She just wanted to finish her assignments and relax for the rest of vacation.

"Jeremy, that boy from St. Thomas I danced with at the mixer. His parents have a house here in Paris, but they're going to be at their vacation house in the Riviera this weekend. Since he's going to have the Paris house to himself, he's throwing a big spring-break party."

Chloe tossed her hair. "I don't know, Gi'. My mom keeps bugging me about going out to dinner with her this weekend. She keeps saying there's someone important she wants me to meet, but she won't tell me who it is." She picked at a hangnail. "I bet it's some new client she's trying to win over. I hate when she drags me along on her business appointments."

"Why don't you just tell her you have other plans?"

"Yeah, like that would go over. All Mother would say is that I'm underage and as far as she's concerned, she'll decide what my plans are."

Gigi gripped Chloe's arm in a pleading gesture. "Come on, Chlo'. It'll be a lot of fun." Gigi paused, grinned and added, "And François will be there."

Chloe stiffened, overcome with a mixture of excitement and wistfulness, remembering her first crush and the pain of seeing him with that blond girl last summer. "How do you know he'll be there?"

"'Cause I called Gaston and invited him and told him to spread the word to some of our old friends from the Lycée, including François."

Chloe stared at Gigi incredulously. "You invited your 'Paris boyfriend' to the party being thrown by some boy you met in London?"

"Yeah, if things don't work out with one, I've got a backup," Gigi said, as if the explanation were perfectly logical.

"I don't want to see François. Don't you remember he was with some other girl when we were at the movies last summer?"

"Who cares about that blond bitch? This is your chance to win him back. I mean, with us away nine months of the year, when are you ever going to get to see him again?"

Chloe twirled a strand of hair, mulling Gigi's argument. "Let me think about it."

Gigi got up and picked up the phone next to her bed. "We're going. Call your mother and ask her if you can stay over here this weekend."

Chloe stared at the receiver like it was an alien life form. "What am I supposed to tell her?"

"Tell her that this is your last chance to have fun before they ship us back to that women's prison. Lay on the guilt. It works every time."

Maxine looked up from the bridal gown sketches splayed across her desk when her assistant, Henri, tapped on the door.

"Your daughter's on Line One," announced Henri, standing in the doorway in his head-to-toe, Paris-chic black uniform.

"Could you tell her I'll call her back later? Mademoiselle Thibault is coming in with her mother and wedding planner this afternoon to get fitted for her gown and I'm in the middle of going over the sketches."

"Chloe said it was important," Henri said, holding the door ajar, letting in the noise generated by Maxine's team of young designers going about their work in the studio behind him.

Maxine sighed and picked up the phone. "Okay, I'll take it. Thanks, Henri."

Maxine took off her earring and cradled the receiver between her ear and shoulder, waiting on her assistant to transfer the call. Chloe usually didn't call Maxine at work unless it was something pressing.

"What's up?" Maxine said when Chloe came on the line.

"Can I stay over Gigi and Simone's this weekend?"

"What? I've already made reservations for dinner on Saturday."

Chloe took on the whiny tone Maxine recognized from the occasions when her daughter asked her for something out of the ordinary. "But Mother, there's a party this weekend with some of our friends from the Lycée, people we never get to see anymore since you and Simone sent us away."

Pangs of guilt stabbed at Maxine like pins pricking one of her handmade dress patterns. The words "you sent us away" resounded in her mind. Chloe was going for the jugular.

"You know there's someone very important I want you to meet at dinner Saturday night," Maxine pressed.

"Can't I meet whoever it is when I come home for summer break? This is the only chance I have to see my friends before I go back to school."

Maxine didn't respond right away, trying to decide if she should indulge her daughter or assert her parental authority.

"We haven't really had a chance to spend any time together since you've been home. I've been so busy with work, as usual, and I was looking forward to this weekend."

"I'll be back on Sunday," Chloe reasoned.

"But we'll barely have any time before I have to take you to the airport."

"Forget it," Chloe huffed. "I'll just tell Gigi I can't make the party."

Maxine read the disappointment in Chloe's voice and finally gave in. "Okay, you can stay over and go to the party." Reasserting her parental authority, she added, "But only if you come home and straighten up your room before you go."

Chloe cheered and Maxine heard Gigi clapping in the background. She concluded the call by telling Chloe she loved her, then immediately dialed Jacques at work.

"I have some bad news," she told him. "I let Chloe talk her way out of dinner on Saturday. There's a party with some of her friends that night, so it looks like I won't be able to introduce you to her this weekend, after all."

Jacques was characteristically understanding. "She's at that age. It's okay," he said, speaking over the sounds of his company's loading dock in the background. "I'll have plenty of time to meet her this summer."

Maxine massaged a crick in her neck. "Sorry to blow our plans for the weekend."

"Just because your daughter has other plans, that doesn't mean we can't still get together. Why don't we go away for the weekend? St.-Tropez is beautiful this time of year. We can go for a sail on my yacht and I can introduce you to the most important person in *my* life – my mother."

Maxine stared out her office window, trying to decide how to respond. Things were progressing quickly with Jacques, and although she had developed feelings for him, her natural instinct was to put on the brakes.

"Can I let you know?" she said finally. "I really need to get caught up on paperwork."

"Take all the time you need, *amour*."

Maxine hung up and continued to stare out the window. She started when the door swung open.

Simone entered, her arms loaded with papers, which she proceeded to dump on Maxine's desk. "I need you to sign off on these." She leaned forward, steadying her hands on the desk. "What's with you? I've only seen that faraway look in your eyes a few times before."

Maxine waved away Simone's concern. "Chloe called and cancelled on dinner with Jacques. I said she could stay over your place and go to that party Saturday night with Gigi – against my better judgment."

"Gigi's been harassing me about that party ever since she got home. I figured she'd want Chloe to tag along."

"Jacques was totally understanding when I called and gave him the news." She began flipping through the papers Simone placed on her desk. "He invited me to go away with him to St.-Tropez this weekend."

Simone looked confused. "And the problem with that is? If a rich, handsome man wanted to sweep me away to St.-Tropez for the weekend, I'd be out the door before you saw the back of my head."

"Things are just moving so fast," Maxine said, reclining in her chair. "I'm not sure if going away with him is the right thing to do, especially with Chloe home from school."

Simone settled into a chair in front of the desk. "Maxine, you've got to accept the fact that Chloe and Gigi are growing up. They're not children and they don't need us anymore, not the way they did when they were little. They have their own friends and their own lives. And we've got to live ours."

Maxine nodded, conceding Simone's point. "Still, I don't want to rush things with Jacques. I told him I'd let him know about this weekend."

Simone stood and picked up the telephone receiver. "You're going to call that man right now and tell him to come pick you up." She pointed the phone in Maxine's direction. "If you don't, I'm going to do it for you."

Maxine hesitated, then took the receiver.

10

Maxine clutched Jacques' hand as they peered out the windows of the private plane he'd chartered. "Oh, Jacques, it's lovely."

The flight into St.-Tropez gave a breathtaking bird's-eye view of the popular Mediterranean resort in the French Riviera. With its sun-drenched beaches and verdant hills, Maxine could understand why the famous writer Colette once praised the picturesque fishing village as "the town one never wants to leave."

Jacques' leased chalet had a prime view of the marina where his yacht was docked. Sheets covered the furniture and wall hangings in the front room and Maxine sneezed from the dust that indicated Jacques hadn't been here since last summer.

"This place has a lot of potential," Maxine said, setting her suitcase down when Jacques opened the door to the small stucco structure. She walked to the center of the front room and rotated, holding her hands out as if she were a movie director envisioning a scene. "I'd redo this room in pastels and ship in handmade furniture from Italy, a tapestry from Spain. I could redecorate this entire house in three weeks – a month, tops."

"Now, Mademoiselle Bareaux, there'll be no talk about work," Jacques said, taking her suitcase. "We're here to relax."

"Relax? I think I forgot how to do that," Maxine said, laughing.

"I'll be happy to refresh your memory." Jacques moved close and kissed her.

"That was nice," she said, wrapping her arms and his neck and savoring the kiss. "I could get used to that."

Jacques grinned mischievously, running his forefingers along Maxine's arms. "That was just a preview of what's to come later this evening."

She affected a coy tone. "Why, M'sieu Chevalier, you know I'm a lady. You promised we'd have separate rooms."

"Okay, come on," Jacques said with exaggerated disappointment, pulling away. "I'll show you to the guest room." He led Maxine to the stairs and began lugging her suitcase up the steps with great effort. "God, woman, what have you got in here, rocks?"

"How do I look in this?" Gigi said to Chloe as they tried on clothes in the dressing room at Reciproque, the funky thrift shop that was the last stop on the girls' Saturday afternoon shopping spree.

"You look great, Gi', but of course you looked great in the thirteen other outfits you tried on," Chloe said, standing behind Gigi in the mirror. The low-cut blouse Gigi wore showed off her womanly cleavage, paired with tight jeans that accentuated her full, round derriere – assets Chloe had not yet developed.

"Will you just pick something already so we can go?" Chloe added with a sigh.

"I'm not tall and thin like you," Gigi said, tugging at her jeans as if to emphasize the difficulty she had wedging herself into them. "I could never pull off that outfit you're wearing."

Chloe adjusted the belt on the jeans she'd matched with an asymmetrical top, the first outfit she'd tried on and the one she'd decided on while Gigi struggled to make up her mind.

"But you have curves and I don't," Chloe said, realizing they admired in each other what was lacking in themselves. "You look amazing in that outfit. Why don't you just go with that?"

"I can't rush this. I have to look my best," Gigi said, looking herself over in the mirror like a doctor examining a patient's suspicious skin discoloration. "I know there's going to be a lot of other girls at the party, and I want to keep Jeremy's attention."

Chloe crossed her eyes. "I'm going to hurl if I hear that name one more time," she said, hoisting an armload of the garments Gigi had discarded on the floor and beginning to place them back on their hangers. "Why are you acting like this guy is the king of England or something?"

"His dad *is* England's ambassador to France, remember? He's someone important – not to mention the cutest boy at St. Thomas."

Chloe shook her head at Gigi's reflection. Why did Gigi always have to go for the boy from a rich family or the best athlete? It was as if winning the affection of "someone important," as she put it, was validation that she mattered.

"I don't get it, Gi'," Chloe said, running her hands over a plush cashmere sweater Gigi had cast aside like an outdated magazine. "Gaston really likes you. Why not just hang out with him while we're home on break?"

"I *am* going to hang out with him. He'll be at the party tonight."

"I know, and I still don't get why you invited him."

Gigi turned to look at Chloe directly. "Because when Jeremy sees that another boy is interested in me, I'll have him right where I want him," Gigi said, her eyes flashing with mischief. "Boys are competitive by nature, especially two jocks like Jeremy and Gaston. What could be better than having two guys fighting over me?"

Chloe tsked and continued to hang up clothes, placing them neatly on the hook on the back of the dressing room door. "You've got two boys fighting over you, but I'd be satisfied just to be with François."

Chloe shuddered, anticipating running into her longtime crush at the party.

What if he was with that other girl she'd seen him with at the movies last summer?

"Girl, you've got a lot to learn about how to make men want you," Gigi said, turning to look at herself in the mirror again and sounding like an older, experienced woman, rather than Chloe's peer. "Speaking of which, I don't think this outfit is the right one, after all."

"You've got to be kidding me, Gi'. I don't want to be here all day."

"Give me this," Gigi said, plucking the cashmere sweater from the pile Chloe was in the process of hanging up.

"You already tried that on, remember?"

Gigi ignored Chloe, pulled off the blouse she had on and slinked into the sweater. She peeled off her jeans, extracted a black leather mini skirt from Chloe's arms and stepped into it.

"This is it. I'll have Jeremy *and* Gaston panting after me when they see me in this."

"That sweater makes your boobs look big."

"*Exactement*, my dear," Gigi said, sticking her chest out and grinning at herself in the mirror.

"I still don't get why you're going to all this trouble to try to snag Jeremy," Chloe said, picking up the blouse Gigi had thrown on the floor and hanging it up.

"I love a challenge, you know that. I'm going to make him love me."

Chloe took the garments off the back of the door and left the dressing room to return them to the rack. She was through trying to talk sense into Gigi. When Gigi got it in her head to try to get the attention of some boy, there was no reasoning with her. Having Gaston was not enough. Once Gigi won over a boy, she grew bored and moved on to the next conquest. No matter how much male attention Gigi got, it was as if there was some deep, dark hole inside of her that could never be filled.

Maxine surveyed the narrow streets lined with quaint villas as Jacques drove their rented car up a winding hill.

"We're here." He stopped in front of a white stucco carriage house that was surrounded by a picket fence and put the car in park.

Maxine took out her compact and made last-minute adjustments to her hair and makeup. "I have to admit, I'm kind of nervous about meeting your mother. I hope she likes me."

Jacques placed his hand over hers. "She's going to love you." He leaned over and kissed her.

"I hope you're right," Maxine said, opening the car door and getting out.

Jacques helped her out of the car. "I know you and *Maman* are going to hit it off," he said, closing the car door.

Maxine steadied herself on her high heels, which she now regretted wearing, and followed Jacques through the gate. She took note of the flowerboxes blooming with bougainvillea and the well-manicured lawn. This was obviously the residence of someone who took pride in her home.

Claudette Chevalier greeted them at the door, looking spring-crisp in a white blouse, tan slacks and a teal sweater slung around her shoulders. Her shoulder-length black hair, graying at the temples, was pulled back and clipped into a ponytail with an oversize barrette. Though wearing full makeup, Claudette had delicate features that had been only slightly ravaged by time – faint lines above her lips and around her sea-green eyes. Jacques' mother was a well-preserved beauty and Maxine immediately noticed the resemblance with her handsome son.

Maxine nearly quaked in her heels as Jacques exchanged hugs and affectionate greetings in French with his mother. Maxine hadn't been this nervous to meet someone's mother since her first boyfriend in high school. She hoped Claudette could see that her feelings for her son were genuine, that Maxine was self-sufficient and wasn't out to get her hands on Jacques' bank account or take the place of his late wife.

"*Maman*, this is Maxine," Jacques said, putting his arm around Maxine's waist as he made the introduction.

"*Enchanté.*" Maxine smiled at the older woman, who regarded her with a polite yet guarded expression. Maxine recognized the protective maternal instinct, the same instinct that kicked in whenever a stranger came around Chloe.

"I've heard so much about you. Won't you come in?" Claudette offered her hand. "I'm making lunch."

Maxine took in the well-coordinated yet homey surroundings. Following Jacques and his mother through the front room, she took note of the overstuffed chairs and sofas and tables bearing knickknacks and family photos. When they reached the airy kitchen, Maxine sat on a stool next to Jacques at a breakfast bar as Claudette finished up the lunch preparations.

Maxine felt something furry tickling her ankles and looked down to see a fluffy white Bichon Frisé snuggling up to her.

"He's adorable," Maxine cooed, scooping up the small dog. "What's his name?"

"It's a *she*," Claudette replied, a bit curtly, with a scolding glance that Maxine interpreted as a warning not to let the dog in the kitchen. "That's Coco."

"She's a spoiled brat, aren't you?" Jacques tickled the dog, who sprawled in Maxine's arms as if relishing the attention.

"She always begs for scraps when I'm cooking." Claudette tossed a piece of shrimp on the floor. "Here, Coco. Go play."

The dog leapt from Maxine's arms and devoured the scrap. Suddenly, as if distracted by a noise, the dog took off running through an open patio door and galloped through the backyard.

"Jacques, go fetch her, *si'l vous plait*," Claudette said, wiping her hands on her apron. "She's so bad, running off like that."

Jacques obeyed his mother and Maxine fought off panic, being alone with Claudette and not knowing what to say.

"Can I help you with something?" Maxine rose and stood next to the older woman at the kitchen island.

"Why don't you cut these cucumbers for the salad?"

Claudette handed Maxine a bag of vegetables and Maxine picked up a knife and began chopping.

"Be sure to wash them first," Claudette said, as if speaking to a child who needed instruction in the simplest task.

"Oh, right," Maxine said, going to the sink. With her demanding work schedule, Maxine normally ate on the go and often had dinner delivered now that Chloe was away at school. It had been months since she had prepared a meal from scratch.

Upon returning to the island, Maxine observed Claudette at work, the way she handled food like an experienced chef. Maxine surmised the older woman had cooked and cleaned her whole life, and she remembered Jacques saying his mother had worked as a housekeeper to supplement his father's meager fisherman's income. Though her nails were painted a ladylike shade of red and decorated with several rings – including a weathered wedding band despite the fact that Jacques' father had been dead for years – Claudette's hands were slightly swollen and covered with age spots. Hers were not the hands of a pampered St.-Tropez widow, but those of a lifelong working woman. Claudette's hands reminded Maxine of her own mother, who had worked as a domestic after her voice began to fail and her singing career faltered.

Claudette placed a copper pan on the stove. "I'll let that simmer for awhile," she said, adjusting the heat.

Maxine gazed out the kitchen window. "Coco must have run pretty far."

Claudette nodded, taking off her apron and wiping her hands on a dishtowel. "Jacques was right when he said she's spoiled. She's like my second child."

"Does Jacques get down to see you often?"

"When he can. He's always off on some adventure. He loves that boat of his. He takes after his father." Claudette plopped the dishtowel on the counter. "Let me show you something."

Maxine followed Claudette to the cozy sitting room at the front of the house. Maxine studied a framed black-and-white photo of a young Claudette, her hair as black as it was today and flowing over her shoulders, hugging a youthful Jacques in a schoolboy uniform.

Maxine touched the gilded frame. "You were so beautiful." She quickly corrected herself. "I mean, you still are. I can see your features in Jacques' face. He was such a cute little boy."

"This is his father, Laurent." Claudette stood next to a small glass table, holding a photo of a dashing man with dark, wavy hair in a military uniform. "He was in the Foreign Legion. He fought in World War II."

Maxine moved closer to Claudette. "He was very handsome. Jacques has his eyes."

"We were married for fifty-one years. He was the love of my life," the older woman said wistfully, staring down at the photo. "Jacques reminds me so much of him."

"Found her."

The women turned to see Jacques cradling the dog in his arms.

"She led me on quite a chase, trampling through all the neighbors' yards in search of a squirrel or a chipmunk or some other critter," he said with a laugh as the dog licked her chops with an indifferent expression.

"Why don't you go get cleaned up, son?" Claudette gently returned the photo to the table. "Maxine, will you help me set the table, *cher*?"

"Sure." Maxine followed Claudette back to the kitchen. She sensed that the older woman had softened toward her during the intimate moment reminiscing about Jacques' father. Though they came from different backgrounds and generations, their love for Jacques was a common denominator.

11

Chloe recognized several former classmates from the Lycée when she and Gigi entered a lavish chateau where teenagers clutching plastic cups and beer bottles congregated in cavernous rooms decorated with priceless art and antiques.

"Gigi! So glad you could make it," said Jeremy, the boy from St. Thomas who was throwing the party, approaching Chloe and Gigi. He hugged Gigi, slapping her on the fanny. "Who's your friend?"

"This is Chloe," Gigi said, nearly shouting over the rock music that boomed from a state-of-the-art stereo system. "Chloe, this is Jeremy."

Chloe shook the boy's hand and scoped the crowd. She saw no sign of François.

"We have a keg," Jeremy said, motioning toward a barrel-like object in the middle of the room that looked as though it contained nuclear waste. He filled a cup with beer, handed it to Gigi and offered one to Chloe.

"No thanks. I'm not thirsty," she said, watching Gigi gulp hers down like lemonade on a hot summer day.

"Make yourselves at home," Jeremy said. "I'm going to go say hi to some people. Be back later."

Gigi had barely finished her drink when Gaston, her "Paris boyfriend" and another former classmate from the Lycée, entered. Chloe noticed François wasn't with him and she felt a mixture of disappointment and relief.

"Thanks for coming," Gigi said, kissing Gaston on the cheek. "Where's François?"

"He'll be here a little later. He had lacrosse practice this afternoon."

"Aren't you on the team, too?" Gigi asked.

Gaston shoved his hands in his pockets, looking sheepish. "Yeah, but I skipped practice because I knew you'd be here."

Gigi touched his cheek. "Aren't you sweet?"

"Excuse me. I don't think we've been properly introduced." Jeremy approached, eyeing Gaston suspiciously, as if sensing he was a competitor for Gigi's affection.

"Jeremy, this is Gaston," Gigi said. "We used to go to school together here in Paris."

Jeremy stepped closer to Gigi and put a protective arm around her shoulder. "Pity, you must not see much of each other anymore, since you're in school in London now."

Gaston narrowed his eyes at Jeremy. "Judging from your accent, it sounds like that's where you're from."

"Yes, and proud of it. I'm a senior at St. Thomas, which is, of course, right down the street from Our Lady of Chastity." Jeremy smirked at Gaston.

Gigi, who seemed to be enjoying the two boys jockeying for her attention, held out her drained cup. "I need more to drink. Would someone mind getting me a refill?"

"I'll get it," Jeremy and Gaston said in unison, reaching for the cup at the same time.

"I'm the host. Allow me," Jeremy said, triumphantly taking the cup as if it were the trophy in a grudge match. "Might I suggest something a little stronger than beer? I just cracked open my parents' best bottle of bourbon."

Gigi smiled. "Sounds awesome. While you're getting that, I'm going to go freshen up in the little girls' room. Chloe, you wanna come with?"

"No, I'll wait out here." She wanted to keep an eye out for François. She knew it was silly, but she had continued to think about him all school year and her pulse quickened at the thought of seeing him again – even if he *had* been with another girl the last time she'd seen him.

Chloe found a vacant spot on a white leather sectional and Gaston followed her, sinking to the cushion beside her like a sidelined player in an important lacrosse match. She made small talk with Gaston and got caught up with a couple of old classmates while waiting for Gigi to return.

Nearly half-an-hour later, Gigi was nowhere to be found. Chloe was about to get up and search for her friend when she spotted Gigi being led upstairs by Jeremy. Chloe glanced over at Gaston, who had also seen them, judging by the dejected look on his face.

"I'm going to go get something to drink. Something strong," he said, rising. "You want something?"

Chloe gave him a sympathetic look. "Some punch would be nice."

As Gaston retreated to the kitchen, Chloe looked up and saw François entering. On his arm was the same blond girl she had seen him with last summer at the movies. Chloe got up and darted to find the restroom. She couldn't let him see her. She couldn't face him. She never should have let Gigi talk her into coming here.

Claudette seemed to warm to Maxine even more over a scrumptious lunch of *Sole Meunière* – filet of sole with potatoes and julienne vegetables – which Claudette served on the patio overlooking the Mediterranean. Claudette shared stories from Jacques' childhood and the three laughed heartily at the dog as she stood on her hind legs, rolled over and did other tricks to be rewarded with table scraps.

"Coco is my baby," Claudette said, taking the pooch into her lap after serving dessert and coffee. "Or, should I say, my *other* baby." She reached out and clasped Jacques' hand.

Jacques' cheeks colored. "You're embarrassing me, *Maman*. I'm a grown man."

"You'll always be my baby." Claudette patted his hand. "A mother never lets go of her child."

Maxine nodded in agreement. "I know what you mean. I have a teenage daughter, Chloe, and it seems like she's growing up so fast."

"Do you have a photo?" Claudette asked.

Maxine took out her wallet and displayed Chloe's latest school picture.

"*Comment beau* – how beautiful," Claudette said, admiring the photo. "She takes after you."

Maxine smiled. "*Merci*."

Jacques took Maxine's hand and squeezed it, and Maxine took it as a gesture confirming that his mother had indeed warmed to her.

"We better be getting on if we want to get a sail in this afternoon," Jacques said, glancing at his watch.

"Thanks so much for lunch, Madame Chevalier," Maxine said, rising along with Jacques and Claudette.

"So nice to meet you, *cher*," Claudette said. She placed her hand on Maxine's shoulder. "And, please, call me *Maman*."

In true motherly fashion, Claudette prepared a care package for Jacques and Maxine to take with them in the form of a picnic basket filled with delicious leftovers, wine and cheese. She embraced her son at the front gate, chastising him to visit more often.

"And you're always welcome, too, *cher*," Claudette added, hugging Maxine.

The exchange was interrupted by the dog yelping and pawing at Maxine's legs. Maxine bent to pet her and Coco offered her paw, as if shaking goodbye.

"You're so cute!" Maxine said, petting the dog's head. "I'd love to have a little companion just like you."

"That can be arranged," Jacques said. "*Maman* knows a good breeder."

Claudette lingered at the gate as Jacques loaded the car. "I haven't seen him smiling this much since Marguerite was alive," she said to Maxine. "You're good for my Jacques."

"Thank you," Maxine said, touched. "Thank you, Madame."

Claudette shook her finger in a scolding motion. "Ah-ah, it's *Maman*."

"Thank you, *Maman*. Thanks for everything." Maxine hugged the older woman one last time and got in the car as Jacques opened the door for her. Once they were settled in the car, Jacques pressed the gas pedal and Maxine turned back to Claudette, who stood at the gate waving them on.

Chloe studied her reflection in the bathroom mirror, the sounds of the party muffled by the heavy oak door. She had locked herself in nearly fifteen minutes ago. The humiliation of seeing François with that blond bitch must have been her punishment for canceling out on Mother's dinner plans.

Someone knocked at the door. "Hey, I'm wasted and I think I'm gonna throw up. I need to use it," a slurred male voice said from the other side of the door. "What are you doing in there, moving in?"

The bathroom was the size of a small apartment and, with its hot tub and other amenities, was certainly luxurious enough to live in. But Chloe took one last look at herself in the mirror, splashed cold water on her face and opened the door. The drunken boy immediately ran past her and kneeled at the toilet, making disgusting heaving sounds.

Chloe closed the bathroom door and proceeded down the darkened second-floor hallway. She was determined to find Gigi and get the hell out of here. She didn't care if her friend was trying to score with the boy from St. Thomas or not.

Chloe stopped at the first door she encountered and, seeing light streaming from underneath, knocked lightly. Hearing no response, she knocked once again and waited a few seconds.

"Gigi?" she said, swinging the door open.

She gasped in horror when she saw a couple going at it on the bed, each of them half-naked.

"Do you always barge your way in places?" the unfamiliar girl snapped at Chloe, her legs wrapped around the guy writhing on top of her.

"Sorry. I knocked, but there was no answer." Chloe shielded her eyes from the debauchery unfolding before her and backed out of the room, securely closing the door.

She tried to shake the image of the copulating couple from her head as she proceeded to the next door, which was cracked just enough to hear voices coming from inside the room. Chloe recognized Gigi's unmistakable French accent mingled with Jeremy's British one. She lingered at the door, trying to find the right moment to knock and tell Gigi she was ready to go.

"Let me help you take that off, baby," Chloe heard Jeremy saying.

"I can get it," Gigi said.

Chloe stepped closer to the door and peeked through the crack. Gigi was sitting next to Jeremy on the bed, pulling her sweater over her head. "I think it snagged on my bra."

"Here. I'll get it," Jeremy said, yanking on the sweater and tossing it on the floor.

Chloe stared at the cashmere sweater lying in a heap on the floor – the sweater that had taken Gigi all afternoon to pick out.

Jeremy scooted closer to Gigi and feverishly kissed her neck like a hungry dog mauling raw meat.

Gigi backed away. "Let's take it slow." She laid her head on his shoulder. "Hold me."

Jeremy put his arm around Gigi, and Chloe saw him slip his hand down Gigi's back to unlatch her bra. "I can't wait, baby. I need you now."

"Let's talk," Gigi said, taking his hands.

Jeremy wrenched his hands away. "I didn't come up here to talk."

Gigi looked hurt. "Is that all you think I'm good for, sex?"

"Well, you do have a reputation. Why do you think I brought you here? The word around campus is Gigi Cartier puts out."

Gigi slapped Jeremy and stood up. "Fuck you, you *connard*. Fuck you."

Gigi grabbed her sweater off the floor and struggled back into it. Chloe stepped away from the door and moved quickly through the hallway and down the staircase. As much as she was ready to get out of this place, Chloe wanted to spare Gigi the embarrassment of knowing she had witnessed the ugly scene.

Chloe decided to return to her spot on the living room sectional, but upon entering the room she saw François sitting there with his arm around the blond girl. She turned on her heels in attempt to exit the room as swiftly as possible without him noticing her. This night was turning out to be a disaster.

Before she was all the way out of the room, she heard François call her name. She pretended like she didn't hear him and scrambled to the front door.

"Chloe, is that you?" she heard him calling as she reached the front lawn, where several partygoers stood in clusters drinking and laughing. "Hey, wait up."

Chloe stopped in her tracks, knowing she couldn't outrun him. She kept her back turned while François jogged to catch up with her, hoping she wouldn't lose her composure when she turned and saw his face.

"Hey, Chloe. I thought that was you."

She turned to look at him, and he was as handsome as ever in a clingy polo shirt that showed off his muscles and cargo pants. She inhaled his scent, a mixture of soap and Joop! cologne, and felt her breath quickening. Why did she have to like this boy so much?

"Where are you running off to?" he said, now face to face with her. "I just got here not long ago, and Gaston said you and Gigi were here."

Chloe stared at François, and before she could say anything, the blond girl appeared on the front stoop.

"François, what are you doing out here?" the girl said, her eyes darting over at Chloe, then back to François.

"I'll be back in a minute, Daphné," François said, turning to the girl. "I'm just saying hi to an old friend from school."

Chloe winced, not so much from the chill in the early-April air but from the bland way he had described her. After all these years of pining for him, that's all she was to him, just an "old friend?"

Seemingly satisfied with François' explanation, the girl turned to re-enter the party and was nearly mowed over by Gigi rushing out of the house.

"Come on." Gigi, her face streaked with tears, grabbed Chloe's hand. "We're getting out of here."

"Going so soon?" François said as Gigi dragged Chloe to the front gate.

"It was nice to see you again," Chloe said over her shoulder, smiling forlornly at him. Despite the fact that he was with some other girl, she couldn't just turn off the feelings she harbored for him.

He held up his beer bottle, as if toasting her. "Yeah, it was good seeing you guys. Maybe I'll see you around this summer."

Maxine stood at the bow of *Nathalie*, Jacques' yacht, sipping Dom Perignon while Jacques steered. The evening sunlight cast gold shimmers on the water and a warm breeze rippled through her light, strapless dress.

"Having a good time?" Jacques said, turning the wheel.

"Wonderful." Maxine turned to face him, noticing his weathered sailor's hands that were rougher than the manicured hands of most men who ran companies and did nothing but sit in boardrooms. "It took me a while to get my sea legs, but this is very relaxing. I could get used to this."

"I'm so glad you could join me this weekend. *Maman* was quite taken with you, I could tell."

"She seemed a bit standoffish at first," Maxine noted, "but I think we connected when you were out chasing the dog. She showed me a picture of your father. She seems like a lovely woman and I'm glad we finally hit it off."

Jacques grinned. "Any time Coco takes a liking to someone new, it's always a good sign."

Maxine turned to look out over the water again, enjoying the sea breeze tickling her skin.

"You know, standing there with the wind rippling through your hair and your dress like that, it reminds me of the night we met." Jacques stepped away from the wheel and stood next to Maxine at the railing. "You looked like an angel in that white gown you were wearing, and when I saw you out on the patio looking so beautiful, I made it my business to get to know you."

"Oh, so you had a plan?" Maxine teased.

Jacques gripped the railing and looked out at the sea. "If there's one thing I've learned, it's not to rely on plans when it comes to life. Marguerite and I planned to be together for the rest of our lives…"

Jacques' voice cracked and he fell silent, staring out at the sea, and Maxine touched his hand to comfort him. He put his hand over hers and turned to her.

"Maxine, you have no idea how happy you've made me since you've come into my life. I feel alive again, something I haven't felt since my wife passed away."

Maxine sipped her champagne, not responding right away. Jacques, in his gentle way, had also awakened feelings she'd never thought she'd have for a man again after Chloe's father, but she didn't know how to articulate her thoughts.

To her relief, Jacques continued to talk, and she was happy to listen.

"I've been doing a lot of thinking about us lately." He moved closer. "Maxine, I know it might sound crazy, but I want to spend the rest of my life with you. I've always prided myself on my instincts – it's what's helped me succeed in business – and this feels right."

Maxine held onto the railing for support, feeling lightheaded. She wasn't sure if it was the champagne or the things Jacques was saying. It sounded like he wanted to move their relationship forward – and fast. He was interested in some kind of formal commitment, from everything he'd said, and the thought both excited and scared her. Maxine had been a single mother for most of her adult life, an independent woman capable of taking care of herself and her daughter. She wasn't sure she was ready to give up her self-reliance.

"I know this is a lot to throw at you right now," Jacques said, as if sensing her reticence, "but you're the best thing that's ever happened to me. I'd like for us to be together, really be together."

Maxine set her glass on a nearby tray. "What are you suggesting?" Her breath grew shallow in anticipation of what he would say next.

"Maxine, marry me," he said, taking her hands. "There's this great little chapel that's not too far from my chalet. *Maman* goes to Mass there every Sunday. I know the priest, Père Bertrand, very well and I could call him tonight. We could be married in the morning and be back in Paris in time for you to see your daughter off to school."

Maxine looked away, staring blankly at the water, not knowing how to respond. "Jacques, this is going so fast. I haven't been in a serious relationship since Chloe's father, and we've only been going out a few months. You haven't even had a chance to meet Chloe yet."

Jacques smiled. "If she's anything like you, I know we'll get along great, just like you and *Maman*. I've always wanted children."

Maxine backed up, letting go of his hands. "Jacques, this is just too much too soon." She put her hand to her forehead, overwhelmed. "I need some time to think it over."

Jacques refused to let up. "Come on, what do you say? Marry me. I'll call *Maman* and she'll be thrilled. You're the only woman she's taken a liking to since Marguerite, and you saw how excited she was when you showed her the picture of Chloe. She's always wanted grandchildren. You saw how she babies that dog."

Maxine laughed in spite of herself, recalling the fun they'd had afternoon playing with the dog and talking to Jacques' mother. This weekend had been a nice getaway, but it didn't erase the reservations she had about jumping into such a big commitment.

"I'm sorry, Jacques. I need time."

The wind picked up and a wave rocked the boat. Maxine pitched forward, nearly stumbling in those damn high heels she insisted on wearing, and Jacques caught her.

"See," he said, holding her. "God is trying to tell us something."

12

"This is terrible, Gi'."

Chloe sat at the desk in the girls' dorm room at Our Lady of Chastity, looking over Gigi's end-of-school-year report card. While Chloe had made the honor roll once again, Gigi had barely managed to pass her classes and advance to the eleventh grade. Gigi had never mentioned the encounter with Jeremy at the spring-break party and soon found a replacement for him, and St. Thomas boys continued to be her favorite extracurricular activity. As much as she snuck out of the dorm past curfew, it was no wonder that her grades were suffering.

"The only class I care about is art, and even that's lame sometimes," Gigi said, transferring underwear from her dresser drawer into a suitcase that lay open on her bed, in preparation for the journey back to Paris for the summer. "I'm so sick of studying the so-called 'masters.' If I'm forced to look at another Renaissance painting by an old, dead white guy, I'll vomit." Gigi shut the suitcase with a thud.

"Did you get the summer reading list?"

Gigi, bobbing up and down on the suitcase, groaned. "Are you crazy? I have no intention of cracking open a book during our vacation from this joint. Summer's supposed to be fun." She got up and began struggling to zip the suitcase. "Speaking of which, I want to go shopping as soon we get home. I need some new outfits for the summer. I can't wait to get out of these prissy uniforms."

Chloe got up to finish packing her own suitcase. "Amen to that. I need a new pair of designer jeans."

"Why don't we hit Galeries Lafayette and go to the movies when we get back to Paris?"

"I wish I could." Chloe carefully placed her teddy bear, Mr. Buttons, on top of her clothes inside the suitcase. "But Mother's insisting that I come straight home. She's sending a car to the airport to pick us up and drop you off first. She keeps saying there's something important she has to tell me."

"Why couldn't she just tell you over the phone?"

"That's what I said, but she keeps insisting it's something she has to tell me in person. She's been acting weird ever since Easter break."

Gigi picked up her suitcase and opened the door, leading the way out of the room. "I don't get our mothers sometimes. Don't you wish you had a father to go to when your mom starts bugging out?"

Chloe followed Gigi out of the room, struggling under the weight of her heavy suitcase. "Yeah, I guess," she said, closing the door behind them.

As the car that picked Chloe up from the airport pulled up in front of Chez Maxine, she noticed workers carrying boxes and furniture from the loft apartment above the shop. Some of that stuff looked like hers!

Chloe got out of the car and raced up stairs to the apartment, passing moving men carrying out various items that belonged to her and her mother. Upon reaching the top of the stairs, she was greeted by Maxine.

"Hi, *ma chérie*. How was your flight?" Maxine pecked her on the cheek.

Why was Mother acting like nothing out of the ordinary was happening?

"What's going on?" Chloe demanded.

"Darling, there's something I've been meaning to tell you."

A strange man appeared in the doorway next to Maxine.

"Chloe, this is Jacques." Maxine locked arms with the man. "We got married – a few months ago. We're starting a new life together, and we're moving to his chateau."

Chloe listened in stunned horror as Mother described her whirlwind courtship and subsequent wedding to this man. Granted, he was nice-looking and well-dressed, but with his salt-and-pepper hair, he looked significantly older than Mother.

"When did all this happen?" Chloe asked incredulously.

"Jacques was a client of mine. He hired me to renovate his chateau, and our business relationship evolved into..." Maxine looked at Jacques, who nodded as if encouraging her to continue. "Something more. One thing led to another and we eloped in St.-Tropez, when you were home for Easter break. That last weekend when you stayed over Gigi's, Jacques invited me to go away with him, and it just kind of happened on the spur of the moment. Neither of us planned it that way."

Chloe could not believe what she was hearing. Why hadn't Mother ever mentioned the new man in her life in any of her calls or letters? Why didn't she ever bother to *consult* Chloe about this? No wonder Mother had been acting so strange.

Jacques smiled at Chloe and extended his hand. "*Bonjour*, Chloe, I've heard so many good things about you."

"I wish I could say the same," she said curtly, not returning Jacques' handshake.

Maxine had went out and hog-tied some man without even bothering to inform Chloe. It figured. Typical Mother behavior.

"I can't believe you didn't tell me we're moving," Chloe said to Maxine, setting down her suitcase. "I spent all afternoon packing up my dorm room, and now I have to pack all over again."

"I'm sorry, honey," Maxine said. "I wanted to wait to introduce you to Jacques in person, and it doesn't make sense for you to unpack your school things here. We've outgrown this apartment. Jacques has a beautiful chateau with lots of room for all of us. You're going to love it."

Chloe pouted. "I don't even get a say-so in this?"

"We've already made all the arrangements," Maxine said firmly. "I've leased the apartment to another tenant. We have to be out of here today."

"I don't feel like moving on my first day home from school," Chloe whined. "I want to go shopping for summer clothes. I need a new pair of designer jeans." She had given up shopping for Lent, and now that that dreaded, masochistic season was over, she was ready to binge and splurge.

"Chloe, you have a whole closet full of designer jeans."

"But, Mother –"

Maxine's attention was drawn to a worker who bumped into her, clumsily lugging a box of dishes out of the apartment.

"Be careful with that, young man. That china is older than you are," Maxine called after the worker, following him out the door.

Chloe found herself alone in the front room with her new stepfather, who gave her an apologetic smile.

"Jacques, I could use your help with these boxes," Mother called from the hallway.

He turned to fulfill Maxine's request and Chloe trudged down the hallway to her room, lugging her suitcase like a sack of boulders. Mother had already begun disassembling the room and Chloe dropped her suitcase and plopped on her barren mattress. She unzipped the suitcase, retrieved her childhood teddy bear and cradled Mr. Buttons while looking around the room, trying to memorize every detail. She couldn't believe she was being forced to abandon the place where she had taken her first steps, fantasized about François, and dreamt of being in the movies one day.

She rose from the bed and began sluggishly taking down posters, Gigi's sketches, snapshots and other mementos she had tacked to the walls. She may as well accept the inevitable. When Mother made her mind up to do something, there was no convincing her otherwise.

She located an empty box and began packing up her desk. She picked up a photo of her, Gigi and their mothers that had been taken at a school function when the girls were younger and everything seemed simpler.

She set the photo down and went to the window, taking in the view of avenue Montaigne one last time. She sensed someone else in the room and turned to see Jacques standing in the doorway.

"Look, Chloe, I know you must be angry, having all of this thrust upon you all of a sudden," he said. "I wish Maxine had told you about us before today. I tried several times to convince her to talk to you, but she insisted that it was best to wait and make the introduction in person."

Chloe said nothing, turning to stare out the window again, her back to Jacques. This was too much to digest at once. First, her mother shipped her off to boarding school and now Maxine was uprooting her from the only home she'd ever known to move in with some strange man.

"It really isn't fair, having to move out like this with no notice, but Maxine has everything planned," Jacques continued. "I've discovered that when she decides to do something, there's no stopping her."

Boy, this Jacques really has gotten to know Mother, Chloe mused.

"I don't expect you to call me 'Daddy' or think of me as your father," he went on. "At least not right away."

Chloe remained silent. It had been just her and her mother all these years and she was used to having Maxine's attention to herself. She wasn't sure if she was ready to share her mother's scarce time outside of work with this new man, even if he did come across as kind and understanding.

"This marriage is going to take a lot of getting used to, I'm sure, for all of us," Jacques said. "Until you can get comfortable with the idea of me being married to your mother, just think of me as a family friend. That's all I want from you, Chloe – to get to know you and hopefully be your friend. I'm not here to try to run your life or fill in for your father, wherever he may be. I'm not going to try to tell you what to do. That's your mother's job."

This guy talks a good game, Chloe thought. *No wonder he won Mother over*.

"So what do you say, Chloe? Do we have a deal? Can we be friends? Will you at least give me a chance?"

Chloe faced Jacques and he entered the room, holding out his hand. She paused, studying his face and trying to gauge his sincerity, then cautiously met him in the middle of the room and shook his hand.

"I think we're going to get along nicely," he said, smiling. "And say, I know no one wants to do anything strenuous on the first day of summer. I'm sure you've been studying hard all year and just want to let your brain go on vacation."

Pretty perceptive, she thought, *not bad*.

"I can have the movers finish packing up your room. Here," Jacques said, reaching into his pocket, taking a huge wad of cash from a solid gold money clip and stuffing it into her hand, "go buy yourself those designer jeans."

Chloe could barely hold the small fortune Jacques had placed in the palm of her hand. There was enough to buy a whole new wardrobe, let alone one measly pair of blue jeans.

"Go ahead. Run along before your mother comes back."

"I can't," Chloe said hesitantly, her eyes darting from the cash in her hand to Jacques and back again. "I'll get in trouble."

"Don't worry, I'll take the blame. I'll tell Maxine I told you to go amuse yourself and stay out of the movers' way. Hurry now, *ma biquette*, before I change my mind." He made a shooing motion. "Hell hath no fury like Maxine's wrath," he added with a laugh.

Chloe stuffed the cash in her purse and slowly proceeded to the door. She turned and glanced tentatively over her shoulder at Jacques, who smiled and winked. She returned the smile.

13

Chloe awoke in darkness and sat upright in bed, startled by unfamiliar surroundings. It took her several moments to realize she was in her new bedroom at the Chateau de Chevalier, the house she and her mother now shared with her new stepfather.

She got out of bed and padded to the window. The first signs of daylight were just beginning to puncture the summer sky and the view of the grounds from her window was veiled by a heavy fog.

She pried open a cardboard box sitting on the window ledge. "Where are you, Mr. Buttons?" she said to herself, rummaging through the books, photos and other artifacts from her old room. The fact that her childhood teddy bear had somehow been misplaced in the move was symbolic of the loss of all that was familiar to her.

Abandoning the search for Mr. Buttons, she stumbled past the enormous four-poster bed, stubbing her toe on one of its gilded legs on the way to the connected bathroom. With its oversize, antique furniture, the room was more suited to an eighteenth-century monarch than a contemporary teenage girl.

She turned on the bathroom light, and admitted that it was nice having her own bathroom. There was a small basin next to the commode and when she turned the handle, a stream of water splashed out. She couldn't figure out if this contraption was a place to soak one's feet at the end of a long day or a sink that had been built for a diminutive ruler like Napoleon.

"That's a bidet."

Chloe turned to see a fiftyish, stout woman with dark hair and eyes standing in the doorway. With her hair pulled into a neat chignon and crisply starched housekeeper's uniform, she had an air of efficiency.

"A bee-what?" Chloe asked.

"A bidet," the woman said, her voice magnified by the acoustics as she entered the room. "People used it to wash their hind parts in olden times."

"Oh," Chloe said, her cheeks flushed with embarrassment.

"Allow me to introduce myself. I'm Marie l'Espée, the head of the household staff," the woman said, offering her hand. "You must be Chloe."

"Yes." Chloe shook her hand.

"I've heard a lot about you. You and your mother are all M'sieu has been talking about since they got married. It's nice to have you here."

Marie smiled at Chloe, her eyes radiating warmth.

"I know it must be hard adjusting to a new place," Marie continued. "Why don't you get dressed and I'll show you around, then I'll whip up something for breakfast."

Marie gave Chloe a tour of the sprawling estate. She recognized her mother's decorating touches throughout the main house. Louis XVI and Provencal furniture anchored hand-stitched rugs in the cavernous rooms. Renaissance paintings and tapestries hung from the walls, and crystal chandeliers dripped like frozen rain drops from the cathedral ceilings. The most exquisite chandelier hung in the large ballroom, where Jacques was known to give the best parties in Paris, Marie said.

"Hey, everyone, this is Chloe," Marie said when she introduced her to Lisette and Sophie, the maids who helped Marie around the house; Louis, the driver Jacques hired for Chloe and Maxine; and Bernard, the groundskeeper. They seemed friendly, nodding and tossing a jovial "*bonjour*" to the new occupant as they went about their jobs.

"Nice to see we have a beautiful young girl around here. Marie, you've got a little competition now," Bernard said with a twinkle in his eye.

"Behave yourself," she scolded, and Chloe picked up on the flirtation between the two.

When Marie reached the carriage house, she showed Chloe her modest room.

"This is my family," Marie said, handing Chloe a framed photo.

Chloe studied the photo, which looked as though it were taken ten or fifteen years ago when Marie was in her thirties. She was standing next to a man and two teenage children.

"That's my son, Jean-Luc, and my daughter, Irène. And that's my husband, Albert. He used to own a bakery. We ran it together."

"What's he do now?"

"He passed a few years ago."

"Oh, I'm sorry," Chloe said, handing the photo back to Marie.

"It's okay. I like to remember him." Marie lingered a moment, staring at the photo before returning it to the stand next to her bed. "Come on. I'll show you the stables and the rest of the grounds."

As they left the room, Marie crossed herself underneath the crucifix that hung above the doorway, one of the many religious symbols that decorated the devoutly Catholic woman's domicile.

After the stables, where Jacques kept two horses, the next stop on the tour was the swimming pool and cabana, which contained a shower, changing room, and well-stocked bar. Next to the pool was the guest house, where Jacques occasionally entertained out-of-town clients, as Marie related.

On the way back to the main house, Marie paused and said, "Let me show you something."

Chloe followed Marie to the entrance of the wine cellar.

"It's a little dusty down here," Marie said, handing Chloe a handkerchief and opening the cellar door.

Chloe placed the handkerchief over her mouth as she followed Marie into the dank cavern, which was lined with wine racks and dozens of bottles.

Marie took a lantern from the wall and lit it. "There, that's better," she said as the flame illuminated the cellar.

Chloe sneezed.

"Are you okay?" Marie said, holding the lantern near Chloe's face.

"Yeah. I'm just allergic to dust, and I'm kind of claustrophobic."

"We'll be out of here soon. The reason I brought you down here was to show you the secret passageway."

"Really?"

Marie handed the lantern to Chloe and she watched as the older woman pushed on one of the wine racks, which gave way and revealed a concealed doorway leading to a long, dark corridor.

"This way," Marie said, taking the lantern.

Chloe looked around in awe. Oil paintings in solid gold frames, gold goblets, furniture, coins of all denominations lay scattered along the stone walls, covered in cobwebs.

"What is this place?"

"It was a hideout," Marie said, her face eerily white in the glow of the lantern.

"For who?"

"The French Resistance," Marie said as they continued to walk through the passage. "In World War II, this was one of the stops during the Occupation. Rumor has it that the marquis whose family built this chateau provided aid to the Underground, and this was where they stored their valuables and passed along secretly-coded messages and hid Jews from the Nazis."

Chloe imagined the brave comrades and their secret missions. It was like something out of one of the spy movies she and Gigi took in at afternoon matinees.

"What happened, after the war, I mean?"

"Before the war ended, the Gestapo raided the compound and arrested everyone. Except for the Marquis and Marchioness Depres."

Chloe looked into Marie's eyes as the lantern's flame flickered. "What happened to them?" she said, almost afraid to ask but unable to stand the suspense.

"They were executed by Hitler's henchmen, put before a firing squad."

Chloe heard a sharp inhalation of breath, realized it was her own, and put the handkerchief to her mouth. "That's terrible."

"Yes, but they died nobly." Marie lowered her lantern to a row of paintings propped against a wall. "That's them."

Chloe studied the portraits of the Marquis and Marchioness Depres. Joséphine Depres was a regal-looking woman with delicate features, her hair cropped in thirties-style waves, her manicured, dainty hand resting in a ladylike gesture on the cream lace of her collar. Edouard Depres was a stern-looking man in an austere suit, his small mouth twisted into a scowling expression under a neatly-trimmed pencil moustache. There was a forlorn, doomed look in his eyes, as if portending the solemn events of the future.

"Before their execution," Marie continued as they began to walk again down the corridor, "the Depres family hid all these treasures down here. The Gestapo never did discover this passageway."

"What's Jacques going to do with all this stuff? It looks valuable."

"He hasn't decided yet. He and Madame Marguerite, God rest her soul, acquired this house through auction. It sat vacant for years and was scheduled to be demolished, but he was able restore it. With your mother's help, of course."

Chloe smiled. It felt good to know that her mother had helped restore a property with such historic value.

They reached the end of the passage and Marie took out a ring of keys and unlocked another door, which led to Jacques' study inside the main house. Chloe marveled at the wood-paneled room, with its large mahogany desk and rows of book shelves. She ran her hand along the leather-bound editions of Voltaire, Molière and Dumas.

"Wow," Chloe said, thumbing through an elaborately illustrated version of Dumas' *The Three Musketeers*. "Do you think Jacques would mind if I took this up to my room and read it?"

"Of course not, child. That's what they're there for."

Chloe was startled when a cuckoo sprang from behind a small door in a clock on the wall and loudly announced the time.

"I better get breakfast started," Marie said, extinguishing the lantern and hanging it on a wall. "Do you mind giving me a hand? I heard your stomach rumbling."

After a breakfast of Marie's homemade croissants, sausage and eggs, Chloe perched on the window seat in her room and immersed herself in *The Three Musketeers*. She was enthralled in Dumas' epic when she heard mewing and looked down to see a fuzzy white kitten clawing at the window seat's wooden base, as if begging to be picked up.

"Where did you come from?" Chloe said, setting the book aside and scooping up the kitten.

"I thought you might like a housewarming gift."

Chloe looked up to see Jacques standing next to Mother in the doorway.

"Maxine told me you've never had a pet because your apartment was too small," he said, putting his arm around Mother and leading her into the room, "so I figured now was a good time to get you one since we have plenty of space."

Chloe nuzzled the kitten, which responded by purring and licking Chloe's nose. "I know exactly what to call you. Bizou."

"'Little kiss,'" Maxine said, speaking the meaning of the French phrase and stroking the kitten's soft fur. "Perfect name."

Chloe dropped to the floor to play with the kitten. Mother and Jacques sat on the window seat, watching her and laughing, and it occurred to Chloe that they really did look like a couple. Instead of just a single mother, for the first time in her life she actually had parents.

Maxine stood on a stepladder in the renovated parlor, running a feather duster over the "Chateau de Chevalier" sign she had hung above the fireplace just a few months ago. Back then, she never dreamed that she'd be married to Jacques and that she and Chloe would be living here. Having poured her creativity and countless hours into the renovation of this room and the rest of the restored wing, she felt a sense of ownership and pride in the house.

Maxine stepped down from the ladder and studied the sign, making sure it hung evenly. She felt something furry at her ankles and looked down to see a Bichon Frisé, identical to the one Jacques' mother owned, nestling her legs.

"The kitten was a housewarming gift for Chloe and I thought you'd like a house pet, too," Jacques explained, entering the room.

"Is it a boy or girl?" Maxine asked, cradling the puppy.

"He's a boy. *Maman* referred me to her breeder."

"I think I'll call you Beeshie." Maxine set the dog down and he scurried off. "You know, I've been so consumed with building my business all these years that I've barely had time to take care of myself and Chloe, let alone a pet."

Jacques gripped her shoulders. "Well, now you have me to take care of you both," he said, punctuating the statement with a kiss. He took the feather duster from her and set it on the mantle. "You don't have to clean, you know. That's what Marie and the household staff are for."

"I know, I'm just so used to doing everything myself. I guess I'll have to learn to give up some control." Allowing herself to be cared for by Jacques both thrilled and frightened Maxine. She was still getting used to her married name – Madame Chevalier.

"By the way," she said, "I was looking at the books in your study and found the secret passageway leading down to the wine cellar. I was thinking maybe we could auction off all those old paintings and antiques down there. We could make a small fortune to donate to the orphanage."

"I think that sounds like a great idea. I've been meaning to clean out that old cellar. And that's coming down tomorrow." He nodded toward the painting of his late wife that hung over the sofa.

Maxine touched his hand. "Oh, no, Jacques. You need something to remember her by."

"I have my memories. I'll always have them. I'm shipping the portrait to Marguerite's family in Rouen."

They stood side by side looking up at the painting. "What will we put up there to cover the empty space?"

"I've commissioned an artist to do your portrait. You're the lady of the house now. You and Chloe have made this house a home." He pulled her close. "Of course," he added, "the challenge will be in getting you to sit still."

At first light, Chloe got out of bed and, trailed by Bizou, her new kitten, tiptoed down the stairs, so as not to wake Mother and Jacques. She went through the kitchen door that led outside and surveyed the grounds, which were thick with mist and shrouded by fog. She loved this time of day, when everything was awakening.

She walked to the stables and petted Starr, the Appaloosa Jacques let her pick out and name. She had been taking riding lessons with a private instructor over the last month since she and Mother had moved in. She had gotten pretty good and was thinking about trying out for the equestrian team when school started in the fall.

Starr neighed as Chloe brushed her mane.

"I'll be back this afternoon to saddle up," she said, petting the horse's head.

She left the stables, went to the swimming pool and dipped her foot in. It was too early for a swim; the water was cool. She would come back later after she rode Starr and maybe invite Gigi over.

Chloe watched the sun rise from a gazebo overlooking the garden. She loved this spot. It was like her secret garden, a place where she could escape for several undisturbed hours to read, write poetry, or just sit and think. She had come to love everything about the Château de Chevalier.

That first night in the house, which she had spent crying and longing for the familiarity of her old room, seemed long ago. The house that at first seemed cold and museum-like now felt as though she had been living here her whole life. She was looking forward to her first summer in the "new" house. Except for a photo shoot with Parisian teen magazine *Jeune et Jolie* and a few other modeling assignments she'd booked for extra spending money, the summer was hers to explore her new surroundings.

On her way back to the main house to shower and get ready for breakfast, she stopped upon seeing a fawn munching dew-sweetened grass next to the gathering of trees that bordered the back lawn. Apparently realizing it was being spied on, the fawn looked up at Chloe and dashed back into the forest.

Upon reaching the main house, the smell of Marie's crepes made Chloe's mouth water. After breakfast, she might go back to bed, snuggle under the covers with a book and maybe catch a couple more hours of sleep. She was home.

"Okay, that should do it," Marie said, instructing Chloe on how to use a pastry bag to put the finishing touches on éclairs for breakfast. "Why don't you grab a tray, *chouchou*, and help me take it out to the table?"

"Sure thing."

Chloe had come to enjoy hanging out with Marie in the kitchen. She had grown fond of the housekeeper, who, aside from Gigi, had become her closest confidante. Chloe felt she could tell Marie almost anything, and the older woman gave the best advice. Marie was a great listener, unlike Gigi, who sometimes dominated the conversation with incessant talk about boys, clothes and other superficial topics. It was nice to have someone to talk to who had more maturity and life experience than Gigi, but was less judgmental and strict than Mother.

"This looks delicious," Jacques said as Marie set a tray down on the screened-in porch where the newly-established family unit often ate breakfast.

"Chloe helped me make everything," Marie said, taking the tray from Chloe and giving her the okay to have a seat. "Does anyone need anything else?"

"No, I think we're good," Jacques said, fanning his napkin into his lap.

"*Merci*, Marie," Maxine said as Marie exited.

"So what do you have planned this afternoon, *amour*?" Jacques said to Mother.

"I have to go into the office for a while. Simone and I are meeting with a new client."

"That's too bad," Jacques said. "I was hoping we could all go riding this afternoon."

"How about tomorrow?" Maxine said. "My schedule's clear this weekend."

Mother had cut back on her hours since she and Chloe had moved in with Jacques and usually made time for them to eat at least one meal together.

"I should probably go into the city myself," Jacques said. "I'm working on a big deal with Pierre Rousseau."

"Isn't that the Belgian financier you were telling me about?" Maxine said, sipping her coffee and thumbing through the morning paper.

"Yeah," Jacques said, "If he signs on as an investor, I can pay off the second mortgage I took out on the house to buy that new cargo ship."

Maxine looked up from the paper, alarmed. "You mortgaged the house?"

Jacques gripped her hand. "No need to worry, *amour*. I've paid down most of it. We're in no danger of being out on the street."

Maxine put her other hand on top of his. "Why don't you let me pay off the second mortgage? Business has been brisk at the shop lately, and I have my savings –"

Jacques put his finger to Maxine's lips, silencing her. "I won't hear of it. It's *my* place to take care of you and Chloe, remember?"

He beamed at Chloe and she smiled at him. She was getting used to having a stepfather. It felt nice having someone around who looked out for her but wasn't smothering like Mother.

"This deal I'm working on is all but done," Jacques continued. "I've been in negotiations with Rousseau for the past six months and he might be coming to the house some time this summer so we can wrap up the deal."

"A houseguest?" Marie said, coming in carrying a coffeepot. "Please give me some advance warning, M'sieu Chevalier, so I can get the guest house ready and prepare a special menu."

"Of course, Marie," Jacques said, steadying his cup as Marie refilled it. "To be perfectly honest, I'd rather not have Rousseau stay here, but we've got a lot of details to hash out and it would be impractical to put him up in a hotel in the city and have to drive back and forth every day while he's in Paris. He's a shrewd businessman, but there's something about him, something that doesn't seem quite on the level."

"You're probably just nervous about the deal," Maxine said.

Jacques nodded. "You're probably right." He thanked Marie for the refill and, after she went back to the kitchen, turned to Chloe. "So I guess you've got the house to yourself this afternoon since your mother and I will be working."

"I might take Starr out for a ride and then go out to the gazebo and read for a while," Chloe said, nibbling on Marie's crepes.

"What are you reading?" Jacques asked, lighting up one of the Cuban cigars he occasionally smoked, especially after meals.

"*The Three Musketeers.* I hope it's okay I borrowed that leather-bound edition from your study?"

"Of course. I love Dumas. He's one of my favorite authors."

"Mine, too," Chloe said. "I especially love the sword-fighting scenes."

"You know, I fence a little myself. Picked it up when I was in the military." Jacques got an excited look on his face. "I'd be happy to give you a demonstration some time."

"Oh, no," Maxine said. "I don't want the two of you getting carried away and one of you getting hurt. And please put out that nasty cigar. You know I can't stand the smell."

Jacques obliged Maxine with a good-natured grumble, snuffing out the cigar in an ashtray. "I'll just show her a few basic moves, nothing too dangerous."

"That sounds like fun," Chloe said. She could already picture herself slicing away like a character in one of Dumas' swashbuckling epics.

"I don't know," Maxine said. "First the riding lessons, and now this. It'll be a miracle if you make it through the summer in one piece."

"I don't mean to interfere," Marie said, reappearing with a tray and beginning to clear empty plates, "but it wouldn't hurt for a young lady to learn to defend herself."

Maxine looked thoughtful. "That's true."

"And if I get good enough," Chloe spoke up, "I could join the fencing team at school."

"Okay," Maxine finally relented, "but you two be careful."

Chloe let out a cheer, raising her arms above her head.

"We'd better get go going if we're going to make it into the city in rush-hour traffic," Jacques said to Maxine, looking at his watch.

They excused themselves and Chloe began helping Marie clear the dishes.

"You know," Marie said, taking the tray from Chloe, "since you guys moved in, I think this is the happiest I've ever seen M'sieu Chevalier."

14

"En garde!"

Chloe charged toward Jacques, who was also wearing a fencing mask and was poised with one arm raised and the other with his foil pointed in her direction. Their swords clinked as they made contact and she struggled to meet every swipe of his blade with her own. Jousting not only provided a vigorous physical workout, it was mentally taxing, as she was discovering. Anticipating the opponent's next move was like chess.

After several minutes of sparring, she saw a moment when Jacques let down his guard and she thrust forward with her foil, jabbing the buttoned tip into his chest.

"*Aaargh!*" Jacques dropped his sword and fell to the mat, groaning like a pirate and holding his chest in a melodramatic gesture as if he were a dueling rival who had been struck down.

"You got me," Jacques said, lifting his fencing mask, his face contorted in a mock expression of agony. "You got me again."

Chloe took off her mask, shook out her ponytail, and smiled at her stepfather. "You let me win again." She extended a hand to help him to his feet.

"Not so, my dear," he said, taking Chloe's hand and picking up his sword. "You're getting good at this. I've taught you everything I know, and pretty soon you're going to out-master the master. You're a quick study."

"I learned from the best," she said, helping Jacques roll up the mat and return the swords to their hooks on the wall.

This room – the artillery room – was her least favorite. The marquis who had previously owned the chateau was an avid hunter, as Jacques explained. Marquis Depres collected antiques swords and rifles that hung on the walls along with the heads of bears, moose, deer and other animals he had taken down in the forest surrounding the grounds. Every time Chloe saw the deer head, she couldn't help but think of the fawn she had encountered that early-summer morning when she was exploring the grounds.

"I'm glad you're learning to defend yourself," Jacques said, putting a fatherly arm around Chloe as they left the artillery room. "You take after your mother – you have her beauty – and there are a lot of men in the world who will try to take advantage of you. I want you to be prepared."

She smiled at him, enjoying having a father figure to look out for her.

"Fencing is hard work. I'm burning up." She mopped her brow. "I think I'm going to take a dip in the pool to cool off."

"Okay, my sweet," Jacques said, giving her a paternal kiss on the top of her head, "but don't linger too long. The man I'm negotiating that big deal with is coming this afternoon and I want to introduce him to my family."

Chloe reluctantly emerged from the pool and toweled off. It was a sultry Saturday afternoon. All she wanted to do was play like a fish and stay cool, but Jacques' business associate from Brussels was due any minute.

She showered in the pool house and slipped into a floral-print summer dress. She took her time strolling to the main house. She didn't want to be all hot and sweaty when she met Jacques' associate. By the time she made it to the screened-in porch, Maxine and Jacques were already having iced tea with the man.

"Here she is now," Jacques said as Chloe timidly entered the room.

She hated meeting strangers. She felt even more shy and ill-at-ease than usual.

"We were just talking about you, Chloe," Jacques said.

The man stood to greet her. He was odd-looking, with a reddish-pink complexion like a baby who had flustered himself crying for a bottle. He was bald and had a big nose, beady little eyes and a potbelly that hung over his trousers.

"Pierre, this is my daughter, Chloe," Jacques said to the man.

Chloe liked how Jacques never added the "step" when introducing her to people. It made her feel even closer to him.

Turning to her, Jacques said, "Chloe, this is my friend and business collaborator, Pierre Rousseau."

"Business collaborator, yes. Friend, maybe. We'll see how the deal turns out," said Rousseau, guffawing at his own joke.

Jacques and Maxine humored him by joining in the laughter. Chloe smiled politely.

"So nice to meet you, M'sieu Rousseau," she said, extending her hand and barely making eye contact.

Rousseau took her hand and cradled it in his chubby, chapped hands, which resembled lobster claws. His skin felt like sandpaper. He raised her hand to his lips and kissed it. Chloe suppressed the reflex to yank her hand away. This man was nauseating.

"Chloe," Rousseau said, still clasping her hand, "such a beautiful name for such a beautiful girl. I'm pleased to make your acquaintance."

She looked away shyly, fighting the urge to crawl out of her skin and seep out of the room.

"Chloe just finished her sophomore year at Our Lady of Chastity. She got straight A's," Maxine proudly reported.

"You must be a very intelligent young lady. Brains and beauty. That's a killer combination," Rousseau said, rubbing Chloe's hand with his thumbs.

Are you going to take my hand off and use it to stir your tea? Chloe wondered, managing to disguise her discomfort with a forced smile.

"Why don't we ladies leave you men to discuss business," Maxine said, prying Chloe's hand from Rousseau's grip. "We'll go check on how Marie's coming along with dinner. Leg of mutton is your favorite, right, Pierre?"

"Jacques, this wife of yours is a gem. Wherever did you find her, and are there anymore like her?"

"Sorry," Jacques replied, "when they made Maxine, they broke the mold."

"Nice to meet you," Chloe repeated in a mumble to Rousseau as she followed her mother to the kitchen.

"The pleasure was all mine," he said, holding her gaze a second too long.

She quickly turned her head.

"There's something *off* about him," Chloe said in an undertone to Maxine as they walked down the hall to the kitchen. "I don't like him. He makes me feel weird."

"He's not the best-looking man I've ever met," Maxine conceded, "but he seems personable enough so far."

Chloe thought Rousseau was about as personable as a rattlesnake.

"Do you mind if I skip dinner tonight? I'm really not that hungry," she said.

"I won't hear of it. You can't be rude to Jacques' guest. You know how important this deal is."

Chloe sighed in resignation and followed Maxine into the kitchen.

Chloe suffered through the five-course meal, created by the masterful Marie and served by her helpers Lisette and Sophie. There were so many dishes that one person couldn't carry them all out. Despite the succulent main course of steak *au poivre* (pepper steak) and raspberry mousse cake for dessert, Chloe just picked at her food, repulsed by Rousseau's presence.

Pierre, a real *béni-bouftou*, or glutton, as the French said, liked the meal so much he demanded to meet the chef. Marie came out, and he lavished compliment after compliment on her cooking, telling her that she would put Alain Bisson, the famous bistro owner, to shame. Marie thanked him and excused herself, visibly embarrassed by all the attention. She was a humble person, as Chloe had come to know, and preferred for dinner guests to show their appreciation by asking for seconds rather than expressing verbal praise.

Halfway through the meal, Maxine's new dog Beeshie and Chloe's kitten Bizou came bounding into the dining room, disturbing the meal as the dog chased the cat under the table, trampling over everyone's feet. Maxine was mortified and apologized profusely to Rousseau, who thought the scene was hilarious. Tiny specks of food flung from his mouth as he snorted. Chloe saw this as her chance to make a getaway. She shooed the animals out of the room and excused herself, saying she was going to confine them, and escaped into the kitchen to talk to Marie.

"Of all the clients M'sieu Chevalier has entertained, he's the one I dislike the most," Marie said in a lowered voice to Chloe, making sure no one in the dining room would overhear. "And believe me, there have been some obnoxious people that have parked their feet under that table. There have been people who belched and passed gas and condemned my cooking, but that man is the worst. He is a complete phony."

"Oh my god, you feel that way, too?" Chloe said in an equally hushed tone, relieved that someone else in the house shared her apprehension. "I can't stand that man, and I don't even know him. He makes me squirm. He was staring at me all through dinner, like he wanted me to be the main course."

A worry wrinkle appeared on Marie's forehead – an expression Chloe had seen before when the older woman was fretting over a recipe that refused to come out right or some other household snafu.

"You steer clear of him, child, do you hear me?" Marie cautioned. "I show respect to whomever M'sieu Chevalier invites into this house. But I have good instincts, and something about Pierre Rousseau doesn't sit right with me."

Chloe was forced to sit through more of Rousseau's unfunny jokes and long-winded stories when Marie served after-dinner coffee in the parlor. As Rousseau rambled on, Chloe struggled to keep her eyes open.

"I think it's time for you to turn in, dear," Maxine said before Chloe committed the ultimate act of rudeness – falling asleep on a guest. "We're

93

going to early Mass in the morning. Go upstairs, lay out your clothes and get ready for bed."

"I think I'll turn in, too," Rousseau said, setting his coffee cup on the antique end table next to his chair. Marie rushed to pick up the cup so as not to leave a ring.

"It's been a long day," Rousseau continued, yawning and stretching dramatically. "I still have jetlag from my flight. There was a lot of turbulence, and I'm going to have to have my corporate jet looked at when I get back to Brussels."

Marie, on her way back to the kitchen with the sterling silver coffee service, gave Chloe a knowing eye roll, as if to say, "This man is so pretentious." Rousseau had been bragging all night about the trappings of his success. As if anyone cared that he had a private jet at his disposal. *Big whoop.*

"Marie had Lisette and Sophie make up the guest house for you," Jacques said to Rousseau. "I hope you'll find everything to your liking."

"I'm sure I will. You all have taken such good care of me, I may not want to leave."

Rousseau's loud, obnoxious laugh set Chloe's teeth on edge. Maxine and Jacques humored the houseguest once again with jovial laughter, but Chloe remained silent. She couldn't bear the notion that Rousseau would never leave.

Tossing a collective "goodnight" to the room, Chloe slipped out. She could feel Rousseau's eyes fixed on her back as she left the room. She hurried upstairs and locked herself in her room.

After a long, hot shower Chloe felt much better. It was as if she had washed away all the discomfort of being around that ghastly stranger all day and became herself again. She knelt by her bedside and said her prayers the way Maxine had taught her as a child. Before sliding under the cool sheets, she decided to sneak downstairs to fix herself a late-night snack. Having picked at her dinner, she was now starving. She'd heard the door to the master bedroom close when she was stepping out of the shower. Mother and Jacques were probably fast asleep. Chloe figured she'd grab a sandwich, some cookies, and a tall glass of milk, bring it back up to her room, and watch TV until she fell asleep.

She threw a robe on over her pajamas, stepped into her slippers, tiptoed to the door, unlocked it, and slowly turned the knob. The door creaked open. She jumped when confronted by the figure of a man standing in her doorway. The night light in the hallway illuminated his haggard features. It was Rousseau. He was standing right in front of her, staring her in the face like a goblin.

"I just wanted to give you something before you go to sleep," he said in a half-whisper.

What, a heart attack?

"Close your eyes," he instructed.

Too afraid to refuse, she obeyed.

"Now open your hand."

She gulped, her throat suddenly dry, and held out her right hand. Rousseau placed something cold and metallic-feeling in her palm and enveloped her hand in his.

"You can open your eyes, but don't open your hand until you're back in your room," he said. "I want what I gave you to be the last thing you think about before you go to sleep."

Chloe stood there staring into Rousseau's cold, beady eyes, petrified. She couldn't see his face well, but she swore it looked like he was staring at her developing breasts through her lightweight robe and flimsy pajamas.

"Well, see you in the morning," he said after a moment, easing her fears that he was going to invite himself into her room. He placed a sloppy kiss on her cheek. She stiffened, suppressing the urge to pull back. He stepped out in the hallway, into the darkness.

Chloe immediately closed the door and locked it. She opened her hand. Lying in her palm was a shiny gold necklace with a tiny diamond embedded in the center. She dropped it in her wastebasket and jumped in bed, pulling the covers over the head. She wanted to run down the hall and get in bed with her mother the way she used to when she was little and had a bad dream, but she didn't want to venture beyond the locked door.

"That was just a nightmare. I was sleepwalking," Chloe said aloud in an effort to calm herself. "When I wake up, I'll have forgotten all about Pierre Rousseau and he'll be gone."

To her dismay, Chloe found Rousseau was still in the house the next morning. When she reported to the screened-in porch for breakfast, she found him sitting at the table, drinking coffee and inhaling bacon and eggs. Luckily, Jacques decided to take on Rousseau in a game of early-morning tennis while Maxine and Chloe attended Mass at St.-Jean l'Evangéliste, one of Paris' historic cathedrals. Chloe got a chance to tell her mother about last night's incident in the car on the way to church.

"He was just being friendly," Maxine said, sounding as though she were trying to reassure herself more than Chloe. "He's just trying to woo Jacques and his family. He'll do anything to get him to sign the deal."

"Mother, the man came to my bedroom last night and made a pass at me."

"Giving a child a gift and kissing her goodnight hardly qualifies as making a pass. Pierre's just an older man who's good at business but lacking in social graces. Believe me, *ma chérie*, if Pierre ever does anything inappropriate, he'll be gone so fast you won't even remember what he looks like."

"I wish. And I don't want him to get the chance to do anything inappropriate."

"Chloe, you know this deal is very important to Jacques. Once the negotiations are done and he gets those contracts signed, he can pay off the second mortgage and send Pierre on his way."

Chloe looked out the window at the storefronts passing by. Why wasn't she getting through to Mother? She had been overprotective Chloe's whole life, not even letting her date, but Rousseau seemed to have Mother fooled with his fake charm.

"I know you don't like Pierre, for whatever reason," Maxine continued, "but can you at least tolerate him until he leaves?"

"You don't understand –"

"Chloe, promise me. Please. I'm trying really hard to make this new family of ours work, and I want this deal to be a success for Jacques. I know you haven't known him long, but I trust his judgment and I know he'd never expose us to someone we couldn't trust."

Maybe Mother was right. Maybe Chloe was just being silly. She'd hadn't been able to gain François' attention, and none of the boys at St. Thomas seemed interested in her. Why would a grown man waste his time trying to win the affections of a teenager who hadn't even had her first kiss?

"I promise," Chloe said finally, her slumping posture reflecting her act of submission.

Maxine patted her hand. "Good. That's my girl."

"I don't like that, I don't like that one bit," said Marie, up to her elbows in flour as she kneaded dough in the kitchen, after Chloe told her about Rousseau coming to her room the other night.

The man was like a bad rash that wouldn't go away. He kept giving Chloe gifts. Every time she turned around, he was slipping some trinket in her hand, a ring or a pin or a pair of earrings. Either he knew Jacques Chevalier had a teenage daughter before he arrived or he was a walking jewelry store. Chloe tried to courteously decline the gifts, but he insisted she take them. His presence made her want to retch. Whenever she looked up, he was staring at her. All she could do was look away and pretend she was invisible.

Chloe hoped Mother was right, that Rousseau was just being friendly in an attempt to win Jacques' favor. She decided, however, to talk to Marie and get her opinion. She would often sit in the kitchen while Marie was stuffing a

Cornish hen or tenderizing a steak and tell the older woman all of her teenage problems. Marie should have been a psychologist, because she gave the best advice.

"Do you think I'm being silly?" Chloe asked.

The worry wrinkle reappeared on Marie's forehead and she continued to knead the dough, not responding right away. "I'm sure your mother knows what's best for you," she said after a moment, sounding as though she were choosing her words carefully. "If she says M'sieu Rousseau is harmless, then hopefully he is. Luckily he's flying back to Brussels tomorrow morning. Until then," she added, lowering her voice, "keep your distance, child."

15

It was unbearably hot. Chloe tossed and turned; sleeping in this smoldering weather was impossible. Air conditioning was one of the few modern luxuries that hadn't yet been installed in the rustic chateau, and all the ceiling fan was doing was circulating humidity. She kicked her covers off, sprung out of bed, and flung open the window. She sat on the sill, fanning herself.

"I'm melting. It can't be this hot on the sun," she muttered to herself.

Moonlight danced around the grounds. The shimmering waters of the pool beckoned, and she couldn't resist its call. She quickly changed into her two-piece and padded out of the house, down to the pool. She jumped in, immersing herself in the cool, placid water. Heaven on Earth. She swam a couple of laps and decided to take a refreshing shower.

She got out of the water, entered the pool house, and stripped off her bathing suit. She stepped into the shower stall, pulled the knob and luxuriated in the invigorating sensation of the icy jets of water caressing her skin. After several celestial minutes, she reluctantly turned off the water and stepped out of the shower, slipping back into her bathing suit and bundling herself in a white terry-cloth robe. She had been roasting alive just under an hour ago but suddenly felt a chill.

She began drying her hair with a towel as she looked in the mirror over the sink. She dropped the towel and gasped. For a moment she thought she saw Rousseau. She rubbed her eyes and looked in the mirror again. Sure enough, there he was, standing right behind her. His shirt was unbuttoned, revealing a paunch, and his belt buckle was undone. What was left of his grayish hair was standing all over his head and he had a crazed expression.

"You scared me half to death," she said as she turned to face him, so stunned she barely managed to get the words out. "What are you doing in here, M'sieu?"

"This is the opportunity I've been waiting for all along. Just you and me, alone," he said with a crooked smile.

Every muscle in her body tensed. She could tell Rousseau wasn't interested in going for a swim.

"I have to get back to the main house. I told Mother I wouldn't be long. She's waiting up for me," she improvised.

"Now, now, it's not nice to tell lies," he said mockingly. "I just checked the master bedroom. Your mother has her sleep mask on and Jacques is snoring. The lights are all out in the servants' quarters as well. It's just you and me. I'd like to show you something. Come with me."

He grabbed her hand and led her into the next room, which contained the wet bar and several lounge chairs. The moonlight reflected off the pool, casting a ghostly reflection on the walls through the glass panels.

"Sit down," Rousseau ordered.

Chloe did as she was told. She figured if she humored him for a couple of minutes she could maneuver her way back to the main house to get help.

Rousseau got two glasses from the bar and poured Scotch into both of them. He offered one to Chloe.

"Have a drink," he said.

She studied the amber liquid. "I'm not old enough to drink."

"Just this once won't hurt. Take it," he said firmly.

Chloe slowly took the glass from his hand.

"Have a sip. I won't tell," he said in his mocking tone.

She gripped the glass, her fingers turning white from the fear pulsing through her body. "I'd really rather not."

"I said drink it!" he shouted.

Chloe put the glass to her lips and let some of the strong-smelling liquid ooze down her throat. She coughed, the alcohol burning her throat. "This is too strong," she panted, hitting herself in the chest.

"You'll get used to it."

Rousseau retrieved a large book from atop the bar and sat down next to Chloe, handing the book to her. "Open it," he commanded. She complied and realized it was a photo album. The first page was blank.

"Go ahead. Look through it," he said, nudging her.

Chloe set the drink aside and thumbed through the album. It contained dozens of pictures of nude girls. Some of them were tied to beds and all of them had terrified looks in their eyes, as if they were being forced to do something against their wills.

"These girls are all around your age," he told her. "It's a very impressive collection, wouldn't you say? All of them desired to become women. At first they acted shy and innocent like you, but deep down they longed to experience the pleasure only a man can bring. And do you know why?" He didn't wait for her to respond. "Because all little girls like you are whores. You may fool your mother and Jacques with that innocent act, but I know you want it."

Chloe may have been inexperienced when it came to sex, but she was wordly enough to know what "it" meant.

Rousseau pointed to a picture of a dark-skinned girl whose wrists were handcuffed to a bedpost. She had a gag in her mouth and a blindfold over her eyes.

"She looks a lot like you, doesn't she?" Rousseau said, running his rough hands along her cheeks. "I'm going to do to you exactly what I did to her."

Something came over her, and she suddenly lashed out. "The hell you are, you sick bastard!" She slammed Rousseau's hand in the photo album and dashed for the door.

"Get back here!" he yelled, jumping up, grabbing her and slapping her to the floor.

He took a knife out of his pocket and pulled her up by her hair. He gripped her neck so hard she thought she was going to choke.

"Look here," he said, holding the knife to her throat, "you do what I say or I'll slit your throat. Do you understand me?"

She didn't respond, struggling to catch her breath.

"I said, do you understand me?"

She spat in his face. He slapped her to the ground again. She tried to scramble for the door, but he forced her up and threw her onto a lounge chair. She struggled to break free, but he was too strong. Rousseau pulled the string from her bathrobe and tied her hands to the chair. She screamed until she was hoarse, but he got on top of her and muffled her cries.

"You scream again and I'll slash that pretty little face of yours," he threatened.

She had no choice but to lie still as Rousseau straddled her. His jagged fingernails dug in to her tender flesh as he tried to tear off the girdle-like bottom of her bathing suit. She had to act fast.

"You're right. I want you," she said, imitating the seductive tone she'd seen movie heroines using on the opposite sex. "Kiss me."

Rousseau's hideous features contorted into a crooked smile again. "I knew that's what you wanted all along." He brought his face closer to hers, sticking his tongue out as if he planned to ram it down her throat.

She waited until he was as close as possible and kneed him in the groin. Rousseau cried out and fell to the floor. Chloe pulled at the rope around her wrists until the hastily-tied knot came loose. She ran to the door, out of the pool house and sprinted to the main house.

Upon reaching the house, she threw open the cellar door, closed it firmly behind her and crouched in the underground passageway Marie had shown her. She leaned against the cement wall in the d–ark, grasping her knees and trying to catch her breath. She kept her eyes on the door, moonlight streaming in through cracks in the wooden slats. Her breath quickened when she heard footsteps at the cellar door.

Chloe did her best to hold her breath, hoping Rousseau would just go away if she hid out long enough. Dust began tickling her sinuses and, before she could cover her mouth, she sneezed. The cellar door flung open and she screamed at the sight of the outline of Rousseau's lumpy frame in the doorway.

"I'm not going to let you get away," he snarled as he began chasing her through the dark passageway.

Chloe ran as fast as she could, stumbling on the hem of her robe and at one point dropping to her knees, scraping them on the floor. She got up and turned back to see Rousseau just inches away, looking even more ominous, silhouetted by the moonlight.

Breathlessly, she threw open the door that led into Jacques' study and closed it behind her, temporarily trapping Rousseau in the cellar.

"Help!" she screamed. Her voice was muffled in the wood-paneled room. This wing of the chateau was so far from the master suite that it was unlikely that Mother or Jacques would hear her.

She turned to see books dropping from the shelves that camouflaged the entrance to the cellar as Rousseau threw his weight against the door. He would break through within seconds and she needed to think fast.

She took off running again, frantically searching for a hiding place. In the dark hallway outside the study, she paused, deciding whether to go right or left. Seeing the shadow of a stuffed bear standing on its hind legs in the artillery room, she bolted in its direction. If she could just get her hands on one of those swords, she could defend herself as Jacques had taught her.

She made it inside the room just as Rousseau caught up with her.

"It's not nice to run off like that," he said, panting and approaching her, his sweaty paunch spilling out of his unbuttoned shirt and unbuckled pants. Light reflected off the knife he brandished.

She grabbed a rapier from the wall. "Don't come any closer." She pointed the sword at him, her hand trembling.

He continued to inch forward, looking even more crazed in the shards of light filtering in through the latticed windows. "A little girl shouldn't play with knives." He held the knife out. "She might get hurt."

Chloe extended the sword, recalling the strike position she'd learned in her fencing sessions with Jacques. "I'm warning you. Don't move another step or I'll slice you in half."

Rousseau's laughter, the same grating sound she'd endured the past few days, pierced the air. He stepped forward with the knife, challenging her. When he was within striking distance, she looked him in his beady eyes and chopped the air with her sword, slicing him across the face.

"*Salope!*" he cried, pressing his free hand to his bloody cheek.

Chloe aimed, ready to strike again, but was distracted by the sudden shrill of the cuckoo clock echoing from the study down the hall. Rousseau grabbed her and she dropped the sword, startled by his swiftness.

He wrapped his arm around her like a boa constrictor and held the knife to her throat. She froze, anticipating his attack. But he simply muttered in her ear, his hot, foul breath searing her cheek.

"You better not tell anyone about what happened tonight. If you so much as utter a word, I'll have your mother killed. I know people in the Mafia who'll do it. Your mother is a dead woman if you don't keep your mouth shut. Nod if you understand."

Chloe shook her head up and down stiffly, her movements restricted by the knife at her jugular. Despite his menacing tone, she sensed she had wounded him seriously enough to cause him to back down – like the coward he was.

"You remember what I said," Rousseau said, releasing her.

She dropped to the floor on her bloody knees, her entire body buckling.

Giving her one last ominous glance, he fled. She heard his clumsy footsteps thudding down the corridor and growing faint as he exited through the secret passageway in the study. Once certain he'd left the house, she collapsed in sobs.

Chloe lay awake in bed for hours, determined not to fall asleep in fear that Rousseau would pick her lock and invade her room. Shortly before dawn, she drifted off to sleep but was soon jarred awake. She dreamt that Rousseau was standing over her with a knife, threatening to rape her.

The swine was sitting at the breakfast table on the screened-in porch when Chloe came downstairs in the morning, shoveling in Marie's crêpes as if nothing had happened last night. He had a large Band-Aid on his cheek. He gave Chloe a dirty look as she sat down at the table, a reminder to stay silent.

"Good morning, *ma chérie*," Maxine said. "What's wrong with your face? It looks a little puffy."

Chloe paused before responding, fearing that if she told the truth, Rousseau would make good on his threats to kill Maxine.

"I tripped and fell on my way back from taking a dip last night," she said, looking down at the table.

"That's funny. Pierre scraped his face on a branch on his way to the

101

guest house after dinner," Maxine said, nothing in her voice seeming as if she detected the two events were connected.

"I hate to rush things," Jacques interjected, "but I had my attorneys draw up the last of the paperwork yesterday, if you're ready to sign, Pierre."

"Of course." Rousseau wiped his sticky mouth with the back of his hand and accepted a fountain pen from Jacques. He scribbled his name on the array of papers arranged on the breakfast table.

"I'll have all the paperwork forwarded to your office today so you can have your attorneys look over everything. Here's to success," Jacques said, raising his glass of orange juice in a toast.

"To success," Rousseau repeated, also raising his glass.

Maxine picked up her glass to join in and nudged Chloe to do the same. Rousseau gave Chloe a look that said, "Remember our little secret," as their glasses touched.

Chloe felt an overwhelming sense of relief when the driver arrived with the car that would transport Pierre Rousseau to the airport and out of her life forever. Before he left, he managed to corner her in the parlor one last time.

"Remember," he whispered, his hot breath brushing her cheek and turning her stomach, "not a word or..." He made a throat-slitting motion with his index finger, punctuated by a gurgling sound.

Jacques and Maxine entered the parlor before he could say anything else.

"Pierre, it's been a pleasure having you stay with us," Maxine said, shaking his hand. "I'd accompany you to the airport along with Jacques, but I'll let you two discuss the last few details of the new deal."

"You are a most gracious hostess, Madame Chevalier," Rousseau said, kissing Maxine's hand. "And what a lovely daughter."

He approached Chloe and kissed her on the cheek. It took all of her might not to vomit all over his shoes.

"We better leave now. Your plane departs in less than an hour and we have a long drive," Jacques said.

"*Au revoir*," Maxine called out to Pierre as he and Jacques left the room.

Giving Chloe one last clandestine, menacing look over his shoulder, he responded, "*Au revoir*."

16

Chloe felt like she was dying inside. Keeping the brutality she had suffered at the hands of Pierre Rousseau a secret was killing her. She had to let it out.

She considered telling Gigi. She tried to work up the nerve, but every time she was close to confessing, Gigi started babbling on about boys and how she was dreading going back to school in the fall. She wasn't mature enough to understand. Besides, Gigi had a big mouth. She'd more than likely tell Simone, and Simone would tell Mother. Then Mother would tell Jacques, and Jacques would try to have Rousseau arrested. In retaliation, Rousseau might make good on his threat to have Mother killed. Chloe had to get her feelings out, though, or she would go insane.

She longed for her *grand-mère*, Mama Louise, and her cure-all Creole voodoo. Mama Louise always said she considered herself a good Catholic, but she also believed in the mystical power of black magic. If anyone messed with Chloe when she was growing up, Mama Louise would promise to put a hex on them. If Mama Louise were still around, Chloe could pour her soul out to her grandmother and she would make it all better. Mama Louise would make a doll of Rousseau, stick pins in it, he'd drop dead, and that would be the end of it.

Finally, Chloe decided to confide in Marie and swear her to secrecy. Marie had shared her premonitions about Rousseau and would understand how she felt.

One afternoon, Chloe was hanging out in the kitchen as she usually did when Marie began preparing the evening meal. Chloe grabbed an apple from a bowl of fruit sitting on a counter and plopped on a stool. Marie was dropping lobsters into boiling court-bouillon broth. Chloe bit into the apple, trying to think of a way to tell Marie about the awful things Rousseau had tried to do to her. Luckily, Marie spoke first.

"Is something on your mind, child? You seem preoccupied."

"What makes you say that?" Chloe said, unsure of how to proceed.

"Usually you're bouncing all around the kitchen, running off at the mouth a mile a minute. Come to think of it, you've been too quiet for the past couple of weeks. Something's troubling you, I can tell."

"I don't know. I guess so."

"You guess so? What is it? You know you can tell me anything."

Chloe inhaled deeply. "Well, you know how I told you Rousseau made me kind of... uncomfortable?"

"Yes. He made me uncomfortable, too. I abhorred him from the moment I laid eyes on his ugly face."

"Well, remember when I told you that he came to my room that one night and gave me that necklace and kissed me?"

"Yes. And?" Marie prompted.

"There's something else he did that I didn't tell you about. I haven't told anybody, as a matter of fact. It happened the last night he was here."

Marie released one last lobster to its watery death, wiped her hands on her apron, and gave Chloe her full attention. The worry wrinkle appeared on her forehead again. "What did he do to you, Chloe?"

"He... he... Oh, never mind." Chloe got up, but Marie gently pushed her back on the stool.

"Tell me what he did to you or I'll be worried sick," Marie insisted.

Chloe paused, grappling for words to describe Rousseau's abuse. "He tried to attack me."

"*Bon Dieu!* Oh dear God!" Marie exclaimed. "I knew something was wrong with that man. The way he looked at you... It wasn't normal. I started to say something. I started to speak up to M'sieu and Madame Chevalier, tell them that he shouldn't be here, but I figured I was only a servant. Who was I to tell them to kick out a guest? I should have spoken up. My instincts are never wrong. Tell me exactly what happened."

Chloe picked at the half-eaten apple. "I was taking a late-night swim and he snuck up on me when I was showering in the pool house. I got away before he could do anything."

"Still, he tried to take advantage of you. It's wrong. He's probably done it before."

"He has. He showed me pictures of other girls he raped."

"That man has to be stopped. It's not right that scum like him is walking around free. He should be locked up, he should be executed. I'm going to have to tell your parents. If we don't do something now, God only knows when he'll strike again."

"Marie, no! You can't do that. He said if I told anyone he'd have Mother killed. He has Mafia connections."

"Child, don't you know that's just something he said to scare you? He probably said that to all his victims to keep them quiet. He was able to intimidate them, but thank God you had the sense to speak up."

"Marie, I'm begging you, please don't tell Mother or Jacques. I don't know what Rousseau's capable of."

"I'm sorry, Chloe. I have to tell. It's my duty."

"Marie, you can't. You just can't."

Marie placed a comforting hand on Chloe's shoulder. "Have I ever done wrong by you in the time you've known me?"

"No."

"Okay, then. You're going to have to trust me on this one. I have to tell."

"I never should have said anything." Chloe ran up the back stairs to her room. She threw herself on her bed and cried. Why hadn't she just kept her big mouth shut? Her confession to Marie was going to cost her mother her life.

Only a couple of minutes passed before Maxine was banging on Chloe's door like the house was on fire. "Chloe, let me in, please! Marie told me what happened."

"Please go away," Chloe sniveled. "I can't see anybody right now."

"I'm not going to go away until you let me in."

Chloe knew her mother wasn't kidding. Maxine would knock the door down if she had to, so Chloe reluctantly unlocked her door and opened it. Her mother rushed in and threw her arms around her, tears streaming down her face. "Honey, I'm so sorry about what happened to you," Maxine whimpered.

"Nothing happened."

"Marie told me Pierre tried to take advantage of you. Did he hurt you?"

"He hit me a couple of times and held a knife to my throat."

"That bastard!" Maxine screamed. "He's going to pay for this! He's going to pay!"

"Mother, please don't go to the police. Nothing happened, okay? He said he'd kill you if I told anyone."

"Oh, Chloe. Nothing's going to happen to me. I'll never let anyone take me away from you. I'm not going to let some slimeball get away with trying to force himself on my daughter."

"Don't do this. You never listen to me. If you would have listened to me when I first told you he made me uncomfortable, this never would have happened."

Fresh tears streamed down Maxine's face, streaking her mascara. "You're so right, *ma chérie*. I should have listened to you. I know this isn't the first time I've failed as a parent. There were so many times I was off chasing my dreams and wasn't there for you when you needed me. Can you ever forgive me?"

"The way you can fix everything is by just letting it be. It's over."

"No, it's not over. It won't be over until that man is behind bars – or dead. It's going to take a long time before we can put this behind us. Honey, do you want to go to a psychiatrist? Do you feel like you need to talk about this with a professional?"

"Great, Mother, now you think I'm crazy." Chloe flopped on her bed. "No, I don't want to go to some shrink. I just want to forget about it, and I wish you would, too."

"I'll never forget it. You can mess with me but don't mess with my baby. As soon as Jacques gets home, I'm telling him what happened and we're going to take the appropriate actions."

"I wish you wouldn't. Pierre Rousseau will *kill* you!"

"No he won't. Mommy won't let him."

Chloe sighed and put a pillow over her face. Mother's logic was impossible.

Maxine touched Chloe's leg. "Come on downstairs. Dinner will be ready soon."

"I'm not hungry. I just want to be alone," Chloe said, her voice muffled by the pillow.

"Okay, you rest and we'll talk later." Maxine affectionately ran her hand over Chloe's hair and left the room, closing the door behind her.

Chloe pushed the pillow on the floor and sat up. "Please don't do this, Mother. I don't want to lose you."

Chloe drifted off to a dreamless sleep, and was awakened by the hall light filtering into her dark room as the door opened. She sat up and squinted at the figure entering. It was Jacques, carrying a tray of food.

"I brought you a little snack since you didn't come down for dinner," he said, setting the tray on the nightstand beside Chloe's bed.

"Don't turn on the light," she said, rubbing her eyes. "My eyes aren't adjusted." She also didn't want Jacques to see her. She knew Mother had told him about what happened and Chloe was embarrassed to face him. He might think she had done something wrong, that she was a bad girl, that she had somehow led his business associate into thinking he could have his way with her.

Jacques hovered at her bedside. "May I sit down?"

"Sure."

Chloe scooted over and made room. Jacques smelled like cigar smoke, as usual. He had probably been reading the paper in his study and smoking before he came upstairs to get ready for bed, his nightly ritual.

"Your mother told me what happened," he said, the light from the hall highlighting his sympathetic expression.

Chloe nibbled on a carrot stick. "Figures. I asked her to keep her trap shut, but she never listens to me. Pierre Rousseau is going to kill her if you guys try to have him put away."

"Listen, darling, Pierre Rousseau isn't going to harm a hair on your mother's head, and I promise he'll never be able to hurt you again, either. I'm going to see to it personally."

"He's an animal. I don't think anyone can stop him."

"You underestimate me, my dear. I know a lot of people in high places. I wish you would have come to me and told me about how you felt about him after I introduced you. If you would have come to me first, I would have put him on the first plane back to Brussels."

"Mother said he was an important client and to just put up with him."

"Your mother has a lot to learn about me," Jacques said. "I never put business above family. I've already ripped up the deal I signed with Rousseau.

I don't want to do business with that *fumier*."

Chloe sat up straighter in alarm. "But what about the loan you took out on the house, Jacques? Don't you need the money from this deal with Rousseau to pay it off?"

Jacques looked pensive. "You know, this whole experience has taught me a thing or two. First of all, I don't want to do business with unscrupulous people. I should have done some more investigating before I invited that snake-in-the-grass into our home." He stroked the stubble on his chin, as if deep in thought. "Your mother is going to advance me the money to pay off the second mortgage and expand my fleet. I should have accepted her help when she first offered it, but I let my macho pride get in the way. I'm still adjusting to the fact that we're a team, a family. And I'm not going to let anyone hurt my family." He clasped Chloe's hand for emphasis. "Especially not a piece of *merde* like Rousseau. I'm going to make sure he pays for what he did to you."

"But I have no proof that he did anything. Nothing really happened." Chloe appreciated Jacques' protectiveness, but she still feared for her mother's safety.

"That's beside the point," Jacques said. "Pierre Rousseau is going to have to answer for what he tried to do to you and for what he's done to those other girls."

Chloe set her plate aside; she still didn't have much of an appetite. "I'm just worried that he'll get to Mother when you're not around."

"Don't worry yourself anymore. I'm going to handle everything. I promised your mother I'd take care of you both when we got married, and that's a promise I intend to keep."

"I'm so glad we have you." She wrapped her arms around her stepfather and nestled her head in his chest.

"You get some rest," he said, patting her back. "You must have had trouble sleeping since the attack."

"I feel much better now, but I'm still scared something's going to happen to Mother."

"Nothing's going to happen to your mother. Just leave everything to me. *Bonne nuit*, sleep well." Jacques lavished a fatherly kiss on her forehead, his five o'clock shadow slightly abrasive against her sensitive skin. "Now get some sleep, *ma ange*," he added tenderly, getting up. "I'll leave your door cracked in case you get scared. The hall light's on."

As Jacques reached the door, Chloe quickly uttered, "I love you." This was the first time she had ever felt compelled to say that to someone other than her mother.

He smiled softly, lingering in the doorway. "I love you, too, Chloe. I'm so glad you and your mother came into my life."

*****

Chloe bounced down the stairs, taking the back way to the screened-in porch to join Mother and Jacques for breakfast. It was the first day of the last week of summer, and Chloe was actually looking forward to going back to school and seeing all her friends again. She had put the night of terror with Pierre Rousseau to the back of her mind after finally talking it over with Gigi on the phone last night. Things were pretty much back to normal, except that her mother was even more overprotective now.

When Chloe reached the table, she found Mother and Jacques had already eaten and were savoring the last few sips of their morning coffee before they headed off to work.

"Good morning," Chloe chirped, kissing her mother and stepfather and plopping in her usual chair.

Mother and Jacques murmured replies, both absorbed in different sections of *The International Herald Tribune*. Jacques was filling the room with the smoke from one of his Cuban cigars. Maxine had all but given up on trying to break him of the "filthy habit," as she called it. She had at least made him cut down to smoking only after meals.

"Marie made muffins. Help yourself," Maxine said, thumbing through the fashion section.

Chloe plucked two plump blueberry muffins from the basket in the middle of the table and smothered them with butter and jam. She poured herself a glass of freshly squeezed orange juice and dug in. She was starving and had a long day of black-belt shopping ahead of her. She had plans to meet Gigi in the city, take in an afternoon matinee and hit Galeries Lafayette and all the other chic department stores. Not that they needed any new clothes since they would soon be donning Our Lady of Chastity's uniforms for nine more months, but shopping was always fun nonetheless. Jacques had given Chloe a credit card of her own to use at her leisure. "Charge" was her new favorite word.

"Are you sure you don't want to reconsider and come to St.-Tropez with us this weekend?" Maxine said to Chloe.

"*Maman*'s been wanting to meet you, plus it's the last big sailing weekend of the summer," Jacques added, "and I promised I'd show you *Nathalie* before you went back to school."

"Who's Nathalie, a friend of yours?" Chloe asked, biting into one of Marie's succulent muffins.

"*Nathalie*'s my favorite lady – other than your mother, of course," Jacques said with a playful gleam in his eye, patting Maxine's hand.

"*Nathalie* is Jacques' yacht," Maxine said, elbowing him good-naturedly. "He proposed to me on that boat. It's beautiful, has all the comforts of home."

"Can't we go sailing next time I'm home on break?" Chloe said. "I told Gigi she could sleep over this weekend."

Maxine's face puckered in concern. "I'm not sure I'm comfortable with that. You know Marie's going out of town this weekend to visit her daughter in Avignon, and I don't like the idea of you and Gigi being here by yourselves."

"We'll be fine, Mother," Chloe insisted. "I mean, I just turned sixteen and I'll be a junior this year."

Maxine looked at Jacques, as if pleading for backup. "Maybe we should reschedule the trip. We could always take a long weekend once Chloe's back at school."

Jacques clasped Maxine's hand. "She'll be fine, *amour*. She's growing up. We have to trust her." He turned to Chloe. "And don't worry. We can go sailing anytime. It'll probably be too cold next time you come home from school, but we'll have every spring and summer for the rest of our lives to take old *Nathalie* out on the water."

Chloe smiled at Jacques, appreciating having an ally.

"I guess you're right," Maxine said to Jacques. Giving Chloe one of her stern, motherly looks, she added, "But you make sure you call and check in."

"Honestly, Mother. I'm not twelve anymore."

Marie came out with coffee and orange juice refills and Maxine and Jacques went back to reading the paper.

"I just came across an interesting tidbit on the front page," Jacques said, rustling the paper.

"What's that, dear?" said Maxine, adjusting her reading glasses.

He read the headline aloud: "'Brussels Businessman Found in Pool of Blood.' It seems our good friend Pierre Rousseau was discovered dead in his Belgian office. Apparently some unknown assailant slit his throat."

"So sad," Maxine said with no emotion.

"So sad indeed." Jacques lowered his newspaper and winked at Chloe.

She nearly choked on her muffin. She had miscalculated her stepfather's power; he had vowed Rousseau would be brought to justice. At least she knew he was a man of his word.

17

"Free at last!" Chloe exclaimed to Gigi, slamming the front door when the car had disappeared down the drive.

Before leaving for St.-Tropez, Maxine made Chloe feel like she was back in grade school by ticking off a long list of "do's" and "don'ts" and making her recite emergency numbers. Jacques had flashed Chloe a sympathetic look while carrying luggage out to the car, and finally got Maxine to let up by tugging on her sleeve and telling her the private plane he'd chartered was on a tight schedule.

Marie had left for Avignon on the train earlier in the day, and Chloe and Gigi finally had the house to themselves.

"We're going to have so much fun!" Gigi exclaimed, clasping Chloe's hands and jumping up and down.

Chloe locked her arm with Gigi's, leading the way up to her room. "I was thinking we could toast marshmallows over the stove and bring our sleeping bags down to the parlor and stay up all night watching movies and telling ghost stories."

Gigi smacked her lips. "Girl, please. This is not summer camp. I invited a couple of guys over."

Chloe stopped in the middle of the staircase, nearly knocking Gigi over. "No company" had topped Mother's "don't" list.

"Gi', you didn't."

Gigi grinned, slinging her backpack over her shoulder. "Of course I did."

"I had to beg Mother to let us stay here by ourselves this weekend, and she only gave in because Jacques talked her into it. I'll get in big trouble if she finds out we had boys over."

"These aren't just any boys. Gaston and François are already on their way over."

Chloe clutched the banister, suddenly feeling lightheaded. The mere thought of seeing François, the boy she'd had a crush on since their freshman year at the Lycée, made her queasy.

"I've been promising Gaston all summer I'd hook up with him." Gigi galloped up the steps. "Besides, I know you can't wait to see François again."

Chloe reluctantly followed Gigi up the stairs, unable to rebut her last statement. She didn't know whether to thank her best friend or strangle her.

Chloe's bed was cluttered with clothes by the time she and Gigi finished getting ready. They raided Chloe's closet and tried on a million outfits before they found just the right ones. Gigi had settled on a pair of skintight jeans and a T-shirt that said *Oui* – a little too suggestive, Chloe thought, but the norm for Gigi. Chloe had decided on a denim wraparound skirt and a short-sleeve blouse. The outfit was summery but not too revealing. She didn't want

François to think she was too forward.

The doorbell rang around eight, and Chloe trembled with anticipation. "How do I look?" she asked, applying another coat of lip gloss as she stood next to Gigi in the bathroom mirror.

"*Fabuleux*, my dear, but loosen up a little." Gigi unfastened the top button of Chloe's blouse.

"I don't know, Gi'," Chloe said, holding the top of her blouse together. "I don't want to give out the wrong impression."

"Come on, girl, don't be such a prude."

The doorbell rang again.

"Let's go get 'em!" Gigi proclaimed.

Chloe and Gigi stampeded down the stairs and raced to the front door.

"We shouldn't seem like we put too much effort into getting ready for them. Act natural," Gigi cautioned before opening the door.

That's easy for her to say, Chloe thought, catching her breath.

Gigi opened the door and Gaston stepped forward. Chloe craned her neck, looking for François, but she couldn't see around Gaston.

"Hi, babe." Gaston handed Gigi a bouquet he had hidden behind his back and planted a quick smooch on her glossy lips.

"You're so sweet," Gigi said, sniffing the daisies and running her index finger up the fine blond hairs on his arm. "So, where's François?"

Chloe heard a car door slam and within moments, François appeared on the doorstep. He looked even better than she remembered, if that was possible. A snug T-shirt and shorts showed off his athlete's body and summer tan. His curly brown hair brushed his boyishly handsome face. His dark brown eyes probed Chloe's, and her mouth went dry.

"Chloe, it's so good to see you again," François said warmly, stepping inside.

A timid "hi" was all she could muster.

Gigi shut the door, ushering the boys inside. "Did you have any trouble finding the house?"

"A little, since it's so secluded," Gaston said. "You really can't see it from the road."

"This is Chloe's new house. We'll give you the grand tour," Gigi volunteered.

Before Chloe could protest, Gigi began leading the boys through the chateau. Chloe trailed behind the rest of the group, feeling awkward, clumsy, and almost feverish in François' presence. She kept tripping over her own feet and bumping into him. Her cheeks grew hot every time his skin touched hers. She became even more self-conscious when Gigi showed the boys the bedrooms.

"Why don't we go down to the ballroom and listen to some music," Chloe quickly suggested when Gigi flung open the door to Chloe's room. She didn't want the boys seeing her personal space. To think of François seeing the bed where she sometimes thought about him while touching herself between her legs was just too much.

"What music do you guys have?" Gaston inquired as the foursome made their way downstairs.

"I think my stepfather has the speakers in the ballroom programmed with his favorite jazz albums," Chloe said, feeling the hairs on the back of her neck stand up at the feeling of François' warm breath behind her.

"We have some CDs in the car," François offered, "all the really cool American rock 'n' roll: Radiohead, Bush."

"Actually, those are English groups." Chloe had become familiar with the British music scene while attending Our Lady of Chastity. She often checked out the BBC's variety show *Top of the Pops* when she had finished her homework and didn't have a good book to read.

Gigi elbowed her, an admonishment for acting too smart around boys, something she was always chiding Chloe for at mixers with St. Thomas. "Why don't you guys go get the CDs, and Chloe and I will make us some snacks."

"Cool," François said, following Gaston to the door. He turned and looked at Chloe over his shoulder as he walked out, and she felt weak when his eyes met hers.

"You have to admit having the guys over is much more fun than camping out in the parlor," Gigi said once they were in the kitchen. She reached into a cabinet and pulled out a Lalique crystal bowl.

"No, Gi'. That's Marie's favorite bowl."

Gigi dumped a bag of potato chips into the priceless antique. "I'll wash it and put it back and she won't even know we used it."

Vowing to keep an eye on the precious item, Chloe opened the refrigerator and began loading soda cans onto a sterling silver tray. "Do you think François likes me?"

"Are you kidding? I've noticed how he looks at you." Gigi balanced the bowl on her hip and opened Chloe's collar on her way out of the kitchen. "I think we're going to get some action tonight."

Chloe shook her head and followed Gigi through the swinging door, not sure if "action" was a good thing or not.

Chloe and Gigi and their dates danced to rock 'n' roll in the chateau's ballroom, cranking the built-in stereo system to full blast. Chloe was a good enough dancer, and she did all right as long as the songs were fast and François kept a safe distance.

As the night wore on, Gigi dimmed the lights and put on slow music. Gaston and François pressed their bodies up against the girls, rocking them back and forth to the rhythm. Being touched by the boy she had fantasized about, Chloe could hardly breathe. She swore she could feel his thing, hard as a rock, mashing up against her leg every time he moved too close. She didn't like how things were progressing. It was a little overwhelming – too much too soon. François' hands were moving up and down her back and grazing her butt and his face was caressing hers.

When the last slow song faded, Gaston took Gigi's hand and led her to one of the divans positioned around the room. As they sat down, Marie's glass bowl went tumbling to the ground, sending crumbs and a large chunk from the bowl's ornate rim scattering across the floor. Chloe winced, but Gaston and Gigi began making out as if they were too turned on to notice the accident.

Chloe was wringing her hands and trying to figure out how she would explain the mishap, when François took her hand and whispered in her ear.

"You want to...?"

Chloe knew what he was proposing, but didn't say yes or no. She simply followed him to a vacant seat and hoped she'd be able to control herself. She closed her eyes as François' lips met hers in the darkness. Her first kiss. His lips were full and moist, and the kiss was everything she had dreamed of and more.

François rubbed her back, and she didn't stop him as he kissed her and blew in her ear. She loved how he smelled, the spicy scent of his Joop! cologne filling all the air around her and driving her crazy. She was getting worked up, but she didn't know how to tell him that she didn't want things to go too far. She didn't know what to do when he put his hand on her breast and started squeezing. She held his hand and stroked it gently in order to get it off her boob.

François' attention was briefly drawn away when Gigi stood up and began to lead Gaston out of the room.

François looked at Chloe. "Come on, *bébé*," he said in a low, sexy growl.

Chloe's inner voice was telling her to be a good girl, to do what her mother would expect her to do and get up, turn on the lights, and tell François that it was time for him and Gaston to go home.

Why should I do what Mother expects me to? She's not even here.

Right then and there Chloe made up her mind that it was time for her to explore the uncharted waters of sex. Newly sixteen, she was still a virgin. Most of her friends had lost their virginity ages ago. She was probably the only girl who did justice to the name of her school – Our Lady of Chastity. Chloe longed to experience having François hold her, but she knew she could end up getting hurt by sleeping with him too soon – or even worse, pregnant.

Chloe could hear Gigi and Gaston reaching the top of the stairs. François was waiting for an answer.

Before Chloe could surrender herself, she had to know if François was still seeing the blond girl he'd been with at the movies last summer and at the spring-break party just a few months ago.

"What about that girl?" Chloe said.

"What girl?" François said, sounding as though he had no idea what she was talking about.

"That girl you were with at the party over spring break."

"Oh, her. Daphné." He paused, looking down. "She's just a friend. She's nobody. She means nothing to me." He ran his fingers over Chloe's cheek. "It's you I want."

She looked into his eyes. She wanted believe him. She wanted to believe he cared about her as much as she cared for him.

"Let's go," she said in a breathy whisper. She took his hand and let him lead her upstairs. She would have so much to tell the priest at her next confession.

This was going to be easy, Chloe thought. All she had to do was pretend she was a sexy character from one of those romantic old love stories she watched on TV. She was Dorothy Dandridge seducing Harry Belafonte in *Carmen Jones*. She was Catherine Deneuve acting out her repressed sexual fantasies in *Belle de Jour*. She was Valérie Bourdain casting a spell on her leading man.

Chloe and François seemed to float up the staircase like Fred Astaire and Ginger Rogers in one of those MGM musicals. Chloe directed her would-be lover down the dark hallway and stopped at the door to her room, ignoring the sounds of Gigi and Gaston moaning and groaning in the guestroom across the hall.

Chloe opened the door to her room and hovered in the doorway, still deciding whether she wanted to go through with this.

"Chloe, *bébé*, I don't think I can hold out much longer," François sighed.

He started undressing. Before she could blink he was standing in the hallway in nothing but his underwear.

"François, maybe you should –"

"I can't wait, Chloe. Come on." He darted past her, strewing his clothes in a trail behind him.

This is all wrong, Chloe said to herself. *This isn't how my first time should be. It's supposed to be special.*

Ignoring her inner voice, Chloe followed François into her room. He was lying on the bed with his hands folded behind his head, his erection poking through his underwear like a flagpole.

Chloe moved closer to the bed. He sat up on his knees and started kissing her and rubbing her all over. Before she knew what was happening, she was naked from the waist down and under the covers with François. She couldn't believe this was really happening, the moment she'd fantasized about so many times. Somehow this didn't seem how she'd imagined it.

François was panting like he was about to have an asthma attack.

"Are you all right?" she asked.

"I'm fine," he gurgled. "I just want you so bad, that's all."

He kissed her so hard it felt like was biting her lips. He wriggled out of his jockey shorts and flung them across the room. As he reached under the covers and took hold of himself, she squeezed her eyes shut and hoped it would be over quickly.

Suddenly, visions came to haunt her, visions that were sometimes there when she closed her eyes at night. As François writhed on top of her, the image of Pierre Rousseau trying to force himself on her in the pool house came back in a violent rush.

Chloe pushed François away.

"What's wrong, *bébé*? I have a rubber in my wallet, if that's what you're worried about."

Oh, so he came prepared, expecting something.

"No, that's not it."

"Then what is it?"

Chloe heard Gigi's voice echoing in her head: *Come on, girl, don't be such a prude.*

Chloe stroked François' small sprout of chest hair. "Nothing, forget about it. I'm ready."

He moved closer, grinning seductively. "I thought so."

He started kissing her again, slobbering all over her neck like a vampire trying to sink his fangs. She closed her eyes again, and the terrifying visions reappeared. She pushed François away again, this time with a force that said she meant business.

"What's wrong now?" he sighed in frustration.

"This whole thing is wrong. I can't do this, François."

"Why not?"

"Because I wanted my first time to be... I don't know, special."

"You're a virgin?"

"Yes."

His expression turned sympathetic. "Well don't worry. I'll make it good for you."

She put her hand on his chest, holding him at bay. "No. I don't want to. I'm not ready yet."

"Trust me. Just let me show you."

He started kissing her again. He slipped his hand under her blouse and tried to unhook her bra.

"No, François."

"Shhhh," he said, as if hushing a whining infant.

"Stop it," Chloe said as he tried to get her bra loose. He ignored her and kept fiddling with it. "I said stop," she said louder.

"Just relax. Let me show you how good it can be."

"Stop!"

François persisted, trying to mount her like a groom breaking in his inexperienced new bride.

"Get off me or I'll scream," she said finally, scratching his face.

"Damn it!" he yelled. He rolled off of her and touched his reddened cheek. "If there's a scar I'll –"

"You'll what?"

François softened his tone. "Chloe, what's the matter?"

"I told you. This just isn't how I wanted my first time to be."

Anger flashed in his dark eyes again. "You fucking tease! You wanted to do it just as much as I did. You and Gigi are the ones who invited us here. You brought me upstairs. I didn't make you do anything."

She sat up, pulling the covers over her half-open blouse. "Get out."

"Fine." He got up and searched for his clothes.

Watching him fumbling in the dark, she started to feel guilty. Maybe he was right. After all, she was the one who had said yes in the first place.

"Look," she said as he sat on the edge of the bed and roughly pulled on his underwear, "just because I didn't want to do it tonight doesn't mean I don't want to see you anymore. Maybe we could go out next time I'm home for break. I'll give you my number at school and maybe –"

He swung his head around. "I want nothing to do with you. You're crazy. First you get me all excited, and then at the last minute you act like I'm trying to rape you or something. I'm sorry we even came here tonight." He stood, gathering his clothes in a bunch under his arm. "At least Gaston's getting something. I'm going to call Daphné. I know *she* won't say no." He stomped out of the room, pounded down the hall and the stairs, and slammed the front door so hard the windows rattled.

Chloe turned over and cried. The only boy she had ever loved had pierced her heart with a dagger. He'd made it clear that the only reason he'd paid attention to her was to satisfy himself. And he'd obviously lied about Daphné only being a friend. He was probably going to trash Chloe to Gaston and all their friends. Gigi had a reputation as a flirt, but being a tease was far worse.

Chloe put a pillow over her head and sobbed. She just wanted this night to be over. Her schoolgirl crush hadn't panned out, it had only brought her pain.

18

Gigi stood on her bed in the girls' dorm room, tacking a centerfold from a teen magazine above her headboard while Chloe lay on her bed turning pages in her chemistry book and listening to music.

The ballad by Latin pop star Sergio Reyes about a relationship gone sour perfectly expressed what Chloe was feeling. Since seeing this handsome young Spanish singer crooning his first crossover hit on *Top of the Pops*, Chloe had nearly worn out the CD, listening to it over and over as she thought about François. The sense of loss and rejection was overwhelming.

"Are you still pouting over François?" Gigi said, stepping back to observe the poster with her artist's eye.

Chloe shut her book and sat up. "I can't stop thinking about him. I don't think I'll ever get over the pain of losing him."

Gigi adjusted the knobs on the CD player that sat on the nightstand between their beds, turning down the volume on the somber ballad that had been the soundtrack to Chloe's life since returning from summer break. "Girl, will you stop being so dramatic? Do you know how many other boys there are out there? There's a whole school full of them just down the road."

Chloe bit the tip of her pencil, her mind drifting once again to the disastrous encounter with François. "I don't care about those boys at St. Thomas. François was the only boy I ever loved."

"You'll get over it. I've already forgotten Gaston." Gigi kissed her hand and touched the poster above her bed. "Montana Blake is my new love."

Chloe tilted her head and studied the poster of the pouty, tanned and toned guy posed in a tank top and faded, ripped blue jeans. His stringy, dark hair partially masked intense blue eyes that were framed by girlishly long lashes. He was more pretty than handsome. "Who's he?"

Chloe was soon sorry she asked, uttering an occasional "uh-huh" as Gigi blathered on about her latest crush. Chloe absentmindedly flipped through her chemistry book again while Gigi cited nearly verbatim the article in that ridiculous fan 'zine about the American teen idol. Montana Blake had risen to fame as a child star on a family sitcom, launched a bumble-gum singing career as a teen, and was now, in his early twenties, trying to conquer the overseas market with a new album produced by a famous European club DJ/dance-pop maestro.

"No offense, Gi'," Chloe said once Gigi had finished ranting about this new sensation, "but it doesn't exactly make me feel better just because you've gone ga-ga over some star you'll never meet."

Gigi gestured toward the poster of Sergio Reyes that Chloe had pinned above her bed, similar to the one Gigi had just tacked up of Montana Blake. Judging from the poster, which had been tucked inside Sergio's CD jacket like a Cracker Jack prize for fans, the Latin hunk's dark, smoldering looks would certainly catapult him to international sex-symbol status just like Montana.

"You have your pretty-boy crush, I have mine," Gigi reasoned. "Besides, Montana's not just a pretty face. He's a serious actor and musician."

Chloe gathered her books. "Whatever. We better get to class."

"You'll see: I *will* meet him someday," Gigi said, stepping down from the bed and grabbing her book bag.

"Right," Chloe said sardonically, following Gigi to the door. "And I might as well pick Sergio Reyes as my rebound romance. I have just as much chance of meeting him as you have of meeting your new pinup boy."

The fall semester at Our Lady of Chastity zoomed by. Chloe continued to excel in academics and even joined the equestrian club and newly-formed fencing team. Those summer riding lessons and "dueling" sessions with Jacques paid off and earned her a trophy in one particularly challenging fencing meet with another British all-girls' academy.

Gigi's performance in school, on the other hand, plummeted. She was too busy keeping time with boys from St. Thomas. She had gotten caught and punished numerous times for sneaking in after lights out. Gigi's rationale was that until fate improbably brought her face to face with her teen idol, Montana Blake, she was biding her time with the academy boys.

In no time at all, seemingly, the Christmas season rolled around. Chloe and Gigi made it home in time for a big Christmas Eve party that Maxine and Jacques hosted in the Chateau de Chevalier ballroom. Melodies played by a live string quartet mingled with the sounds of laughter and buzzing conversation among Maxine and Jacques' diverse group of friends.

"Help yourself, girls," Marie said, approaching Chloe and Gigi with a tray of beignets fresh out of the oven. "Thanks for helping me bake this afternoon."

"Our pleasure," Chloe said, chomping into a delicious cookie. She had also enlisted Gigi to help Marie and the household staff decorate the ballroom with giant red bows and other seasonal favors.

"You know," Marie said, watching Maxine and Jacques greet guests who were still arriving, "I think this is the happiest I've seen M'sieu at the holidays since Marguerite passed on."

Chloe smiled at Marie's sentiment and, along with Gigi, followed her into the kitchen to fill punch bowls with homemade eggnog.

"I think this occasion calls for my favorite crystal bowl," Marie said, reaching into a cabinet above the stove.

Chloe quickly looked at Gigi, remembering the accident in the ballroom that ill-fated summer night with François and Gaston. Chloe and Gigi had hastily glued the chipped bowl and put it back on the shelf, hoping Marie wouldn't notice.

"Why don't you let me get that," Gigi said, maneuvering in front of Marie and reaching for the bowl. "You've got so much other stuff to do."

Marie paused, sizing Gigi up for a moment in which Chloe held her breath and prayed the older woman wouldn't see through their cover-up.

"Okay," Marie said finally, wiping her hands on her apron, "but be careful with that bowl. It was a wedding gift when I married my beloved Albert, God rest his soul."

Chloe breathed a sigh of relief as Marie went about filling a tray with hors d'oeuvres. She helped Gigi fill the fragile bowl with eggnog and carried it out to the ballroom.

"That was close," Chloe said once they had set the bowl on the refreshment table.

"I told you she'd never find out," Gigi said coolly.

"I think we should reward ourselves by exchanging gifts."

"Now that's a plan."

Chloe retrieved their gifts from under the Christmas tree, which was so tall that it brushed the ballroom's cathedral ceiling. Each girl anxiously tore the wrapping paper off their gifts, though neither was surprised since they had exchanged detailed lists.

"How'd you know? Just what I wanted," Chloe said humorously, holding up a DVD of one of her favorite Valérie Bourdain movies.

Gigi admired the pastels and sketchpad she had requested. "I'm going to start a new sketch tomorrow on the way to my grandparents' farm. It'll give me something to do on the long car ride other than hear Simone babble on."

Chloe chuckled, watching Simone flirting with a handsome man on the other end of the ballroom and musing about how alike mother and daughter were.

Throughout the evening, Jacques proudly introduced Chloe as his daughter to friends and business associates. As Chloe stood between Maxine and Jacques, greeting guests at the ballroom entrance, a handsome, middle-aged man with gray-flecked, reddish-brown hair and a plump yet attractive brunette approached.

"Renaud, so glad you could make it," Jacques said, robustly shaking the man's hand. He turned to the woman, kissing her on either cheek. "Henriette, you look lovely as always."

"You know we'd never miss the boss's Christmas party," the man replied, grinning.

"Renaud is the foreman at the loading docks," Jacques explained to Maxine and Chloe. He added jovially, "And Henriette is his devoted wife and the mother of his five children who puts up with me working her husband such long hours."

"Pleasure to meet you both," Maxine said, shaking hands with the couple and nudging Chloe to do the same.

"I'm glad to finally meet the two pretty girls from the photograph on Jacques' desk," Renaud said upon shaking Chloe's hand, his rough palms indicative of a man who had spent much of his life working in the elements. "The three of you make a beautiful family."

After Renaud and Henriette Mercier made their way into the ballroom, a succession of Maxine's longtime friends and clients arrived. Upon seeing Chloe, several uttered the refrain "My, how you've grown," and she had to keep herself from groaning. She bit her lip to keep from giggling as Gigi crossed her eyes and made faces while Chloe endured repetitive questions about school and boring small talk.

One of the highlights of the evening was meeting Jacques' mother, Claudette, whom Jacques had flown in from St.-Tropez for the evening.

"So nice to finally meet you, Madame Chevalier," Chloe said, offering her hand to the well-preserved older woman who was clad in a stylish Chanel suit.

"You can call me *Maman*. Your mother is Madame Chevalier now," the woman said with a kind smile. She released Chloe's hand and pulled her into an embrace. "Welcome to the family. I've always wanted a grandchild."

Gaining a grandmother was a nice Christmas present. Chloe had missed having that connection since Mama Louise passed away.

Later that evening, when most of the guests had cleared out, Simone approached Chloe and Gigi. "You ready to go, Gi'?"

"I've *been* ready to go for the past hour," Gigi whined. "I swear, Simone, it turns my stomach watching a woman your age flirt and carry on with men the way you do."

Simone wagged her finger. "You better watch your mouth, little girl, or Santa's not going to bring you anything but a lump of coal."

"Oh, please." Gigi popped her gum and looked unfazed.

Simone glanced at the doorway of the ballroom, where Jacques and Maxine thanked departing guests. Jacques had his arm around Maxine, and they looked like the two happiest people in the world.

"I'm so thrilled for Maxine," Simone said. "She's finally found the right man."

"Yeah," Gigi interjected, "you could learn something from her instead of hanging out with the losers you do."

Simone grimaced. "I should've made you stay with the nuns over Christmas break." She pulled on her coat and fanned her long, flaming hair over the fur collar. "Come on, let's go. We've got a long drive to *Maman*'s and Papa's in the morning."

"'Night, Chlo'," Gigi said as Simone pulled her toward the door. "I'll call you tomorrow night when we get back."

Chloe waved. "'Night, you guys."

"*Bonsoir*, dear," Simone called over her shoulder.

After everyone had left and *Maman* Chevalier had adjourned to the guestroom, Jacques, Maxine and Chloe changed into their robes and pajamas and retreated to the parlor. Chloe sat in a chair, across from Mother and Jacques in the loveseat, admiring the tree that was smaller than the enormous one in the ballroom and was decorated with ornaments that both Jacques and Maxine had acquired over the years. Chloe had placed the star on the top – a craft she had made in first grade and a tradition she was happy to continue in the home she and her mother now shared with Jacques.

"If there's nothing else you need," Marie said, appearing in the doorway with a tray of hot cider and cookies left over from the party, "I'm going to retire. I have a long train ride to Avignon in the morning. Everyone's getting together at my daughter's and I can't wait to see my new grandbaby."

"'Night, Marie," Jacques said, waving. "Thanks for everything."

"Merry Christmas," Maxine said, taking a steaming mug from the tray and raising it as if in a toast.

Marie nodded. "*Joyeux Noël.*"

A comfortable silence enveloped the room as Chloe sat with her mother and stepfather, drinking cider, admiring the blinking lights and listening to the fire crackling in the fireplace. The sound of the grandfather clock ringing in midnight echoed throughout the house.

"Well, it's Christmas," Jacques said, putting his arm around Maxine.

"This is so exciting," Maxine said. "Our first Christmas together. I can't wait to go to Mass in the morning and come home and open all the gifts."

Chloe eyed the cache of gold- and silver-wrapped boxes glistening under the tree. "Can I open one now?" she pleaded like a preschooler, not attempting to disguise her eagerness.

Jacques and Maxine looked at each other, as if conferring.

"It's technically Christmas," Chloe added to persuade them, "and I won't be able to sleep if I have to wait 'til morning. Please, just one?"

Mother looked at Jacques again, then at Chloe. "You can open as many as you want, *ma chérie*." She put her hand on Jacques' knee. "But there's something we'd like to talk over with you first. We were going to wait until tomorrow after church, but now seems like as good a time as any."

"What's up?" Chloe said, bracing herself for some startling revelation.

"Since we're a family now," Maxine said, "we want to make it official."

"Okay," Chloe said in confusion, not sure where this was going. Was Mother going to announce she was pregnant?

Jacques glanced at Maxine, who nodded for him to pick up where she left off. "Your mother and I have discussed this, and, if it's okay with you, I'd like to formally adopt you and give you my last name."

Chloe was so surprised and overcome with emotion, she didn't know what to say.

"I know this is all happening so fast – your mother and I running off and getting married and you guys moving in here," Jacques said. "If the adoption is too soon, if you want to keep your family name, I understand."

"No," Chloe spoke up, her eyes welling with tears, "I'd like that. I'd love to be a Chevalier."

"I'm so glad." Maxine clasped her hands together. "Now we'll all have the same last name."

"I'll have my attorney draw up the papers and we can go to probate court and finalize everything next time you're home from school," Jacques said.

Chloe got up and threw her arms around her mother and stepfather. "This is the best Christmas present."

As eager as Chloe was to open gifts, material things weren't the best part of this Christmas. The best part was spending the holidays in a real house, and feeling like she was part of a real family for the first time.

19

Maxine sat in her office at work, gazing out the window and admiring the spring buds.

"Good news," Simone said, rapping on the open door as she entered. "The Rocheforts just called. We got the account." She set a manila folder on Maxine's desk. "Just sign the work orders and we can get going on their redecorating project."

Maxine scooted up to the desk and thumbed through the paperwork. "I'm so glad we're finally closing this deal. Two months of wining and dining and finessing this client finally paid off." She signed the papers and handed them to Simone.

Simone flipped the file closed and headed for the door. "By the way, are you going to send a car to pick the girls up on Friday, or should I swing by the airport myself?"

Maxine glanced at her desk calendar. "God, I can't believe it's Easter break already. Why don't Jacques and I go by the airport and pick up the girls?"

"It's hard to believe you two have been married for a year. What are you doing for your anniversary?"

The thought of the romantic weekend Jacques planned brought a smile to Maxine's face. "He made reservations at Alain's tonight. That's where we had our first date."

Simone pursed her lips, looking impressed. "Mmm. *Romantique.*"

"I know, and we're going to St.-Tropez this weekend for the first sail of the season," Maxine added. "We're going to take Chloe so she can go sailing with us. This will be her first time on that boat Jacques loves so much."

Simone leaned on the doorframe with a wistful expression. "You know, I envy you. Not only do you have a good man by your side, but Chloe's such a good kid and she and Jacques really seemed to hit it off."

Maxine nodded. "He's made plans to formally adopt her and give her his last name. We're going to probate court and take care of all the formalities while Chloe's home for break."

"That's so sweet. You lucked out with Jacques, but I'm still on and off with Pascal."

"Well, maybe that's because Pascal has the attention span of a high school student," Maxine said, adding facetiously, "and the same birth date, too."

Simone scowled. "Very funny. But seriously, I'd like to find someone mature and responsible like Jacques. Gigi needs a male influence; I can't handle her on my own. Her report card came in the mail the other day and she's on academic probation – *again*. I wish Chloe would rub off on her."

Maxine beamed. "She made honor roll again. I'm so proud of her. She'll have no trouble getting into a good college." She began straightening her desk, preparing to leave for the day. "You know, everything's been going so well lately, I'm almost afraid to let my guard down. Business is booming, Chloe's doing well in school, Jacques is going to adopt her, and we're celebrating our anniversary. I know it's silly, but I keep worrying that something bad has to happen to balance out all the good things."

"That *is* silly. As much as I envy you, I'm glad to see you happy. You give me hope that maybe I'll find happiness someday."

"You will, and I know I'm being silly. It's probably just that old Creole superstition my mother instilled in me." Maxine reclined in her chair. "I'm still learning to relax and enjoy my blessings."

Henri, Maxine's assistant, came up beside Simone in the doorway. "Sorry to interrupt," he said to Maxine, clutching a large ream of paper, "but do you have time to sign off on these invoices?"

Maxine picked up her briefcase and stood. "Sorry, Henri. That'll just have to wait 'til Monday."

"We hope this is to your liking, Madame Chevalier," the graying, bespectacled man behind the counter at the Tiffany boutique said, handing Maxine a platinum man's watch.

She examined the custom-made piece, turning it over to read the engraving: "To Jacques – Max."

"This is perfect," she told the clerk, "just what I was looking for. It's an anniversary gift for my husband. He's going to love it."

The clerk smiled and placed the item in a box. "*Tres bien.* I hope M'sieu Chevalier gets many years of enjoyment out of it."

Maxine happily handed over her gold card. "I'm sure he will."

Upon leaving the store, she decided to take a stroll before summoning her driver. It was a gorgeous, sunny afternoon. Springtime in Paris was her favorite time of year. She enjoyed watching the flowers bloom in the Jardin du Luxembourg and seeing lovers stroll hand in hand in the April rain down boulevard Victor Hugo and exchange passionate kisses in the Place des Voges, Paris' oldest and most beautiful square.

At an intersection, Maxine waited for the walk signal and stepped into the street. Suddenly, she heard tires squealing and looked up to see a car speeding toward her. A young man behind her pulled her back onto the curb and she nearly dropped her bags, she was so shaken.

"Are you okay, Madame?" the bystander asked her in French.

"Yes, thank you," she replied, straightening her suit jacket. "I'm fine. Thank you so much."

She stared in the direction of the speeding car and tried to make out who was behind the wheel of the sleek black Mercedes, but the tinted windows shielded the driver from view. Before she could make a mental note of the license plate, the car rounded a corner and disappeared.

She took a moment to collect herself, then looked both ways and proceeded through the intersection when the signal changed again. She shrugged off the rude driver; she had more important things to focus on. Tonight was her anniversary.

"I love it, Maxine," Jacques said. He held up the Tiffany watch and the platinum reflected the candlelight at their favorite table at Alain's.

"I had it custom-made," Maxine proudly reported. "It's engraved on the back."

Jacques read the engraving, kissed Maxine, and put on the watch. He then slid a gift-wrapped box across the table. "Your turn."

Maxine tore the wrapping paper with the excitement of a child at her first birthday party and gasped at the sight of a diamond choker encrusted with sapphires that shimmered against the red satin interior of a Van Cleef & Arpels box. "Jacques, it's beautiful." She held her hands to her cheeks in astonishment. "You know I love diamonds."

"M'sieu Chevalier, I didn't know you thought so highly of my cooking! You didn't have to get me such an extravagant gift." Alain Bisson, the incorrigible restaurateur and chef, approached the table and gestured toward the choker.

"It's for my wife, wise guy," Jacques replied in the same good-natured, comical tone.

"Ah, allow me." Alain reached for the choker and fastened it around Maxine's neck. He stood back, admiring the necklace. "That shiny thing is not half as stunning as Ma-*dam*."

Maxine nodded appreciatively, chuckling at the chef's Gallic way with women.

"Okay, enough flirting with my wife," Jacques interjected. "Don't you have other customers to pester?"

"Of course I had to stop by and visit my favorite people first," Alain replied, winking at Maxine. "We haven't seen you in a while. What's the occasion?"

"It's our anniversary," Maxine said with a broad smile, opening her menu.

"You should've told me. I'll have Cédric bring out our best champagne." Alain snapped his fingers at the waiter.

"I can see you're trying to clean my wallet out," Jacques teased.

The chef waved his hand, as if dismissing something trivial. "It's on the house."

The waiter came up and placed a bottle of Perrier-Jouët to chill in the wine bucket next to the table and muttered something in the chef's ear.

"I better get back to the kitchen," Alain said. "There's a minor emergency with a soufflé that just collapsed." He kissed Maxine's hand and slapped Jacques on the back. "Enjoy your anniversary. I'm glad you chose to spend it here."

When Alain turned to retreat to the kitchen, Jacques reached for the chef's hand.

"In all seriousness, thank you for all the years of hospitality," Jacques said to the chef in a tone that was much more serious than their usual banter. "I appreciate your kindness."

The chef looked taken off-guard, as if he didn't know how to respond. "M'sieu Chevalier, why do you talk as though you'll never dine here again? You'll be here next year to celebrate your second anniversary, and many times in between."

Maxine looked at Jacques, not sure what to make of her husband's unexpected outpouring.

"Still," Jacques said, "I just wanted to say thanks while I had the chance."

Alain patted Jacques' hand and backed away from the table, uncharacteristically at a loss for words.

"What was that about?" Maxine said after the chef had returned to the kitchen.

"Nothing, *amour*." He fanned his napkin in his lap. "Tonight's our night."

Maxine reached across the table and took his hand. "Honey, something's bothering you. Talk to me."

Jacques looked down at the table, then up at Maxine, the candlelight accentuating the gold flecks in his eyes. "I didn't want to bring this up tonight because I didn't want to spoil the mood, but there's something going on I should probably tell you about."

She grasped his hand tighter, trying to anticipate what he was going to say. "What? You can tell me anything, you know that."

He shifted in his seat. "Do you remember that ugly episode with Pierre Rousseau last summer?"

Maxine stiffened at the mention of the name of the scum who had tried to attack Chloe. "Of course. How could I forget?"

"I should have done more due-diligence in checking him out. I thought he was a credible financier, but it turns out he was nothing but a glorified loan shark. I didn't know he was involved in the underworld, or I never would have done business with him."

Jacques massaged his forehead with his thumb and forefinger, looking old for the first time since Maxine had known him.

"I was hoping it would all be over after I had him done away with," he continued in a weary tone, "but I'm afraid his henchmen have been coming after me in retaliation."

Maxine let go of Jacques' hand and sat up, trying not to panic. "What do you mean, coming after you?"

"There have been a couple of instances when I was driving and noticed someone following me. Whoever it is tried to run me off the road." He stared at the candle, his face contorted in distress. "At first, I thought I was just being paranoid, but there's only one person who could have set these events in motion." He looked her in the eye. "And my biggest fear is that if they can't get to me first, they're going to go after you and Chloe."

Maxine thought back on the incident from earlier in the day when she was nearly mowed down by the speeding car.

Her concern must have shown on her face, because Jacques took her hand and said, "What is it, *amour*? Did something happen to you?"

"No, not exactly," she said, trying to reassure her husband and allay her own fears.

"What? What happened?" Jacques pressed. "Tell me."

She didn't want to further alarm him, but she had to be honest if she expected the same from him.

"It's nothing, really. This afternoon, when I was leaving the boutique after picking up your gift, I stepped out in the intersection and a car kept going through the light. Whoever it was almost hit me, but another pedestrian pulled me back onto the curb."

Jacques let go of Maxine's hand and slammed his fist on the table, clattering the silverware and water glasses and attracting stares from nearby tables. "Goddamn that Rousseau. He's like a roach. You snuff him out and he still comes back."

"Jacques, why don't we go to the police and tell them everything?"

"But of course, I'd have to confess the role I played in Rousseau's death."

"They should give you a medal for taking such a menace to society off the streets," Maxine said, her maternal, protective instinct evident in the intensity of her voice.

Jacques looked pensive. "I thought I was doing the right thing by taking the law into my own hands. I thought that thug I hired would just rough Rousseau up a bit, put the fear of God into him and make sure he left us alone. But things got out of hand when Rousseau fought back, and the goon ended up slitting Rousseau's throat."

"Poetic justice, if you ask me."

"I agree, but I'll be linked to Rousseau's murder if we go to the police."

"Jacques, we have no other choice," Maxine reasoned. "We'll explain that we had no way of proving what Rousseau tried to do to Chloe. It would have been her word against his."

He sighed heavily, his weariness showing in his tired eyes. "I'm sorry I got you guys into this mess. If we go to the police and word gets out about my involvement in Rousseau's death, the bad publicity would ruin both our businesses. And if they lock me away, who would be around to protect you and Chloe?"

Maxine remained silent for a moment, trying to make sense of it all. "We'll get through this," she said finally. "We'll find a way to get through this if we stick together and refuse to be intimidated. We'll hire twenty-four-hour security, send Chloe to school with a bodyguard."

"That's no way to live, under constant fear," Jacques said. "It's me they want, and you and Chloe aren't going to be safe until I'm out of the picture."

Maxine leaned forward and touched her husband's face. "Honey, don't say that. You're the best thing that ever happened to Chloe and I."

"Look, Max, I'm going to take every precaution possible to make sure we're all safe, but I've set things up so if something does happen to me –"

"Don't talk like that."

Jacques clasped her hand. "Just hear me out, *amour*. I've updated my will and my insurance policies so that my business and all of my assets will go to you. I've also set up a trust fund for Chloe. That's another reason why I wanted to adopt her – to make it easier to list you both as beneficiaries on all of my policies. I want to make sure you're both taken care of if I ever get sick or if an accident or something terrible happens – heaven forbid."

Maxine choked back tears. "Nothing's going to happen to you. We're a family now and I'm not going to let anyone break us apart."

Jacques caressed her cheek. "Let's just enjoy tonight."

He reached for the champagne, popped the cork and filled their glasses. He picked up his glass and she did the same, forcing a smile.

"To us," he said, intertwining his arm with hers.

She looked into his eyes, trying to humor him and savor the moment. "To us."

Maxine awoke to find Jacques' side of the bed empty. He had left a note on his pillow: "Ran out to take care of last-minute business at the office before we leave for St.-Tropez, didn't want to wake you. Be back soon. *Je t'aime* – Jacques."

Maxine lay there for a moment, reflecting on the previous night and the disturbing talk about the repercussions from the messy Rousseau episode.

Shifting her thoughts to the relaxing weekend in St.-Tropez that lie ahead, she sprang out of bed and slipped a silver satin robe over her matching nightgown. She plodded down to the kitchen for a cup of coffee to give herself a jolt of energy to complete the cumbersome chore of packing.

"Good morning, Marie," Maxine said upon entering the kitchen, still a little groggy but buzzing with excitement about the weekend getaway with Jacques and Chloe.

"*Bonjour.*" Marie looked up from her rolling pin. "I just brewed a fresh pot of coffee. Just let me rinse my hands and I'll pour you a cup."

Maxine retrieved a mug from the cabinet. "No, that's okay. I'll get it."

Marie nodded. "*Merci.* I wanted you and M'sieu to have a good breakfast before you leave for the airport, so I'm making my homemade croissants."

"Sounds delicious."

Maxine filled her coffee cup and sat at the counter, thumbing through the morning paper and tuning out the background noise from the small countertop TV that Marie had tuned to her favorite cooking show. Both women looked up and turned their attention to the screen when the program was interrupted by a news bulletin.

"We've just got word that there has been a fatal car accident on the Alexandre III bridge," the female newscaster said in French over footage of a mangled vehicle smashed into a light pole.

Maxine rose, noticing the familiar license plate. *No, it can't be,* she thought, fighting off panic.

The newscaster continued: "Police have identified the driver as shipping magnate Jacques Chevalier."

Marie screamed and Maxine dropped her cup, sending scalding liquid and porcelain shards flying in every direction.

20

Maxine was only going through the motions during the funeral. The altar of St.-Jean l'Evangéliste cathedral resembled the Chateau de Chevalier's gardenia beds. Arrangements and wreaths had been sent by every friend and business acquaintance Jacques had made during his lifetime. The man had been loved by many and was going to be missed by everyone whose life he had touched – especially Maxine and Chloe.

"He loved you both dearly," Marie, tears streaming down her face, said softly to Maxine and Chloe after paying respects at the closed casket.

Maxine nodded, her gauzy crepe veil shielding her face, and told Marie she was grateful to her and Simone for handling most of the arrangements. Marie lingered for a moment, then took her place at the end of the pew. Maxine continued to accept condolences from well-wishers and thanked them for their kindness. She felt as though she were outside of her body. She couldn't believe that she had lost the love of her life, the only man she had ever really cared for, other than Chloe's father. Maxine didn't even have a chance to say goodbye, to kiss his cheek one last time. She hadn't been able to cry; she felt numb inside.

A smiling photo, the way Maxine remembered her husband, sat atop the casket. There were a couple of times she felt like breaking down during Monsignor Guillaume's eulogy, but she fought back the tears. She had to be strong for Chloe and for *Maman* Chevalier, who were sitting on either side of her in the front pew. Maxine put her arm around her daughter and gripped her mother-in-law's hand. She and *Maman* were sources of support and solace for each other and banded together to comfort Chloe.

Toward the end of the eulogy, when the pallbearers were preparing to carry the casket out of the sanctuary, Maxine got a strange sensation that she was being watched. She looked over her shoulder and noticed the shadowy figure of a man standing at the back of a church. For an instant, she thought she recognized the man as Jacques.

She was staring at the figure in shock, trying to figure out if her eyes were deceiving her, when she felt a hand on her shoulder and heard someone call her name. She turned and saw *Maman* Chevalier looking at her with concern.

"Are you all right, Maxine?"

Maxine glanced back and saw that the man, whoever he was, had left the church. He was gone as quickly as he appeared.

"Yes," Maxine said, her voice gravelly with emotion. "I'm okay. I was just thinking about Jacques."

Maman Chevalier's expression softened. "It's time to go to the cemetery, *cher*."

Maxine nodded, appreciating her mother-in-law's ability to retain her composure despite the nearly unbearable grief with which they were all dealing. Maxine took Chloe's hand and they trailed *Maman* Chevalier behind the pallbearers as they carried the casket down the aisle.

As they descended the steps of the cathedral and made their way to the long black limousine waiting to take them to the cemetery, Maxine gripped Chloe's hand tighter. She had to martial her strength and keep up appearances.

Maxine helped *Maman* Chevalier into the limousine and slid in next to her. When Chloe settled beside her, Maxine put her arm around her. Though Maxine felt a wave of sadness washing over her, triggering the urge to sob uncontrollably, she held it in. She had her daughter to think of.

*****

Chloe stood between Maxine and *Maman* Chevalier at Jacques' graveside in the Père-Lachaise Cemetery. Chloe shivered in the chilly April rain, not really listening as Monsignor Guillaume read Bible verses. She glanced over at Gigi, who stood next to Simone and gave Chloe an encouraging nod.

If it weren't for Gigi, Chloe didn't know how she could get through this ordeal. The whole experience was unreal. It was Gigi who had been there for Chloe when the bad news came. The girls had been packing to return home for Easter break when Mother Superior summoned Chloe to her office. The headmistress' tone had been uncharacteristically delicate as she related that Chloe needed to call home on an urgent matter.

Chloe nearly collapsed when she reached Maxine, who said there had been a terrible accident. Chloe instinctively knew what her mother was going to say next.

Chloe's initial reaction was denial. There had to be some mistake, the police must have misidentified the body. Maybe Jacques was in the hospital and the doctors were still working to revive him. But Mother was gently insistent that Jacques was gone.

When reality finally set in, Gigi had taken Chloe in her arms as Chloe screamed and cried, her body wracked with sobs. Gigi had shown maturity beyond her years, rubbing Chloe's back and telling her everything was going to be all right.

Chloe looked around the cemetery at the ornate headstones and mausoleums and towering statues of saints and angels. It seemed just yesterday that the girls had toured the historic site on a school field trip as freshmen at the Lycée. Scanning the graves of French literary legend Marcel Proust and American rock star Jim Morrison, death had seemed so far away to Chloe, so far removed from her own youthful existence. But tragedy had unexpectedly touched her life and claimed the life of the closest person to a father she had ever known, and there was no going back. A layer of innocence had been stripped away.

As the priest concluded his remarks and Jacques' casket was lowered into the ground, *Maman* Chevalier uttered a small cry and faltered and Maxine caught her, the older woman leaning on her daughter-in-law for support. Chloe wished she could have a similar breakdown, which would be a release, but the tears had dried up. She silently followed her mother, *Maman* Chevalier and the rest of the mourners out of the cemetery.

Later during the reception at the Chateau de Chevalier, Mother came over when Chloe was sitting in a corner of the ballroom by herself, a half-eaten plate of food in her lap.

"Hey, *ma chérie*, you haven't said much all day," Maxine said, sitting on the divan next to Chloe.

"I know." Chloe pushed her plate aside. "All I keep thinking is that the last time we were in the ballroom, it was the Christmas party."

Everybody was laughing and singing and dancing then, but this was such a somber occasion. This wasn't how Chloe was supposed to be spending her spring break. Instead of hitting the department stores with Gigi to use the shiny new charge card Jacques had given Chloe, she had accompanied her mother to buy a plain black dress for his funeral. Today was the day they were supposed to go downtown to finalize the adoption papers, the day she would have taken Jacques' last name and officially became his daughter. But he had been taken away before the act could be consummated. It was so unfair.

"I never even got to see his yacht," Chloe said, tears stinging her eyes. "Remember that weekend last summer when you guys went to St.-Tropez and he wanted me to come with you so he could take me out on his yacht? I should have gone instead of staying here so Gigi could sleep over. He loved the open water so much, and now he's gone and I'll never get a chance to go sailing with him."

Chloe hadn't cried all day, feeling oddly disconnected during the funeral proceedings, but now the tears burst forth and she sobbed profusely. Maxine took her in her arms and cradled her the way she used to when Chloe was little.

"He loved you like his own, you know," Maxine said after a moment, still rocking Chloe back and forth. "I'm so sorry he passed before we could go through with the adoption. But he set up a trust fund for you. We talked about it right before he ..." Maxine stopped short. "You'll get the first payout when you turn eighteen."

Chloe, resting her head on her mother's bosom, said nothing in response. Eighteen, when she would become a legal adult, was just over a year away but seemed as distant and out of reach as the concept of death once had.

"If it makes you feel any better, nothing's going to change around the house," Maxine said. "When you come home for summer break, everything will be the same."

Chloe remained silent. Nothing would ever be the same again.

Maxine brushed the bangs out of Chloe's eyes. "Are you okay?"

"Yeah, I'm okay," Chloe mumbled, sitting up and pulling away from Maxine. "I just don't really feel like being around people. May I be excused?"

"Of course. I'll come up and check on you later."

On the way up to her room, Chloe hugged Gigi and Simone and thanked them for their support. Finding Marie collecting empty plates and glasses, she offered to help her clean up.

"No, *chouchou*, you rest. I just wish you'd eat something to keep up your strength."

"I don't have much of an appetite."

Marie hoisted a tray of dirty dishes. "I understand. We all loved M'sieu Chevalier."

Chloe stood there for a moment, reflecting on Marie's comment, then retreated upstairs. Leaving the ballroom, she noticed the framed photo of herself with Mother and Jacques that had been snapped during the Christmas party. Those happy times seemed like a lifetime ago.

Trudging up the stairs, Chloe reasoned that she might as well accept the fact that she was a victim of circumstance just like everyone else. All of her life, she had to deal with things beyond her control: never knowing her biological father, being uprooted when Mother ran off and married Jacques without her knowledge, and now the sudden death of the man she had come to adore and think of as her father.

Reaching the top of the steps, Chloe spied Maxine seeing off a friend of Jacques' and thanking them for coming. Chloe marveled at how Maxine continued to keep up her tough façade, never showing a trace of weakness.

Alone in her room, Chloe lay on her bed and gazed at the family photo on her nightstand. She reached out and touched Jacques' face. She wished he was still around to watch out for her and her mother and kiss her goodnight. He was gone forever, and so was her hope of ever being part of a real family.

Maxine sat at Jacques' desk in the company he had built from the ground up, sorting through his things.

Simone entered, cradling a large banker's box. "I think this is the last of his personal papers. You ready to go?"

Maxine hesitated, gripping the armrests of Jacques' leather chair. "I don't know if I'll ever be ready. I keep flip-flopping back and forth on whether selling the company is the right thing to do."

Simone approached the desk, setting down the box. "Max, you had no other choice. You can't run our company and his, too. That foreign investor's offer is more than generous, and retaining a seat on the board of directors will allow you to make sure the company keeps the Chevalier name and continues to grow."

Maxine reclined in the chair. "You're right, I know. It's just that…" She stared out the window overlooking the shipping yard and docks that lined the Seine. "This just feels so permanent. There's a little part of me that keeps hoping Jacques will come back to me, that some kind of miracle will happen. It's foolish, I know, but I'm still not convinced that Jacques' death didn't have something to do with that whole mess with Rousseau. The last night I saw him, when we went out for our anniversary, Jacques told me he believed Rousseau's people were out to get him. And there was that incident when that car almost ran me down outside the jewelry store."

"You saw the police report. They found no evidence of foul play," Simone reasoned. "No one ran him off the road; he was simply rushing to get home and lost control of the car."

Maxine twirled Jacques' monogrammed Mont Blanc pen. "I know that's what the police are saying, but there's a little part of me that still doesn't believe Jacques' death was accidental. It's probably just that old Creole superstition again." She leaned back in Jacques' chair, sighing wearily. "And because I never got to ID his body, I don't feel like there's any closure."

"Well, there wasn't anything you could do about that. His body was burned beyond recognition in the crash. The dental records matched Jacques', at least that's what the coroner's report said."

"I just keep going over everything Jacques said at our anniversary dinner before he died."

"You could petition the authorities to conduct an inquest, but who knows how long that could drag on. And, of course, they might have to exhume his remains."

Maxine stared out the window at the setting sun, thinking of how distraught *Maman* Chevalier had been when Maxine had called and told her that her only child was dead. And Chloe had been nearly catatonic until the post-funeral reception, when she finally broke down.

"I don't think it would be right to put Jacques' mother through that, not to mention Chloe. She's been through enough, losing him so suddenly." Maxine flipped through the papers in the box Simone placed on the desk. "But if I move forward with selling the company, it's like I'm letting go of Jacques for good and I'll never know the truth."

Simone reached across the desk and took Maxine's hand. "Honey, you have to let go. If you don't, you'll never be able to move on."

Maxine put her other hand on top of Simone's in a gesture of appreciation, her eyes welling with tears. "You're right."

Simone slowly released Maxine's hands and picked up the box again. "Do you want me to give you a moment alone before we close up the office?"

"Please."

Simone shifted the box to her hip. "I'm going to lug this down to the car. I'll be waiting there. Take as long as you need."

Once alone again in the office, Maxine sifted through a bag containing Jacques' personal items that the police had retrieved from the wreckage. She fingered the Tiffany watch she had given him as an anniversary gift and reflected on their last night together.

She looked out the window again at the rippling waters of the Seine, the waning early-evening sunlight casting golden shimmers on its surface. She watched a cargo liner bearing the familiar logo "Chevalier Logistics International" push off from the dock. A pang of uncertainty about selling the company seized her once again.

A knock at the office door startled her.

"Maxine?"

She looked up and recognized Renaud Mercier, Jacques' second-in-command who had been running the company since the accident.

"Yes?" she said, clearing her throat and wiping away a tear.

"I just wanted to say *merci* for arranging for the new owner to allow me and the rest of the employees to keep our jobs." Matted hair clung to his forehead as he took off his newsboy cap, acknowledging the presence of a lady. The gesture was reminiscent of Jacques and that gentlemanly, French way of his.

"It's the least I could do to make sure you guys are rewarded for all your years with the company. It's the way Jacques would have wanted it," she said, struggling to keep her voice steady.

Renaud pursed his lips and looked down, as if acknowledging the truth of her statement. "Sorry again for your loss. Jacques was a great boss and, more importantly, a great man. We all miss him." He stood in the doorway, clutching his hat in his hands. "Would you mind if I looked in on you and Chloe from time to time? I've worked with Jacques since he started the company and I think he'd appreciate it if I made sure his widow and stepdaughter are doing okay."

Maxine smiled in spite of her sadness, appreciating the loyalty that her late husband engendered even in death. "That would be nice, Renaud. Please do stay in touch."

He put his hat back on and tipped it at her as he turned to leave.

"Oh, I almost forgot," he said, turning back to her. "I've been asked to relay a message from the attorney representing the new owner."

"Yes?" She thought she'd taken care of all the details and just wanted to be done with the complex transaction.

"The new owner wanted to know if they could have *Nathalie*?" Renaud said.

"Nathalie?" Maxine repeated, having no idea what Renaud was talking about. Did Jacques have some long-lost daughter he never mentioned that someone in the investment group wanted to adopt for some odd reason?

"Jacques' yacht," Renaud said.

"Oh, right." How could Maxine have forgotten the name of the vessel where they were supposed to celebrate their anniversary, where they'd had so many good times sailing in the Riviera?

135

"I believe they're offering a substantial increase in the purchase price if you throw in *Nathalie*," Renaud continued.

Maxine looked at him curiously. "That seems like an unusual request. Jacques' yacht isn't a commercial vessel. What do they want with it?"

"I don't know. Maybe for use as a corporate vehicle to entertain clients. The attorney said they need an answer before the deal is finalized."

Maxine turned to look out at the Seine again, recalling the first time she and Jacques had gone out on his yacht during that weekend in St.-Tropez. The weekend he proposed.

She had so many good memories of sailing with Jacques, but she hadn't even thought about what to do with the yacht since he'd passed away. It was still docked at the marina in St.-Tropez and she knew she'd never set foot on it again. Not without him.

"Okay," she said, turning back to face Renaud again. "They can have it."

"*Tres bien.* I'll notify the attorney," Renaud said, excusing himself.

Maxine set about finishing the task of packing up Jacques' office. She rummaged through his desk drawers to find any last remnants. She gasped upon discovering that one of the drawers had a false bottom. Lifting the piece of wood, she discovered nautical maps with routes to Corsica and the Cayman Islands. She studied the maps, trying to figure out why Jacques had them. He was probably planning a family vacation on the yacht when Chloe would be home from school. That was so much like Jacques – so thoughtful and full of surprises.

Buried under the maps was a stash of those goddamn Cuban cigars he'd promised to give up. Maxine held the cigar box to her nose, inhaling the scent that brought back so many memories of her dear Jacques. She suddenly regretted having harassed him over his one bad habit that gave him so much pleasure.

She put her heels up on the desk and reclined, lighting one of the cigars. "This is for you, *mon amour*," she said, holding the stogie aloft. "Wherever you are."

21

Chloe climbed the steps of the Métro station and shaded her eyes from the sun. If only the brightness of the early June afternoon would lift her spirits. She missed Jacques terribly and was hoping lunch with her mother would chase away the loneliness she felt in each of the vast rooms of the Chateau de

Chevalier, which now seemed so empty.

Opening the front door to Chez Maxine, Chloe spotted her mother conferring with a young designer at a drafting table.

Maxine looked up from the dress sketch she was marking up with corrections. "Oh, hi, *ma chérie*." She greeted Chloe with a kiss. "What brings you here on this gorgeous day? I figured you'd be at home lounging in the pool or riding your horse and enjoying your first week of summer vacation."

Chloe frowned. "We have a lunch date, remember?"

Maxine smacked her forehead. "Honey, I completely forgot. I have to meet with a client this afternoon."

Chloe followed Maxine to her office, trailed by Mother's ever-present assistant, Henri. "But I took the train all the way into town. What am I supposed to do now?"

"I'll make it up to you, sweetheart, I promise," Maxine said, sitting behind her desk and beginning to look over papers Henri placed before her.

"You say that all the time," Chloe mumbled.

Since Jacques had died, Mother seemed more preoccupied with business than ever. Throwing herself into her work seemed to be Maxine's coping mechanism.

When they'd moved to the chateau last summer, Jacques had coaxed Maxine into leaving work each evening in time for the three of them to sit down to dinner together as a family. But now Mother was back to her workaholic habits, eating lunch at her desk and working long hours in the evening and leaving Chloe to feast on Marie's extravagant meals all by herself.

After Chloe had returned to school in London after Jacques' funeral, she often called home, only to be informed by Henri or Marie that Maxine was tied up on another line negotiating with a vendor or meeting with a client. Chloe had come home for the summer to find that Mother had indeed held true to her word to keep everything at the chateau just as it was before Jacques died. But Maxine's presence was the missing factor. Even when she was physically present, she was absorbed in paperwork and her focus was elsewhere.

At sixteen going on seventeen, Chloe was at an age when she normally would be shunning her mother's company. But, strangely, she found herself craving Maxine's maternal attention.

"Since I have all this time on my hands now," Chloe said, testing whether Maxine was paying attention, "maybe I'll go shopping and max out my credit card."

"Okay, dear," Maxine said, not even looking up from the stack of papers on her desk, confirming Chloe's impression that she wasn't listening.

"Hey, Chlo', good to see you," Simone said, whisking into the office in a clingy summer dress that showed off her voluptuous figure. She kissed Chloe on the cheek. "I would think a girl your age would have better things to do on a beautiful summer day than hang around this stuffy office."

"Mother and I were supposed to have lunch, but she backed out. As usual." Chloe glanced at Maxine, who was still preocuupied with her paperwork.

"I keep telling Maxine she's got to stop spending so much time here." Simone placed a file next to the papers Maxine was going over and turned back to Chloe. "Why don't you go see what Gigi's up to? She's at home working on a new art project. I'm sure she could use some company."

Chloe twirled a strand of hair. "Maybe she'd be up for catching a matinee. I guess I'll take the Métro over to your place."

Simone took Chloe's arm. "I'll give you a ride. I'm on my way home. I'm taking the rest of the afternoon off to go on a picnic with Pascal."

Chloe raised an eyebrow. "You and Pascal are on again?"

"Yeah, believe it or not. I'd have thought one of those sexy young artist's models at the Sorbonne would have turned his head by now, but he keeps coming back to me. He always says, 'There's nothing like a mature woman,'" she said, making her voice sound deep and gruff, apparently imitating her young boyfriend.

Chloe clutched Simone's arm, wishing she had the easy ability with the opposite sex that Simone had passed on to Gigi.

"If there's nothing else, Maxine," Simone called over her shoulder, leading Chloe to the door, "I'm off."

Maxine finally looked up from her work. "I don't remember giving you the afternoon off."

"I'm giving myself a break, and you should, too."

Chloe swung the door open to Simone and Gigi's flat, her arms loaded with bags from the market.

"Just set those down on the counter, if you wouldn't mind," Simone said, equally loaded down and fumbling with her keys.

Chloe followed Simone to the kitchen. "Do you need some help putting everything away?"

Simone retrieved a picnic basket from a cabinet and began filling it with wine, cheese and French bread. "That's okay, *cher*. I'm just going to toss everything in here. Why don't you go see what Gigi's up to? It's mighty suspicious that she's shut up in her room. I get nervous every time she's quiet for too long."

Chloe giggled. "I know what you mean."

She traipsed down the hallway to Gigi's room, calling her friend's name. She rapped on the closed bedroom door. "Gigi?"

Hearing no response, Chloe took that as her cue to enter. "Hey, Gi', Mother stood me up for lunch." She mindlessly flung the door open and made her way into the room. "You wanna catch a movie?"

Chloe stopped short, startled to see Simone's boyfriend, Pascal, hunched over Gigi at her desk.

"Hi, Chlo'. Pascal was just showing me some watercolor techniques," Gigi said matter-of-factly.

Chloe stared, speechless. There was something about the intimate way Pascal was huddled against Gigi that seemed... Inappropriate.

"What's going on here?"

Chloe turned to see Simone standing behind her in the doorway. She turned back to see Pascal immediately step away from Gigi.

The next thing Chloe knew, she was standing next to Gigi in the hallway of the apartment building as Simone tossed Gigi's things out the front door and screamed obscenities. Simone, her fiery temperament matching her flaming hair, was shrieking so loudly in French that Chloe could barely make out what she was saying. Chloe caught the phrases "How dare you try to steal my man?" and "I knew I never should have left you alone with him," punctuated by "little whore." Gigi gave as good as she got, shouting back that her mother was a "paranoid old *vache*" – cow.

Chloe stood there witnessing the ugly scene play out like a bystander watching a car accident in progress, unable to do anything to stop the impending wreckage. Like Chloe, Pascal seemed caught in the crossfire. He pleaded with Simone to calm down, that he was just helping Gigi with her art project and the fact he was in her room wasn't what it looked like. The more he told Simone to calm down, the angrier she got, yelling even louder and causing an elderly neighbor lady across the hall to poke her head out of her front door.

The screaming match ended when Simone threw the last of Gigi's clothes out the door along with a suitcase.

"Get out and don't come back!" Simone bellowed in English, slamming the door.

Gigi pounded her fist against the door. "Fine! Why would I want to stay here with you, you crazy bitch!" She turned to the neighbor lady. "What are you looking at, you old bag?"

Gigi made a face at the horrified woman, who quickly ducked back in her apartment. The sounds of the neighbor lady's locks turning echoed throughout the hall along with the muffled strains of Simone and Pascal's heated arguing.

Gigi fell to her knees and began furiously stuffing her belongings into the suitcase. Chloe crouched to help her collect her things, not knowing what to say in consolation.

"Everything'll be okay once she cools down," Chloe ventured. She helped

Gigi snap the overstuffed suitcase shut. "But I guess in the meantime, you're going to need a place to stay?"

"And then she accused me of trying to steal her boyfriend and kicked me out," Gigi whined to Maxine over breakfast the next morning on the screened-in porch at the Chateau de Chevalier.

"I know. Simone gave me the blow-by-blow on the phone last night," Maxine said with a note of frustration, as if she was sick of hearing about this latest drama. "Now she's not speaking to me, because she thinks I took your side by taking you in."

Chloe gave her mother a sympathetic look, sharing her frustration. She knew that Maxine, as Simone's closest confidante, often got caught in the middle, just as Chloe did in Simone and Gigi's volatile arguments. Their mother-daughter fights had grown in frequency and intensity since the girls entered high school.

"You were there, Chlo'," Gigi said to Chloe. "You know Pascal and I weren't doing anything wrong. You saw us. We were just working on a painting, right?"

Chloe paused before replying, recalling her initial reaction that Gigi and Pascal did look a little too cozy. But she wanted to give her best friend the benefit of the doubt.

"I think Simone jumped to a conclusion," Chloe said after a moment's reflection.

"It's so unfair," Gigi continued. "I didn't *do* anything."

"I've got to get to work." Maxine drained her coffee cup. "Gigi, you're my favorite goddaughter – my *only* goddaughter – and you know I love you like a niece. You're welcome to stay here as long as you want."

"Thank you, *Tante* Maxine."

"I'm sure this'll all blow over by the end of the week when Simone calms down."

"I'm never going back there," Gigi asserted. "I'm not speaking to her ever again."

Maxine shuffled papers into her briefcase. "You say that now, but I know you'll be missing your mother in a couple days. I think you're both acting like silly girls." She put her hand on Chloe's. "I'd never let a man come between me and my daughter, but then again, I'm not Simone."

Chloe nodded, acknowledging the truth of Maxine's statement.

"And since I'm not Simone," Maxine continued, giving Gigi a pointed look, "I'm laying down some ground rules while you're here. Boys are not to call the house after dark, and don't even think about sneaking anyone in – or sneaking out, for that matter. You'll have an eleven o'clock curfew, just like Chloe."

"Yes, *Tante* Maxine," Gigi recited in a mechanical tone that indicated she knew she had no choice but to comply.

Maxine continued ticking off a list of rules and regulations that reminded Chloe of the first day of school when Mother Superior lined up her pupils in the gym and laid down the law.

"You girls are to clean up after yourselves," Maxine said, waving away a refill when Marie came out with the coffeepot, "and help Marie out in the kitchen and mind her while I'm at work."

Marie playfully walloped Gigi on the back of the head. "That goes double for you, you little rapscallion." Gigi looked up at Marie, who gave her an encouraging wink.

Maxine stood, snapping her briefcase shut. "Do I make myself clear?"

Gigi folded her hands and affected an innocent look, the same look Chloe had seen Gigi put on numerous times at school when being interrogated by the nuns. "Yes, *Tante* Maxine."

Later that night, Chloe was getting ready for bed when there was a knock at her door.

"Come in," Chloe called, slipping into her pajamas.

Gigi entered in an oversize, paint-splattered T-shirt that Chloe recognized as her friend's favorite nightshirt. "I just wanted to say thanks again for asking your mom to let me stay here."

"No problem." Chloe flopped on her bed and slid under the covers. "It'll be nice having you right across the hall, just like we're real sisters."

Gigi lingered in the doorway. "Yeah. Well, goodnight."

"'Night, Gi'."

Gigi stood there for another moment, then turned to leave.

Sensing that Gigi didn't feel like being alone, Chloe called out, "Hey, Gi', if you want, you can sleep in my room tonight."

Without hesitation, Gigi turned back around and took a running leap onto Chloe's bed like a little girl coming to sleep with her mother when she'd had a nightmare.

Chloe turned out the light and the two snuggled under the covers. They lay in silence in the darkness, staring at the ceiling.

"You know," Chloe said after a moment, "everything's going to be okay with Simone. She'll come to her senses sooner or later."

"Thanks for always being there for me," Gigi said quietly, her silhouette illuminated by the moonlight, "and for being such a good friend."

141

Chloe remained silent, reaching under the sheets to clutch Gigi's hand, the way they used to cling to one another when they were little and would spend the night over each other's houses.

Chloe had almost drifted off to sleep when Gigi spoke again.

"You know, nothing happened between me and Pascal. He was just showing me some brushstrokes," Gigi said in a raspy whisper. "I didn't do anything wrong."

Chloe squeezed Gigi's hand. "I know," she said reassuringly, suddenly feeling guilty for suspecting that Gigi was engaged in something untoward with her mother's boyfriend. "I'm sure Simone's just being irrational."

"I didn't try to steal her stupid boyfriend. I know I'm no angel, but I wouldn't do something like that, not to my own mother." Gigi's voice trembled. "It really hurts that she thinks so little of me."

She started sobbing, and Chloe released her hand and put her arm around her. Gigi buried her face in Chloe's chest and cried until they both fell asleep.

22

Chloe, in a couture gown and thousands of dollars of jewelry, posed between two male models on a lawn overlooking the Eiffel Tower as celebrated fashion photographer Claude Leblanc snapped shots.

"Boys, move in a little closer," Leblanc directed, angling his lens.

The male models, in Valentino tuxedos with shirts unbuttoned to reveal their chiseled torsos, sandwiched Chloe. She did her best to smile for the camera and disguise her discomfort as the older boys invaded her personal space. She glanced off-camera at Gigi, who was sitting in one of the director's chairs set aside for Chloe and the other models. Gigi smiled and gave Chloe a thumbs-up, and Chloe envied her friend for being able to watch the action from the sidelines while leisurely doodling on a sketchpad. While the prospect of being in French *Elle* was exciting, Chloe would much rather be hanging out with Gigi and enjoying the lazy days of summer.

"Chloe, move your hands down their chests," Leblanc said, taking his camera off its tripod and moving in close. "You're supposed to look like you're enjoying this."

Chloe did as told, looking from one boy to the other with the best coy expression she could feign and stroking their oiled chests. She hated that, on the verge of seventeen, she was still so uncomfortable with male attention. After that disastrous night last summer with François and the near-rape at the hands of Pierre Rousseau, Chloe had good reason to be wary of the opposite sex.

"No, this is all wrong." Leblanc returned his camera to the tripod. "Chloe, you're too stiff and it's coming across on camera. You need to loosen up. Why don't you take five and try to shake off your nerves. I'm sure we could all use a little break."

Chloe retreated to the empty director's chair next to the one where Gigi sitting.

"You're doing good," Gigi said.

"I'm sorry you have to sit through this," Chloe said while a makeup artist ran a makeup brush over her forehead and a hair stylist fussed with her pinned-up curls. "You must be bored out of your mind."

"Nah, I've been sketching. You and those two hot guys make good subjects."

Gigi held up the sketch, which depicted Chloe standing in between the male models with a regal expression, as if she were a queen and the boys were her acquiesent attendants. Chloe looked firmly in control in Gigi's sketch, and wished she could only summon that kind of confidence in real life.

The male models sat down next to Gigi and the one closest to her took off his shirt so that the makeup artist could apply more oil to his chest. Chloe averted her eyes, while Gigi grinned at him.

"Hi, there," Gigi said flirtatiously.

The guy smiled back at her seductively.

Chloe knew she could never be that brazen. Those male models were probably in their early twenties, but Gigi had no problem interacting with them as though they were peers.

"I'm going to get something to eat," Gigi said, turning her attention away from the shirtless male model and to the craft service table. "You want something?"

"Something light, please," Chloe said. "The bustier of this dress is already cutting off my circulation."

Chloe barely had an opportunity to sip a cup of tea and nibble on a strawberry before the photographer called everyone back to the set.

"This is probably going to take a couple more hours. If you want to take off, that's cool," Chloe said to Gigi, getting up from the director's chair and fluffing the skirt of her poofy gown. "We can meet up later."

"Okay. I'll probably go to Trocadéro to watch the breakdancers and do some more sketching," Gigi said, stuffing her sketchpad in a backpack.

Chloe waved goodbye and lifted the hem of her skirt, taking baby steps toward the set in high heels.

"Hey, Chlo'."

She turned back toward Gigi. "Yeah?"

Gigi held up a large black book. "I was looking through your portfolio earlier. Do you mind if I have this picture?" She flipped the book open to a headshot that was plain in comparison to the glamour poses that filled out the book.

"I guess," Chloe said. "There are better photos than that one, though."

"No, I like this one."

Chloe shrugged. "Take it; it's yours. I have other copies at home. Why do you want it? You doing another sketch or something?"

A sly grin spread across Gigi's face, the same look Chloe had seen countless times when her best friend was plotting something. "Something like that."

Chloe watched Gigi slide the photo into her backpack, sling it onto her shoulder and walk away.

When Chloe and Gigi arrived at the chateau later that evening, they found the family driver, Louis, loading Maxine's hefty suitcases into the trunk of the car.

"Where are you going, Mother?" Chloe asked, dropping her duffle bag in the foyer.

"I'm redecorating a villa for a new client in Milan," Maxine explained, directing Louis to be careful with her bags. "I'll be gone over the weekend and most of next week while I go over the plans with Signor and Signora Rossi."

"But we were supposed to go visit *Maman* Chevalier in St.-Tropez this weekend."

Chloe hadn't seen much of Jacques' mother since his death and she couldn't wait to visit her cottage. *Maman* Chevalier treated Chloe as if she were her own grandchild, doting on her and giving her candy, as if Chloe were a toddler.

"Gigi and I were looking forward to hanging out at the beach," Chloe added, realizing she indeed sounded like a toddler who was begging her mother to take her to the playground.

Gigi nodded, confirming Chloe's statement.

Maxine flipped through her daily planner, dividing her attention between Chloe and a travel checklist. "We'll have to do it some other time. I already called *Maman* and cancelled."

"Why didn't you tell me you were going away? It's not fair to back out of our plans like this at the last minute," Chloe argued, reflecting on the irony of the situation. Her classmates at Our Lady of Chastity couldn't wait for their parents to leave town so that the kids could finally cut loose and have a good time without the restrictions of parents or nuns.

But Jacques' death had triggered a clinging instinct in Chloe. Secretly, she feared that her mother could be snatched from her in an instant like Jacques, making it important for her to spend as much time with Maxine as possible while home from school. But Mother seemed to care only about work these days.

"I don't have time to get into this right now," Maxine said, flipping her planner shut and slipping it into a carryon bag. "I'm already running late. This assignment came up unexpectedly, and it's a big account. I promise I'll make it up to you guys. We have the rest of the summer to hang out in St.-Tropez."

Maxine hooked her carryon over her shoulder and Chloe and Gigi followed her to the car.

"Madame Chevalier! Don't forget this!" Marie came running out of the house with a brown paper bag.

"What's this?" Maxine said when Marie handed her the bag.

"It's – how do the Americans say? A doggie bag. I made you a nice dinner to take with you," Marie said. "I know how you hate airline food."

"Thanks, Marie. You think of everything." Maxine turned to Chloe and Gigi. "I want you girls to be on your best behavior and don't give Marie any trouble while I'm gone."

"We're going to be seniors in high school in a couple of months, Mother," Chloe said, not appreciating Maxine's condescension. "I think we're perfectly capable of looking out for ourselves."

"Don't take that tone with me. Do you understand what I told you?"

Chloe huffed and looked away, disgusted that Mother had the nerve to cop an attitude when she was the one who had ruined their weekend plans.

"I said, do you understand me?"

Gigi stepped forward and kissed Maxine on the cheek. "Yes, of course we understand, *Tante* Maxine."

"Good. I'll call when I get there." Maxine got in the car, closed the door, and Louis sped off.

"I guess I'll go finish up dinner," Marie said, wiping her hands on her apron and climbing the front stoop.

"Smells good, whatever's simmering," Gigi called.

When Marie was inside the house, Gigi turned to Chloe and gave her that familiar sly grin. Chloe couldn't help thinking that Gigi had something of her own simmering.

Chloe sat next to Gigi at the kitchen island, chopping vegetables for the ratatouille Marie was making for dinner.

"No, you have to cut zucchini into smaller pieces or it won't come out right." Chloe, who knew Marie's preferences, demonstrated proper cutting techniques for Gigi.

"Whatever." Gigi carelessly plopped a handful of zucchini slices into a bowl. "When I'm a famous artist, I'll have my own personal chef."

"Still, it never hurts to learn the right way to do things," Marie interjected while clanging copper pots around on the stove. She put on her oven mitts and retrieved a tray of fresh-baked beignets from the stove. "These are for later," she said, setting them on the counter to cool.

"Those smell so good, I don't know if I can wait," Gigi said, reaching for one of the pastries.

"I said they're for later." Marie slapped Gigi's hand. "What did Madame Chevalier say about minding me while she's gone?"

"Oh, come on, *chérie*, lighten up a little," Bernard, the chateau's groundskeeper, said, entering the kitchen through the backdoor. "I smelled these babies all the way outside."

He reached for a pastry, but Marie swatted his hand with a spatula.

"You're worse than the girls," she scolded. "And what have I told you about tracking mud into my kitchen?"

"You know no one can resist your beignets," he said, coming up behind Marie and tickling her on either side.

Chloe looked at Gigi and they giggled at Bernard's double-entendre as Marie chased him out of the kitchen with her spatula.

"You know, he's kind of cute and I bet you guys are the same age," Gigi said to Marie once she'd shooed Bernard out the backdoor. "Have you ever thought of hooking up with him?"

Chloe chuckled at Gigi's cheekiness.

"Young lady, why don't you mind your own business?" Marie snatched the knife from Gigi. "And you're cutting the zucchini too big again."

Marie began chopping the zucchini with expert efficiency, as if the task was a welcome diversion from Gigi's intrusion into her personal life, but her culinary lesson was interrupted by the ringing phone. Chloe continued to give Gigi pointers on slicing and dicing, but her attention was drawn to Marie's phone conversation when she heard concern creep into the older woman's voice.

"That doesn't sound too good," Marie said to whoever was on the line, the now-familiar worry wrinkle appearing on her brow. "*Merci*, Dr. Hermant. Thanks for keeping me informed. I'll try to get out to see her when I can."

Marie quietly hung up the phone and began filling a large pot with water, not saying anything.

"What's wrong, Marie?" Chloe asked.

"It's nothing," Marie replied, her head down.

"Come on, Marie," Chloe persisted. "I've known you long enough to tell when something's wrong."

Marie hoisted the heavy pot out of the sink and placed it on the stove. "My mother's taken sick," she said, wiping her hands on a dishtowel. "That was the doctor who's treating her at the hospital. She's come down with a nasty bout of pneumonia and the doctor thinks it would be a good idea if I came to see her. I'm an only child – my father passed away a few years ago – and *Maman* keeps asking for me."

"Go see her," Chloe urged. "Why wait?"

"Because she lives in Gascony. That's a long train ride away, and I can't leave you girls here alone. I promised Madame Chevalier I'd look after you while she's in Milan on business."

"We're old enough to take care of ourselves," said Gigi, who had begun stirring cake batter for dessert, licking icing from her fingers.

"I'm not sure if I can trust you two to be left alone, quite frankly," Marie said, beginning to add the chopped vegetables and other ingredients to the simmering pot.

"Of course you can trust us," Gigi said in the same exaggerated, innocent-sounding tone she had used earlier on Maxine.

Marie stopped stirring and folded her arms, giving her young charges a fierce look. "I have evidence to the contrary."

Chloe and Gigi exchanged nervous looks.

"What do you mean?" Chloe said in a shaky voice, afraid she already knew what Marie was referring to.

Just as Chloe feared, Marie went to a cabinet, pulled out her Lalique crystal punch bowl, and set it on the island like a prosecuting attorney presenting damning evidence.

"Did you think I wouldn't notice my favorite bowl was chipped?" Marie said, tapping her fingers on the counter like a cross-examiner interrogating a hostile witness.

Chloe glanced at Gigi, who looked as clueless as she about how to explain the chipped bowl. Chloe thought they had done a decent enough job Super-Gluing the chipped piece back on after that ill-fated get-together with François and Gaston last summer.

"I have a sneaking suspicion you two decided to have a little party that last weekend of summer last year," Marie continued, staring Chloe and Gigi down. "My educated guess is you used my bowl and dropped it, then tried to hastily glue it back together so I wouldn't notice."

"That's – that's absurd," Gigi stumbled. "We would never –"

Marie held up her hand. "Don't even try it, Miss Smarty Pants. I'm on to you."

147

Chloe, ever the guilt-ridden Catholic girl, spoke up. "Marie, I'm so sorry. We had company over and served snacks. I knew we shouldn't have used your bowl, and one of our friends knocked it over. It was an accident. Can you ever forgive us?"

"I've already forgiven you. I was young once, and I raised two teenagers of my own. I know accidents happen. I discovered the chipped bowl months ago, but I didn't tell Madame Chevalier because I knew she'd overreact." Marie paused, pacing the kitchen like an attorney summing up her closing argument. "But I have no intention of leaving you two to get into mischief again."

"Marie, I promise we won't have anybody over this time," Chloe pleaded. "Don't let our stupid mistake keep you from visiting your mother in the hospital. You'd never forgive yourself if something happened, God forbid."

Marie hovered at the stove, stirring her pot, as if pondering Chloe's words. "You're probably right. Out of the mouths of *not-so-innocent* babes, as the Americans say."

Chloe and Gigi laughed at Marie's play on words.

"I'll call Madame Chevalier after dinner and ask if it's okay if I go see my mother this weekend." Marie turned up the heat on the burner. "But I want you two to promise me you'll stay out of trouble."

Chloe and Gigi looked at each other, then held up their right hands as if being sworn in to testify. "We promise," they said in unison.

"You sure you're just taking these two little bags?" Chloe carried Marie's suitcase to the family car while Gigi followed, lugging a tote.

"Yes, that's all," Marie said, directing the girls to place the bags in the backseat of the car.

"Mother takes more than this when she's going somewhere and not even spending the night," Chloe said with a laugh.

"Well, of course I'm not as glamorous as Madame Chevalier," Marie said. "I'm so grateful she's giving me time off to go see my mother."

Chloe knew Maxine would immediately agree to let Marie go when the loyal housekeeper called and said her mother was sick. Marie had given the phone to Chloe, and Maxine told her that this weekend of freedom would be a gauge of the girls' maturity.

Repeating Maxine's instructions, Marie stood in the driveway briefing the girls on rules and safety guidelines while Louis, the driver, ran a squeegee over the windshield and checked the oil.

"Be sure to lock all the doors at night and turn on the security system," Marie repeated for what seemed like the umpteenth time.

"Yes, Marie," Chloe and Gigi chanted like they did when taking orders at school from Mother Superior.

"There's plenty of food in the refrigerator. I prepared enough meals to last you and Gigi through the weekend. All you have to do is heat them up."

"Yes, Marie."

"I left the number to my mother's house, where I'll be staying, and the direct line to her room at the hospital. Make sure you call me if there's an emergency."

"Yes, Marie."

"Remember: no company. You girls behave yourselves."

"We'd never dream of doing otherwise," Gigi said.

"Yeah, I bet," Marie said, narrowing her eyes at Gigi, as if wondering what evil the satanic imp would conjure without adult supervision. "Just remember, if the two of you get into trouble, Madame Chevalier is going to hold me accountable."

Louis took his seat behind the wheel and honked.

Chloe kissed Marie on the cheek. "You're going to miss your train. You better get going."

Marie directed one last warning glance at the girls and crossed herself before getting in the car.

"We'll be praying for your mother," Gigi called out as Louis started the engine.

Marie ducked her head out of the window and gave Gigi the evil eye once more as the car took off. "I'm the one who'll be praying."

Chloe sprawled on her bed, thumbing through a movie magazine while Gigi fiddled around in the adjoining bathroom. "So, what do you want to do this weekend?" Chloe asked, raising her voice over the sound of Gigi's hair dryer.

They'd heated up the burgers and delectable homemade fries Marie had left in the fridge and put away the lunch dishes. Chloe felt like spending the lazy Saturday afternoon lounging in her room, reading, but something told her Gigi had other things on her agenda.

"I was thinking maybe we could go to a movie or something later on," Chloe said.

The hair dryer clicked off. Gigi emerged from the bathroom, the dark spirals atop her head glistening and fruity-smelling from nearly emptying Chloe's new bottle of shampoo. "I didn't just spend two whole hours doing my hair so we could sit in some dark movie theater where no one will see us."

Chloe sat up. "What did you have in mind?" she said, not sure she was ready for the answer.

Gigi went to the mirror above Chloe's dresser and began fluffing her curls. "Oh, not much," she said in an affected, nonchalant tone. "It's just that one Montana Blake is going to be doing a show tonight to kick off the European release of his new album."

Chloe's cat, Bizou, leapt onto the bed and stretched out and Chloe obliged, scratching the feline's stomach. "Montana *who*?"

Gigi took the towel from around her shoulders and snapped Chloe on the arm with it. "Montana Blake, you ninny. You know, the guy who hangs above my bed in our dorm room, the one I kiss every night before I go to sleep."

Chloe groaned. "Oh, yeah, *that* Montana Blake. The pinup boy. How could I forget?"

"He's performing at Club 69, and I can't miss it."

"Club 69? That's the hottest nightclub in Paris, and it's twenty-one-and-over. They'd never let us in."

The edges of Gigi's mouth twisted into the sly expression Chloe knew so well. "That's why I got these," Gigi said, retrieving two plastic cards from her purse and handing one to Chloe.

Chloe examined the card, which displayed her picture alongside a falsified name and birth date. "Fake IDs! So that's why you asked me for that headshot from my portfolio. How'd you manage to get these?"

"Let's just say I have friends in high places," Gigi replied with a knowing smile.

Chloe looked down at the fake ID, smiling at her friend's cunning. Knowing Gigi, she had probably wheedled the IDs from some unwitting male at the license bureau.

"We could get in big trouble if we get busted trying to get in the club with these," Chloe reasoned. "And we promised Mother and Marie we'd stay *out* of trouble."

"No, we promised not to have company over again. And, we won't," Gigi argued. "We'll be going out."

Chloe shooed Bizou off the bed and tucked her legs underneath her. "I'd rather go to the movies. Valérie Bourdain's new movie just came out. It's getting great reviews. I was just reading about it."

"How about a compromise? I'll go to a matinee of that new movie with you tomorrow afternoon if you'll go to the club with me tonight."

Chloe gave Gigi a skeptical look. "This better not be one of your schemes that backfires, like that time you talked me into going to that exhibit opening with you in London because you wanted to meet that famous artist and Mother Superior caught us violating curfew. My knees are still sore from having to kneel and repeat the Act of Contrition."

"Oh, come on, Chlo'," Gigi nagged, plopping on the bed. "How often do we get a chance at freedom without our mothers around to dictate our every step?"

Chloe paused, recalling the cavalier way Mother had backed out of their weekend plans. "Okay, but if we're going to do this, let's do it right." She got up and retrieved a bankbook from underneath a pile of sweaters in one of her dresser drawers.

"What's that?"

"Let's just say it's my little piggy bank," Chloe said, waving the bankbook as if it were a passport to an exotic paradise. "I've been squirreling money away ever since I started modeling."

"You've got a secret stash?" Gigi said excitedly, jumping off the bed.

"Yes. I've been saving up for an emergency, and this is definitely an emergency. We need hot outfits for tonight."

Gigi grinned. "Now you're talking."

23

Chloe and Gigi went on a scavenger hunt in search of the perfect outfits for their big night out on the town. With Chloe's secret stash on hand, they made the rounds at Galeries Lafayette and other department stores and boutiques. They were convinced they had tried on every garment in Paris by the end of their shopping spree.

Chloe finally decided on a fitting black tank dress she found on the sale rack at Comme des Garçons. Gigi chose a super-short, sequined red mini-dress from Le Garage. They took the train back to the Chateau de Chevalier and spent hours doing their hair and make-up and squeezing themselves into their dresses.

"How do I look?" Gigi asked, fluffing her curly hair with a pick as the two excitedly primped and prepped in Chloe's bathroom. The flashy, red-hot number she had on did wonders for her already well-developed figure.

"You look like you could pass for about twenty-one," said Chloe. "What about me?"

"You don't look a day over twenty-three, my dear."

Chloe checked out her reflection, impressed that she looked less like a high school girl and more like a woman in her little black dress. Gigi had helped Chloe do her hair in a new style: her shiny raven locks hung loose for a change instead of in the usual bangs-and-ponytail style she wore at school.

The girls invented new identities to match the made-up names on their fake IDs. Chloe was Stéphanie and Gigi was Brigitte. They were background singers for Sting's European tour and were only in town for the night. They posed in the mirror, trying their new, older identities on for size.

Gigi opened her purse and retrieved a pack of Galouises, taking out two cigarettes and handing one to Chloe. "A ciggy for you and a ciggy for me," she said. "It'll make us look more sophisticated."

They practiced holding their cigarettes between their index and middle fingers, trying to look grown-up and sexy. They were going to be a more dangerous duo than the scheming women in the classic French film *Les Diaboliques*.

"Well, you ready to paint the town rouge?" Gigi said, applying one last stroke of eyeliner to the already racoon-like mask that encircled her eyes.

Chloe studied their reflections in the mirror above the sink. "We look like a couple of streetwalkers."

Gigi pulled down the top of her dress, exposing more cleavage. "I hope that means Montana will notice me."

When the girls stepped out of a cab in front of Club 69, there was a line around the block.

"We'll be standing out here for hours," Chloe said, shivering in her little black dress, an unseasonable chill slicing the night air. "And then there's no guarantee they'll let us in."

"Let me handle this." Gigi took Chloe's arm and led her past the throng to the front of the line, eliciting angry looks and more than a few expletives from the club-goers who were patiently waiting their turn.

"What are you doing?" Chloe whispered to Gigi as they neared a beefy security guard standing watch at the front door behind a velvet rope.

"Just leave it to me."

"Ladies, you'll have to step to the back of the line," the security guard said in French.

Gigi straightened her posture and stuck out her ample chest. "We're with Montana Blake's entourage. We should be on the guest list."

The guard's face remained impassive. "Names?"

Gigi produced her ID and nudged Chloe to do the same.

The guard took the IDs, looked down at the cards and then up at Chloe and Gigi. It was hard to tell what he was thinking, since his eyes were covered by shades even though it was ten o'clock at night, but his expressionless face seemed to convey that he was unconvinced by the fake IDs and Gigi's accompanying story.

"I'm sorry," he said, flipping through papers on a clipboard without even glancing down. "I don't see no Brigitte Carbonnel or Stéphanie Beauvais on here."

"Are you sure? We're *really* good friends of Montana's." Gigi leaned forward, giving the security guard a full-on view of her cleavage.

Feeling Gigi pinching her, Chloe did her best to imitate her friend, striking a sexy pose on the concrete in front of the club and feeling like a complete fraud. Freezing in the night air, she felt about as sexy as a root canal.

The guard continued to stare straight ahead, not showing any emotion. Chloe tensed up, worried that the guard was going to summon the police and tell them to throw these two underage groupies in jail for trying to get in with fake IDs.

After a long interval, the guard finally gave Chloe and Gigi back their IDs and, without saying a word, unhooked the velvet rope and stepped aside to allow the girls to pass. Chloe stared in disbelief, amazed they were actually being admitted to the ultra-chic club.

Gigi grabbed Chloe's arm and began leading her through the doorway and into the abyss of flashing strobe lights and throbbing dance beats. "Thanks, baby," Gigi said cheekily to the guard as they passed.

Once inside, Chloe surveyed the surroundings. Club-goers in trendy threads pressed their sweaty bodies against each other on the dance floor, gyrating beneath a giant disco ball. A black velvet curtain covered the stage where Montana Blake was to perform.

"Come on," Gigi said, taking Chloe's hand. "Let's get some drinks."

Chloe reluctantly followed Gigi to the bar, not sure what this night had in store. Gigi pushed through the crowd at the bar, flashed her fake ID and ordered two energy drinks doused with vodka like an experienced drinker.

Following Gigi's lead, Chloe cradled her drink and tried to look older as they hovered at a table near the dance floor.

"This tastes like cough syrup," Chloe said after taking a big sip and nearly spitting it out.

Gigi swished the alcohol around in her glass, holding it like a brandy snifter. "It's an acquired taste."

Two punk rockers with spiky, multi-colored mohawks and leather outfits accented with oversize safety pins and zippers approached.

"You w-wanna d-dance?" one of the guys stammered, a stud in his lower lip impeding his speech.

Chloe looked the guys over like wilted lettuce at a salad bar. "Uh, no thanks —"

"Actually, we'd love to." Gigi set her glass down and took Chloe's hand. "You've got to loosen up," she said to Chloe, dragging her to the dance floor. "How often do we get to enjoy a night out on the town without a curfew?"

Figuring Gigi was right, Chloe did her best to keep up with the punk rockers' spastic movements, which seemed to be in sync with the synthesized techno beats throbbing from the speakers. Chloe's dance partner kept rhythmically bumping into her, going through the steps of some kind of bizarre slam-dance.

By the end of the song, Chloe was sore and feared she was bruised. "I've got to take a breather," she said, retreating to the ladies' room.

Gigi followed and they jockeyed for position in front of the mirror to check their hair and makeup in the crowded bathroom. Chloe examined her arms and legs and was glad to see the slam-dancer hadn't left any bruises.

Upon leaving the restroom, the stage curtain parted, the houselights went down and Montana Blake took the stage. Gigi screamed excitedly and pulled Chloe through the crowd until they were directly in front of the stage.

Chloe had an up-close view of the young actor-turned-pop-star's crotch, which he proceeded to thrust toward his adoring fans for the next hour. As Montana lip-synched his way through snippets from his new album, assisted by two lithe female dancers, Gigi and other fans shrieked, jumped up and down and pulled at their hair. Chloe watched in disbelief. It reminded her of vintage clips she'd seen on the BBC of the Beatles performing.

"Thank you, Paris, goodnight," Montana said at the end of the show, blowing a kiss to his fans and stepping behind the velvet curtain.

"I've got to get backstage," Gigi said once the curtain closed.

Chloe looked at the guard standing watch at a curtained entryway leading backstage. "How are you going to manage that?"

"Watch me."

Chloe watched Gigi nudge her way to the front of a line of scantily-clad girls with laminates that read "Radio Contest Winners" hanging around their necks. Gigi briefly exchanged words with the guard, who extended his arm as if motioning for her to go away.

"Damn," Gigi said when she returned to Chloe's side. "I tried to sweet-talk my way back to see Montana, but that goon said no one gets in without a backstage pass."

"Gigi, why don't we just go home?" Chloe reasoned. "I'm tired of standing around in these high heels. We got in and you got to see him perform. Can't you be satisfied with that?"

"I fantasize about him every night. When am I ever going to get the chance to get this close to him again?"

Gigi's dejected look wore Chloe down. She knew that if she got an opportunity to meet her idol, Valérie Bourdain, she'd probably be just as star-struck.

"I have an idea," Chloe said. "Follow me." She took Gigi's hand and led her to the bar.

"What are you going to do, get me drunk so I'll forget about not getting to meet Montana?"

"Just follow my lead," Chloe said. She turned to the bartender. "Two martinis, *si'l vous plait.*"

Gigi watched with a curious expression as Chloe took a sip of her martini, slipping the olive under her tongue. Using her untapped acting talents, Chloe began feigning choking sounds and clutching at her throat.

Gigi looked at her like she was crazy, then finally caught on. "Help! Somebody, please help us! My friend, she swallowed an olive!"

Chaos ensued and the club staff, including the security guard assigned to the backstage entrance, rushed to Chloe's aid. While the men encircled Chloe, Gigi ran to the backstage entrance. She paused, smiled at Chloe, then disappeared behind the curtain.

Chloe stood in a dark alley outside Club 69's stage door, waiting for Gigi to emerge. Since her "choking" performance – which ended with one of the beefy security guards giving her the Heimlich, nearly breaking her ribs until she spat out the olive – the club had closed. Chloe huddled with the paparazzi and the faithful few admirers who hoped to catch an up-close glimpse of Montana exiting and grab an autograph. The same guard who had earlier kept Gigi from going backstage stood watch at the door, keeping the lingering fans at bay.

The heavy metal door swung open and Chloe craned her neck along with the other hopefuls, praying it was Gigi. No such luck. A redhead in a halter top and miniskirt clomped into the alley in six-inch stilettos. She was followed by a procession of girls who were dressed – or *un*-dressed, as it were – in much the same fashion.

If Gigi had been able to maneuver her way to Montana Blake's dressing room, she had steep competition. Not only did these girls look older and more worldly, the hardened glaze in their eyes telegraphed that they would do *anything* to get close to a star.

The door swung open one last time and Chloe recognized Montana, flanked by two tall, muscle-bound security guards and a phalanx of hangers-on. The young pop star held up his hands to block the frantic camera flashes, even though he was wearing dark shades. The guards ushered Montana, who seemed shorter than when he was onstage, to an awaiting limo. Trailing the entourage was none other than Gigi.

"Girl, where have you been?" Chloe grabbed Gigi's arm. "Do you know how long I've been standing in this alley, waiting on you?"

"I got to meet him!" Gigi gushed. "He is *sooo* cool. He invited me to come back to his hotel. He has the presidential suite at Hôtel de Crillon."

Chloe tightened her grip on Gigi's arm. "Are you crazy? It's almost three in the morning. You're not going off to some hotel with some strange American and his posse. You could get gang-raped. Anything could happen to you." She began leading Gigi through the alley. "I've had enough of this nonsense for one night. We're getting out of here."

Gigi ripped her arm away. "I'm going with Montana."

Chloe stopped and glared at Gigi. "Stop fooling around. If you don't come on, we're going to miss the last train home."

Gigi stood between Chloe and the limousine, where a security guard held open the door to the backseat, as if waiting for Gigi to get in before the car took off. The guard held the door open with one arm and fighting off the swarm of hormone-crazed girls trying to get at Montana with the other.

"Gi', please don't do this," Chloe said, switching tactics. The forceful approach never seemed to work with her best friend, so the only other recourse at this insane hour was cajoling. "You know we're both going to be in big trouble if Mother finds out we snuck out to a nightclub with fake IDs. You got us into the club, you got to see Montana perform, you got to go backstage and meet him. Isn't that enough?"

Gigi inched closer to the limousine, demonstrating her intentions. As Chloe had discovered all too often, "enough" was never enough with Gigi.

"I'm sorry," Gigi said, rushing to the limo. "This is the chance of a lifetime. I can't pass it up. I'll be home before Marie gets back. I promise."

With that, Gigi hopped into the limo and the security guard slammed the door. The car sped off into the night, leaving Chloe standing in the alley.

24

"Yes, Mother, of course we cleaned up after ourselves." Chloe cradled the kitchen phone receiver between her ear and shoulder while she washed the dishes she and Gigi had accumulated over the weekend.

"Good," Maxine said long distance from her hotel suite in Milan. "I don't want Marie coming home to a big mess. She's dealing with enough with her mother being sick. What did you guys do while she was gone?"

Chloe turned on the faucet and claimed she couldn't hear Maxine over the sound of the water – stalling for time. She didn't want to lie to her mother, but she didn't want to implicate herself, either.

"I said, what did you and Gigi do while Marie was gone?" Maxine repeated, undeterred.

Chloe turned off the water and leaned against the sink. "Not much." She nervously twirled the phone cord around her finger. "We went shopping."

That was a partial truth, at least.

"You didn't run up your charge card did you?" Maxine pressed.

"A little bit, I guess," Chloe hemmed, not wanting to reveal her secret "piggy bank" to her mother. "We got some new outfits."

"Chloe, I told you not to use that card while I was gone unless it was an emergency."

Not surprisingly, Maxine launched into a diatribe about the responsible use of credit. Chloe was glad for once to be besieged by a motherly lecture, since the topic distracted Maxine from further inquiring about last night's activities. Chloe began drying the dishes and zoned out until she heard Maxine ask to speak to Gigi.

"Uh, she's…" Chloe grappled for an explanation. It was early Sunday afternoon and Gigi still hadn't returned from her ill-advised excursion to Montana Blake's hotel suite. She'd called earlier to say she'd be back "later than expected" and would fill Chloe in about her "amazing night" with Montana upon her return.

"She's indisposed right now," Chloe said finally, trying to invent a good excuse for Gigi's absence.

"Indisposed? What could be so important that she can't come speak to the woman who's putting a roof over her head?"

Chloe wiped around the rim of a glass in a repetitive, agitated motion, like a gerbil in a wheel. "She's… in the bathroom."

"Call her to the phone. It's important that I check in with her. Even though Simone's still not speaking to me, we're communicating through my assistant and she expects progress reports on how Gigi's doing. She still cares about that girl, no matter what she says. They're both so stubborn."

"You're right about that, but you know how long Gigi takes in the bathroom. Can't you talk to her tomorrow?"

Chloe just prayed Gigi would be back by then.

"I should probably go, anyway," Maxine said, to Chloe's relief. "I have another meeting with the Rossis later this afternoon. Oh, speaking of which, I'm going to be here a little longer than anticipated."

"How much longer?"

"I'm not sure yet."

Chloe slammed the towel on the sink, detecting Maxine was being as evasive with her about her stay in Milan as Chloe was about Gigi's absence. "But you're supposed to be back on Wednesday."

"I know, *ma chérie*, but this redecorating project's much more extensive than I initially realized. After meeting with Signor and Signora Rossi this weekend, I saw how involved this project is and realized it's going to be too difficult for me to try to manage the project from Paris."

"Do you have any idea when you're going to be back?" Chloe huffed. She didn't like the sound of this indefinite extension of Maxine's business trip. The longer she was gone, the longer they would have to put off the trip to St.-Tropez that she and Gigi had been looking forward to.

"Honey, quite honestly, I might have to camp out here for a few weeks. I can't exactly oversee the renovation of an eighteenth century villa long-distance. Besides, I've been thinking about opening an office in Milan, and I can do some location-scouting while I'm out here. Henri's going to drop by the house tomorrow to gather some more of my things and ship them to me here."

"Mother, I can't believe you're doing this. It's not fair. What about going to St.-Tropez to see *Maman* Chevalier?"

"Chloe, I don't want to get into this now, not over the phone."

"Of course not. Everything happens on your timeline, when it's convenient for you. Why don't you just admit it? The reason why you spend so much time at work, why you're never home anymore, is because you miss Jacques. Well, I miss him, too."

Maxine fell silent and Chloe stood still, holding the phone and saying nothing, her chest heaving with emotion. The sound of someone knocking on the door of Maxine's hotel room broke the silence.

"Hold on a minute, *ma chérie*," Maxine said softly, setting the phone down.

Chloe heard Maxine open the door, followed by a man saying in an Italian accent, "Your car is ready, Signora Chevalier." Maxine replied, "Okay, I'll be right down. *Gratsi.*"

When Maxine returned to the phone, she said, "Honey, I have to go. My clients are waiting. I'll call you later this evening when Marie's back. You girls be good and mind her while I'm gone. I love you."

Chloe hung up without saying "I love you, too." She stood there for a long time, staring out the kitchen window at the light rain that had begun to fall. The rain intensified the loneliness she felt, just like when she was a little girl and she was left in the care of a nanny while Maxine was away at work.

Chloe walked around the parlor, fluffing throw pillows and running a feather duster over every surface so that the house would be spotless when Marie got back. She glanced nervously at the grandfather clock. It was going on seven p.m. and not only was Marie due home any minute, but Gigi still hadn't returned from Montana Blake's hotel. Gigi had already broken her promise to spend the afternoon with Chloe, going to the movies and catching the matinee of the new Valérie Bourdain film Chloe wanted to see.

Sighing, Chloe threw down the feather duster and picked up the phone. This latest escapade of Gigi's had gone too far.

"Yes, Hôtel de Crillon. May I help you?" the concierge said upon answering.

Chloe twisted her hair around her index finger. "Yes, I'm trying to reach a guest named Montana Blake."

"I'm sorry, Madame, we cannot give out that information."

She slammed the phone down and paced the room, trying to decide her next course of action. Anything could have happened to Gigi – molestation, kidnapping, a brutal beating at the hands of the groupies salivating to get close to Montana. The time had come to report Gigi missing.

Chloe dialed the phone again. "Yes, operator, I need the police." As she was waiting to be connected, she heard a car door shutting in the front drive. "Uh, never mind," she said into the receiver. "False alarm."

She slammed the phone down again and raced to open the front door. She nearly fainted with relief at the sight of Gigi, her sequined red mini-dress covered by a man's blazer, ascending the front stoop as a stretch limousine zoomed out of the long gravel driveway.

Chloe grabbed Gigi's arm and pulled her out of the rain and inside the house. "Will you get in here? Where the hell have you been? I was about to send the police out looking for you."

Gigi leaned on the doorway and smiled serenely. "Montana is so awesome," she swooned, as if blissfully unaware of Chloe's anxiety. "He was a total gentleman. He gave me his jacket to keep me warm." She wrapped her arms around herself. "We stayed up all night talking. Then he took me out to lunch at Les Deux Magots, and time just got away from us. I looked up and it was after six, so he had his limo drop me off." She twirled in the foyer, like a character in a movie who'd fallen in love, dripping water everywhere. "Girl, I have so much to tell you. He invited me to –"

"I don't want to hear it, there's no time. Get upstairs and change." Chloe pointed at the staircase like a mother scolding a child who had sullied her Sunday dress. "Marie'll be home any minute and I don't want her seeing you dressed like some cheap hooker."

Chloe was pushing Gigi toward the stairs when the family car drove up with Marie in the backseat. Marie got out and approached the house before Chloe had a chance to close the front door and shoo Gigi up the stairs.

"Quick, get back there." Chloe motioned for Gigi to hide behind the front door.

As Marie entered the foyer, Chloe put on her sweetest smile and kissed Marie on the cheek. "Hi. How's your mother?" she said, standing so that she was blocking Gigi's hiding place behind the door.

"She's doing much better, thanks. The doctor expects her to make a full recovery," Marie said, setting down her carryall. "I'm so glad you convinced me to go." She took off her scarf and raincoat and went to hang them up on the rack behind the door.

Chloe grabbed the items. "Let me get that for you. You've had a long journey and you need to get some rest. I'm sure you want to go to your room and lie down."

"*Mon Dieu*, do I ever. Where's Gigi?"

Chloe shifted her weight to one foot. "She's… around. But don't worry about us. We did just fine while you were gone."

Marie looked at Chloe for a long moment, as if deciding whether to believe her. "I should hope so." She picked up her bag. "Well, I guess I *will* go rest up from the train ride. It's been a long weekend."

"You can say that again," Chloe muttered as Marie turned to walk away.

Gigi started to come out from her hiding place behind the door, but ducked back just in time when Marie unexpectedly turned to face Chloe again.

"Say, I saw a limo coming out of the drive just before Louis turned in to drop me off. Who was that?"

Chloe stared blankly at Marie, grappling to invent an explanation. "Uh, Gigi and I ordered pizza for dinner and that was the deliveryman."

Marie wrinkled her brow. "A pizza deliveryman in a limousine?"

"Yeah," Chloe ventured, "it's this new gourmet pizza company that only delivers to mansions." She punctuated the incredulous statement with a forced smile and hoped Marie didn't notice the sweat trickling down her neck.

Marie put her hand on her hip. "You know I'm not buying that line of crap you just fed me, young lady, but I'm too tired to investigate. As long as you and Gigi are both in one piece and didn't break anything in the house, I'm going to let you slide."

Marie turned to walk away again and Chloe leaned against the door in relief.

"And you can come out from behind the door, Gigi," Marie called as she walked away.

"And she didn't even offer to send for me so I could visit her in Milan," Chloe, sprawled on her bed, said to Gigi, who was in the bathroom getting ready to turn in for the night.

Chloe grew increasingly angry at Maxine as she related the phone conversation from earlier in the day.

"I'd be glad if I were you." Gigi came out of the bathroom in a short silk robe, toweling her damp curls. "I'd love to send Simone's old ass to a foreign country."

"That's not the point." Chloe cradled Bizou in her lap and buried her fingers in the cat's soft fur. "We were supposed to spend time together this summer as a family, but it's obvious Mother's gone back to being a workaholic as a way of avoiding dealing with her grief over Jacques."

"Don't you see?" Gigi held up her hands, as if begging for acknowledgement. "The fact that *Tante* Maxine's going to be away for most of the summer is a blessing in disguise."

"What are you talking about?"

Gigi flopped on the bed next to Chloe. "If you hadn't been so busy whining about your mommy for the past fifteen minutes, I could have told you all about my exciting time with Montana."

Chloe groaned and fell back on the bed. "If I have to hear the name Montana Blake one more time, I'm going to hurl."

Gigi swatted her with a pillow. "Hey, how often does a girl get to get up-close and personal with her idol?"

Chloe sat up. "Okay. Tell me all about it."

"Well, the best part is Montana invited me to visit him on the set of his new music video that he's filming in Monaco later this month." Gigi started bouncing up and down on the bed, causing Bizou to hiss and leap to the floor.

"That's pretty cool," Chloe acknowledged. "Is his record company going to fly you down for the day?"

"You don't understand. He's going to be staying at the Hôtel de Paris down there for several weeks while he's promoting his new album around Europe."

Chloe shrugged. "And?"

Gigi stood excitedly. "And, he invited me to stay at the hotel with the rest of his entourage and bring a friend. We're going to Monaco!"

Gigi jumped up and down and screamed, causing Bizou to retreat to a corner and stare at the crazy girl. Chloe shushed Gigi, lest she wake Marie and the rest of the household staff.

"There's no way we can run off to Monaco for the rest of the summer," Chloe reasoned. "Sneaking off to the Riviera isn't the same as sneaking into a club with fake IDs."

"Don't you get it? That's why I said it's a blessing in disguise that your mother's going to be away in Milan for the next few weeks. While she's over there, we'll be down in Monaco."

"Uh-uh." Chloe shook her head. "We'd never get Marie to agree to cover for us."

"She won't have to. Let me take care of that."

Chloe eyed her suspiciously. "What are you cooking up now?"

"I worked it all out in my head while I was in the shower." Gigi paced back and forth, like a filmmaker pitching an idea to a studio head. "We'll tell Maxine and Marie that I decided to reconcile with Simone and move back home. Of course, I asked you to come stay with me so I'll have an ally while Simone and I patch things up."

Chloe sat up, intrigued. "But what if Mother calls Simone? Our cover will be blown instantly."

"Didn't you say *Tante* Maxine told you she's only been communicating with Simone through her assistant? They're still not speaking to each other since Simone thinks *Tante* Maxine took my side."

Chloe nodded slowly, still not convinced they could pull off Gigi's plan. "What if Mother comes home early?"

"We'll call her from the hotel in Monaco every day to check in and see how her remodeling project is going. She'll have no idea where we're calling from. We can say we're at Simone's."

Chloe frowned, her face mirroring her lingering doubt. "Sounds like you've thought of everything, but I still think it's too risky. I'm sorry. You can count me out of this one."

"You sure you don't want to reconsider?" Gigi said, sounding as though she was tempting a chronic dieter with a delicious dessert. "Montana said we could be extras in his video."

Chloe played with the tassels on a pillow, uninterested. "Big deal."

"This isn't just any music video. It's more like a short film. Montana said the record executives think this is the album that could make him a big star in Europe, so they're pulling out all the stops. They hired this big-time director, René Lormier, to shoot the video."

Chloe perked up at the mention of the respected French avant-garde filmmaker who had discovered Chloe's idol, Valérie Bourdain, and recently directed her in what was being hailed as one of her best performances to date.

"And," Gigi added, "as part of the promotion of his album, Montana's going to be presenter at the World Cinema Awards. He said he could get us tickets and we could walk the red carpet with him."

Chloe squealed, unable to disguise her excitement. The World Cinema Awards were second only to the Cannes Film Festival in prestige. Chloe had read in a movie magazine that Valérie Bourdain was going to be attending the ceremony, where her new film with René Lormier was nominated for the top prize. The thought of walking the red carpet and brushing shoulders with her idol filled Chloe with awe.

"God, how can I say no to that?" Chloe grasped strands of her hair as if she was going to rip them out in anxiety.

"Okay, then, let's start packing." Gigi turned to head to the guestroom.

"Not so fast," Chloe said. "I said, 'How can I say no?' Unfortunately, I *am* going to have to say no."

"Girl, are you crazy? How many times are we going to get an opportunity like this?"

"I'm just thinking of Marie. Mother expects her to look out for us while she's away in Milan. If something went wrong and we were found out, Mother would hold Marie responsible. I can't have that on my conscience."

"You're right," Gigi said, coming back into the room. "We should be good little girls and behave ourselves and do exactly what your mother tells us to." She paused for effect. "This is the same woman, as you pointed out, who's such a selfish witch that she didn't even offer to send for you to join her while she's away."

Chloe bit her lip and stared at Gigi, contemplating her words.

"You know," Chloe said after a long moment, "you're right. Why should be hanging around the house all summer while Mother's off gallivanting in gorgeous Milan for God-knows-how-long?"

Gigi raised her arms triumphantly. "Monaco, here we come!"

25

Chloe sat across from Gigi at an open-air cafe in Monaco. They were surrounded by cameramen, crew members and other extras who had been cast in Montana Blake's new music video.

"This is so exciting," Chloe said to Gigi, "to be on the set of a real production. I know it's just a video, but it feels like a movie. I can't wait 'til they start filming and I can see how the director works."

Gigi set aside the sketchpad she was doodling on to kill time while the technicians adjusted the light and sound equipment. "Aren't you glad you let me talk you into coming to Monaco?" she said with a broad smile.

A hush fell over the set when Montana made his entrance, accompanied by René Lormier, the acclaimed director.

"*Pleeze*, seemmer down," Lormier said in his thick accent, raising his hands to hush the extras and crew like a principal taking control of rowdy students at an assembly. "We have a lot of setups to do today, so I'll need everyone to take zeir places."

Gigi waved and blew a kiss at Montana and he returned the gesture.

"Isn't he sexy?" Gigi gushed.

"Quiet on zee set!" Lormier called, putting on headphones and taking his seat on a camera crane that overlooked the scene.

When the director called "Action!," Chloe did her best to look like she was casually making conversation with Gigi, like the other extras positioned at tables throughout the cafe. Ignoring the background action, Montana lip-synched the lyrics of his new single and executed dance steps along with actors who were dressed in chic garb like the Monaco jet set. The artsy scene matched perfectly with the tone of "Runaway Love," a dance song about pursuing an elusive lover around the world.

Chloe was doing her part to blend into the background with the other extras, but Gigi kept breaking character and gazing dreamily at her crush.

"Cut!" Lormier called. The camera crane lowered to the ground and he stepped off, raising a bullhorn to address the extras. "People, I need you to look like you're eating and making conversation at your tables. Pleeze don't look directly at zee camera and, *pleeze*, don't stare at Montana while he's performing. Eets distracting."

Chloe could have sworn Lormier was looking at their table and directing his comments toward Gigi.

"We're extras. We're not supposed to call attention to ourselves," Chloe whispered to Gigi, who cracked her gum and went back to doodling on her sketchpad.

A team of stylists touched up Montana's hair and makeup, and the action resumed. When he started lip-synching and doing his trademark pelvic thrust, Gigi looked up from her sketchpad and gazed at him again.

"Cut!" the director called again, coming down from his crane.

Chloe watched with interest as the director huddled with Montana and several crew members. They kept looking in the general direction of where Chloe and Gigi sat. When the impromptu sidebar disbanded, Montana and Lormier approached the table.

"I told you we weren't supposed to call attention to ourselves," Chloe said under her breath to Gigi. "I bet they're going to ask us to leave."

"Montana wouldn't do that," Gigi said, smiling at him. "He told me I'm his inspiration."

"Yeah, whatever."

When Montana and the director arrived at the table, Gigi jumped up and hugged the young pop star. "Thanks again for inviting us to the set. Chloe and I are having so much fun being here!"

Montana took Gigi's hands, holding her at arm's length. "I'm glad you're here, baby," he said, smiling weakly. "There's just a small problem."

Gigi looked confused. "Problem?"

"Zee scene eez not working," Lormier said, crossing his arms.

Chloe looked at him with a pleasant expression, trying to disguise the intimidation she felt in the presence of such an accomplished filmmaker.

"I told Mr. Lormier the scene would work better if I was singing *to* the girl I'm talking about in the song," Montana said. "We need someone to play that girl."

Gigi looked gleeful. "Oh my god, of course I'll do it! I'll go get into hair and makeup right away."

She started toward the wardrobe trailer, but Montana stopped her. "Uh, baby, it's not you he wants. It's your friend."

Montana and Lormier looked intently in Chloe's direction and she turned to look behind her, certain they were talking about someone else.

"*Me?*" she said when they continued to stare.

"*Oui*, mademoiselle," Lormier said. "You have a look. Have you ever acted before?"

"Uh, no, not... not exactly," Chloe stammered. "I've done some modeling."

Lormier smacked his hands together. "I knew it. You have zee look of someone who would take direction well. Go get into costume."

Chloe glanced at Gigi, who was staring at Chloe with her mouth agape.

"Uh, sorry, sir," Chloe said, not wanting to offend Gigi. "My friend and I are just here hanging out. I wasn't prepared to do any acting."

Lormier waved away Chloe's comment. "Zees eez a music vee-deo, not real acting," he said, inciting Montana's famous pout.

Chloe searched for an excuse. Being recruited for a part in a music video by a top director was beyond flattering, but she didn't want to hurt Gigi's feelings. And, if Chloe were totally honest with herself, she was terrified of being the center of attention and wasn't sure she was up to the challenge.

"I really think it's best that I stay back here," she mumbled, shifting uncomfortably in her seat, "as an extra."

"Nonsense," the director said firmly. "You'll get into costume and I'll show you how to heet your marks. Eets very simple, you'll see. You'll be fine once we get rolling, and we'll get zees scene in zee can."

Chloe looked back at Gigi, who still looked like she'd been electrocuted.

"I'm sorry, sir. I just can't –"

Lormier cut Chloe off. "I don't have time to stand here and argue. We've got to keep moving and stay on-budget. Go to zee wardrobe trailer."

Before Chloe could protest further, Lormier slung his arm around Montana's shoulder and shepherded the young star away. Chloe watched the duo walking away, looking as though they were engrossed in a very important director/star tête-à-tête.

"I'm sorry. I don't know what to say," Chloe said, turning to Gigi with a helpless expression. "I was just sitting here, minding my own business. I wasn't trying to call attention to myself – I was doing the opposite, you know that."

"I know," Gigi said, beginning to regain her composure. "It's okay."

"I won't do it. That part should be yours. You're the one Montana invited to the set. I'm just tagging along."

Gigi took Chloe by the shoulders and stood her up. "You're going to get your ass over to that trailer and do this, or I'm going to drag you over there myself."

"What are you talking about, Gi'? I can't do this. I'm not a professional actress. I've only done a little bit of modeling."

"Will you shut up and stop making excuses? How long have you been talking about breaking into acting? Well, this could be your big break. You just happened to be in the right place at the right time."

Chloe nodded, acknowledging Gigi's point. "You sure you're not mad?" She probed Gigi's eyes for signs of jealousy.

"Mad? You're my best friend, Chlo'. I know you'd want the same for me if the situation were reversed." She paused, smiling. "Besides, I'm the one who gets to hang out in Montana's hotel suite at the end of the day."

Chloe clasped Gigi's hands. "Thank you for letting me do this, Gi'. I won't let you down."

"Go on, get out of here and get into wardrobe before that temperamental director has a tizzy fit."

Chloe gave Gigi once last big smile, then headed toward the wardrobe trailer, feeling the envious glares of the other female extras stabbing her in the back.

"Hey, wait a minute," Chloe said, stopping and turning back to Gigi.

"What now?" Gigi said impatiently, as if *she* were the director.

"What if Mother or Simone sees this video? Then we'll be busted for sure."

Gigi folded her arms, lowered her chin and looked askance at Chloe. "Yeah, right. Like our mothers watch MTV."

Acknowledging once again that Gigi had a point, Chloe turned and made her way through the crowd of extras, film technicians and stylists – feeling every bit the movie star she hoped to one day become.

"Could you pass the suntan lotion?" Gigi, sporting a yellow polka-dot bikini and Dolce & Gabbana shades, said as the girls sunned themselves in deck chairs beside the hotel pool.

Chloe, in a baby blue one-piece and Chanel sunglasses, passed the Bain de Soleil. "Here you go."

Gigi slathered herself. "No matter how long I stay in the sun, I'm always so pale," she lamented, holding a silver sun reflector under her neck. "I wish I could turn a nice brown like you."

Chloe flipped through a fashion magazine. "I'm thinking about going home."

Monaco was the playground of movie stars, chart-topping rappers and rockers and the European aristocracy, but Chloe wasn't having as much fun as she thought she would.

"Are you crazy?" Gigi said.

"When you pitched the idea of coming here, it sounded like a really cool summer vacation, but this is the first day I've had off in the week we've been here." Chloe sighed listlessly and reclined in her lounge chair. "When I agreed to play Montana's love interest in the video, I had no idea they'd want me to be in *every* scene."

"Poor thing. Aren't you the put-upon little movie star?" Gigi teased. "Do you know how many girls would die to be you? You got to *kiss* Montana in that scene yesterday."

"It wasn't all that," Chloe said, shrugging.

Gigi was being such a good sport, and had even coached Chloe on how to make the screen kiss look realistic. While Chloe filmed her scenes, Gigi stood off-camera beaming like a proud stage mother – cheering Chloe on, giving her constructive criticism on her performance, and encouraging her to get over her nerves. Instead of jealous or competitive, Gigi seemed honored that Montana had chosen her best friend to be his "video girl." Gigi, in fact, was enjoying the experience more than Chloe.

"I'm exhausted, and we haven't even had a chance to do any sight-seeing," Chloe continued. "What's the point of being in Monaco if we don't get to get out and see anything? I'm so tired at the end of the day filming that all I can do is drop into bed. If I had known I was going to be working so much, I'd have stayed in Paris and had my agent book a whole bunch of modeling assignments."

"There's only a few days left of filming, then we can relax and hang out at the beach and do some shopping. There's a lot of museums and galleries I want to check out." Gigi was right at home in the Riviera, which had been the muse to Matisse, Chagall and other famous artists.

"As soon as M'sieu Lormier says, 'That's a wrap,' I'm out of here," Chloe insisted.

"You'll blow our cover if you go back now."

"I don't know how much longer we can pull off this scheme."

The girls had been lucky so far, phoning to check in every day with Maxine, who apparently suspected nothing. But Chloe feared their luck would soon run out.

"I want to go home. I'm sick of room service. I miss Marie's cooking.

I miss my cat, I miss my horse," Chloe said, reclining in the deck chair and reflecting wistfully on the comforts of home. "And let's be real. When the video wraps, you're going to be spending all your time with Montana and I'll be sitting alone in the hotel room, bored."

Gigi grinned. "Montana needs me. He's going to be shooting a new movie when he goes back to America in the fall. I'm kind of filling in for his acting coach while he's here. He bounces lines off me."

Chloe scowled. "I've seen his trailer rocking. I bet that's not the only thing he bounces off you."

Gigi used her sun reflector to spank Chloe's leg. "Look, all I'm asking is that you give it another week. If you still want to go home by the end of next week, I'll go with you. Deal?"

Chloe hesitated, weighing the consequences of sticking around and possibly getting caught. "Let me think about it."

She went back to flipping through her fashion magazine. She felt a little depressed looking at all these girls and their perfect bodies. She hadn't been watching what she ate since they arrived in Monaco, grazing at the craft service table between takes on the music video, and her bathing suit was a little snug. She promised herself she'd go on a crash diet the minute she got home.

A cabana boy approached, carrying a tray that held an exotic drink with a little umbrella. "*Pardon*, mademoiselle, here's your virgin daiquiri."

"*Merci.*" Chloe didn't look up from her magazine as she took the drink and began to nurse it through a tiny straw.

"Will that be all, mademoiselle?"

A tip. She almost forgot. She reached into her beach bag and shoved a couple bills in the guy's hand. "That'll be all for now, *garçon.*"

"If you need anything else, anything at all…" He paused, adding, "I'll be around."

Chloe finally looked up from the magazine, detecting something in his tone, something a bit… *Flirtatious*? She lowered her shades to get a better look and was dazzled at the sight of the handsome, brown-skinned cabana boy, who looked like he could be mixed-race. Clad in a white polo shirt and khaki shorts that revealed an athletic physique, he flashed gleaming, even teeth and ran a hand through his curly black hair. Tray at his side, he turned and walked away, providing an excellent view of his firm backside.

Gigi smiled mischievously, as if picking up on Chloe's instant crush.

"You know, I've thought it over," Chloe said, trying her best to sound nonchalant while flipping through her magazine, "and maybe I'll stick around for awhile."

26

"Yes, I agree, it's great that Gigi and Simone made up," Chloe said, speaking to Maxine on the phone as she paced the living room of the plush suite at the Hôtel de Paris. The irony of the hotel's name wasn't lost on Chloe, since she and Gigi were actually supposed to be in Paris instead of cavorting around Monaco.

"What have you and Gigi been doing while I've been gone?" Maxine said over the sound of workers moving furniture in the Italian villa where she was overseeing the renovation project.

"Not much." Chloe wrapped the phone cord around her finger, then unwrapped and began pacing again, trying to avoid one of her mother's all-out interrogations. "Shopping, hanging out. You know, just the usual summer stuff."

Chloe glanced out the window at the sun-drenched seascape and longed to be out on the beach, lying on the shore and letting the warm waters of the Mediterranean wash away the guilt of lying to her mother.

"Could you put Simone on the line? I need to ask her if she received the invoices I faxed over for this renovation."

"Um, Simone's not here right now."

"It's after six. Where is she?"

Chloe could hear a hint of concern in Maxine's voice, and she needed to come up with an excuse fast for why Simone couldn't come to the phone.

"She's... she's... Working late at the office. She's been working really hard to keep things running smoothly since you've been gone."

"I knew I should stop worrying and just let her handle things in Paris while I'm gone," Maxine said, sounding relieved. "It's probably best that we continue to communicate through our assistants, or else she'll think I'm checking up on her."

"You're absolutely right. You shouldn't call Simone while you're away. That would be a really, really bad idea." Chloe bit her lip, wondering if she had said too much.

A loud thud sounded in the background on Maxine's end of the line.

"Hey, be careful with that vase!" Maxine called to one of the workers. "Honey, I'd better go," she said, speaking to Chloe again. "I turn my back for one moment and everything goes haywire."

"Okay, Mother. I understand. I'll call you tomorrow."

Chloe was winding down the conversation, glad that she didn't have to resort to more lying, when someone knocked on the door of the hotel suite and yelled, "Room service!"

"What was that?" Maxine asked. "It sounded like someone said, 'Room service.'"

"Uh…" Chloe paused, looking nervously around the room, as if a plausible explanation would jump out at her. She glanced down at the bearskin rug and got an inspiration.

"Uh, no, they said 'groom service,'" Chloe improvised, running her bare foot over the furry rug. "I brought Bizou with me to stay here at Gigi and Simone's, and that's the cat groomer."

"Oh," Maxine said, sounding as though she bought it. "Well, give Simone and Gigi my love."

The waiter continued knocking loudly on the door and repeating, "Room service!"

"I will. Gotta go. Love you," Chloe said, slamming the phone down and rushing to the door.

Chloe took the tray of chocolate-covered strawberries she'd forgotten she'd ordered, tipped the waiter and nibbled while staring out the window. She caught sight of the handsome cabana boy. He and his co-workers were horsing around while off-duty, splashing water on each other in the pool. The cabana boy had his shirt off, his rippled chest gleaming in the evening sun.

She sighed, watching him. She'd been checking him out the past couple of days, but she was too shy to approach him. Every time he looked her way, she looked away bashfully. When she was lounging poolside and he came up and asked her if she needed anything, she would think, *Yeah, I need you.* But she would reply in a soft voice, "No thank you," and gaze longingly at him as he walked away.

The one good thing about her preoccupation with this new guy was that she'd finally gotten over François.

She continued to stare out of the window when she was jolted by a tap on her shoulder.

"BOO!"

She screamed and jumped in shock, then relaxed when she saw it was Gigi, who was convulsing in laughter.

"What were you looking at?" Gigi asked when she finally regained her composure.

Chloe closed the drapes. "Nothing."

"Don't give me that innocent routine." Gigi flung the curtains open. "Ah-hah. Now I see what you were looking at." She spotted the cabana boy. "Checking out the merchandise, huh?"

"Shut up," Chloe said, closing the drapes and pulling Gigi away from the window.

"So, you like the pool guy, do you?"

"No, Gigi. I don't like him, okay?"

"Oh come off it, Chlo'. I saw you salivating over him."

"You are so juvenile! Get out of my face." Chloe flopped on the plush, white velour sofa.

Gigi sat down next to Chloe and started tickling her. "You've got the hots for him, admit it."

Chloe playfully kicked Gigi onto the floor, and Gigi hit her head on the coffee table. "Ouch!"

"That's what you get for sticking your nose in other people's business."

Gigi stood up and dusted herself off. "I don't have time for this. Montana's performing at Le Clique tonight and he got us all-access passes. No fake IDs for us tonight, we're going to get the star treatment all the way."

Chloe plucked another chocolate-covered strawberry from the tray. "No thanks. The video just wrapped this afternoon, and I'm pooped. I just want to pig out on room service and stay in tonight."

"What, and fantasize about your little cabana boy?"

Chloe threw a pillow at Gigi, who ducked just in time.

"Seriously, Chloe," Gigi said, picking the pillow up and tossing it back on the sofa, "if you like that guy, just go up to him."

"And say what?"

"That you want his body."

Chloe groaned and threw another pillow at Gigi. This time it hit her in the face. The girls started play-fighting, punching each other and pulling each other's hair. The game ended at the sound of fabric ripping.

"See what you've done," Gigi bristled, standing up, one of her sleeves hanging by a thread. "Now I have to go change."

"Ha ha. That's what you get for teasing me," Chloe said, biting into another strawberry.

Gigi snatched the strawberry out of Chloe's hand and tossed it back on the tray. "You're not going to sit in this hotel room stuffing your face. You could do that at home. It's taken too much effort for us to be here," she insisted. "We have an extra ticket for Montana's show tonight, and you should bring a date. You should ask that cabana boy out."

Chloe picked up the half-eaten strawberry and nibbled. "I'm not asking him out. I'm not in the mood to go out tonight."

Gigi picked up a pillow and walloped Chloe upside the head. "No more excuses. Go get dressed and meet me in the lobby in a half-an-hour. Montana is sending a limo to pick us up."

Chloe paced the hotel lobby in a burgundy halter dress and heels. Gigi was supposed to have met her fifteen minutes ago, but was taking forever getting ready, as usual. Chloe tugged at the top of her dress, which she thought was too short and nearly see-through, but had consented to wearing upon Gigi's coaxing.

"*Pardon*, mademoiselle, do you have the time?" a graying man in a business suit said, approaching Chloe.

Chloe glanced at her watch. "Seven-fifteen."

"*Merci*," the man said. "I have an hour before I'm to meet my wife for dinner. Would you care to join me in the lounge for a drink?"

The man looked at Chloe with a lusty expression, and it soon dawned on her that he must have been mistaking her for a call girl.

"No, M'sieu, *merci*," she said graciously, her cheeks flushing. "I have another engagement."

He gave Chloe a knowing look. "Ah. I understand. Call me if your schedule clears."

The man slipped Chloe a card, which she promptly tossed in the trash. This encounter convinced her that she should go change into the more demure dress she had picked out and tone down her makeup. She sprinted to the elevator, fumbling in her purse for her keycard, and bumped into someone.

"Are you all right?" the guy asked, putting his hand on her bare back.

Chloe looked up and saw it was him. The cabana boy. He was touching her.

"Y-yeah. I'm okay. Thanks," she stammered, looking down at her feet. "Oh shit." The contents of her purse had spilled everywhere. A tube of lipstick was rolling under a chair and change clattered all over the tiled floor.

"Let me help you."

The cabana boy helped her pick up all the junk and stuff it back in her purse.

"Thanks so much," she said, snapping her purse shut.

"No problem."

He smiled at her, and she noticed he had traded his uniform for casual clothes. He was dressed in jeans, a white button-down shirt open at the collar and tennis shoes.

"My shift just ended," he explained.

"Oh."

A question made its way into her brain and she knew she had to ask it. If she didn't, she would hate herself forever.

"Listen," she started, almost muted by the lump in her throat, "me and a c-couple of friends of mine are about to go out. Wanna come along?"

When he didn't answer immediately, she assumed he was going to turn her down. She had been a fool for thinking an older boy would give her the time of day.

"I'd love to."

She wasn't sure she'd heard him right. She gaped at him, expecting him to change his mind.

"Are you sure you're all right?" he asked.

She nodded affirmatively. She wanted to do cartwheels in the lobby, which probably wasn't a good idea since she was wearing lacy panties.

"Where were you and your friends planning on going?"

"Actually, my friend has VIP passes to Montana Blake's show at Le Clique."

"Le Clique? That's the hottest club in Monaco. They have a strict dress code. They'd never let me in without a jacket."

"Why don't you go change? I'll wait."

"I'm just working here for the summer. I didn't bring any dressy clothes with me."

"Oh, okay. Well, maybe next time." Her shoulders stooped. She couldn't disguise her disappointment.

"Hey wait a minute," he said after a moment. "I'll be right back."

She watched him go to the front desk and whisper something to the clerk. The guy at the front desk looked at Chloe, then took off his jacket and handed it over to the cabana boy.

"Problem solved. Frédéric lent me this for the evening," the boy said, slipping on the jacket as he came back to where Chloe stood. "I'm Dominique, by the way. Dominique St.-Denis."

She extended her hand. "Chloe. Chloe Bareaux."

They stood there smiling at each other, until the doors of the elevator parted and Gigi entered the lobby in a hot pink number that was even shorter and lower-cut than Chloe's dress.

Gigi smiled at Dominique and said, "So, who do we have here?" She flashed a look at Chloe as if to say, "Not bad."

Chloe made the introductions.

"Let's go," Gigi said. "Our limo awaits."

"Do you think I'll be okay wearing tennis shoes?" Dominique asked, lifting the cuff of his jeans to reveal his Nikes.

Gigi reached into her purse and flashed the all-access passes. "Who cares? We have VIP tickets," she said, leading the way to the limousine parked in front of the hotel.

Dominique held his arm out to Chloe. "It's my honor to escort you this evening, ma-*dam*," he said, as if imitating one of the hotel's high-powered guests.

Chloe glanced at Gigi, who gave a clandestine thumbs-up as she piled into the limo ahead of Chloe and Dominique. Chloe smiled and locked her arm in his.

When the trio arrived at Le Clique, they found a long line of people waiting to get in, just like at the club where Montana had performed in Paris. Chloe had to concur with Gigi that it felt good to step out of the limo and be ushered past the velvet ropes like Hollywood royalty.

"These are really awesome seats," Dominique said once they were situated at a table in the VIP section that had a prime view of the stage. "This show's been sold out for weeks. How did you manage to get these tickets?"

Gigi looked at Chloe, grinned, then replied, "Let's just say I'm with the band."

"I wonder if they have virgin daiquiris here," Chloe said, opening the drink menu. "The ones they serve at the hotel are delicious."

Dominique smiled. "They are pretty good, aren't they?"

Gigi took the drink menu from Chloe and returned it to the stand in the middle of the table. "No virgin daiquiris tonight; it's Cristal all around. Montana's record label is picking up the tab. He told me to spare no expense."

"This is really cool," Dominique said, raising his voice over the loud club music. "This is the first chance I've had to go out to a disco all summer." He took Chloe's hand under the table. "I'm glad I could be here with you."

Chloe's palms became sweaty as he held her hand, but the moment was soon interrupted when Gigi yanked Chloe's other hand.

"Let's go to the little girls' room and freshen up," Gigi suggested, grabbing her purse. "I want to look my best when Montana comes onstage."

"I'll be right back," Chloe offered apologetically to Dominique as Gigi pulled her in the direction of the ladies' room.

Just before they reached the entrance, Gigi stopped suddenly and stared straight ahead, as though she caught sight of something gruesome.

"What's wrong?" Chloe looked around to see what Gigi was gawking at.

"It's that awful boy from St. Thomas. He's coming this way." Gigi stepped behind Chloe. "Quick, hide me."

Chloe surveyed the crowd and noticed a boy with blond curls and too-tight jeans heading in their direction. She squinted, trying to remember where she had seen him before, and finally recalled that he was the ambassador's son who had thrown that alcohol-saturated, spring-break party a couple of years ago. What was his name? Jason, Justin? Jeremy, that was it. He was the asshole who'd insulted Gigi when she wouldn't put out.

Chloe and Gigi tried to duck inside the restroom as he neared, but the boy spotted them.

"What are *you* doing here?" the boy said, looking Gigi up and down reproachfully.

Gigi stood up straight. "Not that it's any of your business, but Chloe and I are here as guests of Montana Blake."

"Yeah, right. I bet you two snuck in here like a couple of groupies." He brushed past them, snickering with his friends.

Chloe turned to Gigi, who looked shaken. "Forget about him," Chloe said. "He's a jerk."

"Come on," Gigi said sullenly, taking Chloe's hand and leading her into the restroom. "Let's get ready for the show."

An hour later, immersed in Montana's performance, Gigi seemed to have sloughed off the unfortunate encounter with the beastly boy from St. Thomas. For his part, Dominique was a good sport, popping his fingers to the beat despite the fact that Montana's music was obviously geared toward young girls. Every time Chloe looked over at Dominique and he smiled at her, she couldn't believe she was actually out on a date with the boy she'd been admiring from afar.

"I'm going to slow it down a little," Montana said, taking a stool after performing "Runaway Love," the dance number to which Chloe knew every word, having co-starred in the video. "I'd like to dedicate this next number to someone special in the audience tonight, and she knows who she is."

Montana blew a kiss in Gigi's direction. Chloe glanced at Gigi, whose flattered expression quickly turned to annoyance at all the other girls who crowded near the stage and screamed, "I love you, Montana!"

The lights dimmed and Montana began crooning a sensitive ballad, taking Chloe by surprise with an impressive vocal range.

"God, he's a dream." Gigi propped her head on her fist and looked starry-eyed. "And he's all mine."

Couples began filling the dance floor, swaying to the slow jam.

Dominique extended his hand toward Chloe. "Would you like to dance?"

Chloe looked over at Gigi, who gave her an affirmative nod.

"Sure," Chloe said, taking his hand. "I'd love to."

Dominique led Chloe to the dance floor and draped his arm around her waist. Being so close to him, feeling his body next to hers, felt so right.

Unlike François, who had grinded against her when they danced in the ballroom of the Chateau de Chevalier that horrendous night last summer, Dominique kept a gentlemanly distance. Chloe closed her eyes and imagined that she could stay in his arms forever.

When Montana wrapped the song, Chloe and Dominique remained on the dance floor, holding hands. She wondered if he felt the same attraction to her.

"Thank you, Monaco. I love you. Goodnight," Montana called from the stage as the glaring houselights came on. The club erupted in chaos, with girls swarming the stage and jockeying to touch him. The girls, all of whom had to be at least a couple of years older than Chloe and Gigi, acted like unruly kindergartners grappling for the last piece of Valentine's candy. Security guards formed a human chain in front of the small stage, but the girls pushed past them and shoved each other, tugging on Montana's pants leg, grabbing at his shirt, even pulling his hair.

Dominique continued to grasp Chloe's hand and led her through the crowd, to where Gigi stood at the backstage entrance.

"I need to get back to see Montana," Gigi told a security guard, whose face remained expressionless behind mirrored shades.

"Sorry, no one gets back until we clear the venue," said the guard, a clone of the one at the Paris club where Montana had performed.

Were a pair of shades, a thick neck and a bad attitude prerequisites for getting hired as a bouncer? Chloe wondered.

"But I have an all-access pass." Gigi raised the laminate dangling from her neck.

"Sorry," the guard repeated. "No one gets back."

Chloe stood next to Dominique and Gigi, watching as a bodyguard ripped Montana away from the groping mob and ushered him behind a curtain. The girls continued to yelp and paw at the empty stage, as if Montana would reappear if they made enough commotion.

Gigi turned back to the guard. "Can I go back now?"

He shook his head. "I'm sorry, mademoiselle. I'm going to have to ask you to leave the venue."

Gigi raised her laminate again, shaking it in the guard's face. "But I have a backstage pass."

The guard's face remained impassive. "Sorry, mademoiselle. I'm going to need you to step away."

With a defeated expression, Gigi took a reluctant step backward and Chloe placed a supportive hand on her shoulder. Upon turning to follow the rest of the club-goers who were being ushered out, the trio encountered the jerk from St. Thomas and his gaggle of sycophants.

The boy shook his head disdainfully, as if busting Gigi in an unlawful act. "Nothing but a groupie, just like I figured." He and his friends broke out in mocking laughter and headed for the door.

"Forget them," Chloe said.

"Yeah," Dominique chimed in, "who cares what they think?"

Gigi said nothing, until they had reached the outside and the limo waiting at the curb. "Why don't you guys take the limo back to the hotel? I'm going to hang out here for awhile and wait for Montana."

"By yourself?" Chloe said, touching Gigi's arm. "You going to be okay?"

"Yeah, you guys go ahead. I'll be all right."

"You sure you don't want us to wait with you?" Dominique offered.

"Please," Gigi said, looking away and lighting a cigarette. "Go on ahead without me."

"Okay," Chloe said, inching toward the limo, sensing Gigi wanted to be alone, "but you call me as soon as you get backstage and let me know you're safe."

The chauffeur opened the door of the passenger compartment and, before stepping in, Chloe gave Gigi a hug.

"Here, take this," Dominique said, taking off the jacket he'd borrowed and placing it around Gigi's shoulders. "That sea breeze can whip around pretty strong at night and I wouldn't want you to catch a chill."

"Thanks," Gigi said, puffing on the cigarette.

Chloe gave Dominique an appreciative smile, impressed with his chivalrous act. Once seated next to him inside the limo, she rolled down her window.

"If you need us to come back and pick you up, call me," Chloe said to Gigi, raising her voice over the din that the other patrons were making while chattering and laughing in front of the club.

Chloe watched through the back window as the limo pulled away, saddened by the sight of Gigi standing alone on the curb.

"You sure your friend's going to be all right, waiting outside the club all by herself?" Dominique asked, walking Chloe down the hotel corridor that led to her suite.

"Yeah, I think she'll be okay. Gigi's nothing if not crafty. She'll get back in to see Montana one way or another – even if she has to spill blood to do it," she said, laughing. They arrived at the door of her suite. "This is me."

"Thanks so much for inviting me," Dominique said, flashing that sexy smile of his. "I had a great time."

"Me, too. I'm glad you could join us."

A moment of silence passed with Chloe and Dominique standing in the hallway staring at one another. *Is he going to kiss me or what?* she wondered.

As if interpreting her thoughts, he began inching toward her. She instinctively closed her eyes. She quivered as his lips – soft, full and moist

– brushed against hers.

"Well," he said after they separated, "I guess I'll see you around."

"Uh, yeah," she sputtered. "See you around."

Was that it? He was just going to walk away?

"Have a good night," he said, turning and throwing up a hand in a half-wave.

She nodded, overcome with disappointment that he hadn't made some gesture indicating that he was interested in seeing her again. She thought she was going to cry as she watched him walk slowly down the hall.

Unexpectedly, he stopped and faced her. "Say, what are you doing tomorrow?"

She leaned against the doorframe. "Not much. I hadn't really planned anything," she said, not wanting to sound too available.

"Tomorrow's my day off. You wanna hang out?"

She couldn't suppress a smile. "Sure. That sounds like fun."

"Have you had a chance to do any sightseeing?"

"No, not really. I've been so busy shooting Montana's video that I haven't had a chance to see anything."

Dominique's eyes widened. "You got to be in his video?"

"Yeah, for the song he opened with tonight," she said, slouching against the door. "I guess I forgot to mention that."

"That's really cool. Do you have to be on the set at all tomorrow, or are you free?"

"I'm free. We wrapped earlier today – or I guess I should say yesterday," she said, looking at her watch.

"Cool. I'll pick you up on my scooter and I'll show you around."

"I'd like that."

"I'll have Freddy at the front desk give me the number to your room and I'll call you."

"Great. I'll be waiting to hear from you."

Dominique waved goodbye and started down the hall again.

Chloe held her hand aloft, lingering in the doorway and watching him walk away. When he was out of sight, she let herself in the suite, took a pillow from the couch and screamed into it. She couldn't wait for Gigi to get back so she could give her a full report.

27

Chloe stepped out of the hotel lobby and into the early-afternoon sunshine. She was greeted by the sight of Dominique on a sporty European motor scooter.

"Hi, there. Hop on."

She straddled the bike and wrapped her arms around his mid-section, cherishing the feeling of being so close to him.

"Hold on tight," he said, revving the bike's handlebars. "And don't let go."

The bike took off with a jolt and she gripped him tighter, clutching at his shirt.

"Don't worry," he said, glancing back at her. "I've got you."

He maneuvered the bike through the crowded streets of Monaco, giving Chloe an opportunity to take a good look around for the first time since she and Gigi had arrived. Since Monaco was so compact, less than a square mile, it was possible to take in most of it in a day, he explained.

They rode through the Monaco-Ville neighborhood, past the Grimaldi Palace and the Cathèdral of the Immaculate Conception; motored through the Fontvieille section, where a capacity crowd filled the stands of the Louis II Stadium to cheer their favorite soccer teams; and stopped at the Oceanographic Museum to marvel at hundreds of fish species squiggling around in oversize tanks.

Chloe clung to Dominique as they rode along the Grand Corniche, the winding highway that stretched over the cliffs bordering the Mediterranean.

"It's beautiful," Chloe said, taking in the bird's-eye view of Monaco and the sea, which lay more than a thousand feet below.

"When I said I'd show you around, I meant it," Dominique said with a grin.

That breezy afternoon scooter ride was the start of Chloe getting to know Dominique over the course of the next few weeks. While Gigi was away, accompanying Montana on his promotional tour of Europe, Chloe spent her days lounging around the pool, content to sit and watch Dominique work. He brought her free drinks and snacks and made funny faces at her while serving the hotel's moneyed, pretentious guests.

After his shift ended each evening, he would either come to her suite or she'd visit him in the bungalow where the hotel's seasonal help stayed. They'd take walks on the beach and watch the sun set.

"Wow, I can't believe you guys are actually getting away with that. It takes a lot of nerve, pulling something like that off," Dominique said one evening on the beach after Chloe confessed the circumstances of her and Gigi's visit to the Riviera. "That's pretty bold – lying to your mothers like that."

"It was Gigi's idea," Chloe said, looking out over the water and avoiding eye contact with Dominique, shame washing over her like the waves lapping at their feet.

He squeezed her hand. "Hey, I think it's pretty cool what you guys are doing. If you didn't have the guts to sneak away, we probably never would have met, even though we both live in Paris."

"Yeah, and I'll be going back to school in London," she said, wishing summer could last forever.

"And I'll be starting at the University of Paris in the fall. My parents are paying my tuition, but they insisted I get a summer job to pay for books." He paused, looking into her eyes. "Paris is such a big city, full of strangers. I'm glad we met down here."

He cradled her face in his hands and kissed her. They stood hand in hand, listening to the sound of the waves crashing against the sand and the seagulls crying.

"You know," Chloe said after a few minutes, "one of the reasons I wanted to run away is because my mother is never home anymore. I figured, she's away on business anyway and she'd probably never miss me."

He looked sympathetic. "Why do you say that?"

"It's a long explanation."

"I've got time."

They sat next to each other on the sand and she explained Jacques' sudden death and Maxine's subsequent emotional withdrawal.

"I miss Jacques so much sometimes. He was the only father I ever had – especially since I never knew my biological father," Chloe said, hugging her knees and feeling small against the vastness of the sea. "You're so lucky that your parents are still married."

Dominique traced a line in the sand. "I suppose. They've been together so long, I couldn't imagine them without each other – even though my mom's black and from America and my dad's French."

It was comforting to know that Dominique was also of mixed heritage. They had so much in common, it was eerie.

"How'd your folks meet?" she asked.

"My mom was a model back in the day. She grew up in New York and started coming over to Paris for assignments. My dad's a photographer, and they hit it off. They hooked up and here I am." Dominique grinned and held his arms aloft, as if presenting himself as a gift-wrapped surprise.

Chloe laughed. "Do you ever visit your mom's side of the family in New York?"

He nodded. "All the time. We always go there on holidays. I have a lot of fun hanging out with my cousins, especially since I'm an only child. I usually spend the summer at my grandparents' brownstone in Brooklyn, but this year Mom and Dad said I should get a summer job and save some money since I'll be starting college."

Chloe rested her chin on her knees. "You're so lucky to have extended family and to know where you come from. I've never really had that."

She fell silent, and Dominique put his arm around her and gently kissed her. She leaned into him, feeling warm and protected. He moved his hand down her body, grazing her breast. She shivered at his touch, aroused.

"I'm sorry," he said softly. "I didn't mean to –"

"It's okay. It's just that…" She grappled for words to describe how she felt – excited and frightened at the same time.

He took her chin in his hand. "I understand, Chloe. It's all right. I don't want to make you do anything you're not ready to."

She kissed him, then propped her head on his shoulder and they spent the rest of the evening watching the sun set over the Mediterranean.

"Dominique's a dream," Chloe sighed, sitting across from Gigi at the breakfast table on the terrace of their suite.

Gigi flung a grape across the table. "And you tease me when I talk about Montana like that."

"He's so nice, but not in a nerdy way," Chloe gushed. "And he's *so* cute. God, every time he comes near me, I get all shaky and I fantasize about what it would be like to lay beside him."

Gigi raised an eyebrow. "*Fantasize*? You mean you two still haven't done it?"

Now it was Chloe's turn to throw food. She tore a piece of her croissant and tossed it at Gigi. "Not everyone's like you and Montana, going at it all the time."

Gigi grinned. "Montana says I'm the hottest girl he's ever known – in America or Europe. He said none of those groupies that mob him everywhere he goes can compare to me and what we've got." She leaned back and sighed dramatically. "He's so sweet."

"I know how you feel, now that I've got Dominique. I'm going to ask him to be my guest at the World Cinema Awards this Sunday."

Gigi grimaced. "There's a slight problem with the tickets."

Chloe picked at her croissant. "Oh? What's wrong? I thought Montana could get as many tickets as he wants."

"Yeah, that's what I thought, too, but as it turns out, the awards show has gotten bigger every year and they're saying this is going to be the biggest year ever. It's going to be broadcast live around the world. International media are going to be on the red carpet, and the VIPs are only getting two tickets – one for themselves and one for a guest."

"I want you to go, Gi'," Chloe said without hesitation.

181

"No, Chloe, I want you to go. You're the one who wants to act. You've wanted to be an actress every since we were little, as long as I've wanted to be an artist. You have to be there. This could be your only chance to meet your idol, Valérie Bourdain."

"I'll have other chances to meet her – one day when I'm a star myself." Chloe stuck out her chin and put her hand on her hip, mimicking the pose of a pampered movie star. "Besides, there's another reason I think you should go."

Chloe scanned through the newspaper with her index finger until she located an item. "This gossip column item says that the British ambassador to France and his wife, Sir Nigel and Lady Clarice Dutton, are on the board that chooses the winners at the awards show."

Gigi looked confused. "And? What's that got to do with me?"

"They're the parents of that jerk we ran into at the club the other night – Jeremy Dutton from St. Thomas."

Gigi stared out over the balcony. "Oh yeah, him. Why'd you have to remind me?"

"This article says the Duttons are making their little shit get a summer job and volunteer as an usher at the awards show."

Gigi laughed sardonically. "Some summer job. He'll be slaving away, showing all those glamorous movie stars to their seats. Who gives a shit? I still don't get what that has to do with me."

Chloe reached across the table and put her hand on Gigi's. "What that has to do with you is, you're going to find the most expensive couture gown in Monaco and go to that awards ceremony on the arm of Montana Blake – the hottest young star on either side of the Atlantic. You're going to step out of a stretch limousine on the red carpet and have the paparazzi snapping photos of you with Montana." Chloe paused for effect, adding, "And then, when you reach the end of the red carpet, you're going to make that asshole show you and Montana to your seats – like he's a servant who works for you."

Gigi was silent, as if it took a moment for the magnitude of Chloe's words to sink in.

"You know, *ma amie*," Gigi finally said, "I think that sounds like a plan."

"Are you sure this dress looks right on me?" Gigi said to Chloe as they stood before a three-way mirror at Loudron's, one of the most exclusive boutiques in Monaco's ritzy Monte Carlo district. Gigi tugged at the couture gown's lacy bustier and turned this way and that, examining the long, billowy skirt.

"I modeled this gown for *Elle*," Chloe said, taking Gigi by the shoulders and turning her toward the mirror. "This is from Jean-Paul Gaultier's collection. Trust me, you'll get a lot of attention when you wear this to the World Cinema Awards."

Gigi turned sideways, looking skeptically at herself over her shoulder. "You sure I don't look ridiculous?"

Chloe aimed Gigi toward the mirror. "You look hot. I've gotten to know a little about fashion since I started modeling, and this dress accentuates all your curves. You're going to rock this dress on the red carpet and have all the paparazzi shouting your name and pointing their lenses at you." She added with a groan, "I just hope Mother and Simone don't catch any of the press coverage."

"I doubt that, with *Tante* Maxine away on business. And all Simone cares about is her boyfriend." Gigi looked away from the mirror and directly at Chloe. "Thanks again, Chlo', for being a good sport about the tickets."

"*Laissez tomber* – forget it. I'll still get to watch from the sidelines." She turned Gigi toward the mirror once again. "You know what's going to make me happy? Seeing you stride down that red carpet on Montana's arm like you own Monaco and show that little snot Jeremy you're no groupie."

Gigi threw her arms around Chloe. "Thanks for being such a good friend, and for helping me pick out this dress. I would never have known what to wear without your help."

Chloe pulled away, looking at Gigi's reflection in the mirror. "It was my pleasure. After all, that expense account the record label gave Montana wasn't going to spend itself, was it?"

"This is really awesome," Dominique said to Chloe, shouting to be heard over the hoards of screaming fans gathered around them behind a barricade along the red carpet outside the Grand Théâtre de Monte Carlo.

"Sorry we're so far back," Chloe said, "but I wanted this to be Gigi's night to shine, so I let her have the extra ticket."

"Are you kidding? This is great," Dominique said, looking around at the long line of stretch limousines and the eager press waiting to snap photos and shove microphones in the faces of the celebrities who would emerge. "We can see all the action."

Chloe and Dominique "oohed" and "aahed" along with the rest of the crowd as movie stars, directors and their hangers-on stepped out of the limousines and made their way down the red carpet.

"This is like being at the Oscars," Dominique marveled, his arms around Chloe's waist.

Every time a star would turn and wave to the crowd, the fans would scream even louder. The young girls in the crowd went crazy when Montana made his entrance, Gigi on his arm looking like a Hollywood starlet in her Gaultier gown and gold jewelry purchased, appropriately, from a Cartier boutique. Just as Gigi had stood graciously behind the scenes when Chloe shot the music video with Montana, it was now Chloe's turn to watch from the sidelines with pride.

Just as Chloe predicted, the photographers aimed their lenses at Gigi, jockeying for photos of Montana's new Parisian flame. Following Montana's direction, Gigi stopped and posed for the photographers, illuminated by the camera flashes and obviously drinking in all the attention.

A beautiful female television reporter pointed her microphone at Montana. "Who's your escort this evening, M'sieu Blake?"

He turned and smiled at Gigi, clasping her hand. "This is Gigi, Gigi Cartier of Paris."

Montana said Gigi's name like she was a social-climbing debutante or up-and-coming young actress, and Gigi played the part, preening for the cameras.

"I love you, Gigi!" Chloe shouted from behind the barricade.

Gigi caught sight of Chloe and waved enthusiastically before being pulled along down the press line by Montana's handlers.

"Your friend looks gorgeous," Dominique said, "like a real star."

"I picked out the dress," Chloe said, beaming.

Gigi and Montana were clearly the talk of the red carpet, and Chloe's excitement for her best friend culminated when the glittering couple reached the end of the red carpet and were greeted by a shocked Jeremy Dutton. As Montana handed the tickets to the arrogant St. Thomas boy, Gigi gave him a contemptuous glare, as if putting a peon in his place. Chloe snapped photos, capturing the delicious moment on film for Gigi to savor later.

Chloe was reloading her camera when the crowd erupted in screams again. She looked up to see Valérie Bourdain exiting a limousine, looking every bit the star she was. Her auburn hair was swept up in an elegant French twist and subtle blond highlights glimmered in the evening sun, complementing the beaded gown and tasteful jewelry glinting on her ears, neck and fingers. Her creamy skin was as radiant as when she was onscreen, bathed in the warm glow of camera flashes and floodlights lining the red carpet. Chloe couldn't believe she was standing just several feet from the legend she'd watched on the big screen all these years.

"Who's that?" Dominique asked.

Chloe gave him a bemused look. "Valérie Bourdain, only one of the most famous French actresses ever."

He shrugged. "My parents are always saying I should know more about the arts and culture, but I guess I'm more into sports."

Chloe finally got the film loaded and began frantically snapping photos. The notoriously press-shy star gracefully walked past the television and print interviewers, but paused for the paparazzi. The veteran performer looked unflappable in the July heat as photographers shouted her name, craning her gorgeous face in each direction like a true pro to give the shutterbugs equal time.

Chloe watched mesmerized from behind the barricade. For one magical instant, Valérie Bourdain turned and looked in Chloe's direction. Time seemed suspended as Chloe made eye contact with her idol, entranced by the woman's famous violet-blue eyes. Chloe smiled admiringly at her heroine. To Chloe's surprise, Valérie smiled back and winked. But as quickly as the moment happened, it was over, and an official-looking man wearing a headset ushered Valérie out of Chloe's sight line and into the auditorium.

Valérie had made one of her headline-grabbing, fashionably late appearances – the *ne plus ultra* of the frenzied red carpet experience. With only a smattering of B-list stars left to work the press line, the media and fans began to disperse and the excitement died down.

"You ready to go?" Dominique said, taking Chloe's hand.

"Yeah." She stuffed her camera in her purse. "Gigi said she and Montana'll meet us back at the hotel after the show."

Chloe followed Dominique in silence to his scooter.

"Did you get some good shots of that movie star?" he asked, climbing on.

She straddled the bike and hugged his mid-section, her now-familiar position. "I think my shots'll come out okay; I just wish I could've gotten closer."

Dominique took off and Chloe glanced back at the auditorium, studying a blown-up poster of Valérie's latest movie that was nominated for the top prize.

"I know I'll meet her someday," Chloe said, snuggling up to Dominique. "I just know it."

After the awards ceremony, Chloe and Dominique joined Gigi and Montana for an unofficial "after-party" on the beach. It was a beautiful night. A gentle breeze rippled the waves of the Mediterranean onto the sand and there were more stars out than Chloe had ever seen. Everyone sat around a bonfire, toasting marshmallows and watching the dancing flames.

"This is much more fun than those pretentious industry parties," Montana said, his arm slung around Gigi.

"Still, being there was a blast," Gigi said, leaning into him. "It's a night I'll never forget."

Gigi looked at Chloe, and they shared a conspiratorial chuckle about the revenge they had exacted on the jackass who'd dissed Gigi.

Montana took out his acoustic guitar and began strumming.

"I just wrote this song," he said to Gigi. "You're my inspiration."

Gigi rested her head on Montana's shoulder while he strummed and sang the lyrics to a song called "You're the Only One I Need." Chloe joined Gigi and Dominique in applauding when Montana wrapped the impromptu performance, taken with the clarity of his voice sans studio wizardry and the surprising nimbleness of his arpeggio guitar picking.

"That was beautiful, Montana," Gigi said, kissing him.

"Let's go back to my suite," he said. "It's getting chilly out here."

Montana rolled up the wicker mat they'd been sitting on and slung it on his back, along with his guitar.

"'Night, you guys," Gigi said, waving to Chloe and Dominique and vacating the beach with Montana.

Dominique put his arm around Chloe and they cuddled under an army blanket.

"You know, I have to admit, I misjudged Montana at first," Chloe said. "I thought he was an empty-headed pretty boy, but he's turned out to be a nice guy. That song he wrote for Gigi wasn't half-bad." She curled her toes in the sand. "I'd love it if someone wrote a song just for me."

"Well, I can't sing, but I can whistle." Dominique whistled a bonfire song and Chloe laughed and punched him good-naturedly in the shoulder.

They looked up at the stars.

"That's Perseus and there's Andromeda," Dominique said, pointing upward. "And Pegasus is over there."

Chloe nodded, impressed. "How do you know so much about astronomy?"

"I've had a telescope since third grade." He wrinkled his face. "Okay, I admit it, I'm a science geek."

She laughed. "I don't think you're a geek at all." She kissed him and they moved closer under the blanket.

Dominique pointed out more constellations and she gaped at them. She'd learned about the galaxy in science class but this was the first time she'd seen them up close, igniting the universe like the torches of the gods.

As they gazed up at the night sky, the only sound that could be heard was the crackling flames of the bonfire and waves splashing the shore. The full moon reflected off the waves, shining down on them.

"I think I love you," Dominique said, breaking the silence.

Chloe responded slowly. "I love, you too." She relaxed against him, glad he'd said it first.

He kissed her, then paused, his eyes boring into hers. He spread the blanket out on the sand.

"I'm yours," she whispered, lying next to him on the blanket and running her fingers through his hair. He caressed her face and looked into her eyes one more time. And then he made love to her underneath the stars.

28

Simone lit a Gauloise. The time had come to bid *adieu* to her pubescent paramour. Pascal Vilatte lugged boxes of his things out of her apartment. He had turned out to be no-good, just like all the other younger men she'd been with. He was leaving her for some twenty-year-old waitress he'd met at one of those outdoor cafés that young artistic types and college students frequented. They were moving in together.

Pascal lingered in the doorway of her bedroom, a blank canvas and paint-splattered palette tucked under his arm. "I wish things could have worked out differently."

Simone blew out a puff of smoke and flicked an ember in a bedside ashtray. "I'm not the one boinking some *connasse*." She closed the top of her robe tighter around her neck. No need to give Pascal a free sample of what he was giving up. "Tell me, what's she got that I haven't got?"

Pascal looked stricken. "Jesus, Simone, maybe we could've worked things out if you weren't so insecure. Every time I even looked at another woman, you thought I was having an affair."

Simone took another drag on her cigarette. "Sure, put all the blame on me."

"I'll miss you, Simone," Pascal said forlornly. "Take care of yourself."

Was that pity she detected in his expression? How dare he!

"Get out of my life."

Pascal took his cue and turned to leave. He stopped short and turned to her again. "Just for the record, I never tried to seduce your daughter. She's a talented artist. I saw the potential in her and tried to give her some pointers, that's all."

Simone narrowed her eyes, trying to decipher if he was sincere. Without another word, Pascal left, closing the door behind him.

She snuffed out her cigarette and went to the mirror above her dresser.

She examined herself, pulling back her skin to stretch out the fine lines that were beginning to form under her eyes and around her mouth.

"I look pretty damn good for my age. I'm not even forty yet," Simone said aloud, opening her robe and pushing up her breasts. "I keep myself in shape." She turned and studied her profile, then closed her robe, her shoulders sagging in despair. "All those goddamn sit-ups and early mornings at the spa I put in for Pascal, a waste."

Simone felt like having another nervous breakdown, her third of the morning. But why should she? This was going to be the last time. She was giving up younger men for good. They were too unstable, hopping from one thing to the next – or one bed to the next. Sure, they liked to have their fun with an older, sophisticated woman like her, but when they got bored, they tossed her out like a used canvas that had been painted over too many times. Simone had let herself be hurt and used by men, but no longer. It was time she took control of her life. After all, she had a lot to live for. She was still a vital, attractive, desirable woman. People still mistook her for Gigi's sister.

Gigi. Her little girl. The little girl she had neglected and whose trust she had breached. Her sweet Gigi, her baby.

Simone frowned at herself in the mirror, her expression reflecting her regret at accusing her daughter of trying to steal her man. Gigi was the innocent victim in the situation. She knew Gigi was no angel, but maybe Pascal was telling the truth when he said there had been nothing improper going on between the two.

Simone hadn't realized just how much she missed her daughter until now.

She sat on her bed and pulled the princess phone from her nightstand into her lap. She dialed the number to the Chateau de Chevalier, let it ring once, then slammed the receiver down. She couldn't. She just couldn't apologize. When she told Gigi about Pascal leaving, Gigi would rub it in.

Simone caught sight of herself in the mirror, sitting on her bed all alone, and dialed again.

"Hello."

The voice on the other end sounded familiar, but it wasn't Marie's.

"Maxine? Max, is that you? What are you doing home?" Simone had expected her to be away in Milan for at least a couple more weeks.

"I got a lot accomplished in a short amount of time," Maxine said, speaking over the sounds of Marie clattering pots in the kitchen in the background. "I was able to finish the Rossi project ahead of schedule. I'm back. I'll be in the office today."

"I'm glad someone has good news."

"What's the matter, Mo'?"

"It's Pascal," she said, her voice cracking. It was all she could do to keep herself from breaking down over the phone. "He left me."

"Oh, hon', I'm so sorry to hear that."

"I feel like a fool. I was wrong to accuse Gigi of trying to seduce him. He's a *troufignard*. I'm glad he's gone. I want my daughter back. Is she around?"

"What do you mean? I thought you and Gigi reconciled weeks ago. I thought she and Chloe were spending the rest of the summer with you."

"What? I haven't seen or talked to Gigi since I kicked her out. Chloe called me a couple of days ago and told me everything was okay and they were getting along well at your place."

"And I talked to her just yesterday. She called to check in like usual and told me she and Gigi were having fun staying at your flat in the city. Where in hell could they be?"

"I have no idea."

"Simone, call the office and tell them neither one of us will be in today."

Chloe showered and dressed with a smile. She had finally lost her virginity, and with a boy she truly loved. Her first time had been perfect. It was all she had hoped it would be.

She sat on her bed, opened her journal and studied a photo she pasted in that she and Dominique took on the beach. They had plans to spend the day together and she couldn't wait to see him.

She was bursting to tell someone about her wonderful night with Dominique and how she was going to love him for the rest of her life. Gigi hadn't yet returned from Montana's suite, where she had spent the night as usual, so Chloe decided to call Marie. She would enjoy telling her about her new love. She wouldn't reveal too many details, of course, but she would tell her she had met a great guy while hanging out near Simone and Gigi's apartment in Paris. Marie would be so happy for her.

The voice that answered at the Chateau de Chevalier sounded like... *Oh no!*

"M-mother, what are you doing home so soon?" Chloe stuttered, almost tripping over the phone cord.

"Chloe Yvette Bareaux, I don't know where in creation you are, but you get your butt home right this minute!"

Chloe tried to come up with an explanation but the only sound that came out of her mouth was a tiny squeak. The phone almost slipped out of her instantly-sweaty palms.

Gigi entered the suite and ambled into the living room. "What's with you?"

Chloe put her other hand over the mouthpiece. "They know. We're screwed."

Gigi reached for the phone, looking unfazed. "Don't worry. Let me handle this."

Chloe held the phone out of reach. "I think you've done enough."

"Breaking it off with Montana was no big deal. He took it really well," Gigi related to Chloe as they packed their suitcases and prepared to vacate the lavish suite that had served as their summer home for the past two months.

Chloe stuffed a handful of clothes into her already-bulging suitcase. "You think you'll ever see him again?"

"He invited me to run off to L.A. with him and move into his condo. I was flattered, but I turned him down," Gigi said matter-of-factly, as if rejecting an international pop star were an everyday occurrence. "It would have been over soon, anyway."

Montana was good-looking and talented and all, Gigi continued, but she was beginning to tire of him. His fifteen minutes of fame would most likely be drawing to a close in a year or two. He would probably become a drug addict and/or convicted felon and be relegated to reality shows and infomercials. Gigi declared that she was ready for a new challenge. Now that she had conquered the once-impossible task of seducing her teen idol, she was ready to move on to something else – like a toddler tossing aside a toy that no longer held her attention.

As Gigi prattled on, Chloe half-listened, slowly placing the rest of her things in her suitcase and trying to savor the last few moments of their time in Monaco. It may have been easy for Gigi to slough off her summer fling with Montana, but Chloe wanted to cherish the special moments she'd shared with Dominique. She flipped through the pages of her journal, studying the passages she'd written about her first real boyfriend and the photo she'd pasted in, before carefully placing it in her suitcase.

Before leaving for the airport, she and Dominique shared one last walk on the beach. They promised to stay in touch and stay forever devoted to one another. But something in her heart told her she would never see him again. In less than a month, they would both be back at school – in different countries, nonetheless. His first day at college, he'd probably meet some sexy co-ed and forget all about the shy, inexperienced high school girl he'd spent the summer with in Monaco.

Gigi stood at the edge of the beach, motioning to Chloe, who was standing on the shoreline with Dominique, the waves rushing over their bare feet.

"We have to go *right now* or we're going to miss the plane!" Gigi shouted.

"I guess this is it," Chloe said to Dominique.

"Look, before you go, I have something to give you." He dug into his pocket and took out a small box. "I was going to give this to you today anyway..." He trailed off, looking boyish in that adorable way of his, then added, "Because I was going to officially ask you to be my girl."

She was speechless as Dominique opened the box, revealing a gold pin in the shape of Pegasus, the winged horse from Greek myth whose constellation he had pointed out to her last night on the beach.

"It's beautiful, Dominique," she said, her eyes misting.

"Want me to put it on for you?"

"Please."

He pinned her, kissed her one last time, and they lingered in an embrace.

The moment was interrupted by Gigi bellowing, "Come on, already!" She waved her arms frantically. "We're in enough trouble already," she added, gesturing like an air traffic controller guiding in a jumbo jet.

Chloe slowly pulled away from Dominique. "I have to go."

"I understand."

"I'll never forget you," she said softly, kissing him on the cheek.

She made her way up the beach to join Gigi, turning to him and waving. The vision of him standing next to the sea, waving goodbye, grew smaller and smaller and almost faded from sight, as if it were a mirage.

Chloe hung her head when Marie opened the front door of the Chateau de Chevalier. She had violated Marie's trust and undoubtedly lost her respect.

Marie said nothing as she directed Chloe and Gigi to the parlor, like a prison matron leading inmates to the gas chamber.

Chloe and Gigi found their mothers suited up for combat, emotional swords drawn like the suits of armor in the artillery room.

Simone stood next to the fireplace, puffing on a Gauloise. "You girls have a lot of explaining to do." Her emerald eyes smoldered like the end of her cigarette.

"That's the understatement of the year," said Maxine, sitting on the loveseat and clutching a coffee mug.

"I can explain everything," Gigi said, striding into the room with her usual defiance.

"Don't even try it," Maxine said, slamming her mug on the coffee table and standing. "Since you girls were grown enough to lie to us and poor Marie, you're grown enough to face the consequences."

Maxine and Simone took turns launching verbal assaults, tag-teaming and battering their daughters with rebukes for lying, deceiving Marie, making them worry and stressing them out.

Chloe and Gigi had no choice but to turn in full confessions and beg for leniency. Maxine and Simone were apparently in no mood to plea-bargain, grounding the girls for the rest of the summer. They weren't allowed to use the phone and were even barred from watching TV. It was like a life sentence with no chance of parole.

Chloe bided her time by holing up in her room, curling up with her cat and writing letters to Dominique. Every morning, she would get up and rush to the mailbox, only to be disappointed. She never got a single reply. Her fears that Dominique would forget about her had unfortunately come true. She gave up writing letters to him after a couple of weeks, realizing that she simply had to accept the fact that her tender relationship with her first real boyfriend had ended.

Maxine relented on the strict punishment after a couple of weeks, telling Chloe she should stop dragging around the house and get some fresh air. But all Chloe felt like doing was sulking in her room, writing melancholy poetry. She dedicated a poem to Dominique in memory of their prematurely ended affair, "Summer Lover." Each stanza of the poem was punctuated by a somber refrain:

You broke my foolish heart
But I'd rather die than love another
So long, farewell, goodbye…
My summer lover

29

"But there's only a few weeks left in the summer, Marie. Can't you put off your vacation until Chloe goes back to school?"

Chloe stood in the dining room, straining to hear Mother and Marie's conversation through the swinging door that led to the kitchen. Chloe had been on her way to grab a snack when she stumbled onto the conversation.

"I'm sorry, Madame Chevalier, but my mother took a nasty fall and I really need to go check on her," Marie said, chopping carrots and celery on the island. "I'm the only one my mother has to rely on."

Chloe peeked through the circular window of the kitchen door and saw

Maxine nodding her head in understanding with Marie's last statement.

"I know how you feel. My mother fell very ill before she passed away when Chloe was younger. I know what it's like to have an ailing parent." Maxine paused, refilling her coffee cup. "It's just that we all need you. I guess I've come to depend on you a lot since…"

Maxine didn't finish the sentence, but Chloe knew she was referring to Jacques' death.

Marie nodded, indicating that she understood, just as Maxine had done earlier. "I appreciate that, and I wouldn't ask for the time off unless it was absolutely necessary. To be honest, I really need a break. I've been up to my ears in *merde* this year."

Chloe flinched at Marie's uncharacteristic swearing. She had only heard her use profanity on the rare occasions when she burned something in the kitchen.

"First, M'sieu Chevalier passed away so suddenly, then my mother took ill," Marie continued. "Just when I thought my mother's health was improving, she falls and is rushed back to the hospital."

"We've all been through a lot this year," Maxine said, gazing introspectively at her coffee cup. "I understand that you need some time off. How long do you think you'll be gone?"

Marie said she'd probably be out the rest of the summer. She was planning to take her *maman* on a spiritual sojourn to Lourdes, where, as legend had it, the Blessed Virgin had appeared and where miracles of healing were known to take place. Besides, Marie added, getting away from Paris would be a nice sabbatical. After nursing her mother back to health, she could drop in on her son, Jean-Luc, in Lyon and her daughter, Irène, in Avignon.

"My daughter and son-in-law called me last night to tell me my grandbaby just said her first words. I've been meaning to get out to visit them, but I haven't been able, with all my responsibilities here."

Maxine touched Marie's hand. "I appreciate all you do for us. You're invaluable. I don't know how we'll get along with you."

Marie finished chopping vegetables and placed them on a plate along with a sandwich, then stashed the plate in the refrigerator. "I'm sorry for taking off on such short notice," she said, wiping her hands on her apron, "but I need to get away. Especially after the stunt those girls pulled, sneaking away to Monaco and lying to everyone." She tugged at the gray wisps at her temples. "It's a wonder my hair isn't completely white!"

Chloe's head fell to her chest in shame. Mother's strict grounding after the Riviera incident had not been nearly as severe a punishment as the guilt Chloe felt every time she came in contact with Marie. Up until the Monaco adventure – or *mis*adventure, as it were – she had been able to tell Marie anything and everything. But now every time Chloe ventured into the kitchen, Marie averted her eyes and responded with monosyllabic grunts whenever Chloe attempted to make conversation. Chloe felt horrible for exacerbating Marie's stress level, and was determined to somehow win back her trust and friendship.

"Take as long as you need, and you know your job will be here waiting for you whenever you return," Maxine told Marie. "I just don't know how I'm going to find someone to fill in."

"Thanks for understanding, Madame Chevalier. If you don't need anything else right now, I'm going to start packing."

Chloe watched Marie exit through the backdoor that led to the carriage house. Mother picked up the kitchen extension and began what sounded like a long and involved business call, and Chloe figured it was safe to enter. She pushed through the swinging door and immediately headed for the refrigerator. While Mother gabbed on the phone, Chloe flung open the refrigerator door and scanned the contents, trying to find a snack to tide her over until dinner. She spotted something wrapped in cellophane and picked up the plate, which contained a sandwich, carrots, celery sticks and a note in Marie's neat handwriting that read "For Chloe."

She closed the refrigerator and stood there for a moment, holding the plate. She ran her fingers over the note, reflecting on how nice it was for Marie to continue to leave treats for her even when she was obviously still angry. Chloe knew she would miss these little kindnesses while Marie was away.

Later that evening, after dinner, Chloe ventured to Marie's room. She knocked lightly on the half-open door and entered tentatively when Marie said nothing and simply continued neatly folding clothes into a suitcase on her bed.

"I just thought I'd come up and say goodnight and wish you a safe trip," Chloe said, taking a hesitant step into the room.

Marie went to her closet and retrieved an armful of blouses without looking up or acknowledging Chloe's presence.

"And, for what it's worth," Chloe added, "I'm sorry, again, for the whole Monaco episode. I never intended to lie to you or get you in trouble with Mother, since you were responsible for looking out for me and Gigi."

Chloe paused while Marie began taking the blouses off their hangers. She appeared to be absorbed in the task, as if Chloe weren't in the room.

"It was Gigi's idea," Chloe continued. "I don't know why I let her talk me into it. Running away like that was really stupid." She took a breath, then proceeded. "Actually, that's not true. I can't put all the blame on Gigi. I guess the truth is, part of the reason I ran away with Gigi is because I wanted to get back at Mother for being gone and for working so much. It seems like ever since…"

Chloe trailed off, trying to marshal the courage to verbalize the feelings she'd kept buried for so long. She eyed the blouses in the suitcase, noting that Marie's practical, unpretentious wardrobe reflected her reliable, sturdy character.

"Ever since Jacques died," Chloe continued, leaning on Marie's bureau for support, "Mother has gone back to being a workaholic. I really resented her for taking that business trip to Milan and for leaving me here in Paris. I guess running off to Monaco was my of showing her I was mad at her for leaving me behind and that I could do the same thing." She shrugged. "It was childish, I know, and I'll never do anything like that again. I promise."

Marie, still keeping her eyes averted, approached Chloe. For a moment, Chloe thought Marie was going to confront her, but she reached past Chloe and retrieved a hairbrush from the bureau.

"Well, I just thought I should tell you how sorry I am, again, for everything, since I don't know if I'll see you before I go back to school in September."

Marie remained silent, placing toiletry items in her carryall, and Chloe turned to go.

"Oh, and Marie," she added, stopping and facing her again, "I know I don't say it often enough, but I want you to know I don't take you for granted. I appreciate everything you do for me and Mother."

Chloe's last statement, just like her earlier statements, seemed to have no effect. Marie's expression remained blank as she began zipping her suitcase. Chloe hovered in the doorway momentarily, then turned again to leave.

"Sit on it."

Chloe turned back, not sure if she had heard correctly when Marie finally spoke.

"I'm sorry?" Chloe gingerly entered the room again.

Marie finally looked up and made eye contact. "I said, 'Sit on it.'"

Chloe gave Marie a confused look.

"Sit on it," Marie repeated, gesturing toward her overstuffed suitcase.

Realizing that Marie was not insulting her with an American put-down, but actually wanted Chloe to sit on the suitcase so that it would close, she sprang forward and followed the command. Marie grunted and struggled to zip the suitcase while Chloe sat on top.

Finishing the task, Marie stepped back and dusted her palms. "*Ça alors!* Gee, am I glad you were here to help me with that. *Merci.*"

Chloe nodded and scooted off the suitcase, onto the bed. "You're welcome. It's the least I could do, after all the trouble I caused you this summer."

Marie continued taking items off her bureau and loading them into her carryall. "You know, when I was your age, my parents sent me away to convent school here in Paris. For my father, sending his oldest daughter to boarding school in the big city was a big accomplishment for him. But I didn't want to go. St. Agnès sounded like a prison sentence to me – just like Our Lady of Chastity probably seemed to you and Gigi at first."

Chloe nodded, impressed as always with Marie's insight into the teenage psyche.

"The main reason I didn't want to go off to convent school was because I had a boyfriend back in the village where I grew up," Marie said, reclining on the bureau like a stool. "Well, when it came time for me to leave for school, I packed up my things and acted like I was headed off to school. But I had Olivier meet me at the train station and we took off on his motorcycle." Marie grinned, her eyes twinkling with mischief.

"Wow," Chloe said, marveling at Marie's revelation. "You actually did that?"

"Oh, yeah. I had a life before I was a wife and mother and a housekeeper."

Chloe pulled her legs underneath her, settling in to hear more about Marie's former incarnation as an adventurous young woman. "What happened when you ran away with your boyfriend?"

"We spent a couple days riding around the countryside on his motorcycle and camping out under the stars."

Chloe looked down at the floor, reflecting on the times she'd had with Dominique in Monaco.

"Anyway," Marie said, "the school called my parents when I didn't show up and Papa set out in his pickup truck and tracked me and Olivier down." Marie shook her head, as if recalling the frightening confrontation. "I thought Papa was going to kill Olivier, but he just lectured us and deposited me at school."

"Gosh, Marie, that was pretty bold of you."

Marie looked pensive, as if thinking back on her youth. "*Oui*, I suppose so. I knew I would get in big trouble, but I was so in love with Olivier at the time, I was willing to do anything to be with him." She directed her gaze at Chloe. "I know Gigi talked you into running away with her because she was chasing some boy, and judging from the way you've been moping around with that lovesick expression, I have a sneaking suspicion you met someone in the Riviera, as well."

Chloe looked away, ashamed to admit that Marie was right. "His name's Dominique. I was going to tell you about him that last day I called from Monaco, when Mother picked up and made us come home."

"Have you stayed in touch with him?"

Chloe shifted positions, hugging her legs and propping her chin on her knee. "That's kind of hard, since Mother banned me from using the phone." She grew quiet for a second, then added, "I've written to him, but he never wrote back."

Marie touched her finger to her chin, looking wise and thoughtful. "Ah, your first love broke your heart – just like me and Olivier. After I was sent off to convent school, we lost touch." She stepped closer, cradling Chloe's chin in her palm. "I know it hurts right now, but you'll get over it eventually and love again. You're so young." She added with a playful smack against Chloe's head, "But I'll make sure you don't live to see eighteen if you ever pull another stunt like the one you and that little instigator Gigi did, running off like that and worrying me and your mothers sick."

Chloe laughed and pulled Marie into an embrace, placing her head on Marie's shoulder. "I'm going to miss our talks while you're gone." She squeezed her arms tighter around Marie. "I'm going to miss you so much. Sometimes I feel like you're the only one who understands me."

Marie kissed the top of Chloe's head. "I'll be back before you know it, *chouchou*. And your mother's a very resourceful woman. I'm sure she'll find someone suitable to fill in while I'm gone."

"Could you hand me the file for the Navarre account?" Simone said to Maxine as they sat in Maxine's office at work, going over the books. Stacks of papers and file folders littered Maxine's desk, along with Chinese takeout cartons and diet soda cans.

Maxine didn't respond, but continued to gaze out at the streetlights lining avenue Montaigne.

Simone peered at Maxine over the rims of her reading glasses. "I said, could you hand me the Navarre file?" she repeated, waving her hand before Maxine's face.

Maxine looked blankly at Simone. "Huh? Oh, here you go." She reached beneath a stack of papers and finally gave Simone the file she'd requested.

Simone opened the file and began tapping the tip of her pencil on the buttons of an adding machine. "What's with you tonight? We have a whole stack of invoices to go through, and we're barely making a dent. I haven't seen you this distracted since Jacques…" Simone stopped short, then touched Maxine's hand. "I'm sorry, *cher*. I didn't mean to bring up –"

"No, it's okay. You're right. I have a lot on my mind." Maxine picked at her lo mein noodles, then nudged it aside. "Marie's taking some time off, and it's reminded me how much I've come to depend on her since Jacques passed away." She turned to stare out the window again. "I still dream about him, and I always wake up crying when I realize he's not next to me."

Simone rubbed Maxine's back. "Sweetie, I know you're still grieving, but you've got to accept the fact that Jacques isn't coming back. You've got Chloe to think about, and you need to carry on for her sake."

Maxine began sorting the papers on her desk. "You're right. I need to stay focused. And the first order of business is finding a temp to fill in for Marie." She massaged her forehead. "God, I have no idea where to start. Marie runs the house so efficiently, there's no way I can find a replacement."

"The girls will be leaving for school in a few weeks. Can't you and Chloe just wing it until then?"

"If it were just me, that'd be easy. But since we've been working so many hours lately, I'm afraid to leave Chloe unsupervised ever since the scheme she and *that one* of yours pulled over on us."

Simone shook her head. "I still can't believe the nerve of those two," she said, running her index finger down a row of figures on a spreadsheet. "Gigi topped herself with that one."

The late-night work session quickly devolved into a gripe fest as Maxine vented about how it was next to impossible to find someone who was willing to run the kitchen, prepare meals and supervise her teenage daughter.

"You know what your problem is? Your standards are too high," Simone said, picking up her chopsticks and nibbling on fried rice.

"I can't entrust the myriad responsibilities of an enormous estate like the Chateau de Chevalier to just any Tom, Dick, Harry or Jane that answers my ad," Maxine said.

"I just think your expectations are a little unrealistic." Simone washed down a bite of egg fu yung with a swig of Diet Pepsi. "Marie leaves this weekend, right? So you have a couple of days, tops, to interview replacements. In that short amount of time you expect to find someone who can move in for the remainder of the summer who's not only a gourmet chef but also a teen guidance counselor like Marie? That's not going to be easy."

Maxine propped her elbows on the desk. "You can say that again."

"Say, have you considered posting notices at a couple of colleges? I'm sure there's some student who could use room and board and a little extra spending money. Why don't you find yourself an au pair girl?"

"I'm supposed to turn over the keys to an eighteenth century estate to some kid straight out of high school?" Maxine gave Simone a skeptical look.

"A lot of college students are very mature. You'd be surprised, Max."

"Yes, and you ought to know, Mo', seeing as how you've dated so many of them."

Simone clucked her tongue disdainfully in response. "You can put me down if you want, but think about my suggestion. You don't have much time."

"Thanks for reminding me." Maxine glared at Simone.

"Don't look at me," Simone said, returning to the task of crunching numbers on the adding machine. "I'm not going to do your books and your windows.

30

"I don't understand why I need to sit through these interviews," Chloe said, pacing before Maxine in the parlor. "This whole thing is ridiculous. I just turned seventeen and I'm going to be a senior in high school in a few weeks. I don't need a babysitter."

Maxine calmly sipped her tea. "*Au contraire*. The fact that you and Gigi ran off for several weeks and lied not only to me, but Simone and Marie, shows me that you *do* need adult supervision."

Chloe huffed and plopped on the loveseat next to her mother. "Are you ever going to let me live that down? How many times do I have to say, 'I'm sorry'? Haven't I been punished enough? Making me sit through these babysitter interviews is a complete waste of time."

It was a gorgeous mid-August day, and Chloe could be out riding her horse or taking a dip in the pool. But Mother had forced her to put on a formal dress that Chloe normally wore to church and join Maxine for a round of interviews with the candidates who had applied to sub for Marie.

"You brought this on yourself. You and Gigi and that little scheme you pulled are part of the reason why Marie needed to take a sabbatical." Maxine returned her teacup to the silver tray on the coffee table and looked at her watch. "The first interview should be arriving any minute."

The doorbell rang, as if underscoring Mother's annoying tendency of always being right.

"Ah, that should be Madame Le Prieur," Maxine said, reading from a list of names on a legal pad. "Why don't you go let her in?"

Chloe got up and trudged to the front door, opening it to find a stern-looking woman with gray hair pulled back so tightly in a bun that it made her eyes bug out.

"I'm here for the interview with Madame Chevalier," the woman said in a prim, upper-crust accent, looking Chloe over like a board of health inspector examining an offending sample of tainted meat.

"Yes, I'm her daughter, Chloe." She adjusted the straps of her Sunday dress in a self-conscious gesture, as though *she* were the one interviewing. "Right this way."

Chloe led the woman to the parlor, where Maxine introduced herself and invited the interviewee to have a seat. There was something schoolmarmish about this woman, and Chloe felt the need to sit up straight and cross her legs at the knee – the way she did in class at Our Lady of Chastity to appease the nuns.

"I see here you have previous experience as a nanny," Maxine said, skimming the woman's résumé. "Tell me, what are your philosophies on child rearing?"

"I believe children should be free to express themselves," the woman replied.

Chloe relaxed her posture a bit, relieved that maybe her first impression of the woman as harsh and dictatorial was unfair.

Chloe immediately stiffened again, however, when the woman puckered her face into a sour expression and added, "But I also believe children flourish under structure and rules." She looked at Chloe with those bugged-out eyes, as if seeing through to her very core. "*Firm* rules."

Maxine jotted notes on a clipboard. "I couldn't agree more."

Chloe glared at her mother. As far as Chloe was concerned, Maxine should send this Mary Poppins reject packing.

The graying dominatrix was followed by a succession of similarly nightmarish interviews. There was even a freaky punk rocker with a purple Mohawk who admitted, under Maxine's relentless drilling, that she had no babysitting or housekeeping experience and was only interested in the job as a quick way to score some cash. Not surprisingly, Maxine cut the interview short with a curt "Thank you, that will be all," and promptly showed the punk rocker the door.

"Well, I may as well call Madame Le Prieur and tell her she's got the job," Maxine said upon closing the front door on the last interviewee. "She's the only one I saw today who's got the qualifications to fill in for Marie."

"You can't be serious," Chloe said, filling with dread at the thought of being at the mercy of the stern taskmistress for the last few weeks of summer. "There's no way you can hire her."

"Her résumé came with excellent references. Why shouldn't I hire her?"

"I didn't like the way she looked at me, like I'm some problem child she plans to whip into shape."

"After the worry you and Gigi caused," Maxine said, affectionately tweaking Chloe's nose, "that wouldn't be such a bad thing, now would it?"

"Why'd you make me sit through these stupid interviews if you weren't going to listen to my input?"

Maxine left the question unanswered, and Chloe resignedly turned to follow her mother back to the parlor. They stopped short when the doorbell rang.

Maxine flipped the pages on her clipboard. "That's probably the last interview, but she's late. She was supposed to be here a half-hour ago, before the last one I talked to."

Chloe followed her mother back to the front door, prepared to witness one of Maxine's infamous tongue lashings. Tardiness was something she never tolerated.

Maxine opened the front door to an attractive blonde in her early twenties. The late-summer sun had given way to overcast, drizzly skies, and the blonde stood on the front stoop in a short gray trench coat that was dripping-wet.

"Hi," the blonde said in an American accent with cheerleader perkiness, flashing gleaming white teeth worthy of a toothpaste model. "I'm Daniella Webster. I'm here to interview for the au pair position." She reached into her pocket and produced a crumpled flier that Maxine had her assistant, Henri, post on bulletin boards and lampposts around the University of Paris campus.

"Ah, yes." Maxine made a grand gesture of looking at her watch. "I had you scheduled for four-thirty, but it's after five now. I'm sorry, but the position has already been filled."

The blonde's smile faded and she looked as though she were going to dissolve into tears, as though her rain-streaked mascara portended an emotional collapse. "I'm sorry I'm late, but I accidentally took the wrong train. And then it took me forever to find a cab to bring me the rest of the way."

Chloe looked at Mother, trying to read her reaction to the young woman's litany of excuses. Maxine looked unimpressed, and Chloe assumed her mother had chalked up the young woman's lateness to American arrogance. When she serviced the occasional client from New York or another big U.S. city, Mother complained that white Americans treated her like she was their maid instead of a professional. Chloe surmised that Maxine saw this young woman showing up half-an-hour late and expecting the same treatment as the other, prompt candidates as further confirmation of the privileges white Americans took for granted.

"I'm sorry for all your trouble in coming out all this way," Maxine said in a diplomatic tone, "but quite frankly, if you can't be on time for the interview, how can I trust you can handle the job?"

The blonde looked crestfallen. "You're right. I'm sorry for wasting your time, Madame. It's just that I'm a student and I had a big test today and I had just enough time after class to rush to the train station and –" She stopped mid-sentence, as if realizing her excuses weren't making a good impression on the prospective employer. "I understand. Sorry again for wasting your time."

Chloe stared at the young woman, trying to gauge her sincerity. It was possible that she was just making up lame excuses, but something about her seemed genuine. Chloe watched with pity as the young woman plodded down the front stoop, lugging her oversize designer purse and looking like a chic baglady.

Just as the young woman left the shelter of the front awning, the downpour intensified and she was pelted by rain.

"Oh, come on, Mother." Chloe looked pleadingly at Maxine. "Why don't you cut her a break?"

Watching the young woman slog down the graveled drive in the pouring rain, Maxine's expression softened. "Uh, miss, why don't you come back?" she called. "We'll do the interview really quick, then I can have my driver take you to the train station."

The blonde promptly jogged back to the front door. "Thank you so much, Madame," she said as Maxine stepped aside to let her in.

"Call me Maxine." Mother extended her hand. "And this is my daughter, Chloe."

"Nice meeting you both." The young woman smiled broadly, pumping their hands.

"Let's get you out of that wet coat before you catch cold." Maxine took the interviewee's trench coat and held out the damp garment as if it were a mangy pelt from a dead animal.

Chloe took the coat and hung it up on the rack beside the door while the young woman smoothed her pink and gray, checkered suit.

"Nice suit," Maxine said.

"Thank you," the young woman said, adjusting the gold chain-link belt around her waist. "Vintage Chanel."

Maxine nodded, looking impressed. "Chloe, why don't you get – Danielle, was it?"

"Daniella."

"Chloe, please get Daniella some hot tea and then join us in the parlor." Maxine hooked her arm in Daniella's and began leading her down the hall. "So, tell me all about yourself."

Maxine had already begun her interrogation of the young woman by the time Chloe brought out a fresh pitcher of hot water from the kitchen.

"*Merci*," Daniella said when Chloe handed her a steaming cup.

"You're American, I take it?" Maxine said to the young woman as Chloe took a seat on the couch.

"*Oui*. I'm from L.A."

Chloe looked at the young woman with renewed interest, perking up at the mention of the moviemaking capital of the world.

"What brings you to Paris?" Maxine asked.

202

Chloe glanced at her mother, trying to read her body language and discern what she thought of this latest interviewee. Daniella delicately sipped her tea, legs crossed at the knee in ladylike fashion – manners that were sure to score points with Maxine.

"I'm an exchange student at the University of Paris," Daniella said. "I'll be a senior at Columbia, in New York, in the fall. Spending the summer semester here in Paris is something I've always wanted to do."

"What are you majoring in?"

Maxine's tone was friendly, but Chloe had seen enough from the previous interviews to know this was Mother's stealthy way of exacting information about the interviewee's character.

Daniella set her teacup on its saucer, cradling it in her lap. "I was thinking about majoring in psychology, but I've decided to go pre-law. I know it may sound a little corny, but I want to help the disadvantaged."

"I think that sounds noble." Maxine quickly turned matters back to business. "Now, about this position, there's no cleaning involved. Sophie and Lisette take care of that. What I need is someone to cook and run the kitchen. Do you have any experience in that?"

Daniella looked cautious. "Does taking home ec in high school count?"

Maxine laughed, which eased the tension in the room. Chloe laughed as well, appreciating Daniella's sense of humor. There was something about this girl that made Chloe want to root for her – not the least of which was the fact that she grew up near Hollywood, which Chloe couldn't wait to ask her about.

"Actually, I'm a pretty good cook," Daniella continued. "I spent a lot of time hanging around our housekeeper, Consuelo, when I was growing up." She grinned, adding, "In fact, my Spanish is better than my French."

Chloe laughed again, prompting Maxine to reach over and pat her hand, as if quieting an unruly child who was interrupting a grownup conversation.

"I need someone to watch over Chloe until she leaves for school in London in a few weeks. Do you have any childcare experience?"

When Maxine wasn't looking, Chloe crossed her eyes – a jab at her mother referring to her as a "child."

"I've been baby-sitting since eighth grade." Daniella directed a small, conspiratorial smile in Chloe's direction while Maxine scribbled notes on her clipboard.

"Do you have any references?"

Daniella looked slightly panicked at the question. "None here in Paris, but I could give you the number of a couple back in L.A. that I baby-sit for whenever I'm home from school on break."

Maxine studied the young woman. "Tell you what, why don't I give you a call in a day or two after I've had a chance to review the other applicants?"

Daniella sat up and set her teacup on the coffee table. "Is there any chance you could let me know about the job any sooner? To be honest, I'm kind of in a bind. I was mugged the other day."

"Oh, no," Maxine said, looking sympathetic. "What happened?"

"It all happened so fast, I don't really know myself. I was out sightseeing on the Champs-Elysées and this guy came up behind me and snatched my purse."

As Daniella went into detail about the incident, Chloe had to restrain herself from yelling at her to shut up. She had already given Mother enough reason to think she was flaky and not cut out for the job, and this confession would probably only reinforce the impression.

"Everything was in my purse: my money, my credit cards, my traveler's checks, you name it," Daniella continued. "My parents are financing my trip, and I still haven't told them. They weren't thrilled about me spending the summer in a foreign country. If they find out I was mugged, they'll make me come home." Looking pointedly at Chloe, she added, "They're very overprotective."

"Parents do tend to worry," Maxine said, sounding as though she could relate.

Daniella leaned forward and folded her hands in her lap. "Ma'am, I really need this job. All the student positions at school are filled. I promise you, if you give me a chance, I'll work my butt off – excuse my French. I won't let you down."

"Why don't you just try her out, Mother?" Chloe spoke up.

Maxine didn't respond, but looked down at her clipboard as if in deep thought. "You know, I was your age when I first came to Paris." She looked up at Daniella. "I was mugged, too. I was so shaken up, I considered going back home to my mother, but I was determined to make it on my own."

"So am I. I want my parents to know I'm responsible enough to be on my own."

"This is a live-in position. I need someone who can move in immediately," Maxine said, as if issuing one last test.

"Just say the word and I can go get my stuff from the dorm. I'm sharing a room with three other girls." Looking around the well-furnished room Maxine had decorated, Daniella added, "Staying here would definitely be a step up."

"Go back to your dorm and start packing." Maxine stood and offered her hand. "You're hired."

"Thank you so much, ma'am. I promise I won't let you down." She shook Maxine's hand and flashed Chloe her California smile.

*****

Chloe knocked on the half-open door of the guestroom down the hall where Daniella was unpacking. "Need any help?"

"I think I'm pretty much settled in," Daniella said, closing a dresser drawer.

Chloe leaned on the doorframe. "I just wanted to apologize if Mother came across as a little harsh at first. She has high standards, and she can be pretty intense sometimes."

"No sweat," Daniella slid her suitcase under the bed. "Actually, I admire your mom. I'm sure it's not easy running a business and being a single parent. My mother could learn a thing or two from Maxine. All my mom does all day is get pedicures and figure out new ways to spend my dad's money."

"What's your dad do?"

"He's a 'plastic surgeon to the stars,' as he's fond of telling people."

"Really?" Chloe said, inching into the room, her curiosity heightening.

"Yeah. You know those actresses who used to be so beautiful but now they all look like they have duck lips?" Daniella demonstrated by affecting an exaggerated pout.

Chloe giggled. "Yes. I've seen them in magazines."

"Dad's handiwork."

"Get out of here!"

"I kid you not. Growing up in L.A., I went to school with the sons and daughters of a lot of movie stars, so I've seen them up close. The men have plugs and the women have all had 'nips and tucks.' L.A. is *so* superficial!"

"What was it like? Growing up around the entertainment industry, I mean. I've always loved the movies."

Daniella swept a pile of clothes off the bed, clearing a space. "Why don't you cop a squat and I'll tell you?"

Born and raised in the upscale Toluca Lake section of the San Fernando Valley, Daniella was an all-American girl.

"I went to Bradley, which is this prep school for rich kids that's like something right out of *Beverly Hills 90210*," Daniella said, sitting across the bed from Chloe.

"Sounds pretty exciting," Chloe said, lying on her belly and wagging her feet.

"Ah, not really. Growing up in that environment, you sort of take everything for granted." Daniella took out a manicure kit and began filing her nails. "Don't get me wrong, I had fun in high school. I was popular. I got straight A's and I was homecoming queen – the whole nine. I was a class officer and a cheerleader, and I actually dreamed of becoming a Laker Girl at one point."

"Really?" Chloe rested her head on her fist, visualizing Daniella cheering for the popular NBA team whose games were often attended by celebrities.

"Yeah, I guess I took my idol worship of Paula Abdul a bit far." Daniella laughed, as if making fun of herself.

Chloe liked the fact that although this girl grew up pampered, she didn't take herself too seriously.

"Anyway," Daniella said, applying a fresh coat of nail polish, "that dream quickly faded. I knew skipping college wasn't an option, not with all the money my parents paid to put me through Bradley. All my friends go to UCLA, but I applied to Columbia in New York so I could get as far away as possible from my parents. They're so overbearing."

Chloe nodded, empathizing. "Tell me about it. I love my mother, but she can be smothering sometimes."

Daniella took off her socks and started on her toenails. "I know what you mean. Anyway, when I heard about the exchange-student program, I thought it'd be a fun way to knock out my foreign language requirement and spend the summer abroad. I'm so glad your mom took a chance and hired me. I don't know what I'd do if I had to go home and tell my folks I got mugged and lost everything."

"I think it's pretty brave of you, coming to a foreign country all alone. I don't know if I could do it, although I've always wanted to visit the States. That's where Mother's from originally, and I was born there."

Daniella curled her toes and placed cotton balls between them. "So, what's stopping you? If you want to go to America, just hop on a plane."

Chloe leaned forward, hugging a pillow. "I wish it were that simple. I keep asking Mother to plan a trip to New Orleans, where she's from, and New York, where she lived when I was born, but she always finds some excuse."

"Parents can be so weird." Daniella took Chloe's hand and examined her cuticles. "You want me to do your nails?"

"Yeah, that'd be great." Chloe sat up eagerly. "And if you don't mind, could you tell more about growing up in Hollywood?"

31

"I'm so glad our moms are letting up off the punishment and letting us hang out again," Gigi said to Chloe as they tromped down the back stairs leading to the Chateau de Chevalier's kitchen.

"I guess they trust us again, since Mother hired this new temp to fill in for Marie. She's really cool. You have to meet her."

The girls entered the kitchen, where they found Daniella twirling like a ballerina at the sink and singing along at full volume to a song playing on her CD Walkman while she did the lunch dishes. She was able to arrange her schedule at the University of Paris to have all of her classes in the morning. She made breakfast before taking the train into the city each morning, and after school she made it back to the Chateau de Chevalier just in time to fix lunch. When Marie returned, she would surely be glad to see that her kitchen had been operating in the same efficient, spic-and-span order in which she left it.

While Daniella sang as she dried the dishes, Chloe and Gigi looked at each other and cracked up at the sight of the young woman's private concert.

"What are you listening to?" Chloe asked, approaching Daniella.

The volume on the Walkman was apparently up too loud, because Daniella continued singing to herself.

Chloe tapped her on the shoulder and repeated the question in a near-holler. "*What are you listening to?!*"

Daniella jumped and fumbled with a dish, which Chloe caught just before it crashed to the floor.

"Good save," Daniella said, taking off her headphones and placing the recovered dish in the rack to dry. "Sorry, I didn't hear you guys come in. I'm listening to a new CD by this Latin pop star, Sergio Reyes. He's a real hunk, and he can sing, too. My parents' housekeeper, Consuelo, always listens to him when she's cooking. His music is as spicy as her tamales." She offered the headphones to Chloe. "You wanna listen?"

"Are you kidding? I love Sergio Reyes!" Chloe exclaimed, excited to have something in common with the new au pair girl.

"I'm glad we have the same good taste in music," Daniella said, handing over her headphones.

Chloe pressed the headphones to her ears and closed her eyes, taking in Sergio's melodic voice. She pictured him standing before her, singing directly to her.

"I wanna listen, too!" Gigi clamored, tugging on Chloe's sleeve.

"I take it you're a friend of Chloe's?" Daniella said, smiling at Gigi.

"I'm sorry," Chloe said, taking off the headphones. "I got so caught up in the music, I forgot to introduce you guys."

After Chloe made the introductions, Daniella transferred the CD to the radio that sat on the kitchen counter.

"Come on, you guys, join me," Daniella said, turning up the volume and singing along to the salsa-flavored dance track.

Chloe and Gigi merrily joined in Daniella's sing-along, and the three girls danced around the kitchen like a conga line. Chloe was used to the sound of Marie's sublime humming while she worked in the kitchen, and no one could ever replace her, but this all-American girl was already turning out to be a lot of fun.

Over the next few weeks, Daniella proved to be not only a capable au pair girl, but a trusted friend and advisor. Whereas Marie spoke from life experience when Chloe came to her for advice, Daniella was old enough to have learned from a few mistakes but was still young enough to relate to Chloe's teen angst.

Maxine and Simone seemed pleased that Daniella turned out to be a good influence on Chloe and Gigi. Daniella let them hang out in her room, giggling and gossiping with the girls and tutoring them on American pop culture, and even taught them how to play pool on the billiards table in the den (a skill she confessed she'd picked up in campus bars).

As much fun as Daniella was, she took school seriously and emphasized the importance of hard work and education – and laughed when she said she realized she sounded like her parents when she spoke to the girls. She often stayed cooped up in her room for hours after she'd fixed dinner, cramming for tests and banging out research papers.

Chloe interrupted one of Daniella's marathon study sessions on the next-to-last evening before they would both leave Paris for school in their respective cities.

"Can I come in?" Chloe said, rapping on the door and pausing before entering Daniella's room.

"Sure. Come on in." Daniella, sprawled on the bed surrounded by textbooks and crumpled notes, sat up. "I was just studying for my French final. What's up?"

Chloe sat on the floor next to the bed and pulled her legs underneath her. "Nothing. I just wanted to talk, seeing as how we'll both be leaving in a couple of days."

Chloe had come to value these late-night girl talks with Daniella and would miss having someone close to her own age to talk to other than Gigi.

"These last few weeks have flown by," Daniella said. "I can't believe summer's almost over."

"I know," Chloe sighed. "I'm not really looking forward to going back to a daily routine, but at least I had a little adventure this summer."

Daniella giggled. "From what you and Gigi told me, that was *quite* an adventure you guys had in Monaco. I still can't believe Gigi hooked up with Montana Blake. He's a real hottie."

"Yeah, but Gigi'll find someone else as soon as we get back to school, knowing her." Chloe played with the fringe on the bedspread, reflecting on the events of the past few months. "I wish I was more like her – not caring about anything. I'm still pining for Dominique."

Daniella shifted positions on the bed, looking thoughtful, as if she could relate to the concept of lost love. "Guys are different than girls. We get more emotionally involved. I had a boyfriend at school before I came to Paris, and we promised to stay in touch over the summer, but he stopped e-mailing me back after a couple of weeks." She shrugged. "That's men for you."

Chloe and Daniella put their bitch-fest about the opposite sex on pause when Maxine entered, carrying a tray of tea and cookies.

"I thought you could use a study break," Maxine said to Daniella. Upon noticing Chloe, she added, "Oh. If I had known you had a visitor, I would have brought enough snacks for two."

"It's okay," Chloe said. "We were just talking."

"Don't keep Daniella up too late. You know she has finals in the morning," Maxine said to Chloe, setting the tray on the nightstand next to the bed. Mussing Chloe's hair on the way out, she added, "And you need to finish packing to go back to school."

Chloe groaned. "I *know*, Mother."

As Maxine exited, Chloe crossed her eyes at Daniella, who offered a sympathetic chuckle.

"I know Maxine can be a bit much at times," Daniella said when Maxine had left the room, "but she means well. I've actually come to see her as a role model."

"Really?" Chloe said, nibbling a vanilla wafer.

"Yeah. I had to do a paper on a local entrepreneur for my business class, and your mom let me shadow her at work the other day. It was really cool seeing how she's so on top of things, but she's also very understanding and feminine. That's how I plan to be one day when I'm a famous attorney." Daniella struck a self-important pose, holding her cookie aloft.

"But seriously," Daniella added, "it's nice to see an example of someone who's successful other than my parents. Your mom does so much for charity. When I was shadowing her, she was planning a charity ball for an orphanage."

"That's how she met my stepfather, Jacques – at a charity ball he hosted here in the ballroom," Chloe said, looking mournfully at the floor as she remembered him.

Daniella touched her hand. "I know you still miss him, but your mom seems like she's really got things under control. I like how she gives back, unlike my folks. All they seem to care about is trading their Mercedes in for the latest model and planning their next vacation to Club Med." She reclined on the bed and stared at the ceiling. "I swear, I'm never going to end up like them."

"Have they always been like that?" Chloe asked, beginning to see her own mother in a new light as Daniella described her parents' materialistic quest for the American dream.

"No. I don't know what happened. I've seen pictures of them before I was born. They were both big-time activists when they were in college. That's how they met – at a no-nukes rally. But, I dunno." Daniella took out her nail kit and began touching up her manicure. "I guess after they graduated and got married and settled down, they took on a mortgage and had me and my brother and all their big ideals went out the window. They became yuppies, just like the rest of their friends."

Chloe screwed up her face. "What's a yuppie?"

Daniella laughed. "That's right. I keep forgetting you weren't raised in America. Suffice it to say, a yuppie's something I never want to be. When I get to be a big-time lawyer, I'm going to take on cases that really mean something – fair housing and discrimination cases. I'm going to go to work for the Legal Aid Society or the Southern Poverty Law Center and do pro bono work. I'm going to help people."

Chloe pulled down the corners of her mouth, impressed. "I think that's admirable – something to aspire to."

"And what about you?" Daniella took Chloe's hand and began filing her nails. "Have you started thinking about college yet?"

"Not really," Chloe said as Daniella filed, "but Mother practically has my future all planned out. She wants me to go to the University of Paris, then med school. I'm going to be the next Marie Curie, if she has anything to do with it."

"What do *you* want?" Daniella filed harder, as if applying pressure would get Chloe to open up.

"Honestly?"

Daniella nodded, barely looking up from the task of Chloe's impromptu manicure.

"What I really want to do is go to New York and study acting. I've wanted to be an actress ever since I was little." She paused, not sure if she should have revealed her far-fetched dream to the level-headed, practical Daniella. Maybe wanting to be an actress sounded frivolous to someone who was about to enroll in law school and do important work. "That's really silly isn't it?"

"No, not at all." Daniella set the file down and fanned Chloe's fingers out, admiring her handiwork. "You know, I thought about getting into acting once."

Chloe's eyes widened, excited to find that someone she looked up to had shared her dream at one point. "For real?"

"Yup. Who grows up in L.A. and doesn't think about going into the entertainment business at one point or another? Of course, that was a passing phase – right before my Laker Girl phase."

Chloe joined Daniella in laughing at the whimsical notion.

"But seriously," Daniella added, "I really thought about going into acting when I was in high school – right around your age. I was at the mall and this guy came up to me and said he was a casting agent and that I have a really commercial look and asked me if I wanted to try out for this sitcom he was casting. He gave me his business card, but I thought he was a perv' and threw the card away."

Chloe sat up, intrigued by the story. "Oh my god. The same thing happened to me a couple years ago. Gigi and I were hanging out after school in Trocadéro, near the Eiffel Tower, and this guy came up and said he was a photographer and he wanted to take me to New York for a shoot. But of course Mother said I was too young."

"She was probably right. Who knows, that guy could have been Jack the Ripper or something – same with that man who approached me in the mall." Daniella glanced down at her nails. "But sometimes I can't help but think, 'What if?' What if I had my parents check the guy out? He might have been legit'. I could have been the next big teen star like Molly Ringwald."

Chloe screwed up her face again. "Who?"

Daniella chuckled. "Sorry. A little bit before your time." She yawned and stretched. "I guess I better get back to hitting the books. I have to get up early for my final."

Chloe got up and headed for the door. "Daniella?" she said, pausing in the doorway.

"Yeah?" Daniella looked up from her textbook.

"I just wanted to say thanks for everything. I really enjoyed hanging out with you this summer. You're like the big sister I always wanted."

Daniella closed her book. "Come here, kiddo." She pulled Chloe into a hug.

Chloe lingered a while longer in Daniella's room, talking about their plans for the future. She gave Chloe the number and address of her dorm at Columbia, and they both promised to write and call each other as often as time, money and their studies would allow. Daniella said she had fallen in love with the City of Light and planned to make it back whenever she could.

Just before midnight, Chloe finally said goodnight and went back to her own room. As she finished packing to return to school in London, she reflected that Daniella Webster had made a lasting, positive impression on her in a few short weeks. She was sure their paths would cross again one day.

32

Chloe lay on her dorm room bed, listening to music and thumbing through the syllabi for her senior-year courses. It was hard to believe that she and Gigi were entering their final year at Our Lady of Chastity and would graduate in nine short months. The prospect of leaving behind the cloister of the all-girls academy and entering adulthood was exhilarating, and yet it also filled Chloe with panic. As much as she hated to admit it, a part of her didn't want to grow up.

The sound of hammering disrupted Chloe's thoughts. She turned to see Gigi standing on her bed, tacking up a new poster to replace the newly discarded pinup of Montana Blake. Chloe turned up the volume on her CD player to drown out Gigi's commotion.

Chloe hummed along with Sergio Reyes' catchy new single, his CD jacket splayed out among the syllabi, while jotting down the books she needed to check out from the library for English lit' class. Right at the best part of the song, Gigi hammered louder and ruined the experience.

"Will you keep it down over there? I'm trying to get a head start on my class schedule," Chloe huffed, taking off her headphones.

Gigi set the hammer aside. "I'm done now." She planted a smooch on the lips of her new pinup boy. "Isn't he a cutie pie?"

Chloe cocked her head and examined the poster, which depicted a shirtless soccer player with bulging abs propelling a ball through a goal. Chloe recognized the exotically handsome young man as Justin Bradshaw, a rising young star with the Kensington United. The son of a British Parliamentarian and a Nigerian mother, Justin had young girls swooning all over the U.K., where "footballers" were worshipped like rock stars. With his pretty-boy looks and mop of shoulder-length, blondish-brownish dreadlocks, Justin looked more like the lead singer of a reggae or ska band than a serious athlete.

"So, he's your new man, huh?" Chloe said, still eyeing the poster. "You've kicked Montana Blake to the curb?"

"Montana *who*?" Gigi balled up Montana's poster and tossed it in the wastebasket.

Chloe laughed. "You'll never change, Gi'. We haven't even been back at school a whole week and you've already found a new toy boy to drool over."

"And what about you?" Gigi leapt from her bed and snatched the CD jacket from Chloe. "*Oh, Sergio, I love you. I'll run away with you to Madrid*," Gigi moaned in an exaggerated Spanish accent, holding the CD jacket to her chest.

"Give me that!" Chloe grabbed at the CD jacket, but Gigi held it out of reach.

"Your Latin heartthrob has quite the body," Gigi said, unraveling the inside of the CD jacket to reveal Sergio in a shirtless pose similar to the footballer's poster hanging above Gigi's bed. "You made fun of me for drooling over a pinup boy, when you're doing the exact same thing."

"I was not drooling over him." Chloe finally managed to snatch the CD jacket from Gigi. "I respect him as an artist, that's all."

"Yeah, right." Gigi pursed her lips in a cynical expression.

"For your information," Chloe said, discreetly folding the CD jacket and tucking it back in its case, "his music helps me concentrate when I'm studying. I recommend you do the same – studying, that is. You do want to graduate on time and get out of here, don't you?"

"Of course," Gigi said, standing on her bed again. Smoothing the edges of the footballer's poster, she added slyly, "But you know me. I plan to have some fun in the process."

On the first day of classes, Chloe walked into drama class and was pleasantly surprised to be greeted by Sister Maureen's smiling face.

"Welcome back. How was your summer?" Sister Maureen said as Chloe entered.

"Great." Chloe approached the chalkboard, where the young nun was writing the day's exercise. "Are you subbing today?"

"I'm a full member of the sisterhood now and I just got my first permanent teaching assignment. I'm going to be teaching drama and English lit' from now on."

Chloe clapped her hands excitedly. "Congrats! What happened to Sister Georgina?" she said, referring to the stern, older nun who normally taught drama and directed the school's productions.

"The parish offered her early retirement," Sister Maureen said, setting down the chalk and dusting her palms. Lowering her voice, she added conspiratorially, "And not a day too soon, I might add."

Sister Maureen laughed, prompting Chloe to do the same.

"Would you do me a favor?" Sister Maureen said, retrieving a pile of papers from her desk.

"Sure," Chloe said, approaching the desk, eager to assist.

"Could you pass out the syllabus for me while I finish writing out today's assignment on the board?"

"No problem."

Chloe set about the task of placing a syllabus on each desk, glad when she noticed that instead of having Chloe and the other girls read age-old British plays like Sister Georgina always did, Sister Maureen's assignments included a lot of in-class dramatization exercises to give the students an appreciation for live theater.

"What's that song, dear?" Sister Maureen said when Chloe had placed the syllabus on the last desk.

"Huh?" Chloe said, turning around to look at the young teacher. She didn't even realize she'd been singing aloud to the tune in her head.

"That song?"

"Oh, it's the new single by this singer I like named Sergio Reyes," Chloe said shyly, her cheeks growing warm, embarrassed that Sister Maureen had overheard her.

"It's very catchy, whatever it is," Sister Maureen said, smiling. "I remember when you worked in the library, you'd hum to yourself when you filed books. You have a nice voice, very pleasant."

"Thanks," Chloe said, looking down at her feet.

"Why don't you take a seat, dear," Sister Maureen said as the other students filed in.

"Sister Georgina had us seated alphabetically. Should I take my old desk, or did you change the seating assignments?"

Sister Maureen sat on the edge of her desk and opened her lesson plan. "Sit wherever you like. I don't bother with assigned seats."

"I'm glad you're here," Chloe said, taking a seat in the front row.

Sister Maureen smiled warmly. "Me, too. I think we're going to have a fun year."

By Christmas break, Chloe was certain about what the future held. The constancy of planning for life after high school kept at bay the terror that in a few months she and Gigi would enter the adult world.

Fear mingled with excitement over the prospect of sharing an apartment with Gigi while she attended the Sorbonne and Chloe was a student at the University of Paris. Chloe had already applied and was eagerly awaiting the acceptance notification that was due in spring.

Chloe was confident she would be accepted, with her excellent transcript. She continued to excel academically, especially in Sister Maureen's English and drama classes. Whereas other teachers forced Chloe and her classmates to memorize and regurgitate dry facts, Sister Maureen made her classes lively. Chloe took part in spirited group discussions about the themes of the classic literature they read and why some of the books were considered controversial at the time. Acting out scenes from Shakespeare, Molière and other classic playwrights further whet Chloe's appetite to become an actress – after college, of course.

While Chloe was doing her part, Gigi was falling further behind and had again been placed on academic probation. As other students made plans for skiing vacations and shopping expeditions over Christmas break, Gigi had to lug home a heap of books to catch up.

When Chloe arrived home on the first day of Christmas break, she found Marie in the kitchen, humming while she pulled a fresh batch of her famous beignets from the oven. The whole house smelled wonderful, just the way Chloe remembered when she'd left for school in the fall.

"It's so nice to have you home from sabbatical," Chloe said, kissing Marie on the cheek. "Do you mind if a steal one?"

"Go ahead, but just don't spoil your dinner, *chouchou*. I made these for you and Madame Chevalier to have with my homemade eggnog after dinner."

"Where *is* Mother?" Chloe poured herself a glass of milk to go with her cookie. "I thought she'd be home from her business trip by now."

Marie set the tray of cookies aside to cool and began rinsing dishes. "She's stuck in Zurich. A bad storm just blew in there. She said she'd call back when she finds out when her flight departs."

The phone rang and Chloe raced to answer the kitchen extension, expecting news from Maxine.

"Hello, *ma chérie*. How was the trip home?" Maxine said over the scratchy connection from the busy Zurich airport. She was barely audible, nearly drowned out by an announcer speaking in French over an intercom, people conversing in other languages, and assorted background noise.

"The trip was fine, I guess," Chloe said, leaning on the counter. "When are you coming home?"

"Actually, that's what I was calling about. We're snowed in here, and the airline is going to put me and the other passengers up in a hotel for the night. I probably won't be home until tomorrow morning – maybe the afternoon – when the weather lets up."

"But, Mother, it's Christmas Eve," Chloe said, not even trying to hide her disappointment. "We always spend Christmas Eve together."

"I know, dearest, but there's nothing I can do about it. Your gifts are under the tree. You can get started opening them, if you want."

"But it's not the same. And this is our first Christmas without Jacques…"

Chloe choked up, her eyes tearing as the impact of spending the holidays without him hit her. She'd been so busy with finals and getting ready to come home for break that she hadn't stopped to think about how much she would miss her father figure this season. And now that harsh reality was worsened by the fact that Mother wouldn't be around.

"If there was any way I could be there, you know I would," Maxine said finally.

Chloe didn't respond, just held the phone and choked back tears. She was determined not to break down; she was almost eighteen and didn't want her mother to mistake her emotional state for immaturity.

"Would you put Marie on the line, *ma chérie*? I need to tell her a couple of things about the house, since I won't be there," Maxine said after a few moments of silence.

Chloe turned to Marie, who gave her a look of concern. Remaining silent, Chloe handed Marie the phone and retreated to the ballroom. Watching the lights blinking on the massive Christmas tree, the urge to cry subsided, replaced by a dull, empty feeling.

"Are you okay, *chouchou*?"

Chloe started, seeing Marie standing at the entrance of the ballroom. Chloe had been so lost in thought, she hadn't heard Marie enter.

"Yeah, I'm okay," Chloe said flatly. "Thanks for asking."

"Madame Chevalier assured me she'd be home for Christmas tomorrow, after the snowstorm clears up," Marie said, slowly coming to stand beside Chloe.

"Yeah, that's what she told me, too," Chloe said, her voice thick with skepticism.

Marie placed a comforting hand on Chloe's shoulder. "Your mother loves you. Please don't be cross with her. It's not her fault all the flights were canceled."

Chloe looked at the floor. "I know. It's just that this is our first Christmas without Jacques."

Marie pulled Chloe into her arms. "We all miss him. It's okay to be sad."

Still fighting back tears, Chloe allowed herself to be cradled in Marie's bosom for a minute, then pulled away. "You better get ready to go to the train station," Chloe said, wiping her eyes. "Aren't you going to see your mother?"

"My daughter's picking her up, and I had planned to spend the holidays with my family," Marie said, speaking slowly, as if treading lightly with Chloe's fragile emotions. "But I can stay here with you until Madame Chevalier gets back. I don't want you to be alone on Christmas Eve."

Chloe shook her head. "No, Marie, I can't ask you to do that. Go be with your family."

"You *are* my family, *chouchou*." Marie affectionately pinched Chloe's cheek. "Besides, this is a tough time for all of us – the first Christmas season without M'sieu Chevalier."

"I'll be okay, Marie, really. I'm a big girl now. I can take care of myself," Chloe said, trying to convince herself as much as Marie.

"I just don't like the idea of you being all alone in this big house by yourself. All the other household staff have left for the holidays. Why don't I have Louis drop you off at Simone and Gigi's house on the way to the train station?"

"They already left for Gigi's grandparents' house in Aurillac."

The familiar worry wrinkle appeared on Marie's brow. "You sure you'll be okay here, all by yourself?"

"Yeah, I'll be fine. I have a lot to keep me busy. I still have to unpack, and I have some wrapping to do."

"Speaking of which, I left a gift for you under the tree."

Chloe smiled. "I got you a little something, too. I still have to wrap it, though."

"Why don't we plan to do our gift exchange when I get back? I'll be back Sunday afternoon, and we can ring in the New Year together. I'll fix a big, traditional New Year's dinner."

"That'd be fun, something to look forward to."

Bernard, the groundskeeper, appeared at the ballroom's entrance. "Are you ready for me to take you to the train station?" he said to Marie.

"I'll just be a moment." Marie turned to Chloe. "I guess I better get a move on. I'll call to check on you as soon as I get to my daughter's."

"Thanks, Marie."

"Chloe, you're not staying here all alone, are you?" Bernard said.

"Yes. Mother's stranded in Zurich."

"Well, I don't live too far away," he said. "Don't hesitate to call if you need anything, you hear?"

Chloe smiled appreciatively at Bernard. It was a bit strange to see him more subdued than his usual, jovial self, as if he sensed Chloe's melancholy mood.

"I'll wait for you in the car," Bernard said with a lingering glance at Marie that reminded Chloe of how a boy her own age would gaze at someone he had a crush on.

"You know he's sweet on you, don't you?" Chloe said to Marie after Bernard had left the room.

"I'm not thinking about him," Marie said with a dismissive wave in the direction Bernard had exited. "It's you I'll be thinking about on Christmas."

"I'll be thinking of you, too. My mouth's already watering; I can't wait for our New Year's feast."

Marie mussed Chloe's hair, then slowly backed out of the room. "Oh, I almost forgot," she said, turning to face Chloe again. "A package came for you earlier today. I put it under the tree with the rest of the gifts."

"Who sent it?" Chloe wasn't expecting any packages. She and Gigi had exchanged gifts in their dorm room before they left school.

"Whoever sent it didn't put their name or address on the package. I guess you'll have to open it to find out."

Chloe shrugged. "Oh, okay. Thanks again, Marie. Merry Christmas."

"*Joyeux Noël.*"

After seeing Marie off, Chloe changed into her pajamas, fixed a steaming cup of hot chocolate and a heaping plate of Marie's beignets and returned to the ballroom to open a couple of gifts before snuggling under the covers in her room to watch Christmas movies.

Noticing the unmarked package Marie mentioned earlier, Chloe reached for it and tore it open, unable to stand the suspense. Inside the box lay two voluminous poetry collections, one in English and another in French, with works by some of Chloe's favorite writers.

The tears Chloe had suppressed earlier now flowed easily. This is exactly what Jacques would have gotten her for Christmas. She rifled through the Styrofoam chips inside the package, but there was no card. Mother had probably sent this gift to cheer Chloe up, perhaps anticipating that her business trip would run long and ruin the holiday.

Chloe's cat, Bizou, padded into the ballroom and Chloe pulled her onto her lap. She sat there in front of the Christmas tree, stroking Bizou and thinking back on the good times – remembering first moving into the chateau when Bizou was just a kitten, fencing and horseback riding with Jacques, laughing with Gigi at last year's Christmas party in the ballroom, and sitting with Mother and Jacques in the parlor afterward when he proposed the idea of adopting her. Those happy times were now just a distant memory.

33

Chloe sat in the downstairs lounge of her dorm at Our Lady of Chastity, staring out the window at the driving rain pelting the newly opened spring buds that dotted the campus. Her attention strayed from the trigonometry book in her lap and she didn't even hear her dormmates' chatter and the latest episode of *Top of the Pops* blaring on the large-screen TV across the room. Her mind wandered as she watched the rain.

"Why do you look so down?" Gigi said, coming up and flipping Chloe's textbook shut.

Chloe sat up and shifted on the sofa, the rough, plaid fabric scratchy against her legs. "I was just thinking about Jacques. It'll be the one-year anniversary of his death in a few weeks."

"I'm sorry. I didn't realize." Gigi sank to the sofa next to Chloe, setting her books between them. "I have good news that'll take your mind off it."

Chloe braced herself. Whenever Gigi had "good news," it was usually something that involved bending or outright breaking campus rules.

"What?" Chloe said, preparing herself for the latest diabolical scheme.

"I landed some tickets to Kensington United's big game at Wembley Stadium this weekend. They're taking on Real Madrid, their big rival."

Chloe looked at Gigi blankly, confused as to why this rated as "good news." "Why would I care about going to some stupid soccer game?"

"For starters, I want you to be there with me when I get to see my cutie up close." Gigi held up her binder, on which she had plastered a photo of Justin Bradshaw, the soccer star she had a crush on.

"Oh, yeah, him." Chloe mumbled, opening her book again. "You'll have to go to the game without me, Gi'. I don't have any time to go out this weekend. I'm going to be studying for that big trig final that Gottlieb is giving before spring break, and you should do the same."

Chloe planned to throw herself into her schoolwork to forget about how badly she missed Jacques. Gigi, however, continued to neglect her studies and was doing worse than ever, in danger of not graduating on time. Fraternizing with St. Thomas boys, her only extracurricular activity other than painting and sketching, certainly wasn't helping her academic standing.

"Oh come on, it'll be fun. Some other girls from our dorm are going. We can all take the train into the city together." She grinned mischievously, adding, "Maybe we'll meet some cute boys at the game."

"I don't think I'm ready to date again," Chloe said with a sigh, looking out at the rain again. "I still haven't gotten over Dominique."

"Dominique? That was last summer. You've got to get over him, girl."

"I'm not like you, Gi'. I can't just jump from one boy to the next."

"The only way you're going to get over Dominique is to get out," Gigi reasoned. She reached over and shut Chloe's book again. "All you do is study. Our senior year is almost over. You have to have fun some time."

"Going to some crowded soccer game where everyone's yelling and acting like a maniac isn't my idea of fun. Haven't you seen those fans on TV? They're *crazy*." Chloe reopened her book and shifted in her seat again, settling in to study. "I'll be at the library Saturday night, studying."

"Studying on a Saturday night? You're the crazy one," Gigi said, as if Chloe had said she planned to jump from the top of Big Ben with no parachute. "Come on, Chlo', I don't want the extra ticket to go to waste. Besides, if you go with me to the game, there's something in it for you."

Chloe looked up from her book. "What are you talking about, Gi'?" she said wearily, just wanting to be left to her studies.

Gigi picked up the remote off the coffee table and turned up the sound on the TV. "Look, your Latin hottie's shaking his ass on *Top of the Pops*."

Chloe turned her attention to the TV. Sure enough, Sergio Reyes was gyrating his hips, inciting shrieks from the girls in the studio audience. Chloe had been so distracted, thinking about Jacques, that she had forgotten about the reason she had moved her study session to the lounge – to catch Sergio performing his new hit on TV.

"What has Sergio Reyes got to do with the soccer game?" Chloe asked.

"He's the half-time entertainment. Being from Spain, he's a big supporter of his hometown team, Real Madrid, of course. You should know that. What kind of fan are you?" Gigi opened her binder and took out the tickets she'd scored. "Sure you don't want to reconsider going to the game?" Gigi dangled the tickets before Chloe, as if enticing a fussy child with a favorite pacifier.

Chloe glanced back at the television, where Sergio was taking a bow to wild applause. "Okay," she said finally, "but we have to be back by curfew."

"Of course we'll be back by curfew," Gigi said, not sounding at all convincing.

"I'm going to hold you to that. This is our more semester, and I don't plan to spend it on probation." Chloe opened her book again and retrieved a pen and notebook from her bookbag. "Now, if you don't mind, I've got studying to do."

"Knock yourself out." Gigi gathered her books and got up to leave. "I'm going up to our room to pick out an outfit for the game. I've got to look my best in case Justin notices me in the stands."

Seeing that Gigi had left the tickets lying on the sofa, Chloe picked them up and held them out. "Don't forget these."

"Oh, yeah. Thanks." Gigi took the tickets and turned to leave again.

"Hey," Chloe called to her, "how'd you manage to get your hands on those, anyway? I bet that game's been sold out for weeks."

Gigi paused in the doorway, clutching her books. "Let's just say there's a boy from St. Thomas I've been seeing who's a big fan." Her familiar mischievous grin spread across her face again as she added, "A *very* big fan."

"Spare me the details," Chloe said, holding up her hand. "I don't want to know."

Maxine stared out her office window, watching a couple strolling by hand in hand. It had been a year since Jacques had died and she missed him more than ever. The fact that his fatal car crash happened the day after their anniversary made his absence all the more painful.

"Are you okay?" Simone slowly entered the office, her arms loaded with files.

Maxine swiveled in her chair. "Yeah, I'm all right, thanks," she said, plucking a tissue from the box on her desk and dabbing at her eyes. "The anniversary of Jacques' death is coming up, and I've been thinking about him a lot."

"I'm so sorry, Max." Simone set her files on the desk and touched Maxine's hand. "He was such a great guy. We all miss him."

"I try not to think about him being gone, but the strangest thing happened."

Maxine opened a desk drawer and pulled out a small gift box.

"What's that?" Simone asked, peering at the box.

Maxine flipped the box open, revealing a crystal dome filled with water, a tiny gold sailboat floating inside. "This came to the house yesterday in an unmarked package. It's exactly the kind of gift Jacques would have picked out to remind me of when he proposed on his yacht. There was no note, but it's really strange that someone sent it to me right around what would have been our two-year anniversary."

Simone picked up the paperweight. "This is exquisite. Someone has good taste. Maybe Jacques' mother sent it to you. You're still close with her, right?"

Maxine studied the paperweight thoughtfully. "Yes, you're probably right. I'll have to call her later and thank her. I've been meaning to send her flowers. I'm sure this is a difficult time for her, too."

Simone carefully placed the paperweight back in the box. "You know what we should do? We should get dressed up and go have dinner at that restaurant where Jacques took you on your first date and your anniversary. That'd be a nice way to remember him."

Maxine smiled faintly, thinking back on that happy occasion with the man she thought she'd spend the rest of her life with. "That'd be nice," she said, not wanting to hurt Simone's feelings by telling her going back to Alain's would be too painful.

"Well, listen," Simone said, standing, "if you're feeling up to it, your four o'clock appointment is here. The Lamberts."

Maxine glanced at her desk calendar. "The Lamberts?"

"Yes, you remember, don't you? They're that couple from Haiti who just moved to Paris. They made an appointment to talk about redecorating the chateau they're moving into with their kids."

"Oh, yeah. Send them in, but can you give a minute?"

Simone pursed her lips in a sympathetic expression. "Sure."

Once alone in her office, Maxine pulled out her compact and touched up her makeup. She fluffed her hair and straightened her suit jacket. She had to pull herself together. She had a business to run.

She stood and offered her hand when the well-dressed couple entered her office. She noticed that Yves Lambert, an even-featured but not particularly handsome dark-skinned black man, had rough hands – hands that seemed coarsened by manual labor. Madeleine Lambert, in contrast, had smooth, manicured hands that matched her fair complexion and petite figure. Maxine surmised that Yves had worked his way up from Haiti's sugarcane fields and built his own business through toil and sacrifice, and Madeleine was the light-skinned trophy wife accustomed to a life of leisure.

"So nice to meet you, Madame Chevalier," Yves said, shaking Maxine's hand.

"Yes, thank you for seeing us," Madeleine added.

"Please, won't you have a seat?" Maxine motioned to the chairs in front of her desk. She took a seat and opened the file Simone had prepared detailing the couple's redecorating project.

While the couple droned on about the extensive work they wanted done to their chateau on posh avenue Foch, Maxine caught sight of the gift box she'd forgotten to put away and had to fight the urge to break down in tears. No matter how hard she tried, she couldn't forget about Jacques and the impending anniversary of his death. But she managed to get through the appointment by doing what she'd been doing ever since she'd become a widow: putting on a pleasant face and convincing the world, if not herself, that she was in control.

Chloe and Gigi and their friends from school chatted away and giggled on the train ride into the city, en route to Wembley Stadium for the big soccer match. Although many of their friends came from different countries and backgrounds, the drama that teen girls faced seemed to be the same the world over. The ethnic diversity of Chloe and Gigi's group of friends was testament to the fact that Our Lady of Chastity was a world-class institution that attracted students from all around – some of whom weren't even Catholic.

Being around Gigi and their girlfriends lifted Chloe's spirits and took her mind off missing Jacques. She admitted that this all-girls outing – window shopping at chic stores in London's fashion epicenter Carnaby Street and hanging out in funky record stores in the West End on their way to the stadium – was a hell of a lot more fun that being cooped up studying in her dorm room.

The girls' last stop before hopping a double-decker bus to the stadium was a huge bookstore near Soho Square. Browsing the "Human Sexuality" section, the girls erupted in uncontrollable giggles again while ogling the illustrations in *The Joy of Sex* and were shooed away by a disapproving clerk.

Upon migrating to the newsstand section, the girls thumbed through *Seventeen, YM* and other teen-oriented publications to catch up on the latest fashions.

"Hey, Chloe, isn't this you?"

Chloe looked up from her copy of British *Vogue* to see Enid Agu, a Nigerian classmate whose parents were foreign diplomats, holding up a photo in *Cosmo Girl* that Chloe had posed for last summer.

"Oh, yeah," Chloe said, flipping her magazine shut and putting it back on the rack. "I model sometimes when I'm home from school."

Enid's deep-set, brown eyes grew larger. "Really? Wow. That's pretty cool. How come you never mentioned it before?"

"I dunno. It's not that big a deal, really," Chloe mumbled, suddenly embarrassed and burying her nose in another magazine to deflect attention.

She flipped through the music magazine she'd picked up and scanned a profile on Sergio Reyes. Spying photos from his current world tour made Chloe even more excited to see him perform live during half time at the game.

"Aren't you glad you came?" Gigi said, brushing by Chloe and glancing over her shoulder at the spread on Sergio.

"Yeah. I can't wait to see him onstage."

"Our seats are kind of far up, but I packed the binoculars," Gigi said, patting her backpack.

"Hey, guys, the *Times* has a big cover story about the game."

Chloe and Gigi turned to see Emily Chen, a classmate who was the daughter of a prominent Beijing scientist, holding up one of the daily newspapers with the headline "Thousands to Pack Wembley For Season Opener." The girls huddled around the paper, ogling photos of the buff soccer players, like their rowdy cohorts from the neighboring all-boys academy drooling over a girlie magazine.

"I like Number Thirty-six," Anastasia Thornhill, the only Anglo in the bunch, said in her British lilt while pointing to a photo of a blond goalie. "He's a babe."

"Number Nineteen's my guy," Gigi said, beaming over a shot of Kensington United's star forward in action.

"This article says he's been suspended a couple times for yelling at the refs and picking fights with players who foul him," Chloe said, skimming the story.

"He also has a reputation for hard partying. He's always in the gossip pages," Anastasia said, plucking one of London's notorious tabloids off the stands and thumbing through it. "He's had a couple of arrests for disorderly conduct and driving under the influence."

"I can't believe you read that trash," Gigi said scornfully to Anastasia, scolding her classmate like one of the nuns at school.

"You sure this guy is someone to emulate?" Chloe said, concerned Gigi would get carried away with her bad-boy crush.

"'Emulating' would be the last thing on my mind if I ever got close to him, if you know what I mean," Gigi said, eliciting another round of giggles. "I don't care if they arrest me, I'm going to find a way to get back to the locker room after the game. I've got to meet him."

Chloe tsked at Gigi. "You promised me you wouldn't do anything crazy."

"No, I promised we'd make it back to campus by curfew. And don't worry, we will." Gigi took the newspaper from Emily and returned it to the shelf. "We better get going. Kick-off's in twenty minutes."

34

Maxine strode down a grand front staircase in the Lamberts' avenue Foch chateau, flanked by her two new clients.

"This wallpaper is amazing," Maxine said, running her hand along the textured floral print as she descended the staircase with Yves and Madeleine. "I'm guessing the original owner put this up, but it's been kept in such good condition."

"It's old and dingy," Madeleine said dismissively upon reaching the landing. "I want it stripped and replaced with something modern."

Maxine said nothing as she scribbled notes on her clipboard. Madame Lambert had proved herself to be a typical hard-to-please customer during this initial walk-through, giving Maxine ample reason to decline taking on the redecorating project. But she willed herself to remain professional, keep her opinions to herself for the time being and give the Lamberts a fair assessment.

"This chandelier is nineteenth century gilt-bronze." Maxine motioned toward the ornate light fixture hanging in the foyer.

"I want that monstrosity taken down immediately," Madeleine said without so much as glance upward. "It's so gaudy, it hurts my eyes."

"But it's an antique – priceless," Maxine couldn't help interjecting. "It was probably installed when the house was built. It gives the foyer so much character."

"This is our house now, and I plan to put my personal stamp on every corner," Madeleine declared. "My taste is contemporary."

Maxine looked at Yves, who held his hands out as if to say, "What my wife wants, my wife gets." Maxine had noted how Madeleine always used "I" and "my" when speaking about the house, and Yves seemed resigned that redecorating their new abode was his wife's pet project and he was present only to find out how much her expensive taste was going to cost him.

"Won't you join us for tea?" Madeleine, standing in the doorway of an old-fashioned drawing room, said to Maxine. "We can go over all the details and get to know one another a little better."

Maxine tucked her clipboard under her arm and followed the couple into the drawing room, taking one last glance over her shoulder at the antique chandelier.

The girls screamed and hooted in the stands at Wembley Stadium, cheering along with the crowd as the Kensington United players took the field. The fact that the girls' seats were way up in the "nosebleed" section and they had to use binoculars to see the field didn't dampen the excitement.

Gigi screamed louder than anyone upon seeing Justin Bradshaw. "God, I can't wait to see him up close and personal," she said, training her binoculars on her favorite footballer as the announcer called his name. "He's so hot, I might just rush down to the field and jump on him."

Chloe laughed at the preposterousness of Gigi's remark. "Behave yourself, Gi'. You don't want to get us thrown out of here before the game even starts."

When the opposing team took the field, the crowd booed and made obscene gestures, and it was apparent that these rabid fans were not going to grant a genteel British reception to the home team's rivals.

Throughout the first half, the rowdy crowd whooped and whistled whenever Justin's team scored a goal and roared profanities whenever the opposing team advanced. The score was tied at one point by the end of the first quarter, when the referee made a call that all of the fans disagreed with, judging by the commotion. The guy in front of Chloe blew an air horn to express his disapproval, and she stuck her fingers in her ears to block out the clatter.

The ref called "foul" and penalized Justin, who responded by yelling in the ref's face. Chloe was startled by how quickly the smiling, charismatic player transformed into a red-faced brute, veins protruding from his forehead and neck.

"I'd hate to be that ref," Chloe commented, watching the action on the field through her fingers, as if shielding herself from a grisly scene in a horror movie. "It looks like Justin might punch him out."

"That call sucked," Gigi said, watching the confrontation through her binoculars. "Justin's just standing up for himself."

Before the encounter with the ref could further escalate, Justin's coach pulled him away and benched him. The young athlete spent the rest of the first half on the sidelines with a towel around his neck, his handsome features twisted into a scowl.

Just before half time, the opposing team scored a goal, taking the lead. The crowd groaned and Gigi screamed, "No!" as if witnessing a loved one being shot.

"I'm going to the bathroom," Gigi said, getting up. "I think I might be sick."

"Do you want me to go with you?" Chloe said, with an anxious glance at the field, where the stage was being set up for Sergio Reyes' half-time show.

"No, that's okay. I know you want to see Sergio perform. That's the whole reason you came."

"I'll go with you, Gi'," Emily volunteered. "I need to freshen up myself."

"I'll come, too," Enid spoke up. "I might get something from the concession stand."

"Me, too." Anastasia stood up and grabbed her purse. "I'm going to see if they have any posters of the goalie I can buy to hang above my bed."

Chloe wrinkled her nose, as if smelling something foul. "You still want a poster of him, even though they're losing? He hasn't done such a hot job of protecting his team's goal."

Anastasia shrugged. "That's the kind of stuff only guys care about. I just think he's cute."

Chloe giggled and nodded in agreement.

"Do you want us to bring you something to eat?" Gigi said to Chloe as she and the other girls filed out.

"No, I'm fine, but can you toss me the binoculars?"

Gigi handed them over. "I knew you couldn't wait to see Sergio shake his ass."

Chloe shooed Gigi away and settled in to watch the show. The opening was like one of those Brazilian Carnival celebrations Chloe had seen on TV, with dancers in multicolored, Caribbean-style costumes and jugglers on stilts twirling around the stage. When Sergio Reyes came on, the crowd went wild and Chloe finally allowed herself to shout with abandon like the rest of the fans.

The opening number was an upbeat, Latin-flavored dance tune that was obviously designed to rev up the crowd. Chloe kept the binoculars trained on the stage while Sergio swiveled his hips and stepped to the beat with the backup dancers. She had to admit Gigi was right – she did enjoy watching him shake his behind.

When the number concluded, Chloe leapt to her feet and applauded and whistled with the rest of the crowd.

"*Gracias*. Thank you," Sergio said breathlessly. "I would now like to perform a song from my new album. This is dedicated to all the ladies out there."

At Sergio's announcement, a throng of female fans poured out of the bleachers and flocked to the edge of the stage. The women screamed so loud they nearly drowned out the subdued instrumental start of the romantic ballad.

"Girl, what are you still doing up here?"

Chloe looked up to see Gigi filing into the row along with the other girls, arms loaded with snacks and souvenirs.

"He's about to sing a love song," Chloe said, directing the binoculars to the center of the stage, where Sergio had taken a seat on a stool in preparation for the number.

Gigi snatched the binoculars. "Get down there."

"Are you nuts? I'm not fighting my way through all those crazy girls." Chloe tried to yank the binoculars back, but Gigi held them behind her back.

"I didn't drag you all the way out to Wembley Stadium so you could sit in the stands while all those groupies get close to him." Gigi pulled on Chloe's arm, forcing her to stand up. "Now get down there."

Chloe glanced at the other girls, who nodded enthusiastically for her to venture down to the field. She slowly descended a few steps, then turned back to look at Gigi, like a child looking to her mother for reassurance when going down the slide at the playground.

"Move it, before the song's over!" Gigi bellowed, cupping her hands around her mouth like one of those soccer fanatics yelling at the players not to bungle an important scoring opportunity.

With Gigi and the other girls prodding her, Chloe made her way down to the field. By the time she reached the stage, Sergio was well into the chorus.

Her view blocked by the hordes of women who surrounded the stage, Chloe told herself this was silly. She should have just stayed in the stands, where she could have had an overhead view of the performance.

Just as she was about to turn around and head back to her seat, Sergio stood up and looked in her direction. She glanced behind her, wondering if he was singing to someone else. But he began inching closer, seeming to make eye contact. She began moving forward, as if drawn to him by a magnetic force, and the crowd parted deferentially as she took each step.

"*All my life I've been looking, looking for a love with someone true,*" he sang, "*and now I've come to realize that someone is you.*"

Chloe was now standing at the edge of the stage, staring into Sergio's seductive brown eyes. The moment was unreal, made even more dreamlike when he concluded the song by plucking a red rose from a bouquet one of the fans had tossed onstage and handing it to her.

His hand brushed hers and she trembled, instantly forgetting Dominique and François and any other male she'd ever had feelings for. In that instant, it was as though everyone else had disappeared and it was just her and Sergio connecting.

The trancelike state Chloe had fallen into was shattered when the fans surrounding the stage screamed and applauded as the band wound up the song. Sergio blew a kiss, then dashed across the stage to conclude the half-time show with another high-energy number.

Drifting back to her seat, Chloe could feel the envious stares of the other female fans. Climbing the steps to rejoin Gigi and the other girls in the stands, it was as though she were walking on clouds.

"I saw the whole thing through the binoculars," Gigi said when Chloe took her seat. "Aren't you glad I made you go down there?"

"It was amazing," Chloe said quietly, sniffing the rose Sergio had given her.

"I can't wait to tell everyone at school Sergio Reyes sang to you!" Anastasia exclaimed, accompanied by shrieks from the other girls.

Gigi leaned in to Chloe, nudging her out of her reverie. "See, I told you, you wouldn't regret this."

"So, what brought you to Paris?" Maxine said, sitting across from the Lamberts in the couple's stately drawing room.

Yves' normally jovial expression turned serious. "We were forced out of Port-au-Prince, like everyone else accused of being sympathizers to the Duvaliers."

Maxine flinched. She had read numerous articles in *The International Herald-Tribune* about Dr. François "Papa Doc" Duvalier and his son, Jean-Claude "Baby Doc" Duvalier, in which they were portrayed as ruthless dictators who exploited their own people until they were ousted in a bloody coup.

"We were good friends with Jean-Claude and his wife, Michèle," Madeleine said. She picked up a framed photo from an end table and handed it to Maxine.

Maxine studied the photo, which showed Madeleine and Yves sitting next to Jean-Claude and Michele Duvalier at a lavish banquet table. "Where was this taken?" Maxine asked, setting her teacup down upon realizing it was rattling in her hand. The image of her potential clients fraternizing with such reviled figures was unsettling.

"That was at one of the fabulous state dinners they used to throw at the presidential palace in Port-au-Prince," Madeleine said, as if describing a family vacation to Disney World. "That was in the '80s, a few years after our oldest, Jean-Baptiste, was born."

"Then they turned their anger on all of the Duvaliers' associates, and burned our sugar-cane plantation to the ground." Yves stared at the wall opposite Maxine, as if recalling the harrowing episode. "My father was a sharecropper and built that plantation with his own two hands. I grew up helping him plow the fields, and when he died, he passed it on to me. All of those decades of hard work and struggle went up in flames in a matter of minutes."

Maxine listened intently as Yves described how he, Madeleine and their older children narrowly escaped the vengeance of the angry masses. The field hands turned on the family, came after them with sickles and torches, setting fire to the sugar-cane stalks.

Madeleine placed her hand on her husband's, the contrast between her smooth, fair complexion and his rough, dark skin more pronounced. "Yves put me and the children on the first boat out of Port-au-Prince while he stayed behind to salvage what he could. Thank God he managed to rescue the bank statements and jewelry from the safe." She punctuated the statement with a frantic wave of her bejeweled hand.

"The Duvaliers went into exile in France, but we decided to try our luck in the States," Yves said. "We set sail for Miami and stayed there for years."

"Yves set up a restaurant-supply business and did quite well," Madeleine said. "We could have stayed in the States, but we noticed our children were becoming too Americanized. They almost never spoke French or Creole around the house, and even though we sent them to private schools, they picked up all kinds of horrible slang and bad manners from their classmates."

Maxine nodded. "I know what you mean. I sent my daughter, Chloe, off to boarding school in London so she could get a better education," Maxine said, happy to change the subject to child rearing and away from dicey political matters.

"We didn't want our kids to lose touch with the old ways, the way we did things back in Haiti," Yves interjected. "In America, we saw that our kids were becoming materialistic, they were getting lazy and didn't want to work for things the way I did. My oldest son, Jean-Baptiste, asked for a sports car for his sixteenth birthday." Yves shook his head in disgust and sipped his tea.

"That's why we decided to move to Europe, where there's less of an emphasis on capitalism," Madeleine said. "We wanted to be in a place where we could speak French again."

"America, for all of its talk of being a melting pot," Yves added, "doesn't seem very accepting of foreigners or different cultures."

"You're so right," Maxine said thoughtfully. "I grew up in the deep South – New Orleans. America still has its problems, which is why I haven't been back in years. I've come to think of Paris as my home."

"So do I. My grandfather, Cyrille, was a white Parisian, you know," Madeleine said with a look of pride, confirming Maxine's initial impression that Madame Lambert had been raised in Haiti's light-skinned aristocracy. "He started my family's business that shipped sugar cane all over the world and did business with Yves' father, which is how Yves and I met. It was an arranged marriage."

Maxine raised an eyebrow at the antiquated notion.

"He always promised me we'd live in Paris someday," Madeleine continued, patting her husband's hand, "and now we're here."

"I just invested in a winery in Bordeaux," Yves said. "So far, our children seem to be doing much better here in France."

"How many children do you have?" Maxine asked.

"Four girls and two boys. Can you imagine?" Madeleine said in an exasperated tone, pressing her hand to her forehead in mock exhaustion.

"No, I can't. I stopped at one," Maxine said with a laugh.

It was hard for Maxine to envision the impeccably groomed, dainty Madeleine going through the agonies of labor six times, but the evidence was indisputable when Madeleine handed over a family photo.

"You have a beautiful family," Maxine commented, studying the photo of children of various ages. From their large brood, it was apparent that, like most Haitians, the Lamberts were Catholic and practiced the ineffective rhythm method.

"Here's our youngest now, just up from her nap," Madeleine said when a girl in pigtails who looked to be about nine or ten pattered in.

"Ariane, say hello to Madame Chevalier," Yves instructed his daughter, who was busy climbing onto Madeleine's lap.

"*Bonjour*, Madame," the little girl said, groggily rubbing her eyes.

"You're adorable," Maxine said, smiling at the little girl. "You remind me of my Chloe when she was your age."

The sound of the front door opening and closing sounded throughout the house.

"That must be our oldest," Madeleine said. "He enrolled at the University of Paris and usually gets home around this time."

"Son, come greet our guest," Yves called.

A strikingly handsome young man with a backpack slung over his shoulder appeared in the doorway. Like his sister, he had curly light brown hair and a tawny complexion that was somewhere between his mother's and father's skin tones. He had Madeleine's hazel eyes and Yves' height, although he was much leaner than his brawny father.

"This is Madame Chevalier," Madeleine said, motioning for her son to enter the room. "We've been talking to her about redoing our house."

The young man looked at Maxine with a bored expression, and she took note of his untucked shirt and sagging pants. With his slumping posture and sneering expression, he certainly had the air of an Americanized youth who eschewed his immigrant parents' traditional values.

"Don't just stand there. Introduce yourself, son," Yves chastised.

The young man held his hand out to Maxine in a grudging gesture. "*Bonjour*, I'm Jean-Baptiste," he mumbled, barely making eye contact.

"Jean-Baptiste's majoring in business," Yves said, standing and putting his arm around his son. "I'm grooming him to become my second-in-command at the winery when he graduates."

Jean-Baptiste stared at the floor with the same blasé expression while his father described expansion plans for the family vineyard.

"How do you like the University of Paris?" Maxine asked, trying to engage the young man. "My daughter's going to be a freshman there in the fall."

"Really?" Madeleine spoke up. "Maybe Jean-Baptiste can show her around some time."

Maxine glanced at the young man, sipping her tea and silently evaluating his overall irreverent demeanor.

"Yes," Maxine said finally, forcing a smile and setting her tea aside, "that would be nice."

35

Nearing the end of the fourth quarter, Kensington United was still tied with the opposing team. The crowd gasped when one of the home team's stars players attempted to make a goal, missed and fell, twisting his ankle.

"I don't think I can watch anymore," Gigi said, covering her eyes and handing Chloe the binoculars while medics surrounded the player.

"If there's a tie and it goes into overtime, we won't be able to stay to see who wins because of curfew," Anastasia said, munching on popcorn.

"Still," Chloe spoke up, "the half-time show was worth it."

"C'mon," Gigi said, shoving Chloe playfully. "This is serious."

A collective moan arose from the crowd as the medics carried the star forward off the field on a stretcher, but the moan turned to a loud cheer when the coach replaced the downed player with Justin.

"*Yeeesss!*" Gigi yelped. "My baby's finally getting another chance!"

Chloe laughed at Gigi's possessiveness of a guy she'd never met. "Let me guess," she said, handing Gigi the binoculars, "you want these back?"

Gigi focused the binoculars on Justin as he sprinted to take his place on the field, waving to the cheering fans. Apparently buoyed by the crowd's enthusiasm, Justin played with renewed vigor and soon took possession of the ball. A hush fell over the crowd as Justin surged toward the opposing team's goal, tension heightened by the clock running out.

Chloe scooted to the edge of her seat, her lack of interest in soccer overridden by the suspense. Just before the buzzer rang, Justin kicked the ball into the goal, pushing his team into the lead. Chloe jumped to her feet and howled with Gigi and the other girls. The jovial demeanor Justin had originally exhibited returned as his teammates hoisted him on their shoulders, fists raised above his head in a champion's pose.

Fans began pouring out of the stands, onto the field, and Gigi climbed over Chloe and began descending the steps to follow the stampede.

"Gi', where are you going?" Chloe called.

Gigi paused and turned to face Chloe. "Since they won, they're going to be signing autographs."

Chloe pointed to her watch. "But we have to leave now to make the train back to campus. You promised me we'd make curfew."

Gigi waved her hand dismissively. "You guys go ahead. I'll catch up. This might be my only chance to meet Justin."

"I'd love to have the goalie sign my poster," Anastasia said, unfurling the poster and taking a step down the bleachers toward Gigi. She stopped, glancing at the field. "But we'll never get through that crowd in time to make the train."

"Go on, you guys," Gigi said.

"We can't just leave you," Chloe said. "It's not safe for you to take the train by yourself after dark."

"I'll be fine," Gigi insisted.

"Are you staying with us or going with Gigi?" Enid said to Anastasia.

"Yeah, we gotta leave *now*," Emily spoke up.

Chloe looked at Anastasia, who stood hesitantly on a step between Gigi and the rest of the girls. Chloe darted her eyes at Gigi, who was buffeted this way and that by the crowd while peering impatiently at Anastasia.

"Sorry, Gi'," Anastasia said finally, rolling up the poster and slipping it into her backpack. "I can't risk violating curfew this close to graduation."

"Fine, be a wuss, but I'm not letting this opportunity pass me by," Gigi said, turning to descend the steps again.

"Be careful, Gi'," Chloe called.

The other girls began filing out of the stadium, but Chloe hovered on the steps, watching with concern as Gigi reached the field and was swallowed by the crowd.

Maxine watched the sun setting through her office window. As the last strains of daylight filtered in, she reflected on her encounter that afternoon with the Lamberts and their disturbing alliance with the deposed Haitian dictator.

The sound of a knock at the door jarred Maxine from her thoughts.

"Sorry, didn't mean to startle you," Simone said, entering. "How'd the walk-through go with the Lamberts?"

"It went okay." Maxine turned toward Simone. "They have a big family – six kids, can you believe it? Their baby girl, Ariane, reminds me of Chloe when she was little and I met their oldest son, Jean-Baptiste. He's a senior at the University of Paris, and when I mentioned that Chloe's enrolling there in the fall, I kind of got the impression that Yves and Madeleine wanted to play matchmaker. He seems kind of bratty, and they probably want to marry him off."

Simone chuckled and sat in one of the chairs in front of Maxine's desk. "Knowing you like I do, no one's good enough for Chloe. I'm sure if it was up to you, she'd live at home 'til she's forty." Simone stretched, slipped off her heels and propped her stocking feet on Maxine's desk. "So, what kind of shape is their house in?"

"Not bad. It has a lot of antique fixtures, but I can already tell Madeleine is one of those people who wants to redo everything with her own decorating taste. She wants to rip everything out and start from scratch."

"That sounds like a big undertaking. You sure you're up for it?"

"I don't know, quite honestly." Maxine stared past Simone, her mind drifting to memories of Jacques. "To tell the truth, I could use a big project to dig my hands into, to take my mind off the anniversary of Jacques' death."

Simone put her feet on the floor, sat up and reached for Maxine's hand. "I know the pain is still fresh. I'm so sorry, *cher*."

"I know I'm supposed to stop mourning at some point and get on with my life, but I've been thinking about him nonstop ever since I got that mysterious package." Maxine nodded toward the paperweight with the sailboat that sat on her desk next to a framed photo of herself, Jacques and Chloe in happier times.

"Why don't you get rid of it, since looking at it bothers you so much?" Simone said, eyeing the object like it was some kind of voodoo charm meant to conjure spirits of the dead.

"It doesn't bother me, really. Actually, it makes me feel peaceful, since it reminds me of Jacques." Maxine stared at the paperweight, thinking of the last time they'd gone sailing in St.-Tropez.

"Well, if taking on this remodeling job for the Lamberts will help you get over Jacques, then I say go for it," Simone said, rising and making her way to the door. "I'll draw up the contract first thing in the morning."

"Not so fast. I'm going to give myself tonight to sleep on it."

Simone paused in the doorway. "What's the problem? Did they not agree to the price you quoted?"

"No, it's not the money. It's just that…" Maxine paused, grappling for the right words to describe her consternation over the Lamberts' association with the Duvaliers. "Back in Haiti, they were friends with Baby Doc."

"You mean *the* 'Baby Doc'?" Simone said, closing the office door again as if to keep the employees from overhearing.

"Yes," Maxine confirmed. "Madeleine showed me a photo of her and Yves at a state dinner with Baby Doc and his wife."

"You mean Michèle? The one they called 'Her Dragon Lady Excellence'? That woman was a notorious spendthrift."

"I think Madeleine felt competitive with her, and is determined to match or even exceed that kind of extravagance with this renovation." Maxine let out a sigh of fatigue and massaged her forehead. "Part of me says I should turn the Lamberts down for ethical reasons, since much of their fortune no doubt came from Baby Doc funneling government sugar cane-exporting contracts to Yves." She paused, staring at the wall again. "But another part of me says go ahead with the renovation, obscenely overcharge them and donate all the money to charity."

Simone leaned against the door. "That's a big dilemma. We don't really need the business, if that's what you're worried about. It's slow right now, but you know how things go in cycles. Things'll eventually pick back up."

"I'm not worried about the business." Maxine glanced at the sailboat paperweight, running her fingers around its pedestal. "With the anniversary of Jacques' death, I just really need something to occupy my time."

Simone didn't immediately reply. "Why don't you take tonight to sleep on it, like you said," she said after a moment, opening the door again. "Just let me know what your decision is in the morning. Whatever you decide, I'll back you." Stepping out of the office, she added, "You are the boss, after all."

Maxine smiled at Simone's comment and turned her chair to the window again to look out at the streetlights that were beginning to blink on along the avenue.

Chloe sat at the desk in her dorm room, trying to concentrate on a chapter on the Crimean War in her world history book. She reached up and turned the clock to face her. It was going on midnight and Gigi still hadn't returned from the stadium. Chloe should have known better to trust Gigi when she promised to make curfew.

Chloe closed her book and rubbed her tired eyes. Trying to study was pointless. She got up and paced, wondering if Gigi had been in some kind of accident or had been mugged at the train station on her way back to school.

Pausing in front of her bed, Chloe glanced at a photo of Sergio Reyes she'd taped to her wall. His performance had been electrifying, but she was unsure if the thrill of seeing him in person was worth the anxiety she was going through now.

"Okay, I'll give Gigi ten more minutes," Chloe said aloud, sitting down at the desk again and reopening her book. "Then I'm reporting her missing."

Just as she began scribbling notes, she was distracted by the sound of something brushing against the window. Thinking it was just the wind rustling through the trees, she went back to studying. But she was interrupted again by an object hitting the window, this time louder than before.

Springing to her feet and rushing to the window, she looked out to see Gigi standing below, hurling pebbles.

"What are you doing?" Chloe called in a panicked tone that was somewhere between a whisper and a shriek, pushing the window open. "Get in here!"

Gigi climbed the trellis and, with a hand from Chloe, hoisted herself through the window.

"Where the hell have you been?" Chloe chided as Gigi smoothed her clothes and plucked leaves from her hair. "I was just about to go to Mother Superior and have her send the police out looking for you."

"I got to meet Justin!" Gigi cooed, plunging on her bed and ignoring Chloe's concern. "I waited around 'til he signed autographs for all the other fans, then I went up and introduced myself and congratulated him on that winning play. He not only signed my poster and my ticket, he invited me to come to the team's after-party at Byrne's Tavern."

"Are you crazy? You went to some pub with a bunch of drunken footballers? How'd you even get into that pub?"

"I have my fake ID on me at all times," Gigi said nonchalantly. "Besides, I was with Justin. He's twenty-one, and he got me in with no problem. The team goes there after every home game, and the bar staff never cards the players' guests."

"Is that beer I smell on you?" Chloe said, knowing she sounded like a harassing parent.

Gigi grinned. "Justin bought a round of Guinness to celebrate."

"Staying out until all hours, coming in smelling like alcohol. Do you know what could have happened if Mother Superior had caught you? You could've been expelled." Chloe paused and took a breath in an attempt to quell her mounting anger. "You couldn't have called? I was so worried I couldn't even concentrate on studying."

"Chill out. Everything's cool," Gigi said, changing into her pajamas. "I made it back all right."

"Yeah, but only because I helped you sneak in the window like some kind of cat burglar," Chloe said, shutting the window and drawing the curtains.

"It was totally worth it. We both got something out of it: You got to see Sergio perform," Gigi said, throwing a pillow at Chloe, "and I got to meet Justin. He gave me his number and told me to call him to hang out after practice some time."

"Oh, god, Gigi, not again," Chloe said, flopping on her bed. "I thought you were through chasing after celebrities when you had your little fling with Montana last summer."

"Montana's ancient history. Justin's the one for me now." Gigi stood on her bed and planted a kiss on the star player's poster.

"At least Montana was a nice guy. Justin seems like he has a bad temper." Chloe pulled back the covers and began getting ready for bed. "It was really scary when he fouled that other player and got up in the ref's face. If he gets that bent out of shape when a crowd of people are watching, I wonder what he's like in real life when something pisses him off."

Gigi hugged her pillow like a lover. "He's a real sweetheart. He just takes his work really seriously."

"Yeah, maybe," Chloe said, getting up to turn off the desk lamp, "but be careful. If the way he acted in the game is any indication, he's got issues."

36

Chloe sat in Sister Maureen's drama class, riveted as the young teacher read a passage from *Othello*. Her English accent gave the perfect treatment to Shakespeare's words, her inflection rising and falling at just the right moments like a trained stage actress.

"Okay, that's enough of me." Sister Maureen closed her book and sat on the edge of her desk. "Who'll volunteer to read Desdemona's soliloquy?" She looked at Chloe. "How about you, dear?"

Chloe looked around at her classmates to see if anyone else had raised their hands. "Me? I'd rather just follow along while someone else reads."

Chloe sank down in her seat. As much as she loved Sister Maureen's class, she still got shy getting up in front of people. She knew she would have to get over her reticence if she were to become an actress someday, but she figured she had plenty of time to build her confidence when she was older.

"Come on up here," Sister Maureen urged. "That's what you get for sitting in the front row."

Hesitantly, Chloe got up and stood in front of Sister Maureen's desk, facing her classmates. She scanned the girls' faces, certain they were sneering at her and judging her and silently willing her to stumble over her words. She wished Gigi were here for moral support, but fifth period was when Gigi took her elective – art appreciation, of course.

Chloe looked down at her book, the pages shaking in her hands. Why did she get so nervous? After all, wasn't it her goal to "perform" for a captive audience?

"Whenever you're ready, dear," Sister Maureen said.

Chloe glanced back at the teacher.

"Go ahead, let 'er rip," Sister Maureen added jovially. "You have nothing to worry about. If you mess up, we'll just make you scrub Mother Superior's toilet with your toothbrush, that's all. No pressure."

The class laughed at Sister Maureen's joke, and Chloe relaxed a bit. She smiled at the teacher, who had a way of putting her students at ease with her easygoing manner and surprisingly irreverent sense of humor.

Chloe looked down at her book again and began reading. It was not long before she got lost in Shakespeare's words and allowed the poetry to transport her to another time and place. She forgot that she was standing before her classmates and became the character of Desdemona.

When the bell rang, Chloe closed her book, concluding her "performance." Her classmates applauded and she curtsied, fanning out her uniform skirt like an opera diva's petticoats.

Sister Maureen patted Chloe on the back. "Very good, I must say. That wasn't so hard, was it?"

"It was fun, thanks," Chloe said, returning to her desk and gathering her books. She tossed a hurried "see you tomorrow" at the teacher and began to file out of the room with the rest of the girls, but Sister Maureen stopped her.

"I need to speak with you a moment, dear, before you rush off to your next class," the teacher said. "It'll only take a second."

Chloe hovered next to Sister Maureen's desk, wondering if she had done something wrong. The teacher reached into a drawer and handed Chloe a book.

"*Les Miserables*?" Chloe said, reading the title on the cover. "Did you want me to read this for English lit'? I read this before, actually, when I was in ninth grade at the Lycée Américain back in Paris."

"Why don't you skim through it again? A little brush-up on Victor Hugo never hurt anyone," Sister Maureen said, going to the chalkboard.

"Do you want me to turn in a book report for extra credit or something?" Chloe turned the book over in her hands, glancing over the synopsis on the back cover.

"No, nothing that formal. I just want you to familiarize yourself with the character Cosette. I'm in charge of the school's spring production this year and I was able to get the rights to *Les Miz*. I think you should try out."

"For Cosette?" Chloe said, a tinge of panic causing her voice to tremble. "But that's the female lead."

"I know," Sister Maureen said matter-of-factly, her back to Chloe as she wrote notes for the next class in her neat script.

Chloe grappled for an excuse to avoid the audition. Our Lady of Chastity's plays were joint productions with St. Thomas, which supplied boys for the male roles. The prospect of failing in front of a coed audience filled her with dread.

"But, but…" Chloe stammered. "But I can't sing."

"You can carry a tune," Sister Maureen said, continuing to write on the board with her back turned and sounding unconcerned. "I've heard you humming around the library and singing to yourself when you help me out before class. You're no Mariah Carey, but you have a decent enough voice for a high school play."

"But I've never acted before, not really. Every time I auditioned for a speaking role when I was at the Lycée, I always got buried in the chorus." Chloe swallowed, her mouth suddenly dry. "I get really nervous in auditions."

Sister Maureen set the chalk down, dusted her palms and turned to face Chloe. "My dear, all you're doing is coming up with excuses, and if there's anything I have in common with Mother Superior, it's that I never tolerate excuses. Now I want you to take that book back to your dorm, memorize a scene and recite your lines at the audition next week. It's quite simple, nothing to be afraid of."

"I'm just not sure…" Chloe shuffled her books in her arms and looked down at her feet. "I'm just not sure if I can do it."

Sister Maureen placed her hand on Chloe's shoulder. "Watching you read today, I could see you have real potential. And you ask more questions than anyone in class, so it's obvious you have a natural interest in drama. Out of all the girls in this school, if anyone could play Cosette, it's you. You're French, after all."

Before Chloe could protest further, the bell rang again, announcing the start of the next class period.

"You better skedaddle. I don't want Mother Superior coming down on you for being late to your next class," Sister Maureen said, opening another drawer and taking out a pad. She wrote out a tardy excuse and handed it over.

"Thanks, Sister Maureen," Chloe said, clutching her books as she backed out of the room.

"Remember what I said." Sister Maureen wagged her finger at Chloe, as if reinforcing a set of instructions. "No one's going to buy you as Cosette, or any other character for that matter, until you start believing in yourself."

"He's cute," Gigi said to Chloe as they sat in the second row of Our Lady of Chastity's auditorium watching a boy from St. Thomas ascend the steps leading to the stage for the *Les Miserables* auditions.

Chloe shoved Gigi's shoulder. "Can't you keep your hormones in check for five minutes? You're here to support me, not flirt."

"Oh, come on, I've got to have *some* fun. And you will, too, if you stop being so uptight."

"That's easy for you to say," Chloe sighed, opening the book Sister Maureen had given her and going over her lines yet again. She hadn't gotten a wink of sleep last night, staying up reciting her lines in the mirror ad nauseum.

Chloe tuned out Gigi, who batted her eyes at the St. Thomas boys who'd shown up for the audition. When Chloe heard Sister Maureen announce it was her turn to take the stage, she froze.

"Chloe, you're up," Sister Maureen repeated from her seat in the front row, setting aside her notepad and turning around to look at Chloe.

Gigi elbowed Chloe. "Go on, you can do it."

Realizing all eyes were on her, Chloe put down her book, stood and smoothed her skirt.

"Just remember, if you get nervous, just imagine all these boys in their jockey shorts," Gigi whispered.

Chloe ignored Gigi, convinced that the image of half-naked teenage boys would only make her more nervous. Climbing the steps to the stage, Chloe felt as though she were being led to the guillotine.

After what seemed like eons, she finally reached center stage. She stood there, looking out over the footlights at the students scattered throughout the auditorium.

"Any time you're ready, dear," Sister Maureen prodded, picking up her notepad.

Chloe stared out at her classmates, who seemed to be staring back with hostile expressions that said, "Hurr`y up and get on with it." She swallowed, trying to moisten her parched throat. She opened her mouth, but the words wouldn't come. Her throat tightened, rendering it impossible for her to recite the lines she had so painstakingly memorized.

"Chloe, honey, are you all right?"

Chloe blinked, looking down at the young teacher, who was sitting forward in her seat, clutching her notepad with a look of concern. Chloe's eyes drifted to Gigi, who was sitting behind Sister Maureen, smiling like she had every confidence in the world that Chloe could ace this audition.

"Chloe, do you want to go through with the audition or not, dear? There are other students waiting for their turn," Sister Maureen said in a patient yet firm tone.

Chloe scanned the crowd and, instead of taking Gigi's suggestion and imagining the boys in their underwear, came up with her own technique. She envisioned her peers not as the children of the elite who could afford to send their offspring to exclusive boarding schools, but as paupers from Victor Hugo's classic tale of woe, begging on the streets in dirt-smudged rags.

She cleared her throat and nodded at Sister Maureen. "I'm ready."

She began speaking, her voice cracking a bit at first, but as she continued to set the scene in her mind, Hugo's words came out as though they were her own.

When Chloe had finished, Sister Maureen jotted notes. "Thank you, Chloe, you may sit down now," she said without looking up.

Chloe came down from the stage and sat next to Gigi. "She didn't say anything," she whispered to Gigi, examining the back of Sister Maureen's head, as if it held the answer to whether she'd gotten the part or not. "I wonder what that means?"

"Don't worry," Gigi said, "you did great. That part is yours."

Chloe sat back in her seat and looked up at the empty stage. Gazing at the lights, she longed to be up there again.

"And remember," Sister Maureen said as the bell rang, announcing the end of drama class, "we're going to be discussing *A Streetcar Named Desire* on Monday, so you'd best read the play over the weekend."

Instead of groaning over the assignment like her classmates, Chloe eagerly slid the textbook with the Tennessee Williams play in her bookbag. She couldn't wait to read the play that was set in New Orleans and learn more about her family's city of origin.

"Chloe, before you go, stop by my desk," Sister Maureen said while the students filed out. "I want to discuss something with you."

Chloe waited until the room was empty, figuring Sister Maureen had bad news to deliver about the *Les Miz* audition. If Chloe had won the part of Cosette, she reasoned, Sister Maureen would have cheerfully informed her when she arrived for class instead of waiting until the end when no one was around.

"Yes?" Chloe said. "Have I done something wrong?"

"No, my dear, quite the contrary," Sister Maureen said, writing in her lesson planner. "I just wanted to let you know you're excused from the weekend assignment."

Chloe furrowed her brow, confused at why Sister Maureen was letting her slack off. "You mean I don't have to read *A Streetcar Named Desire*?"

"No, not unless you want to," Sister Maureen replied simply, not looking up as she wrote and revealing nothing about the reason for the special dispensation.

"Well," Chloe ventured slowly, still baffled, "I was kind of looking forward to reading it, since it's set in New Orleans, and that's where my mother's side of the family is from."

Sister Maureen closed her lesson planner. "If you want to learn about New Orleans or any other place, it's best to visit and experience it firsthand. Besides, your time will be better spent this weekend learning your lines for *Les Miz*." She reached into a desk drawer and handed Chloe a script.

"Does this mean…" Chloe trailed off, flipping through the script with shaky hands. "Does this mean I got the part?"

Sister Maureen smiled. "Most certainly."

Chloe suppressed the urge to scream. She couldn't believe she actually got it, her first real part.

"Thank you, Sister Maureen," she said, her voice quivering with excitement. "Thank you so much! I won't let you down."

"I know you won't, dear. I have faith in you; that's why I cast you." The teacher held out her hands in a shooing gesture. "Now, off you go to your next class. I'm fresh out of tardy excuses."

Chloe thanked Sister Maureen again and tucked the script in her bookbag. She was still beaming when she reached the hallway, where Gigi was waiting to walk to their next class together.

"Are you going to keep me in suspense?" Gigi asked, poking Chloe in the arm "Did you get the part or what?"

Chloe erased the smile from her face, wanting to keep Gigi guessing and draw out for as long as possible the delicious experience of announcing the good news. "Let's put it this way, you know that new exhibit you wanted to see at the National Portrait Gallery this weekend?"

"Yeah?"

"Sorry, but I won't be able to go. I'm going to be busy learning my lines."

"You got it! Oh my god! Why didn't you tell me?! I knew you could do it!"

Chloe joined Gigi in squealing their delight, drawing one of Mother Superior's withering glances as they passed the headmistress in the hallway.

37

Backstage on opening night of *Les Miz* reminded Chloe of her first runway assignment in Paris, with a swarm of girls running around frantically trying to squeeze into their period costumes. The dressing room was just as chaotic as that of a fashion show, with the added distraction of the boys in the cast trying to sneak peeks at their half-dressed co-stars.

Chloe sat in front of a mirror, applying stage makeup while her friend Anastasia, who had been cast as an extra, fought off an advance from at St. Thomas boy.

"Get out of here, Trevor, and go back to the boys' dressing room right now, or I'm going to tell Sister Maureen you were trying to look at my boobs!" Anastasia bellowed, hitting the offending boy over the head with a hairbrush and shoving him out the dressing room door.

"What's going on here?" Sister Maureen said, entering the dressing room.

"The boys keep sneaking over here to peep us in our knickers," Anastasia reported in her funny-sounding accent.

"I'll keep an eye on them. You finish getting dressed," Sister Maureen said, giving Anastasia a push in the direction of the wardrobe rack.

"Sorry to interrupt, Sister," a short girl in pigtails and overalls said, entering the room and gingerly approaching the teacher, "but one of the stagehands just dropped a sandbag on Tom."

"Oh, no! Is he all right?" Sister Maureen said, putting her hand on the girl's shoulder.

The girl nodded. "I think so, but he says he's seeing spots and he doesn't think he can go on."

Sister Maureen sighed heavily. "I can't believe I'm going to have to replace my lead actor on opening night. Now I have to go track down his understudy. For the love of Saint Pete, if it's not one thing, it's another." She turned to face the other girls and loudly clapped her hands together. "Girls, I want you all in costume. Fifteen minutes to curtain."

Before leaving the room, the teacher crouched next to Chloe and asked, "How are you doing, dear?"

"Okay, I guess, but I've got jitters," Chloe said, setting down the eyeliner pencil and shaking her ice-cold hands to bring back feeling.

"That's perfectly normal on opening night. Don't let your nerves get the best of you. I need you more than ever now that I'm going to have to replace Tom with his understudy."

"Don't worry, Sister Maureen. I won't let you down."

"That's my girl," the teacher said, patting Chloe's back. "I knew I could count on you."

Chloe ruminated on Sister Maureen's words and tried to tune out the chaos surrounding her in the dressing room while she finished applying her makeup, focusing on going over her lines. As strong as her passion was for acting, she had an overwhelming urge to run away. What if she forgot her lines? What if her voice gave out and she couldn't sing? What if she fell flat on her face walking across the stage or a piece of scenery came loose and knocked her out, like the unfortunate mishap that befell the boy playing Jean Valjean, the main character?

She was still sitting in front of the mirror, nearly paralyzed by all the hypothetical disasters that kept playing themselves out in her head, when the dressing room had emptied out and all the other girls had taken their cues.

"Chloe, Sister Maureen told me to tell you need to take your place," the girl in the overalls said, peeking her head in the dressing room again. "Five minutes to curtain."

"Okay, thanks."

Chloe took a deep breath and stared again at her reflection. When there was another knock at the door, she turned around and smiled at the sight of Mother, Simone and Gigi entering.

"I brought them back so they could wish you good luck before you go on," Gigi said, leading their mothers into the room.

"I'm so glad you could make it!" Chloe rose and threw her arms around the women, never so glad to see her mother and godmother. "Thanks for coming."

"Are you kidding? There was no way we'd miss your big stage debut," Simone said, holding Chloe at arm's length and checking out the costume that had transformed Chloe into a pre-revolutionary waif.

"Marie sends her love," Maxine reported. "She wanted to come, but you know how she hates flying. She gets so anxious."

"I know how she feels," Chloe moaned, shaking her still-clammy hands. "I figured I'd have opening-night jitters, but I'm terrified."

"I know you're going to do great, *ma chérie*. We'll be in the front row cheering you on," Maxine said, wiping a dirt smudge from Chloe's cheek.

"Thanks, Mother, but that smudge you just wiped off was part of my costume."

"Can't stop being a busybody for five seconds, can you?" Simone scolded, taking Maxine's arm. "Come on, let's get out of here and let the kid finish getting ready in peace."

"Break a leg, Chlo'," Gigi called, ushering the women to the door.

"I know that means good luck, but you probably shouldn't say that, the way things have been going so far," Chloe said with a laugh, returning to her seat in front of the mirror to touch up her makeup. In the reflection, she noticed Mother lingering in the doorway.

"I just wanted to say that I know acting's something you've wanted to try for a long time," Maxine said, "and no matter how the show turns out, I'm proud of you."

Chloe dabbed at her eyes with a cotton swab, welling up with emotion at Maxine's words. "Thanks, Mother, that means a lot."

Maxine sniffled, her own eyes misting. "You know, looking at you sitting there putting on your stage makeup, it reminds me of the first time I danced at the Moulin Rouge when I came to Paris. I wasn't much older than you," she said, her voice cracking. She stared wistfully at Chloe, as if her daughter were the living embodiment of her younger self. After a moment, she added, "I'll leave you alone now. Go out there and knock 'em dead, sweetheart."

After Maxine left the room, Chloe looked at herself in the mirror.

"Chloe, we need you to get in place right now," the girl in the overalls said, reappearing in doorway. "The curtain's about to go up."

"Okay, I'll be right there."

Chloe took one last look at herself, then rose to take her place. She strode to the stage with a new sense of confidence, emboldened by her mother's stamp of approval.

When the curtains parted and the applause died, Chloe hesitated.

"Go on, dear, it's your cue," Sister Maureen whispered, standing beside Chloe in the wings.

Come on, we've rehearsed this a dozen times, Chloe told herself. *Just step out there and do it.*

Inhaling and crossing herself, Chloe took a step and mechanically walked centerstage, as if in a trance. She turned and stared out over the audience, temporarily blinded by the footlights.

The band students played the cue for Chloe to begin singing her part, then played the section again when she continued to stand silently in the middle of the stage. Although surrounded by dozens of students who'd been cast as extras, she felt all alone in the spotlight – a sensation that terrified her.

This can't be happening, Chloe thought. She was seized by the paralysis she'd initially felt during the audition.

Chester, the lead actor's understudy, whispered Chloe's opening line under his breath, but she just looked at him blankly, unable to find her voice. Her eyes glided over the faces of the audience, who leaned into each other and whispered while looking at her like she was an escapee from an asylum who had crashed the show.

Just as she was about to give into the urge to run offstage and out of the auditorium, she caught sight of Simone, Gigi and Maxine huddled in the front row. Seeing the three most important people in her life reminded her that they would be there for her whether she stole the show or bombed.

"I love you," Maxine mouthed.

Heartened by Mother's presence and remembering that Jacques was watching over her from above, Chloe finally opened her mouth and the most miraculous thing happened: sound came out. She sang, softly at first, but as she heard her own voice and realized she was actually on key, she sang louder, getting into character. She glanced offstage, just long enough to see relief washing over Sister Maureen's face, then began following the stage directions the teacher had choreographed.

Just as in her audition, Chloe visualized herself in the play's setting. The painted backdrops morphed into the Paris streets she knew so well and she was swept away to nineteenth-century France, resolving to take the audience with her.

Something strange and wonderful seemed to overtake her. For two magical hours, she escaped from the everyday monotony of tests and homework and dorm life and inhabited the spirit of a waif who was beaten and exploited by her cruel caretaker, but had something to say, something to teach the world.

When the curtain closed for the final time and she returned with the rest of the cast to take their bows, she looked out over the audience again and saw Maxine, Simone and Gigi hopping to their feet to lead a standing ovation. One of the stagehands from St. Thomas presented Sister Maureen with a bouquet of roses and another student handed Chloe an identical batch.

"That's my girl!" Gigi yelped, whistling and hooting louder than when she was cheering on her favorite footballer at the soccer game.

Chloe beamed and blew kisses at her and Simone and Maxine. At Sister Maureen's direction, Chloe took one last bow with her castmates. While the other students filed offstage, she lingered for a moment in the spotlight, drinking in the last strains of applause. She knew exactly what she wanted to do with the rest of her life.

Chloe mingled with castmates and their parents at the opening-night cast party in Our Lady of Chastity's gym, which was decorated with balloons and streamers and a large banner that read "Congratulations, Mizzies!"

"I'm so proud of you, *ma chérie!*" Maxine said, planting a smooch on Chloe's cheek.

"You were the star of the show, baby. You certainly earned these," Simone said, sniffing the roses Chloe was still cradling.

"You were awesome," Gigi said. "You rocked."

"You did such a great job, dear," Sister Maureen added, approaching Chloe's group. "I have to admit I was a bit concerned when you first came onstage and seemed to choke up, but you pulled it together and performed beautifully." Patting Chloe's back, she added, "Just like I knew you would."

"Thanks, Sister Maureen," Chloe said, hugging her. "By the way, let me introduce you."

"I'm sure you're quite proud of your daughter, Mrs. Chevalier," Sister Maureen said, shaking Maxine's hand.

"You bet," Maxine said, putting her arm around Chloe. "I think it's great that she has such a productive hobby to keep her busy when she's not studying."

Chloe glanced at Sister Maureen and took note of the confused expression that registered on the young teacher's face.

"I think Chloe's interest in acting is more than a hobby," Sister Maureen said after a moment. "I have several students who talk about wanting to be actresses, but I think Chloe is one of the few who could actually do it professionally. She has a level of talent that's really something special, and I think you saw that tonight."

"Yes, she did very well tonight, and I'm proud of her," Maxine reiterated in that tone that Chloe recognized from when her mother was determined to have the last word, "but she's going to be starting college in the fall. She won't have much time to act with her course load."

"She could major in drama, of course."

Maxine laughed, as if the teacher had suggested Chloe major in underwater basket-weaving. "Maybe drama could be a minor, but I want her to major in something practical so she'll never have to rely on a man. I never got to go to college, and I want Chloe to have all the opportunities I never had."

Chloe flashed Maxine a dirty look. She hated it when her mother spoke about her like she wasn't in the room. She would be eighteen in a few months, but Mother still insisted on treating her like a child.

"Yes, well I certainly think you have noble goals for your daughter," Sister Maureen said after a thoughtful pause, as if realizing that debating a parent about her daughter's future was pointless.

Chloe had seen the teacher respectfully retreat like this before, when acquiescing to some unreasonable edict from Mother Superior.

"Sister Maureen, the cast wants you to say something," said Chester, the boy who had stepped into the lead role at the last minute, approaching the women.

"Okay," the teacher said with a look that conveyed relief at having an excuse to exit from the conversation with Chloe's opinionated mother, "and by the way, good job pinch-hitting tonight. You really came through for us."

The boy grinned and led his co-stars in chanting "Speech! Speech!" while raising their Styrofoam cups in the direction of the young teacher who had skillfully directed them to opening-night success.

"It seems my work is never done," Sister Maureen said, offering her hand to Maxine and Simone. "It was a pleasure meeting you both. Will you excuse me?"

"No problem. You better say something to these kids before they start rioting," Maxine said with a laugh, lifting the tension.

"You have a very talented and special daughter, Mrs. Chevalier," Sister Maureen added, clasping her hands and pointing her forefingers at Chloe. "I hope you'll support her in whatever she decides to do."

Maxine tightened her grip around Chloe's shoulder, pulling her in closer. "Of course I will."

38

"I still can't believe how awesome you were in *Les Miz*," Gigi said to Chloe as they walked across campus to their next class. "That was the best performance I've ever seen, better than Justin scoring that winning goal in the soccer game."

Chloe eyed Gigi skeptically. "Cut the crap, Gi'. Just tell me what you want."

"Can't a girl compliment her best friend on her big stage debut without having an ulterior motive?"

Gigi affected an innocent look, but Chloe detected she was up to something again. "Out with it."

Gigi paused beneath a statue of Saint Ursula, the patron saint of schoolgirls, her devious grin contrasting with the statue's serene expression. "Kensington United is playing Manchester Saturday night and I need you to cover for me if the game runs into overtime and I can't make it back by curfew."

"No, Gi', I'm not going through that again," Chloe said, walking away. "You know we have an early Mass for Palm Sunday before we go home for Easter break, and Mother Superior is going to be extra vigilant Saturday evening in making sure everyone's in on time for lights out."

"If she checks our room, you could just say I'm down the hall in the bathroom."

"I can't lie to Mother Superior. It's like she has a truth detector straight from God or something."

Gigi put her hand on Chloe's shoulder. "Chloe, please, just this once. I swear I won't ask you to cover for me again. It's just that if I don't see Justin this weekend before we go home for vacation, who knows when I'll see him again. He has a bunch of away games after this, and I probably won't get to see him much before the end of the school year."

Chloe hesitated, trying not to let herself be swayed by Gigi's sad brown eyes. "Okay," she said when the bell rang, knowing she didn't have time to debate Gigi if she was going to make it to class on time. "I'll cover for you this time, but this better be it until graduation."

"Thanks, Chlo'," Gigi called as she scooted off to her class, sad eyes replaced by a broad smile. "I owe you big time."

Before reporting to class, Chloe looked up at Saint Ursula and offered up a silent prayer.

Chloe closed her trigonometry book, turned off the desk lamp and rubbed her tired eyes. She glanced at the clock, which read quarter 'til ten.

"Come on, Gi', you still have time to make it back before curfew," Chloe said, going to the window and peeking through the curtains at the moonlit campus, but there was no sign of Gigi.

At the sound of a knock at the door, Chloe started.

"Open this door." There was no mistaking Mother Superior's gruff voice.

"Oh *shit!*" Chloe whispered, then reflexively covered her mouth to chastise herself for swearing with the head nun close by. She rushed to Gigi's empty bed, pulled back the spread and rumpled the sheets.

"Miss Bareaux? Miss Cartier?" Mother Superior called again from the other side of the door, turning the knob. "You know you're not to lock the door until I've completed my rounds. Open this door at once."

"Uh, just a minute," Chloe called, pounding her fist into a pillow to make it look as though Gigi's head had been resting there.

"Open the door *now*, young lady." Mother Superior's knocking was insistent.

Chloe heard the jangling of keys and dashed to the door, opening it just as Mother Superior was about to put her master key in the lock.

The headmistress, in her flannel robe and kerchief, appeared slightly less intimidating than in her severe black habit. "What took you so long?" she said, peering past Chloe into the room, as if looking for contraband.

Chloe leaned on the doorframe, trying to block Mother Superior's view. "I was just studying and didn't want to lose my place."

Mother Superior glared at Chloe with her piercing, gray-blue eyes, as if she found the explanation circumspect, and pushed past her into the room. "Where's Miss Cartier?" she said, surveying Gigi's empty bed.

Chloe paused, momentarily blinded by the overhead light glinting off the gold crucifix around Mother Superior's neck. Chloe's eyes darted around the room, trying to ignore the religious symbol and muster the strength to lie to the headmistress.

"She's, uh... She's in the bathroom."

"No she's not," Mother Superior shot back. "I just checked the lavatory and no one's in there."

Chloe swallowed hard. Trying to outwit Mother Superior was like jumping in the boxing ring with the heavyweight champion of the world.

"Oh, really?" Chloe said, stalling. "Maybe she got hungry and went down to the kitchen to get a bedtime snack."

Chloe's latest explanation didn't seem to mollify the headmistress, who proceeded to run her hand over Gigi's rumpled sheets like an astute detective examining a crime scene.

"These sheets are cool." Mother Superior directed a scrutinizing gaze at her pupil, like a cop interrogating a reluctant witness.

Chloe remained silent, her muscles tensing and sweat beginning to bead on her forehead. Maybe if she just kept quiet and played dumb, Mother Superior would lose interest and move on to the next room.

"If Miss Cartier had been in bed like she's supposed to be, the sheets would be warm," Mother Superior stated with the expertise of a school administrator who had decades of experience in tracking the misdeeds of disobedient charges.

"Uh..." Chloe's mouth gaped open while she grappled for another explanation. Her stuttering was interrupted by the sound of an object pinging against the window. She groaned inwardly, figuring it was Gigi trying to get Chloe's attention and help her climb in the window, since curfew had now officially past.

"What was that?" Mother Superior, despite the strands of gray that peeked from underneath her kerchief, spun toward the window with the agility of a cheetah.

"What?" Chloe said, hoping that if she didn't confirm she'd heard the noise, too, Mother Superior would shrug it off.

"That sound."

"What sound?"

"Shhh." Mother Superior held her finger to her lips in the reprimanding gesture Chloe had grown accustomed to. "I just heard it again."

Sure enough, the sound of something hitting the window was louder this time. There was no way Chloe could get away with acting like she hadn't heard it.

"Oh, that?" Chloe said, inching toward the window, trying to beat Mother Superior there. "That's probably just this frisky squirrel that tries to get in our window at night. I'll go shoo him away."

Chloe dashed to the window, pulled back the curtains and saw Gigi standing below, pebble in hand. With her back to Mother Superior, Chloe quickly raised her hand and slid it across her throat, giving Gigi the "cease" signal. But Chloe was too late and the sound of the pebble thudding against the window reverberated throughout the room.

"That's no squirrel," Mother Superior said, approaching the window and shouldering Chloe out of the way. "What's going on here?"

Chloe stepped aside and squeezed her eyes shut, a reflexive attempt to avoid the agony of witnessing Gigi getting caught in the act of violating curfew. Mother Superior's intolerance for rule-breakers was the stuff of campus legend, not unlike the wrath of the vengeful, "eye for an eye" God of the Old Testament.

"Miss Cartier, get inside this instant," the headmistress said, throwing open the window with a force reminiscent of Moses parting the Red Sea, her crucifix gleaming in the moonlight like Gabriel's sword. "You know you were supposed to be in bed by ten for early Mass in the morning. This behavior is unacceptable."

Mother Superior slammed the window shut and barreled to the door. "Get dressed and meet me down in the commons area, where I will dispense swift punishment to you and Miss Cartier. I'm very disappointed in you, Miss Bareaux, for aiding Miss Cartier in her devilment."

When Mother Superior exited, Chloe peered out the window and mouthed "sorry" to Gigi, who stood with her arms wrapped around herself in her skimpy outfit, shivering in the dark.

"Screw this. I'm not cleaning one more goddamn thing." Gigi tossed a sponge into a bucket and kicked it down the aisle of the campus cathedral, where she and Chloe were performing their "act of contrition." Mother Superior had punished the girls by forcing them to stay up and wipe down the pews and get the church ready for early Mass.

Chloe looked up from her position on a kneeler in the next pew, where she was dusting off hymnals. "I know you're frustrated, Gi'," she said, pushing a wisp of hair out of her eyes with the back of her hand.

"It's so unfair. I was only a few minutes past curfew." Gigi leaned against a pew, folding her arms and pouting. "This sucks."

Chloe finished dusting the book she was holding and gently returned it to the holder on the back of the pew, not responding to Gigi's comment. Considering the headmistress's reputation for harsh discipline, Chloe thought the punishment was actually pretty lenient.

"Let's just get this over with," Chloe said finally. "We only have two more rows. Why don't you take this side and I'll do the last two pews on the other side?" She doused a rag with furniture polish and handed it to Gigi.

Gigi began furiously scrubbing a pew like she was trying to strip the wood, griping all the while. "If this bullshit cleaning assignment wasn't enough, what sucks even more is that Mother Superior isn't going to let me go home for Easter break."

Chloe stopped cleaning and glanced over at Gigi, startled by her announcement. "What? When did she say that?"

"She'd already sent you off to get started here, but she held me back to lecture me some more. She thinks she's going to break me, but I'll show her." Gigi threw her rag on the pew's seat, as if to illustrate her defiance.

"Wow, that really does suck. Mother promised me we'd all fly down to St.-Tropez to visit *Maman* Chevalier, and I was hoping we'd get to hang out at the beach."

"Forget it. I'll be trapped here all week," Gigi sighed, picking up her rag and violently rubbing it against the pew, as if taking out her frustration. "I swear to God, I hate this place. I can't wait to get out of here."

Chloe pulled down the kneeler and began wiping down the leather kneepad. "I know this really blows, but hang in there," she said, crouching to attack a hard-to-reach spot with her rag. "We only have a couple more months 'til graduation."

"I'm not going to graduate on time."

Chloe put down her rag, stood and faced Gigi. "What are you talking about? Did Mother Superior tell you that?"

Gigi shook her head, not looking at Chloe. "She didn't have to. I failed math and science again last semester. I won't have time to take them over before June."

Chloe approached Gigi, who was still scrubbing the pew, her back turned.

"Gosh, I didn't realize, Gi'. I got so caught up in doing the play that I didn't know you'd fallen that far behind."

"It doesn't matter, anyway. I might as well drop out. That way, I won't have to sneak out to be with Justin." Gigi stopped scrubbing and finally faced Chloe, her angry expression turning to a smile. "When I saw him at the game last night, he asked me to join him on the road for his away games. He said he likes having me around, like a good luck charm."

Chloe could see the same fascination that had danced in Gigi's eyes when she'd talked Chloe into running off to Monaco to be with Montana Blake, and Chloe knew she needed to stop Gigi before she got carried away again.

"I know you really like this guy, Gi', but you can't just drop out. What about your dreams of being an artist? What about getting into the Sorbonne?"

Gigi's expression turned somber again. "A rejection letter came in the mail last week. I didn't get in."

Chloe wrapped her arm around Gigi and pulled her into a hug. "I'm so sorry, Gi'. Why didn't you tell me?"

"I was too depressed to bring it up. I knew my grades weren't good enough, but I was holding onto to some sliver of hope that they'd be so impressed with the portfolio I submitted that they'd let me in." Gigi slouched against the pew. "Who was I kidding? School just isn't for me, so I might as well drop out now and get it over with."

Chloe stared sympathetically at Gigi, not knowing what to say. "Things aren't going as planned, I know," she said after a moment, "but you know what we need? A plan."

Gigi looked confused. "What do you mean?"

"Remember when we were kids and we wanted to do something that our mothers wouldn't let us do? Like that time when we were in eighth grade and we wanted to go to Euro Disney on the class trip, but our mothers said no because I didn't turn in my science fair project on time and you were flunking math, just like you are now?"

Gigi rolled her eyes. "Thanks for reminding me."

"Don't you remember what we did? We made a plan and stuck to it so we'd get to go to Euro Disney. I tutored you in algebra, so you passed the final, and you helped me with my science fair project."

Gigi laughed, her mood seeming to lift momentarily. "God, I still remember staying up all night painting those Styrofoam balls we made look like planets. That was worse than polishing these damn pews."

"I brought that up just so you'll remember that we've been through tough times before and we got through it." Chloe squeezed Gigi's shoulder and added, "Together."

Gigi pulled away and began scrubbing again. "We were kids then. Even if you tutor me in algebra and chemistry, I'm still not going to graduate on time."

"Like I said, what we need is a plan." Chloe picked up her rag and helped Gigi finish up the pew she was working on. "Why don't you make up the two classes you failed in summer school here, and then you can come back home, get a part-time job and save some money for a couple of months, and start at the University of Paris in winter semester. You can get your required classes out of the way, keep working on your portfolio and reapply to the Sorbonne."

Gigi stopped scrubbing and looked at Chloe skeptically. "I don't know if I can stand being here over the summer. It's bad enough I'll be stuck here over Easter break."

"The time'll fly by, you'll see. Maybe it was a blessing in disguise that you didn't get into the Sorbonne right away. Just think how much fun we'll have going to college together. We can share a dorm, or even get our own apartment." Chloe put down her rag and touched Gigi's hand, excited about the prospects for the future. "It'll be so much different than rooming together here – no more sneaking in past curfew. We'll be able to come and go as we please. We'll both be eighteen by then, legal adults. We'll be free."

Gigi stared at the floor, as if considering Chloe's proposal.

"Come on, Gi', this plan will give us both something to look forward to over the summer. Do we have a deal or not?" Chloe held up her pinky, enticing Gigi to lock fingers, the way they always did to seal a pact.

After a moment, Gigi held up her pinky and interlocked it with Chloe's, a smile slowly spreading across her face. "Deal."

The girls' moment of joy was quickly squelched when Mother Superior appeared, seeming to materialize out of the shadows and looking like the Angel of Death in her stark black habit.

"Mass will be starting in one hour. I don't remember granting permission to take a break, ladies," the headmistress said in her austere tone, hands clutched behind her back. "Finish up while I inspect your work."

Chloe and Gigi hurriedly broke apart and began scrubbing the pew again. The clapping of the headmistress' black leather boots against the marble floor echoed throughout the cathedral as she made her way down the center aisle, examining each pew for the smallest speck of dust. While Mother Superior's back was turned, Gigi made a sneering face, prompting Chloe to cover her mouth to keep from giggling.

"I saw that, Miss Cartier," the headmistress said, her voice booming as if delivering a message from On High. "You'd do yourself a favor if you took this task seriously. The whole purpose is to make you think about your actions." Mother Superior paused in front of Gigi, her normally grave expression softening. "You're a smart girl with a God-given gift for art. If you spent as much time developing your talent and studying as you did chasing boys, you'd be graduating with the rest of the class."

Chloe stopped, surprised at Mother Superior showing the slightest hint of compassion, even if it was cloaked in criticism. She glanced at Gigi, whose expression remained defiant.

39

"And remember to review Shakespeaere's sonnets for the final tomorrow," Sister Maureen said just before the bell rang at the end of the next-to-last English lit' class for Chloe and the other seniors. "It's been a great year. Let's end it on a high note tomorrow."

While the other girls gathered their books and gabbed excitedly about graduation, Chloe slowly approached Sister Maureen's desk. She promised herself not to get too emotional in thanking the teacher who had given her her first acting opportunity and provided invaluable guidance and support.

"Sister Maureen, I just wanted to say thanks for everything."

"Thank *you*, dear," Sister Maureen said, smiling. "It always gives me great joy to see a student blossoming and realizing her potential. And you've certainly done that this year."

"I owe it all to you. I can't thank you enough for giving me the part in *Les Miz*. It was a big confidence boost."

"I didn't *give* you the part, dear, you earned it," the young teacher said, patting Chloe's shoulder in an affirming gesture. "I hope you continue on with drama. You're very talented. What are your plans for college?"

"I was accepted at the University of Paris. I start in the fall."

Sister Maureen took a seat behind her desk. "Will you be majoring in drama?"

Chloe shrugged, ashamed to admit that she hadn't yet given that much thought to her future. "I'll probably go pre-med or major in business or something, to keep my mother happy."

Sister Maureen opened her lesson planner and wrote something, not responding right away. "You know, you remind me a lot of myself when I was your age," she said, looking up at Chloe. "Pleasing my parents was a big deal to me, too. Believe it or not, they were *not* happy when I told them I wanted to join the sisterhood."

"Really? I think my mother would be thrilled if I became a nun. She's so strict, I might as well be one now," Chloe said, laughing.

"I come from a big Irish family. All my sisters got married and had kids right out of high school," Sister Maureen said. "My parents expected me to do the same, and they were really disappointed when I told them I wanted to take a different path."

Chloe studied the floor tiles, taking in what Sister Maureen was saying but not sure what she was getting at.

"The reason I mention that," Sister Maureen said, as if picking up on Chloe's uncertainty, "is that I can tell you're conflicted about what direction to go in life. You're at a crossroads, that tender age where you all of a sudden have to grow up and decide what you want to be. I'm sure part of you wants to be a good girl and do what your mother expects, but another part of you would like to be adventurous and explore the world and all it has to offer. I just beg of you, consider all of your options before you go down a certain path just to please your mother."

"I know my mother comes across as overbearing, but she means well, she really does," Chloe said, surprised to find herself defending Maxine with such vehemence. "She just wants what's best for me."

"I'm sure she does," Sister Maureen said. "But what about what *you* want?"

Chloe didn't respond, caught off-guard by Sister Maureen's question. She'd been so busy getting ready for graduation and dealing with Gigi's latest catastrophe that she hadn't really had time to stop and do any soul searching.

"You don't have to answer that. It's not a pop quiz," Sister Maureen said, joking. "But if you don't mind, would you help me sort out the test booklets for tomorrow?"

"Sure."

Chloe took an armload of booklets and began helping Sister Maureen place them on the desks, still mulling the question the teacher had posed.

"I always encourage my students to pray and think about what God's plan is for their lives," Sister Maureen said, setting about the task of straightening a row of desks. "Maybe it's going to college and getting a degree in something sensible like your mother expects you to, or maybe it's taking some other avenue."

Chloe paused, looked out the window and surveyed the campus she would soon leave, then said, "I guess if I really thought about it, what I'd really like to do is go to New York and study acting." Her hands shook as she placed the next test booklet, nearly trembling with the mix of delight and terror at verbalizing such a big dream.

Sister Maureen looked unflustered. "So what's stopping you? There are plenty of good schools in New York. The Tisch School of the Arts at NYU has a first-rate drama program. I'd be happy to write you a letter of recommendation."

Chloe hesitated, choosing her words carefully, not wanting to seem ungrateful for Sister Maureen's generous offer. "But I've already been accepted at the University of Paris. Gigi's going to be starting there in winter semester and we're going to room together."

Sister Maureen dropped a handful of booklets and Chloe rushed to help her pick them up.

"Thanks, dear," Sister Maureen said, tucking a stray curl back under her headscarf.

There was silence as Chloe and her teacher returned to the task of placing the booklets on desktops.

"Are you sure Gigi's going to be able to start college in January?" Sister Maureen said when they'd finished the task. "I thought she was being held back."

"She just has a couple of classes to make up in summer school," Chloe said, following Sister Maureen back to her desk. "After a couple of semesters at the University of Paris, she's going to reapply to the Sorbonne."

"That would be a great place for her. I've seen her artwork and she's brilliant," Sister Maureen said, tidying her desk. "But as much as I like Gigi, she reminds me of so many students who have loads of talent but lack motivation. Her focus seems to be on boys, not school."

Chloe gave the teacher a knowing smile. "So you heard about her sneaking in after curfew?"

Sister Maureen nodded. "Word travels fast around here. All the nuns were whispering about Gigi's brazenness. Look, I know she's your best friend, but sometimes friends end up going in different directions. When I was your age, I had a really good friend named Sabrina. We were as close as you and Gigi. But when I decided to join the sisterhood, Sabrina and I grew apart." The teacher threw up her hands, as if in surrender. "It happens. But we still write occasionally. She lives in Manchester and has a whole brood of kids. She sends me pictures and Christmas cards every year and always invites me to drop in. I keep meaning to get up there, but with my teaching schedule and responsibilities with the church, it just never seems to happen."

Chloe took a moment to digest what Sister Maureen had said. Chloe hadn't really considered that the teacher had a life before she'd entered the sisterhood.

"Gigi's had a rough couple of semesters, but she's really trying," Chloe said finally, realizing she was defending Gigi as adamantly as she'd defended Maxine earlier. "We've worked out a plan and we're both looking forward to being college roommates next year. I figure I'll get my degree out of the way and there'll be plenty of time to pursue acting when I finish school."

"Okay, dear, well you know I wish you the best," Sister Maureen said in the same tone of resignation she'd reverted to when discussing Chloe's future with Maxine after the school play a couple of months ago. She extended her arms. "Come give me a hug in case we don't get a chance to speak after the final tomorrow."

Chloe hugged her teacher, holding on a bit longer than normal, as if clinging to the security that the all-girls academy represented. She was excited yet frightened about the prospect of leaving the school's protective bubble.

She finally broke away and slowly walked to the door to go to her next class. "Sister Maureen?" she said, pausing in the doorway.

"Yes?" The teacher looked up from grading papers.

"Thanks again for everything. I really appreciate your advice."

Sister Maureen nodded. "Any time. And make sure you stay in touch and let me know what you're up to. Whatever you choose to do, I know you're going to be a success."

Graduation came like a whirlwind. When Mother Superior called her name at the commencement ceremony, Chloe strode across the auditorium stage, where she had made her acting debut in *Les Miz* a mere two months ago. The headmistress' usually stern expression was replaced by a warm smile when she handed Chloe her diploma. Chloe nodded respectfully and shook her hand. Despite the nun's harsh demeanor, Chloe appreciated the discipline the headmistress had instilled.

Chloe was going to miss Our Lady of Chastity. The school's rigorous curriculum had taxed her mentally, but it had also enriched her as a person. She felt more well-rounded and knowledgeable than she had four years ago. The academy's hallowed halls had been host to some of the best times in her young life, times she would never forget. She would miss all of her friends. They would be scattering to various destinations to build their respective futures, and she knew she would never see most of them again.

Continuing her walk across the stage, greeting teachers who bid her good luck, Chloe glanced out at the auditorium. She caught sight of Gigi, sandwiched between Maxine and Simone, studying her nails and cracking gum. Chloe stared at Gigi, trying to send her positive vibes to stay strong even though she wasn't graduating with the rest of the class. But the telepathic energy that had flowed between the girls since they were children seemed to fail this time and Gigi never looked up.

Reaching the end of the line of faculty, Chloe stopped upon seeing Sister Maureen. She gave her favorite teacher a big hug and choked back tears, thinking of how much she'd miss the young nun's guidance – and how much she'd miss this place that had shaped and molded her. A phase of her life was ending and she was transitioning into an uncertain area where she wasn't fully adult and yet no longer a girl. She just hoped she'd find her way and be able to realize all her dreams.

Descending the steps on the way back to her seat, Chloe looked over at Gigi again, but she never once made eye contact.

After the ceremony, Chloe hung around outside the auditorium saying goodbye to friends and promising to keep in touch.

"Let's take a picture," suggested Anastasia, one of the girls who'd accompanied Chloe and Gigi on the Wembley Stadium outing.

Chloe and Anastasia rounded up Enid and Emily, recruited one of their dads to hold the camera and huddled together.

"Come on," Chloe said, motioning to Gigi. "We want you in the picture."

"No, that's okay," Gigi said, walking away. "I'm just going to go back to the dorm and unpack my summer clothes, since I'll be stuck here."

Chloe smiled for the camera, but her focus shifted to Gigi, who was trudging back to the residence hall. After posing for a couple more snapshots, Chloe finished saying her goodbyes and rushed to catch up with Gigi. Elbowing her way past girls dragging overstuffed trunks and suitcases out of the dorm, Chloe found Gigi curled up on the sofa in the lounge, watching television.

"Mother and Simone want to take us out to dinner in the city," Chloe said. "You coming?"

"Nah, you guys go ahead," Gigi said without looking up from the TV. "It's your day. There's not much for me to celebrate."

"Come on, Gi', don't be like that. Mother and Simone flew in to support both of us."

"Yeah, right. I'm not in the mood to be around my mother right now. I can't stand to hear one more lecture about how I'd have gotten to walk across the stage and get my diploma today, too, if I'd only have applied myself."

"You're going to be getting your degree at the end of the summer. Remember our plan?"

When Gigi didn't respond, Chloe repeated the dinner invitation.

"Mother made reservations at St. Germain, one of the best French restaurants in London. They have *coq au vin*, your favorite."

"I'm not hungry. I'll probably grab something from the kitchen later and take it up to the room," Gigi said, her eyes still fixed on the TV.

Chloe peered around and looked at the screen. "Oh, I see why you want to hang around here. That's Justin's team, isn't it?"

"Yeah, and I wish I could be there to cheer him on. Getting to hang out with him this summer is the only thing that makes the thought of being trapped here bearable."

"It's probably not a good idea to be spending so much time with him. You should concentrate on your classes this summer," Chloe said, realizing she was taking on the very nagging, motherly tone that Gigi had complained about from Simone. "So you can finish up your degree and start at the University of Paris in January, like we talked about."

Once again, Gigi didn't respond, so Chloe stepped in front of the TV to get her attention. "You do remember our plan, don't you?"

"Yes, I remember," Gigi said impatiently. "Now will you move?"

Chloe took a reluctant step toward the door. "You sure you don't want to come out to eat with us? This is the last time we'll all be together for a couple of months. Mother and Simone'll be disappointed."

"They'll get over it. All Simone cares about is getting back to Paris so she can be with whatever man she's banging."

Chloe remained silent, not sure that Gigi's cynical attitude toward her mother was entirely wrong.

"I'll bring you back a doggy bag of *coq au vin*," Chloe said, looking over her shoulder at Gigi on her way out of the room.

Gigi turned up the sound and trained her attention on the television screen. "Don't bother. It'll just remind me of Paris."

40

"You're hurting me," Chloe said, standing on a pedestal in Chez Maxine's fitting area.

"Stop fidgeting and moving around so much or I'm going to draw blood," Maxine said, reading glasses perched on the tip of her nose and needles dangling from her lips as she pinned the bottom of a dress pattern.

Chloe picked at the itchy dress pattern. "Can't we do this later?" She had just come back from an exhausting photo shoot for French *Elle*, and the last thing she felt like doing right now was being poked and prodded.

"Just hold still for a few more minutes. I want this ball gown for your society debut to be perfect."

"This is all about what *you* want."

Mother was insisting on throwing a big debutante ball at the Chateau de Chevalier for Chloe's eighteenth birthday in a couple of months. She didn't even bother consulting Chloe on what she wanted, just hired an event planner and forged ahead.

Chloe thought the whole deb-ball concept was a joke, an archaic tradition, torture her mother insisted on putting her through. She didn't feel like a debutante. She was herself, a regular girl. She wanted to celebrate her eighteenth birthday *her* way – fly to London and hang out with Gigi, go out for pizza and to the movies. But Mother wouldn't hear of it.

"This is going to be so exciting," Mother said, ignoring Chloe and babbling on about the deb ball as if it were *her* birthday. "I've enrolled you in charm school to get ready for your big debut."

"*What?!*" Chloe nearly shrieked her displeasure with Mother's latest stunt, prompting the designers and seamstresses toiling away at drafting tables and sewing machines to turn and to see what the commotion was about.

"Why in the world did you enroll me in some stupid charm school, for chrissake?" Chloe said, lowering her voice. "I'm supposed to be relaxing this summer before I start college."

"You just need a little brush-up on etiquette before you're presented to society, that's all," Maxine said. "I signed you up with Madame Eloise de Tornquist, who runs one of the oldest and most respected finishing schools in Paris."

Chloe looked down at Maxine. The only good thing about this fitting was seeing Mother in a rare submissive position.

"I already have a slew of modeling assignments lined up this summer. You know that. How am I supposed to squeeze in charm school on top of everything else?" Chloe whined, realizing she sounded like a fussy four-year-old whose mother was forcing her to go to preschool instead of letting her go outside to play.

Maxine sat back on her haunches, made one last adjustment to the hem, then stood. "You're only going to turn eighteen once," she said, taking off her glasses and setting aside her needles and thread. She cupped her hands, as if in prayer, adding, "Please just do this one thing for me. Mama Louise would have been so proud if she could have seen you graduate, and this is what she would have wanted for you if she were still around."

Chloe tugged at the top of her dress, falling silent at the mention of her late grandmother.

"When I turned eighteen, Mama wanted me to be in the big cotillion for Creole girls they had every year at the Hotel St. Marie in the French Quarter. It's a tradition, and Mama Louise did it when she was your age, which is where she met Papa," Maxine said. She paused, walking around Chloe and inspecting the dress pattern. "Papa died when I was still in high school and we ended up leaving New Orleans and moving to New York before I could make my big debut." She spun Chloe to face the three-way mirror. "I just want you to have all the things I never had."

Looking in the mirror and noticing the tears welling in her mother's eyes, Chloe looked away, feeling suddenly ashamed that she'd thrown a mini-tantrum over something that obviously meant so much to Maxine.

"All right," Chloe said after a moment, looking Maxine in the eye again, "I'll go along with the deb ball. I'll even go to charm school." Getting an inspiration that she could use this opportunity as leverage, she added, "But when I turn eighteen, no more curfews. I *am* going to be starting college, after all."

"Deal." Maxine put her hands on her daughter's shoulders and straightened Chloe's posture. "Now stand up straight and stop slouching, *ma chérie*. This is why I'm sending you to finishing school."

"And one and two and three and four."

Chloe and a procession of other soon-to-be debutantes struggled to keep up with the steps of the minuet as their elderly etiquette tutor, Madame de Tornquist, tapped her cane on the dance studio's hardwood floor. For the past six weeks, Chloe had hopped the train every day to the crone's studio in the Tuileries Quarter to sit through hours of tedious lessons in "comportment, couture and congeniality" – the three "Cs" of being a "proper lady," the catch phrase Madame de Tornquist had coined and posted all over the studio. Chloe was relieved that this was the final class and she would have a few weeks of leisurely summer relaxation before the big debutante ball on her birthday on August twentieth.

"*Excusez-moi,*" muttered Chloe's dance partner, a girl named Charlotte Fournier whom she knew from the Lycée, trampling Chloe's feet.

"That's okay," Chloe whispered back. She flashed Charlotte a pained expression that related she couldn't seem to get the steps right, either – especially not in the murderously high heels the directress forced them to wear in order to inure themselves to the high price of beauty.

"When will we ever use this stupid dance?" Charlotte said under her breath.

"Tell me about it," Chloe said. "What is this, 1893?"

Chloe spun Charlotte around and made a face that made the girl giggle. These lessons were such a drag and so useless, a total waste of money. Nothing the old spinster taught would be applicable in the "real world" – the cold, harsh place waiting to gobble Chloe up that Maxine was always lecturing her about. And moreover, Chloe already knew how to sip tea without slurping, which fork to use at the dinner table and that you weren't supposed to drink out of the finger bowl, and had been taught at Our Lady of Chastity how to cross her legs in her uniform skirt without her panties showing.

"That will be all for your final dance instruction," Madame de Tornquist said, turning off the old-fashioned phonograph. The directress looked as vintage as the record player, with her neatly waved blue-gray hair and classic black Yves St. Laurent dress with frilly white collar and cuffs. "Please take out your texts for the elocution lesson."

Chloe was pleased to find that instead of the usual inane verbal exercise, such as reciting "twixt this and six thick thistle sticks" or some other silly phrase over and over to perfect their English diction, the directress planned for the girls to read a theatrical monologue. Chloe selected Queen Gertrude's monologue from Shakespeare's *Hamlet*, one of her favorite scenes she had acted out in Sister Maureen's class.

Chloe had no choice but to go first, since the directress always assigned tasks in alphabetical order and there were no "A" surnames in the class. The girls pulled their chairs into a semicircle, creating an audience for Chloe as she stood before them.

"All right, Mademoiselle Bareaux," Madame de Tornquist said with an imperious tap of her cane, pacing behind the seated girls, "you may begin."

Chloe nervously thumbed through the text, rankled by the anxiety that gripped her whenever she had to speak in front of people or perform before an audience, no matter how small. She looked up, feeling the intensity of the gaze of the other girls and the directress as they waited for her to begin.

She began reading, but stopped short when her voice cracked. "I'm sorry," she said, swallowing to moisten her throat. "Can I start again?"

Madame de Tornquist furrowed her brow and flared her nostrils in the chastising expression that had become familiar. "Yes, you *may* start again. Why don't you take a sip of water, *cher*?"

Chloe walked on wobbly legs to a nearby table, poured herself a half-full glass of water with shaky hands, gulped it down and returned to her position in front of the class. She found her place in the text again, but her throat was still dry and her hands were shaking so badly that she wasn't sure if she could go through with it.

She scanned the faces of the other girls. They were all pampered trust-fund babies, true debutantes who came from old money and two-parent homes. None of them had been raised by a single mother, none of them were fatherless or mixed-race like she. They were thoroughbreds and she was a mutt. These spoiled girls were all judging her and hoping she'd trip over her words, Chloe told herself.

"Mademoiselle Bareaux, please begin," Madame de Tornquist said in an impatient tone. "I want to give the other girls an opportunity to read before class ends."

Chloe nodded. "*Oui*, Madame."

She cleared her throat, placed her finger in the text to mark her place and opened her mouth, but the words still wouldn't come. Panicked, she looked up and caught sight of Charlotte, whose eyes signaled compassion. Chloe pursed her lips in a small smile, signaling she appreciated Charlotte's support. She was the only girl in the class, other than Chloe, whose parents came from humble beginnings.

Still nervous, Chloe's eyes darted around the room and she saw a photograph on the opposite wall that she'd never noticed before. Hanging along with snapshots of other esteemed alumni of Madame de Tornquist's Finishing School was an early publicity still of Valérie Bourdain, Chloe's favorite French actress. Chloe had been so preoccupied with learning dance steps that she'd only glanced occasionally at Madame de Tornquist's "wall of fame," blurring together the faces of all the well-known actresses, television personalities and parliamentarians the directress had schooled in the art of etiquette.

With her idol smiling down at her, Chloe felt newly empowered. As Chloe had seen her do so often onscreen, Valérie Bourdain would take command of this situation and recite her lines with authority, not allowing anyone to intimidate her. Inspired by her idol, Chloe began reading with a fresh surge of confidence and soon became lost in the poetry of Shakespeare's words. The snobby French girls transformed into seventeenth-century British peasants who were huddled onto rickety benches in the Globe Theatre to witness a performance of the Bard's latest work.

Concluding her reading, the girls applauded and Chloe curtsied graciously, happy to return to her seat and give someone else the spotlight.

"I hope that you young ladies will carry the lessons I've imparted to you here into society and the world at large as you embark on life's journey," Madame de Tornquist said at the end of class in one of her grand speeches. "Please keep me informed of your progress."

When the directress dismissed the class, Chloe hugged Charlotte and invited her to attend her deb ball. Excited to be done with charm school and finally have some time to herself, Chloe changed out of the punishing heels and into comfortable tennis shoes, hurriedly gathered her backpack and headed for the door. She halted at the sound of her name being called.

"Mademoiselle Bareaux, may I have a word with you?"

Chloe slowly turned to face the directress, leery that she had inadvertently breached the code of "ladylike" behavior by tromping out of the studio and would be made to stay after class and do some tedious exercise as punishment.

"Yes, Madame?" Chloe said sheepishly.

The directress gracefully leaned on her cane and lowered herself to a chair. She motioned for Chloe to join her. "Have a seat."

Chloe walked across the studio with measured steps and sat next to the directress, taking great care to cross her legs in the ladylike manner in which the crone had repeatedly instructed the girls.

Nodding approvingly, Madame de Tornquist began speaking in her refined accent. "I've watched you over the course of these past several weeks," the directress said, her heavily made-up black eyes keeping consistent eye contact with Chloe, as she had told her pupils to do. "You've blossomed."

Chloe nodded thanks, not sure where the directress was going with this. "Thanks – I mean, thank you. *Merci*."

"That elocution exercise at the end of class showed your potential. Have you ever thought about performing professionally?"

Chloe was so taken aback by one of Madame's sparsely meted-out compliments that she didn't know how to respond. "Uh, yeah – I mean, yes. *Oui*. I had the lead in *Les Miserables* at school this spring."

"I think you have the ability to go further than a school production, much further," Madame said with a wave of her jangled wrist, a gesture apparently meant to indicate the grandness of her statement. "You remind me of a young Valérie Bourdain."

The directress pointed at the photo of Chloe's idol hanging above them, and Chloe's cheeks grew hot at the comparison. She was beyond flattered that the stern taskmistress would see any fleck of potential in Chloe that reminded her of the international movie star.

"Like you, Valérie was shy and tentative at first," Madame continued. "When she was an ingénue – just getting started and very uncertain of herself – the studio sent her to me for some polishing. I had to work with her for months to break her tendency to slump her shoulders and speak in whispers, but even with those bad habits, I could detect a glimmer of the star she would one day become." Madame de Tornquist paused, looking at Chloe more intently now. "And I see the same potential in you."

Chloe was so overwhelmed that she absentmindedly uncrossed her legs and slumped forward. With a scolding gaze from Madame, she quickly corrected her posture and muttered, "Thank you," not knowing what else to say at such high and unexpected praise.

Madame raised her immaculately painted brows. "How many times have I told you not to mumble?"

Chloe cleared her throat and sat up straighter. "Thank you, Madame," she repeated in a louder, clearer tone.

"Most of the girls I get are just taking my course as a last-minute brush-up before they become the wife of a powerful businessman or politician. But every now and then I come across a girl who has a very real possibility of making something of herself. Valérie Bourdain was one." Madame lifted an impeccably manicured hand toward the photo again. "And you, *cher*, are another."

Chloe nodded, unable to verbalize her appreciation.

"I can tell you're not going to be one of those girls who just goes to college to bide her time until the right marriage proposal comes along," the directress said. "Whatever you do, whether you choose to go into the performing arts or another career path, don't just settle. Do you understand what I'm saying to you?"

Chloe nodded and looked up at the photo of Valérie Bourdain, hoping that she could take Madame de Tornquist's instruction and realize her potential as magnificently as the glamorous star had done.

"You may go now," the directress said with a dismissive wave of her cane. "Enjoy the rest of your summer."

"Thank you, Madame, thanks for everything," Chloe said, hastily rising and slinging her backpack on her shoulder. "You're coming to my deb ball, aren't you?"

Madame de Tornquist flashed a smile that revealed just a hint of straight, even teeth (dentures, no doubt), another trick she'd taught her girls. "*Bien entendu*. Of course. I always enjoy seeing the fruits of my labor."

Chloe thanked the directress again for taking the time to speak with her personally and jogged to the door, hoping not to miss the next Métro.

"Uh-uh-uh," Madame tsked from across the room. "We don't clomp across the floor like a stampeding cow. Slow down and walk like a lady."

Chloe turned to acknowledge the direction. "*Oui*, Madame," she said, taking smaller steps.

"Oh, and Mademoiselle Bareaux?"

Chloe paused in the doorway and faced the directress again. "Yes?"

Madame smiled again, but this time her expression was more playful. "My hearing's not what it used to be, but I overheard you and Mademoiselle Fournier complaining that you'll never use the minuet in real life. Don't be so certain of that." Her eyes twinkled, matching her understated jewelry. "You never know when a young man may ask you to dance."

"*Oui*, Madame." Chloe tipped her head respectfully and left the old woman's studio for the last time.

41

The delicious smells of Marie's ratatouille greeted Chloe when she opened the front door of the Chateau de Chevalier upon returning from her final charm lesson and she headed directly for the kitchen. Sputtering around a dance studio in high heels for hours trying to learn the minuet, a girl could work up a voracious appetite.

Chloe greeted Maxine and Marie with kisses on the cheek upon entering the kitchen.

"How was your lesson?" said Maxine, sitting at the counter while she went over household bills and receipts.

Immediately forgetting everything she'd learned over the past six weeks, Chloe slumped against the counter and helped herself to one of the carrot sticks Marie was chopping to add to her simmering pot. "I still don't have the minuet down pat," Chloe said, gnawing a carrot stub, "but we had to read a monologue for elocution and Madame de Tornquist kept me after class and said some very nice things. She told me I could be a professional actress. She said I –"

"That's nice, *ma chérie*."

Chloe hadn't even finished describing the confidence-boosting encounter with Madame de Tornquist when Mother, clearly not listening, cut her off. Chloe glanced at Marie, who gave her an understanding look while plopping a pile of chopped vegetables in the pot.

"It's almost finished," Marie said, stirring the wonderful-smelling stew. "Do you want me to fix you a bowl?"

"Save your appetite for the event tonight," Maxine said. "There'll be plenty of food there."

Chloe waved the carrot stick in her hand to indicate her confusion. "What event?"

"You know, the open house. I told you about it weeks ago. I just finished doing a house for my clients, the Lamberts, and they're having guests over tonight, kind of like a housewarming."

Chloe shuddered, thinking of all the pretentious people she would have to greet. "Do I absolutely have to go, Mother?"

"Yes, you do. My clients are Haitian Catholics and they have a big family and I told them I would bring my daughter. Now go get ready. It's a formal affair, so put on one of your good dresses."

Chloe began trudging up the back stairs, dreading getting ready for this event. After a long day of being put through the paces by Madame de Tornquist, she just wanted to change into jeans and a T-shirt, camp out in front of the TV and veg' for the rest of the evening. She was half-way up the steps when Marie called her to the phone.

"Chloe, it's Gigi on the line."

Chloe turned around and bounded back down the stairs to pick up the kitchen extension, anxious to catch up with Gigi. Chloe had been so preoccupied with charm school and modeling assignments that she hadn't had much chance to monitor Gigi's progress in summer school. She was bursting with excitement, thinking of all the fun they'd have in just a few short months when they'd be attending the University of Paris together and sharing their very own apartment.

When Chloe picked up the phone, she began telling Gigi about her day in one big jumble of words, like when they were kids and something interesting had happened at school.

"Hi, Gi'! Guess what? Madame de Tornquist told me I remind her of Valérie Bourdain and —"

"Really? That's pretty cool."

Gigi had interrupted Chloe with a cajoling comment before she finished her feverish rant, just as Maxine had done earlier.

"Did you catch the soccer match this afternoon?" Gigi said.

"Uh, no, I had my last charm lesson today, like I said. Anyway, like I was telling you —"

"The game was between Justin's team and France. It was here in London, at Wembley, and I had to be there, of course. I've gone to every home game Justin's had this summer. He always says I'm his lucky charm, and it must be true, because they won! At first I didn't know who to root for, since it was Justin's team facing off against France. But my loyalty's with Justin now. He scored the winning goal. He was brilliant. You should have seen him."

Chloe zoned out while Gigi went on and on about Justin's prowess on and off the soccer field. She had apparently been spending most of her time when she wasn't in summer school with the footballer.

As Gigi blathered on, Chloe shifted her weight from foot to foot. "Uh-huh," she muttered periodically, studying her nails, so Gigi would know she was still on the line. It occurred to her that this conversation was the exact opposite of how her talks with Gigi used to be, when one of them would listen attentively and give honest feedback while the other opened up about some boy-related dilemma or problem at school. Now it seemed neither one had much interest in hearing about what was going on in the other's life. Had their time apart over the summer created that much of a gulf?

"Hey, Gi', sorry to interrupt," Chloe said after several minutes of nonstop chatter. "But how's school going? That *is* why you're there, after all."

"Oh, fine," Gigi said in a tone that sounded more nonchalant than convincing. "I only have class a couple of hours a day, which leaves the rest of the afternoon to spend with Justin. He officially asked me to be his girlfriend. Can you *believe* it?"

Gigi let out such a piercing shriek that Chloe held the phone away from her ear.

"That's great," Chloe said, knowing she didn't sound as thrilled for Gigi as she should. "He can be your date to my deb ball. You are coming, aren't you?"

"Of course. I got the invitation this morning. That's the reason I called: to RSVP."

Chloe wanted to further inquire about Gigi's classes, to ensure she would earn her diploma at the end of the summer, as planned, but Maxine interrupted to tell Chloe to get off the phone and get ready for the open house.

"Listen, Gi', I have to go get ready for this thing Mother's making me go to" – another guilt-inducing glance at Maxine missed its target – "but I'll call you back later tonight."

"I won't be in my room. I'm going out with Justin later on to celebrate his victory."

Chloe sighed and shifted her weight again. "Right. Well, have fun," she said and hung up.

"How's Gigi doing?" asked Marie, who was now ladling steaming bowls of her delectable stew to serve to the household staff.

"All right, I guess," Chloe said, dragging her feet on her way to the back stairs. "All she could talk about is her new boyfriend."

Marie chuckled, wiping her hands on her apron. "It's good to know that even being away at summer school by herself hasn't changed her."

Chloe gave a half-smile, appreciating Marie's attempt to lighten the mood with humor, and retreated to her room to get ready for Mother's event.

A valet opened the door and helped Chloe and Maxine out of the car when they arrived at the Lamberts' chateau. Simone was waiting for them on the front steps, on the arm of her new boyfriend, an older man named Jules Fabré. It was as though after her breakup with Pascal, Simone had sworn off younger men. White-haired yet spry, Jules appeared to be in his late fifties. While not as handsome or well-preserved as Jacques had been, he was nice-looking and well-dressed and Chloe could see why Simone was attracted to him.

"It's so nice to finally meet you both," Jules said, smiling and nodding at Maxine and Chloe.

"Likewise," Maxine said, taking Chloe's arm and leading her up the steps, following Simone's lead. "Come on, I'll introduce you to my clients."

"You've outdone yourself again, Maxine," Simone said, marveling at the red-and-gold, Chinoiserie wallpaper lining the walls of the foyer.

Chloe followed Maxine, Simone and her date as they took their place in the receiving line to greet the host and hostess. Yves and Madeleine Lambert kissed Maxine on either cheek.

"This is my daughter, Chloe," Maxine said.

"What a beautiful girl. She looks so much like you," Madeleine exclaimed, clasping her lacquered, ringed hands and addressing Maxine as if Chloe were a small child who had not yet learned to speak. "We must introduce her to Jean-Baptiste!"

Summoned by their parents, a seemingly endless parade of children of varying heights and ages filed in one by one. The appearance of the sixth child confirmed Mother's description of the family as strict Catholics.

"This is Jean-Baptiste," Madeleine said when the eldest child approached.

In contrast to the well-scrubbed guests, the twenty-something guy's shirt was untucked, hands shoved in the pockets of his sagging khakis.

Despite his casual appearance, Chloe extended her hand to the young man and said, "*Enchanté*," plying her etiquette training.

Instead of shaking her hand, he kissed it and looked up at her with seductive hazel eyes.

"Why don't we show you all around," Yves suggested. "They just finished painting the master suite this morning, Maxine, and I don't believe you had a chance to see it after the final walkthrough."

Chloe was glad for an opportunity to pry her hand away from the Lambert boy. She ditched the group as they climbed the stairs and decided to show herself around. Jibing with Mother's frequent complaints while finishing up the massive redecorating project, the house had an ultramodern, museum-like feel that was mismatched with the home's old-style architecture. The only room that radiated warmth was a large drawing room, which had Mother's subtle touch, painted in soothing earth tones and lined with family photos. She recognized Jean-Baptiste in a school portrait. He appeared to be about eleven or twelve, on the verge of puberty, but was staring at the camera with the seductive smirk he'd directed at her earlier.

"That was back in Haiti."

Chloe turned to see the young man standing in the doorway. "I'm sorry," she sputtered. "I was just looking around."

"No need to be sorry. That's why we threw the party – to show off the house." He seemed to stare straight through her.

She turned her back to him and examined photos from the family's homeland. "Do you miss it?"

"Miss what? Haiti?"

"Yes."

"Sometimes." He leaned on the doorframe. "Most of my brothers and sisters are too young to remember much about Port-au-Prince, but I remember everything."

Chloe studied a photo of Jean-Baptiste and his siblings on what appeared to be a family picnic on the grounds of their old plantation. "That must have been hard, leaving everything you knew."

He shrugged. "We had to do what we had to do. I like it here. I'm a senior at the University of Paris."

"You are? I'm going to be starting there in the fall," she said, turning to look at him with renewed interest. "What's your major?"

"Business. I'm going to work at my father's company after graduation. He said he's going to leave the winery to me when he retires."

"Really?" She said, turning to peruse the photos again. She got the feeling he was trying to impress her and, in the reflection of the glass of one of the picture frames, saw him coming closer.

"Do you want to get out of here and take a ride in my new Fiat? My folks bought it to bribe me into improving my grades."

She felt his breath on the nape of her neck and faced him once again. He was dangling car keys in one hand, his other hand resting on the wall beside her in a stance that was too intimate, considering they'd just met.

"I should really go find my mother." She inched closer to the wall, pinned in by him. "She's probably looking for me."

"Don't you ever go anywhere without your mother?" he said, sounding as though he were taunting her.

"Of course."

"So, how about taking a ride me with me?" he said cockily, waving the keys, as if offering her the grand prize on a game show.

Was this his way of asking her out? He was cute, but he seemed a bit stuck on himself – always a turnoff. She didn't want to offend her mother's clients, and she grappled for a way to politely rebuff their stuck-up son.

"Tonight's not good – I promised my mother I'd hang out here – but I'm having a party in a couple of weeks," she improvised. "Actually it's for my eighteenth birthday, a deb ball. Would you like to come?"

Inviting him to her debutante ball would not technically be considered a date, since there would be dozens of other people there. The last thing she wanted was to lead him on.

He looked skeptical. "Do I have to dress up?"

"It's black tie. You might want to wear a tux."

He stood there for a moment not saying anything, penetrating her again with his stare.

"Okay, I'll come," he said finally, as if his presence were some rare and treasured commodity. Eyes gleaming mischievously, he added, "On one condition."

She took a step further back, flush from his warm breath on her cheeks. "Yes?"

"I get to have the first dance."

"Okay," she agreed, just wanting to get away from him. She wriggled out from under his arm and backed out of the room. "I'll send you an invitation," she said over her shoulder.

That seductive smirk spread across his face again. "I look forward to seeing you again."

Chloe was getting ready for bed later that night, with the TV on as background noise, when her ears perked up at an anchorman's mention of Gigi's footballer boyfriend.

"This just in from London. Justin Bradshaw, forward with London's Kensington United, was rushed to Queen Mary's Hospital after crashing his sports car following a night of bar-hopping to celebrate the team's win over France," the anchorman said as Chloe stood transfixed in front of the screen.

The news cut to a reporter at the scene of a wrecked vehicle that had smashed into a tree. "Amazingly, Bradshaw walked away from the accident unscathed," the field reporter said, motioning toward the wreckage. "This ill-fated night of carousing is just the latest episode in a long string of near-calamities involving Kensington United's resident bad boy."

Chloe rushed to the phone and dialed Gigi. Her mind raced with horrifying thoughts: Had Gigi been in the car? Had she been able to escape with her life intact, or were the news reports going to simply dismiss her as some nameless victim who happened to be in the wrong place at the wrong time?

"I'm okay," Gigi said when Chloe finally reached the dorm at Our Lady of Chastity.

Chloe sunk to the bed, nearly fainting in relief. "I saw the news. What happened?"

Gigi's explanation was punctured by sobs. "I don't know. He dropped me off on campus after we went out to celebrate and he must have crashed on his way home." She took a deep breath, let out a small whimper and continued. "I thought he'd had too much to drink and offered to sneak him into my room to sleep it off, but he insisted he'd be all right. He said he'd driven home dozens of times before when he was drunker than he was tonight."

"Gosh. Is he okay?"

"Yeah, he's all right, just a few scrapes and a gouge on his forehead. He was worried about his kicking leg more than anything else, but they bandaged his head in the emergency room, sent him home and said he could be back on the field next week."

"What about the police? Aren't they going to arrest him for drunk driving?"

"I doubt it," Gigi said, blowing her nose. "There were no other cars involved. And besides, they're not going to lock up one of Kensington United's biggest stars, especially not after their victory today. They have another big game next week and if they put him in the clink, he'd miss it." She sighed. "I just wish I could go see him, but I'm trapped here, as usual."

"Are you sure it's a good idea to keep seeing this guy?" Chloe said, treading lightly, not wanting to upset Gigi anymore than she already was.

"I could never leave him, especially not now," Gigi said, sounding as overemotional as Chloe had anticipated. "You don't know him like I do. No one does."

Chloe leaned against one of the oversize posters of her bed, spent. "Maybe you're right," she said wearily. "It's just that after seeing that horrible wreck on TV, I freaked out, thinking you were in the car. I'd hate for anything to happen to you. I couldn't take it. Especially not after what happened to…" She couldn't finish the sentence. *Especially not after what happened to Jacques.*

"Justin would never put me in danger. He'd never hurt me."

Chloe's knuckles tightened around the receiver, a physical manifestation of her concern. "I hope you're right."

42

The big night came around quicker than Chloe expected. She always thought she would instantaneously feel like a woman when she turned eighteen, but she felt no different from the day before when she was still a seventeen-year-old girl.

She stood in front of the full-length mirror in her bedroom, preparing to make her grand entrance. Despite the fact that Mother had forced her into this affair and posing for the gown was tedious, she had to admire Mother's work.

Chloe felt like Cinderella, pretty in pink in her silky, off-the-shoulder ball gown that flared out like a bell at the bottom, white gloves that came just above her elbows, and satin slippers. Mother's diamond choker and bracelet reflected the light in the room, making rainbows on the walls.

There was a knock at the door. "Come in," Chloe called, tugging at the gown.

Mother and Marie entered. It was unusual seeing Marie out of her housekeeper's uniform. She was wearing the conservative black dress she saved for special occasions, with a single strand of pearls tucked under her prim, white lace collar, and sensible shoes. Maxine, in contrast, was resplendent in a gold lamé, Givenchy gown, with matching gold jewelry adorning her ears and neck. They made their way into the room and took stock of Chloe's appearance.

"My god, what a vision," said Marie, placing her hand over her heart. "I'm so proud of you, *chouchou*."

"Thanks, Marie," Chloe said, hugging her.

Marie handed Chloe a large box exquisitely wrapped in gold paper that matched Maxine's gown.

"Marie, you didn't have to do this," Chloe said, accepting the gift.

"Actually, I didn't," Marie said with a chuckle. "I don't know what's in there, but I'm sure my gift is much simpler. That came by messenger this afternoon."

Chloe examined the heavy box, but there was no tag with the sender's name. "Who's it from?"

"I don't know," Marie said. "Why don't you open it and find out?"

Chloe glanced at Maxine, seeking permission to open her birthday gift just like when she was a child.

"Go ahead," Maxine said. "I'm just as curious to know what's inside as you are."

Chloe set the box on her bed, tore off the wrapping paper and flung the flaps open. Inside she found a leather-bound set of Dumas' novels and cast-iron bookends in the shape of a pony-tailed female pirate holding a sword aloft.

"This is so amazing," Chloe said, taking the volumes from the box and running her hands over their shiny covers. "This is every book I love, from *The Three Musketeers* to *The Count of Monte Cristo*."

"You can take those to college with you in the fall," Maxine said, peering at the books over Chloe's shoulder.

"Did you get these for me, Mother?"

"No, but whoever did is very thoughtful. You've almost worn out those copies in the study downstairs."

"Is there a card?" Marie asked, inching toward the bed.

Chloe shook the box. "No, nothing." She began carefully placing the books back in the box, as if handling fragile antiques. "This is the kind of gift Jacques would have gotten me. He knew how much I love Dumas. That's why he taught me to fence, like the characters in these novels. I wish he were here tonight."

Silence enveloped the room, as if Chloe, Mother and Marie were each acknowledging the pain of Jacques' absence.

"If he *were* here, he'd be so proud of you," Maxine said, affectionately sweeping a wisp of hair out of Chloe's eyes.

"I'll give you two a moment alone," Marie said, dabbing at her eyes with a lace handkerchief and exiting the room.

Chris Bournéa

Chloe put the box away and returned to the mirror, making sure, with her mother's help, that every stitch of her gown was in place.

Maxine pressed her cheek against Chloe's, standing next to her in the mirror. "You look like a princess," Maxine said. "You are a princess, *my* princess. And what princess would be complete without her crown?"

Maxine brought out a black velvet box and handed it to Chloe. "Happy birthday, *ma chérie*," she said.

Chloe opened the box. A diamond tiara sparkled against the lavender satin interior. "Oh, Mother, it's beautiful."

"I'll help you put it on." Maxine positioned the tiara in Chloe's elegantly swept-up hair, adding the finishing touch. Chloe was ready for her debut.

"My baby's all grown-up," Maxine said, tears welling in her eyes. She took a step back, examining Chloe's reflection. "I think it's time I gave you this." She took off one of her diamond rings and slid it over the gloved ring finger of her daughter's right hand.

"I love it," Chloe said, fingering the ring and admiring the way it shone in the mirror.

"It was your *grand-mère*'s wedding ring. Take good care of it."

Chloe placed her ringed hand over her bosom, honored to take possession of such a treasured heirloom and reminder of her beloved Mama Louise. "I will. Always. I love you, Mother."

"I love you, too, baby," Maxine said, pulling Chloe into an embrace. Maxine pulled away, sniffling and rubbing her eyes. "I'm getting myself all flustered. My mascara is going to run and my eyes are going to get all puffy if I don't get it together." She wiped her eyes with a tissue while the string quartet she hired began to play. "I think it's time. You ready?"

Chloe inhaled sharply. "As I'll ever be."

Maxine fussed over Chloe in her maternal way, making last-minute adjustments to the gown she'd designed and sewn herself. "Take my hand," she said finally, aiming Chloe toward the door.

Maxine led her daughter to the top of the winding staircase. She kissed Chloe on either cheek and smiled.

"I'm shaking all over," Chloe said.

"Just do it like we rehearsed and you'll get through it," Maxine said reassuringly.

She gave Chloe one last hug and released her daughter's hand, going downstairs, and leaving her standing by herself. Just like when she was a child, Chloe was going to have to take those first, uncertain steps on her own.

When Maxine reached the bottom of the staircase, she nodded at an emcee holding a microphone, giving him the cue. "*Mesdames et Messieurs,* announcing Mademoiselle Chloe Yvette Bareaux."

274

Chloe began her slow descent down the winding staircase as the string quartet played. When she reached the middle step, she paused, realizing all eyes were on her. She stiffened, seized by performance anxiety, that dreaded phenomenon that rose like a gator's head in a swamp whenever she was the center of attention. She shot a panicked look at her mother, like when she was little and was about to fall off a swing at the playground. Maxine smiled, prodding Chloe to continue her descent.

Chloe tried to move, but it was as though her feet were welded in place. Her biggest fear was that she was going to trip, tumble down the stairs and land at the bottom with her dress over her head.

She scanned the faces of the guests assembled in the ballroom – mostly Maxine and Simone's work acquaintances and clients, but a few friendly, familiar faces scattered here and there. Chloe caught sight of Marie and Simone, who were standing side by side with identical "you can do it" expressions. She noticed Madame de Tornquist, her etiquette tutor, nod at her from her position in a corner, a gesture of confidence in Chloe's ability to command the room like her famous alumna, Valérie Bourdain.

Recalling Madame de Tornquist's supportive words, Chloe began moving down the staircase again. She concentrated on what Valérie Bourdain would do in the situation, and descended the stairs like the screen siren making a grand entrance in a splashy party scene. As Chloe placed one foot in front of the other with renewed self-assurance, the guests gathered around the landing, "oohing" and "aahing" as she came into view.

Careful, one step at a time. Don't rush it and you'll be fine. Chloe silently repeated the rhyme she'd made up to get her through this ordeal. It seemed to take forever to reach the landing – like a slow-motion sequence in a movie. She actually felt like a movie star when a photographer from *Le Monde*'s society section snapped her picture. Standing next to the photographer at the bottom of the staircase was Jean-Baptiste Lambert, who was waiting for her with his hand outstretched. In contrast to his disheveled appearance at his parents' open house a few weeks ago, he looked dapper in a sleek tux, his wavy hair slicked back.

He may have looked like Fred Astaire, but he murdered her feet as he led her in a waltz around the ballroom. She immediately regretted making good on her promise to let him have the first dance. Her new shoes were tight and now her feet were killing her. She couldn't have been happier when the dance was over, but, true to her etiquette training, she graciously curtsied to his bow and caught a glimpse of Madame de Tornquist smiling approval in the background.

Chloe was glad to escape from Jean-Baptiste when Mother yanked her away to the greeting line. Chloe felt like the honoree at a bat mitzvah as she acknowledged guests and well-wishers, making sure to shake hands firmly and make eye contact as Madame de Tornquist had instructed.

"You and Jean-Baptiste looked so graceful together when you were dancing," Madeleine Lambert said to Chloe as she and Yves approached.

Chloe bit her lip to keep from blurting that Madeleine must be blind if she couldn't see how out of sync Chloe was with her son.

"You two looked like a couple of young newlyweds dancing at your wedding reception," Madeleine added, looking fondly at Jean-Baptiste, who was now raiding the buffet table.

Flabbergasted, Chloe glanced at her mother, sure that Maxine would indulge her with a conspiratorial eye roll over such an absurd statement. Maxine, however, simply thanked the Lamberts for coming and excused herself to direct the caterers, along with Marie, who was supposed to have the night off.

Left alone with the Lamberts, Chloe panicked. She was eighteen now and hated to admit that she still needed her mother. She didn't know what to say to these people without Maxine there to fill in the gaps of awkward silence. She should have paid more attention when Madame de Tornquist was going over the finer points of "making conversation in social settings."

Simone came to Chloe's rescue by whisking her away from the greeting line. "I'm so happy for you, *ma bellotte*. You're handling it all so well," Simone said, planting a kiss on Chloe's cheek and affectionately wiping away the lipstick smudge with her thumb.

"Thanks. I was so nervous coming down the stairs, I almost peed my panties."

Simone chuckled. "You did great, dear."

Jules Fabré, the well-kept older man Simone was dating, approached, carrying two wineglasses. "Here you go, *cher*," he said, handing a glass to Simone.

"*Merci*. Oh, Jules, you've got to introduce Chloe to your daughters."

"*Tres bien*." Jules summoned two tall, blond, super-slim girls who appeared to be in their early twenties, each clad in couture halter dresses that looked to be size "zero." Chloe had seen them numerous times before in the society pages of *Le Monde*.

"Chloe, this is Mimi and Paulette," Jules said when the girls meandered over.

Jules' daughters glanced at Chloe with an air of disdain. Each tossed a barely audible "nice to meet you" in Chloe's direction before turning back to nurse their martini glasses and scan the room with bored expressions, as if they had been dragged here by their father and were waiting for someone more important to arrive. Chloe saw Madame de Tornquist walking by in her elegant stride, gawking in mortification at the short, low-cut handkerchiefs the girls were passing off as acceptable formalwear.

These bitches could use a few charm lessons, Chloe thought.

"Say, you seen Gigi yet?" she said to Simone, paying no mind to the pretentious Fabré sisters.

Simone sipped her wine and shook her head. "I haven't spoken to her all summer. She never calls, and every time I try to reach her, the dorm monitor says she's out. I know she's coming, though. She wouldn't miss your debut."

Simone peered around the ballroom, then pointed out Gigi arriving on the arm of her soccer-player beau. Justin's mop of dirty blond mini-dreads was swept back in a ponytail and he was wearing a cocktail jacket, dress shirt open at the neck and baggy jeans, like a rock star attending a hip industry function rather than a young lady's escort to a debutante ball.

"*Oh my god!* Is that Justin Bradshaw?" Mimi exclaimed, her vacant stare replaced by a spark of interest.

"What's *he* doing with her?" Paulette said in an imperious tone, scowling in Gigi's direction.

Chloe saw motherly anger flash in Simone's eyes, and Jules rubbed her shoulder with a soothing motion, seeming to placate her for the moment.

Clutching Justin's hand and guiding him past fawning women of all ages, Gigi came over to Chloe and the rest of the group. Chloe noticed his gate was wobbly, as if he'd gotten the party started by cracking open a six-pack during the limo ride over. But she was so thrilled to see her best friend after nearly an entire summer apart, she overlooked Justin's sloppy demeanor.

While Justin stopped to shake hands with a couple of men who were apparently big soccer fans, Chloe seized the opportunity to have a moment alone with Gigi.

She threw her arms around Gigi and then took her by the shoulders, checking out her red and white striped designer shift, which was just as short and low-cut as the ones the Fabré sisters were wearing. "You look great, Gi'!"

"So do you." Gigi handed Chloe a gift. "Sorry I missed your entrance."

"Don't worry about it. I'm just glad you're here."

Looking Gigi over once more, Chloe noticed red marks in the shape of fingerprints on her arm, like someone had grabbed her. "What happened?"

Gigi glanced down at her arm, self-consciously sliding her hand over the bruise. "Oh, this? Justin had a little too much to drink in the limo on the way over," she said, confirming Chloe's suspicion, "and he had to hold onto me for support when we were getting out of the car."

Before Chloe could question Gigi's explanation, she looked up and saw Jean-Baptiste invading her personal space.

"Hey, Chloe, you wanna dance with me again?"

She noticed his parents watching from a corner, as if this was a child's birthday party and they'd encouraged him to make nice with the guest of honor.

"Uh, maybe later," Chloe said, annoyed that he'd interrupted her reunion with her best friend in that singularly obnoxious way of his.

"Whatever. There's plenty of other girls here to dance with," he said smugly, walking away, as if depriving Chloe of some grand privilege.

"That's the guy I was telling you about the last time we spoke," Chloe said, turning to Gigi. "The one that hit on me at his parents' open house."

Gigi smiled knowingly. "Cute, but stuck on himself."

The girls shared a laugh at Jean-Baptiste's expense, and it felt good to giggle over a boy like they were in high school again.

"I can't wait to introduce you to Justin," Gigi said as her companion made his way past several more adoring fans.

"Well, well, the prodigal daughter returns," Simone said, putting her hand on her hip as she approached. "Since you haven't called or written me for two months, I don't know whether to hug you or scratch your eyes out."

"Hello, Simone, you're looking well," Gigi said, addressing her mother formally, as though speaking to a distant acquaintance.

"What happened to your arm?" Simone said, her angry tone turning to concern when she saw the bruise Chloe had noticed earlier.

"It's nothing," Gigi said. When Justin finally reached her side, she took his hand and introduced him to Simone.

"This is your mum?" Justin slurred, reeking of alcohol. "She looks like your sister. What a babe."

Simone was clearly flattered. "So pleased to meet you, Justin." she said, shaking his hand and tossing her long red tresses in that unmistakably flirtatious way Chloe recognized. "Gigi, I'm glad you finally get to meet Jules and his daughters, Mimi and Paulette."

"I've heard so much about you, I feel as though I know you already." Jules smiled at Gigi.

"I wish I could say the same," she replied, giving him a skeptical once-over.

"Oh my god. I'm your biggest fan," Mimi said, completely ignoring Gigi and stepping forward to gush over Justin.

"Would it be too much to ask to get a picture?" Paulette fluffed her frizzy blond mane, took a camera from her purse and shoved it at her father.

"'Course not, luv." Justin, obviously used to the female attention, grinned while the two girls flanked him. He seemed to lean on them for support, as if he could fall over any moment in his inebriated state

"Why don't you get in the picture, Gigi?" Jules said in a cordial tone.

"No, that's okay," Gigi said, looking Mimi and Paulette up and down like they were cheerleaders for Justin's rival team.

"Come on, babe." Justin beckoned Gigi over with a bob of his head.

As if obeying his command, Gigi smoothed her dress and sandwiched herself between Justin and Paulette, looking like a dwarf next to the leggy girl. "Chloe, why don't you join us? It's your party."

"I don't really feel like…" Chloe began to protest, knowing she was going to have to pose for dozens of other photos this evening, but acquiesced when she saw Gigi's pleading expression. It was obvious she wanted to deflect attention from the Fabré sisters, so Chloe handed Gigi's gift to Simone and wedged herself between Justin and Mimi.

While Jules fumbled with the camera, trying to activate the flash, Chloe saw Paulette glare at Gigi's dress like it was a dust rag. "Is that a Fabrice Morel?" the girl said to Gigi in an undertone.

"Yes," Gigi replied, looking straight ahead at the camera and not making eye contact with the girl. "It was a gift from Justin."

"I have one of those in the back of my closet from last season," Paulette said, affecting a saccharine smile as her father snapped the photo.

Gigi looked over at Chloe, and they exchanged a glance that communicated their instant loathing for the snooty Fabré girls.

"I could use some champagne," Gigi said once the group broke apart.

"I could go for something stiffer," Justin said, tottering and taking a step back as if to steady himself. "Where's the bar?"

"Why don't you come with me, son?" Jules said, handing Paulette back her camera and taking Justin's arm. "I'll walk with you, so we can get to know each other."

Chloe admired the magnanimous way Jules ushered the stumbling Justin, so as to spare him from embarrassing himself and Gigi. Jules seemed nice, Chloe thought, but it was too bad it didn't rub off on his daughters.

"We're going to go freshen up," Mimi said, grabbing her sister's arm as soon as their father was across the room.

"Those two emaciated bitches are probably going to stick their fingers down their throats," Gigi said when they were out of earshot.

Simone looked pained. "Look, I know they come across as a little bratty, but they're daddy's girls. Their mother died when they were young and they're used to having Jules all to themselves. They're not used to sharing their father with me." She paused and added, "Or with you, for that matter."

"Why would they have to share their father with me?" Gigi said with a baffled expression. "I've been away at school, and knowing how you go through men, he'll be history by the time summer's over."

"Not this time. Jules and I are pretty serious."

"Yeah, right. That's what you always say."

"It's different this time." Simone drained her wineglass and handed it to a passing waiter. "Where are you staying?" she said to Gigi. "Can you come over for dinner tomorrow?"

"Sorry. Justin and I are leaving on an early flight in the morning. He has a home game tomorrow."

"I really need to talk to you," Simone pressed. "How about coming over after the ball?"

"I'm really exhausted. It's been a long day. Justin and I are just going to go back to the hotel. He needs to rest up for the game tomorrow."

Sobering up wouldn't be a bad idea, either, Chloe thought.

"Besides," Gigi added, "whatever you have to tell me, you can tell me now."

Simone glanced at Chloe and handed Gigi's gift back to her. "I'd really rather not go into it right now. This is Chloe's night."

"Hey, I'll give you two a moment alone." Chloe backed up, remembering to balance herself on her heels the way she'd learned in finishing school.

"No, stay," Gigi said. She turned back to Simone. "We're all family here. Anything you have to say to me, you can say in front of Chloe."

Chloe stood still, her eyes darting between Gigi and Simone, not sure whether to stay or go.

"Fine." Simone looked over to the bar, where Jules was conversing with Justin, then turned to Gigi and said, "Jules proposed. I asked him to give me time to think about it and talk it over with you, but I've pretty much made up my mind I'm going to say yes. I'm tired of being alone, and Jules is a good man."

Chloe took another step back, wishing she'd left Simone and Gigi alone to talk over the sensitive subject. Chloe studied Gigi's face, trying to gauge her reaction, but Gigi just stared open-mouthed at her mother.

Maxine came up and broke the awkward silence. "Why's everyone looking so down? This is my baby's coming-out party," she said, putting her arm around Chloe. "Liven up, for heaven's sake."

As if responding to Maxine's dictate, they jumped at the sound of a loud thud across the room, which caused the string quartet to abruptly stop playing. The musicians looked over, along with the other guests, and saw Justin on the floor on his butt. He had apparently knocked over one of the buffet tables in his drunken state and was surrounded by broken plates. Gigi rushed to his side.

Chloe watched from across the room as Gigi and Jules helped Justin up, and Maxine, in her typically efficient manner, directed the catering staff to clean up the mess. The guests gawked and whispered among themselves at the spectacle. The Fabré sisters had returned from the restroom just in time to see Justin fall on his ass. They turned away and now shunned the young soccer star they had drooled over just minutes earlier – lest they be associated with someone who had committed the *über*-sin of social faux pas, no matter how hunky or famous he was. Madame de Tornquist observed the action from a corner with a look of pity, as if she felt for the young man who was sorely lacking in social graces.

Watching Gigi and Jules struggle to help Justin stand, Chloe bit the inside of her cheek. She knew the incident would undoubtedly make the papers, since Mother had also insisted on inviting *Le Monde*'s society columnist, who was busy scribbling notes. Despite the fact that Justin's ruckus had disrupted her deb ball, Chloe's only concern was that Gigi would be embarrassed. As much as Chloe had reservations about Gigi's relationship with the rowdy young footballer, she knew Gigi loved him, as she demonstrated by the way she came to his aid.

"Just a minor spill, nothing to be concerned about," Maxine announced from the center of the ballroom as the wait staff swept up the broken dishes. Taking command of the situation as usual, she cued the musicians to play again. "This is a party. Everyone, go back to enjoying yourselves."

Chloe watched Jules and Gigi leading Justin out of the ballroom.

"Come on, son," Jules said in a fatherly way to Justin. "Let me help you upstairs to lie down and sleep it off."

Simone took Gigi's hand as she passed, pulling her aside. "Where are you going?"

Gigi looked at Simone as if her mother had lost her mind. "To help Justin. Where else?"

"Let Jules handle that." Simone nodded at Jules' back as he continued to guide Justin out of the room, the young man's arm slung lazily around the older man's shoulders. "We need to talk. And not just about my pending engagement. That Justin obviously isn't good for you, judging from the way he just made a total ass of himself."

Gigi yanked her hand from Simone. "You have no right to judge, not with your track record with men," she said, sounding indignant. "And now you've found some geezer to be your sugar daddy. Well, good for you. But don't you dare try to tell me how to live my life."

"I'm your mother, remember? And I want you to give Jules a chance. We're going to be a family."

Chloe, witnessing the ugly exchange from the spot where she was anchored, saw a mean streak shine in Gigi's eyes. Chloe had seen this omen dozens of times before, when Gigi was about to say or do something to get back at her mother.

"A family, huh?" Gigi said, her voice laced with sarcasm. "I don't need to be part of your little family. I'm going to have a family of my own."

Simone furrowed her brow. "What are you talking about?"

Gigi glanced at Chloe. "I wasn't going to say anything tonight either, since this is Chloe's party, but since we're on the topic…" Gigi held up her hand, flashing a rock the size of Mount Olympus. "On the way to Paris, Justin and I stopped off in Monte Carlo and eloped."

Time stopped. Gigi's words rang in Chloe's ears like an alarm. Chloe stood frozen in her pink satin slippers like a petrified tree, dumbfounded. Gigi, Chloe's best friend since... since forever, married? This was not happening. It simply could not be happening.

The color drained from Simone's face. "You ran off and got m-married without my permission?"

Gigi looked satisfied, as if she'd sufficiently one-upped her mother. "Don't forget I'm eighteen now. I'm a legal adult. I don't need your permission."

"My daughter's married, and I wasn't even invited to the wedding? Why doesn't this surprise me? Well, I guess you beat me to the altar. I can't believe you ran off and married that boy without even consulting me. I may not have been the best mother in the world, but I've been around enough to spot trouble when I see it, and it's plain to see he's not right for you."

"You don't even know him. I'm proud to call him my husband."

My husband. Those words sounded like a foreign language coming out of Gigi's mouth, Chloe mused. Gigi was always the wild one, the one who claimed she never wanted to be bound to just one guy, and now she was somebody's wife. This was unreal.

Maxine approached, once again breaking an uncomfortable silence. "I'm glad that little mishap is taken care of," she said, dusting her palms. "I had Marie make up the guestroom for your boyfriend, Gigi, so he can sleep it off."

"He's not her boyfriend, he's her husband. My daughter's married," Simone said robotically, staring blankly at a spot on the wall, as if catatonic.

"What? What are you talking about?" Maxine said, looking back and forth from Simone to Gigi.

"I'll explain later. First, I need a drink." Simone put the back of her hand to her forehead, like she was feeling faint.

Maxine glanced sideways at Gigi, then led Simone away to the bar, leaving Chloe alone with Gigi. Normally, they would have been gabbing away after so much time apart, but Chloe had no idea what to say to Gigi anymore.

"I'm sorry I had to break the news this way, Chlo'," Gigi said after a long moment. "I was going to tell you, but it was kind of a spur-of-the-moment thing."

Chloe tried to part her lips, but her jaw was clamped shut.

"I'm going to move in with Justin. He just bought a big estate outside London that used to belong to some duke and he's renovating it," Gigi continued, prattling on as if she and Chloe were housewives dishing over coffee. "You're going to have to come visit us before summer's out."

"What about school?" Chloe mustered the strength to say.

"I dropped out."

Gigi's latest announcement hit Chloe like a fist in the gut. The anticipation of being college roommates with Gigi in a few months had kept Chloe going over the long, lonely summer.

"But what about... What about trying to get into the Sorbonne and all your dreams of being an artist?"

"Who was I kidding? That's never going to happen. I don't have what it takes, never did. Look, Chlo', I wasn't completely honest when we spoke a few weeks ago. I failed my remedial courses. I was going to flunk out sooner or later, anyway, if I didn't drop out."

"You gave up, just like that? What about our plans?" Chloe said, her bottom lip trembling.

"We were just kids when we made those plans, foolish kids."

Chloe hugged Gigi's gift like a security blanket. "I didn't think our plans were foolish."

"I know, but things just haven't turned out like I thought they would."

"You can say that again."

"When Simone marries Jules and moves in with him and his two bitchy daughters, there'll no place for me in their little family. And school, I don't belong there either."

"Come on, Gi'. Don't be so hard on yourself. You're smart, you just don't try hard enough. I've told you that all along. How much time did you really spend studying this summer, and how much time did you spend goofing off and hanging out in the locker room with your boyfriend – I mean, husband?" She barely managed to say the word, stumbling over it like a terminal diagnosis that shouldn't be uttered in polite company.

"I'm not like you, okay?" Gigi said, her voice high-pitched, as if pleading for forgiveness. "Do you know how envious I've always been of you? You have it all: looks, brains, money. You get to model and you ace classes and all the teachers love you. Your mother owns a company, but mine just works there. And you get to live in this big, beautiful chateau. Do you know how many times I've wished this house was mine? That I was the one who got to ride your horse and have my own bathroom?"

Chloe twitched, stung by Gigi's admission. She had no idea Gigi felt this way. "You know you're welcome here any time."

"It's not the same."

Chloe sighed in frustration. Trying to reason with Gigi was proving increasingly futile. "Gigi, please, think about what you're doing. After the crash and the way Justin behaved tonight, are you sure running off and marrying him was a good idea? I know you're in love, but you could probably get an annulment since it was on the spur of the moment –"

"No, that's not an option." Gigi stepped forward, lowering her voice. "Chloe, don't repeat this because I don't want Simone to know just yet –"

"What?" Chloe braced herself, not sure she could take any more bombshells.

"I'm pregnant."

She stared in shock at Gigi, then bolted from the ballroom, up the stairs, and locked herself in her room. She ripped off her diamonds and tiara, kicked off her shoes, flung Gigi's gift aside and threw herself on the bed.

"I hate her!" she sobbed.

She was so hurt, so betrayed. Gigi was so selfish. She was ruining everything, all their dreams. All Gigi had to do was stick to their plan and everything would have been all right, but she gone and thrown it all away because she couldn't keep her legs closed. Simone was right. Gigi was nothing but a whore.

The sound of footsteps echoed in the hallway. "Chloe, are you mad at me?" Gigi said from the other side of the door, knocking lightly.

"Go away!"

"Chloe, please try to understand. I know I've screwed up again – that's what I'm good at – but just please try to understand."

"I have nothing else to say to you."

Chloe heard Gigi hover at the door for a moment, then the sound of retreating footsteps grew faint.

Wiping away tears, Chloe hoisted herself off her bed and crouched in a corner, where she had tossed Gigi's gift. She tore away the silver wrapping paper and red ribbon and opened the box. Inside, surrounded by billowy tissue paper, was a music box. Atop the box, a porcelain mime clutched a bouquet of balloons that threatened to whisk him away. Gigi had painted the balloons lavender, Chloe's favorite color. A tear ran down the mime's frowning face. Chloe cranked the box and watched the mime spin to a forlorn melody.

43

Chloe pushed pasta around her plate while Maxine and Simone talked shop around the dinner table on the Chateau de Chevalier's screened-in porch.

"I'm going to London next week to meet with a new client. Why don't you come with me," Maxine said to Simone. "We can stop in and visit Gigi and her husband."

Chloe set her fork down, relieved Mother had broached the subject. Chloe was still in shock at what Gigi had done, but it hurt more not to talk about it.

Simone didn't look up from her plate. "I'm not talking to Gigi."

"I know you're upset about her running off and getting married without your blessing, but she needs you now," Maxine reasoned.

"Yeah," Chloe piped up. "Don't you want to be there for her and the baby?" Her hand reflexively shot up and covered her mouth. She had let Gigi's little secret slip.

"Oh my god. I'm going to be a grandmother and I'm not even forty." Simone fumbled for her wineglass.

Maxine continued sawing her steak. "I guess I can't say I'm surprised," she said, sounding blasé, as if Gigi's pregnancy was bound to happen. "I've been telling you for years to get that girl some birth control."

Chloe grimaced. Why couldn't Mother ever pass up an opportunity to say, "I told you so"?

"I've done all I can do for Gigi." There was a flatness in Simone's voice Chloe had never heard before. "It's time for her to live her life and for me to live mine."

Chloe threw her napkin down on the table. She couldn't believe Simone. Chloe was still mad at Gigi, too, but how could a mother be so cold to her own daughter when she needed her now more than ever? "May I be excused?"

Without waiting for Mother's approval, Chloe rose and stomped off to the kitchen to talk to Marie.

"It's almost ready," Marie, who was icing a carrot cake, said when Chloe entered.

"I'm not hungry." Chloe plopped on a stool.

Marie wiped her hands on her apron. "You still upset about Gigi?"

"Yes, and Simone's being a bitch. I just let it slip that Gigi's pregnant and she acted like she didn't even care. She turned it around and made it about her, like she always does, and how she doesn't want to be a grandmother."

Marie rinsed her hands in the sink and wiped her hands on a dishtowel. "You know, it takes time to adjust to news like this. Everybody has their own way of dealing with things."

"I still can't believe Gigi's married. I can't believe she's going to have a baby."

"I met that Bradshaw boy at your party. If some handsome soccer star gave me the time of day when I was your age, I probably would have run off with him, too." Marie smiled, obviously trying to cheer Chloe up.

"She says she loves him."

"Sometimes young girls can't tell the difference between love and infatuation."

Chloe rested her elbow on the counter and propped her chin up with her palm. "Everything we talked about since we were kids, all our plans, all our dreams. Down the drain."

Marie picked up the pastry tray. "Gigi has made her choices," she said, walking to the dining room door. "Now you have to make yours."

Chloe stood in line at the University of Paris registrar's office, trying to tune out the loud indie rock blaring through the headphones of an Asian guy cradling a battered skateboard in front of her. The music intermingled with ringing phones, chatty students and office workers clacking away on computer keyboards. The historic building apparently had not been equipped with air conditioning, and a whirring ceiling fan circulated a sweltering mix of body heat and late-summer humidity around the cramped room.

While waiting to sign up for fall classes, Chloe scanned a display case with brochures advertising interesting-sounding electives. She picked up a leaflet on learning to play piano – something she'd always wanted to do but knew she had no aptitude for – and browsed another course description on alternative religions of the world. The latter sounded like a welcome reprieve after three years under Mother Superior's iron rule.

"Next," the middle-aged woman with a bad perm and a librarian's fashion sense called in French from behind the registration desk. The Asian skateboard dude stepped up, finally turning off his radio and mercifully lowering the decibel level in the overcrowded office.

Chloe replaced the brochures and began fumbling in her purse for her identification, when another leaflet caught her eye: "Study Abroad in New York City." Bold red script beckoned above a photo of the Statue of Liberty, torch raised against a cloudless blue sky.

Snatching up the brochure, Chloe devoured every detail about the city where she was born – the museums, Broadway theaters and avant garde performance spaces, arts and culture brimming on nearly every street corner. For the first time since she'd graduated, Chloe reflected on Sister Maureen's suggestion that instead of matriculating to the University of Paris as Maxine expected, she should venture out and realize her dream of studying acting in New York.

"Next."

Chloe looked up from the brochure, disoriented. She had been so absorbed reading up on New York that it was as if she had been momentarily transported there and was shocked to find herself standing in the drab registrar's office, surrounded by rickety file cabinets and pimply-faced teens who were gawking at her as if she were an extraterrestrial.

"Mademoiselle, are you next?" The lady behind the registrar's desk leered at Chloe with her false eyelashes.

Chloe moved to take a step forward, but it was as though she were cemented in place. She glanced around at the unsmiling faces and the room began to shrink, as if the stale air was causing everything to constrict.

"Please come forward, mademoiselle," the admissions lady repeated impatiently.

Chloe continued to peer at her surroundings, feeling like the fawn she'd glimpsed munching dew-laden grass on her first morning at the Chateau de Chevalier. Like the fawn, Chloe felt exposed, vulnerable.

School had always been her anchor, the place where she excelled no matter what was going on in her home life. But for the first time, she felt totally out of place in this academic setting.

"Mademoiselle?" The lady behind the desk raised a painted brow, glaring at Chloe like she belonged in a psych ward instead of an institution of higher learning.

Becoming short of breath, as if suffocating, Chloe stepped out of line and bolted from the room. She ran out of the building, down the steps and all the way to the Métro station. It was only when she had boarded the train that would take her home that she exhaled.

As the subway took off, she glimpsed herself in the window opposite her seat, hair plastered to her sweaty forehead. She glanced down and realized she was still clutching the brochure on New York. She took one last look at it, then stuffed it in her purse.

Chloe sat on a stool at the kitchen island, helping Marie snap peas for the evening meal.

"Okay, out with it," Marie said, tossing a handful of peas into a pot.

"What do you mean?" Chloe pushed a strand of hair out of her eyes with the back of her hand.

"Usually you'd be running off at the mouth while we work, but you've been quiet ever since you got back from campus."

Chloe dropped the pile she'd been working on into the pot and stared past Marie, through the kitchen window, looking out over the grounds. She had no idea how to communicate what she was feeling. "When I went to register this morning, I don't know, something came over me and I couldn't go through with it," she said after a long pause.

"Mmm-hmm." Marie, deftly snapping bunches of peas at a time, didn't look up, but her contemplative expression indicated she was listening.

"Up to now, my whole life's been laid out for me – go to school, get good grades, get into college. But ever since Gigi got knocked up and ran off and got married, nothing seems certain anymore."

Without answering, Marie got up and took the pot to the sink, filling it with water. She wiped her hands on her apron and returned to her seat across from Chloe. "What are you saying, that you want to put off college for a while?"

Chloe nibbled on a pea, staring out the window again. "I guess. I don't really know what I want anymore." Putting college off did seem appealing. An extended break without the confines of exams, papers and having to be somewhere every day at a certain time would give her an opportunity to clear her head and put the situation with Gigi into perspective.

"You know, my daughter Irène went through something similar at your age." Marie reached for a mound of dough and began kneading it. "When she graduated from high school, she wanted to put off her first semester of college and spend some time backpacking around Europe with her friends, just going wherever their fancy led them, camping out under the stars and staying in youth hostels."

"That sounds like fun." Chloe imagined herself hitting the road with nothing but the bare essentials strapped to her back, visiting Hemmingway's old haunts and treading down the winding streets of Pamplona, Spain, for the annual Running of the Bulls.

"Of course, my husband Albert, God rest his soul, wasn't having it," Marie continued, running a rolling pin over the dough. "He had an old-fashioned work ethic and believed young people with too much time on their hands were courting trouble."

"Sounds like he and Mother would've gotten along," Chloe said with a laugh. "So what happened?" She listened for Marie's response with anticipation, as if finding out Irène's fate would help her determine her own.

"I tried to convince him that we should let Irène take some time off, but he yelled and harangued that we didn't work and scrimp and save to send her and her brother through parochial school for her to go prancing off with a group of hooligans. He was a good man, but, *mon Dieu*, did he have a temper." Marie shook her head, as if recalling how obstinate her husband could be. "Anyway, Irène eventually gave in to shut her father up and enrolled at the University of Paris, where you're going."

"And?" Knowing Irène had attended the school where she was supposed to enroll further piqued her interest in the story.

"What do you think happened? She failed all of her classes and ended up running off to join the Peace Corps." Marie chuckled. "She's a good girl, though, and eventually went back and got her master's in social work.

288

She's settled and married now and, as you know, has given me two adorable grandbabies. Albert would be so proud."

"So what do you think I should do?" Chloe asked as Marie placed the dough on a baking sheet.

"It's not my place to tell you what to do," Marie said, going to the double oven and placing the bread in the lower compartment, "but from my experience with my daughter, sometimes young people have to find their own way. If that means putting off college for a while, then so be it."

Chloe slouched, shrinking at the frightening prospect of telling Maxine she wanted to postpone college. "Mother's going to have a conniption. I know she's worked really hard and given up a lot for me, just like you and your husband did for your kids. I don't want to let her down."

"You can't live your life to please your mother," Marie replied, her back turned as she adjusted the temperature dials.

"Are you saying I should defy my mother?" Chloe said, as if receiving Marie's permission would embolden her to do just that.

Marie said nothing at first, wiping down the counter and tidying the island, as if choosing her words carefully. "I'm saying you should follow your heart," she said finally. "I know Madame Chevalier loves you more than anything in the world, but if there's one thing I've learned over the years, it's that no one can live your life except for you, Chloe. No one."

Chloe smiled appreciatively. "Thanks, Marie. It's a comfort to know I can always count on you for good advice."

Marie's words registered with Chloe and helped her make up her mind. She was now convinced herself that putting off college was for the best. Now the hard part would be convincing Mother.

This was the night. Maxine was home for dinner on time, a rare occurrence. Chloe knew that if she didn't approach her mother this evening about her plans to postpone college, she might never find the right time.

This certainly wasn't going to be easy, Chloe thought as she sat down across from Maxine on the screened-in porch. She was so nervous she thought she was going to combust. She had to excuse herself and go into the kitchen to get encouragement from Marie.

"I can't do it, I just can't," Chloe told Marie.

"Yes you can, Chloe," Marie said firmly, setting aside a spatula.

"She'll be so disappointed in me."

"Madame Chevalier is a strong woman. She'll get over it. Now, go back out there. I'll be right here if you need me."

Chloe stood still, hesitating.

"Go on," Marie said, giving Chloe a little push.

Chloe resumed her seat at the table and tried to collect herself. She rehearsed what she was going to say in her head as Marie served the main course.

"This smells wonderful, Marie. You outdid yourself once again," Maxine said, digging into her *la médiatrice,* a delectable oyster dish and one of Maxine's favorite Creole recipes that Marie had learned to prepare.

Marie set Chloe's plate in front of her with a reassuring smile and went back in the kitchen.

"You seem fidgety," Maxine said as Chloe shifted in her seat. "Is something wrong?"

Here was the opportunity. Chloe took a deep breath, trying to work up the nerve to say to her mother what she knew she had to say.

"Oh, I forgot to mention that a letter from the University of Paris came the other day," Maxine said before Chloe could utter a word. "They said you haven't registered for fall semester yet. Don't keep putting it off, dear. I told you to do it last week, remember? The letter said competition for classes can be pretty steep."

At least Chloe didn't have to bring up the subject. The gods must have been working in her favor.

"Mother, I have something to tell you."

"What?" Maxine said, sounding unconcerned as she attacked her plate.

"It's sort of like this..." Chloe fiddled with her fork, clanking it against her plate. "I'm going to college –"

"Of course you are," Maxine interrupted, dabbing at her mouth with a napkin.

"Will you let me finish?"

"Go ahead. I'm listening."

"What I was going to say was that I'm going to college, just not right now. I'd like to take some time off." She sat back, the relief of having finally gotten it out washing over her.

Maxine swallowed, took a sip of wine, and pushed her plate aside with an expression that said she was evaluating Chloe's announcement. "College is a big step. If you want to take a semester off to prepare yourself, I guess nothing's wrong with that. I could even find something for you to do at the shop so you can get some practical work experience before you start school."

"I want to take more than a semester off."

Maxine scooted closer to the table, her expression turning more serious. "How much time are we talking about?"

"I don't know. Maybe a year."

"Out of the question," Maxine said without hesitation.

"Hear me out, Mother. Look, Gigi really threw things off course when she got pregnant and married that guy. We had a plan, but now everything's changed. I feel like I need to get away to think things through and figure out what I want to do with my life."

"There'll be plenty of time for that once you finish college."

"I've always done what's expected of me. I need a change."

Maxine blinked, as if trying to bring everything into focus. "Let me get this straight. Are you telling me that you just want to throw away twelve years of private-school education? That's ridiculous. Eat your dinner, *ma chérie*. It's getting cold."

"I'm an adult now. I can do what I want." Chloe was surprised by the words coming out of her mouth. She had never spoken to her mother like this before. But it was true, she was eighteen, a legal adult.

Mother, however, still insisted on treating her like a minor. "You may think you're grown, young lady," she said in the condescending tone she'd taken since Chloe was little and would challenge her with some childish act of rebellion, "but as long as you're living here, you're going to listen to me." She spoke as though she were reasserting her role as the head of the household.

Marie entered, carrying a pitcher of water, but quickly backed up, as if repelled by the force of Maxine's outburst. Before returning to the kitchen, Marie nodded at Chloe, prodding her to continue despite Maxine's resistance.

Encouraged by Marie, Chloe marshaled her strength. She could see the aggressive approach wasn't working, so she tried Plan B. She took her mother's hand and said calmly, "This is something I have to do, Mother. If you'd only listen to me for once."

Maxine snatched her hand away, ripped her napkin across her mouth, and threw it on the table. "I won't hear another word of this foolishness – skipping college and running off to do god-knows-what," she said, storming away from the table. She stopped in the doorway, turned to Chloe and, her voice softening, added, "I know this little stunt was inspired by Gigi dropping out of school, but you're not going to end up like her, not if I can help it."

With that, Maxine retreated into the house, leaving Chloe alone to reflect on the encounter and wonder what she was going to do now.

44

"If you'll just sign these invoices, that should wrap everything up," Maxine said, sitting across from Yves and Madeleine Lambert in their newly-decorated drawing room, handing them the last of the paperwork related to their chateau's renovation.

"The open house last month was such a big hit," Madeleine raved, gold bracelets jangling as she clasped her hands. "We're thrilled with your work."

"*Oui*," Yves interjected, scribbling his signature on the invoices, "everything couldn't have turned out better if we had done it ourselves."

"I'm so glad you're pleased with the end result."

Maxine sat back in the plush velvet chair she had upholstered and sipped her tea, regarding her soon-to-be-former clients. While the Lamberts' one-time association with Haiti's deposed dictator had initially unsettled Maxine, she had to admit the couple had grown on her. Over the past several months of working with them, she had found numerous things in common with Yves and Madeleine. Not the least of which was their traditional values.

"If there's ever anything we can do for you," Yves added, handing over the signed paperwork, "please let us know."

"You know what would be a big help? Pass my name on to all of your friends. That's how I get most of my business – referrals."

"We hope you don't mind if we stay in touch and call on you socially from time to time," Madeleine said. "We've grown quite fond of you and your lovely daughter. How is Chloe?"

Maxine sighed, thumbing through the paperwork to ensure every "X" had a signature. "Don't ask. She's talking about putting off college so she can take time to 'find herself.'" She threw up her hands. "Children. What can you do?"

"We know what you mean," Madeleine said, placing her hand on her husband's. "Our oldest, Jean-Baptiste, is on the verge of flunking out."

Maxine looked up from the paperwork. "Is he having trouble in his classes?"

"He might, but he'd have to show up first," Yves said, chuckling and shaking his head.

"Going to high school in America did him no good," Madeleine explained. "He picked up that lazy attitude of his American peers – studying only when he feels like it and spending too much time partying."

"I've tried to set a good example and pass on my work ethic, but it just hasn't sunk in," Yves said, sounding frustrated. "The more I lecture him, the more intent he seems on doing his own thing."

"It's not your fault. I'm sure you've both done the best you could as parents," Maxine said, empathizing.

"You know what our Jean-Baptiste needs? A nice young lady to settle down with, someone like your Chloe." Madeleine looked at Maxine as though she possessed the power to set Jean-Baptiste on the right path.

"Uh, whoa, guys," Maxine said, setting down her teacup. "You're very nice people and I'm sure you want the best for your son, but if you're talking about playing matchmaker to our children, I don't think –"

"Think about it," Madeleine interjected. "You just said Chloe wants to put off college, and at the rate he's going, Jean-Baptiste probably won't finish. If we got them together, they could be good for each other."

"Madeleine has a point," Yves said. "Settling down might be just the thing our Jean-Baptiste and your Chloe need to straighten them out and make them more responsible."

Maxine opened her mouth to speak, but was so flabbergasted she didn't know what to say. She hadn't even allowed Chloe to date seriously up to this point, let alone coerce her into a relationship.

"I'm not sure I'm following," Maxine said cautiously, fixing her gaze first on Yves, then Madeleine. "Our children barely know each other. Are you proposing some kind of arranged marriage?"

Yves and Madeleine looked at one another, squeezing each other's hands.

"It's very common back in our country," Madeleine said. "It worked out for Yves and I."

"I was so focused on work and making something of myself when I was a young man," Yves said, "I never would have taken a bride if my parents hadn't had the foresight to choose one for me."

"And do you think I would have chosen *you*? A dark-skinned farm boy?" Madeleine laughed, affectionately cradling her husband's chin. "I had far more high-minded plans for my future. My head was full of fantasies. I used to dream of running away to Hollywood and becoming a model or an actress. From the time I was a little girl, everyone told me how beautiful I was, and it went straight to my head."

Maxine said nothing, wondering if the same were true of Chloe.

"Madeleine's the best thing that ever happened to me," Yves said, patting his wife's hand. "As beautiful as she is, I resisted marrying her at first. I knew our parents had an interest in us being together, since my father worked the land and her father distributed our crops."

Maxine glanced down at the paperwork in her lap, thinking that the way in which Yves and Madeleine came to be husband and wife was as cold and commercial a transaction as these invoices.

"But I'm so glad I listened to my father and married Madeleine," Yves continued. "She's given me six beautiful children. And now I want Jean-Baptiste to settle down so that he can take over the winery in Bordeaux someday, just as I did with my father's plantation."

As though he detected his parents were plotting to curtail his youthful rebellion, Jean-Baptiste rudely announced his entrance by thrusting open the

293

front door and stomping past the drawing room.

"Jean-Baptiste, where are your manners? Aren't you going to greet Madame Chevalier?" Madeleine called after her son, who proceeded to ignore her and barrel up the stairs, slamming the door to his room. Within seconds, bass-heavy hip-hop music began rattling the windows, disrupting the previously tranquil house.

"Please excuse our son," Yves said. "We trained him better than that, but lately he seems out to prove that we can't control him."

Maxine nodded, thinking the same was true of Chloe. "It's okay. He's at that age, I understand. I should be going, anyway." She slid the paperwork into her briefcase, stood and offered her hand to the Lamberts. "I've enjoyed working with you both. Please do stay in touch."

"Think about what we said." Madeleine rose along with her husband to shake Maxine's hand. "Jean-Baptiste obviously needs some reining in –"

"*Oui*," Yves spoke up, picking up his wife's point in the familiar way of long-married couples, "and it sounds like your Chloe could use some, too."

Maxine and Simone huffed and puffed frenetically, moving in sync along with a dozen other sweaty women to the disco beat booming from the dance studio's oversize speakers.

"And that's a wrap!" the dance instructor announced from her position on a platform at the front of the class. "Make sure to hydrate and get in a good stretch before hitting the showers."

Simone reached for her water bottle. "Thank God *that's* over!" she grunted, toweling off her sweaty chest, her heaving bosom straining the contours of her leotard.

"I've never seen you work out that hard before," Maxine commented, wiping perspiration from her forehead and panting, but not as heavy as her pack-a-day smoker best friend and business partner.

"I'm not kidding myself. Jules is marrying me because he wants a young trophy wife."

"'Young,' of course, being a relative term," Maxine teased.

"Very funny." Simone slung her towel over her shoulder and slid her hands under her bosom, examining her figure in the studio's mirrored walls. "You think I should get a breast lift?"

"You're talking crazy," Maxine said, lifting a leg onto a dance bar and beginning to stretch. "You shouldn't go cutting on yourself. You don't even turn forty until next year."

"Thanks for reminding me. God, I can't believe I'm going to be a grandmother at thirty-nine."

Maxine bent over in a graceful ballet stretch, displaying the flexibility from her younger days. "Have you talked to Gigi?"

"No, and I don't plan on it."

Maxine switched legs, stretching her opposite side. "Simone, I know you're still angry at her, but you had Gigi when you were young, too. Can you imagine how scared she must be? Why don't you pick up the phone and call her?"

Simone didn't reply. She was too busy examining the area under her eyes. "I could probably use a nip and a tuck. Years of smoking have not helped my crow's feet." She sighed, releasing her skin and patting her hand under her chin, as if checking for sagging flesh. "I wish I had your coloring. 'Black don't crack,' as they say."

"Good genes are priceless," Maxine concurred, bending over and touching her toes. "But seriously," she said, standing upright again, "why don't you give Gigi a call? I'll be happy to give you some time off to spend with her in London, talking things over."

"Max, I know you're trying to be helpful, but from what you told me about Chloe wanting to skip college, it sounds like you've got enough to worry about in your own household."

"You've got a point there," Maxine said, looking down as she flexed first her right foot and then her left in a calf stretch. "This is the first time as a parent that I can honestly say I don't know what to do. Chloe's eighteen now. What am I supposed to do, take her by the hand and drop her off at school like I did when she started kindergarten?"

Simone picked up her gym bag, tossing in her towel and water bottle. "I wish I knew what to tell you, but I'm the last one to be dishing out motherly advice. I have my doubts about that footballer or whatever he is that Gigi ran off with, but at least she's got her own life now instead of constantly wreaking havoc in mine. Marrying her off was probably a blessing in disguise."

As Simone left the studio to report to the locker room, Maxine turned to stare at her image in the mirror, reflecting on what Simone just said.

Chloe ripped the page she was scribbling on from her notebook, balled it up and tossed it in the heap on the floor next to her bed. Her notebook was full of poems that made no sense. She couldn't focus. There was too much on her mind – Gigi's shotgun marriage, starting college in a few weeks and being thrust into a new environment where she knew no one.

Chloe had resigned herself to the fact that her plot to postpone college was irrational, just as Mother said it was. She may as well sign up for classes at the University of Paris and throw herself into her studies, make the best of the situation. After all, she had worked hard for her grades at the Lycée and Our Lady of Chastity. Going straight to college was the sensible thing. As always, Mother was right.

"Why can't growing up be easy?" Chloe said to her cat, Bizou, who was perched at the foot of her bed and responded to her query with a yawn. "I should probably get to sleep, too. I have to get up early tomorrow and go register for classes. I guess I'll actually go through with it this time."

Setting aside her notebook, Chloe got up to go to the bathroom to get ready for bed and bumped her foot on the leg of a chair. Feeling restless earlier in the day and worrying about all the confusing choices she faced, she had rearranged her furniture to keep herself occupied and was now paying the price with a bruised big toe.

Instead of taking an aspirin when she reached the bathroom, she took a bottle of sleeping pills from the medicine cabinet. With all that was on her mind lately, she was having trouble falling asleep and Mother's doctor had prescribed these pills.

Chloe screwed off the top and held the open bottle over her free hand. She glanced at herself in the mirror, suddenly realizing how easy it would be to gulp down all the pills and never have to wake up again. She could just lie down, close her eyes and never again have to think about how Gigi had ruined their lives. She would never be forced to make another agonizing decision – choosing to indefinitely delay her dreams and "do the right thing" and go to college as Mother expected.

Chloe hovered at the sink, considering whether to empty the bottle, when the sound of meowing snapped her back to her senses. She looked over and saw Bizou crouched in the doorway with an accusatory look, as if the cat somehow sensed that her owner was considering abandoning her by taking her own life.

"Don't worry, Bizou," Chloe said. "I'm not going anywhere. You're stuck with me."

She shook one pill into her palm, washed it down with a sip from the faucet, and put the bottle away. Returning to her room, she picked up Bizou and nuzzled her. When she set the cat on the bed, she accidentally knocked onto the floor the university's course catalog, which she'd been thumbing through earlier. Upon picking up the catalog, the brochure on the study-abroad program in New York fell out. She opened it, poring over the glossy photos of the Statue of Liberty, the Empire State building and other landmarks she longed to see up-close. Gazing at the photos, she felt a longing, as though the city where she was born was beckoning to her.

A knock at her door startled her and she slid the brochure under a pillow. "Come in," she called.

Maxine, in her robe and nightgown, entered and sat down on the bed next to Chloe. "I've been thinking, *ma chérie*," she said in a subdued voice that was a stark contrast to her angry tone the other night. "If you don't want to go to college right away, I guess I can't make you."

Chloe, beyond perplexed, didn't respond. Her mother's attitude had made an about-face this drastic in a couple of days?

"If I forced you to go, your grades would only suffer," Maxine continued, "and what good would that do?"

Chloe stared at Maxine, suspicious of her coming in here, acting as if everything was settled all of a sudden, but she didn't let on. "Thanks for understanding," she said quietly, shrinking away from her mother in fear that she would change her mind again and revert to ranting and raving.

Instead, Maxine leaned over and kissed Chloe on the cheek. "Get some sleep. We can talk about all this later. There's plenty of time." She got up and let herself out.

Now Chloe was more confused than ever.

45

"I'm glad you joined me, *ma chérie*," Maxine said, locking arms with Chloe as they ascended the steps of the Opéra de Paris Garnier. "Seeing Kathleen Battle sing the lead role in *Tosca* is going to be so exciting."

Chloe smiled but said nothing. She, too, was excited about seeing the African-American opera diva perform, but she was suspicious of how unusually cheerful Mother had been the last few weeks. Mother was usually stressed and grouchy this time of year, gearing up for the busy fall season. Whatever the reason, Chloe was glad that Maxine hadn't pushed the subject of college lately.

As Maxine led her inside, Chloe admired the ornate architecture of the Baroque theater, which had been the setting for Paul Leroux's classic play *Phantom of the Opera* – which, of course, later because became a world-famous Broadway musical.

On the way to their box seats, Maxine greeted friends and clients. When Mother waved to someone across the theater, Chloe noticed the Lamberts sitting in the box directly across from theirs. She saw Jean-Baptiste, his arms crossed and his legs extended in an unruly pose that indicated attending the opera with his parents was not his idea of fun. He turned and stared at her with those penetrating hazel eyes. Giving a quick wave, she popped her gold-plated theater goggles into place and trained her attention on the stage so that she wouldn't have to make eye contact. There was something about the way he looked at her, as if he owned her.

When the curtains parted, Chloe forgot about Jean-Baptiste and lost herself in the production. Maxine, in an effort to pass on her lifelong love of arts and culture, had toted Chloe to the opera before. In the past, Chloe had been bored numb by the nonstop warbling of Italian lyrics she couldn't understand. But having starred in her school's production of *Les Miz*, she had a new appreciation for the stage.

Peering through her goggles, Chloe marveled at the elaborate sets and costumes, the painstaking attention to detail. And most impressive of all was Kathleen Battle's command of the stage, making the audience believe that instead of a black woman from Ohio, she was the ill-fated Italian songstress Tosca. And that voice was like a force of nature. Chloe knew she had done only a passable job singing her lines in *Les Miz*, but Ms. Battle's voice was like a finely-tuned instrument, alternately high-pitched enough to shatter glass and low and subtle at just the right dramatic moments. Chloe could only hope to bring such passion and emotion to the stage someday when she realized her dream of becoming an actress.

Partway through the second act, Chloe's concentration was disrupted by the odd sensation that someone was watching her. She looked up from her goggles and saw Jean-Baptiste staring at her again. She immediately focused on the stage once again, but she could feel his eyes on her throughout the rest of the first half.

At intermission, Maxine excused herself, saying she was going over to greet the Lamberts. Chloe thought it odd that Mother didn't insist on dragging her over as well, but she was just glad she didn't have to make forced conversation with Yves, Madeleine and their creepy son.

Chloe flipped through the program to pass the time, and whenever she glanced up, Mother and the Lamberts were looking in her direction while talking feverishly. She tried to read their lips, but she couldn't glean what the conversation was about. All the while, Jean-Baptiste continued to stare at her with that self-satisfied smirk, as if he had some inside information to which she wasn't privy.

A wave of relief washed over her when the theater darkened and the curtains parted again just as Maxine returned to her seat. Chloe tried to concentrate on the action onstage, but throughout the rest of the show, she could feel Jean-Baptiste's piercing glare.

"I don't understand why you're making such a big deal about me going out with him." Chloe stood in front of her bedroom mirror in a slip, trying on dresses for a date with Jean-Baptiste that Mother and his parents had orchestrated.

"It's not a big deal. I just think he's a nice boy and you should give him a chance," Maxine said, picking a formal black dress from the closet that Chloe sometimes wore to church.

Chloe took the dress and held it against her frame. "Why didn't he just ask me out himself? It's weird that he had his parents ask you if I'd meet him for dinner."

"I think it's old-fashioned and sweet – the parents setting everything up. That's how they do things down in Haiti. It reminds me of New Orleans – very Creole."

Chloe hung the black dress on the edge of the mirror and selected a more modern one with a colorful print. "I don't like the way he looks at me. He kept staring at me the other night at the opera."

"He's probably just shy and didn't know how to approach you."

Chloe held the dress up in the mirror, modeling again. "Jean-Baptiste, shy? I get the impression he's anything *but* – full of himself is more like it."

Satisfied with the dress she chose, Chloe began wriggling into it.

"Is that what you're wearing?" Maxine looked at Chloe with disdain. "What about the one I picked out?"

"It's too dowdy."

"It's not dowdy. It's formal. The restaurant Jean-Baptiste is taking you to is upscale. You want to be properly dressed."

"Mother, you don't have to lay my clothes out for me like I'm in grade school. I'm eighteen now, remember?" Chloe said in disgust. "And for someone who's so busy playing matchmaker, you're sure trying to make me look like a nun."

"Call me old-fashioned," Maxine said, helping Chloe pull her arms through the dress's billowy sleeves, "but I just think a young woman should look demure on a first date."

"I wouldn't even be going on this so-called date if you weren't pushing that Lambert boy off on me," Chloe said, flipping her hair over the back of the dress. "Up until now, you've been so strict about me dating. Why are you so insistent that I go out with him?"

Maxine began smoothing the dress and dusting off pieces of lint – insistent on babying Chloe. "Just give Jean-Baptiste a chance, *ma chérie*. I never would have married Jacques if I hadn't kept an open mind."

Chloe looked away, not meeting Maxine's gaze in the mirror so that her mother wouldn't see tears welling up as she thought of her late stepfather. She still missed him so much. Now more than ever, she wished she had a father figure to talk to and give her guidance.

"Okay, okay, I'll go on this stupid date," Chloe finally relented. "But I'll meet him there instead of having him pick me up so I can make a quick escape if he starts getting on my nerves."

Maxine placed her hands on Chloe's shoulders, making one last motherly inspection. "Makes sense. I'll have Louis give you a ride."

"And if he annoys me as much as he has the past few times I've been around him, I never want to see him again."

Maxine went to Chloe's jewelry box, chose a gold necklace, and handed it over. "Whether you see Jean-Baptiste again or not is entirely up to you."

Chloe strode into La Maison Bleu and immediately wished she had worn the more formal gown Maxine had picked out. Chloe nervously tugged at her off-the-rack dress as the maitre d' showed her past tables where smartly-clad diners spoke in hushed tones amid soft music and glanced askew at her.

There's no way a college student could afford to bring a date here, Chloe thought, observing the authentic Matisse and Cézanne paintings adorning the walls. *Mommy and Daddy must be picking up the tab.*

When Chloe reached the table, she saw Jean-Baptiste slouching in his chair the way he had done at the opera. In his baggy jeans, shirt open at the collar and casual blazer, he looked more like an American hip-hop star hanging out at a nightclub than the son of a well-to-do immigrant family on a date at a high-class restaurant. Instead of rising to greet her, he simply glanced up at her with that smirk of his.

"*Merci*," Chloe said as the maitre d' seated her and handed her a menu.

"You look nice," Jean-Baptiste murmured, his eyes focusing on the V-neck of her dress that revealed the slightest hint of cleavage.

"Thanks." She held the menu up, self-consciously shielding her bosom from view.

Jean-Baptiste continued to stare at her without saying anything, so she attempted to make conversation.

"This is a nice place. You come here often?"

"No, never been here before. My parents picked this place."

Just as I thought, Chloe said to herself, *his folks set this whole thing up.*

When the waiter came over, Jean-Baptiste ordered without bothering to ask her what she wanted. The thoughtless gesture reinforced her impression of him as self-centered.

When the waiter brought out the first course, Chloe hungrily attacked her salad, glad to fill her mouth so as not to have to make forced small talk with Jean-Baptiste. He didn't exactly wow her with stimulating dinner conversation, continuing his irritating habit of staring at her silently.

"So, how's school going?" Chloe said to break the awkward silence when the waiter had cleared their salad plates.

"Not too well, I guess."

"Oh? Not hitting the books enough?" Chloe said, feigning interest. She resisted the urge to tell him to sit up straight, the way her etiquette tutor, Madame de Tornquist, would have. He had committed every major gaffe at the dinner table other than drinking from the finger bowl.

"Nah. I guess I like partying too much. My parents say I need culture," he said, leaning back in his chair, hand resting between his legs, as if illustrating his parents' point. "And to be exposed to a better class of people than the ones I hang out with at school, which is why they dragged me to the opera the other night."

"Hmmm." Chloe looked around the restaurant, having run out of things to say. She was in no position to criticize Jean-Baptiste's poor study habits, having put off college herself.

"You know, *Maman* and Papa keep saying I should find a nice girl and settle down," he said, sitting up and looking lively for the first time. "They were married and had me by the time they were my age, and they say I should do the same, that it would give me some direction in life."

Chloe squirmed under the intensity of Jean-Baptiste's now-familiar but still disconcerting glare. "Oh, really?" she sputtered, sipping her water to calm the jitters that suddenly overcame her. "Maybe you'll meet someone."

Jean-Baptiste smirked again, as if amused by Chloe's subtle rejection. "My parents say they want me to find someone to start a family with and carry on the family name. Actually, they threatened to take away my car keys and cut off my allowance if I don't 'get it together,' as they say."

Chloe looked Jean-Baptiste up and down, trying to determine if he were joking. She thought it was absurd that someone his age still got an allowance. Her part-time modeling income gave her at least a measure of independence.

"I know how my folks are," he continued. "They won't settle for just any girl for their eldest son. They want someone special." He leaned in, reached over and ran the tips of his fingers over her cheek. "Someone like you. A Creole girl – not too dark, not too light."

Chloe reflexively bristled, not only at him invading her personal space and touching her, but at his despicable words. He spoke to her as if she was auditioning to be his future wife, selecting her on superficial criteria, as if she were a wall hanging that would enhance his parents' redecorated chateau.

She saw an opportunity to make her escape when the waiter brought out the main course.

"You know what? I'm not really hungry," she said, scooting her chair back from the table. "I better get going. I've got an early call tomorrow."

Jean-Baptiste opened his eyes beyond their usual half-mast postion, intrigued. "An early call?"

"Uh, yeah. I model every now and then and I've booked a couple of assignments tomorrow. I probably shouldn't be eating all this heavy food. I don't want to look bloated on-camera." She punctuated her improvised excuse with a nervous laugh, thanking God she'd insisted on meeting him here rather than having to endure a long ride home and being subjected to more of his bullshit.

"Oh, come on, even models have to eat. You've got to try this veal." Jean-Baptiste speared a portion of his dish and waved it at her with a flirtatious grin.

"Tempting as that is, I've really got to go. I should get to bed early. I always try to be on time. Modeling's just a way to earn extra money right now, but I take it pretty seriously."

Jean-Baptiste broke his smug expression by laughing out loud, holding his stomach as if he'd just heard the funniest punch line ever.

"What's so funny?" She stared at him in the imperious way he'd been looking at her all night.

"Nothing, sorry," he said through chortles. After nearly a minute of uncontrolled laughter, drawing scornful glances from other diners, he finally composed himself and took a sip of water. "It's just that every pretty girl I've gone out with has this silly notion in her head that she's going to be a famous model or actress."

Chloe could feel her breath going shallow, her nostrils flaring with contempt. How dare he mock her dream? He didn't even know her. And the more he spoke, the less desire she had to get to know him.

She threw her napkin on the table and rose to leave. "I've got to go."

46

"Bonjour, *ma bellotte*," Simone said, throwing open the door of her apartment and embracing Chloe. "Come on in."

"Thanks for letting me stay here while I'm working in the city," Chloe said, lugging an overnight bag over her shoulder as she made her way inside.

"No need to thank me. You know you're always welcome," Simone said, stepping aside to welcome Chloe in and looking youthful in a T-shirt, jeans and a paisley scarf tied over her flaming tresses. "It makes total sense to stay here while you're doing your modeling assignments, rather than trekking all the way back home at the end of a long day. A young girl shouldn't be riding the Métro alone at night." She began padding toward the kitchen in her bare feet. "I was just doing some cleaning and was about to take a break. You want something to drink?"

Chloe tossed her bag on an empty chair and followed, taking note of the boxes that littered the floor. "You moving?"

"Yeah. I'm going to be moving in with Jules after we get married," Simone said, opening the refrigerator.

"Oh yeah, that's right, I almost forgot," Chloe said, pulling up a chair at the dinette set where she used to eat breakfast with Gigi during their girlhood sleepovers. "I've been so preoccupied with the whole ordeal of convincing Mother to let me put off college."

"Maxine hasn't talked much about that lately, and I've been afraid to ask. How'd that go?" Simone set a diet soda on the placemat in front of Chloe and joined her at the table.

"Okay, I guess. That's why I've lined up these modeling jobs – to put some money away until I decide what my next move is." Chloe cracked open her soda and took a sip, reflecting on Maxine's seemingly abrupt change of heart on the issue. "She went ballistic when I first told her I didn't want to start school in the fall, but then she changed her mind all of a sudden and said it was okay for me to take some time off."

Simone, straddling her chair backwards like a dance-hall girl, nodded knowingly. "That's Maxine. Moody as can be – a tempest one minute, gentle rain the next. That's why I usually hole up in my office and stay out of the storm." She laughed, sipping her soda through a straw.

"Have you noticed she's been acting kind of strange lately?" Chloe probed. "I mean, more pleasant than usual, considering this is you guys' busy season."

"Hmm. No, can't say that I have." Simone looked thoughtful, reaching under her scarf and scratching her scalp. "But then again, I haven't been paying close attention. I've been too busy planning my wedding and getting ready to move. *Mon Dieu!* You never know how much stuff you've got until you have to pack it all up!"

Chloe stared out the kitchen window at the Seine. "I can't help thinking Mother's up to something. She's just been too calm, and it makes me nervous."

The ringing phone interrupted the conversation.

"That's probably Jules," Simone said, getting up to answer the kitchen extension. "Why don't you make yourself at home? You know where everything is – if I haven't packed it away already!"

While Simone conversed with her fiancé in French, Chloe retrieved her bag from the front room and traipsed down the hall to Gigi's old room, where she'd be staying.

Upon opening the door, an incredible feeling of sadness swept over her. The space that was once filled with laughter and animation was now morbidly quiet and still – the opposite of Gigi's colorful personality.

Chloe went to Gigi's desk, where her childhood friend used to sketch and paint, and looked over some of her drawings that were pinned to the wall. She picked up a scrapbook from the desk, sat on the bed and began flipping through it.

Chloe smiled in spite of the melancholy she felt, reflecting on fond memories as she looked over school memorabilia, ribbons and certificates Gigi had won in art contests, and candid shots of the girls and their mothers at various stages of their lives. Happening upon a snapshot of herself and Gigi with Montana Blake and Dominique on the beach in Monaco, Chloe shook her head in disbelief. The photo was taken only last summer, but that experience seemed like eons ago. So much had changed since then – Gigi was married and expecting a baby and Chloe had deviated from the college-preparatory track Maxine had placed her on as soon as she could read.

Studying the photo, Chloe ran her finger over Gigi's face, as if touching her image would bring back the free-spirited, rambunctious girl depicted in the photo.

"I miss her, too."

Chloe looked up to see Simone standing in the doorway, arms wrapped around herself as if she were cold, even though Paris was still in the throes of oppressive summer heat.

"Have you talked to her?" Chloe said softly.

"No. I guess I've been waiting for her to make the first move." Simone entered the room and sat beside Chloe. "You know how it is with me and Gigi: stubborn pride."

Chloe nodded, looking down at the scrapbook.

"I've been meaning to pack up her stuff and send it to her in London," Simone said after a moment, "but I don't even have her new address."

"I can give it to you. I have a stack of letters she sent me with her return address."

"How's she doing?" Simone said eagerly. "What'd she say in the letters?"

"I don't know. I haven't opened them." She paused, taking a long look at the photo of her and Gigi with their boyfriends last summer. "I started to open them last night so I could get her new phone number. I had this really bad date that Mother set me up on with the Lambert boy, and when I got home, all I wanted to do was call Gigi and tell her all about it and talk about boys for hours on end like we used to." She sighed, her shoulders slumping. "But somehow it just didn't seem like it would be the same."

Simone put her arm around Chloe. "You know, *cher*, Gigi and I have issues that are not easily resolved, so I understand how you feel, but I hope you don't give up on her. If there's anything Gigi needs right now, it's a friend."

Chloe's gaze drifted around the room, pondering Simone's words while scanning the teen-idol posters, album covers and other remnants of youth that lined the walls. "I still can't believe she's married and about to have a baby. And if you would have told me this time last year that I'd be putting off college, I'd have said you were crazy." She leaned into Simone's embrace, as if acting as Gigi's proxy for her mother's stingy affection. "Things have not turned out at all like I thought they would."

"*C'est la vie*, my dear," Simone said, massaging Chloe's shoulder. "You think you have things all planned out, but then the unexpected happens. If you'd have told me this time last year that I'd be marrying an older man with two grown daughters, I'd have laughed in your face."

Chloe was quiet for a moment, appreciating the fact that Simone, the closest thing to an aunt, seemed to understand where she was coming from – even if Mother didn't.

"Do you remember this trip?" Chloe said, sliding the scrapbook halfway onto Simone's lap and pointing out snapshot they'd taken with Gigi and Maxine.

"*Oui.* That's when Maxine and I agreed to be chaperones on you and Gigi's eighth grade trip to Euro Disney. What a day that was." Simone smiled. "You girls were about to become teenagers, but for that one day, Gigi seemed like a kid again and we laughed and squeezed each other's hands when we rode the roller coasters." Tears formed in Simone's eyes. "That wasn't that long ago, but now Gigi's going to have a kid of her own."

"I wish I could roll back the clock to that time and stay there forever. Things were so much less complicated then." Chloe stared at the photo, as if willing it to open up and let her and Simone step inside. She looked up at Simone and added, "I know, you don't have to say it. Learning to cope when things don't go as planned is a part of growing up, right?"

"Actually, that's not what I was going to say. What I was going to say is that even though I'm twice your age, we have something in common."

Chloe gave Simone an intrigued look. "We do?"

"Yes. We both want to stay young forever." Simone pulled back the flesh of her face, imitating a bad facelift. To further lighten the mood, she tickled Chloe like she used to do when she and Gigi would jump in her bed to wake her up when they had sleepovers.

Chloe briefly forgot about her increasingly complicated, grown-up existence and broke up laughing.

*****

Chloe's lips quivered as she posed for the camera, standing atop a skyscraper. She was doing her best to look grownup and sexy in the couture gown she was modeling, but keeping her composure was torture. It seemed as though the first strong wind would sweep her off the ledge and send her plunging to her death.

"Hold still, *cher*," Marjorie Malveaux, the photographer, directed. "You're shaking again."

Chloe's cheeks ached from twisting her face into various expressions and her legs felt like they were going to buckle from standing all day, but she did her best to honor the photographer's request.

Marjorie had a way of coaxing models into taking risks, having been one herself. Athletic and strong with an untamed mass of brown curls, Marjorie was of the breed of 1980s "glamazon" that was the antithesis of the stick-thin waifs who dominated the industry these days. Marjorie had reinvented herself as an in-demand photographer, and Chloe wanted desperately to win her approval.

"Let's try something else," Marjorie said, stepping away from the camera and wringing her hands. "Can you step closer to the ledge?"

Chloe swallowed and took a small step backward, trying to hide her fear.

"A little further back." Marjorie waved at her as if directing a truck driver pulling up to a loading dock.

Chloe backed up to the ledge and stood, frozen.

"Sandrine, can you fix her hair?" Marjorie said to the stylist, who promptly rushed to rearrange Chloe's windswept hair and run a makeup brush over her face.

"That's good." Marjorie waved the hair and makeup artist out of frame. "Chloe, *cher*, can you prop your arms on the ledge?"

When would this nightmare end? She did as she was told, placing her trembling elbows on the ledge, feeling like an acrobat venturing out on a tightrope.

"Can you spread your arms so I can see the bracelet?"

Chloe's knees knocked, not so much from the high-altitude breeze but from the knowledge that just a piece of stone separated her from tumbling backward to the traffic zooming by below. She managed to obey once again, spreading her arms on the ledge, defying her fear.

"You look tense." Marjorie had stepped behind the camera and was looking through the viewfinder. "Relax your face, *amour*."

Easy for you to say. She tried to do as she was told, spreading her arms out further and feeling like she was posing for a Crucifixion scene rather than a fashion spread. Her wrist scraped against the stone, unfastening the latch on the gold bracelet she'd been given to wear. The bracelet went sailing over the ledge and she reflexively glanced over her shoulder, watching it fall.

"Don't worry about that bauble. That's what insurance is for," Marjorie said. "I need you to look at me."

Chloe heard Marjorie's command, but her gaze was fixed on the sixty-story drop. She already felt lightheaded from skipping breakfast, and the sight of the busy street far below made her dizzy.

"Chloe, *cher*, I need you to focus."

She swallowed her fear and turned to the camera. She could do this. If she were to succeed at acting, she would have to get used to coming out of her comfort zone.

Marjorie snapped off a few shots. "Tell you what. Why don't you sit on the ledge and prop up one foot? You're laughing at the skyline in the distance. You own the city." Like the veteran supermodel she was, Marjorie demonstrated the pose she wanted Chloe to enact.

Before following Marjorie's direction, Chloe glanced back again at the terrifying drop. *I can do this*, she told herself again. *No, I have to do this.*

She saw this challenge not only as an opportunity to overcome her fear and cement her newfound adulthood, but as an opportunity to prove she could truly act. In the photos, she was playing a character, that of a carefree socialite with such an unrestrained approach to life that perching on the ledge of a skyscraper meant nothing.

She carefully hoisted herself to a seated position on the ledge, imitating Marjorie's demonstration and making sure not to look down. Slowly, she lifted the hem of her dress, raised her left leg and placed the heel of the Dior stiletto she was wearing on the ledge.

"Loosen up a little," Marjorie said. "Try to look natural."

Chloe leaned forward, resting her elbow on her knee. Looking natural would be a quite a feat, considering that every muscle in her body was tensed.

Marjorie waved her hand, directing her movements again. "Can you move back just a hair?"

When Chloe went to comply, her heel slipped off the ledge and she lost her balance. She screamed, nearly flipping over the ledge.

Marjorie lunged forward, catching Chloe just in time, her camera dropping to the roof's asphalt surface and breaking. "You okay?" Marjorie said, pulling Chloe away from the ledge with her strong swimmer's arms.

Terrified and shaking violently, Chloe was unable to speak, and simply nodded.

"Hey, I know you're a new model," Marjorie said, holding Chloe by the shoulders, as if to steady her, "but you don't have to do everything the photographer tells you to. You can always say no. Even to a crazy former model like me."

Chloe appreciated Marjorie's attempt at levity and tried to return her grin. "Yeah. Sorry. About your camera." Chloe's words came in staccato bursts, her jaw feeling like it was held together with iron pins.

Marjorie waved dismissively at the broken camera, as she'd done earlier with the bracelet. "It's just a tool. I have a dozen others. We can salvage the film. Let's wrap. It's been a long day."

While Marjorie and the crew began dismantling the lights and equipment, Chloe stood in place, shivering despite the still-potent, late-afternoon sun. She thanked a stylist who handed her a robe, but her teeth chattered.

Before leaving the rooftop with the rest of the crew, Chloe ventured to the ledge and took one last look down. With the forceful wind rippling through her hair, all she could think about was the gruesome demise she had narrowly escaped.

47

Chloe was still shaken up from her near fall from the skyscraper when she got home.

"Mother?" she called, throwing open the front door of the Chateau de Chevalier. Instead of going back to Simone's apartment as planned, all she wanted was to rush to her mother's side and tell her all about her day, like when she was little and scraped her knee at the playground.

Seeing a light coming from the parlor, Chloe rushed down the hallway. "Mother? Mother, you'll never guess what happened to me today," she said, rounding the corner leading into the room. Her words came in an excited rush, just like when she was a kid and had some important bit of news to report. "I was doing a shoot on the top of this building and –"

Upon entering the room, Chloe stopped short, noticing that Mother was having coffee with Yves and Madeleine Lambert.

"*Excusez-moi.* I didn't realize you had company." She began backing out of the room. Drained from the harrowing shoot atop the skyscraper, the last thing she wanted was to make forced conversation with the Lamberts. Especially after the horrible date with their obnoxious son.

Madeleine turned to Maxine and began muttering in Creole, while looking at Chloe. How rude. How many times had Maxine told Chloe that it was impolite to whisper about people in their presence?

"Won't you join us, *s'il vous plaît?*" Yves said, gesturing toward an empty seat on the sofa next to Maxine.

"Thanks, but I just got back from a really long modeling shoot and I'm exhausted," Chloe said, continuing her slow retreat toward the door. "I'm just going to grab something to eat and go straight to bed."

"There's something we need to discuss with you, *ma chérie*." Maxine patted the cushion next to her. "Come on in and have a seat."

"I had a really bad experience today, Mother, and I just want to –"

"Have a seat."

The firmness in Maxine's tone gave Chloe pause. She recognized her mother's serious expression as a signal that further protests would not be tolerated. She sat next to Maxine, glancing at Yves and Madeleine. They were looking at her like she held the clue to a treasure hunt. She looked at Maxine, who was shifting in her seat as if preparing to deliver a speech, and wondered what was going on.

"Yves and Madeleine and I have been discussing this for a while now," Maxine said, setting aside her coffee mug and taking Chloe's hand, "and we think you and Jean-Baptiste getting married would be the best thing for both of you."

Chloe said nothing, not sure she had heard her mother correctly. Instead of English, French or Creole, it was as if she had spoken in some completely foreign dialect.

"I'm sorry," Chloe said, looking at her mother intently. "Come again?"

"We were hoping you two would hit it off at that date you went on," Madeleine said. "He's very taken with you."

"He couldn't stop raving about how beautiful you are when he got home," Yves added, beaming at Chloe like she was the bearer of his future grandchildren.

"I - I'm flattered," Chloe fumbled, blindsided by all this talk about marriage. She'd gone on one lousy date with Jean-Baptiste, and now their parents were acting as though she were engaged to him. "But I'm not ready to get married. I just turned eighteen. I'm not even sure what I want to do with my life just yet."

"That's entirely the point. You're in need of some direction in life, and so is Jean-Baptiste." Maxine looked at Yves and Madeleine, who responded with confirming nods. "You've decided to skip college, and he's on the verge of flunking out."

"Look, this is moving way too fast. This is absurd." Chloe stood up, growing more outraged with each breath. "I can't talk about this right now. Please excuse me."

She rushed out of the room and up the stairs. Still nauseous from the dizzying experience atop the skyscraper, she went straight to the bathroom and vomited. Panting, she splashed water on her face and lay down on her bed, trying to collect herself and make sense of what had just transpired.

Maxine burst into Chloe's room. "The Lamberts just left," she said. "I told them you're not feeling well. That was rude, walking out like that."

She was being rude? Mother had auctioned her off like some prize heifer, and she had the nerve to accuse Chloe of bad form?

"You can't do this to me." Chloe sat up, holding her still-queasy stomach. The prospect of a life of wedded servitude to that moron made her wish she had thrown herself off that skyscraper.

"Chloe, don't be difficult," Maxine said, sitting down on the bed. "Marrying Jean-Baptiste is the only way to deal with this situation."

"What situation? I'm not pregnant, if that's what you think. I never slept with him. I wouldn't even let him kiss me goodnight."

"I know you're not pregnant, but since you've decided that college isn't for you, this is the best alternative," Maxine said, as if she sounded perfectly logical.

"This is crazy," Chloe said, her voice growing quieter, realizing that arguing with her mother on this topic was getting her nowhere. She didn't feel up to a shouting match, but she was determined not to back down. Maxine couldn't just marry her off without her consent. An arranged marriage? Mother was acting like they were back in turn-of-the-century New Orleans, promising her fertile young Creole daughter to some French aristocrat.

"I could never be happy with Jean-Baptiste, don't you understand?" Chloe said after listening to Maxine go on and on about the merits of marrying into the Lambert family. "I don't love him, and I never could."

"You can learn to love him."

Chloe shook her head. "Never."

"Chloe, I've had only two wishes for you since the day you were born: the first was that you would get a good education, finish college like I never did, and the second was that you would marry well. And let me tell you, the way you've been acting lately, one outta two ain't bad."

Chloe stifled the urge to scream. Mother just didn't get it. "How many times do I have to tell you? I don't want to be married. Not to him. Not to anyone. And you can't make me," she said, her juvenile tone betraying her attempt at asserting her rights as a legal adult.

"I've done the best I could as a single parent. God knows it hasn't been easy," Maxine said, getting up and going to the door. She paused in the doorway. "In order to make it to where I am today, I had to beg, borrow, and steal everything I could. I promised myself that my daughter would never have to beg for anything. Nothing was handed to me the way things have been handed to you, and you're not going to make a shambles out of your life." Before leaving the room, she added, "Not if I have anything to do with it."

Chloe stared blankly ahead at the engagement photo as she stood on a pedestal in the fitting area at Chez Maxine, two seamstresses positioning her arms and legs like a mannequin as they made alternations to her wedding gown. The photo was splashed on the cover of the *Le Monde* society page, which Mother had proudly tacked to a bulletin board. "Scion, Debutante to Wed," the headline read.

"Stand up straight, dearest," Maxine said, putting her palm on the small of Chloe's back. "I want everything to be perfect."

Chloe mechanically followed her mother's orders, as she had been doing for the past few weeks. At first, she'd argued nonstop with Mother about the insane plan to marry her off to Jean-Baptiste. Chloe had tried every weapon in her arsenal to talk sense into her mother, from outright refusing to marry the Lamberts' son to recruiting Marie and Simone to intervene on her behalf. Simone was too preoccupied with her own wedding plans to get involved and Marie's attempts to talk to Maxine were met with a polite yet firm directive not to overstep her bounds. For reasons that were still unclear to Chloe, Maxine was hell-bent on Chloe becoming the new Madame Lambert.

Just like when Chloe was little and she refused to swallow bitter medicine or do something else her mother deemed "for your own good," Maxine's forcefulness wore her down. Chloe's adamant protests eventually gave way to resignation. It was true, as Mother kept pointing out, that Chloe had no idea at the moment of what she planned to do with her life. Having no concrete plan for the future, it was hard to counter Mother's relentless arguments.

Chloe slouched on the pedestal, feeling utterly powerless. She could run away, but she didn't know where to go, and the prospect of fending for herself alone in the world frightened her as much as being trapped in a loveless marriage.

Maxine was orchestrating every detail of the whirlwind wedding. The marriage of Chloe Bareaux and Jean-Baptiste Lambert was going to be the second biggest social event of the year in Paris – after Chloe's debutante ball, if Maxine got her way. As always, Maxine took control, designing the gown, personally addressing each invitation and coordinating the catered reception, which was to be held in the Chateau de Chevalier's ballroom.

"Hard to believe in less than twenty-four hours you'll be a married woman," Maxine said, examining the seamstresses' work as the women put away their pins and tape measures.

"I'm so glad you decided to stop fighting me on this. I only want what's best for you, *ma chérie*."

While Mother pulled and tugged at the dress, making sure each seam was to her specifications, Chloe stood on the pedestal, staring ahead and saying nothing. Just a few months ago, she had stood in that very spot, being measured for her deb-ball gown. And now she was to be married. A wedding was supposed to be the most important day of a young woman's life, but Chloe couldn't have felt more detached. She was being forced to marry a boy-man she didn't love.

In the car on the way home, Mother continued to blather on about the guest list, the menu for the reception and other trifles. Chloe just stared out the window, watching dusk envelop the City of Light and cast eerie shadows on statues and street corners. Sainte-Chapelle, the cathedral where Chloe was to marry Jean-Baptiste the next morning, loomed against the darkening sky like a forbidding medieval fortress.

Once they got home, Mother got on the phone in the kitchen to go over last-minute details with Yves and Madeleine. Marie had left dinner in the fridge, but Chloe had no appetite. She went up to her room and sprawled on the bed, which was covered with congratulatory cards and letters from people she either didn't remember or had never met. It was all a sham, a cruel hoax.

Chloe began tidying up to get ready for bed and came across the engagement announcement again. She skimmed the society columnist's summation of her pending nuptials to Jean-Baptiste: "The union joining the offspring of Jacques Chevalier's widow and the heir of the Lambert vineyard enterprise will be a merger of fortunes and family names."

Chloe balled the newspaper up and stuffed it in a drawer. She didn't recognize herself in that story. It was as though they were describing someone else.

Dumping the pile of cards and letters on her desk, she caught sight of an envelope with Gigi's new address in London. She hadn't opened any of Gigi's letters, since she was still angry at her for derailing their plans, but curiosity got the best of her this time and she ripped open the envelope and read the card:

Dear Chloe,

I heard about your wedding and just wanted to say congratulations – if congratulations are in order, that is. I wish I could be there, but I understand if you're still mad at me.

I hope we'll be able to talk things over and see each other again some time soon.

Love Always,
Gigi

Chloe sunk to her bed, clutching Gigi's card and breaking down in tears. She had been so busy going through the motions of Mother's wedding-planning frenzy the past few weeks that the enormity of everything was just now hitting her. The malaise she'd been feeling since she stopped speaking to Gigi had mushroomed into a full-blown depression.

Wiping her tears, she got up and tossed Gigi's card in the trash and swept the rest of the correspondence off her desk and into the wastebasket as well. There was no point in inviting Gigi to the wedding. Even if she made up with Gigi, this was not going to be a happy occasion she wanted to share. Gigi had no way of comprehending what Chloe was going through. Gigi had chosen her fate, while Chloe was being pushed into marriage by overbearing parents.

Going to the bathroom, Chloe stared at herself in the mirror. She was still trying to figure out where everything went wrong. She was supposed to be an independent college student, experiencing her first taste of freedom and living it up as roommates with her best friend. Instead, Gigi had gone and gotten herself pregnant and jumped head-first into a quickie marriage. And it would soon be Chloe's turn to walk down the aisle.

She opened the medicine cabinet and retrieved a bottle of sleeping pills, staring at it like it held the answers to the convoluted mess her life had become. She slowly unscrewed the lid and titled the bottle slightly, so that a single pill fell into her palm.

Bizou, Chloe's cat, appeared in the doorway, mewing at her as if she knew what Chloe was about to do and was begging her to reconsider.

"Sorry, Bizou, but this seems like the only way out."

She took one last look at herself in the mirror before emptying the rest of the bottle and washing it down with a glass of water.

Returning to her room, she took out her wedding gown, stepped into it and turned out the light. In the darkness, Bizou's glowing eyes glared at her, as if indicting her for the mortal sin she'd just committed.

Chloe shooed her cat off the bed and lay back, crossing her hands over her chest, covering the gaudy ring Jean-Baptiste had given her. She might as well go out dramatically, like Juliet stabbing herself with her lover's dagger.

Chloe pulled the tulle veil over her face like a shroud and waited silently for the pills to take effect. All she wanted was to go to sleep and never wake up.

48

The sun intruded its way into Chloe's room, searing through her gauzy veil and dancing on her eyelids, refusing to leave her alone until she opened them. Jarring awake, she looked around the room, disoriented. At first, she didn't know where she was or even what day it was. Then it all came back to her like a recurring nightmare. It was her wedding day.

She sat up, clutching her aching stomach. The suicide attempt had failed. She had been foiled by some ruthless force in the universe that wouldn't let her die.

"I guess you're stuck with me after all, Bizou," she said in a groggy voice to her cat, who glared at her from her favorite position at the foot of the bed.

Groaning and still holding her cramped stomach, Chloe swung her feet to the floor and sat on the edge of the bed for a minute, summoing the strength to get up and go on. Finally, she got up, took off her veil and stepped out of her gown. She managed to shower, put on a slip and waddle down to the parlor, where she would be dressed by a team of Chez Maxine stylists.

"You don't look so good, *chouchou*," Marie said, carrying in a tray with croissants, strawberries and freshly-squeezed orange juice. "You need to eat something."

Chloe waved the food away, not wanting to speak and further irritate her dry, raspy throat. Food was the last thing she wanted. Her mouth felt like she'd inhaled a whole bag of cotton balls, her temples were throbbing and her intestines felt as though she had swallowed ground glass.

"You seem sluggish this morning, *ma chérie*," Mother said. Observing the crumpled gown Chloe had slung over her arm, she nearly gasped. "What in the world did you do to your dress, sleep in it?"

Mother began flitting around the room, issuing polite orders and outright commands to the stylists as they steamed the wrinkles out of the gown and attended to Chloe. Mother kept talking, saying things Chloe couldn't understand. Everybody's voices sounded like they were at the end of a long tunnel. Her vision was blurry. She was in a fog and couldn't seem to snap out of it.

Maxine's hairdresser, Gérard, curled Chloe's hair and fashioned baby's breath on either side of her face. She caught a glimpse of herself in the full-length mirror someone had brought down from her bedroom and barely recognized herself.

"Turn around and let us get a good look at you," Mother said, taking

Chloe by the shoulders and twirling her to face the small army of stylists.

At Mother's direction, the seamstresses made a few last minor alternations to Chloe's gown – an intricate tapestry of French silk and Chantilly lace. A train the size of Monaco followed behind her like a stray dog when she walked, trying her best to balance herself on her crystal-beaded, silk-satin sandals.

The wedding party rode to the cathedral in a caravan of limousines. The groom wasn't allowed to see the bride before the ceremony because it might bring bad luck. That was fine with Chloe. She wished she never had to see him again, ever.

Maxine, Simone and Marie got emotional before the ceremony began, crying and hugging Chloe, whose brain was in such a thick haze that all she could do was stand still, her arms dangling limply at her sides as the women embraced her.

Simone seemed the most distraught. "First Gigi, now you," she wept into a handkerchief. "You girls have grown up too damn fast. It makes me feel old."

"Stop cursing in church," Maxine scolded, crouching to the floor to adjust Chloe's train. "And don't forget, we'll be crying over you in a couple of months when you marry Jules."

Marie pressed the back of her hand to Chloe's forehead. "You feel feverish and your color's not so good. I told you, you should've eaten something this morning. I packed a little snack for you. I'll just go back out to the limo and grab it."

"We don't have time for that," Maxine said, standing. "The ceremony's about to start."

It was just as well. Chloe's stomach was still so cramped, if she ate anything, it would surely come right back up.

At the sound of the wedding march beginning, the women finally stopped fussing over Chloe and took their seats.

"I love you, *ma chérie*," Maxine said, kissing Chloe on the cheek before pulling down her veil. "This is all for you. Please remember that."

Maxine lingered at Chloe's side for a long moment, clutching her daughter's hand and dabbing at tears, until an usher showed her to her seat.

"Are you ready, dear?" Yves Lambert said, appearing at Chloe's side and offering his arm.

Chloe stared at him through her veil. Monsieur Lambert was standing in for Jacques by walking her down the aisle. She knew her stepfather would never go along with this farce if he were still alive. She wished he were around to talk sense into Mother and put an end to this charade.

"Chloe, *cher*, are you ready?" Yves repeated in a patient tone.

She dutifully took his arm, grateful at least that he could help her steady herself. She still felt out of it and wasn't sure she could make it down the aisle without stumbling.

The congregation uttered a collective sigh as the doors of the sanctuary slowly opened. The photographer Maxine hired began snapping photos and Chloe noticed the *Le Monde* society columnist who had covered her debutante ball scribbling notes. Chloe was glad her thick veil hid her expression, that no one could read the absolute dread on her face.

She silently coached herself as she put one foot in front of the other, the way she had done when she made her entrance at the deb ball. She could get through this, too, she told herself. But her lilies-of-the-valley bouquet trembled in her unsteady hand and her feet felt like lead as she neared the altar, where Jean-Baptiste was waiting. To calm herself and try to loosen the knot that had coiled like a cobra in her stomach, she pretended she was an actress playing the part of a joyful bride. But rather than a romantic comedy, she was trapped in a bad horror flick.

When she finally reached the altar after what seemed like a journey of miles, Yves took her hand and presented it to Jean-Baptiste, as if handing over the keys to a shiny new sports car to his spoiled son. Chloe glanced over at the front row, where Maxine, Simone and Marie were beaming at her with tear-streaked faces, then took Jean-Baptiste's hand and knelt beside him at the altar.

As Monsignor Gabriel began the ceremony, she tried to shift her thoughts to other things. The only image that came to mind was dozens of white doves being released as she and her new husband descended the steps of the cathedral. She couldn't get the sound of cooing doves and ringing bells out of her head. She could almost feel the sting of being pelted with rice by hundreds of cheering guests.

She was barely coherent throughout the ceremony. The priest sounded as though he were underwater. He was speaking in French, she could decipher that much. When he came to the vows, the part about Chloe and Jean-Baptiste loving each other 'til death did them part, her knees seemed to give out. Having knelt for nearly half an hour, her legs became wobbly, as if they could support her weight no longer. She was burning up all over and was short of breath.

Jean-Baptiste enthusiastically responded to his vows, punctuating his last response by directing one of his familiar smirks at her – as if smugly confident that he would soon have her under his legal control. Monsignor Gabriel turned to Chloe and began asking her the same questions. She didn't know if she was going to make it through the ceremony. Her chest heaved and her breaths came in shorter and shorter gasps.

When she looked up and saw Monsignor Gabriel nodding at her, she realized she had been letting her mind wander again. Apparently it was her turn to answer, commit to her wedding vows in front of God and man.

"I...I..." She knew what she was supposed to say, but the words wouldn't come – *I do*.

Dead silence enveloped the cathedral. She turned to Jean-Baptiste, who, instead of smirking, was now looking at her with a mix of confusion and contempt, like he was mad at her for embarrassing him in front of all of his parents' hoity-toity friends.

She tried once again to complete her vows, but all that came out was asthmatic wheezing. She felt lightheaded, as if she could fly away, an angel in white ascending to the heavens.

"I... I..."

Before she could finish the sentence, she lost consciousness, collapsing at the altar. The last sounds she heard were loud murmurs arising from the crowd and Mother screaming for a doctor as she rushed to Chloe's side.

When Chloe came to, she was in the back of an ambulance, surrounded by a team of paramedics.

"Don't worry, Madame Chevalier, we'll take good care of her," one of the men said while pumping a blood-pressure band attached to Chloe's arm. "She's going to be fine."

Maxine was at her side, holding her hand. "I'm here, *ma chérie*. Mommy's here."

Chloe tried to sit up, straining to see her mother's face, but the paramedic gently pushed her head back onto the gurney. Why was everything fuzzy? Although she heard voices, she couldn't distinguish any of the faces around her or see her feet. The skirt of her gown was pushed up to her waist. She stared at the seams of the lace, tracing its complex pattern with her eyes, a form of self-hypnosis. She was getting sleepy, very sleepy.

She couldn't keep her eyelids open anymore. She surrendered, letting the fog wash over her and carry her back to that silent, pitch-black place.

Chloe awoke in darkness, uncertain of her surroundings. A door opened and light flooded the room.

"Rest, dear, you're home now. Everything's going to be okay." It was Mother's voice, sweet and soothing – a stark contrast to the harsh, commanding tone she'd taken the past few weeks. Maxine ran her hand across Chloe's hair. "I'll be up for a while. If you have a nightmare or anything, my door will be open..." Mother's voice faded as she left the room.

Chloe felt good knowing she was back in her own bed. Her pillows and sheets felt so soft. It was as if her senses had been heightened and only pleasant stimuli filled her environment. She turned over and fell into a deep sleep.

The next few days were difficult. Chloe was weak and couldn't hold anything down. Her abdominal muscles locked and she vomited when she even thought about solid food. Maxine and Marie nursed her, spoon-feeding her warm broth.

One morning when Chloe finally felt well again, she bathed, put on clean pajamas and her favorite robe. Before leaving her room, she noticed the brochure for the University of Paris study-abroad program in New York and leafed through it. Thoughtfully, she placed it in a drawer and went downstairs. Taking the stairs one by one, she felt pensive and vulnerable, like an accident victim hobbling through physical therapy.

Mother was sitting at the table on the screened-in porch, attacking a half-grapefruit with a serrated spoon. Chloe had regained her strength as well as her appetite. She was, in fact, starving. Her cells craved nourishment. Not having eaten much for several days, she was in the mood for down-home, New Orleans-style cooking like her grandmother, Mama Louise, used to make. She wanted Cajun-spiced eggs doused with hot sauce, biscuits and gravy, hash browns and sausage. The more grease, the better.

"I'm glad to see you're up and about. You look much better. The color has returned to your cheeks," Maxine said as Chloe took a seat at the table. "How're you feeling?"

"Pretty good, still a little out of it." She generally felt better, but there was still a distant throbbing in her temples.

"I'll tell Marie to whip you something up next time she comes out," Maxine offered. She set a glass in front of Chloe and began pouring orange juice into it.

"I can do it," Chloe said, taking the pitcher. She finished pouring the juice as Maxine shuffled through the morning paper.

"The doctor wants to see you one last time to make sure you're fully recovered," Maxine said, putting on her reading glasses.

"So what exactly happened?" Chloe asked, confused about what caused her mysterious illness. She had been in a daze and had trouble sorting out the events that took place the night before the wedding.

Maxine put the paper down and took off her glasses. "You fainted at the altar during the wedding ceremony. Someone called an ambulance and you were rushed to the hospital."

Now Chloe remembered. How could she have forgotten? The sleeping pills. They didn't kill her, but they had caused her to become violently ill. She couldn't believe she had fainted in front of the entire church. She was more embarrassed than anything, ashamed that she had disgraced her mother in front of all those important people. The *Le Monde* society columnist at the wedding probably had her photographer capture it all on film as the paramedics carried her to the ambulance. The story was probably splashed all over the papers: "Debutante's Wedding Cut Short by Fainting Spell" or "Bride Leaves Groom Standing at the Altar."

"I'm sorry for ruining the wedding." Chloe picked up her glass and sipped, not making eye contact with Maxine.

"You don't have to apologize, *ma chérie*," Maxine said, reaching across the table and taking Chloe's hand. "Your health was my main concern. There can always be another wedding, but I can never get another you."

Chloe sat back in her chair, relieved Mother wasn't angry.

"Your stomach had to be pumped. They found traces of sleeping pills. A lot. Almost a whole bottle," Maxine continued. "I've just got to know one thing, Chloe. Why? What possible reason would you have to kill yourself?"

Maxine may as well have been asking Chloe to explain the Theory of Relativity. What she had done was stupid, she realized now, but it seemed like her only option at the time. If there was one reason why she did it, there were a thousand. There were endless reasons why she felt imprisoned and isolated and alone and frightened. She didn't even know how to begin to explain it all to Mother.

"You could never understand, no one could ever understand these feelings I have. There's something inside me, something so strong, I feel like there's something out there calling to me," Chloe said, hoping she didn't sound crazy. "When I said I wanted to put off college for a while, I didn't mean I just wanted to play hooky from school for a few months. I feel like I need to find my place in the world."

"Your place is right here. I've already begun making arrangements to reschedule the wedding, but if you don't want to go through with it, I'd like for you to go back to school and become what you were meant to be – a college-educated professional."

"That's your dream for me, Mother, not mine."

"Then what do you plan to do with your life, Chloe?" Maxine said in a huff. "Tell me."

Chloe paused, recalling the events of the past several months. Her mind was suddenly flooded with images from the University of Paris study-abroad brochure, co-mingled with her high school drama teacher's words about having the courage to strike out on her own and pursue her dreams of becoming an actress. Her brain had been muddled lately, but everything now seemed clear.

"I want to go to New York, Mother," she said finally. "I want to try to get into acting."

"Do you have any idea how dangerous New York is for a young girl on her own?"

"You skipped college and left home at seventeen. I'm a year older than you were."

"Yes, but that was a different time. The world was a safer place. You have chances I never had at your age. You can achieve anything you want."

"And what I want is to act. You know that's all I've ever wanted to do since I was little."

"Why can't you try to do some acting here, in Paris? I can have the modeling agency line up some commercials for you."

"If there's anything this disastrous experience with the wedding has shown me, it's that I need to get away from Paris. I need to be on my own."

The prospect of leaving the cocoon Mother had created had once scared Chloe, but facing death seemed to have awakened something fearless inside.

"You can't just run off to New York with no plan," Maxine argued. "Just how do you plan to support yourself in that rat-infested city?"

"What about the trust fund Jacques set up for me before he died?"

Now that she was eighteen, she was due to receive the first disbursement any day now. The money would be plenty to tide her over until she got herself established in New York.

Maxine shook her head. "Jacques put that money away for your future. He wouldn't want you squandering it, chasing some crazy pipedream."

"How do you know what he'd want?" Chloe said, raising her voice. "He's dead, Mother, and he's not coming back. He put money away for both of us so we could move on, and maybe if I leave home, you'll finally get a life of your own and stop trying to control mine."

Maxine fell silent, her pained expression reflecting the sting of Chloe's words.

Feeling guilty for lashing out, Chloe took her mother's hand. "I'm sorry," she said, softening her tone, "but I need to get away. I promise I'll put the money from my trust fund to good use. Once I get settled in New York, I'll be frugal and spend wisely, just like you taught me."

Maxine pulled her hand away and scooted back from the table, as if preparing to go into attack mode. "I'm the executor of Jacques' estate and I will not have you wasting your trust fund. If you want to be a grownup and go off on your own, act like it."

Chloe stared incredulously at Maxine. But maybe Mother was right. Maybe it was time that she grew up and learned to take care of herself.

"All right, Mother, if that's the way it has be, fine." Chloe got up from the table. "Forget the trust fund. I'll make it on my own."

49

Chloe stuffed a sweater into the already bulging Louis Vuitton suitcase that lay on her bed, surrounded by mounds of clothes. She didn't have room to pack all her stuff, but she needed a selection of heavier and lightweight garments since she would arrive in New York in late October. She'd read in the travel guide she'd bought that fall weather in New York, like Paris, could alternate between chilly and unseasonably warm.

Going to her dresser to get one last armload of clothes, Chloe picked up a framed childhood photo of herself in her mother's arms. Maxine didn't have much to say since the confrontation at the breakfast table the other day when Chloe had announced her plans to leave Paris. In fact, the two had stopped speaking altogether. Clutching the photo, Chloe considered placing it in her suitcase. Instead, she put the photo back and retrieved a bankbook, her private piggybank, from underneath her jewelry box.

Maxine thought she had stumped Chloe by cutting her off from the trust fund Jacques had set up. Unbeknownst to Maxine, Chloe had been squirreling away the money she'd earned from her modeling assignments. It wasn't a fortune, but it would sustain her until she found a job in New York. Other than modeling and library duties at school, Chloe had never held a real job, but she would survive somehow. She was determined to show Mother she could make it on her own.

When she tried to zip her suitcase, Bizou jumped on the bed and kept pawing at her hand, as if trying to stop her from going.

"I'm not leaving you, Bizou," Chloe said, picking her up and cuddling her cheek against the cat's soft white fur. "Marie promised to take good care of you, and I'll send for you as soon as I'm settled."

Choking back tears, Chloe set the cat down on the bed. This was different than when she left for school after each vacation; this time it was permanent.

Having finished packing, Chloe sat down at her desk and looked out over the grounds. There was so much to think about. All her dreams were just a heartbeat away. The prospect of the new opportunities and choices she would soon face was almost overwhelming.

She flipped through the New York travel guide, her pulse quickening at the sight of each landmark she would soon take in with her own eyes. She had seen dozens of movies set in New York. She hoped the saying "It's a nice place to visit, but I wouldn't want to live there" wasn't true, especially since she would be living in that huge metropolis all by herself. She couldn't believe it was finally happening.

She closed the travel guide and took out a pen and paper. After staring pensively out the window for a moment, she began to write:

Dear Jean-Baptiste,

I'm giving you back the ring, because I don't feel right keeping it. I'm sorry if I embarrassed you by fainting during the ceremony, but I just couldn't go through with the wedding. It's nothing personal. I'm just not ready to be married.

I'm sorry things didn't work out between us. I'm moving to New York, so we probably won't see each other again.

I'm taking a big step by leaving home and striking out on my own, and I hope it's not too bold of me to say this, but you'd probably do well to do the same. I wish you all the best.

Sincerely,
Chloe

She considered adding her last name to the closing line, but she figured that might be rubbing it in. As much as Jean-Baptiste got on her nerves, a part of her felt sorry for him. She sensed that his smug air was just a façade and he didn't have the courage to take the scary step toward independence that she was taking. Jean-Baptiste would probably find some other girl to marry who was "not too dark, not too light," who met with his parents' approval. Chloe had seen right through his rebellious act, pretending like he couldn't care less what his conservative parents thought, and that he would ultimately be bound by tradition and do exactly what they expected. He'd eventually settle down, go to work at the family business and be financially dependent on his parents and, thus, under their control, for the rest of his life.

She opened a drawer and took out the engagement announcement from *Le Monde*, skimming it over before tearing it up and tossing the shreds in the trash. She held out her hand and took one last look at the shiny diamond engagement ring before sliding it off her finger and slipping it into an envelope along with the letter.

Later that evening, she rode the Métro out to Jean-Baptiste's house and placed the letter in the mailbox next to the front door, taking care not to alert anyone of her presence. Glancing back at the chateau as she descended the front steps, she caught sight of Jean-Baptiste's baby sister, Ariane, peeping out the window at her. Chloe froze, afraid the little girl was going to summon her parents, who would surely berate Chloe for the shame she'd brought to their family by leaving their precious, firstborn son at the altar. Instead, Ariane simply waved goodbye with a forlorn expression. Chloe waved back with a faint smile, pausing a few seconds on the steps before exiting the front gate.

Walking back to the Métro station, Chloe buttoned her jeans jacket, shivering from the slight evening chill. She kept replaying the sad look on the little girl's face, and was suddenly filled with regret that she hadn't married into the Lambert family, after all. Since she had no siblings, it might have been fun to be part of a large family with young children.

On the subway ride home, Chloe wondered if she was doing the right thing by calling off the wedding and running off to New York. When the train came to her stop, she took her time getting up, realizing this was one of the last times she would go home to the Chateau de Chevalier.

Before her departure, Chloe embarked on a "farewell tour" of Paris. She walked down the Champs-Elysées, taking the same route she and Gigi used to take when walking home from the Lycée. She paused in front of a poster advertising the latest movie starring Valérie Bourdain and envisioned herself in her favorite actress' sultry pose, her head resting seductively on the shoulder of her handsome leading man.

Next, Chloe dropped by Monique Lillier's office to inform the formidable modeling agent that instead of taking her usual hiatus for the school year, she was leaving the agency for good.

"I hate to see you go," Monique said, sounding genuinely disappointed to lose one of her most promising "finds." "But if you decide to get back into modeling in New York, give me a buzz. I have connections there. With a little coaching to bring you out of your shyness, you have the potential to become a top model."

Chloe thanked Madame Lillier for her words of encouragement, but silently dismissed them. The assignments Monique's agency had lined up over the years had given Chloe valuable experience in front of the camera, but it was *acting* she was looking to break into in New York. She had to stay focused.

Chloe's last stop was at the building that housed Chez Maxine. She stood on the stood sidewalk, peering up at the loft above the shop where she had spent her childhood.

On a whim, Chloe opened the side door and climbed the dimly lit, narrow staircase that led to the loft. She knew the new owners had converted the apartment into a seamstress shop and it most likely no longer resembled the place where she'd grown up, but she had the irrepressible urge to see the space again before she left.

She raised her hand to knock on the door, but thought better of it and turned to leave. This was silly. She couldn't disturb total strangers for some ridiculous nostalgia trip.

Just as Chloe was about to head back down the steps, she heard the door creaking open and turned to see a middle-aged Asian woman standing in the doorway, staring at her with a bemused expression.

"Oh, sorry," Chloe said hesitantly, hovering on the steps. "I used to live here and I just wanted to take a look around. But you're probably busy. Sorry I bothered you."

The woman looked Chloe over. "You're the landlady's daughter, aren't you?" she said in a thick Chinese accent.

"Yeah." Chloe nervously shifted her weight to the opposite foot. "How'd you know?"

The woman smiled. "You look just like Madame Bareaux." She stepped aside, opening the door wider. "Come on in."

Chloe took a tentative step forward, still unsure if she was disturbing the woman from important work. She relaxed when the woman extended an arm to welcome her inside.

She smiled appreciatively at the woman, passing her in the doorway. "Thanks. I won't be long."

Once inside, Chloe glanced around at rows of sewing machines that lined the space that used to be the living room. She barely recognized her old apartment, which had been returned to its roots as an industrial loft by the new occupants. A sign hanging on one of the walls read "Madame Wong's Custom Tailoring" in French and Chinese characters, and Chloe assumed the woman that had let her in was the business' namesake.

"I'm going to get back to work," the woman said, sitting at one of the sewing machines. "Feel free to have a look around."

Chloe nodded at her and walked slowly through the front room. As she passed one of the sewing machines, a young Chinese woman looked up, her large eyes probing Chloe, as if Chloe were a visitor from an alien civilization.

"I used to live here," Chloe quietly offered as an explanation, realizing the girl, who was probably the same age as she, didn't understand a word she was saying.

Moving beyond the front room, Chloe slowly walked down the hallway that led to her old room. She opened a door and peeked in the room that used to be Maxine's and saw that it was stacked to the ceiling with colorful fabrics and threads and racks of Oriental-print garments in various stages of completion.

She stared at a table in the center of the room that was overflowing with scissors, tape measures and other supplies. Remembering that was the spot where Maxine's bed use to sit, she recalled occasions from her childhood when she got in bed when she'd had a nightmare and bounced on the mattress when she thought Maxine was out of the room. Chloe laughed softly to herself, thinking back on how Maxine, with that keen, motherly sixth sense of hers, always managed to catch Chloe in the act. But instead of scolding her, Mother would tickle her until her stomach hurt. She sighed, realizing that was back when Maxine was a playful young mom, before she became so serious and business-oriented.

She closed the door and continued her methodic procession down the hallway, stopping in the open doorway of the room that was once hers. All remnants of her childhood were gone. The walls were barren and the floor was covered with boxes stuffed with fabric samples, beads and miscellaneous sewing supplies. She lingered for a moment, trying to memorize every detail of the room as a memento to take with her to New York.

She was turning to leave the room when she caught sight of something familiar-looking poking out of one of the boxes. She stepped into the room and approached the box, noticing that it contained unfinished handmade dolls. Pushing back the cardboard flaps, she saw that the box was like a mausoleum for castoff dolls, one missing an eye, another missing an arm or leg. She squelched an excited yelp upon seeing that nestled in this mound of rejects was her childhood teddy bear, Mr. Buttons. She frantically pulled the teddy bear out of the box like a lifeguard rescuing a drowning child from the deep end of a pool and cradled him to her chest.

"I'm glad you found that."

Chloe spun around to see Madame Wong standing in the doorway.

"Oh, I was just looking around and saw this sticking out of that box." Chloe held the teddy bear behind her back, as if hiding a priceless treasure she'd been caught stealing.

"I found that toy when I first moved in and figured it belonged to Madame Bareaux's daughter," Madame Wong said, smiling kindly again at Chloe. "I kept meaning to take it downstairs and return it, but I must have shoved it in that box and forgot about it all this time."

"Do you mind if I keep it?"

"Of course. It's yours."

Chloe glanced around the room once more, then followed Madame Wong down the hallway. "Thanks again for letting me look around," she said when they reached the front door. "I'm moving to New York and I just wanted to see my old apartment before I left."

"New York?" Madame Wong's black eyes sparkled. "My husband and I lived there for a time before we came to Paris. It's a wonderful city. You'll love it."

Chloe nodded. "I hope so."

"Good luck in your travels."

"Thanks." She held up the teddy bear. "Thanks again."

As Madame Wong wished her well and closed the door, Chloe made eye contact again with the young woman at the sewing machine and wondered if she would end up working a menial job like that in New York. She pushed such thoughts out of her head as she descended the stairs, hugging the teddy bear like a missing child who'd suddenly turned up.

She stopped when she came to the bottom of the stairs, savoring the irony of the experience. By making this very adult move toward independence, she'd inadvertently reclaimed a long-absent piece of her childhood.

"I'm glad to have you back, Mr. Buttons," she whispered to the teddy bear. "You've been sitting in that box all these years, but now I'm taking you on a big adventure to a faraway place across the ocean."

Out on the street on her way back to the Métro station, Chloe heard someone calling her name and swiveled to see Simone standing in the front entrance of Chez Maxine.

"Chloe? I thought that was you. What are you doing here, *cher*? Why don't you come on in?" she beckoned.

Chloe stood on the sidewalk, buffeted by people walking by as she stared warily at Simone.

"Don't worry. Your mother's out consulting with a client. She won't be back for hours," Simone said, as though interpreting Chloe's apprehension. "I just ordered lunch. Come on in and join me."

Relieved that she wouldn't have to have an awkward encounter with Maxine, since they weren't speaking, she took Simone up on her offer and followed her into the building. Over Italian takeout food in Simone's office, Chloe told her about the experience of visiting the loft and finding her teddy bear.

"I know it sounds silly, but I'm glad I'll be able to take Mr. Buttons to New York with me," Chloe said, tweaking the teddy bear's nose, which was peeking out of her backpack. "It's like having an old friend to travel with."

"I don't think that's silly at all," Simone said, ladling spaghetti noodles onto her fork. "You know, when I left Aurillac, the farm village where I grew up, and came to Paris, I wasn't much older than you. I brought Claire with me. She was my baby doll I'd gotten for Christmas when I was six. Claire kept me company. Being all alone in a big city where you don't know anybody can be pretty lonely."

"I figured it would be. I'm really scared about going to New York for the first time by myself, but it feels like I'm doing the right thing."

"It takes a lot of guts to do what you're doing – taking a risk," Simone said. "But you've always been a smart girl and I know you'll do well at whatever you set your mind to."

"Thanks, Simone. It feels good to know you support me, even if Mother doesn't."

Simone waved dismissively in the direction of Maxine's office. "Max'll come around, especially when you've been gone a couple days and she starts missing you like when you were away at school."

Chloe grabbed her backpack. "I better get going," she said, standing. "I have a few more errands to run to get ready to leave tomorrow."

"I want to give you a little something to help you get started in New York." Simone reached into her bosom and retrieved a wad of cash. "That's where Mama always keeps a little stash. You never know when it might come in handy," she said with a wink, handing the wad to Chloe.

Chloe looked down at the roll of bills in her palm. "Simone, you don't have to do this."

"Take it," Simone said, folding Chloe's fingers over the bills. "Look, I know Max cut you off from your trust fund. I heard her on the phone with the attorney handling Jacques' estate the other day. It's not fair; she's just being stubborn, as usual. I know what it's like to be young and on your own in a big city, so I want to do this for you."

Chloe stuffed the wad in her jeans jacket. "Thanks, Simone. I'm going to miss you so much."

Chloe hugged Simone and they held the embrace for a long time.

"I'll call you after my plane lands and let you know how I'm doing," Chloe said, finally pulling away.

"Please do, *cher*. You're the only goddaughter I have and I want to hear from you every day. Call collect."

Chloe promised to check in, hugged Simone one last time and headed for the door.

"Chloe?"

She turned back to Simone, pausing in the doorway.

"I just wanted to tell you how courageous I think it is of you to not go through with the wedding to that Lambert boy and to go off on your own instead," Simone said.

"Thanks. I know taking those pills was a cowardly thing to do, but –"

"You're not a coward, you're strong. Don't ever forget that. It takes incredible strength to do what you're doing. Pursuing your dream takes a lot of courage."

Chloe just looked at Simone, not wanting to speak for fear that she'd get too emotional.

"I'm sure it'll probably be really tough at first in New York and you'll probably get a few doors slammed in your face. That's what happened to me when I first came to Paris and was looking for work," Simone said. "But no matter how discouraged you get, don't give up. Do this for me. Do it for Gigi."

Chloe gave Simone a bewildered look, not sure what she meant.

"I hate the fact that she gave up on being an artist and jumped head-first into marriage with that soccer player. I can tell he drinks too much, just like her dad." Simone's gaze drifted to a painting of a clown hanging behind her desk that Gigi had made for her when she and Chloe were in fifth grade. "Gigi gave up her dream and settled. And if I were to be honest with myself, I'm settling by marrying Jules."

Chloe glanced at a photo on Simone's desk. In the photo, Simone's white-haired fiancé had his arm wrapped around her in a paternal gesture, which emphasized the age difference.

"He's a nice man, but I'm not in love with him. Still, I have to admit it feels good to know I'll have someone to take care of me as I get older, even if his daughters are a couple of mega-bitches," Simone said, laughing. Her expression turned serious as her emerald eyes met Chloe's again. "But you don't have to settle. I'm glad you didn't let your mother force you into marrying Jean-Baptiste. Maxine means well, she really does, but marrying you off to someone you don't love just wasn't right."

Simone ran her hand over a framed photo on her desk of her and Gigi that was taken before the mother-daughter relationship turned combative. "I guess it's not surprising how Gigi's life has turned out, since I haven't exactly set the best example."

Chloe looked away, feeling guilty for all the times she'd judged Simone for being too self-absorbed and consumed with her social life, career and everything other than parenting.

"It's too late for me to save Gigi," Simone added, "but I have high hopes for you and I know you're going to go far, whether it's in acting or whatever you choose to do. I want you to know how proud I am of you."

Chloe swallowed the lump that had formed in her throat. "I love you, Simone," she said softly.

"*Je t'aime.*" Simone blew a kiss. "Take care of yourself, *ma bellotte.*"

Leaving the office, Chloe reflected on everything Simone had said. Chloe refused to believe that Gigi couldn't be saved, as Simone had said. Thinking of her best friend and all the times they'd shared as she walked the familiar route they'd traveled as schoolgirls, Chloe stopped in a gift shop and bought a "thinking of you" card. It was time to break the silence.

She dropped in at Trocadéro, the park near the Eiffel Tower where she and Gigi used to watch breakdancers after school, and sat down to fill out the card. She apologized for being out of touch for so long, wrote about her plans to move to New York, and promised to scrape together enough money to come see Gigi once the baby was born.

Addressing the envelope, Chloe found it odd to write "Mrs. Bradshaw." She dropped the card in a mailbox and stopped to browse the front window of La Galerie Nouveau, where Gigi used to talk about having her paintings displayed. Chloe prayed marriage and motherhood wouldn't completely deter Gigi from realizing her dreams of becoming an artist. Maybe when the baby was a little older, Gigi would eventually go back to school and take up painting again.

Noticing a miniature replica of the Statue of Liberty in a travel shop next to the art gallery, Chloe studied it. Going off to New York with no concrete employment or housing lined up was a vast departure from her usual practicality. But, as Simone said, at least she had the courage to take a chance.

Chloe and Marie shared a tearful goodbye at Charles de Gaulle Airport.

"I'm scared, Marie," Chloe admitted before she boarded the plane. "What if I get lost? What if I don't succeed?"

"What if, what if. What if the world stops turning? You're going to make it. I'm going to be praying for you day and night." Marie wiped her tears with her already soaked handkerchief. "You be careful. Whatever you do, please be careful."

"I will."

Chloe and Marie embraced.

"Your mother is thinking about you, and she still loves you. She'll always love you. She wanted me to give you this."

Marie handed Chloe a sealed envelope. Chloe turned the envelope over, examining it suspiciously, as if it contained anthrax. "What's this?"

Marie shook her head. "She didn't tell me. Why don't you open it when you get on the plane?"

"I'm going to show her," Chloe said, shoving the letter in her jacket pocket. "I'm going to make something of myself. She'll see."

"I know you will." Marie reached in her purse and stuffed a wad of bills in Chloe's hand. "That's for you. Emergency money."

"I can't take this. You didn't withdraw any money out of your retirement fund, did you?" Chloe was sincerely touched, but tried to give back the cash.

Marie pushed Chloe's hand away. "I'm going to be worried sick anyway, but I'll sleep a little easier knowing you have a little something to fall back on." In her maternal way, she added, "You make sure to put that in a safe place. Put it in the hotel safe as soon as you check in."

Chloe nodded, appreciating Marie's well-intentioned nagging, and placed the bills in her purse. "Simone gave me some money, too. I should be set if anything happens." Seeing the familiar worry wrinkle appear on Marie's brow, she hastily added, "Not that anything *will* happen, of course."

The announcement for the last call of the boarding of Chloe's flight came over the intercom.

"You call and write every day, you hear?" Marie said. "And if ever you get homesick, don't hesitate to call. I'll wire you money for a ticket home."

Chloe threw her arms around Marie one last time. "I love you."

"I love you, too, *chouchou*. God bless."

Chloe walked to the boarding gate, Mr. Buttons sticking out of her carryon. She felt like a child going away to camp. The permanence of her decision hadn't yet set in.

Once seated on the plane, Chloe opened the envelope from Mother, which contained a letter:

Chloe,

For what it's worth, I just want you to know I still love you and support you. But I think you're making a big mistake by running off like this.

New York is where I gave birth to you, so for that reason it will always hold a special place in my heart. But it also holds a lot of bad memories. As you know, Mama Louise and I moved there after Papa died and I saw her struggling, losing her voice and working as a domestic to make ends meet.

I vowed my child would never have to struggle like that, the way I had to struggle when I first came to Paris to be a dancer. I don't want that life for you – a life of uncertainty and rejection. That's why I wanted you to marry into the Lambert family, so you'd never have to struggle for anything.

I know I can't stop you from leaving, so go to New York, see everything you're curious to see, and come home. I beg you, please come home.

Love,
Mother

"Mademoiselle, could you please stow your purse in preparation for takeoff?"

Chloe looked up and saw an Air France flight attendant glaring at her. She looked down at her lap and saw her purse sitting there.

"Oh, sorry. *Pardonnez-moi*," Chloe said to the flight attendant, who moved on to the next row.

Chloe opened her purse to place the letter inside and saw the wad of cash Marie had given her. Placing the letter next to the cash, it suddenly occurred to Chloe that Maxine had probably given Marie the money to pass on. That was just like Maxine – finding a way to be motherly without admitting she was wrong for cutting Chloe off.

She saw something glimmering amid the contents of her purse and pulled out her grandmother's wedding ring, which she was taking with her as a good luck charm. She put on the ring, closed her purse and placed it under the seat in front of her.

As the plane began to taxi down the runway, she tightened her seatbelt and braced herself. Commuting back and forth to London for school was a short trip, but flying to another continent felt like a real voyage. Hearing the whoosh of the engines, the impact of the unfamiliarity she was venturing into hit her full-on.

While the plane began its slow ascent, she looked out over the city that had nurtured her and given her license to dream. She reflected on Mother's letter and considered her plea to come back home.

Maybe I am making a big mistake by running off to New York like this, Chloe mused. *But I have to give it a try. I know something's out there for me. And nothing can stop me from getting to it.*

PART II

50

Chloe could hardly contain the butterflies in her stomach as the plane touched down at JFK International Airport. She had finally reached her destination: New York City. It was really happening. The dream she had thought and fantasized and obsessed about for so long was finally a reality.

As she exited the plane and made her way into the airport, she was pushed along and shuffled about by an unrelenting mob of people arriving and departing. She moved slowly, savoring her first few steps on American soil. She considered dropping to her knees and kissing the ground like the pope, but she thought that might qualify as a sacrilegious act.

Surprisingly, she had little trouble retrieving her luggage and hailing a cab. Contrary to what she had heard about the manners of New Yorkers, the cabbie was polite and helped her with her luggage without being asked or offered a tip. In no time, her bags were secure in the trunk of the cab and Chloe was tucked away in the back seat, on her way.

The cab wove in and out of traffic, executing death-defying maneuvers. Chloe was oblivious to the cabbie's crazy driving. She was in her own world. She couldn't stop looking around. It seemed as though the size of the planet had increased tenfold, and she suddenly felt tiny. Skyscrapers towered overhead. Throngs of people of all hues, shapes and sizes crowded the litter-strewn sidewalks, all scurrying to get to wherever they were going.

Chloe marveled with childlike wonder at her new surroundings. Every street corner was abuzz with energy. It was all so vibrant and alive and exciting – and scary.

"Where did you say you was going again, miss?" the Pakistani cab driver said in his garbled accent as he rounded a corner, almost on two wheels.

She knew exactly where she was going – at least for now. During the long plane ride, she had come up with a plan. She figured she would take up residence at the Waldorf-Astoria Hotel, which was highly recommended by her New York travel guide. The Waldorf, the book said, offered luxury accommodations. Lodgings there came with a pretty high price tag, but she had planned to go to New York in style. With the money she'd saved, combined with the gifts from Simone and Marie, her funds weren't due to run out for a long time.

According to her plan, Chloe would ensconce herself in a suite at the Waldorf for a few weeks and take in the atmosphere of New York – the theater, shopping, fine dining, et cetera, et cetera. She deserved to treat herself. She had been through a hell of an ordeal in Paris, attempting suicide and almost being forced to marry a total idiot. She needed to lay low and chill out for a while. After she had a chance to recharge and collect herself, she'd go look for a job. She could surely land a cushy office job as a receptionist or administrative assistant to someone important until her acting career took off.

Once she found employment, she would get an apartment. She knew rent was astronomical in New York, so she planned to move into a small walk-up in one of the trendier sections of the city – Greenwich Village or Soho. She imagined herself mingling with bohemian artists and poets. She had been sheltered far too long, and if she were going to be an actress, she needed experiences, dramatic experiences, to draw upon.

She checked into the Waldorf, unpacked, and soaked in a bubble bath until the mirrors were steamed over and her fingers were wrinkled like prunes. There was nothing like a hot sudsy to refresh and revitalize and make a girl feel like herself again. When she came out of the bathroom, she put on her favorite pajamas, noticing the maid had turned down her sheets and placed a mint and a red, long-stemmed rose on her pillow. *Ah, this is the life,* Chloe thought, smelling the rose. The scent brought to mind the garden at the Chateau de Chevalier and her old room...

"We'll have none of that now," she told herself. "You haven't even been gone that long and you're already starting to look back. Don't go getting homesick on me. I have to concentrate on my new life."

She opened a set of oversize curtains, uncovering French doors leading to a balcony. She threw the doors open and stepped out into the night air, shivering from the slight chill and her newly-minted fear of heights. She inhaled, mustered all of her nerve, cautiously walked to the edge of the balcony, and leaned over the ledge. The vista was breathtaking, like something on a postcard. The Big Apple was living up to its reputation as The City that Never Sleeps. It was nearly one in the morning, but the streets below were ablaze with millions of lights and people.

"New York, here I am!" she declared.

The streets, slicked with a light rainfall from earlier in the evening, seemed to respond to her, greeting her with a chorus of honking car horns and wailing sirens. She could have stood there all night, taking in all the sights and sounds, but she knew she had to get to bed. She had a big day ahead of her tomorrow. There was an entire city to explore.

She closed the balcony doors, said her prayers and slid in between the sheets, clutching Mr. Buttons. She tried to close her eyes, but she just lay there, wide awake. A jumble of thoughts swam through her head. Trying to sleep would be useless; she was too wound up. Who needed sleep, anyway? She was in The City that Never Sleeps.

*****

By dawn, she still hadn't slept. After a couple hours of insomnia, she'd turned on the TV and ordered a couple of her favorite movies. When the front desk delivered the wake-up call she'd requested, she kicked back her covers and ordered room service. She feasted on a hearty breakfast of pancakes topped with blueberries and maple syrup, crisp bacon and orange juice. She needed all the strength she could get; a marathon shopping spree awaited her.

While getting dressed, she came upon the wad of emergency money Marie and Simone had given her. She remembered Marie's admonishment to put the money away in the hotel safe, but instead she rolled it up in a pair of socks and stashed it in a suitcase. She couldn't wait to hit the streets.

She stood in the middle of Times Square, staring up at the flashing billboards and all the lights and the scores of people rushing by. She noticed a billboard advertising a new film starring her idol, Valérie Bourdain, and she vowed that one day her own image would hover above the masses in this exciting center of activity.

"Hey, watch it, kid," a man barked, brushing past.

She felt herself swept along by the movement of the crowd. She could feel the pulse of the city. Paris may have been the seat of centuries of history, but New York was the center of the universe.

All the famous department stores beckoned – Macy's, Bloomingdale's, Saks Fifth Avenue. Noticing a jewelry store window, she thought of Audrey Hepburn in one of her favorite American classic films, *Breakfast at Tiffany's*.

By early evening, her wardrobe had expanded considerably. She'd exercised restraint she never knew she had and got several good bargains and a couple of outright steals. She decided to go back to her hotel suite, change into one of her new outfits, treat herself to dinner and take in a show. She accessorized her new basic black cocktail dress with her grandmother's diamond ring, which made her feel grown-up and sophisticated.

Chloe was mesmerized by the marquees in the theater district. She recognized famous names and imagined her own name emblazoned on a marquee. She stood in line at the box office in the middle of Times Square to purchase her first Broadway-show ticket. She decided on a revival of *Les Miz*. It would be interesting to see a professional production of the show in which she'd played the lead in high school.

Before the show, she dined at a five-star French restaurant that was highly rated by her travel guide. The meal was decent but not outstanding. Marie could have done much better blindfolded. While Marie was on her mind, Chloe remembered to call her and Simone to let them know she'd arrived safely. Since she hadn't yet gotten around to picking up a U.S.-compatible cell phone, she located a payphone near the restrooms. She checked in first with

Simone and then Marie, calling collect like they told her to.

"How is Mother?" Chloe asked Marie.

"Stubborn as ever," Marie replied with a chuckle. She reminded Chloe to be careful and take care of herself once again, after which Chloe said goodbye and went to the ladies' room.

She glanced at her watch when she returned to her table and had no idea it was so late. She didn't want to miss the beginning of the show. When the waiter presented her with the check, she was prepared to leave a substantial tip. Now was the time to break out the plastic. She hated to use a credit card when she wouldn't have anything to show for it later, but she had overspent a little and needed to reserve her cash.

She reached for her purse. Why wasn't it there? She was sure she had hung it on the back of her chair like she always did. She looked all around the table for her purse but couldn't find it anywhere. No, she hadn't placed it on any of the other chairs and hadn't set it on the floor under the table. So where in hell was it!

Don't panic. Calm down, she instructed herself, taking a deep breath. *There has to be a logical explanation for this. When was the last time I had my purse? Did I leave it in the bathroom?*

Wait a minute, she didn't even remember having her purse in the bathroom. The last time she *did* remember seeing her purse was in the cab on the way to the restaurant.

"Oh shit!"

A couple of patrons turned around and looked at her. She smiled at them, pretending everything was okay. But everything wasn't okay. Her purse had everything in it, all of her money and credit cards. She hadn't had time to stop and put some of the money away for safekeeping after exchanging her European currency for American bills at the bank this morning. Now her chic Chanel bag was in the backseat of a cab somewhere, probably on its way to some rough borough like the Bronx or Queens. God only knew if she'd ever see it again.

She tried to convince herself that all was not lost. She'd call the cab company and get her purse back. The driver had probably turned it in to the lost and found.

Fortunately, the maitre d' honored her request to use the phone at his podium, as she didn't even have change for the payphone. Upon reaching the cab company, she didn't get quite the response she was looking for from the garage manager. It was her first experience with a rude New Yorker, and now that she was penniless, it probably wouldn't be her last.

"You don't remembuh the cab numbuh and you don't remembuh the drivuh's license numbuh? Do you even remembuh what he looked like?" the manager said in a heavy East Coast accent that underscored his uncivil tone.

Chloe doubted if the driver spoke much English. This was hopeless. "Are you sure no one turned in a black Chanel purse? Could you please look in your lost and found again?"

"I already looked twice and it's not there, lady," the manager said, sounding as though she were a fly he kept swatting but wouldn't go away.

"Is there any chance you could track it down?"

The manager laughed in her ear. "You want me to track down some little designer bag?" he said through snorts. "Do you have any idea how many cahz we have? Do you have any idea how big this city is? You must be a tourist."

She didn't realize she was that transparent. "Please, sir, this is an emergency. You have to help me out. All my money was in that purse."

"All your money was in that purse? What are you, a retard or somethin', girly? This some kind of prank call? I ain't got no time to waste." The manager slammed the phone down.

She tried to call back, but got a busy signal. She trudged back to her table. She was all alone in this huge city with no money. What was she supposed to do now?

The meal she'd just consumed was her first concern. She had really pigged out, ordered appetizers, soup and salad, virgin cocktails, the most expensive entrée on the menu and dessert. And she had absolutely no way of paying for any of it. What should she do, offer to wash dishes or sleep with the owner? The only viable solution was to sneak out.

When the attention of the maitre d' and most of the wait staff was diverted to a large party that entered, Chloe saw her chance. She got up, slowly pushed in her chair and casually made her way to the door. Just as she reached the exit, the maitre d' returned to his podium.

"Hey! What do you think you're doing, miss!" he yelled as she scrambled for the door.

She broke into a run, taking off her pumps and sprinting down the street in her stocking feet with a busboy in pursuit. Luckily, she was able to duck into an alley and lose him. She felt bad about stiffing the restaurant, but it wasn't her fault she had lost her purse. One day, when she was rich and famous, she would come back and not only pay the restaurant back, but treat all the diners to filet mignon.

She waited for a while in the alley until she was sure the busboy was long gone, then took off the new pair of pantyhose she had ruined and threw them in a dumpster and put her shoes back on. She was glad the theater where *Les Miz* was playing was within walking distance and that she already had her ticket. She needed an escape.

Sitting through the show, however, only reminded her of the predicament she was in. She had only been in New York for shortly over twenty-four hours, but she had already met the fate of the starving street urchins depicted in the show. When she starred in the school production, she practiced crying on cue for hours. But now the tears came easily.

When the show was over, she cleared out of the theater with the rest of the audience. Everyone seemed to have a place to go and a way to get there but her. As she wandered through Times Square, she dog-eared the pages of her theater program, wondering how she was going to get back to the hotel. And wondering what she was going to do with the rest of her life.

51

Exhausted and downtrodden, Chloe got back to the hotel the best way she could. She managed to find the subway and jumped the turnstile. She knew it was dangerous riding the subway by herself, let alone at night, but she had no other choice. She certainly wasn't going to walk the city streets.

There was a curious assortment of weirdos on the subway, all of whom seemed to be challenging her to a staring contest, but Chloe ignored them. She had more important things to think about at the moment. Like how she was going to survive in this strange city all alone.

As the subway rattled on, she considered her options. She glanced down, and something shiny caught her eye. Turning her grandmother's wedding ring around on her finger, it occurred to her that she could pawn it. She quickly squashed the thought. She'd rather sell her body than hock such a priceless heirloom. She would have to figure something else out.

When she finally got back to her suite at the Waldorf, she tumbled onto the bed. Sleep came easily this time. She could contemplate her future in the morning after a good night's rest.

Up before dawn, Chloe showered and dressed. While hastily packing, she discovered the small stash of emergency money Marie and Simone had given her. She had rolled up the wad of cash in a pair of socks and forgotten about it. She would still have to check out, though, since the Waldorf was way beyond her price range now. She was going to have to ration her money until she found a job and a place to stay.

There was no way she was going to be able to pay her hotel bill since her only credit card, which she'd used to reserve the room, had been cancelled when she reported it missing. She splurged on room service one last time, knowing this was the last big meal she was going to get for a while. Bilking the hotel was not going to be easy. Her luggage was too heavy to run with. She was going to have to improvise.

She put on her fanciest designer outfit (acquired on her frenzied shopping spree the day before), went to the front desk and informed them she was checking out. The bill they handed her almost gagged her. She was totally unaware that she had been such a glutton when it came to room service and didn't realize the pay-per-view movies she'd ordered had been so expensive.

She patted herself down, pretending she couldn't remember where she'd stashed her wallet. "Oh, silly me, I must have left my wallet in my suite."

"What was your room number? I can go retrieve it for you, ma'am," a young, eager and kind of cute Hispanic bellhop said with a flirtatious grin.

"I couldn't have you do that. I don't want you to wear yourself out for my sake," she said, batting her eyes at him and surprising herself with her own brazenness. Desperate times called for desperate measures.

"No, ma'am, really, I don't mind. It's my job."

"No, I couldn't have you run all the way upstairs just for me. Besides, I think I left some unmentionables in the bathroom. You know, lady's undergarments and feminine hygiene products."

He turned red, sputtering, "Perhaps I should load your luggage into a cab while you go get your wallet and the rest of your, uh, things."

"You're so sweet." She winked at him. "I'm going to have a big tip for you when I get back."

She pretended to walk toward the elevators. When the front desk staff wasn't looking, she turned and walked in the opposite direction. She had already plotted her escape route; all she had to do was stay calm. She pretended to take a wrong turn and get lost, cutting through the kitchen. The kitchen staff looked at her strangely but didn't say a word as she calmly walked out the back door.

Her heart threatened to jump into her throat as she walked around to the front of the building. The staff was probably starting to get suspicious, thinking she was taking an unusually long time to retrieve her wallet and personal things from the suite. She ran into the bellhop when she reached the front entrance, where a cab packed with her luggage was waiting to whisk her away.

"I didn't see you come out, ma'am," he said.

"Pretty quick, aren't I?" She hoped the perspiration matting her hair wasn't too noticeable.

"Let me help you," the bellhop said, opening the cab door for her.

"You're a dear," she said, stepping into the cab. "Say, you still want that tip?"

He flashed his flirty smile again. "Sure."

She closed the door and blew him a kiss as the cab pulled off.

"Floor it!" she commanded the driver.

When the cab was a safe distance away from the hotel, she sat back. She couldn't believe she had pulled that off. Maybe she would survive in the Big Apple after all.

Chloe temporarily set up camp in Port Authority. The bus terminal had everything she needed at the present time: a place to check her luggage and bathrooms where she could wash up and change to prepare for job hunting. The thought of going back home crossed her mind. She could call Marie and take her up on her offer to wire money for a plane ticket home, but that would be giving up too soon. Leaving her life in Paris had been too much of a big step for her to turn back now, and she couldn't stand seeing Mother gloat. She had to tough it out. Going back home would be her last resort.

Lying to Marie was something Chloe dreaded, but that's exactly what she did the next time she called collect. She said she was doing okay, that everything was fine. Yes, she was still staying at the Waldorf, having a great time. No, she wasn't homesick at all and wasn't ready to come back. She hung up, wincing and remembering how terrible it felt the last time she deceived Marie when she and Gigi ran off to Monaco. But this time the deception was different, as she didn't want Marie to worry or try to persuade her to come home.

Job-hunting was more frustrating than Chloe assumed. Unless an employer was going to hire her on the spot, it made no sense to apply. She had no address and no phone number. After a couple of long, fruitless days looking for work, she returned to home base at Port Authority. Upon changing in the bathroom, she carefully folded the business suit she'd interviewed in and placed it in her suitcase. Before checking it with the rest of her luggage, she retrieved her wad of emergency money and stuffed it in her jeans pocket. She knew keeping the stash on her person was risky, but it comforted her to run her fingers along the bills and remind herself that she had a little something to sustain her until she found employment.

Settling in for another night at the bus station, she curled up in a corner on the floor where passengers were waiting for buses. She had dozed off when a cop came up and jabbed her awake with his nightstick.

"What do you want?" she said groggily, angry that her much-needed rest had been disturbed.

"I been watching you for the past couple of days. You slept here the past two nights," the cop said.

What was he going to do, offer her a pillow so she wouldn't have a crick in her neck when she woke up? "What are you getting at?"

"What I'm getting at, missy, is this is a bus station, not a homeless shelter.

Move along or I'm going to have to take you in for loitering."

Loitering? She was just sleeping. She wasn't hurting anybody, just taking up a little space.

"Look, could you please give me a break? I'm new here. I don't have a place to stay right now."

"That ain't my problem. Now move along, like I said."

Chloe got up and did what the cop said, temporarily abandoning her checked luggage. She couldn't believe she was being tossed out onto the streets. She wandered through Times Square, not knowing where to go. The lights and activity that had seemed so exciting when she first arrived now felt uninviting, almost terrifying. She kept her eyes downcast as she neared a group of women standing on the corner in tight dresses and fishnet stockings.

"Hey, sweetie, you in the life?" one of the women called in a mocking tone as Chloe passed.

She caught a glimpse of herself in a store window and, seeing her disheveled appearance, realized she didn't look that different from the women whose lives had previously seemed so far removed from her own. She kept walking, stepping over broken bottles and discarded condoms and syringes. She pulled the sleeves of her sweater over her hands and crossed her arms, shielding herself from the crisp fall air.

She had somehow managed to stray into a bad section, a dimly lit area that had not yet been cleaned up like the gleaming theater district. A siren howled in the distance and she realized there weren't many people around, except for the homeless sleeping in doorways and pushing shopping carts filled with trash bags down the sidewalk.

As she continued to walk, trying to find her way back to an area with more lights and people, she heard footsteps approaching. She picked up her pace and the footsteps got faster.

Maxine's warnings about New York being a big, frightening place replayed themselves in Chloe's head. She looked back, trying to see who was following her, but couldn't make out the shadowy figure under the busted streetlights. Breathing heavy, she broke into a run and heard the footsteps getting closer. She turned a corner, trying to lose her pursuer, and found herself trapped in an alley. There was no time to catch her breath before a tall, wiry man in a hooded sweatshirt approached her. She backed up against a wall, shaking with terror as he neared.

When she was face to face with the man, all she could see under his hood was the vague outline of a scowling white face distinguished only by a blondish goatee and a pierced lip. He said nothing as he brandished a gun and pointed it at her.

"I don't have anything. Please don't hurt me," she muttered, almost

343

paralyzed with fear as she stared into his cold blue eyes. She squeezed her eyes shut as he came closer. She tensed as he began to touch her, his hands groping her body. Still aiming the gun, he shoved his free hand into her pocket and snatched the wad of emergency money she'd forgotten to stow in her luggage before leaving the bus station.

He shoved the money into his sweatshirt and she held her breath as his face came closer to hers, his rank breath filling her nostrils. She was pinned against the wall, the cold steel of the gun pressing against her neck as his hands groped her body once again. The eerie silence that hung in the air was suddenly pierced by a siren. As quickly as he had appeared, the man turned and ran off.

Chloe sank to her knees, gasping for air. She wanted to call out for help, but the siren passed before she could get the words out.

With great effort, she rose. She began to walk, putting one foot in front of the other without thinking. She was so shaken up, she had no idea in what direction she was going. She knew she should try to find a police station, but she kept walking until she stumbled upon a church.

She entered the sanctuary and took a seat on a pew near the back, trying to collect herself. The building appeared to be empty, except for a janitor pushing a dust mop down the center aisle and an elderly woman in a black lace shawl who was kneeling in one of the front pews. Chloe stared at her, suddenly feeling an urge to go to the kindly-looking woman and have her cradle her in her arms like her grandmother, Mama Louise, would have done. But the woman was muttering to herself and rocking back and forth as she clutched a rosary and didn't seem to notice Chloe.

Votive candles flickered around the sanctuary and Chloe slowly began to warm up. She scanned the faces of saints in the stained glass windows and other iconography, which brought comfort and reminded her of the cathedrals back in Paris and the one at Our Lady of Chastity's campus.

"Is the confessional open?" Chloe asked the old black man who was sweeping.

He looked at her as if to ask if she was serious about baring her soul at such a late hour, but simply replied, "I'll get Father Don."

Chloe kneeled in the confessional. She needed to talk to someone, anyone, make human contact.

"Bless me, Father, for I have sinned," she said, crossing herself when the priest opened the screen. "It's been... I can't remember my last confession."

"It's okay," the priest said in a soothing voice peppered with an Irish brogue. "What brings you here tonight?"

She couldn't stop the tears. All of the anxiety she felt about the events of the past several days came rushing to the surface.

"I just came to the city, not knowing anybody. I'm all alone. I have such big dreams, so many things I want to do. But I've managed to mess everything up. I can't go back home, 'cause my mother's not speaking to me. I don't know where to turn."

The priest offered counsel, reciting the 23rd Psalm and encouraging her to seek guidance in prayer.

"Sometimes when we feel like we've failed, God gives us a sign," he said, "a signal to encourage us to hold on to our faith and keep going."

Chloe thanked the priest and left the confessional. She lingered in the church a while longer, until the elderly woman idled out on her cane and the janitor told her he was going to have to lock up. She knew she should have asked the priest if he could direct her to a shelter or food pantry, but she was too embarrassed.

Back out on the street, she looked for the sign from God the priest had mentioned. But all she saw was the unwelcoming faces of strangers. She passed a travel shop and almost broke into tears when she saw a postcard with a photo of the Arc de Triomphe. She never knew she'd miss Paris so much. She had felt right at home when she arrived in New York, but now she felt like a motherless child. She longed for familiarity, for home, but she didn't even have a place to lay her head. She eventually wandered into Central Park and curled up on a bench.

52

Chloe woke with a start. She had tried keep her eyes open and stay vigilant, but she must have drifted off. It was morning now and the park was full of animation like it usually was in the daytime, with joggers and Rollerbladers whizzing by. She had been fortunate, but she knew she couldn't survive another night on the streets.

She went back to Port Authority, retrieved an item from her luggage and stuffed the object in her pocket. She only had to walk a couple of blocks before she found a pawn shop.

"Mama Louise, forgive me," Chloe said to herself as she stood outside, holding her grandmother's wedding ring. Her empty stomach growled and she went inside.

With the money she got from pawning the ring, she could rent a small room. As soon as she found a job, she would go back and reclaim the irreplaceable heirloom.

Devouring dry croissants and stale coffee at a donut shop, she looked through the want ads. She had given up hope of finding some cushy office position and was willing to settle for anything. She'd scrub floors if she had to. An ad caught her eye: *Figure modeling. No experience necessary.*

Could this be the sign she was looking for? She had plenty of modeling experience. "Figure modeling" probably referred to posing in bathing suits or athletic gear. It was at least worth checking out, since she had no other prospects.

She called the number in the ad from a payphone and scribbled down the address that the man who answered the phone gave her. She had to stop and ask for directions several times, but she finally found the place, a tenement in a run-down neighborhood.

Chloe entered the building and looked on the directory until she found the suite number for Garrett Latham Photography. As she climbed several flights of rickety stairs, she noticed that the hallways were strewn with trash and the walls pocked by graffiti. Strange cooking smells coming from apartments mingled with the smell of alcohol, apparently from the wino she had to step over who had passed out in the stairwell. This place gave her a bad feeling, but she kept climbing until she arrived at the entrance of what appeared to be a claustrophobic photography studio. The door was open.

"Hello?" she said, rapping on the glass window of the open door as she walked in.

An obese man appeared from behind another door leading to what looked like a closet doubling for a dark room. His flabby stomach bulged out over his trousers and his Grateful Dead T-shirt was stained with ketchup, mustard, and sweat. The man stuffed the remainder of a jelly donut into his mouth and wiped his hand on his shirt.

"Somethin' I can do for you, sweetheart?" he said.

"I called earlier about the ad," Chloe said, trying to conceal her revulsion at this gruesome man.

"Which ad?"

She held up the newspaper. "Figure modeling."

He nodded. "Ah, yes. I'm Garrett Latham, the photographer." He held out his hand, then noticing it was sticky with icing from the donut, retracted it and began licking his fingers.

She ignored his vile behavior, hoping to get down to business. "Do I have to audition?" The thought of setting herself up for rejection, especially from this grotesque man, filled her with dread.

"I guess you could call it an audition," Latham said. "Open your blouse. I'll need to see your breasts."

She took a step back. She couldn't have heard him right. "I beg your pardon?"

"The shoot is a nude. I need to see what you have to work with."

"I guess this opportunity isn't for me after all. I'm sorry I wasted your time." She turned to walk out the door.

"Two hundred dollars. Cash. You telling me you couldn't use the money?"

Chloe came to a halt in the doorway. She pictured her grandmother's wedding ring sitting in the glass case at the pawn shop. She turned to face the photographer again. "What are the pictures going to be used for?"

"One of my clients is a crazy artist, real weird guy."

As if he can talk, Chloe thought as she watched him wipe his hand on his stained shirt.

"Anyway," he continued, "this artist dude is putting together some kind of photo collage on the female anatomy. Nothing real graphic – no beaver shots or anything – doesn't even want to see the model's face. He's going to use the pictures in an exhibit at some gallery."

"Which gallery?" She was actually considering taking the job, but first she wanted to make sure her boobs weren't going to be plastered all over a billboard in Times Square.

"I don't know the name. It's some place nobody ever heard of. Trust me, not a lot of people will be seeing these pictures, sweetheart."

Chloe stood there, trying to figure out what to do. She had a choice, the choice between a quick two hundred dollars or letting her grandmother's wedding ring be snatched up by a stranger in that seedy pawn shop.

"So what d'ya say, babe? Two hundred bucks sound good to you?"

Chloe paused, then unbuttoned her blouse, unfastened her bra and exposed her breasts to the photographer. She stared at water spots on the ceiling as his eyes scanned her flesh.

"Hot damn, we're in business!" Latham exclaimed, clapping his pudgy hands enthusiastically. "You got the job, sweetie pie."

She studied the dingy floor tiles while buttoning her blouse. Posing nude was one step up from prostitution – her years of Catholic school began gnawing at her conscience – but she wasn't in a position to turn down cash.

"When's the shoot?" she asked, wanting to get it over with as soon as possible.

"Just give me time to get set up," Latham said. He took a silk kimono off a hook and tossed it to her. "Why don't you go in the bathroom and change into that while I arrange the lights and load my camera."

She noticed a door leading to a tiny bathroom and began walking toward it.

"By the way, what's your name, sweetheart?"

"Gabrielle," she said, inventing a nom de guerre. There was no way she was going to give this slimebag her real name.

"Gabrielle. I like that. Is it French?"

"It's whatever you want it to be."

"I can see we're going to be able to work together just fine, sweetheart. I just need you to do one thing."

She froze in place. "What?"

Latham went to his desk, reached under a stack of contact sheets and empty takeout cartons, and handed her a clipboard with grease-stained papers attached to it. "Just sign this release and we'll be in business."

She hesitated, looking down at the clipboard. "What's this for?"

"Standard procedure. Just gives me and my client the right to use your image, that's all."

She skimmed the document, which indeed appeared to be a standard model's release similar to ones she'd signed when doing assignments in Paris. She picked up the pen and started to scrawl the alias she'd given the photographer.

"I need your real name, sweetheart." He smiled knowingly, as if seeing straight through her. "If you wanna get paid, I gotta have the correct information on file."

She looked past the man to an open lockbox on his cluttered dusk, eyeing the cash. She hesitated for another second, then signed the release and handed him the clipboard.

"Good girl. Now go get dressed – or *un*dressed, that is."

He laughed at his own stupid joke and she turned away from him, going to the bathroom and locking the door. Taking off her clothes in the filthy bathroom didn't boost her confidence. This entire episode was degrading. She knew her mother would be heartbroken if she could see what had become of her daughter, the debutante, living on the streets and posing nude for a couple hundred bucks.

Chloe took off her clothes and slipped into the robe as quickly as she could. The stench in the bathroom was almost unbearable, probably because the toilet was backed up. As she was taking off her shoes, a huge cockroach ran across the floor. She screamed.

"Somethin' wrong, sweetheart?" Latham called from the other room.

"I'm okay." She didn't want him coming in there, trying to console her. Dealing with one big roach was bad enough.

"Then come on out. I'm all set up."

She took hold of the doorknob, paused, then opened the door and went back into the studio. The photographer had set up a gray backdrop and several lights.

"Here, babe, put this on," Latham said, tossing her a long, curly wig. "It'll make you look older."

"I thought you said my face wouldn't be in the pictures."

"It won't. I'm just setting a mood." He added with a crooked grin, "Trust me."

She hesitated, wondering if this was a big mistake and she should walk away. Noticing the cash beckoning from the lockbox on his desk, she pinned up her hair, put the wig on and stood in front of the backdrop, still wearing the robe. Latham turned on the radio, adjusted the lights, white-balanced his camera and took his place behind the lens.

"Okay, doll," he said, "drop it and make love to the camera."

Chloe did her best to follow the photographer's direction, but she was cold and couldn't relax being in the buff in this shabby studio with this fat-ass photographer aiming his lens God knows where.

Latham must have picked up on her tension, because he stopped clicking the shutter and turned off the music. He went to his desk and pulled out a wad of bills from the lockbox.

"This is your pay, sweetheart," he said, flashing the bills. "If you don't work for it, you ain't getting it. I ain't gonna give it to you if you don't give it to me. Now loosen up."

She nodded. "I'll try to do better."

Latham began snapping photos again, but she just couldn't get into it. Thoughts of roaches crawling up and down her skin kept going through her head.

"This ain't no better," Latham sighed. He went to the front door, shutting and locking it. "I guess we're going to have to do something to warm you up."

"What are you talking about?" She wrapped her arms around her naked body as the fat man approached.

"You're as stiff as a board, sweetheart. Maybe you need to *feel* something stiff to loosen you up." He grabbed her hand, placed it on the hard place in his trousers, and tried to kiss her. Chloe's reflexes kicked in. Without thinking, she scratched at his eyes, temporarily blinding him.

"You fucking bitch. I'll kill you for this!" Latham shouted, putting his hands over his bloody eyes and falling to the floor.

She ran to the bathroom, threw on her clothes and ran back out to the studio. Latham hollered obscenities and tried to lash out at her, crazily waving one arm while covering his wounded eyes with the other.

Taking this job had turned out to be a big mistake. This man was obviously some kind of sicko. He had probably put that ad in the paper to bait unsuspecting women to this rattrap so he could force them into compromising positions. But she had held up her end of the bargain and she deserved an honest day's pay for an honest day's – or half-hour's – work. She grabbed a handful of twenties out of the lockbox and fled the studio. Latham stumbled after her, cursing and yelling. She managed to make it out of the building and the neighborhood, unharmed. The obese, blinded photographer couldn't keep up with her.

After nearly fifteen minutes of sprinting, Chloe realized she had no idea where she was. Her stomach was killing her, grumbling loud enough for the whole block to hear. She found a diner near what appeared to be a college campus, ordered enough food to last her another day and ate slowly. Carrying around cash, she might be mugged again, so she had to savor this meal. There was no telling where her next one would come from.

She paid her tab, left a small tip and exited the diner. As she was walking out, someone ran into her, almost knocking her over.

"*Ohmigawd!* I'm so sorry! Are you okay?" the woman said.

Chloe squinted and tried to get a good look at the woman that had nearly plowed her over. All she could make out was a shock of blond hair. But that voice was so familiar.

"Do you need to sit down? Let me help you back inside," the woman said, taking her arm.

No wonder Chloe couldn't see. She realized she was still wearing the wig from the shoot, and the fake hair had fallen in her eyes. She brushed the curly strands back, away from her face, and finally got a good look at the woman.

"Oh my god!" Chloe and the woman shouted at the same time.

"Daniella, Daniella Webster?" Chloe said, not believing who was standing next to her.

"Chloe, it's you! It's so good to see you!" Daniella threw her arms around Chloe, then pulled away. "So," she said, "what in the world are you doing in New York?"

Chloe smiled. "It's a long story."

53

Over several cups of coffee at the diner, Chloe related to Daniella the incredible tale: Gigi's plight, the botched arranged marriage to Jean-Baptiste, her suicide attempt, and leaving Paris. She even told Daniella the part about posing nude.

"Wow," Daniella said with amazement, "if your mother knew you posed nude, she'd have a cow."

"I know," said Chloe, having discarded the wig she'd worn in the shoot, "but I did what I had to do. I'm determined to make it on my own."

"I can't believe so much has happened to you. It's been too long since we spoke."

Neither had done as good a job of staying in touch as they'd promised. Since filling in for Marie that summer in Paris, Daniella had earned her undergrad degree and entered law school at Columbia.

"My first priority is finding a place to stay," Chloe said, scooping more sugar and cream into her coffee.

"The streets of New York are no place for a young girl on her own. Why don't you come stay with me until you can get on your feet?"

"Oh, no, I wouldn't want to impose."

"You wouldn't be imposing. Me and my roommate have lots of space. I stayed with you and your mom when I was in Paris, so I'd just be returning the favor."

"Sure it wouldn't be too much trouble?"

"I insist."

"Well, okay then, if you insist."

Daniella signaled for the waitress to bring the check and paid it. Chloe offered to give her the money for her coffee but Daniella refused.

"It's on me," said Daniella. "Let's get outta here and go get your stuff from Port Authority."

"I really appreciate you taking me in. Who knows what would have happened to me if I hadn't run into you." Chloe felt so relieved. Her guardian angel must have been working overtime.

"This is going to be so fun, being roomies again," Daniella said, hooking her arm in Chloe's as they walked out of the diner together. "Now let's go get Grandma's wedding ring out of hock."

"Just make yourself at home," Daniella said, swinging open the door to her apartment near Columbia's campus on the Upper West Side of Manhattan.

"This looks just like those New York apartments you see in movies," Chloe said, looking around and dragging her luggage in behind her.

The spacious apartment Daniella shared with her roommate, at over three thousand dollars a month, was out of the price range of the average college student. But since both Daniella and her roommate's well-off parents were footing the bills, the place was just right. The building was quite old, with high ceilings and painted-shut windows covered by steel mesh on the outside. There was a window seat under the big picture window in the living room that provided an excellent view of the city. The living room also had floor-to-ceiling bookshelves stuffed with thick legal volumes, feminist literature and classics by Chloe's some of favorite authors. Copper pots hung over the stove in the kitchen and a tea kettle in the shape of a hen sat on the back burner. The apartment had a warm, cozy feel to it, a feminine vibe.

Seated at the roll-top desk in the living room was a pretty African-American girl, around Daniella's age, with skin the color of cinnamon and a close-shorn, well-groomed afro.

"Hi, I'm Muriel," the girl said, rising and extending her hand to Chloe with a big smile.

Chatting with Muriel, Chloe took an instant liking to her. Chloe could see why Daniella and Muriel, who'd met at school, had gotten to be good friends. In addition to being super-intelligent like Daniella, Muriel had a terrific sense of humor. She had big brown eyes that sparkled when she laughed, which was often. She and Daniella were always joshing around.

"I hope you like it here," Muriel told Chloe, "but you might have to get up extra early to take a shower since Daniella's always using up all the hot water." She underscored her point by dabbing her fingers in the coffee mug she'd been sipping from and flicking droplets at Daniella.

"Hey, it's not my fault these pipes are so old," Daniella said, wiping her arm with a napkin. "Come on, Chloe, I'll show you where to put your stuff."

She helped Chloe stow her belongings in a spare room that once was the pantry.

"The couch in the living room folds out into a bed," Daniella told Chloe before they all turned in for the night. "I left some sheets and pillows and blankets out for you. I hope it'll be comfortable."

"Listen, after sleeping in the bus station, on the subway, and on a park bench, that sofa is going to feel like a king-size bed at the Waldorf."

Daniella began walking toward her bedroom. "Well, goodnight, sleep tight."

"Hey, Dan?"

She stopped. "Yeah?"

"Thanks," Chloe said, suddenly overcome with emotion, thinking of the harrowing experiences she'd endured the past couple of days and how glad she was to be in a safe place again. "Thanks for everything."

"Don't mention it. I'm glad you're here."

Chloe smiled appreciatively. She waited until Daniella and Muriel were done in the bathroom and then changed into her pajamas, brushed her teeth and got ready for bed. She then went into the living room, pulled out the sofa bed, made it up with the sheets and blankets Daniella had left out, and propped Mr. Buttons up on the pillows. Before going to sleep, she said her prayers, turned out the lights and sat on the window seat, looking out at the city that sprawled before her like a fluorescent, urban kingdom. If she squinted really hard, she could see the Statue of Liberty in the distance.

The Statue of Liberty, a symbol of independence, donated to America by the French. Chloe started thinking about France, about Paris, the city from which she'd defected. She was overcome with homesickness. She longed to return to Paris, to all that was familiar. And as much as she hated to admit it, she missed her mother. They hadn't spoken since Chloe announced her decision to leave.

As she looked out into the night, she touched the ring that had belonged to her grandmother, which she was relieved to have in her possession again. The ring was her good luck charm and a constant reminder of home. She wondered what her mother was doing and thinking at that very moment. Did she still think of her wayward daughter or had she disowned her? Had she cut Chloe out of her life, the way she had done with Chloe's father, whoever he was?

Clutching Mr. Buttons and rocking back and forth on the window seat, Chloe had an irresistible urge to have her Mother hold her in her arms and soothe her until she fell asleep, the way she did when she was little. But Chloe was on her own now, and Mother was on the other side of the world.

"That can't be. I just spoke to her a couple of days ago and she said she was still staying there."

Marie gripped the phone while stirring a simmering pot in the kitchen of the Chateau de Chevalier, questioning the staff of the Waldorf-Astoria Hotel in New York. They kept saying the same thing. There was no one registered under the name Chloe Bareaux. She had checked out almost a week ago, left without paying her bill.

"There has to be some mistake," Marie said once again. "Will you please check again? The name is Chloe Bareaux. B-A-R-E-A-U-X."

She held while the woman on the other end checked the guest register again. At least this clerk was being patient and helpful. Marie realized the woman was probably having trouble understanding her through her thick accent.

"I'm sorry, ma'am. I checked again. No one here by that name," the woman said after a couple of minutes.

"There has to be some kind of explanation. Maybe she changed suites. I'd like to leave a message for her."

Marie left her name and number, thanked the woman for her assistance and hung up. She tried to go back to preparing dinner, but all she could do was pace and wring her apron. She was really starting to worry. Chloe had made a point of calling her every day, but the phone hadn't rang in a couple of days. And now the hotel said she had skipped out. It wasn't like Chloe to steal or cheat. She was raised with good Catholic values. Something must have happened to her.

Marie debated telling Madame Chevalier about her daughter's strange disappearance. Marie didn't want her to worry, but she had to do something. Anything could have happened to Chloe. New York was a dangerous place.

Maxine looked up from the paperwork she'd brought home when Marie entered the study, looking distressed.

"What is it, Marie?"

Marie stepped in front of the desk, clutching her apron. "It's Chloe."

Maxine took off her reading glasses and listened intently as Marie informed her that she was having trouble tracking Chloe down.

"*Merci beaucoup*, Marie. I know you're concerned about her, and so am I."

"I just thought you should know," Marie said, backing out of the room and closing the door behind her.

Once she was alone in the study again, Maxine slumped on the desk, releasing the anxiety she'd kept in check while talking to Marie. She didn't want to overreact and upset Marie even more than she already was. Damn that daughter of hers. She had told her New York would eat her alive. She was probably lying in a gutter somewhere, her throat slashed and her body defiled. If Chloe had just listened, but she was as fiercely independent and headstrong as her mother.

Maxine contemplated the situation for a moment as she stroked Bizou, Chloe's cat, who had curled up in her lap. She scratched the cat on her favorite spot behind her ears and looked at the family photo sitting on the desk. She sighed, touching the photo and longing for those all-too-brief days when she, Jacques and Chloe were a happy family.

"Jacques, our girl's missing. I was so stupid. I stopped speaking to her when she left, and now I may never see her again."

She ran her finger over first Chloe's face, then Jacques'. It brought her comfort to sit at the antique mahogany desk where he used to make business calls and smoke those godforsaken Cuban cigars.

"I wish you were, *mon amour*," she whispered, her eyes misting with tears. "I need your strength. You'd know what to do to find Chloe."

Maxine gazed at the photo for another moment, then wiped away her tears. She couldn't afford to fall apart. She had to keep it together and be strong, as she had always done.

She brushed the cat off her lap, rose and dialed the number of her personal assistant, Henri.

"I need you to take care of some business for me," Maxine said when she reached him. "I'll need flight reservations to New York, and book me a suite at the Waldorf. Also, find me the name of a private investigator over there."

"Something wrong, Madame?"

"Just do it!" Maxine slammed the phone down. She had no time to play Twenty Questions. There was packing to do. Never mind her disdain for America, she was going to New York to find her daughter.

54

Chloe settled in at Daniella and Muriel's apartment. She found a cheap futon at a used furniture store and moved into the spare room. The windowless space was about the size of Chloe's walk-in closet at the Chateau de Chevalier, but it suited her just fine since the arrangement was only temporary until she found a job and was able to get her own place.

She struck a deal with Daniella and Muriel. They at first refused to take any money from her, but Chloe insisted on chipping in toward the rent. She planned to earn her keep. She gave them a hundred dollars and promised to pay her fair share of the rent when she found a job.

To facilitate the task of job hunting, Daniella and Muriel gave her a crash course in all things New York. They gave her an extensive tour of the city, providing her with a map and dropping her off at certain spots so she could find her own way back and get familiar with street names and significant landmarks. In no time, Chloe was able to find her way around and get from point A to point B with little trouble. It would take her a while to get to know the city backwards and forwards, but she eventually acquired a basic sense of north and south, east and west. She learned the names of all the boroughs and how to reach them on the subway.

Before embarking on an aggressive job search, she rested up for a couple of days to regain her energy. Nearly starving and living on the streets had taken its toll. She spent her first couple of days in her new living quarters sleeping. When she finally got up, showered and dressed, nearly forty-eight hours had gone by without her seeing the sun.

After rising from her nearly comatose slumber, she spent a few days camped out in front of the large-screen television set in the living room watching cable. She had the TV all to herself, since Daniella and Muriel never had time to do anything but eat, sleep, go to class and study. This new discovery was a phenomenon: American cable television. Chloe was astounded that there was so much programming on the airwaves. There was a channel for every activity under the sun: cooking, golfing, fishing and her personal fave, shopping. From trashy talk shows to campy soap operas to melodramatic made-for-television movies with over-the-top acting, it was all entertaining and quite addictive.

She was hooked, like a junkie. She promised herself that when she found her fortune, she'd buy a house with a satellite dish.

Having to tear herself away from the television set, she unpacked, putting her clothes in an old armoire that had been left in the pantry before Daniella and Muriel moved in. The armoire couldn't totally accommodate her extensive wardrobe, and Chloe had to put some of her things in boxes, which she pushed into a corner to keep as much floor space clear as possible. After unpacking, she dropped a line to Gigi on the back of a Statue of Liberty postcard. Chloe wanted her to know that she had found a place to stay in New York and that she would always be there for her.

Realizing she hadn't spoken to Marie for several days, she sat down at the desk in the living room later that evening and dialed the overseas operator to place a collect call. Her heart sank when the operator said there was no answer. Chloe kept forgetting about the time difference. It was just before dawn in Paris and Marie, though an early riser, was probably still asleep. She took out a pen and pad and began writing Marie a letter to send via Fed Ex, omitting the parts about her homeless stint and nude photo session, of course. She wanted to tell Marie that she was doing all right and had found a place to stay, but she didn't want her to know too much. She didn't put a return address on the envelope. Marie meant well, bless her heart, but she might crack if Mother began interrogating her as to Chloe's whereabouts.

Daniella walked in, coming home from class, as Chloe was sealing the envelope.

"Who you writing to?" Daniella inquired, setting her bookbag on the coffee table.

"Marie, the one you subbed for that summer you were in Paris. She's a good friend."

"Next time you write or call, tell Maxine I said hi."

"I'm not speaking to her, remember?"

"You're going to at least let her know where you are, right? She's still your mother. You guys may be fighting, but I know she still cares about you and wants to know how you're doing."

"Dan, you don't understand. Mother's a control freak. She tried to force me to marry a guy I didn't even *like*, for god's sake! It took a lot of courage, me getting away from her, and I don't want her pushing her way back into my life again. The less she knows about what I'm doing in New York, the better. If she really wants to know, Marie can keep her updated."

Daniella threw up her hands. "Whatever you say. It's your life."

Maxine feared she would have to rough it in New York, but her suite at the

Waldorf had all the comforts of home: a maid, room service and satin sheets. For all she knew, Chloe had slept in that very bed when she first arrived in the city.

After checking in at the hotel, Maxine hired the best private eye in New York to track Chloe down and filed a missing persons report with the NYPD. The police weren't as cooperative as she'd expected. The flippant detective she spoke to informed her that missing persons reports were often shuffled to the bottom of the pile of unsolved cases. It was next to impossible finding someone in a city the size of New York.

The detective's cavalier attitude was not acceptable. "You get your men out there on the streets and find my daughter immediately, or I'll have your job!" Maxine pounded on the detective's paper-strewn desk for emphasis.

"Believe me, toots, you don't want my job," the detective said, stuffing the remainder of a calzone into his mouth.

The private eye wasn't much help, either. Maxine checked in with him every hour on the hour, but he had no leads, not a clue, after days of searching for Chloe.

"She couldn't have just vanished," Maxine said when she called the detective after the frustrating encounter at the police station.

After hanging up with the detective, she resolved to take matters into her own hands. Like she had learned one too many times in business, if she wanted something done right, she was going to have to do it herself.

The next morning, she set out on foot to find Chloe. She would traverse every street, every alley of every borough of this godforsaken town if she had to. She wasn't concerned for her personal safety; no one could stop a mother from getting to her child.

After several hours of riding the subway and hopping off at random stops to wander streets in search of Chloe, Maxine sat on the edge of a fountain in a crowded square bounded by skyscrapers. Scores of office workers ringed the fountain, squawking on cell phones and munching sandwiches in the noonday sun. She guessed she was somewhere in Manhattan's financial district, but by now she had lost track of where she was. She hadn't set foot in this city in decades and all the unfamiliar streets and strange faces had blended together. The more she searched, the more futile her efforts seemed.

She slipped off the tennis shoes she'd bought earlier that morning and massaged her aching arches. Even as a former dancer who stayed in shape, her energy – physical and otherwise – was waning.

She had put her shoes back on and was resigned to find her way back to the hotel without having accomplished her mission when a young woman lugging a backpack brushed past her.

"Chloe?" Maxine called.

357

From the back, it looked just like her – head full of thick black hair bobbing through the crowd with Chloe's girlish gait. Continuing to call out her daughter's name, Maxine pushed her way through the crowd, determined to get to her daughter and end this frantic search.

When Maxine finally reached the young woman, she put her hand on her shoulder. "Chloe?"

The young woman turned around, revealing that she was just another stranger.

"I'm sorry," Maxine stumbled. "I-I thought you were someone else."

The young woman turned away with a bewildered expression and disappeared into a busy intersection. Maxine watched the back of the girl's head until she was out of sight.

Back at the hotel, Maxine tossed her purse onto the bed, sighing heavily. She would do anything, give anything, to see her little girl again and know that she was all right. She stepped out on the balcony, looking out over the city. Her daughter was out there somewhere. Maxine knew the fact that she couldn't find Chloe was God's punishment for being so stubborn and trying to force her to marry someone she didn't love, and then turning her back on her daughter when she decided to strike out on her own.

"Where are you, *ma chérie*?" Maxine said, hoping the sound of her voice would travel to wherever her child was. "Where on Earth are you?"

Daniella peeked around the corner. The light in Chloe's room went out. Now was the time. She tiptoed into the living room. Where was that old phone book of hers? She tried to be as quiet as she could as she lifted the cover of the roll-top desk, and finally found her little black book buried in one of the drawers.

She went to the window and thumbed through the pages by the light of the street lamps. Where was that number? Ah, of course, under the Cs – the Chateau de Chevalier.

She picked up the living room extension and dialed. She hesitated, holding the receiver in her hand. Was this the right thing to do? Yes, it had to be. She'd want someone to do the same if she were a parent.

"Is this the overseas operator?" Daniella said, her voice just above a whisper, pressing the receiver to her ear and cupping her hand next to the mouthpiece. "I need to reach a number in Paris."

Maxine slid off her black satin sleeping mask, jarred awake by the ringing phone. She hadn't requested a wake-up call and she started to ignore the blasted thing, roll over and go back to sleep. She needed her rest after a long day of roaming the city in vain for Chloe. Then she remembered. It might be the police, calling to say they'd found her.

Maxine spastically projected her arm, picking up the phone just before it stopped ringing. "Hello? Who is this?"

"*Bonjour*, Madame Chevalier – or I guess I should say '*bonsoir*,' since it's still nighttime over there."

"Marie?" Maxine sat up in bed and turned on the bedside lamp. "Anything to report?"

"*Oui*, Madame. I got a call."

Maxine tightened her grip on the receiver. "Really? From Chloe?"

"No, from Daniella Webster."

"Who?"

"Daniella Webster. Remember the American au pair you hired to mind the house that summer I was on sabbatical?"

"Oh, yes. Yes, of course. But what has that got to do with Chloe?"

"Daniella said she's staying with her."

"Please tell me she gave you her address."

"We're in luck."

Maxine jotted down the information, hung up with Marie and turned to the family photo she'd brought with her and kept on the bedside table. She ran her hand over Chloe's face, then Jacques' – an unconscious habit. Clasping her hands and looking upward, Maxine whispered, "*Merci*."

Chloe let herself in and trudged into the apartment. The day had been just like every other: a total waste of time. Wasn't anyone in New York willing to hire an earnest young girl with no experience or skills? All she wanted to do was take a long, hot bath and get in bed.

The sound of voices wafted from the living room. She recognized Daniella and Muriel's voices, and one other that sounded familiar. Chloe stepped into the living room to see what was going on. She was horrified to see Daniella and Muriel sitting in the living room drinking tea with none other than Maxine.

"Hello, *ma chérie*," Maxine said nonchalantly as Chloe entered the room, as if nothing out of the ordinary had happened in the past couple of months.

"Mother, what are you doing here?" Chloe demanded. "How'd you find out I was here?"

Maxine winked at Daniella. "I have my ways."

Chloe scowled. "Traitor."

"I'm sorry, Chloe," Daniella said, "I know you feel I betrayed your confidence, but I just couldn't sleep at night knowing Maxine might be worrying about you. I would have told you I was going to call her, but I knew you'd either try to stop me or leave, or both."

"Okay, you've had your little rebellion," Maxine said to Chloe. "This game has gone on long enough. It's time to come home."

"I'm not going anywhere."

"Chloe, let's not go through this," Maxine said in a weary tone, as if dealing with a preschooler who refused to get dressed in the morning. "Daniella told me everything. You'll never last in New York. The best thing to do is to come home with me."

Chloe put her hands on her hips. "Mother, I'm not a baby anymore," she said, her childlike stance belying the proclamation. "Maybe I am making a mess out of my life, maybe I'll have to learn the hard way, but I'm the one who has to learn the lesson. It's my choice. You can't protect me from everything."

"Chloe, maybe going back home is for the best," Daniella interjected. "New York is pretty rough."

"Yeah," Muriel added. "Don't make it hard on yourself when you don't have to."

"I can't believe you guys are taking her side," Chloe whined, knowing she sounded immature.

"Listen to reason, Chloe," Maxine said. "Come home."

"When I left, I said I was going to make it on my own," Chloe said, feet planted firmly. "And nothing anybody says is going to make me go back."

"Suit yourself," Maxine replied, setting her teacup aside. "You've always been so damn hardheaded."

"I wonder where she gets it from," Chloe overheard Daniella muttering in an undertone to Muriel, who pursed her lips to keep from laughing.

Maxine got up and put on her coat. "Muriel, it was nice meeting you; Daniella, it was good seeing you again." She turned to Chloe. "You stay here if you want, but don't come crawling back to mama when you realize you made a mistake," she said, retreating to the front door.

"You don't have to worry about that."

"Fine." Maxine stuck out her chin and slammed the door behind her so forcefully, the whole apartment shook.

Chloe mimicked the action, stomping off to her room and slamming the door behind her. The rickety old door creaked open again and when she went to secure it, she heard Daniella and Muriel chuckling in the living room and musing at how alike mother and daughter were.

Later on, after Chloe had a chance to cool down, Daniella knocked on Chloe's bedroom door. Chloe had been lying on her futon, pouting all evening after the encounter with Maxine.

"Can I come in?" Daniella said in a soft-spoken tone.

"If you want."

Daniella entered, carrying a tray. "I brought you a snack, some milk and cookies." She set the tray down next to Chloe.

"Thanks." Chloe sat up, dipped one of the cookies, and began to munch. She was famished, having skipped dinner.

"I just wanted to say sorry again for turning state's evidence, but it's something I felt I had to do," Daniella said, positioning herself on the arm of Chloe's futon. "Your mother helped me out when I was in a bind, and I felt obligated to her. And just so you know, I didn't tell her the part about you posing nude."

Chloe took another bite of the cookie and didn't respond.

"So, you given any more thought to going back home?"

Chloe took a swig of milk, then pushed the tray aside. "Look, I've already made up my mind. Please don't lecture me anymore about how important a college education is and how I'm wasting my life. You and Muriel are starting to sound like my mother. Save your breath, okay? If you don't want me here, I can find someplace else, but I'm never going back home."

"Of course you can stay here," Daniella said, taking a napkin off the tray and wiping off Chloe's milk mustache. "I just want you to think about all your options, weigh the pros and cons and make the best decision you can."

"I already have."

"All right, then. You know me and Muriel are both behind you, whatever you decide. Oh, by the way." She reached into her sweater pocket. "Maxine said she figured you wouldn't go back with her, so she left this for you." She handed Chloe a plain white, sealed envelope.

"What is it?"

"I don't know. I don't open other people's mail. I am going to be a lawyer, you know. I have ethics." Daniella smiled, giving Chloe a playful punch on the shoulder.

Chloe stared at the envelope. "Thanks again, Dan, for taking me in and for being so understanding."

"Don't mention it. I'll get out of here so you can get some sleep. I know you have another long day of schlepping ahead of you." She mussed Chloe's hair in her affectionate, sisterly way and left the room.

Chloe bit her bottom lip, wondering about the contents of the mysterious envelope. She held it up to the light, but the paper was too thick. Unable to suppress her curiosity another second, she ripped it open. Her eyes bugged out as the envelope's contents were revealed. It was a check for twenty-five thousand dollars, the first disbursement from the trust fund Jacques had set up for her in his will. The initial payout was even larger than she thought.

Chloe went into the living room and sat at the desk. She dashed off a terse note to Maxine explaining that she didn't need or want the money and to cease and desist from sending any further disbursements from the trust fund. How dare Mother patronize her, suggest that she couldn't make it without her help.

She stuffed the note and the check in an envelope, grabbed her jacket and ran downstairs and out of the building. Dropping the envelope in the mailbox down the street, she felt even more determined to make something of herself in New York. Maxine thought Chloe would come shambling back home with her head hanging low after a couple of days in the big city. She had vastly underestimated the will to survive and grit and ambition and determination and steel inside of Chloe. Like mother, like daughter.

55

Before Chloe could start going on auditions and begin her acting career, she needed to start bringing in some money. Relentless knocking on doors and pavement-pounding eventually paid off. Her first "real" job was waiting tables at Mario's, an Italian restaurant on Columbus Avenue. The owner, Mario Garavani, a kind-hearted Sicilian immigrant who said he liked giving breaks to young people, must have had a lot of faith in her potential. The first assignment he gave her was tending to Darren Marati, a Wall Street high roller and the restaurant's most important customer.

When Chloe tried to reach over the portly man to place his glass of water – with a slice of lemon and no ice, just the way he liked it – on the table, she accidentally spilled it all over his designer suit. She apologized profusely, dabbing at the water stains with a napkin and offering to pay the dry cleaning bill, but the owner grudgingly yet promptly fired her. She was out the door before she even got to take her first order.

Trying not to dwell on her failed waitressing stint, she was up bright and early the next morning looking for another job. She answered a help wanted sign and was hired as a coat check girl at an exclusive supper club on Park Avenue. Her stint at this gig was also short-lived, however. She made a catastrophic mistake, giving a pricey trench coat to the wrong woman. The real owner, the wife of a well-connected New York senator, was livid and demanded that Chloe be fired. Management granted her wish.

"Serves the old bitty right, losing that coat," Chloe mumbled to herself on the subway ride home. "Ten-year-old orphans in Malaysia probably worked their fingers to the bone in a sweatshop making that rag, and besides, plaid is out."

Sympathizing with Chloe's unemployment blues, Daniella intervened. Through a friend majoring in photography, she secured Chloe a job as a photographer's assistant. Chloe somehow managed to bungle this one on her first day, too. Mistaking the dark room for a closet to hang her jacket, she exposed multiple rolls of film. The photographer complained that her mishap was going to cost him an important account, and he immediately showed her the correct door to the exit.

"What are you doing home so early?" Daniella called from the living room when Chloe returned shortly after noon. "How'd it go?"

"Disastrously. I really don't want to talk about it right now, okay?" Chloe moaned. "My energy's totally sapped."

"Think you have enough energy left to see an old friend?" Daniella said as Chloe came into the living room.

Sitting on the couch was an unexpected visitor – Gigi. The two girls ran to each other and hugged. Chloe clung to Gigi tightly, afraid if she let go, Gigi would disappear.

"My god. What are you doing here?" Chloe said after their long embrace. "I mean, not that I'm not glad to see you. I'm just surprised."

"I don't even know where to start," Gigi said, running her hand through her thick curls and looking as though she'd been through an ordeal.

Chloe glanced down and noticed Gigi wasn't showing. "Is the baby okay?"

Gigi said nothing, looking down at her feet.

Daniella backed out of the room. "I'll leave you two alone so you can talk."

Over steaming mugs of cocoa, Gigi told Chloe all about what she'd been through in the last couple of months.

"I'm surprised you didn't hear about the accident," Gigi said, sitting next Chloe on the couch in the living room. "It was all over the tabloids. At least the ones in London."

Gigi related the horrific car accident a couple weeks ago in which she'd miscarried. Justin had been drinking after soccer practice and, upon picking Gigi up from an obstetrician appointment, insisted on getting behind the wheel despite Gigi's pleas to let her drive home.

"I should have refused to get in the car," Gigi said, sniffling into a tissue. "I should have taken the keys."

"I'm so sorry about the baby," Chloe said, touching Gigi's knee.

"I feel horrible, like I not only screwed up my life, but the baby's, too."

"You've got to stop blaming yourself." Chloe touched Gigi's hair and noticed a bruise on her friend's cheek. "Is that from the accident?" she said, pulling Gigi's hair back to examine the bruise.

Gigi looked down at her mug, plucked a marshmallow floating on top and gnawed on it. "No, it's from before."

Chloe slowly drew her hand away from Gigi's hair. "What do you mean?"

"You know Justin's famous temper?" Gigi said, meeting Chloe's eyes.

"Yeah," Chloe said cautiously, not sure she wanted to hear what Gigi was going to say next.

"Well, he had trouble controlling his temper off the field as well." Gigi paused, looking down at the floor. "The longer I stayed with him, the more I realized how out of control his drinking was. He was usually able to hold it together for the sake of the team, but he started making a lot of mistakes on the field. Eventually, the coach stopped letting him play and benched him. Instead of going out partying after the games like he used to, he would come home and take his frustrations out on me."

Chloe looked at Gigi intently. "You mean he hit you?"

"*Oui*," Gigi said without looking up.

"That bastard," Chloe muttered, anger rising within her. She wanted to hop the first plane to London and beat the crap out of the son of a bitch who'd brutalized her best friend.

"Justin needs help, but it soon became clear to me that I couldn't make him. He got a DUI when the accident happened and he might be forced to go into rehab, but he's got some high-powered attorney and he's trying to fight it. I don't think he even wants to change." Gigi sighed wearily and sipped her cocoa. "Losing the baby in the accident was the wake-up call I needed to get out."

"So what are you going to do now?" Chloe said, trying to be as sympathetic as possible.

"I don't really know," Gigi confessed. "I was reluctant to come here. I thought you still might be mad, even though you sent me that card when you left Paris. After I got out of the hospital, I stayed with some friends from school in London for a couple of days. I've arranged to have the marriage annulled, but I have no idea where I'm going to live."

"I'm sure Daniella and her roommate wouldn't mind if you stayed here for a while, but have you thought about going back home, back to Paris?" Chloe suggested.

"Are you kidding? There's no way I'm letting Simone have the last laugh. If I told her my marriage fell apart and I lost the baby, all she'd do is throw it up in my face."

"I don't think Simone's that heartless. Sure you won't at least consider going back home?"

Chloe felt like a hypocrite. Daniella had been trying to get her to do the same thing, and she had refused, just like Gigi. But Gigi's situation was different. Chloe had at least finished high school, and she had goals, aspirations. She wasn't just coasting along, trying to pick up the pieces.

"I've been through so much, with the accident and the miscarriage and leaving Justin," Gigi said, her eyes welling with fresh tears, "I can't even think straight right now."

Chloe set down her mug, took Gigi's from her and reached over and hugged her friend. "It's okay. You don't have to think right now. Just let it out."

Chloe and Gigi decided to forget about the big questions hanging over their heads for a few days. Chloe abandoned her job hunt, enjoying the reunion with her best friend. It was a lot of fun, a sleepover, just like when they were kids.

"Do you remember when we were younger and I first started modeling?" Chloe said to Gigi one night when they stayed up late watching movies.

"Yeah, what about it?" Gigi said, spooning cookie dough ice cream out of a container as they lounged on the sofa in the living room in front of the TV.

"You encouraged me to go along with that agent my mother signed me up with and save the money I made so we could visit New York together someday." Chloe motioned to the city that sprawled outside the window. "Well, this is it. We're doing it."

Gigi smiled, as if catching on to Chloe's point that despite the uncertainty that loomed over both their lives at the moment, they were realizing a childhood dream.

"Yeah, you're right," Gigi said, following Chloe's gaze out the window to the unexplored world that beckoned. "It took us a long, roundabout way to get here. But we're here."

The girls toured New York and Daniella lent them money to buy Gigi some new clothes, since there was no way she was going back to London to retrieve the rest of her things. She said she never wanted to see her soon-to-be ex again, and Chloe was relieved that that part of Gigi's life was over for good.

Chloe continued trying to coax Gigi into calling her mother, reconciling and going back home. Gigi finally consented, conceding that she had nowhere else to go. She wouldn't place the call herself, but allowed Chloe to contact Simone and fill her in on the situation.

"I'll be on the next flight to come and pick her up," Simone said without hesitation.

When Simone arrived the next day, she and Chloe embraced for almost as long as Chloe and Gigi had.

"It's so good to see you, *ma bellotte*," said Simone, planting a smooch on Chloe's cheek. "We were all worried to death about you. I was so relieved when Maxine told me you were alive and well and staying with Daniella. So, where's Gigi?"

"Just a minute." Chloe went to her room, where Gigi was nervously awaiting her mother's arrival, and knocked on the door. "She's here."

Gigi emerged from Chloe's room, eyes glued to the floor. She came into the living room and froze, seeing her mother again for the first time in months. "Well, Simone," Gigi said in the sardonic tone that Chloe recognized as a defense mechanism. "I screwed up again. You happy?"

"Gigi Michèle Cartier, come here," Simone said forcefully.

Gigi slowly walked up to her mother. Simone threw her arms around her, holding her daughter close to her bosom. "Don't you know I care about you? Don't you know I love you? Don't you know all I ever wanted is for you to be happy? I'll never let anyone hurt you again."

Gigi and Simone began to weep. Chloe joined in. Daniella and Muriel got home just in time to see the tearful reunion and started crying, too. It was like something out of one of those made-for-TV movies Chloe had become addicted to.

Daniella and Muriel fixed a big dinner and everyone ate, drank and talked for hours. After dinner, Gigi packed her things. Simone had already booked two seats on a flight back to Paris.

"Thanks for everything, guys. I love you all," Gigi said, hugging everyone and lingering in an embrace with Chloe.

Before departing with Gigi for the airport, Simone pulled Chloe aside. "Thanks for bringing Gigi and I back together," she said. "I know she never would have called me on her own."

"I'm just glad you're there for her," Chloe said. "She's too stubborn to admit it, but she needs you."

"Well, I know someone else who's stubborn – your mother. And I know she's too proud to say it, but she really misses you. I wish you'd call her and patch things up."

Chloe looked down at her feet, not wanting to confess how much she missed Maxine, as well. "I don't know, Simone. I think I need some distance right now, to prove to her I can make it on my own."

"Just think about calling her, okay? That's all I ask." Simone wrapped her arms around Chloe. "You take care of yourself, *ma bellotte*. And thanks again for all you've done for Gigi and me. You've always been the mediator."

"At least I'm good at something."

Chloe, Daniella and Muriel helped Gigi gather her bags and carry them to a cab that was waiting outside. Before setting off, everyone exchanged hugs and kisses.

"Come on, daughter of mine," Simone said, taking Gigi's hand and leading her out of the apartment. "We're going home."

56

Chloe reveled in the experience of her first Christmas season in New York. The smell of roasted peanuts and the sounds of carolers greeted her as she walked the streets of Manhattan, taking in the flashing lights illuminating every corner of the city as she finished last-minute shopping. The cold nipped at her ears and she pulled down her knit cap and secured her scarf as she joined the crowd admiring the huge tree in Rockefeller Center.

"Merry Christmas," the Salvation Army bell-ringer said with a smile in spite of the cold as Chloe dropped what few coins she had in his basket.

Chloe returned the smile. "*Joyeux Noël.*" Her lapse into French brought to mind the Champs-Elysées, which was always festive and animated with busy shoppers this time of year.

She rounded a corner, clutching her bags as she was consumed by the crowd scurrying up and down the steps of a subway station. Even the faces of the riders seemed less hardened than usual. On the subway ride home, a saxophonist piped out a cheerful if off-key rendition of "It Came upon a Midnight Clear" as the car rattled along on the tracks.

"There's cider on the stove," Daniella announced when Chloe entered the apartment. She was standing on a stepladder helping Muriel hang decorations.

"Thanks. It's freezing out there." Chloe set her bags down, hung up her coat and went to the kitchen to pour herself a tall mug of steaming cider.

"So how'd it go today?" Muriel asked, tacking a row of garland in place.

Chloe pulled a chair next to the humming radiator and slid her numb feet underneath. "I want to work. Is that a crime?" She took a sip of the cider and felt the bubbling liquid warming her insides. "I need something to tide me over until I get my big acting break."

"Sometimes you have to know people," Muriel said with a shrug.

"It seems like that's the case with everything in this town. And to make matters worse, it's two days before Christmas and I just spent the last of my savings on gifts. I hope you guys like what I got you."

"We told you not to get us anything," Daniella said, stepping down from the ladder.

"I couldn't afford anything fancy, but I wanted to get you guys something since you've been so good to me, letting me stay here and freeload off you."

"Girl, will you stop with that already," Muriel said, waving Chloe off. "This is your place, too. We're all family."

"Yes, and since you're part of the family, you must do the honors," Daniella said, handing Chloe a glow-in-the-dark angel.

She placed the ornament atop the wobbly Charlie Brown Christmas tree and joined her roommates for another cup of cider. They clinked mugs and sang along to Mariah Carey's Christmas album. Daniella and Muriel were really in the holiday spirit. They had taken her ice skating at the Sky Rink on the Chelsea Piers and treated her to the big show at Radio City Music Hall, complete with Rockettes. And, of course, no Big Apple Christmas would be complete without attending the New York State Theater's annual presentation of *The Nutcracker*.

"We might as well exchange gifts now since Muriel and I are going home for Christmas," Daniella suggested.

"But I didn't have time to wrap your gifts," Chloe said, fetching her bags from the vestibule.

"We're family, remember?" Muriel called from the kitchen, putting on another kettle of cider. "We don't care about formalities."

Chloe handed Daniella the earrings she'd found in the markdown bin at a discount store and gave Muriel the new Nikki Giovanni poetry anthology that was on sale at Barnes and Noble. She immediately changed into the thick argyle sweater Daniella gave her. Muriel presented her with a box wrapped in colorful paper with an Africentric design.

"Muriel, these are beautiful," Chloe said upon opening the box, stroking the pair of gold butterfly barrettes that lay inside.

"You know how I love poetry. When I saw them, I thought they were the perfect metaphor for you."

"Let me guess," said Daniella. "Chloe being so brave and coming to New York on her own was like a butterfly leaving its cocoon?"

Muriel nodded, grinning.

"I swear, Muriel, you should write greeting cards," Daniella teased. "Could you be any more corny?"

Chloe hugged the box to her chest. "I love them. I'll wear them whenever I need good luck."

After exchanging gifts, Chloe helped Muriel put together a Kwanzaa display as a centerpiece for the dining room table, celebrating the holiday that promoted unity among people of African descent.

"You sure you don't want to come home to Baltimore with me for the holidays?" Muriel asked later that evening as she and Daniella shuffled between their bedrooms, packing and returning pieces of clothing they'd borrowed from each other during fall semester.

"Thanks. I'll be fine," Chloe said, leaning on the doorframe of Daniella's room.

"Oh, come on. It'll be fun. We can take the train into D.C. and I'll show you the White House and the Capitol and all the sights. The Smithsonian has a really great American cinema exhibit going on."

Chloe would have loved to see the nation's capital as well as the exhibit about the movies, but she politely declined, not wanting to further infringe on the girls' generosity.

"How about coming to Cali with me?" Daniella tossed a miniscule bikini in one of her bags. "The weather's great this time of year. A little chilly at night, but nothing like winter in New York. You know what they say – it's always sunny in Southern California." She put on a pair of sunglasses and pranced around the hallway in her socks, imitating the affected mannerisms of a movie star.

Chloe laughed, but said no. She already felt guilty for staying with them rent-free, and she didn't want to mooch round-trip airfare off them as well since they were struggling students – struggling students with deep-pocketed parents, but still. It had been six months since her graduation from Our Lady of Chastity, but Catholic guilt was a corset not easily doffed.

"You sure? My folks are skiing in Aspen. They called to tell me they're leaving the keys to their weekend getaway in Malibu. We'd have the house to ourselves, except for my brother and his beach bums."

Chloe followed Daniella into her room and sat on a suitcase to help close it. "I'm just going to hang out here and see if any jobs open up between Christmas and New Year's."

"We're going to be so worried," Muriel called from her room, "you being here all by yourself."

"Really, you guys," Chloe said, standing up. "I'll be fine."

The next morning, Chloe saw Daniella and Muriel off at the airport and returned home to the empty apartment. She made herself some cocoa and curled up on the sofa to watch TV. It was the day before Christmas Eve. All that was on was old American movies she had seen a million times like *The Bells of St. Mary's* and *Miracle on 34th Street*. The dialogue sounded so different without being dubbed into French. She lingered on a cable channel's back-to-back marathon of *It's a Wonderful Life*, then clicked over to the travel channel. A documentary on Christmas in Montreal caught her attention. When the narrator began speaking in French, she turned the television off.

She wasn't in the mood for TV after all. She had spent Thanksgiving alone, watching the Macy's parade on TV and eating rubbery turkey and soggy stuffing out of a microwave dinner. She didn't relish the prospect of spending another holiday moping around the apartment, bored and lonely.

She perched on the window seat and looked out over the city. A gray, cloudless sky loomed overhead and drops fell from the icicles stuck to the downspout. Seeing the Statue of Liberty in the distance, she picked up the phone on a whim and dialed home collect. Marie accepted the charges.

"Hi. It's me. I know it's really early over there, but I just wanted to call and say Merry Christmas. I know it's not Christmas yet, but…"

Before she could say another word, Marie told her she was wiring her money to come home for the holidays. She wouldn't take no for an answer. It was Christmastime, the season of love and forgiveness, Marie insisted. As far as she was concerned, Chloe and Maxine were going to have to set aside their petty differences. Their feud had gone on too long.

Chloe threw some clothes in a bag and took the subway to JFK, which was swamped with holiday travelers. She made it onto the standby list for a flight to Paris, and made it onto the plane just before takeoff, thanks to a last-minute cancellation. She would make it home in time for Christmas Eve.

She was greeted by the smiling face of Louis, the driver, when she arrived at Charles de Gaulle Airport and she reclined in her seat as they drove to the chateau, happy to be enveloped in familiarity and security for the first time in months.

"Hello?" Chloe called out as she unlocked the chateau's front door and set her bag down. She was almost surprised that her key still worked. At least Mother wasn't vengeful enough to change the locks.

Her footsteps echoed through the front hallway. "Marie?" Chloe entered the kitchen. The mouth-watering smell of sweets baking in the oven lingered in the air, but the room was deserted. She pushed the swinging door leading to the dining room.

"Welcome home!"

Mother, Marie, Gigi and Simone rushed to her and enveloped her in a group embrace. Chloe broke down crying, clinging to Maxine.

"I'm so happy you're here, *ma chérie*," Mother said, stroking Chloe's cheek. Mother cried, too, and said Chloe's homecoming was a pleasant surprise, the best Christmas gift she could have wished for. Their reconciliation was immediate and unspoken, and the estrangement and rancor of the past several months faded like an old scar.

The women got caught up as they gorged on Marie's delicious eggnog and beignets. The household staff, who hadn't yet departed for their respective holiday destinations, also celebrated Chloe's return.

"I'm glad our girl's home," said Bernard, the groundskeeper, entering the dining room after shoveling freshly-fallen snow from the front walk.

"I'm glad, too," Marie said. "And I'll be even happier if you get those soggy boots off the floor I just waxed."

"How about I park them under your bed?" Bernard said mischievously, leering at Marie.

Marie gasped. "Talking like that on the eve of our Lord's birth! Go away and leave us women alone."

Chloe laughed at Marie and Bernard's flirtatious exchange, proof that things around the Chateau de Chevalier had pretty much stayed the same in the few months Chloe had been gone.

After Simone and Gigi headed out to drive to Simone's parents' farm, and Marie left for the train station to visit her family, Chloe settled into her old room, relieved to see that nothing had changed. Her cat, Bizou, leapt into her arms, licking her face and welcoming her back.

Before Chloe turned in, Mother invited her to sleep in her bed, like she did when she was little.

"You all warm and toasty?" Maxine said, pulling the covers up to Chloe's chin.

"Yeah." Chloe snuggled under the covers, careful not to knock off Bizou, who was curled up at the end of the bed. "This is really nice, being home again."

"I'm so glad you came home."

"I made an exception for the holidays, letting you give Marie the money to pay for my ticket," Chloe said. "But I'm serious about making it on my own."

"I know you are, and I didn't mean to offend you when I left that check for you from your trust fund. That's your money. I was wrong to withhold it."

"I appreciate it, Mother, but I want to earn my own money."

"You've got a lot of me in you," Maxine said, brushing the bangs out of Chloe's eyes. "Jacques set up that trust fund because he wanted to provide for you."

Chloe didn't respond, growing quiet at the mention of Jacques. The joy of her homecoming faded upon realizing she and Mother would be spending another Christmas without him.

"Why don't you just take the money and use it to fall back on while you're in New York?" Maxine continued.

"That's the very reason I don't want to take the money – that I'll fall back," Chloe said. "The hungrier I am, the more motivation I have to make it as an actress."

"I don't like that word, 'hungry,'" Maxine said, pulling the cover up further under Chloe's chin in her motherly way.

Chloe pushed the covers down, sticking out her arms. "Mother, I'll be fine. Why don't you take the money and donate it to charity in Jacques' name?"

Maxine smiled softly. "That would be a nice way to keep his memory alive."

In the morning, Chloe and Maxine padded down to the parlor to sit by the Christmas tree and exchange gifts. Mother seemed to appreciate the paperweight with a miniature replica of the Empire State Building that Chloe had picked up at the JFK gift shop.

"I'll put this on my desk," Maxine said, shaking the paperweight and watching the tiny flakes of fake snow descend. She reached under the tree and handed a box to Chloe.

"This is really nice, Mother," Chloe said after tearing off the wrapping paper to reveal a cashmere sweater. She held the sweater up, running her hand over the soft fabric.

"I want you to keep warm when you're out on those New York City streets. Always be sure to button up."

Chloe stuffed the sweater back in the box. "Oh, Mother, really. How many times must I tell you I'm a big girl now?"

"I know. It's just good having you back, even if it's just for the holidays. This has turned out to be such a great Christmas." Maxine fell silent, looking at the Christmas tree lights with a wistful expression. "The only thing missing is Jacques."

Chloe touched her mother's hand. "I miss him, too."

They sat in silence for a few minutes, watching the lights and quietly reflecting on the good times they'd had together as a family with Jacques.

The doorbell ringing punctured the stillness of the house.

"I'll get it," Chloe volunteered, curious to see who had ventured out on a snowy Christmas Eve.

When she opened the front door, she was greeted by the smiling face of Renaud Mercier, Jacques' former employee who had continued on at the shipping company after his death.

"I'm sorry to disturb you on Christmas Eve, but I promised to look in on you and your mother from time to time," Renaud said, his arms loaded with packages.

Maxine joined Chloe at the door. "Renaud, so good to see you. Won't you come in?"

"I've got to get back to my family. I just came to drop these off."

Chloe and Maxine took the packages from Renaud.

"Renaud, you didn't have to buy us all these gifts," Maxine said. "This is far too generous."

"Two of them are from me and my wife. The other two packages were sitting on your front stoop when I arrived."

Chloe examined the two small, unmarked packages she was holding. "I wonder who they're from?"

"Why don't you come in and have some hot chocolate while we open the gifts?" Maxine said to Renaud. "You must be freezing out there."

"*Merci*, but I really must be getting home. We have a family tradition of singing carols with my kids and I don't want to miss it."

"Thanks again for coming out in the cold," Maxine said. "Chloe and I were just talking about Jacques."

"We all miss him," Renaud said. "He was always so generous to everyone at the company during the holidays."

The three fell silent for a moment, and Chloe gathered Maxine and Renaud were reflecting on that last big Christmas party with Jacques, just as she was.

"Well, I better be getting home," Renaud said, turning to leave.

Chloe joined her mother in thanking Renaud once more for taking the time to deliver the gifts, then returned to the parlor to open them.

After they'd open the two boxes from Renaud, which turned out to be colorful tins filled with delicious Christmas cookies baked by his wife, Chloe and Maxine turned their attention to the unmarked boxes.

"Maybe they're from Gigi and Simone," Chloe said, examining the boxes, which were wrapped in plain brown paper. She noticed one box was addressed to her and one was for Maxine, but there was no sender's name.

"Seems like they would have just brought them over when they stopped by, if that was the case," Maxine said, accepting the box with her name from Chloe.

"Wonder what it could be," Chloe said, pressing her ear to her box and shaking it.

"Why don't we open them and see?"

They both tore off the wrapping, eager to see what was inside.

"Oh my god. This is magnificent," Maxine said, reaching into her box and holding up a gold pendant encrusted with diamonds in the shape of a sailboat.

"Mine, too." Chloe showed Maxine the contents of her box, which contained another gold-and-diamond pendant in the shape of a rapier.

"Here," Maxine said, taking Chloe's pendant out of the box. "I'll put yours on you, and you put mine on me."

"Wonder who could have sent these?" Chloe said after they'd fixed the pendants to their robes. The shiny baubles reflected the twinkling Christmas tree lights.

"I don't know, *ma chérie*. You coming home was a Christmas miracle, and maybe Santa paid us a visit."

Chloe smiled at the thought. "You know, it's really good to be home."

57

Chloe sat in a cracked pleather chair in a cramped Manhattan office building, filing tax forms in a rusty file cabinet. Six months of temping and this was all she had to show for it. When she'd envisioned the glamorous job she'd land before her breakthrough acting role came along, she'd pictured herself working as an editor's assistant at a top fashion magazine. Slaving away in some stuffy accountant's office was about as *un*glamorous as you could get.

Finally reaching the bottom of the mountain of tax forms, Chloe shoved and shoved until the file cabinet's rickety metal jaws swallowed the overstuffed drawer. She reached into her purse and retrieved the ad she'd circled in *Variety* calling for actors to try out for a television commercial.

The TV spot for a new shampoo wasn't exactly the grand thespian opportunity to which Chloe aspired, but if she got this gig, it would pay residuals that would enable her to give up temping and pursue acting full time.

"Mr. Morris, I'm through," she said, knocking on the private office door of the one-man shop who'd hired her. "Can I leave now?"

The needle-nosed man with Coke-bottle glasses and an unkempt mustache looked up from his ancient adding machine, glanced at the clock and scowled. "It's only two-thirty. You're scheduled to be here until three today."

Chloe shifted from foot to foot, already nervous enough about the pending audition. "Yes, but you said I could leave early if I finished the filing you gave me, remember?" she said, keeping her tone deferential, not wanting to jeopardize her current and only source of income.

"But what if someone calls?" Morris said, sounding almost panicked, as if he ran a fast-paced 911 call center rather than a dull office where the phone hardly ever rang once tax season was over.

"If you're too busy to pick up, the voicemail will intercept the call," Chloe said slowly, feeling as though she were explaining the wonders of modern technology to a time traveler.

"You sure you finished all the filing?" Morris said, looking Chloe over skeptically from behind his thick lenses.

"Yes, sir," she said, glancing anxiously at the clock.

Morris lowered his glasses, massaged his forehead and sighed dramatically. "I suppose if you've finished your work, you can leave."

"Thank you, sir. I'll be back bright and early in the morning," she said, silently hoping that either this commercial or one of the full-time jobs she'd applied for around town would come through and she wouldn't have to make good on the promise.

As she returned to the outer office to gather her purse, she heard Morris mutter under his breath, "I can't wait 'til Delores gets back from maternity leave."

Me, too! Chloe had to restrain herself from uttering out loud.

She bounded down the back stairs, taking two at a time, not bothering to wait for the snaillike elevator. With barely half-an-hour to make her audition, she would have to hustle. She dashed out of the building and into the muggy June air.

Pausing on a street corner, she studied the address listed in the *Variety* ad. Was she supposed to turn right or left? She asked a mounted policeman for directions and he pointed her toward an address a couple of blocks away. She sprinted the whole way and finally reached her destination. She looked up at the skyscraper, which loomed over her like a schoolyard bully made of concrete and steel. The Wellington Tower. She took a step forward and entered through the revolving door. Stepping onto a glass elevator, she closed her eyes and held her breath, trying not to give in to her fear of heights. She didn't exhale or open her eyes until the elevator stopped on the forty-seventh floor and the offices of Infinity Productions.

Hurrying down a long corridor, she looked at her watch and realized she was five minutes late. In spite of her tardiness, she stopped in the ladies' room and splashed cold water on her face, still shaken from the ascent into the sky on the glass elevator.

"Pull it together," she told herself in the mirror. If she was going to make it in New York, she was going to have to get over this phobia.

Having collected herself in the bathroom, she reported to the receptionist, told her she had a three o'clock appointment with the casting director and muttered a quick, "Sorry I'm late."

As it turned out, her tardiness didn't matter. She had to wait another half-an-hour, thumbing through back editions of *Advertising Age* and other trade journals in which she had no interest. When she was at last called in to see the casting director, she did her best to steady her nerves.

Upon opening a door that led to a production studio, she stood transfixed by the bright overhead lights and the motion-picture camera stationed in the middle of the room. She shivered, since the room was ice-cold.

"Are you Chloe?"

Chloe blinked and noticed a middle-aged woman with graying, shoulder-length hair and a lumpy frame that belied the image-conscious industry in which she worked.

"Yes. Nice to meet you," Chloe said, shaking the woman's hand.

"Hi. I'm Janis Younger, the casting director. Sorry if my hands are cold. They have to keep it below a certain temperature to protect the camera equipment and keep the lights from overheating. I'll introduce you to the director."

Janis led Chloe to a paunchy, balding man who was adjusting the camera.

"We're almost set up," the director said. "Why don't you go get changed?"

"There's a dressing room over there," Janis said, pointing to a door in a corner of the studio. "While you're getting changed, we'll take a look at your audition reel."

Chloe gulped. "Audition reel?"

"Haven't you done any commercials before, hon'?" Janis said, sounding more motherly than condescending.

"Um, not exactly. I've mostly done print modeling."

"That's okay. We're always looking for fresh new talent," Janis said, smiling and handing Chloe a script.

Chloe relaxed a little as she made her way to the dressing room, until she saw that her costume was nothing but a towel. She undressed, used the towel's Velcro tabs to secure it around her mid-section, looked over the script and took her place on the set, which was made up to look like a bathroom. A blindingly powerful light positioned outside the fake window simulated artificial sunlight. Chloe stood as close to the window as possible, as the light provided the only source of heat in the frigid studio.

"This is the product," Janis said, handing Chloe the shampoo bottle. "Just let us know when you're ready and we'll get rolling."

The bottle shook in Chloe's clammy hands as the director told her where to stand. There was nothing to be nervous about, she told herself. She only had a few, easy-to-remember lines.

"I'm ready," she said after one last perusal of the one-page script.

"Action!" the director called.

"My hair shimmers and shines when I use…" she trailed off. How could she forget the name of the product she was holding?

"I'm sorry," she said. "Can I start again?"

The director called, "Cut," and crew members fiddled with the lights. When the camera began rolling again, Chloe cradled the shampoo bottle and affected a smile, trying to keep her teeth from chattering.

"My hair shimmers and shines when I use Herbaltene. It's equipped with essential vitamins and minerals that give my hair bounce." She held the bottle in one hand and ran the other through her hair, as the script called for. The bottle tumbled to the ground and the director angrily called, "Cut!"

"I'm sorry," Chloe said as the casting director came onto the set.

"It's okay, hon'," Janis said, offering her a robe. "Why don't you take a minute and look over the script again?"

Chloe warmed up with a cup of coffee and ran through her lines. This dialogue wasn't exactly Shakespeare. So why was it so hard to do it in front of the camera?

"Sure you don't need some more time? You're the last girl we're seeing today," Janis said when Chloe took off the robe and took her place on set again.

"No, I'm ready."

Chloe tried to picture herself in her own personal bathroom at the Chateau de Chevalier, but when the director called, "Action!" again, she froze up. She stared into the camera, trying to remember her lines, but the words wouldn't come.

"Cut!"

Janis approached Chloe, placing the robe around her shoulders. "I think we've got enough to see how you come across onscreen. Why don't you go get dressed, hon'?"

"Can't I just do it one more time? I know I can –"

"We have your contact information. Thanks for coming out."

"You're hired."

Chloe reached across Bloomingdale's perfume counter and threw her arms around the middle-aged former beauty queen who'd uttered the two words Chloe had been waiting to hear for the past six months.

"Thank you for this opportunity. I promise, I won't let you down," Chloe gushed. She was so happy to get a callback for *something*, even if it was just a retail job, she felt like turning cartwheels in the middle of the store.

"Honey, this is not a chance at the Miss America title," Candy Chandler said in her nasally Buffalo accent, "it's just a part-time job spraying samples on unsuspecting passersby."

"Still, I'm grateful."

Chloe thanked her new manager again and nearly danced out of the department store's revolving door. She could finally give up temping and bring in a regular paycheck, if small, and start reimbursing Daniella and Muriel for their generosity. True, working the perfume counter at Bloomingdale's wasn't an acting job, but at least she felt like she was beginning to get a foothold in New York.

She hummed to herself as she strolled down the street and dropped a coin in the hat of a street musician playing a steel drum. She was a working girl now and could afford to part with a little spare change. She bought a pretzel from a sidewalk vendor and munched on it as she followed the undulation of the crowd moving toward Central Park for a free symphony concert. She sat down on a patch of grass and enjoyed the late-afternoon sunshine. The variety of attractions that the Big Apple had to offer was infinite. When the brutal winter finally came to an end, she spent the spring exploring the city, soaking up the cultural melting pot that was New York. She visited the Bronx Zoo, frequented museums and open-mic nights at funky coffee shops in the Village, took in off-Broadway plays. Daniella and Muriel had taken her to a couple of jazz clubs where the music reminded her of her grandparents. She loved living in a city where there was creativity around every corner.

Upon leaving the park, she stopped to watch a group of breakdancers who were entertaining a small crowd. The scene reminded her of walking home from school with Gigi in Paris, when they would often see breakdancers in the Trocadéro park near the Eiffel Tower, and she realized she hadn't heard from her friend in a while.

Walking home from the subway station, Chloe reminisced, thinking about Gigi and all their adventures. On one street, the sounds of a couple arguing in Spanish near an open window mingled with Middle Eastern music coming from a corner carryout. She never realized there were so many different kinds of people on the planet. Every race on Earth, and every possible variation and hybrid, was represented in New York, all living side by side in cramped apartment buildings. She turned a corner and passed a group of Puerto Rican kids splashing in the water spilling forth from an open fire hydrant. Her first sweltering summer in New York was underway, streets buckling and tempers flaring as the mercury rose.

"Yo, *Mami*," a guy in a basketball jersey draped with gold medallions called to her from a stoop. He made kissing noises at her through his gold teeth, his hand resting on his crotch.

She was careful to keep walking and not make eye contact. She had learned how to ignore come-ons. Daniella and Muriel occasionally set her up on blind dates with the younger brothers of their college friends, but she was having trouble finding anyone who really interested her. Boys her age were so immature. She didn't need to be bothered with them; she enjoyed her own company. Her idea of a good time on a Saturday night was taking a bubble bath or washing her hair, making a bowl of microwave popcorn and curling up with a good book or watching old movies.

She sighed with relief as she opened the door of the air-conditioned apartment building. She checked the mailbox on her way up the steps, plopping the large stack on an end table and hitting the play button on the answering machine once inside the apartment. There was a message from Mother calling to say hi and see how she was doing. She was glad she was on good terms again with her mother, and Chloe also frequently corresponded with Marie.

Entering the kitchen, Chloe saw a note from Daniella under a refrigerator magnet saying she and Muriel were going to be out late with their study group and there were leftovers in the fridge. Daniella and Muriel were like her big sisters, always looking out for her. They were busy with classes, extracurricular activities and internships at law firms, but always managed to make sure she ate right and took care of herself.

While heating up a casserole, Chloe's ears perked up at the sound of a vaguely familiar voice on the answering machine.

"Hi, Chloe. This is Janis Younger from Infinity Productions. We just wanted to call and thank you for auditioning for the commercial, but we've decided to go in another direction with casting. Thanks again for trying out and best of luck in the future."

Chloe slammed the refrigerator door. Her chronic fear of auditioning had sabotaged her again, causing her to freeze up during the commercial audition. The confidence boost she'd gotten from being hired at Bloomingdale's was now trampled by her umpteenth acting rejection in the past six months. She opened the freezer and considered downing a whole carton of cookie dough ice cream, but stopped at the sound of Gigi's voice on the machine.

"Hi, Chlo', it's me. Give me a call when you get in. I'll be up late. I've got great news I can't wait to tell you about."

The knowledge that Gigi was doing well was comforting. Chloe changed out of the business clothes she'd worn to the Bloomingdale's interview and into a T-shirt and shorts and took the phone into her room to call Gigi back, munch on dinner and sort through the mail.

"So what's the big news?" she said between bites of casserole upon reaching Gigi.

"For one thing, I just got my diploma in the mail from Our Lady," Gigi said, her voice sounding slightly scratchy over the long-distance connection. "Believe it or not, Mother Superior was actually pretty cool about letting me finish up my degree through correspondence courses. She even put a little note in with my diploma wishing me well and letting me know she was praying for me to get my life together."

"Guess the old bag has a heart after all." Chloe chuckled. "Who knew?"

"And guess what?"

"What?" Chloe said, setting the mound of junk mail beside her on the futon.

"I got accepted at the Sorbonne!"

Chloe sat up, knocking the mail onto the floor. "Oh my god, Gi'! That's awesome!"

"I know. I'm still in shock. When I submitted my portfolio and application, I thought I'd never hear from them again. But they said they liked my portfolio and I start at the École des Beaux-Arts in the fall."

"I'm so happy for you, Gi'," Chloe said, trying to muster enthusiasm for her friend in spite of the disappointment she felt over losing out on the commercial.

"Are you okay? You don't sound like yourself."

"I'm happy for you, I really am. It's just that…" Chloe picked the mail off the floor, placed it on her lap and reclined on the futon. "I have some good news of my own, and some bad news."

"Bad news first. Let's get it over with."

"Before you called, the casting director of that commercial I tried out for left a message saying they picked somebody else."

"Bummer. I know you really wanted that part."

Chloe sank back against the futon, her slumping posture reflecting her deflated mood. "In the past six months, I've auditioned for every commercial, film and theater role that calls for a breathing female, but I haven't even been cast as an extra."

"That really sucks, but what's the good news?"

"I got hired at Bloomingdale's, so now I have a steady job."

"That's great, Chlo'. At least you'll be able to support yourself while you go on auditions."

"Yeah, but I couldn't make it if it wasn't for Daniella and Muriel. And they're going to be graduating at the end of the summer term and moving out. I don't know what I'm gonna do then."

"Have you given any more thought to going back to school?"

Chloe sifted through the pile of junk mail, pausing when she came upon the New York University application she'd sent for. "I've thought about it," she said. "But honestly, I just don't know if I'm ready for four more years of school right now. I've kind of been holding out for my acting break."

"It'll come. Hey, if I can get accepted at the Sorbonne with my grades, anything can happen."

Gigi laughed, and Chloe joined in, in spite of herself. They chatted for a while longer, getting caught up.

"How are the therapy sessions with Simone going?" Chloe asked.

"Not too bad, actually. I was really skeptical when she suggested we go into family therapy when I first came back home. But the counselor has helped us work through a lot of issues."

Gigi related that she had learned through therapy that a major reason she'd become sexually promiscuous as a teen and was attracted to "bad boys" like her ex-husband Justin Bradshaw was because of growing up without a father. Slowly, she was learning to accept herself and learn from the mistakes she'd made in her young life. She wasn't a screw-up, she was a survivor. She was learning to forgive herself, and was also learning to forgive Simone for not always being there for her when she needed.

"I'm going to be moving into the dorms when I start at the Sorbonne, but I'm glad I've had these past few months to get to know my mother again," Gigi continued. "I never realized how much I missed having a real relationship with her."

"Speaking of relationships, when's the wedding? I thought Simone and Jules had set a date."

"The wedding's off. The counselor helped Simone realize she was only marrying Jules for his money and she broke it off with him, so now I don't have to pretend to get along with those two spoiled bitches of his."

"That's fantastic. Sounds like things are really coming together for you." She tossed the NYU application aside. "I just hope the same will happen for me."

It was unbelievably busy all day at work, and Chloe nearly ran out of Bloomingdale's when it was time to take her lunch break. Stepping out onto the teeming streets, she debated about what to have for lunch. Lox and bagels at her favorite Jewish deli? A slice of world-famous New York pizza with double cheese and everything on it at the pizzeria down the street? She junked both ideas and instead chose a hot dog from a sidewalk stand. Restaurants were always filled to capacity during lunchtime hours. You either had to scream your order or go hungry.

"Do you mind if I ask you a personal question?" the East Indian hot dog vendor said to Chloe.

"I guess not," she said with trepidation, wondering if he was going to make a crack about her voracious appetite since she'd ordered a foot-long chilidog with everything, a bag of chips and a soda.

"Well, I see you walking up and down this street every day and I always wonder what race you are," the man said through his accent. "Your complexion is like the blacks, but your hair is like white people's. I'm from India. You almost look like one of us, but not exactly. What are you?"

Chloe chuckled. "I'm me."

She downed the fattening chilidog and stopped at a newsstand for her weekly ritual of browsing *Variety* and *Back Stage* for audition notices. Catching sight of a fashion magazine, she picked one up and began flipping through it. The slick photography, the fantasy images, the colorful threads adorning glassy-eyed models. It all intrigued Chloe. None of the girls in the high-fashion spreads were prettier than she. Chloe could do what they did; she had done it before, in fact, and was good at it. When she occasionally came across an outdoor photo shoot while walking the streets of New York, she felt a pang for the attention she had received when she had modeled in Paris.

Chloe spent the remainder of her lunch hour thumbing through international editions of *Vogue*, *Elle* and other fashion mags. Skimming the fashion bible, *W*, she became engrossed in a profile of Warren and Barbara Rubinstein, the sixty-something founders of New York's Epitome Modeling Agency. According to the article, the Rubinsteins and their world-famous agency had helped launch the careers of numerous top models. Epitome had established a reputation over the past few decades as an incubator for undiscovered talent, mainly through its annual "cattle call," or open audition, which was coming up in a few weeks.

"Hey, this ain't no library," the newsstand clerk growled at Chloe as she continued to scour the magazine. "Buy it or beat it, kid."

Chloe handed the clerk a few bucks, dog-earing the magazine to mark her place, and dashed back to work. Her break was over fifteen minutes ago. She had been so engulfed by the article on the modeling agency that she'd lost track of time.

For the rest of the day at work, Chloe kept sneak-reading the profile on the Rubinsteins and their modeling agency, hiding the magazine behind a row of bottles on the perfume counter. A blurb at the end of the article gave the details of the cattle call, stating aspiring models would need to bring headshots and be prepared to present themselves in front of a panel of fashion experts.

For some reason, Chloe thought about going out for this upcoming "audition." While the cattle call didn't directly relate to acting, getting back into modeling might be a way to get noticed by directors and producers. She recalled Monique Lillier, her French modeling agent, telling her before she left Paris that she had the potential to become a top model.

Chloe was so preoccupied with the prospect of yet another anxiety-inducing audition that she nearly blinded a potential customer, not paying attention when she sprayed a perfume sample in the woman's face. Fortunately, Chloe's supervisor took pity and instead of firing her, sent her home early since she obviously had something on her mind.

That evening, when Chloe spoke to Maxine on the phone, she casually said, "Mother, when you fly in for your visit next week, would you please remember to bring my portfolio with you?"

"Sure," Maxine said. "What do you need it for, dear? Are you thinking about doing some modeling in New York?"

"I don't know. Maybe."

When she hung up, she found Daniella standing behind her at the desk in the living room.

"What's that?" Daniella asked, peering over Chloe's shoulder at the blurb Chloe had circled in the magazine with the details of the cattle call.

"Nothing."

Daniella picked up the magazine. "You planning on going to this audition?"

With her relentless questions, Daniella was going to make an excellent legal eagle.

"No. It's nothing, really."

"Whatever you say. It's your business. I just wanted to tell you Muriel and I are going out to grab a bite to eat, if you want to come with."

"Thanks, but it's been a long day and I'm kind of tired."

"Want us to bring you something back?"

"No, I'm probably just going to take a bath and go straight to bed."

"Okay."

Daniella took one last curious glance at the magazine and handed it back to Chloe, who promptly closed it and stuffed it in a drawer.

58

For weeks, Chloe flip-flopped: Should she go to the cattle call, shouldn't she go to the cattle call? The dilemma was making her crazy. She was still smarting from being turned down for the commercial she'd tried out for and just wasn't sure if she could handle any more rejection.

The day before the cattle call, she made up her mind. She was going to give it a go. What was she going to do, work part-time at a department store the rest of her life?

Chloe figured the cattle call would last all day. With a prestigious agency like Epitome, there was sure to be extra long lines of models waiting to try out. It was too late to arrange to get the day off work, so she would have to call in sick. She hated lying to Candy, her supervisor, whom she liked a lot and really got along with, but this was a once-a-year, maybe even once-in-a-lifetime opportunity she couldn't afford to pass up. If she didn't go, she would spend the next twelve months – or worse, the rest of her life – kicking herself and wondering what could have been, what might have been, if only... She couldn't do that to herself.

She got little sleep that night. Why was she so nervous? She had done plenty of modeling in Paris. All she had to do was go in there and do her best. If they didn't like her, it was their loss. Then why was her stomach tied up in knots?

She tore her room up in the morning, pulling all of her clothes out of the armoire and spreading them on her bed to get a bird's-eye view of all the possible ensembles. She tried on outfit after outfit, walking back and forth to the bathroom to see how she looked. Every time, the mirror told her that she had no business wearing something that made her look either dumpy and fat, or too tall and lanky.

"What are you doing?" said Daniella, cracking her bedroom door and rubbing her eyes as Chloe made yet another trip from her bedroom to the bathroom.

"Nothing. It's Saturday morning. Go back to sleep." She couldn't risk jinxing her chances by telling someone where she was going.

She finally decided on a conservative black cocktail dress she found buried in the back of the armoire. She had bought the dress during her manic spending spree when she first arrived in New York and worn it on her big night out on the town when she treated herself to dinner and a Broadway show. That was the night she lost her purse and was soon plunged into homelessness.

She took the dress out and held it up, inspecting the garment on its hanger like an archaeologist examining an artifact from a time that seemed long ago. The dress hadn't brought her luck the first time she wore it, but it was the only thing in her closet that was appropriate for a fashion-related audition. Basic black was the perfect choice – not too dressy and not too casual. A late bloomer, she had filled out since high school, and black was slimming, but accentuated her tall yet well-proportioned frame. Black matched her hair and brought out her wine-colored eyes.

She hurriedly slipped into the dress and grabbed her portfolio and the impromptu résumé she'd thrown together. As a finishing touch, she retrieved one of the butterfly barrettes Muriel had gotten her for Christmas and used it to pin her hair back on one side. Maybe the barrette would serve as a charm and counteract any residual bad luck from the dress, Chloe reasoned.

"Well," she said to herself, checking her appearance one last time in the mirror on the way out, "here goes nothing."

Just as Chloe expected, there was a line around the block when she arrived. The cattle call was scheduled to begin at nine, and she was an hour early.

The Epitome Modeling Agency was housed in a big brownstone in Manhattan. Standing in line, Chloe continued reading up on the agency and its founders in *W* magazine.

According to the article, Warren and Barbara Rubinstein were both second-generation Americans and represented the classic rags-to-riches, Ellis Island success story. They both hailed from poverty-stricken, orthodox Jewish families that had emigrated from Russia, fleeing the pogroms of Eastern Europe.

Having met in college in the late '60s – the first in their families to have access to higher education – Warren and Barbara made a dynamic husband-and-wife team. As the article noted, they had a knack for complementing each other's strengths, which is what had sustained their marriage and helped their business grow since its founding in the early '70s. The couple started the agency as newlyweds, combining Warren's business savvy and Barbara's fashion sense. The magazine profile portrayed Warren as easygoing, while Barbara was the "bad cop" of the duo. The Rubinsteins had established a reputation for meticulously grooming their models for success, teaching them all the tricks of the trade, protecting them from the pitfalls of the industry and treating them like adopted children.

As the hours dragged on, Chloe was glad she had grown used to standing on her feet all day, working retail. To pass the time, she struck up conversation with the girl in front of her.

"Hi. I'm Chloe Bareaux."

"I love your name," said the girl, a buxom blonde with boobs to rival Dolly Parton. "Is it French?"

"*Oui.* My mother's Creole." Chloe glimpsed the name on the girl's headshot. "Brandon? That's kind of an unusual name for a girl, isn't it?"

"I know," the girl replied, smiling. "My father wanted a boy. Everybody calls me Brandi."

Chloe thought she detected a Southern drawl. Brandi related she had come all the way from Houston.

"My parents are disappointed I dropped out of college to pursue this crazy dream of modeling in New York. They wanted me to be a Southern belle." Brandi rolled her eyes. "They even threw me this big, outrageous debutante ball when I turned eighteen."

"Oh my god, my mother did the same thing. She's from New Orleans and is totally into that whole Southern gentility thing."

Chloe and her new acquaintance chatted away the hours, finding they had a lot in common.

"Have you always wanted to model?" Chloe asked.

"Yeah, I was in pageants when I was a kid. But if it was up to my folks, I'd marry a military man like my daddy and start havin' babies. I took a big risk by coming up North to try to get into modeling."

Appreciating Brandi's candor, Chloe related her experience leaving the insular world her mother had created in Paris and the run of bad luck she'd had when she first came to New York.

"Gosh," Brandi exclaimed in her drawl, "after all that, you deserve a break!"

It was late afternoon when they made it to the front of the line, and there were hundreds of people behind them.

"I hope you get chosen," Chloe said when Brandi's turn came up.

"I just hope I make it through this audition without falling on my ass, stuttering or looking like a dumb bumpkin."

Chloe laughed, telling Brandi she felt exactly the same. She really liked this girl.

Watching Brandi go through the agency's front door, Chloe's stomach rumbled. The fact that she'd had only a bowl of cereal and skipped lunch waiting in line wasn't the only reason she felt faint. Auditioning always made her queasy. Now she wished she hadn't given up the teen smoking habit Gigi had turned her on to. A shot of nicotine might calm her nerves.

"How'd you do?" Chloe asked when Brandi returned about fifteen minutes later.

Brandi shook her head. "You don't wanna know."

Chloe got her cue to go in.

"Good luck," Brandi called.

"Thanks." Chloe waved. "I'll need it."

As she entered the building, Chloe crossed herself and said a silent prayer. She needed divine intervention if she were going to get through this.

Upon entering the audition room, her stomach began churning again. Seated at a long table were some of the top models, designers, photographers and fashion editors in the industry, people Chloe had read about and seen pictures of in the magazines she browsed on her lunch break. And they were all here to judge her. She noticed Warren and Barbara sitting at the end of the table.

"Come on in," Barbara motioned. "Don't be shy."

Chloe did her best to project confidence, and as she walked in, she felt like Jennifer Beals going before the panel of judges in the climactic audition scene in *Flashdance*, one of her favorite American movies. She walked in and handed her photo and résumé to Barbara, who glanced at them and passed them to Warren. The couple looked exactly as they did in the magazine spread. Warren was white-haired yet looked lean and fit from mornings of tennis at a Park Avenue athletic club, as he related in the story. Barbara's features were elegant, topped off by her trademark ash-blond hair helmet, and Chloe could tell that as a young woman she'd been a great beauty. Barbara had aged gracefully, wearing her subtle crow's feet and frown lines like badges of honor she refused to surrender to the plastic surgeon's knife.

"Why don't you tell us your name and a little about yourself," Barbara said.

Chloe tried to swallow the lump in her throat, intimidated by being in the presence of the fashion baroness who was as legendary in the industry as Eileen Ford.

"My name's Chloe Bareaux. I was raised in Paris and I came to New York last year," she said in one quick breath, her mouth going dry and her cheeks growing hot. "What else do you want to know?"

"Girl doesn't exactly have a bright future ahead of her as a public speaker," a female editor in smart-girl glasses quipped.

The room erupted in howls.

Warren hushed the jeers like a judge calming a disruptive courtroom. "Chloe, would you please step on the runway, walk back and forth and strike a few poses for us? We want to see what you've got."

"I'll bet you do," one of the models cracked. "You men are all the same."

Once again, everyone laughed except for the Rubinsteins.

At Warren's direction, a college-age assistant flipped a switch and techno dance music filled the room. Chloe walked to the edge of the runway, averting her eyes from the panelists who were commenting among themselves and jotting notes, evaluating her. She tugged at the hem of her dress. Why had she worn this? It was too short, too revealing. She felt naked, exposed.

"Come on, hon', don't hold back, show us your stuff," Barbara said, snapping her fingers. "Put some *oomph* into it."

Taking another turn on the runway, Chloe tried to loosen up, but her legs felt like they were made of wood. Recalling her etiquette training in Paris, she tried to keep her chin up and her knees flexible, as Madame de Tornquist had taught her. All she could seem to manage, however, were stiff, jerky movements. The music was loud, but it wasn't loud enough to drown out the panelists' harsh asides.

"She must have pins in her knees. Maybe she's an android," Chloe heard one of the photographers saying.

"And she could stand to lose a few pounds," one of the designers sneered.

Chloe stepped down from the runway and burst into tears. "I don't have to take this," she cried. "I'm getting out of here." She ran out of the room, down the hall, and out of the building. She ran past all of the people waiting outside, down the block and back to the subway. She just wanted to go home and drown her sorrows in a carton of cookie dough ice cream, and she wanted her mommy.

"Those bastards, those dirty bastards!" Maxine bellowed when Chloe called to vent about the disastrous audition. "I have connections in the fashion industry, you know. I can destroy Epitome."

Maxine was being melodramatic, as usual, but Chloe knew she was just trying to make her feel better.

"Thanks, Mother, but I just want to forget all about this day, pretend it never happened."

Chloe simply accepted that fact that she had bombed at yet another audition. It just wasn't meant to be.

Monday morning arrived too soon, as always. Chloe just wanted to stay in bed and pull the covers over her head. She was depressed about making a fool of herself in front of all those fashion experts over the weekend and felt she couldn't face the world in this vulnerable state. She called in sick at work again and spent the entire morning in bed, wallowing in self-pity. She had failed once again.

At noon, she got up, showered and dressed, realizing that falling apart wasn't going to solve anything. She vowed to force herself to sit down and fill out that college application.

The hapless tryout at Epitome had shown her that getting back into modeling wasn't going to happen, and her chronic fear of auditioning was obviously going to keep her from success in acting. So she may as well go back to school and figure out what to do with her life.

She sat down at the desk in the living room and retrieved the NYU application, going through several reams of paper on the essay portion of the application. After ripping up yet another sheet covered with erasures, she finally decided that the honest approach was best. Since high school, she wrote, she had moved to New York, tried new things and gained valuable work experience and she was now ready to further her education.

Sliding the completed application in an envelope, she felt a sense of accomplishment. She was on her way out to mail the application when the phone rang. She turned back.

"Hello?" she said, picking up the kitchen extension.

"Hi, is this Chloe BAH-roy?" said the voice on the other end, thick with a "New Yawk" accent, mispronouncing her last name.

"Buh-ROW. Yes, this is she. Who's calling?"

"I'm with the Epitome Modeling Agency."

Chloe dropped the phone.

"Hello? You still there?" the voice on the other end repeated.

She caught her breath and retrieved the phone "Yes, I'm here," she said, the receiver trembling in her hands.

"My name's Rachel Rubinstein-Gould. I'm Warren and Barbara's daughter," the woman explained. "I'm a booking agent and talent scout here at Epitome. My parents asked me to call and set up an appointment with you."

The offer sounded kind of shady. What did they want? To put her through even more torturous embarrassment? She couldn't subject herself to that again, she just couldn't.

"Look, if they want me to come in and audition again, I'm sorry. I don't think I'll be able to –"

"They're not interested in another audition. They'd like to work out an arrangement with you."

"What kind of arrangement?" What did they want her to do, sign a contract saying she'd never come within a 100-mile radius of their building?

"You can work out the details with them personally," said Rachel. "Can you come in and meet with them tomorrow morning?"

"That soon? What about next week?"

"I have their appointment book in front of me. They're both booked solid for the next few weeks. Tomorrow morning's the only availability."

The nerve of these people, Chloe thought. After the humiliation they had put her through on Saturday, they expected her to just drop everything and come running at their beck and call.

"I have clients waiting. I need an answer now," Rachel, who obviously had plenty of practice in being aggressive, pressed.

Chloe wished she had more time to think about it, but she had to make a decision. "Yes. I can make it."

"Great. Nine o'clock sharp?"

"I'll be there."

59

This time Chloe was going to do things her way. Instead of agonizing over the meeting with the Rubinsteins like she had done with the cattle call, she pushed it to the back of her mind for the rest of the day. She went to bed early and got a good night's rest, rolling out of bed in the morning feeling refreshed, revitalized and ready to take on the world.

She didn't fuss over what to wear, she simply showered and slipped on a white, ribbed T-shirt, a black halter dress and some sandals. She grabbed a small purse and pulled it over her head so that it clung to her hip. Before leaving the apartment, she ran back to her bedroom, located the butterfly hairclip Muriel had given her for Christmas, and fixed it in her hair. It wouldn't hurt to have a good luck charm.

She arrived at the Epitome Modeling Agency a few minutes before her appointed time.

"Good morning. My name's Chloe Bareaux. I have a nine o'clock appointment with the Rubinsteins," she said, smiling at the receptionist.

"Have a seat. Mr. and Mrs. Rubinstein will be right with you."

As she sat on a large sofa that dominated the reception area, Chloe peered at the pictures of models and fashion magazine covers that adorned the walls. She recognized several of the cover girls, including two models who had been snotty to her during her very first runway show in Paris. It was as though they were sneering at her from the framed magazine covers on the wall, looking down at her and telling her she wasn't good enough to be here. Chloe scrunched down in her seat, as if shrinking in the presence of these fashion icons.

Photos of the Rubinsteins also decorated the lobby. There was a photo of Warren shaking the hand of the similarly white-haired Andy Warhol at an exhibition opening in the '80s. In another, celebrated designer Halston had his armed draped around Barbara, who was clad in a '70s Pucci dress and Jackie O. sunglasses. From studying the photos, it was apparent that the Rubinsteins had a long and storied history in the fashion industry.

Chloe played with the braided strap on her purse and tapped her foot, eager to find out what it was they wanted with her. Waiting was a pain. Minutes felt like hours. She tried to kill time by flipping through magazines scattered on the coffee table, but she couldn't help glancing at her watch every five minutes. She wasn't scheduled to go in to work until eleven and figured she'd have plenty of time to meet with the Rubinsteins and catch the subway. But by nine-thirty, she was still sitting in the lobby.

"I'm sort of in a hurry. Are they free yet?" Chloe said to the receptionist.

"They're both tied up right now. They'll be with you shortly," the receptionist said, dismissing Chloe with her brusque tone and a sideways glance.

At nine forty-five, Chloe asked to use the phone.

The receptionist looked up from the switchboard. "Is it a local call?"

"Yes."

The receptionist handed Chloe a receiver. "Make it quick," she said. "We have calls coming in from all over the world."

Chloe took the receiver and stared at the confusing maze of outgoing lines. "How do I dial out?" she asked, feeling stupid.

"What's the number? I'll dial it for you."

Chloe told her the number of her department at Bloomingdale's and the receptionist dialed, clicking over the keys with the agility of a seasoned court reporter. Chloe called in sick from work again. Her boss was probably starting to think she had contracted some incurable tropical virus. Whatever it was the

Rubinsteins had to say to her better be good.

Finally, after having waited for an entire hour, the receptionist told Chloe the Rubinsteins were "ready to see" her and showed her into their office, which was jam-packed with papers and photographs covering nearly every bare surface. Bulging address books and Rolodexes sat in the middle of an antique, leather-covered partners' desk.

Warren and Barbara greeted Chloe with firm handshakes.

"So glad you could make it, dear," Warren said. "Have a seat. Sit anywhere you like."

So glad you could make it? Chloe thought, taking a seat across from their desk. He said it like she had just strolled in five minutes ago.

"Would you care for coffee or tea, a glass of water?" Barbara offered.

"No thank you." She just wanted to know why they had called her back.

"Let's get down to business, then," said Barbara. "We weren't very impressed with you at the audition."

"To say the least," added Warren.

This is what they had called her here for? She had waited around and taken yet another day off work for them to bring her down even further?

"You came off as stilted and mechanical, unsure of yourself," Barbara continued. "We had a brainstorming session with the panel on Sunday. Those so-called experts kept trying to shuffle your photo and résumé to the bottom of the pile, but somehow it kept ending up back on top."

"That's a surprise," Chloe spoke up. "Everyone seemed to hate me." Those so-called fashion experts had really hurt her feelings with their cruel comments.

"If you plan to go into this business, you best develop a thick skin and learn not to take anything personally," Barbara advised.

"So if I did such a bad job, why am I here?" Chloe shifted in her seat. She really wanted them to get to the point.

"Barbara and I talked a lot about you after the auditions wrapped," said Warren. "You know, hundreds of models came out for that cattle call, and every week we get thousands of unsolicited photos from young men and women all over the world. Out of all those submissions, we sign maybe five, ten at the most, a year. We only consider the very best. We've been at this a long time and we know how to spot raw talent. Some of our best girls were the gawkiest at first."

"We looked up some of the European assignments you listed on your résumé," Barbara said, "and there was one thing in particular that swayed us."

Chloe leaned forward. "Really? What was that?"

Barbara picked up a remote control from under a pile of papers and aimed it at an ancient-looking TV/VCR combo situated on one of the overstuffed shelves across the room. Barbara kept pressing buttons, but the only thing that showed on the screen was static.

"Rachel, will you come in here?" Barbara said in an agitated tone, pressing an intercom button. "I can't get this goddamn gadget to work."

Moments later, a thirty-something brunette with Warren's brown eyes and Barbara's ethnic yet regal nose emerged from an adjacent office. "You must be Chloe. I'm Rachel-Rubinstein-Gould," she said, extending her hand. "We spoke on the phone."

Chloe nodded, recalling the conversation from yesterday afternoon. Rachel was prettier than Chloe had pictured her, and seemed friendlier and not as pushy in person.

Rachel, however, once again showed her take-charge personality by seizing the remote from her harried mother. "Here, Ma, let me do it. How many times have I told you, you have to put it in VCR mode to get it to work."

Rachel turned to Chloe. "Parents," she said in a conspiratorial tone, shaking her head, as if Chloe could relate since she was a young person. "I keep telling them they need to computerize, get rid of all this paper and join us in the digital age, but they're hopelessly old-school."

"Thank you, Rachel. That will be all," Barbara said, sounding as though she didn't appreciate being put down in front of someone with whom she was discussing business.

Rachel adjusted the volume on the TV, then exited. Color bars appeared on the screen, signaling the beginning of a tape, and Chloe sat on the edge of her seat, anticipating what was about to play. She felt like she was in a theater, waiting for the opening of a movie she'd been dying to see, but the twist was that the movie was about her.

The color bars eventually faded, replaced by a panoramic shot of a crowded, open-air café in the French Riviera. The setting and the dance beat playing over it were vaguely familiar, and Chloe struggled to recall where she knew them from.

The mystery was soon solved when Montana Blake, the American pop star Gigi had a fling with, appeared onscreen. The music video had been filmed that summer she and Gigi ran away to join him in Monaco. In the video, Montana sang to a girl whose back was turned. The girl turned around, and Chloe was shocked to see herself.

"Oh my god," she gasped, putting her hand over her mouth.

She barely remembered making the video; the memory had faded into obscurity, along with Montana's fleeting, bubblegum career. She propped her chin on her fist, watching the girl dancing around onscreen as if watching a stranger. It was like looking into a time capsule. Was she ever really that fresh-faced? You could see the naiveté and lack of worldliness and life experience in her eyes. She never thought of herself as chubby, but having experienced lean times and been constantly on the go since moving to New York, she had lost a few pounds and the girl onscreen had clearly been coddled on Marie's crêpes and high-calorie, school cafeteria food. So much had transpired since the making of that video, it felt like a lifetime ago.

After the video ended and the screen faded again to color bars, Warren clicked off the TV. "From that video, we could tell you have something, Chloe, something that makes you stand out. Even though you bombed at the audition, Barbara and I saw a lot of potential in you."

"You're like a diamond in the rough," Barbara interjected. "Pure, unpolished. We'd like to hone your potential, bring it to fruition. Under our tutelage, you'll go far."

Chloe sat back in her seat, still weirded out from viewing the blast-from-the-past video. "What are you saying?"

"What we're saying is, we think you have the look, and you're obviously driven and ambitious, or you wouldn't even have braved all the competition and come to the cattle call in the first place," said Barbara. "But you need work. Whenever we sign a new model, we send them to a sort of finishing school, if you will."

"I took charm lessons in Paris when I turned eighteen."

"You don't understand, dear. This isn't charm school," said Warren. "We offer a comprehensive, intensive, modeling and self-development course. You'll relearn how to walk and talk, sit and stand, how to project yourself and stand out in a crowd."

"That's *if* I decide to sign," Chloe said, unsure whether this opportunity was the one she'd been waiting for.

"Excuse the hell out of us. We weren't aware that you had every agency in New York beating down your door," Barbara said, sounding indignant. "At only five-nine and with all that baby fat you're still carrying around, I don't think it's wise to turn us down. We're offering you the kind of chance that only comes around once."

Chloe didn't say so out loud, but Barbara had a point.

"Is this modeling course free?" Chloe asked.

"Oh no, no, no," Barbara was quick to point out. "We hire the most experienced instructors in the world to teach the course. When a new girl or guy signs with our agency and enrolls in the course, they get advice from successful models who have gone before them and get the chance to do photo sessions with some of the leading photographers in the industry. There's no way we could offer that service free of charge."

"Well, how much is it?"

Barbara and Warren exchanged a glance and whispered to each other. Warren jotted a quote on a piece of customized stationery and handed it to Chloe, whose mouth dropped.

"I can't afford this," she blurted. The fifteen hundred dollars for the course was way out of her price range.

"Most of our models can't afford it at first. You can give us a third as a down payment and make installments on the rest," said Warren. "We'll take it out of your first couple of assignments."

"I was always under the impression that when it comes to modeling, you either have it or you don't," Chloe said, glancing down again at the figure the Rubinsteins had quoted.

"That's true to a certain extent, but some models need that extra little push," said Barbara. "Watching the video and looking over the magazine spreads from your résumé, we could tell you're a natural in front of the camera. But we could also tell you never received formal training. The tuition for the course is a small price to pay for what you'll get in return."

Chloe twirled a strand of hair. "Can I take some time to think about it?"

"Do you know how many girls would give their firstborn child, even kill to be in your shoes right now?" Barbara said. She turned to Warren. "You've got to admit, if nothing else, the girl's got chutzpah."

"We'll need an answer as soon as possible," Warren said. "We'll give you until next Monday."

That was less than a week away. Chloe needed more time to make up her mind, but she agreed to the deadline. She thanked the Rubinsteins for meeting with her and promised to get back with them promptly. This wasn't going to be an easy decision. She had just started repaying Daniella and Muriel for the months they'd carried her, and in order to pay for the course she would have to drain her meager savings. And that was just for the down payment. And there was no guarantee she would get any work upon completing the course. It was a risk she wasn't sure she was willing to take.

"If we haven't heard from you by noon on Monday, we'll assume you decided not to sign," Warren said as Chloe left the office. "We hope to hear from you soon."

Chloe tossed the Rubinsteins' offer around. She would decide to sign, pick up the phone to notify them, then change her mind and hang up. This routine continued until Friday, when she broke down and sought advice from her mother.

"You do what you think is best. I learned my lesson. I'm not going to try to run your life anymore," Maxine said when Chloe called her office in Paris.

The one time Chloe really needed her mother's advice, she decided not to tell her what to do. Thanks, Mom.

Still feeling conflicted, Chloe turned to her roommates for guidance.

"Personally, I don't think you should do it," Muriel said as they sat in a circle around a pizza box on the living room floor.

Muriel explained that in her opinion, modeling was a sexist industry that treated women like objects to be bought and sold.

"Furthermore," she added, "no legitimate modeling agency would ask you to pay for some stupid course."

"How would you know?" Chloe asked, taking another piece of pizza from the box and picking at the gooey cheese.

"Well, I don't know that for sure, since I've never modeled and have no desire to," Muriel admitted, sipping her Coke, "but I care about you like my little sister. We're just trying to look out for you. Right, Dan?"

Daniella took a bite of her breadstick and looked thoughtful. "You know, when I saw that magazine with the ad you circled about Epitome's cattle call, I figured you were thinking about getting back into modeling. I was against it, for the same reasons as Muriel, but I decided not to say anything because it wasn't my place. But since you asked…"

"Tell her, Dan," Muriel said between bites of pepperoni. "Tell her about everything we learned in that women's studies class about how modeling and beauty pageants exploit women."

"What I was going to say is, I'm not so sure now that she shouldn't do it."

"What?" Muriel set her plate down and wiped her hands. "What're you talking about?"

"Why do you think I'm taking that job offer at that big law firm in Boston? Corporate law isn't why I wanted to get into the legal profession – I don't want to sell out and become part of the establishment like my parents."

"Then why take the job?" Muriel asked, looking befuddled. "And what has this got to do with Chloe's situation?"

"I'm getting to that. When I sat down and thought about the job, I realized all the good I could do. I could use my position in the firm to go after big corporations that step on the little guy, and I'll be making enough money to do pro bono work for nonprofits and people with good causes who can't afford legal representation."

Muriel took another sip of her Coke. "So what are you saying?"

Chloe remained silent, waiting to hear Daniella's point.

"What I'm saying is," Daniella said, standing up, "is that taking that job at the firm in Boston is a way for me to accomplish my goals and make a difference. I plan to use the firm's resources to further the causes I believe in.

Working for a high-profile firm like Westmoreland & McNeil will enable me to use the system and make it work for me – in a good way. And Chloe can do the same thing with the opportunity at Epitome – it's a means to an end."

"How so?" Chloe said, sitting up.

"You've been trying to get a break in acting ever since you came to New York. It's almost been a year and you've gotten nowhere, right?"

"Thanks for reminding me."

"Just hear me out. Modeling is something you can surely do, and you could use this opportunity to make a name for yourself. You could use it as a steppingstone. Once you've established yourself as a model, you'll have an easier time getting people to consider you for acting roles."

Chloe nodded, buoyed by Daniella's reassurance. "I thought the same thing. That's why I went to Epitome's cattle call in the first place."

"But you're so smart, Chloe," Muriel said, standing as well. "And you went to prep school. With a transcript from a school with an international reputation like Our Lady of Chastity, you'll have no trouble getting into NYU. You could get a scholarship, maybe even a full-ride. Do you know how many kids in the inner city would love to have that kind of opportunity?"

Chloe chewed on a crust, pondering Muriel's persuasive argument.

"I take issue with several of the points you just made, counselor," Daniella said to Muriel, breaking into courtroom-speak. "First of all, Chloe *is* smart, and using this modeling opportunity to get her to the next level is shrewd. Secondly, not just anybody can become a model and be successful at it. Top agencies like Epitome are very selective. They don't just sign up any schlub who walks in off the street. They obviously see potential in Chloe and can give her the backing she needs to make it. And thirdly," Daniella added, gesturing with her half-eaten breadstick, "how many young girls in the inner city would die to have the money and glamour and *attention* that come with a model's lifestyle?"

Chloe turned to Muriel, who appeared to be collecting her thoughts and readying her rebuttal. Chloe felt as though her roommates were arguing a trial, and the verdict would determine her future.

"I just hate to see an intelligent girl like Chloe with so much promise wasting her time on such a shallow profession," Muriel said.

"Oh come on, Muriel. I'm as much of a feminist as you are, but it's a fact of life that all women, no matter what line of work you're in, are ultimately judged by your appearance." Daniella folded her arms and paced around the room. "When I went for the interview at the firm in Boston, do you think I didn't wear that low-cut suit of mine with the short skirt? I didn't go through all those years of cheerleading, developing my calf muscles, and not use them when I needed them. And I'm not above sitting up front in a class and batting my eyes at the professor if it means he'll spend just as much time reading my papers and evaluating my ideas as he does the men in the class. I've done it – I'm not going to say I haven't – and I know you have, too."

"I've never done anything like that in my life." Muriel put her hands on her hips. "I don't need to act like that to get grades. I've never flirted with a teacher."

"Not even with that African-American studies professor you told me about, the cute one with the dreads and the dimples?" Daniella gave Muriel a precocious look. "Come on now, tell the truth just like you'd expect any witness to do under oath."

Muriel grinned. "I plead the Fifth."

Daniella circled the room, as if giving a closing statement. "All I'm saying is, you should use whatever advantages you have. Do whatever gets you in the door, as long as you're not trampling on anyone else. Chloe's been trying to do things the hard way, and maybe this is a shortcut. This modeling opportunity could be an avenue that gets her noticed and makes it possible for her to do other things, the things she really wants to do."

"Well, I rest my case," Muriel said, sinking to the floor next to Chloe. "I hope we haven't confused you even more. We both have your best interests at heart."

"I know, and I appreciate it, but I still can't make up my mind," Chloe said, expelling a gust of air that blew her up her bangs.

"Tell you what: I'll drop by the library on campus this weekend and do a little research," Muriel offered. "I'll give you a full report on Epitome by Sunday night. That way, you can make an informed decision on Monday morning."

True to her word, Muriel handed Chloe a dossier on Epitome after dinner Sunday evening. "Everything checked out," she reported. "They're up there with Elite, Ford and IMG."

Muriel added that the last thing she wanted to do was influence Chloe to sign with a modeling agency, but withholding evidence would be unethical.

"Another thing I found out about Epitome," Muriel said, "is that they have a reputation for launching ethnic and foreign models, unlike other agencies that only represent the 'all-American' type or promote Eurocentric beauty."

"Thanks," Chloe said, skimming the file, "but I still can't seem to make up my mind."

"Look, I don't want to influence your decision," Daniella piped in from the kitchen as she did the dinner dishes, "but do you remember when I told you about that talent scout that approached me in the mall in high school?"

"Yeah, of course," Chloe said, recalling the story Daniella related when she was filling in for Marie at the Chateau de Chevalier.

"You never told me about that," Muriel said.

"Because I was afraid you'd think it was silly," Daniella said, wiping her hands on a dishtowel as she came into the living room. "I've always wondered what would've happened if I would have followed up with that guy. After I threw his card away, I saw his name in the credits when one of my favorite sitcoms came on. Every now and then I think about that and wonder, 'What if?' Don't get me wrong. I've always wanted to be a lawyer, but I've also fantasized about being on television."

"You're certainly very telegenic, Miss California," Muriel teased.

Daniella threw the dishtowel at Muriel. "Look, whatever you decide to do about Epitome," she said, turning to Chloe, "don't do it out of fear. Sometimes you have to take risks. You don't want to spend the rest of your life wondering, 'What if?'"

Chloe closed the file Muriel had given her and got up to go to her room. Maybe it would be easier to make up her mind after a good night's sleep. "Thanks for the advice, you guys." She held up the file and gestured at Muriel. "And thanks again for the background info. I'll give it a thorough read-through before I go to bed."

"No problem," Muriel said. "I just hope you know what you're getting yourself into."

60

Monday morning behind the perfume counter at Bloomingdale's whizzed by.

"It's a few minutes early, but why don't you go ahead and take your lunch break now," Candy, Chloe's supervisor, told her.

Chloe looked at her watch. It was almost noon. She had been so busy all morning that she'd forgotten about the deadline the Rubinsteins had given her. She had five minutes to call them or forever relinquish the opportunity with Epitome. After talking with Daniella and Muriel the night before, she had finally made up her mind. Daniella's story about being approached by the talent agent in the mall had swayed Chloe. She was going to take a risk and sign with Epitome. She couldn't spend the rest of her life wondering, "What if?"

In the break room, Chloe fished her cell phone out of her purse and dialed Epitome with a few minutes to spare. She was intercepted by the ho-hum voice of the receptionist.

"I'm sorry. Mr. and Mrs. Rubinstein are on other lines right now. Would you like to leave a message?"

Chloe didn't want to risk leaving a message that the Rubinsteins may not get until well past the noon deadline. "I can hold," she said.

"It'll probably be quite a while."

"That's okay. I can wait as long as it takes."

An eternity later, the receptionist put Chloe through to Barbara.

"Since we didn't hear from you last week, we thought you had decided to turn us down," said Barbara. "Warren will be thrilled you're going to sign. He's already taken a liking to you. We'll have the papers drawn up today."

Chloe fibbed, telling her boss she had a doctor's appointment, and was able to leave work early to take care of business the next day. She had to go to the bank and clear out her savings account, in addition to several other errands. Daniella skipped a class in order to accompany her to look over the fine print of the contract at the Russian Tea Room, where the Rubinsteins treated Chloe and her "lawyer" to lunch.

"Where do I sign?" Chloe asked after she and Daniella had looked through the contract.

"On the last page," Raymond Andreoff, the Rubinsteins' attorney said, handing her a pen. Chloe had read about the powerful attorney, who was well-known for negotiating deals for famous clients.

"Wait," Daniella said just as Chloe was about to sign the document. "Will you excuse us, please? I need to confer with my client."

Daniella, playing the part of the attorney to the fullest in a tailored suit, led Chloe to the ladies' room, where they convened an impromptu sidebar.

"What's going on?" Chloe asked.

"Well, I'm not majoring in entertainment law, mind you, but I think we should demand that they add a rider to the contract."

"What's that? Someone to pick me up in the morning and take me to my assignments?" Chloe said, snorting.

"No, a rider is an amendment. I think you should ask for one that releases you from any obligations with Epitome in case you change your mind down the road or, for some reason, decide modeling's not for you, after all."

Chloe looked in the mirror and began touching up her makeup. "I don't know, Dan. I feel like I already pressed my luck by waiting until the last minute to sign."

"Like I said, I'm not majoring in entertainment law, but I remember from the classes I took in that area that contracts are usually slanted to the agency or company that's doing business with talent. From what I could tell, Epitome's contract is pretty standard. They have the option to drop you at any time, but you're basically bound to them unless they agree to release you."

"So?" Chloe said, reapplying lip gloss in the mirror. "That's to be expected, isn't it, since I'm an undiscovered talent?"

"First of all, 'undiscovered' is a relative term since you modeled before in Paris. If anything, they're lucking out by getting an experienced model who's appeared in magazines, runway shows and a music video by a major pop star. You could probably demand a signing bonus if you wanted."

Chloe gave herself a doubtful look in the mirror. "I don't know. I don't want to start out with a reputation of being a prima donna. I'm sure there are enough of those in the modeling industry."

"If there's anything I've learned in law school, it's that deal-making is nothing but a big game – like poker. You can raise the stakes as much as you want. If they really want you, they'll agree to your terms. If you're going to get into acting, you're going to be signing bigger contracts eventually. You have to learn how to negotiate."

Chloe bit her lip. "Are you sure about this?"

"Absolutely. The way that contract is written now, if you ever get sick of modeling and decide you never want to take another picture, Warren and Barbara could force you to keep working and bringing in money to their agency indefinitely."

Chloe squinted at Daniella. "You mean like slavery?"

"More like indentured servitude. That's why you need that rider. Trust me on this one. I'm just looking out for you, like a big sister."

Chloe put away her makeup and closed her purse. "Okay."

"Just let me do the talking," Daniella said as she led Chloe back to the table.

The Rubinsteins and their attorney rose to greet them.

"After consulting with my client," Daniella said in her businesslike tone, "we've decided we need more time to look over the fine points."

"We're already past the deadline," Andreoff said. "We've already given your client more leeway than the other models who were selected."

"Signing a contract of this magnitude is a big step," Daniella said, looking unfazed. "I'll take another look at the contract at my office this afternoon and fax you our counter-offer."

Chloe looked at Daniella, impressed with how she had stood up to the Rubinsteins' high-powered lawyer. Daniella kept a poker face as the attorney whispered to Warren and Barbara and scrawled notes to his clients on a legal pad.

"We'll give you until midnight tonight," Andreoff said, turning back to Daniella. "I'll look over your proposal first thing in the morning and, after talking it over with my clients, we'll call you with their decision."

"That's fine," Daniella said, tucking the contract in a manila folder.

"Do you have a card with your office number where I can reach you?" Andreoff asked, as if challenging Daniella's legitimacy.

"I'm fresh out of cards," Daniella replied without a pause, "but I'll put my number on the cover sheet when I fax you. Now if you'll excuse us, I have another meeting across town."

The Rubinsteins and their attorney rose once again. Chloe took note of how Daniella looked Andreoff directly in the eye as she shook his hand. Chloe was impressed with her roommate's unflappable demeanor and ability to think on her feet. She obviously had a bright legal future ahead of her.

"Just remember, I have a stack of photos this high of girls I could call right now who could take your place," Barbara, holding her hand several inches above the table, said to Chloe. "Are you sure you don't want to reconsider and sign right now?"

Before Chloe could say anything, Daniella took her by the arm. "Thanks again for your time, Mr. and Mrs. Rubinstein. As I said before, I'll fax Mr. Andreoff our counter-offer this afternoon."

As Daniella led her to the street and hailed a cab, Chloe asked her if she was sure she knew what she was doing. "What about what Barbara said? I don't want to miss out on this opportunity. What if they think I'm too demanding and decide to sign somebody else?"

"That's just a negotiating ploy," Daniella said, following Chloe into the cab. "If we hold out long enough, they'll cave."

"What are you going to do, fax the lawyer from the campus library or something?"

"I intern at Wycoff, Wycoff & Kaylor in the afternoons, remember? They're one of the most respected firms in New York. When that guy sees my fax with their letterhead, he'll be forced to take us seriously."

"I hope so."

"Relax. I've got this under control. I'll call you after my next meeting."

"You mean your next class?" Chloe said, laughing at Daniella's boldness as the cab sped off.

Just like on the night before the cattle call, Chloe couldn't sleep after the lunch meeting with the Rubinsteins and their lawyer. She tossed and turned, wondering if she was going to lose out on the opportunity with Epitome.

By the next afternoon, she couldn't stand the suspense and nearly pounced on Daniella when she opened the front door of the apartment.

"So? Did they call? What'd they say about the counter-offer?" Chloe asked in a frenzy, following Daniella to the kitchen, where Muriel was making a snack.

"Well, luckily, me and LaTasha, the receptionist, are cool and I told her to transfer the Rubinsteins' lawyer to me when he called," Daniella said, calmly making a sandwich. "I took the call in my boss' office, since I knew he'd be out the rest of the day in court on a big trial."

"You actually sat at Gil Wycoff's desk?" Muriel said, referring to the prominent attorney Daniella was clerking for.

"Yeah. It felt pretty good, propping my feet up on his desk," Daniella said, popping open a Diet Coke.

"Girl, you are too much," Muriel said, chuckling as she poured a glass of orange juice and offered one to Chloe.

"Will you get to the point?" Chloe said, almost spilling her juice as she shook with nerves. "I can't stand the suspense."

"Calm down, will you?" Daniella took a bite of her sandwich and sipped her soda. "It worked, just like I said it would. They agreed to the rider that releases you with no penalty if you ever decide to quit, and they even agreed to a small signing bonus, which will be used as a down payment on the modeling course." She winked at Chloe. "I added that one when I faxed over the counter-offer."

Chloe screamed, jumped up and down and hugged Daniella.

"I was going to order Chinese food, but we'll have to go out and celebrate," Muriel said.

"Thanks, Dan. Thank you so much," Chloe said, hugging her again. "I can't believe the way you held your own with that high-and-mighty lawyer. You're going to go far."

"So are you, my dear," Daniella said, raising her soda can in a toast and clinking glasses with Chloe and Muriel. "So are you."

Tears flowed as easily at Daniella and Muriel's graduation from Columbia Law School, as did the margaritas at the after-party in the girls' apartment. Chloe had a good time laughing and dancing with Daniella and Muriel and their friends until the building's super came up to complain about the noise, threatening to call the cops. These kooky college kids were more trouble than they were worth, he was always saying.

The festivities broke up around one in the morning. Chloe, Daniella and Muriel sat around the living room after everyone had left, munching on left-over chips and salsa. It was like when they used to stay up late on weekends, laughing and sharing girl talk.

Despite the festive atmosphere created by the streamers and other party favors decorating the apartment, the mood was bittersweet. Daniella and Muriel said they were happy to finally have that piece of paper and be on their way to starting their illustrious legal careers, but they also knew they were going to miss each other. Chloe felt an equal mixture of sadness and joy. She was excited about the prospects of her new modeling career, but another phase of her life was coming to an end.

"Well, this is it, the moment our parents have been preparing us for all our lives. We're finally done with law school and passed the bar. *Yiiip-eeeee!*" said Daniella, blowing a noisemaker.

"This is so weird," said Muriel, still wearing her mortarboard and tassel. "I've been working toward this day every since the first grade. Now that it's here, I feel... I don't know. It's not like how I imagined it would be."

Chloe dipped a broken tortilla chip in a bowl of salsa and crunched. She wasn't sure if the spiciness of the salsa or the nostalgic feeling of the moment was causing her eyes to tear up. "I'm going to miss you guys so much."

"Don't start. You'll get me started," Daniella whimpered.

The girls huddled together in their gazillioneth group hug. They stayed up a little while longer, but the law school grads had to get to sleep. They were both catching early-bird flights to their respective destinations. Daniella was off to her new job at Westmoreland & McNeil in Boston, while Muriel was taking an entry-level position at the Department of Justice in D.C.

In the morning, after promising to call and e-mail each other regularly, Daniella and Muriel were off. Chloe was left alone in the deserted apartment, everything packed up in boxes. Before she headed out to her own destination, she perched on the window seat in the living room, thinking about everything she'd experienced throughout the past year and a half in New York.

Peering out the window, she squinted, taking in the view of the Statue of Liberty in the distance one last time. She had managed to survive in the Big Apple. And now she was embarking on a new adventure, reinventing herself again. From the sheltered debutante afflicted with wanderlust, she had blossomed into the independent working girl, and evolved into the starry-eyed hopeful. Her nineteenth birthday only a few days away, she had her sights set on rising to the top of the fashion world.

Her introspective moment was cut short by loud honking from a cab on the street below. The cab was to transport her to the apartment that the Rubinsteins had arranged to set her up in, along with a few of the other aspiring female models who were selected from the cattle call. Her things had already been shipped to the new address.

She got up from the window seat, picked up the suitcase that contained the remainder of her personal items, and slowly sauntered to the front door, reminding herself to turn her key in to the super. She flicked the light switch and stood silently in the darkness of early morning, pausing in the doorway. This apartment, her first refuge after leaving home, would always hold warm memories.

"Well, I'm off," Chloe said aloud, as if bidding goodbye to an old friend.

61

Stepping out of the taxi, Chloe noticed her new apartment building was in a fairly nice Brooklyn neighborhood. Moving again might not be so bad after all. Climbing the three flights of stairs it took to reach the apartment, though, was not so pleasant. She had envisioned the "models' loft" where Epitome was putting her up as a glamorous spread, but the modestly-furnished walk-up reflected the "waste not, want not" values of the ever-practical Warren and Barbara.

Chloe was greeted by a familiar face when she walked in the door. Brandi Baxter, the girl from Texas whom Chloe had struck up a conversation with in line at the cattle call, had made the cut as well. At least one of her new roommates wasn't a total stranger.

"I can't believe I made it," Chloe told Brandi, exhaling as she set down her heavy bags.

"Me neither. Good seeing you again, roomy," Brandi said, patting Chloe on the back.

"Thank God the last girl is finally here," said a statuesque brunette sitting on a windowsill in the corner. "Let's settle up on who gets the big room to herself."

"Hold your horses. Chloe hasn't been properly introduced to everyone," said Brandi, proceeding to do the honors.

In addition to Brandi, Chloe was going to be sharing the apartment with Roxanne Michaels, the brunette, a native New Yorker; Graciela Luisa Teresa Santiago y Santana, a native of Venezuela who mercifully went only by her first name; and an African girl named Ayana Ashanti Kailinya.

"Your name is really pretty," Chloe said to Ayana, who had the high forehead and prominent cheekbones of many Ethiopians.

"Thank you. It means 'beautiful flower' in our language. Your name sounds foreign, too. Where are you from?"

"Here and there."

Unlike Roxy, the daughter of a filthy-rich corporate raider, who made a point of boasting about her family's fortune, Chloe told the girls very little about her affluent upbringing in Paris. Determined to carve out her own identity, she simply said she was raised by a single mother and was struggling to pay her way through the modeling course.

Ayana shared that she, too, was paying her own way. Her hard-working, immigrant parents had scrimped to send her to college and were not pleased that she'd decided not to complete her business degree and go into modeling instead.

"Can we please stop this game of show and tell and get on with the business at hand?" Roxy insisted. "It's burning up in here. Someone's going to have to call Maintenance and tell them to fix the air conditioning. All I want to do is unpack and jump into an ice-cold shower." She pinned her long, dark hair to the top of her head and fanned herself with a magazine.

"Okay, guys, there's three rooms and five of us. We can partner up, but who gets the spare?" said Brandi, already proving to be the mediator of the bunch.

"I say we flip a coin," Graciela proposed.

"How are we going to flip a coin when it only has two sides? There's five of us, remember, or is your math as lousy as your English?" Roxy said in her condescending way, looking down her nose at the Hispanic girl.

"How 'bout we draw straws? Whoever draws the longest straw gets the extra room to herself," Chloe suggested.

"We agreed, everybody?" Brandi called out.

"Agreed," everyone except Roxy chimed in unison.

"Whatever," Roxy added with a dramatic sigh.

Brandi located a box of straws in a kitchen cupboard and cut them into varying lengths. Each girl chose a straw and compared.

"I got the longest straw," Chloe said, holding hers up for all to see.

"This isn't fair," Roxy whined. "How do I know you all didn't rig this?"

"I'm the one who cut the straws," Brandi said. "What would I have to gain by letting Chloe pick the longest straw and have her own room?"

"Yeah, you seem paranoid," Graciela snipped at Roxy.

"I'm *not* paranoid. All I'm saying is, I obviously have the most luggage and the most stuff out of all of us. It's only fitting that I get the most closet space."

"If you're so rich and highfalutin," Brandi said, her Texas accent growing as thick as her obvious frustration with the difficult girl, "why're you sharin' an apartment with four other girls?"

"Because I wanted to get away from my parents and I'm not about to live alone in New York. Call me crazy, but I do not wish to be raped or murdered." Roxy flipped her hair over her shoulders. "Now that I've told all of you my life story, back to the room situation..."

"Maybe we should draw again," Ayana said.

"Maybe she should shut up and stop acting like such a Miss Priss," Graciela purred, rolling her R's and her eyes in Roxy's direction.

"Why don't you make me," Roxy said, getting up in Graciela's face.

"*Chica*, I'm warning you. Get out of my face or I'm going to slap you."

"You do and you'll lose your hand."

"We'll just see about that."

Roxy inched closer to Graciela, who promptly made good on her promise, slapping Roxy so hard that a red handprint appeared on her cheek. Roxy retaliated by trying to pull out a clump of Graciela's wavy, blond-streaked brown hair. Before anyone could stop them, the two were rolling around on the floor like a couple of sumo wrestlers, scratching and biting and trying to tear each other's clothes off. The other girls stepped in and broke it up, after watching Roxy get her butt kicked.

"You better not have scratched my face, bitch!" Roxy yelled at Graciela, taking a mirror out of her purse and surveying the damage.

Graciela bit her hand, shook her fist at Roxy and uttered a string of Spanglish profanities.

"Come on now, y'all," said Brandi, stepping in between the two newly-formed rivals. "It's hot, everybody's irritable and we all just want to put our stuff away."

"Look, I really don't need a room all to myself," Chloe said, just wanting to get the matter resolved. "Roxy, you can have it."

"Don't give in to her," Graciela said. "You won that room by luck of the draw. She's just being selfish."

"No, really, I don't mind. And anyway, Brandi and I have met before. What do you say, want to share a room?" Chloe smiled at Brandi.

Brandi returned the smile. "You sure you don't mind giving up the big one?"

"Positive."

Chloe and Brandi spent the rest of the afternoon cramming their clothes into their room's tiny closet and stowing the overflow in twin footlockers at the ends of their beds. It was a tight squeeze, but they made it work. Sharing a bathroom with four other girls, however, was going to be a true test of the human spirit.

For the next six weeks, nearly every waking moment Chloe had was consumed by the modeling course. When the Rubinsteins said the course was intensive, they weren't lying. Chloe and the other models – which included several guys who lived in a separate apartment – were taught how to properly walk down a runway, how to pose, how to turn. She learned the basics of lighting and photography, the dos and don'ts of a photo session. She actually had homework and tests. An ongoing assignment was to browse through fashion mags, clip pictures and make collages of looks she thought suited her. One of the goals of the course was to help the models develop their own sense of style.

The Epitome models were also given instruction in etiquette and table manners, something that Barbara said would prove invaluable when they had lunch or dinner meetings with clients. Some of the models, the oldest in his early twenties, were severely lacking in social graces. Chloe showed them all up. Madame de Tornquist, her Parisian etiquette tutor, would be proud.

The highlight of the course came when Barbara announced one day that the guys and girls would be taking a "field trip" to NYU's Tisch School of the Arts. The group would get a few pointers from a drama professor that would help them emote on the runway, Barbara said. The session would also help the models hone skills that would assist them if they were ever cast in a television commercial, she added, or, if they were really lucky, crossed over into acting.

"This is so surreal," Chloe whispered to Brandi as they sat in the back of an oversize van, riding over to NYU's campus with the rest of the models. "I was going to apply to the Tisch School of the Arts before Barbara and Warren signed me."

"Really?" Brandi said. "This should be fun for you, then, seeing what you're missing."

Chloe swallowed to moisten her throat as the van pulled into a parking garage. She wasn't sure if she would be able to relax enough to enjoy the condensed acting lesson, since she was terrified of messing up and proving that she really wasn't talented enough to have been accepted to the prestigious drama school.

Walking across the campus, Chloe looked around at the students who were sauntering to classes with overloaded bookbags, headphones plugged in their ears. The college kids laughed and joked, some of them walking along in couples and holding hands. They all seemed so happy-go-lucky, Chloe observed, as if they had years to figure out what they wanted to be when they grew up. Chloe realized she could have been one of these carefree kids instead of jumping headfirst into the cutthroat world of modeling. Being on NYU's campus was like walking through a sliding door and catching a glimpse of the alternate life she could have chosen.

The female drama student who was guiding the Epitome models across campus ushered them into an ivy-covered hall that reminded Chloe of one of the buildings at Our Lady of Chastity. Once inside the hall, the student led them to a midsize lecture hall that was set up like an intimate theater, with seats facing a small stage.

As Chloe and her counterparts filed into the front row, an African-American woman with dark, luminous skin appeared onstage and stood in the spotlight that shone center-stage.

"Hello, everyone, my name is Helena St. John," the woman said.

Chloe recognized the woman's name from the issues of *Variety, Back Stage* and other trade publications she devoured. Helena St. John, in addition to being a tenured NYU professor, was also a respected acting coach who had helped several major actors prep for Tony-nominated Broadway runs.

"I'm going to give you a rundown on the fundamentals of acting today," Helena said in a booming voice that was no doubt a demonstration of how to project on the stage.

Helena was tall and broad-shouldered, with a commanding presence. She was neither fat nor skinny, but had middle-aged "padding" that she carried with confidence. Neat dreadlocks cascaded over a light blue tunic, which she'd paired with black slacks and clogs. She wore several silver rings on each hand, rows of silver bracelets on either wrist and a succession of silver hoops on both ears. She had the look of a former bohemian artist who had transitioned into the stodgy world of academia but retained a dash of individuality.

"Of course, the best way to learn is by doing," Helena said, looking each model in the eye as she spoke. "So I'm going to have each of you come onstage and act out a short scene. Jamie, would you pass out the scripts, please?"

As the drama student followed Helena's directions, Chloe could feel herself tensing up. Getting onstage in front of the other Epitome girls and guys would be difficult enough, but the thought of trying out her unrefined acting skills in front of one of the best coaches in the industry was petrifying.

Always a show-off, Roxy volunteered – *demanded*, actually – to go first. She strode onto the stage and into the spotlight in a designer blouse and jeans and black stiletto boots, looking like a cover girl but nothing at all like a serious acting student.

"Think of your character's motivation," Helena directed Roxy from the seat she'd taken in the second row, behind the models. "You're a mother who's just lost her only son to a violent murder and you're begging the overburdened police detective to give your son's case the attention it deserves."

Roxy closed her eyes for a moment, as if channeling the character, and then began clomping back and forth across the stage in her high-heeled boots. She spouted her lines in a loud voice, gesticulating wildly.

When Roxy finished, Helena paused before saying anything.

"That performance was something you'd see on a soap opera or a Lifetime movie," Helena finally said to Roxy, who stood center-stage with her arms crossed, pouting defiantly as if daring the teacher to criticize her. "When you're doing theater, you need to be a bit more subtle."

"That means she sucks, which is no surprise," Graciela muttered, causing Chloe and Brandi to cover their mouths and giggle.

When Helena finished her critique, Roxy harrumphed "whatever" and stomped offstage, showing a snotty attitude that Chloe found not only rude but embarrassing. How many young people just starting out would give everything they had for invaluable advice from an expert like Helena?

"Next, please," Helena said, seemingly unfazed by Roxy's petulance, as if she were used to dealing with "divas."

Graciela was up next, turning in an overwrought performance worthy of the Latin American *telenovelas* she tuned into whenever she wasn't in class at Epitome. Next came Brandi, Ayana and then the guys, each garnering politely-worded yet firm critiques from Helena. Chloe squirmed in her seat when each model took the stage, unable to work up the nerve to raise her hand and volunteer to go on.

"I think that's everybody, isn't it?" Helena said when the last guy had left the stage.

"Chloe hasn't gone up yet," Brandi spoke up.

"Thanks a lot," Chloe said under her breath, nudging Brandi. "I almost got out of it."

"Take the stage, please," Helena said, smiling in Chloe's direction.

Chloe gripped her dog-eared script and slowly made her way onstage. When she reached center-stage, she shielded her eyes from the glare of the spotlight.

"No need to be nervous," Helena said, as if picking up on Chloe's stage fright. "Just try to think of how you would react in this situation and try to interpret it through the character."

Chloe glanced down at the script. She was supposed to act out a scenario in which a battered woman related the harrowing experience she'd endured to a jaded emergency-room physician as she undressed – an apt situation since she felt naked standing in front of her classmates.

"Start whenever you're ready," Helena said in a patient tone as Chloe hesitated, shifting from foot to foot.

Chloe opened her mouth to speak, but nothing came out. Her throat closed up.

Please, no, she thought. That chronic fear of auditioning was taking hold again. There was no reason to be so nervous, she told herself, since she wasn't actually auditioning for a real part but was just doing an exercise.

"Take your time," Helena said. "If you need to take a minute to get into the scene, that's fine."

Chloe opened her mouth again, but all that came out this time was a squeak. She heard the Epitome guys snickering and tried to ignore them.

She looked down at her feet and was about to tell Helena that she simply couldn't do this, when she looked up and noticed Brandi smiling encouragingly at her from the front row. "You got this, girl," Brandi mouthed.

Buoyed by her friend's support, Chloe opened her mouth again and finally started speaking. The more words she said, the more she loosened up and got into the scene. She began moving around the stage, reciting her dialogue and surprising herself with how naturally it flowed.

When she concluded, she returned to the center-stage position, waiting on Helena's critique.

Instead of commenting on Chloe's performance, Helena stood and said, "Thank you all for coming out this afternoon. I hope this session has been helpful."

Chloe left the stage, overcome with confusion. Did Helena's lack of constructive criticism mean she had totally bombed? The other models had turned in horrible performances, but was she the worst of all?

Gathering her coat and purse, Chloe couldn't stop her bottom lip from trembling. She'd known she would screw up big time. Even if she had applied to NYU instead of signing with Epitome, she probably wouldn't have been accepted since prospective students had to audition. She really didn't have what it took to be a real actress. Her awful performance today confirmed that unfortunate fact beyond any doubt.

When the models began filing out of the classroom, Helena took hold of Chloe's arm.

"Chloe, is it?" Helena said.

"Yes," Chloe said, taken aback that the teacher was addressing her directly.

"Would you mind staying after for a minute? I'd like to talk to you about your performance."

Chloe called for Brandi to tell the van driver to wait up and followed Helena back to the front of the classroom. She braced herself for the tongue lashing that was surely on its way. Helena was probably too tactful to deride Chloe in front of the other models and decided to pull her aside to tell her that she should never step onstage again.

"You're not from the States, are you?" Helena said, seating herself on the edge of the stage and looking totally natural there, as if she were sitting in a comfortable recliner.

"Uh, no, I grew up in Paris," Chloe said, sitting across from Helena in the front row. She was caught off-guard by the unexpected question.

"I could tell you grew up overseas," Helena said, proving herself to be amazingly perceptive. "You have something about you, an unspoiled quality you don't see in American kids." She added with a laugh, "And I should know, since I deal with dozens of them every day in my classes."

Chloe smiled politely, wondering why Helena had asked her to stay after.

"You know, I've made my living for the past twenty years studying characters, and you have to know real people in order to get inside the head of fictional ones," Helena said, looking at Chloe pointedly. "If I had to guess, I'd say you really want to be an actress but you got into modeling as a steppingstone to what you really want to do."

This lady knows what she's talking about, Chloe thought. *I must be transparent.*

"You're right," Chloe said. "Actually, I was going to apply to the program here before I got a callback at Epitome."

"Oh, I wish you'd applied," Helena said, sounding genuinely disappointed to not have Chloe as a student. "Once you got over your nerves, you really did an outstanding job with the scene, better than a lot of my second-year students."

"Thanks," Chloe said, not sure she could believe her ears. Just moments ago, she'd been convinced she should give up her lifelong dream.

"You know, I've coached a few models-turned-actresses before, and making the leap isn't easy," Helena said. "I'm sure most of the other models you came with will try their hand at acting at some point, and some of them might even luck out and have a bit of success. This business is so weird. I know plenty of classically-trained actors who have to wait tables to make ends meet and models who don't have an ounce of talent who get cast in movies and TV shows because of the way they look."

Chloe shrunk down in her seat, wondering if Helena was trying to say that the only way Chloe was going to make it as an actress was if she traded on her looks.

In that uncanny way of hers, Helena vocalized what Chloe was thinking.

"You, my dear, have that rare combination of looks and talent, and that will get you far," Helena said, smiling. "No matter what happens with your modeling career, do me a favor and don't lose sight of your dreams. You have a gift, and I'd hate to see it go to waste."

Chloe sat there, not knowing what to say. A glowing review from such a revered acting teacher was the highest praise.

"Chloe, we have to get back," Brandi called out, appearing in the doorway of the classroom. "The driver said he's going to take off without you if you don't hurry up."

"Don't you just love this town and how impatient everyone is?" Helena said, laughing as she stood to show Chloe to the door.

"I'm still getting used to it," Chloe said, shoving her hands in her pockets.

"Remember what I said," Helena said when they reached the door. "Use your brains and don't just rely on your looks." She gently tapped Chloe on the top of her head, reinforcing her statement.

"I can't thank you enough," Chloe said, shaking Helena's hand. "I'll never forget what you said."

411

62

"Brooklyn Institute of Fashion. How may I direct your call?"

Chloe fiddled with the confusing jumble of knobs and buttons on the switchboard until she was able to transfer the caller to the correct extension – hopefully. The Rubinsteins had forced her to quit her job at Bloomingdale's, and this part-time position as a "creative assistant" at the fashion-design school of an art college required her to juggle the roles of secretary, gopher and all-around girl Friday.

"We want to place you in a job that's less visible," Barbara had explained. "Part of the appeal Epitome girls possess is their sense of mystique. We don't want the general public being able to walk in off the street and have access to you."

When Chloe informed her manager at Bloomingdale's about her new opportunity and apologized for leaving so soon after she was hired, Candy Chandler said that as a former beauty queen she understood being signed by a top agency like Epitome was every girl's dream. Upon Chloe's departure, Candy wished her well and gave her a bit of advice to help her advance in her new career: don't call in sick so much.

When the Rubinsteins said they were going to place her in a "fashion-related position," Chloe assumed she was going to be working as a stylist or as an assistant to a top designer. In her much-less-glamorous new job, however, she was relegated to answering phones, fetching coffee for the instructors and making copies of their lesson plans. She sharpened pencils and made sure caps were placed on felt tip markers so they didn't dry out. She threw out old watercolor chalk and replaced them with fresh ones. And she made trips back and forth to art supply stores and fabric shops. Her feet were always killing her by the end of the day. She failed to see how this was a step up from her previous place of employment.

"Hey, girl."

Chloe looked up from the latest edition of French *Vogue* to see Christy King, a black design student she had become friendly with, approaching the front desk. Brooklyn-born and -bred, Christy was a self-described "around-the-way girl" who had hipped Chloe to rap music and schooled her on hip-hop culture and street slang. Like Chloe, she was raised by a single mother and was working her way through design school, just as Chloe was working to pay off the tuition for the modeling course.

"I love your outfit," Chloe said to Christy, who was wearing platform shoes, bell-bottom jeans and a tie-dyed denim jacket embellished with oversize safety pins.

"You like?" Christy said, extending her arms in a model's pose. "It was inspired by one of Pam Grier's costumes in that seventies movie marathon we went to last week."

Chloe ran her hand over Christy's jacket. "And the safety pins?"

Christy grinned. "I had to add my own *flava*, of course."

"You're so creative. If I had your sense of style, I wouldn't have to pore over these magazines."

Chloe admired Christy's individuality. She'd shown up one day wearing a vintage frock accessorized with a church-lady hat, mesh gloves and an antique purse reminiscent of Joan Crawford in *Mildred Pearce*. Christy said she loved to rummage through thrift stores and create fashion statements out of the discarded treasures she found. She changed her hairstyle as often as she changed clothes, wearing braids one day, pigtails the next, a floor-length Morticia Addams wig on Wednesday, a curly Cher wig on Thursday, and a *Soul Train* afro wig on Friday. The girl was one of a kind.

"Do you want to catch a movie later?" Chloe said. "They're showing *Guys and Dolls* at that revival house in the Village."

"God, I love that movie. I designed the costumes when we did a student production of it when I was in high school."

"You went to the *Fame* school, right?"

"Yeah, the School for the Performing Arts, but nobody broke out in song and started dancing on the tabletops in the cafeteria."

Chloe giggled. "So, what about the movie tonight?"

Unlike Chloe's roommates, who stuck to formulaic "chick flicks" and mindless comedies, Christy shared Chloe's diverse taste in cinema. They often ventured to funky art-houses in the Village to take in foreign films and retrospectives of classics.

"I wish I could go. I really love *Guys and Dolls*. That's the movie that made me want to become a costume designer, but I'm going to be tied up with homework this evening. Graduation's coming up soon, and I'm down to the wire working on my final project."

"What is it?"

Christy reached into her backpack, opened a sketchbook and placed it on the desk before Chloe. "It's a wedding dress."

Chloe studied the sketch, which depicted an off-white, asymmetrical gown that was strategically ripped. "This is really funky, not your conventional wedding gown. I like it a lot."

"Thanks. It was inspired by Miss Havisham's costume in the movie version of *Great Expectations* – the black-and-white one from the '40s ."

"That's one of my favorites, a classic."

413

"I know. I always watch it when it comes on TV, and I was trying to figure out what to do for my final project one night when it was on. I started sketching while I was watching it, and this dress is what I ended up with. I've really put a lot of work into it. I was up sewing all last night, and I'm going to be at it again tonight."

"The design must have been really complicated."

"Not really. I actually finished the dress a couple of days ago, but I keep getting ideas for things to add and making alternations. You know me. I'm a total perfectionist." She sighed, staring at the sketch. "It's a shame that after all this work, the dress will probably just get put away in mothballs after my instructor gives me my grade."

"That really is a shame. A gown like that is one of a kind and shouldn't just sit around in storage." Chloe pulled the sketch toward her, getting an inspiration. "Hey, you know what? You should let me show this sketch to Warren and Barbara at Epitome. They're in the midst of putting together Epitome's annual runway show."

"Really? When's that?"

"In a few weeks. They do it every fall during Fashion Week. It's kind of like a graduation ceremony for the new batch of models they sign every year, kind of like our big coming-out for designers and the fashion press to see Epitome's new faces. The Rubinsteins always get hot young designers with original voices to donate clothes for the models to wear. Your dress would be perfect for the big finale."

Christy propped her elbows on the desk. "Gosh, that would be a great opportunity," she said with a faraway look in her eyes, as if thinking out loud, "but I'd be so nervous, with all those high-powered fashion people judging me."

Chloe nodded in agreement. "Tell me about it."

The upper echelons of the industry would be there – supermodels Epitome had launched, designers, photographers, editors, as well as a host of celebrities and VIPs Warren and Barbara invited to give the event cachet. They would all be staring at Chloe, scrutinizing every pore, evaluating her every move. There would be no room for error. The New York *fashionistas* were legendary for their ruthlessness. It would be like a replay of her cattle-call audition, magnified times ten. The big debut was nearly a month away, but cramps were already twisting her intestines. She got nauseous just thinking about it. At least with Christy around, she'd feel like she had a buddy, in addition to her roommate Brandi, to root for and share in the anxiety.

"So what d'ya say? Do you want me to show the sketch to Warren and Barbara?" Chloe said. "I know it's just what they're looking for, plus I'm sure you could use the exposure. Talent scouts for a lot of the top designers will be there, and you could end up getting hired at one the big houses if the dress goes over well – which I'm sure it will."

"This would be an amazing opportunity, and I'd love to be a part of it," Christy said, quickly adding, "on one condition."

Chloe looked at her, eager to hear what she was going to say. "Yeah?"

"That you're the model who rocks my dress on the runway."

Chloe raised her hand to high-five Christy. "Deal."

The girls chatted about how much fun it was going to be, working together on the runway show, but their conversation was soon interrupted by the buzzing switchboard.

Christy picked up her backpack. "I better get to class and let you get back to work."

Looking down at the switchboard's flashing lights, trying to figure out which line to pick up, Chloe replied, "If you can call it that."

"Hello?" Chloe called, opening the front door of the apartment.

No one answered, so she figured she had the place to herself. Maybe she would have some peace and quiet for a change. It was Friday night, but she was going to have to stay home and prepare for the upcoming fashion show.

It didn't surprise her that no one else was home. When her roommates weren't in class at Epitome, they were out on the town. Chloe couldn't figure out how they made time for a social life. Her airtight schedule, taken up by her hectic job and demanding course work, left little time for herself.

Opening the door to her room, Chloe saw a note pinned to Brandi's pillow explaining that she was out with a new guy she'd met and would be home late. Chloe marveled at the ability of Brandi and the other girls to make time to meet new people. As far as Chloe was concerned, she was too busy to even think about dating. A couple of Epitome's male models hit on her, but she blew them off. They were nothing but empty-headed pretty boys.

The girls Chloe roomed with thought she was a goody two-shoes. She only rarely consented to go clubbing with them and she shunned all drugs and alcohol, not even wanting to experiment. She had to keep her system pure and her mind thinking clearly. She was on a mission.

She fetched her favorite sweats from her footlocker and went to the bathroom to wash up and change. She turned the knob. It was locked. She wasn't alone, after all. Somebody was always in there. Sharing this apartment with the other models was like living in a cramped college dorm.

She started to go back to her room, but she was drawn back to the bathroom door by familiar-sounding music. She put her ear to the door and soon realized it was one of her favorite songs by Sergio Reyes, the Latin pop star whose voice she'd fallen in love with in high school. A melodic female voice co-mingled with Sergio's on the chorus.

Funny, Chloe thought. *I don't remember that song being a duet.*

The door opened suddenly and Chloe nearly fell inside the bathroom.

Graciela helped her up. "I'm just in here doing my hair," she said, setting down her curling iron. "Do you need to use it?"

Chloe motioned toward the CD player sitting on the sink. "I love that song. I've had a crush on Sergio Reyes since high school."

"He's a cutie, isn't he? I was just singing along."

"You're kidding. That was you? Graciela, you can sing. You can *really* sing."

"*Muchas gracias.* I'd love to record a real duet with Sergio someday." She turned toward the mirror and began curling a strand of hair. "I've been singing and dancing my whole life. That's all I've ever wanted to do. What I'd really like to do is be a recording artist."

Chloe handed her roommate the tube of styling gel she was grappling for. "So why are you wasting your time with modeling?"

"For me, modeling is a way to break into what I really want to do. That's why I came to the States. Before I signed with Epitome, I made a demo tape back in my country and sent it to all the labels up here. They rejected me, even the Latin ones. Right now I'm just a nobody from Caracas, but if I make a name for myself as a model, I can get a deal with one of the big American record companies."

"It's good to know I'm not the only one who plans to use modeling to get to the next level. What I really want to do is act."

"Tell you what." Graciela picked up a brush and began teasing her blond highlights. "I'll give you a shout-out at the Grammys, as long as you remember me in your Oscar speech."

Chloe met Graciela's eyes in the mirror. "Sounds like a plan."

63

"Ladies and gentlemen, we present to you young men and women who are the epitome of grace, the epitome of style, the epitome of beauty."

As Barbara Rubinstein finished her opening remarks at Epitome's fashion show, Chloe peeked out from behind the curtain shielding her and the other models from the crowd that had gathered in a heated tent at Bryant Park to witness their debut. The room was packed with celebrities from every area of entertainment. Barbara and Warren worked the crowd, greeting the members of the "fashion police" that were stationed around the T-shaped runway.

Everywhere Chloe looked, there was a famous photographer or model or self-important magazine editor. She noticed Maxine seated in one of the back rows with the rest of the models' family and friends. Chloe waved, glad to see a familiar face, and Maxine blew a kiss.

Returning to the dressing area, she stood up straight and held her breath as a stylist secured the zipper of the couture evening gown she was to wear in the opening number. She hadn't eaten much that morning and her stomach grumbled, more from nerves than hunger. Nudged by Rachel Rubinstein-Gould, who was overseeing the backstage proceedings, Chloe made her entrance onto the runway.

She froze momentarily, peering out at the sea of faces. Blinded by flashbulbs, she proceeded slowly, struggling to remember the choreography she and the other models had rehearsed ad infinitum. *One step at a time, keep going and you'll be fine...* She internally repeated the mantra she had memorized for her society debut in Paris. She looked straight ahead and saw that Roxy, who had been first to take the stage, had already reached the end of the runway.

"Come on, Chlo'. Pick up the pace," she heard Brandi whisper behind her.

Chloe began stepping to the tempo of Prince's "U Got the Look" as it boomed from the sound system. This was one of her favorite songs – she had danced to it at a nightclub in Monaco with Gigi – and she tried to recall the abandon with which she had let her body sway to the music then. She began to loosen up as she fell in step with the beat. When she reached the end of the runway, she paused and stared into an imaginary spot at the back of the tent with that vacant model's expression she had practiced in the mirror. Wobbling as she pivoted on her six-inch stilettos, she made eye contact with her mother. Maxine beamed, the way she had done when Chloe walked across the stage at Our Lady of Chastity's commencement, and Mother's support helped Chloe regain her balance and make it backstage without incident.

She forgot the mandates about posture that had been drilled into her and slouched with relief when she made it to the dressing area, which was in a state of controlled chaos with models scurrying to dress and undress and to take their turns in hair and makeup. She had made it through the first scene. She exhaled and heard the zipper pop. *Uh-oh.* There was no time to worry about it as an assistant pulled the zipper the rest of the way and helped her step out of the gown and into another designer frock.

Before going out on the runway again, Chloe nervously glanced at the backstage entrance, hoping to see Christy entering. She was supposed to have been here hours ago with her funky wedding gown that Chloe was to wear in the finale. But there was still no sign of her friend and Chloe began to worry, as it was unlike Christy to be late or no-show an important engagement.

Chloe's anxiety over Christy's unexplained absence was soon replaced by renewed stage fright as Rachel pushed her back onto the runway. If there was any time to draw on her untapped acting skills, it was now. She psyched herself up by pretending she was a contestant in a beauty pageant. She wasn't Chloe Bareaux, aspiring model and actress, she was "Miss New York," parading before the judges in hopes of securing the coveted title of Miss America. Inventing a character allowed her to concentrate on playing the role instead of obsessing about all these people looking at her.

The pageant scenario she'd concocted in her head got Chloe through her latest turn on the runway and, true to pageant form, the swimsuit competition was next. Backstage, the guys and girls were squeezing themselves into bikinis and Speedos. Breasts and male genitalia of varying sizes were dangling all around her and she was forced to set her modesty aside.

She undressed and went to the clothing rack to retrieve her next change, periodically glancing at the back door. Still no sign of Christy.

"Where the hell is your friend?" Rachel said, tapping her watch and approaching Chloe. "We designed the whole finale around that gown."

"She'll be here." Chloe glanced at the back door again, as if her promise would make Christy materialize. Chloe had risked her own reputation by vouching for the young design student, and Chloe clung to the belief that Christy wouldn't let her down.

"If she's not here in fifteen minutes, we'll have to come up with a backup plan," Rachel said, sounding as harried as she looked. "There's no time to worry about it right now. I have to get everybody on the runway for the swimwear scene. Hurry up and get into your next change."

Taking Rachel's direction, Chloe began wriggling into a designer swimsuit and was nearly mowed down by Roxy and Graciela as they engaged in a tug of war over a strapless one-piece.

"It's mine," Roxy said, yanking on the suit.

"No, it's mine!" Graciela yanked back.

"This is a size four. Need I remind you you're a size eight?"

"So? Latin women have curves, unlike your bony white ass. Now give it to me!"

The two girls went flying in different directions as the suit ripped in half. The mayhem came to a standstill when Barbara appeared.

"That piece of Lycra cost a thousand dollars and will be coming out of both your commission checks when you get your first assignments," Barbara said in measured tones to the two girls at her feet, both still holding separate halves of the torn swimsuit. "Stop this foolishness right now and find something else to put on."

Roxy and Graciela continued to go at it, squabbling over who was supposed to wear what, and had to be pulled apart by Barbara. The older woman seemed undaunted by her models' disruptive behavior. Catfights, while unprofessional, were common at runway shows, Barbara had told the girls during the modeling course. They didn't call it the "catwalk" for nothing.

Fortunately, Roxy and Graciela halted their ongoing feud when they hit the runway and Chloe followed them out. Donning designer shades, she imagined sunning herself on the shores of the Riviera. The more she walked the runway, the more similar to acting it seemed.

When she reached the backstage area once again, she was relieved to see Christy wending her way through the horde of models and stylists with a garment bag slung over her arm.

"I'm so sorry I'm late!" Christy ran up to Chloe.

"I was beginning to worry," Chloe said, hugging Christy, glad she'd shown up just in time. "The finale is up next."

"Sorry it took me so long to get here. After the dress rehearsal last night, I took the dress home to make some last-minute alterations. I ran out of fabric and had to run to the store, and then my sewing machine broke down. I had to finishing sewing it by hand." Christy unzipped the garment bag, revealing the gown in mint condition. "But I got it done."

Rachel approached and took Chloe and Christy by the arms. "Come on, you guys. There's no time to waste. Chloe, we have to get you into that gown."

Christy helped Chloe into the dress, which was gauzy and resembled an intricate patchwork of oversize spider webs. Christy worked with the makeup artist to create the edgy look she'd envisioned. The makeup artist fixed extra-long false eyelashes that looked like spider's legs onto Chloe's lids and pinned a wig to her head that was a jumble of dark, tangled curls and tattered ribbons. The "bridezilla" look was topped off with a ratty veil, strategically torn fishnet stockings, clunky platform sandals and a bouquet of wilted roses.

"You look just like the sketch," Christy said, fluffing the gown as Chloe stood before a full-length mirror. "You're the perfect model for my creation."

"I love this look," Chloe said, examining her reflection and feeling proud that together they had realized Christy's vision of the perfect tribute to Dickens' eccentric Miss Havisham character, updated with cutting-edge fashion.

Rachel appeared to usher Chloe to the runway. "Two minutes. I need you to get in place."

When she reached the steps leading to the runway, Chloe took the arm of her "groom," a male model outfitted to look similarly grungy. They stepped onto the runway to Billy Idol's hard-rock classic "White Wedding." As they began the march down the runway, Chloe tried to conjure another character to get her through this final scene, but walking down the "aisle" unexpectedly brought back haunting memories of her ill-fated wedding to Jean-Baptiste Lambert. It all came flooding back, washing over her like a wave – the scratchiness of her throat after she swallowed the pills, the incessant whirring of the stomach pump as it vacuumed out her insides and left her feeling hollow, the coma-like sleep that had altered time and claimed days she could never get back. Wedding bells rang in her ears, nearly deafening her.

In an effort to push the traumatic flashback out of her head and focus on the task at hand, she took slow, tentative steps, balancing herself on her escort's arm as flashbulbs went off. Almost blinded by the flashes, she looked to the side of the runway and saw a young, light-skinned black man with hazel eyes. She resisted the urge to rub her eyes to make sure they weren't deceiving her. Jean-Baptiste? What was he doing here?

At the sight of the ghost from her past, she tottered on her clunky sandals but regained her footing when the flashes stopped and the man she thought was Jean-Baptiste disappeared from view. She steadied herself by leaning into her escort, following the steps of the meticulously choreographed number. When they reached the end of the runway, she could see Maxine looking up at her with concern, as if she could tell Chloe was distracted. She acknowledged her mother by breaking character and giving her a half-smile, trying to reassure Maxine in spite of the fact that she was the one responsible for the bad wedding-day memories in the first place.

Turning to make the return trip down the runway, Chloe told herself it was almost over. A few more steps and it would all be over. She was a few feet from the curtain when she caught sight of the Jean-Baptiste look-alike again. She squinted, trying to see through her veil and discern if was really him. He was standing next to the stage, staring at her with those piercing eyes, the way he had done that night at the opera. Now, instead of wedding bells playing in her head, a mezzo-soprano raised her voice in a glass-shattering note as the strings built to a crescendo.

Before Chloe could collect herself, her heel caught in the hem of the dress and she went tumbling face first onto the runway, arousing a loud gasp from the audience and setting off a frenzy of flashbulbs once more. She looked up at the man standing next to the runway. It wasn't Jean-Baptiste, but a reporter gawking at her with a curious expression and scribbling notes, cataloging every movement leading up to her embarrassing fall.

The male model at her side helped her to her feet and she did her best to play the mistake off gracefully, as she had been taught to do in class, but she had never been more humiliated.

Backstage, she saw Maxine forcing her way past security. "Are you okay, *ma chérie*?" Maxine said, rushing up to Chloe as she descended the steps of the runway.

"Yes, Mother, I'm fine. Please go back to your seat." Chloe made no attempt to disguise the frustration in her voice. She knew Maxine meant well, but the last thing she needed right now was her mother fussing over her like a child who'd skinned her knee on the playground. It took Chloe a few minutes to convince the still overprotective Maxine that she was indeed injury-free. She insisted that the best way Maxine could help was by returning to her seat so Chloe could get ready to take her curtain call with the rest of the models.

"You sure you're okay?" Christy said, approaching Chloe with a look of consternation. "You took a pretty bad fall out there. I feel horrible. I should've shortened the hem so you wouldn't trip."

"It's okay, Christy. I'm fine. Really. It wasn't the dress. I thought I saw someone… someone I used to know, and I got distracted."

"There's no time to stand around chit-chatting," Rachel said, shooing Chloe back up the steps leading to the runway. "You've got to get back out there."

All Chloe wanted to do was hide from all these important people, but she forced herself to return to the runway with the rest of the models to take their bows. People stood and clapped, with Maxine clapping and whistling the loudest. Chloe was smiling on the outside, but she couldn't hear anything. The applause was empty.

64

"Brooklyn Institute of Fashion. How may I direct your call?"

Chloe sat at the receptionist's desk, familiar enough with the switchboard now that she could coast on autopilot.

"Professor Griffin's not in right now. May I take a message?"

She reached for one of the pencils that jutted from her hair like chopsticks in a Chinese takeout container and began jotting down the caller's number. She got sidetracked from the task by Christy approaching the desk, shouting jubilantly.

"I got it! I got it!" Christy said, twirling in front of the desk in another offbeat outfit.

Curious to find out what Christy was raving about, Chloe wrapped up the call. She quickly realized she hadn't written down the last few digits of the caller's number, but shrugged. If it was important, they would call back.

"What happened, Chris?" Chloe said, hanging up the phone.

"I got the job at Adriano Ferraro."

"The Italian designer?"

"Yeah, he's opening an office in New York. One of his talent scouts was at Epitome's fashion show and they liked my gown so much that they offered me a job."

"That's great!" Chloe stood up, reached across the desk and hugged Christy, genuinely happy for her friend. "I'm glad my screw-up at the end didn't mess things up for you."

"Are you kidding? If anything, it got us more exposure."

Christy was right. Chloe's blunder a few weeks ago got more press attention than anything else that had "went down" at the fashion show. A photo of Chloe tumbling face first onto the runway had been plastered on the *New York Post*'s infamous Page Six with the clever yet cutting headline, "Model's Debut Falls Flat."

While Christy and her considerable design talent had obviously benefited from the extra attention, Chloe had not fared so well. Since completing the modeling course, she had been to go-see after go-see, but none of Epitome's top clients seemed interested in hiring her. At this rate, it seemed as though she would be working part-time at the design school indefinitely and would be forever indebted to the Rubinsteins, making payments on the course.

Maybe signing with Epitome had been a mistake. Maybe taking a risk hadn't paid off after all.

Chloe pushed her anxieties aside and tried to be supportive of Christy, listening intently as the rising design star told her all about her new job. Chloe was glad at least one of them was doing well.

"I got to meet Adriano personally. He said he loves my originality," Christy gushed. "He's giving me an entry-level job in his couture division."

"That sounds like an amazing opportunity, but I thought being a costume designer for the movies was your dream."

"You gotta start somewhere. I figure I'll get a couple years' experience under my belt working in fashion so I can build my portfolio and get noticed by the movie studios. This job is a great head start. And I owe it all to you."

Chloe waved her off. "Get out of here. You're talented and you would have succeeded without my help. All I did was put in a good word for you with the Rubinsteins so they'd use your dress in the show, and then fell on my face while wearing it! What a klutz!"

"Don't sweat it. We'll look back on that incident and laugh one day when you're a famous actress and I'm a successful costume designer. In fact, I'll design the gown you wear to the Oscars."

"That dream seems further and further away," Chloe said wistfully, looking down.

"Don't get down on yourself. You're going to make it."

"I'm not so sure about that. Nothing's been going my way lately." She took off her headset and smoothed her hair. "I'm tired of sitting here, feeling sorry for myself. You wanna go to lunch to celebrate your new job?"

Chloe loved going out to lunch with Christy, whose taste buds were as adventurous as her fashion sense. Chloe had encountered Souvlaki and Szechwan, sushi and squid hanging around her new friend.

"I wish I could do lunch, but the big final exam is this afternoon. Why don't you come over for dinner? My mom's making a celebration dinner with all my favorite Jamaican food."

Chloe's mouth watered, thinking about the fried plantains and curried chicken. She enjoyed visiting Christy's predominantly West Indian neighborhood and learning about other cultures. Christy's mother, a divorced social worker from Kingston, Jamaica, always made her feel welcome. She loved listening to Joyce King's stories about her childhood on the island.

"Count me in for dinner," Chloe said as Christy headed to class.

Still not feeling up to eating lunch alone, Chloe called Brandi.

"I don't think I can make it today," Brandi said when Chloe reached her on her cell. "I have a shoot."

Of course she did. She always had a shoot. Chloe hated to admit that she envied Brandi and the other girls who had begun working steadily. While they were off doing high-fashion shoots and runway assignments around New York and glamorous parts of the world, the only job Chloe had booked thus far was a catalog shoot for a sportswear line in which her co-star, a frisky Labrador retriever, mistook her leg for a fire hydrant. The demeaning episode seemed a metaphor for her stalled career. Being relegated to such low-paying assignments, Chloe could barely manage her share of the rent, and she was starting to become desperate. She would be twenty soon, practically ancient in the modeling industry.

"Okay. I understand," Chloe said, trying to disguise her disappointment. She rarely got to see Brandi now that she was working all the time. "I'll let you go, then."

"Hey, listen, if you don't mind taking your lunch a little late, why don't you come to the studio? These things are always catered. There'll be a real nice buffet to pig out on."

Free lunch. With cash in short supply, the idea didn't sound too bad. The studio where Brandi was going to be shooting a spread for *Vogue* wasn't that far from the design school, and by working through her lunch hour, Chloe was able to get the rest of the afternoon off and meet her there. Hanging out on the set might be fun. If Chloe couldn't work, she would at least enjoy watching her friend doing so.

When Chloe arrived at the studio, she saw Brandi standing before a pristine white backdrop with a group of models conferring with the photographer, who had his back turned.

When the photographer told the girls to take five, Brandi walked up to Chloe and explained the situation. "He's trying to decide which one of us to use for the cover."

Chloe glanced at the photographer, whose back was still turned while he adjusted the camera and lights. "What's the problem?"

"He says he can't find the right look. He ought to use you. You're prettier than any girl in this room."

Chloe laughed off Brandi's compliment. "You've got to be kidding."

"No way. I'm totally serious. He'd love you," Brandi said, nodding in the direction of the photographer.

Brandi had piqued Chloe's curiosity. "Who is he?"

"Grant Herschel."

"Why does that name sound familiar?"

Brandi explained that Grant Herschel was one of the best in his league, a highly respected fashion photographer who was as famous as the models he shot. He could spot perfection from across a crowded room, and he could spot imperfection a mile away. That was apparently why he was having such a hard time finding a subject for the latest *Vogue* cover he'd been commissioned to shoot.

When Grant turned around, Chloe was overcome with déjà vu. She figured he had been in the audience at Epitome's fashion show or maybe she had seen him on TV, since he was as photogenic as his subjects. The photographer was ruggedly handsome, with jet hair, blue-green eyes and the sculpted body of an Olympic athlete. He was dressed in what Brandi described as his photo shoot uniform: blue denim shirt, faded blue jeans and black cowboy boots with silver tips. Chloe's first impression was that he belonged *in front* of the camera.

Grant approached Chloe and Brandi with an intrigued look that seemed to indicate he recognized Chloe, too. She averted her eyes, surmising that he was recalling her now-infamous tumble on the runway.

"How'd she get in here?" Grant demanded from no one in particular.

Chloe started to back away, fearing that he was angry she'd crashed the shoot, but Brandi caught her by the arm. "This is my friend, Chloe."

Grant came closer and Chloe looked away in embarrassment as he scanned her frame with a photographer's acumen. As he studied her, his eyes suddenly registered a flicker of recognition.

"My Parisian discovery!"

"Huh?" Chloe said, dumbfounded. How did he know she was from Paris?

"You don't remember me, do you?"

Chloe said nothing, struggling to recall if they had previously been introduced. The modeling course had been so intensive, with a daily barrage of new tasks and challenges, that Chloe may have forgotten that Grant was one of the photographers she and the other girls had worked with on a series of test shoots.

"You must have been no more than fourteen or fifteen that day I spotted you in the park," Grant said, circling Chloe like a museumgoer examining an intriguing sculpture.

"Do you two know each other?" Brandi said, her eyes darting from Grant to Chloe. She looked as baffled as Chloe.

"Even in that school uniform you were wearing, I could tell you had potential," Grant continued, as if talking more to himself than to Chloe. "I was just a young apprentice working in Paris, but I had an eye for talent even then."

The mention of the school uniform jogged Chloe's memory, and she finally remembered her encounter with Grant years ago while she was attending the Lycée. He had been the handsome young man who had snapped photos of her as a teen while she was hanging out with Gigi after school in Trocadéro near the Eiffel Tower.

"I was really disappointed when you never called. You would have been the perfect model for the project I was working on back then. I figured your parents wanted to protect you from a strange older man who came up to you in the park. I can't say I blame them; I'd do the same thing if I had a daughter – especially as one as beautiful as you." Grant paused, standing before Chloe and smiling at her like she was a long sought-after muse that had finally materialized. "I always wondered what happened to you."

"Chloe's represented by Epitome, too," Brandi interjected. She nudged Chloe, as if confirming her hunch that Grant would take to her.

"Why wasn't she assigned to this shoot? Warren and Barbara need their heads examined. I told them to send over their best girls."

One of the makeup artists interrupted the exchange. "Grant, which one of the girls should I style for the cover?" said the young black guy, who looked like he, too, should be striking poses, with his funky jeans, nightclub shirt unbuttoned to the navel and frizzy afro.

"Go get into hair and makeup, Chloe," Grant said. "I've found my cover girl."

"See! I told you he'd like you!" Brandi whispered to Chloe, clapping her hands excitedly like a kindergartner who'd brought her favorite toy in for show and tell.

"Uh, Mr. Herschel," Chloe called after Grant as he retreated to the set to finish adjusting the lights, "I really don't have that much experience. I've never done a cover before." She could feel that old, familiar insecurity rising inside.

He turned to her. "Call me Grant. And let me tell you something," he said, approaching her and putting his hands on her shoulders like a sergeant addressing a new recruit, "I've been in this business a long time. I know what I'm doing. When I make a decision about a cover, don't question it."

Chloe figured he was right. He probably didn't get to the top of his field by making poor judgment calls. She obediently reported to hair and makeup. When the team of stylists had finished working their magic, Chloe was blown away by the transformation. Her hair was big, her lips were pouty, her eyes were smoky and smoldered with a mature sensuality she didn't know she possessed.

"Tell me the truth. Do you really think I'm cover girl material?" she asked the makeup artist, checking herself out in the brightly illuminated mirror.

"Girl, you better work it," he saucily replied, snapping his fingers. "With a face like that, you belong on the cover of *Vogue*."

In spite of the makeup artist's endorsement, she was shaking with nervous energy as she took her position in front of the backdrop. She did her best to hold still as Grant's assistant held a light meter next to her face. She knew that even with the help of airbrushing, the camera could be unforgiving.

Grant put her totally at ease. He was the ultimate professional. All she had to do was follow his direction.

"There's something missing," he said after snapping a few shots.

Insecurity seized Chloe again. Was she doing something wrong?

Grant fixed his gaze on an object out of Chloe's sight. "That's it. Would you do me a favor and hit that, Keiko?" he said, gesturing to his Japanese-American assistant.

Following Grant's instructions, the young man turned on a wind machine. Chloe's hair began whipping around her face, and she leaned back and pretended she was a glamorous movie star riding in a convertible along the Pacific Coast Highway. Assuming the identity of a character, like she had done at Epitome's fashion show, would get her through this shoot.

"*Perfecto*," Grant said, kissing his fingertips and aiming his lens at her.

When the photographer started clicking the shutter again, she relaxed, channeling the character she'd created in her head. Brandi gave her a thumbs-up and gathered around a monitor with the other models and stylists milling around the studio, watching Chloe's cover debut.

"It's unbelievable," she heard one of the stylists say. "She was so shy when she walked in here, but she's turned into a cover girl."

As Grant told her before she left the studio, a subtle, almost imperceptible change had come over her when he began shooting. With his direction, she came alive in front of the camera. He said he could spot that quality in her that he had pinpointed in other girls who went on to catapult to the top of the fashion world – that indefinable star quality.

The first thing she did when she got home was call her mother and ecstatically tell her about the shoot. Maxine shared her daughter's enthusiasm. Her *chérie* was going to be on the cover of *Vogue*. She apologized for discouraging Chloe from going to New York and said she was proud that Chloe was finally beginning to make it on her own – the words Chloe had longed to hear.

When her cover debut hit the stands, the effect was immediate. The event changed her life forever. She was suddenly in demand. Grant Herschel's latest "discovery" had the industry buzzing. Designers, magazine editors and advertising-agency creative directors who previously told her she wasn't their "type" began calling Epitome nonstop, even calling her at home. Everyone was clamoring for this fresh new face. She had arrived.

65

Chloe strutted down a runway in Madrid's Juan Carlos I Exhibition Centre. An eclectic assortment of international press, European glitterati and celebrities from the design, film and music worlds huddled inside the massive venue for the unveiling of celebrated Spanish designer Nikolai Fuentes' fall collection.

Upon reaching the end of the runway, Chloe paused, teetering on her Miu Miu stilettos. Her shaky equilibrium was not so much from the pressure of modeling for one of the top designers in the world, but from the presence of the devastatingly handsome man seated in the front row. Each time she reached the edge of the runway, he stared seductively at her with those smoldering brown eyes.

She gathered her composure, struck a pose, swiveled on her heels and made her way backstage. Descending the steps leading from the runway to the dressing area, she nearly lost her balance again. Losing control was a metaphor for the craziness that had consumed her life for the past several months.

Her career had skyrocketed since her first *Vogue* cover, and she often felt like her life was controlling her instead of the other way around. It was hard to believe almost a year had gone by since she'd been "discovered" by Grant, and her twenty-first birthday was fast approaching. She had gone from obscurity to worldwide fame literally overnight, and the nonstop work since then had been a blur of first-class flights from New York to Paris to Milan and other fashion capitals, photo shoots, runways and red carpets. Despite the hectic schedule, being in demand felt good after all the months of struggling.

As Chloe regained her balance and entered the dressing area, she was glad to be greeted by a familiar face.

"He's *here*!" Graciela exclaimed, throwing her arms around Chloe.

"I know," Chloe said, giving her former roommate a big hug. "I got so nervous when I caught sight of him at the end of the runway, I almost fell right on my face – *again*!"

"Come on. Let's see if he's still out there."

Graciela grabbed Chloe's hand and excitedly pulled her to peek through a crack in the curtains separating the backstage area from the runway.

"*Dios mio*, he looks even better in person than on his album covers," Graciela sighed, pointing out the target of their surveillance.

"I can't believe the star I've had a crush on since high school is right there in the flesh," Chloe said.

Sergio Reyes, the Latin pop star Chloe had fantasized about endlessly since her teens, was sitting so close that she could reach out and touch him. Doing so would be utterly unprofessional, of course, but Sergio was so hot, she didn't rule out the notion.

"I'm still trying to get my singing career off the ground," Graciela said. "I wish I could find some way to slip him my demo tape."

"Ladies, I've been looking all over for you."

Chloe and Graciela looked over their shoulders to see Nikolai Fuentes, the designer, approaching. They turned to face him.

"I've been searching frantically for you two lovely *mujeres*," said Nikolai, who was swarthy and handsome himself. "What were you doing?"

"Oh, nothing. We were just, uh… checking out the crowd to see how they're responding to your brilliant designs," Chloe improvised, feeling like she was back at Our Lady of Chastity, caught by the headmistress in some act of mischief.

"We have no time for that, ladies," Nikolai said, taking Chloe and Graciela by the hands and leading them back to the dressing area. "The finale's coming up and I need to get you two into your gowns. I want you both to accompany me down the runway when I take my bow."

"We'd be honored," Graciela said, pecking him on the cheek. "Anything for you, Nikolai, *cariño*."

Graciela winked conspiratorially at Chloe, a gesture Chloe interpreted as confirmation that they would work together to find some way to get close to Sergio Reyes before he left the venue.

After being wedged into a low-cut evening gown that evoked Nikolai's sexy, classic style, Chloe joined Graciela in flanking the designer for the final bow. The onlookers rose to their feet, applauded and whistled as the trio made their way down the runway. Reaching the end of the ramp, Chloe again caught sight of Sergio, looking dapper in a black pants suit from Nikolai's men's line.

Her pulse quickened as they made eye contact.

This time, instead of just staring back at her, he stood, reached out and handed her a single red rose. Their hands brushed as she accepted the rose, and she flashed back to his half-time show during the soccer match at Wembley Stadium she had attended while a student at Our Lady of Chastity. He had made the same gesture back then, but this time it felt more intimate, like he was personally extending himself to her rather than randomly acknowledging an anonymous fan.

Out of the corner of her eye, Chloe saw Graciela grinning widely. Rather than jealous, Graciela seemed genuinely impressed that Sergio had singled Chloe out.

Chloe lingered at the edge of the runway, staring into Sergio's eyes. But her line of sight was soon obstructed by flashes from the photographers' bulbs. She felt Nikolai tugging at her arm, pulling her as he and Graciela turned to walk backstage again. Chloe followed Nikolai's lead, glancing over her shoulder to get one last look at Sergio. But the spot where he stood was empty, as if he'd disappeared.

"Girl, that was so amazing!" Graciela exclaimed once they were backstage, having thanked Nikolai for choosing them to accompany him for his bow. "You're the only model Sergio gave a rose to. That must mean he wants to meet you."

Chloe sniffed the rose, then placed it on the dressing table. "He was probably just being nice. I turned to look back at him when we were leaving the runway and he was gone."

"*¡Maldición!* Now I'll never get to give him my demo tape," Graciela huffed, undressing along with the other models. "Oh, well. It was still a blast getting to see him up close. If I were you, I'd keep that rose forever."

Chloe smiled, vowing to do just that. As she was changing into her street clothes, Nikolai came up to her and handed her a note.

"What's this?" she asked.

He grinned. "It's from a friend of mine, Sergio Reyes."

Chloe's hand trembled, clutching the note. She glanced at Graciela, who stopped chatting away in Spanish on her cell phone and gave her full attention to hear Nikolai's explanation.

"We've been friends ever since he agreed to sign on as a celebrity model for my men's line," Nikolai said. "It seems he was quite taken with you during the show and would like to meet you."

Chloe looked at Graciela, who mouthed, "I told you so."

"Where should I meet him?" Chloe said, fumbling for her purse.

"I assume that's what the note says," Nikolai said, placing his hand over Chloe's and folding her fingers over the paper.

Once Nikolai had departed, Chloe slowly unfolded the note, savoring the experience, like opening a bottle of vintage wine.

"Come on, girl!" Graciela prodded. "Hurry up and read what it says."

Chloe glanced over the note's contents, which read: *Señorita Bareaux, would you do me the pleasure of joining me for dinner at my villa? A car is waiting for you, should you accept my invitation.*

"*¡Dígame!* What does it say?" Graciela demanded, sounding as though she were going to burst from anticipation.

Chloe calmly folded the note and slipped it in her purse. "Hey, Graciela, why don't you give me your demo tape?"

Chloe sat in the back of a chauffeured black BMW, en route to her rendezvous with Sergio. She rolled down the tinted window to watch the sun set on the Madrid skyline, her mind wandering.

Slightly less than a year ago, she was struggling to make ends meet while working as a receptionist and scrapping for the sporadic low-end catalogue assignment. Now she was traveling the world, trolling the runways of top designers, and was about to meet the international sex symbol she'd admired since adolescence. As the car drove past the Catedral de la Almudena, one of Madrid's oldest landmarks, Chloe offered up a silent prayer. Her outrageous fortune was almost too good to be true.

The car stopped at the entrance to a gated villa and the driver punched in a code. Chloe watched the gates open, feeling as though she were being ushered into a fantasy realm.

As the car drove down the cypress-lined drive and stopped in front of a Mediterranean-style villa, her skin tingled with anticipation. She just hoped she wouldn't fall apart in Sergio's presence, fawning over him like the gawky teenage fan she wasn't that far removed from.

"Watch your step, Señorita Bareaux," the driver said, opening the door of the backseat for her.

"*Gracias*," she said, getting out of the car and reaching in her purse to tip him generously.

The driver shook his head, refusing the tip. "Señor Reyes is taking care of everything." He extended his arm, motioning toward the villa. "*Por favor*, go right in."

Chloe nodded her appreciation and climbed the steps of the villa, marveling at its magnificence. She could hardly believe the grand *casa* was the residence of the talented young man who was only a few years older than she.

When she reached the front door, a man in a formal butler's suit greeted her with a warm smile. "*Hola*, Señorita Bareaux. Señor Reyes is waiting for you on the terrace. Allow me to show you the way."

Chloe followed the butler's lead, her stilettos clapping on the travertine floor of a hallway that was lined with exquisite paintings by Dalí, Goya and other renowned Spanish artists. She pulled her wrap around her shoulders, hoping the low-cut, strapless red cocktail dress on loan from Nikolai wasn't too revealing. She didn't want Sergio to think she was some groupie who'd come to his villa to allow him to have his way with her – although she wasn't sure she had the strength to resist his abundant sex appeal if that was his intention.

Upon arriving at the entrance to the terrace, the butler excused himself. Chloe took a step forward, noticing a candlelit table set up in the middle of the outdoor sanctuary. Upon closer inspection, she saw the silhouette of a well-toned man in a black silk shirt and black slacks. His back was turned to her as he leaned on the ledge overlooking the manicured grounds. He turned to face her and Chloe immediately recognized Sergio, his slick black hair gleaming in the moonlight.

"Chloe, so glad you accepted my dinner invitation," he said in his adorable accent, flashing that seductive smile that reduced females young and old all over the planet into swooning schoolgirls. He approached the table and pulled out a chair. "Won't you join me, *por favor?*"

She swallowed to moisten her dry throat and clutched her tiny designer handbag, which contained Graciela's demo tape. Finally, she moved toward him, musing that if everything went well, hers wasn't the only dream that would come true tonight.

Chloe entered her lavish hotel suite, not bothering to flick on the lights. She stared out at the stunning nighttime view of Venice and its famous waterways.

She plopped a program from the Venice Film Festival on an end table. It had been fortuitous that her latest runway assignment coincided with the prestigious event. Unlike her teenage excursion to the World Cinema Awards in Monaco, when she'd been just another anonymous fan watching from the sidelines, this time she enjoyed VIP status and the exclusive access it granted her to all the red-carpet events. It was such a rush, interacting with actors and directors whose work she admired. She imagined the day when a movie she was starring in would play at the festival.

Approaching the bed, she started at the sound of a voice whispering her name in the darkness. She turned to see a man emerging from the shadows.

"Chloe, *cariño*, I'm glad we're able to connect again."

A flood of relief, mixed with nervous excitement, washed over her when she recognized Sergio. She'd had several encounters with him since that midnight rendezvous in Madrid a few months ago. She recalled with fondness that night at his villa. As his butler served them *paella* – a delicious seafood-and-rice dish that reminded her of Creole jambalaya – they talked into the wee hours on his moonlit terrace, getting to know each other. In contrast to his reputation as an international sex symbol, he was a total gentleman and didn't even attempt to make a pass at her. Instead, he had politely asked for her number and permission to see her again.

Their relationship was blossoming slowly. They got together whenever she happened to be in Madrid, Barcelona or another European city on assignment and whenever he was in New York performing or promoting his music.

Sergio had wooed her with dinners at the finest restaurants, roses sent to hotels she stayed at around the world. He was clearly well-versed in the art of seduction. But she had been holding back, afraid that if she gave herself to him fully that the experience wouldn't live up to her fantasies.

"What are you doing here?" she asked, inching backward toward the bed as he drew closer.

"I sang at the gala for Pedro Almodóvar, the filmmaker, who's a friend of mine." He stood next to her at the foot of the bed, his custom-made tux hugging the contours of the fit, trim physique that was the object of lust for women across the globe.

Shivering with anticipation, she muttered, "Sergio, I –"

"Shhh. Don't speak," he said, brushing his finger over her lips.

He kissed her, and any shred of resistance she clung to gave way. She stripped him of his jacket, then untied his tie and unbuttoned his collar and sleeves, dropping his gold cuff links to the floor. Her excitement mounting, she tore off his shirt like one of the crazed groupies who stalked him and ran her hands across his rippling chest. She unbuttoned his pants and removed them, leaving him in nothing but his black briefs.

He took his time undressing her, as though he were composing a complex melody that required the utmost care and attention. He slid the spaghetti straps of her black slip gown down her shoulders with his teeth, revealing her lace bra and panties. She kicked off her heels and he caressed her thighs, unraveling her silk stockings.

"Take me now," she said in French, compelled by some primal instinct.

"I, too, have anticipated this moment," he responded, smoothing back the satin sheets.

In the moonlight, he made love to her, stroking her like she was an instrument crafted solely for pleasure. He brought her to climax again and again, causing her to reflect that the reality far surpassed any fantasy.

PART III

66

Chloe and Gigi strode down the Champs-Elysées, swinging their interlocked hands the way they did when they were schoolgirls. Gigi motioned toward a store window, where an advertisement bearing Chloe's image heralded her as the international face of Laurel Cosmetics.

Chloe turned away from the window. "It still freaks me out, seeing my own face staring back at me," she said, "even after all this time."

The four years since her first *Vogue* cover with Grant Herschel had zoomed by, like one of those European bullet trains that whooshed you from one destination to another before you realized the ride was over. Just as Gigi had been expanding her knowledge base during her years at the Sorbonne, Chloe felt like she had also received higher education over the past four years – traveling the world, picking up bits and pieces of different languages and learning about other cultures. She may have skipped college, but Chloe felt like she had been enrolled in an international university with campuses in every major city for the past four years.

In an effort not to be recognized, Chloe pulled Gigi away from the window with the Laurel Cosmetics advertisement. They walked along, chatting and window-shopping as if no time had passed since their school days.

They paused before the front window of La Galerie Nouveau, which was emblazoned with a sign that read in French, "Opening In Two Weeks: The Debut Exhibit by Gigi Cartier."

"It's so amazing that it's actually happening," Chloe said. "When we were kids, you said you'd have your own one-woman show at this gallery, and now it's finally here."

Gigi stared at the sign in the window, as if she couldn't believe she was finally realizing girlhood dream. "It only took four long years at the Sorbonne to make it happen."

"But you stuck with school and finished, Gi', and now look where you are. I think your graduation was the proudest I've ever been."

"I'm *so* glad to be done with school. Hopefully we'll have more time to hang out when you come to Paris for assignments."

They stopped at a newsstand, with Chloe thumbing through *Le Monde* to keep up on the latest news in her hometown and Gigi browsing the magazines.

"Are you taking a date to your gallery opening?" Chloe asked.

"Who would I take? You know school didn't leave me any time to date."

During her years at the Sorbonne, Gigi had done a total one-eighty from her wild-child days at Our Lady of Chastity. Whereas Chloe and Gigi's conversations had once been dominated by Gigi's too-detailed descriptions of her misadventures with the opposite sex, their long-held career ambitions now took precedence. Chloe was impressed that Gigi had finally taken her education seriously. Except for the occasional Saturday night movie date with a male classmate who asked her out, Gigi had really buckled down and focused on her studies, learning her craft and compiling the works that would be on display at her upcoming one-woman show.

"What about you?" Gigi said. "Are you going to bring your *boyfriend*?"

Gigi held up a celebrity magazine with a paparazzi shot of Chloe stepping out of a limousine, clutching Sergio Reyes' hand. Gigi teased Chloe about dating the Latin pop star she had idolized as a teen, the way they used to kid each other about their schoolgirl crushes.

"Put that down," Chloe said, flushing as she snatched the magazine from Gigi and placed it back on the rack.

"You two have been going at it hot and heavy since you met at that fashion show in Madrid," Gigi said, falling in step along the boulevard with Chloe again. "Four years is a long time. I'm surprised you two haven't started talking about marriage yet."

"I doubt if marriage is in the cards any time soon. We're both so busy that we barely have time to see each other, let alone plan a wedding."

Chloe's on-again, off-again relationship with Sergio was like a tango – they would come together, only to push each other away again. Their demanding schedules kept them in different parts of the world – too often, it seemed. They had even gone through a mutually agreed-upon "seeing other people" phase, during which she temporarily set aside the workaholic tendencies she'd inherited from her mother and allowed herself to have a few dalliances. She figured she might as well live it up while she was young. There was the devastatingly handsome French actor who spent more time primping in the mirror than she did. There was the hip, twenty-something African-American music video director who, like her, aspired to make the leap to the big screen. It wasn't coincidental that the men she was attracted to happened to be creative types. If a guy couldn't talk about books and movies, he didn't hold her interest.

Somehow, she and Sergio always seemed to drift back together. But it had been several weeks since she'd since him and she was starting to wonder if the prolonged absences had done irreparable damage to their relationship.

"I still remember how you drooled over him when he did the half-time show at that soccer match when we were in high school," Gigi said.

"You mean the one where you met your ex?"

Gigi grimaced. "God, why'd you have to bring him up? I haven't seen him since the annulment became final, and I hope I never will." She looked down, as if reflecting on the painful episode from her past, then turned her attention back to Chloe. "Enough about me. We're talking about you. When are you and Sergio going to see each other again?"

"He's performing at Madison Square Garden in a few days. He's supposed to take me out while he's in New York for a belated celebration for my birthday." Chloe paused when they stopped at an intersection. "Speaking of which, I have to fly back to New York tomorrow, but I'll be back for your opening. I have a big meeting with the executives at Laurel. This is my annual performance review." She groaned. "I'm dreading it – being evaluated."

"You'll do fine, and I'm proud of you," Gigi said, following Chloe into the intersection once the "walk" signal flashed. "We're both living our dreams."

Chloe wrinkled her nose at Gigi's statement as they neared a movie theater marquee. "You're living your dreams, but I've still got a long way to go."

It was true that Chloe had all the trappings of success – a degree of celebrity, a glamorous lifestyle, even the obligatory "rock star" boyfriend that came with supermodel status. And she had accomplished all of this prior to her recent twenty-fifth birthday. But there were goals she had yet to achieve.

"I still haven't been able to break into acting," Chloe said, stopping in front of the movie marquee and admiring a poster advertising the latest film starring her idol, Valérie Bourdain.

"But modeling has at least helped you get noticed, hasn't it?"

"Sometimes I wonder about that." Chloe made a face. "Sometimes being a so-called 'supermodel' actually seems like a hindrance. People don't take models seriously – at least not in Hollywood. I get sent scripts all the time, but it's all schlock." She stared at the movie poster, trying to envision her own face in place of her idol. "I feel like I'm still waiting to be discovered."

Gigi took Chloe's arm and began ushering her down the street, toward the Musée d'Orsay, where they planned to spend the remainder of the afternoon browsing a new van Gogh exhibit. "It'll happen. You're talented and hard-working."

Chloe leaned into Gigi, appreciative of the support and grateful that their steadfast friendship had endured personal and professional highs and lows over the years.

"And knowing you," Gigi added, squeezing Chloe's hand, "you'll *make* it happen."

Accustomed to crisscrossing time zones by now, Chloe caught a few hours of much-needed sleep on the flight from Paris to New York. A limousine chartered by Laurel Cosmetics picked her up from JFK. Riding past Central Park, she reflected on how far she had come since sleeping on a bench there when she first arrived in New York and lost all her money. It was very gratifying that a major corporation was willing to throw exorbitant sums of money at her to represent them around the world.

En route to her meeting with the Laurel executives, the limousine came to a stop light in Times Square and she rolled down the window to look around the city that she had feared would conquer her when she first arrived as a timid eighteen-year-old. It had not been so long ago when she had wandered the streets of Times Square, cold and hungry and penniless. But now she felt as though she had a firm foothold in the city that had become her second home.

Confirming her newfound confidence, a billboard bearing her image hovered over the city's famous theater district, dwarfing the brightly lit Broadway marquees. In the avant-garde, black-and-white advertisement, her latest collaboration with Grant Herschel, she stood on a balcony with ornate ironwork like those found in Paris and New Orleans' French Quarter. She was dressed in stilettos and a lacy gown, one of the spaghetti straps hanging seductively off one shoulder. Centered at the bottom of the ad was one word in lowercase white letters: *unforgettable*. A television spot, also directed by Grant and featuring the Grammy-winning, father-daughter Nat King Cole/Natalie Cole duet "Unforgettable," would soon begin airing. The spots would promote Laurel Cosmetics' popular fragrance of the same name.

As the limo took off from the red light, she smiled to herself. In four short years, she had gone from hawking perfume samples at Bloomingdale's to being the spokesmodel for a best-selling brand. Not bad for a girl who had arrived in this city not knowing anyone and with little but her dreams to sustain her.

The limo rolled on, and she spotted the gourmet French restaurant where she'd pilfered a meal when she was new to the city. Keeping the promise she'd made to herself, she'd returned after she'd made it big, obscenely overpaid her tab and treated everyone in the restaurant to filet mignon.

When the limo pulled up in front of the location of Chloe's meeting, she peered up at the skyscraper. She trembled, anticipating the long elevator ride to the seventieth floor that would undoubtedly trigger her fear of heights.

"Ma'am, are you all right?" the limo driver asked, holding open the door to the passenger compartment and staring at her with a quizzical expression.

For a moment, Chloe considered cocooning herself in the limo and asking the driver to take her anywhere but here. But she gathered her courage, straightened the lapels of her Armani power suit and stepped out.

Moving through the skyscraper's revolving door, she observed the words "Wellington Tower" written in art deco script and recalled that this building had been the site of her botched audition for the shampoo commercial when she was new to the city. Thinking of the strides she'd made since then made her good about herself and temporarily eased her dread of the upcoming elevator ride into the heavens.

When she reached the bank of elevators, she paused before pressing the call button, her anxiety returning. She considered dashing back to the limo, but finally pushed the button, realizing she was going to have to press on if she were to ever conquer this fear.

When the elevator doors opened, she nearly gasped upon realizing the building had glass elevators that revealed a stunning view of the city. The higher you went, the steeper the view. Swallowing to moisten her throat, she stepped into the car and was dismayed to see no one else getting on behind her. She would have to take this ride alone. With a shaky hand, she pressed the button for her floor and held her breath as the doors began to close.

"Hold the elevator, please!"

Just before the doors shut, a handsome young African-American man wriggled through. For a moment, she stared into his soulful brown eyes before clearing her throat and asking, "Which floor?"

"Sixty-three, please."

She pressed the button for his floor and he stood next to her, the delicious scent of his cologne filling the small space. The elevator whirred into motion and Chloe was mercifully distracted from the temptation to look over her shoulder at the heart-pounding view by studying the man's reflection in the mirrored doors. Staring was impolite, as she had been taught in Madame de Tornquist's etiquette course as a young debutante-in-the-making, but her eyes were drawn to his flawless bronze skin, curly black hair and chiseled frame. He was tall and she savored the rare feeling of not towering over a man when she was in heels.

When his eyes met hers, she looked away. She had no business flirting – she was, after all, taken. And as gorgeous as he was, he probably was, too. But there was something about him, something that made her never want to take her eyes off him.

A loud ding announcing that the elevator was reaching the sixty-third floor brought back her high anxiety like a belch calling up a bad taste. To keep from losing her equilibrium, she gripped the waist-level bar circling the elevator's interior.

"You okay?" the man asked, turning to her.

Her sudden queasiness must have shown on her face. She nodded, unable to find the strength to speak.

The elevator stopped at the man's floor and the doors opened to a busy reception area with the words REGENCY PUBLICATIONS printed on glass double doors. With a nod in Chloe's direction, the man stepped off the elevator and was buffeted by a throng of people getting on. Brushing past someone, a stack of papers fell out of his leather satchel.

"Sir, you dropped something," she called out, kneeling to pick up the papers. She glanced down at the top page of the document, which appeared to be a manuscript of some sort, and a sentence caught her attention: *The young detective pointed her gun at the suspect as Mardi Gras revelers tossed beads from balconies lining the French Quarter.* The reference to New Orleans, her family's city of origin, intrigued her and she wanted to read on, but she politely handed the papers to the man.

"Thanks," he said with a smile.

Before she could respond, the doors closed. Thoughts of the handsome man and his captivating prose occupied her and kept her mind off her fear of heights for the remainder of the elevator ride. When she arrived at her floor, she pushed the thoughts aside, certain she would never see him again.

Chloe stepped off the elevator and into the sleek lobby of IDG Media, the international firm that handled all of Laurel Cosmetics' marketing. The walls were lined with glamour poses of Chloe and other models who had graced the company's advertising campaigns.

Waiting for her was Barbara Rubinstein, who was to serve as her representative and review whatever offer Laurel placed on the table. "You ready, kid?" Barbara said, taking Chloe by the arm and leading her to the boardroom.

"As I'll ever be."

This annual review made her feel like she was back in boarding school obsessing over mid-terms.

"Hello. Thank you for joining us," said Susan Foster, one of the executives, offering her hand to Chloe and Barbara as they entered the boardroom. Clad in a designer suit, with a tall, slender frame and an impeccably coiffed chestnut mane, Susan herself resembled one of the company's spokesmodels.

Chloe and Barbara chatted with Susan and the executives and turned down an assistant's offer of Danishes and other pastries. She was too nervous to eat. It was that old fear of auditioning, that she was being put on the spot and made to prove herself.

After nearly fifteen minutes of unbearably polite small talk, the room fell silent when the CEO entered the room. Maximilian Laurel cut an imposing figure, with his tall, sportsman-like physique. His name was as recognizable as the cosmetics industry's other famous Max – Max Factor.

"Chloe, always a delight to see you," Max Laurel said, gripping her hand with his firm handshake.

"Likewise," she said, sitting across from him as he took a seat at the head of the table.

"I know your and Barbara's time is as valuable as mine," Max said as his secretary spread out a stack of papers before him. "Let's get down to business."

Chloe glanced at Barbara as Max leafed through the papers. Barbara had on her stony negotiator's face.

"You know that every year, we reevaluate our brand's performance and the people we hire to represent Laurel, which my family built from the ground up," Max said.

Chloe nodded. She was familiar with the history of the company, which was started by Max's late mother, Lorraine Laurel, a housewife who started out selling Mary K to make extra money and, by catering to the needs of stay-at-home wives and mothers like herself, eventually built her own cosmetics empire.

"This annual review is a requirement of our board of directors in the report we present to our shareholders each year," one of the male executives spoke up. Chloe recognized him as Bill Bosworth, the head of marketing and communications.

Pudgy, balding and short, the forty-something spinmeister's appearance contrasted sharply with his young, attractive colleagues. Ironically, his appearance was the antithesis of the beauty image Laurel Cosmetics projected. Chloe figured Max Laurel intentionally hired a non-glamorous person to represent the company to the media in order to illustrate Laurel's corporate image of being an ethical business that put people first.

"In anticipation of this meeting, I prepared this presentation," Susan Foster said, clicking a remote and activating a screen with a Power Point presentation.

"Our market research indicates that sales of all of our signature lines increased substantially in the past year," she said, scrolling through several charts. "We're gaining market share over our closest competitor, Luxe Cosmetics."

"This upstart has been trying to siphon off our customers," Bosworth said. "They even chose a name similar to ours, so that our products would be side by side on department store shelves."

"How original is that?" Max said with a roll of his eyes.

Chloe obliged the executives with an affirmative nod. She liked to stay informed, but she was well aware that market forces were largely beyond her control and left the figures to the numbers-crunchers.

"You and our other spokesmodels have represented our company well over the past year," Max said. He took a sip of coffee and cleared his throat. "Unfortunately, we've decided to make a change."

Chloe looked at Barbara, who continued to look impassive. Chloe admired Barbara's ability to never show emotion, especially in business settings.

"After much discussion, we've come to a very difficult decision," Max continued.

Chloe braced herself. Rejection was an inevitable part of the business, but it still was uncomfortable to deal with.

"What I should say is that the decision will no doubt be difficult for all the other models," Max said, looking pointedly at Chloe, "but not for you."

Chloe tried to interpret his cryptic statement. "Oh?" she said, interested to hear more.

"The products that performed the best over the past year are the ones *you* endorsed," Susan said, turning on a slide presentation of ads that featured Chloe modeling Laurel's lipsticks, nail polish and fragrances.

"Based on those figures, we'd not only like to extend your contract for another year," Max said, "we'd like to offer you an exclusive deal."

"What exactly does that involve?" Barbara spoke up.

"To cut to the chase," Max said, "we're dropping all the other models and we want Chloe to be our sole spokesperson." He turned to Chloe. "You have an exotic beauty that transcends racial boundaries, and we'd love for you to serve as Laurel's cultural ambassador around the world."

Chloe inwardly exhaled, feeling a mixture of relief and ambivalence. She had thought Max was going to fire her, but he was offering her a primo deal. While the offer was certainly enticing, she knew that locking herself into an exclusive modeling contract would keep her so busy that she would end up continuing to put off pursuing her acting ambitions.

"We took the liberty of drawing up a contract," Max said, sliding a stack of papers toward Chloe. "All you have to do is sign."

Barbara retrieved the papers. "We'll have our attorneys review the terms and get back to you. Thanks again, Max, for taking the time to meet with us."

Chloe stifled a laugh. Barbara hadn't changed over all these years; she was still all-business.

Chloe and Barbara shook hands with Max and the other executives. Barbara added that they appreciated the offer and would let them know if the compensation was acceptable.

She took Chloe's arm as they stepped into the elevator. "You know, I knew we were doing the right thing when you came to us all those years ago as a slightly pudgy, gawky teenager who was so unsure of herself, and Warren and I decided to sign you and groom you into a star. You've come so far. I feel like a proud mama."

"Thanks," Chloe said, pressing the button for the ground floor. "Luckily I'm secure enough now to accept a backhanded compliment."

"This offer is very generous," Barbara said, "but you don't exactly seem thrilled. I'll back you up if you want to ask for more money. I bet they've already gotten rid of all the other models, thinking you'd sign right away. We've never been in a better bargaining position."

"You're probably right," Chloe said as the elevator doors closed, "but money's not everything."

67

The next stop on Chloe's chauffeur-driven jaunt through Manhattan was a mammoth Barnes & Noble bookstore in Times Square where she and the other Epitome girls would sign copies of a calendar benefiting AIDS research. The cause had become close to Chloe's heart, having lost numerous colleagues and friends in the fashion industry to the epidemic. It was she who had rounded up her former roommates to donate their time to shoot the calendar.

At the entrance of the bookstore, a couple of spectators broke through the barricade and approached Chloe, holding out magazines for her to sign. She told the security guard to relax and politely obliged.

Once inside the store, she changed out of her power suit and into a pair of jeans, a T-shirt and a leather jacket. She took her seat at the autograph table and flipped through the calendar while waiting for the others to arrive. While the other girls' shots were cheesecake poses in lingerie and swimsuits, Chloe's photograph was an old-fashioned, black-and-white glamour pose depicting her as a Hollywood starlet from cinema's golden age. She was dressed in a vintage Chanel gown, revealing a mere suggestion of cleavage.

The shot was in keeping with the classy, sophisticated image she'd crafted for herself with Warren and Barbara's help. She turned down offers to do lingerie shoots, the covers of men's magazines like *Maxim* and *FHM*, and tits-and-ass centerfolds. Chloe Bareaux was high fashion and high class all the way.

Brandi was the next to arrive, looking like an off-duty Dallas Cowgirl cheerleader in a cowboy hat, sleeveless denim top tied in a knot to reveal her diamond-studded belly button, jeans and snakeskin boots. Brandi greeted Chloe with an enthusiastic "Hey, girl!," seated herself at the table and opened the calendar to her photo, a bikini shot taken on a beach in Aruba.

Brandi's buxom frame and ability to tan well made her a *Sports Illustrated* swimsuit edition favorite, having graced the cover twice. Her curves also made her a regular in Victoria's Secret, Frederick's of Hollywood and other lingerie catalogues, and she had her own best-selling pinup calendar. For a quarter of a million dollars, she had revealed her secrets – her favorite foods and movies, turn-offs and turn-ons, pet peeves and pleasures – to *Playboy*. Brandi told Chloe she considered it an honor to don the legendary bunny ears, bow tie and not much else except a come-hither smile.

Chloe caught up with Brandi as one of the bookstore employees stacked copies of the calendar for them to sign. Their banter was interrupted by a flurry of flashbulbs going off outside, followed by excited yelps from the crowd. Chloe looked up to see Graciela making her way to the store's front entrance, the camera bulbs reflecting in her Gucci shades. Dressed in designer jeans, a hot pink, silk-and-lace camisole, faux-fur shrug and stilettos, Graciela looked every bit the superstar she had become.

With Chloe's help, Graciela had realized her goal of landing a recording contract. That night four years ago in Madrid when Chloe first met Sergio at his villa, she waited for an opportune moment and mentioned that she had a friend who was trying to break into the music business. Sergio generously accepted Graciela's demo tape and offered to pass it on to the talent scouts at his record label. With Sergio's endorsement, Graciela was called in to do a showcase for top execs at DMR Records and was signed on the spot to a multi-album deal. The Venezuelan bombshell's spicy dance tracks were huge club hits in Europe and her native Latin America. When she wasn't recording or performing, she was modeling in Spain, Italy, Portugal, Greece and other Mediterranean countries where her sultry looks made her a hot commodity.

"Graciela! Graciela!" the crowd chanted as she neared the bookstore entrance.

She graciously stopped and posed for photos with a couple of adoring young fans. The Hispanic girls donned T-shirts with Graciela's image and had their hair styled just like her, with long, wavy extensions and blond highlights. It was obvious that the girls sought to emulate Graciela, who was second only to Jennifer Lopez as an example of a proud Latina who had garnered mainstream success.

Graciela arrived at the autograph table as a store employee fanned out copies of her latest album. The CD cover bore only the international dance diva's first name, as Graciela had dropped her long surname at the advice of her handlers.

"¿*Que pasa, chicas?*" Graciela said, air-kissing Chloe and Brandi and taking her seat at the table, draping her shrug on the back of her chair.

Ayana was next to arrive, breezing in with her long, elegant stride. Known simply as Ayana Ashanti in the fashion industry, she was dubbed the next Iman. Following the example of the enterprising Iman, Ayana had started her own line of skin-care products for women of color. As she informed Chloe and the other girls, her hard-working, immigrant parents were glad she got to use the business courses she took in college after all.

"I'm so glad to see you guys," Ayana said, exchanging hugs around the table. "We hardly ever get to see each other anymore, since we're all working in different parts of the world."

"I know," Chloe said. "Hard to believe we all used to live together."

Graciela lowered her shades and peered around the store. "Where's Miss Priss?" she said, obviously referring to Roxy.

As always, Roxy was the last to arrive, flinging an indifferent "hello, ladies" at Chloe and the other girls upon taking her seat at the table. She sipped the water the bookstore employee set in front of her.

"This isn't Perrier. Where's my Perrier?" she barked at the man. "I had my assistant fax my requirements this morning, and I clearly asked for Perrier. I *cannot* – no, make that *will* not – drink tap water. I need my Perrier."

"Coming right up, Ms. Michaels. Sorry for the mix-up." The man obediently carried away the offending water glass as if he were Roxy's personal valet rather than an employee of the bookstore.

Chloe and Brandi looked at each other and laughed. Their former roommate hadn't changed. Roxy had a well-earned reputation as Epitome's resident bitch. Her prima-donna behavior was infamous, causing her to become a tabloid fixture. She was known for her outrageous demands, childish tantrums, backstage tiffs with other models and condescending behavior to "the little people" – hotel staff, limo drivers and personal assistants, who sold their stories to the supermarket rags. Roxy's classic, flawless beauty and nearly six-foot height were her saving graces.

When the security guards finally opened the doors to the bookstore, the fans stampeded in and resisted being corralled into an orderly line. The afternoon flew by, with Chloe and the other girls signing calendars, magazines, CD jackets and the occasional bicep or forearm offered up by male admirers.

Between signings, the girls updated each other on their personal lives. Brandi had found wedded bliss with a handsome young rodeo star named Brad Tatum, with whom she shared a thousand-acre ranch outside of Dallas.

"He has a ten-gallon... hat," Brandi giggled, pulling up a photo on her phone of her snuggling with her significant other.

Ayana displayed a photo of her own. "Isn't he fine?" she said, swooning over Malik Yuri, the Jamaican reggae star who'd stolen her heart. She explained that she and her musician beau were building a love nest in the Virgin Islands with miles of white sand and crystal-blue surf stretching as far as the eye could see.

Not to be outdone, Roxy broke out photos of her boyfriend, Shane Rhys, a hot new actor she'd met at a red-carpet event in L.A.

"He just made *People* magazine's 50 Most Beautiful People list," Roxy said, adding with a melodramatic flip of her long, dark mane, "but of course, I made the list before he did."

"Who cares?" Graciela broke in. Reigniting her rivalry with her former roommate, she interrupted Roxy's lengthy monologue about her relationship with an update of her own. She was seriously involved with Jorge Cruz, a Mexican bullfighter – possibly the only man who could handle her hot-blooded temperament – and they commuted between a Manhattan duplex and a beachfront spread in Acapulco.

"What about you and Sergio?" Graciela said to Chloe.

"Come on, details, details!" Brandi said, drumming on the table like a diner patron demanding counter service. "I want to know all about your guy."

Chloe sank down in her seat, shrinking from the attention. She wasn't as glib as the other girls about her relationship. "I wish I had something juicy to tell you guys, but Sergio and I really don't get to see each other that often since we both work so much."

"Speaking of which," Graciela said, "you're coming to the show tonight, aren't you? I'm so excited about getting to perform my duet with Sergio live for the first time – and at Madison Square Garden!"

Graciela gushed that recording the duet with Sergio was the realization of a longtime dream. If it hadn't been for Chloe, Graciela added, she might still be singing along with Sergio on the radio in the bathroom of a cramped apartment.

"Of course I'll be at the show. It's the kickoff of Sergio's U.S. tour," Chloe said. "Unfortunately, it might be the only time I get to see him for the next few weeks."

The girls' chatter was disrupted when a male fan approached the table. "Hey, ladies, will you sign my stomach?" he said, lifting up his shirt to reveal a beer gut.

Chloe broke out laughing with the other girls and joined them in honoring the man's request, following up by posing for a photo with each of their hands on his flabby midsection.

As the autograph session wound down, Chloe glanced down the table at the other girls. It was nice reuniting with her former roommates, but it occurred to her that as much as things had changed, there was a lot that hadn't changed at all. In many ways, she felt like she did when they were starting out. Just as the other girls' modeling careers took off before hers when they first signed with Epitome, she was the only one who wasn't completely satisfied with where she was now. While they all seemed content with the overall direction of their careers and personal lives, Chloe could shake neither the nagging sense that her relationship with Sergio was unraveling nor the disappointment that she hadn't yet been able to accomplish her ultimate goal of becoming a serious actress.

Upon leaving the store, she exchanged hugs and kisses with the girls and promised to stay in touch.

"Do you want to ride with me to the concert hall?" Graciela said as a limo pulled to the curb. "I'm going over to do the sound check. Sergio will be there, of course, and I'm sure he'll be thrilled to see you."

"No, that's all right," Chloe said, turning to walk in the opposite direction. "I think I'm going to take a little walk to clear my head."

Chloe sat in the front row at Madison Square Garden, screaming and clapping with the rest of Sergio's female fans as he performed a dance number. Watching him swivel his hips, she got the same rush of excitement as when she first saw him as a teenager at Wembley Stadium. He was an electrifying performer and sometimes it was still hard to believe that he was her man.

Wrapping up the number, Sergio thanked his fans in Spanish and blew a kiss at Chloe. She beamed, feeling like a schoolgirl with a crush all over again.

"And now," Sergio said, wiping the sweat from his brow, "I would like to bring out a very special guest. Graciela, would please you join me?"

Chloe stood up with the rest of the crowd, greeting her friend and former roommate with a standing ovation. Graciela took the stage in a silver sequined gown, specially designed for her by Nikolai Fuentes, which showed off her ample breasts, hips and backside. She waved to the crowd and aimed her index finger in Chloe's direction as if to say, "Thank you for helping me get here." Chloe gave her a thumbs-up and whistled, cheering her on.

The stage lights dimmed, focusing a spotlight on Sergio and Graciela as they began crooning a sexy duet titled "*Mi Corazón Es El Suyo (My Heart Is Yours)*" that was currently topping the Latin pop charts. Watching Sergio and Graciela draw closer onstage, their voices harmoniously intertwining and their hands interlocking, Chloe felt not a twinge of jealousy. She knew this was all theatrics. She felt a surge of pride, knowing she had helped Graciela fulfill her dream. Chloe flashed back to that day not so long ago when she and Graciela were first starting out as models at Epitome and Chloe came home to discover Graciela singing along with the radio. To see Graciela onstage with the man they had both idolized brought tears to Chloe's eyes. They had both come so far in such a short time.

When the song concluded, Chloe stood to join the audience in giving Sergio and Graciela another standing ovation. Graciela waved at Chloe, kissed

Sergio on the cheek and thanked her fans, making a graceful exit. Chloe flashed her all-access pass at security to go back and congratulate Graciela on an amazing performance and prepare to greet Sergio when he came offstage.

Elbowing her way through the throng of roadies, well-wishers and hangers-on clustered backstage, Chloe reached Graciela's dressing room.

"You were fabulous, as always," Chloe said, throwing her arms around Graciela, who had slipped out of her gown and into a terrycloth robe.

"*¡Gracias! Ay,* performing in a huge arena like this, what a rush!"

Sergio entered the dressing room, knocking before entering like the gentleman he was.

"You were great, baby," Chloe said, kissing him on the cheek.

"I can't take all the credit. My duet partner here helped keep the excitement level up," he said, giving Graciela a brotherly hug.

"I made reservations at Le Bernardin," Chloe said as Sergio put his arm around her. "They're open late and I figure we could have a nice, romantic dinner. It'll be mostly empty by the time we get there and we'll have plenty of privacy."

"That sounds like heaven, *cariño,*" Sergio said, kissing Chloe and sending her heart racing again. "I can't wait for us to spend some time alone. It's been too long. And I owe you a nice dinner since I was performing in Barcelona on your birthday."

"You two are so cute together," Graciela said, grinning.

There was another knock and when the door swung open, Chloe recognized Reynaldo, Sergio's road manager.

"They're calling for you, man," Reynaldo said, putting his hand on Sergio's shoulder. "The fans, they're chanting for an encore. They want you to come back out."

Sergio looked at Chloe, flashing a pleading expression, as if seeking her permission to return to the stage and delay their dinner date.

"Go on," she said, patting him on the back. "You have to give the fans what they want."

"I won't be long, *cariño,*" he said, blowing her a kiss as he was nearly dragged out of the room by his road manager.

"I'd hang around and keep you company until Sergio comes back, but I've got to get going. I've got an early shoot in the morning," Graciela said, slipping into a pair of jeans and a T-shirt. Sans glamour, she looked more like the ordinary girl from a poor Latin American family from when she and Chloe were first starting out.

"Don't mind me," Chloe said. "I'm just going to hang out and wait for Sergio in his dressing room."

"Hmmm. Sounds like you want skip dinner and go straight to dessert,"

Graciela teased, slinging an overstuffed tote bag over her shoulder.

Chloe swatted Graciela on the behind. "Get out of here, will you?"

Half-an-hour later, Chloe was still alone in Sergio's dressing room, nibbling on grapes from a fruit basket an admirer had sent and trying not to spoil her appetite. It seemed Sergio's encore was stretching out longer than he'd anticipated. Chloe could hear the roaring crowd from backstage and apparently the band kept playing, obliging the rowdy fans' demands for more and more of Sergio. She didn't mind sharing him with his adoring fans, but increasingly she found herself wishing she had more of his time to herself. It would be nice to go out to dinner like a normal couple without being mobbed or having to close down a restaurant to be able to enjoy each other's company in peace.

Chloe glanced at the clock on the wall. It was past ten p.m. now and the restaurant would only be open for another hour or so. They would have to tell Sergio's limo driver to ignore every red light if they were still going to make it to dinner.

Finally, the door swung open and Sergio rushed in, drenched in sweat.

"Sorry, baby," he said, toweling his forehead. "The fans didn't want to let me go. You know how it is."

"It's okay," she said, nearly drowned out by the sounds of the band winding down that filtered in through the open door. "We're going to have to hurry if we're still going to keep our reservation, though."

"It'll only take me a minute to change and then we'll leave right away."

Sergio began unbuttoning his shirt as his road manager appeared in the doorway.

"Don't get undressed just yet, bro'. Your fans need you," Reynaldo said.

Chloe looked at Sergio and then at Reynaldo, trying to figure out what he was talking about.

"Show's over, dude," Sergio said, taking off his shirt and revealing his glistening, ripped torso. "I don't have the juice to do another encore."

"I don't mean going out for another encore. There's an autograph session with the contest winners from the radio station, remember?"

Sergio slapped his forehead. "*¡Mierda!* I totally forgot. Chloe and I have dinner reservations. We'll never make it if we don't leave now."

"We can't disappoint the fans, man," Reynaldo insisted. "Standing up the contest winners would make for really bad publicity. Besides, the meet-and-greet is part of our contract with the venue. You don't want to risk a lawsuit, do you?"

Sergio looked at Chloe, his eyes seeming to probe for her reaction.

"It's okay, babe," she said, once again taking on the now-familiar role of the self-sacrificing *novia*. "Go take care of business."

449

"I won't be long," he said, slipping into a clean shirt. "I promise."

She mustered a thin smile, knowing all too well from past experience that his promise would be in vain.

"I know you'll be exhausted after signing dozens of autographs and posing for all those photos, so why don't you go back to the hotel afterward and get a good night's sleep? We can do dinner tomorrow night," she offered. "And instead of going out, I'll throw something together and we can stay in and have a night to ourselves."

"*Gracias, mi cariño.*" He took her in his arms and kissed her passionately.

She lingered in the embrace, sensing that if she let him go, she may never hold him again.

Reynaldo loudly cleared his throat, interrupting the intimate moment. "Sergio, we can't keep the fans waiting," he said, impatiently tapping his watch.

Chloe slowly broke away from Sergio. "Go on," she said softly, releasing his hands.

"*Te amo,*" he mouthed, following Reynaldo to the door.

Before she could respond, he disappeared into the noisy, crowded corridor.

68

Chloe let herself in her Greenwich Village apartment, a bag of groceries and a bottle of merlot in one arm, a copy of her latest *Cosmo* cover tucked under the other. After a long day modeling wedding gowns for *Brides* magazine, she cherished coming home to her own place. She could still remember when she first moved into the commodious loft, which resembled an empty warehouse floor.

"I can't believe it! It's mine! It's all mine!" she had shouted when she signed the lease, hugging the landlord, who said he was already wary of crazy models and their wild lifestyles.

After sharing an apartment with four other girls when she was starting out, Chloe was overjoyed to have her own four walls, her own living and breathing space, and most of all, her own bathroom. Her first apartment was comfy, a place where she could barricade herself and hide from the world after working abroad. It was her sanctuary, a haven from the pressures of her career and the craziness of the world. It was home.

As she plopped her groceries on the kitchen counter, her cat, Bizou, purred at her ankles. She squatted and stroked the cat, which she had brought over from Paris once she had her own place. She freshened the cat's food and water bowls and put on some soft music while getting dinner started. She was certainly no maestro in the kitchen, but she had brought back Marie's recipe for linguine and clams – one of the domestic doyenne's few non-French specialties. Chloe was excited about cooking dinner for Sergio and catching up. She was hoping they'd be able to discuss their relationship and how they could make more time for each other.

She was elbow-deep in flour, rolling out dough for homemade pasta and trying desperately to follow Marie's detailed instructions when the phone rang. She let the machine pick up, knowing Sergio would be arriving any moment, and immediately recognized his sexy accent.

"Chloe, *cariño*, I'm sorry, but I'm going to have to cancel for tonight. There's been an unexpected change in my tour schedule. Tickets sold out in Philadelphia in under an hour and they've added an extra show. I have to leave right away to rehearse with the band and get settled in at the hotel." There was a brief pause before he added, "Listen, the tour bus is leaving now, but why don't I have the label fly you out to Philly for the night? I think we should... get together and talk."

Chloe went to the stove and turned off the steaming pots. She was too used to this all-too-familiar scenario to be disappointed. If it wasn't Sergio backing out on their plans because of a last-minute work commitment, she was doing the same.

She rinsed her hands in the kitchen sink and waited a few minutes before calling him back on his cell phone. Her prayers were answered when his voicemail picked up.

"Sergio, it's me," she said. "Listen, I got your message. Unfortunately, I won't be able to make it out to Philly tonight. I have an early-morning assignment tomorrow. I'm sorry we keep missing each other, but I've come to realize that we're both so busy that it's probably best that we don't see each other anymore." She paused, holding back tears. "*Te amo*," she added quietly, "Goodbye."

She hung up and stood in the middle of the living room, looking at a framed photo of her and Sergio that sat on the bookshelf. She turned the photo facedown. From now on she was going to focus on work. Relationships were just too complicated.

Chloe was in the middle of disposing of the half-cooked meal when the doorbell rang. She opened the door to a handsome, light-skinned black man she'd never met before who was holding a bouquet of gardenias.

"I believe these are for you," he said.

"Thank you." She accepted the bouquet, thinking they were from Sergio, but the card simply said "Happy Belated Birthday," with no signature. "If you hold on a second," she said to the man, "I'll get you a tip."

"Oh, I'm not a deliveryman. Those were lying in front of your door." Apparently picking up on her apprehension over a strange man hanging around her front door, he added, "I'm your new downstairs neighbor. I know this sounds horribly cliché, but I was wondering if I could borrow a cup of sugar?"

Chloe laughed and stepped aside. "Come on in. Any man who brings me flowers, even if he didn't buy them himself, is welcome."

"Thanks so much. I'm Rick, Rick Mitchell."

She shifted the bouquet to her other arm and wiped her palm on her apron before shaking his hand. "Sorry if my hands smell like clams. I was fixing dinner for my boyfriend."

"You know, you look familiar." He stared at her. "Hey, aren't you –"

"Chloe Bareaux. You guessed it."

"Wow," the guy said. "I had no idea a famous model lived in this building. You're even prettier in person."

"Thanks," she said, leading him to the kitchen. "I'll get that sugar for you. Just give me a minute to put these in water."

Placing the gardenias in a vase, she puzzled at the anonymous delivery.

"Those from your boyfriend?" Rick said, standing in the doorway of the kitchen.

"No. I have a secret admirer," she said. "Someone sends me flowers and gifts on special occasions – birthdays, holidays, career milestones."

"I bet your secret admirer could be any one of the millions of men out there who worship you."

She scoffed at the notion, embarrassed.

"You're sweet, but I don't think the men who worship me number in the millions, or else I wouldn't spend so many Saturday nights alone."

She set the vase on the counter stood back, admiring the flowers. It was nice to know someone out there was thinking about her – whoever he may be.

"I'm probably the only person in the free world who adds sugar to pasta sauce," Rick said as she lingered in front of the vase.

Picking up on his polite reminder of the task at hand, she retrieved a cup from the cabinet. "Believe it or not, my friend Marie's recipe for linguine and clams calls for a pinch of sugar." She filled the cup with sugar and handed it to him. "Here you go."

"Thanks," he said. "I'd invite you to join me and my partner for dinner, but it sounds like you already have plans."

Chloe took off her apron and plunked it on the counter. "Actually, my plans just fell through."

Upon entering Rick's apartment, she presented him with the bottle of merlot she had planned to enjoy with Sergio.

"This is a really good year," he said, checking out the label and looking impressed.

"I'm just happy it's not going to waste."

"I'll open this. Come on in and make yourself at home."

Chloe sipped the glass of wine Rick poured for her and looked around the loft as African-American opera diva Denyce Graves cooed an aria through speakers mounted throughout the apartment.

She took note of the paintings covering the exposed brick walls. "You have such great taste in art," Chloe called to Rick, who was busy finishing up dinner in the kitchen. "Who's your dealer?"

"I don't have one. I've been collecting for years," he said, coming to the kitchen doorway, wiping his hands on a towel. "My partner, Dave, is an artist. Some of these pieces are his."

She paused, acknowledging Rick's partner was a "he," not that it mattered. "Really? Which ones?" she said after a moment, looking around at the paintings.

"Well, he did that one," Rick said, pointing to an abstract.

"He's really good," Chloe said, studying the piece. "My best friend Gigi's an artist, too, and she's helped me develop an eye. Dave's work is some of the best I've seen, next to Gigi's. His stuff should be in a gallery."

"Someday. Right now he's teaching and doing the starving artist routine. He's at a class right now, in fact. He should be home any minute."

Shortly after Rick put dinner on the table, Dave, an average-looking white guy with sandy hair and a scruffy goatee, joined them. He apologized for being late and introduced himself.

"Chloe," she said, shaking his hand as he took a seat at the table next to Rick.

Dave looked at her in the probing way that had become familiar. "*The*?"

She smiled. "Yes, *the*." It was still a bit jarring when people recognized her. She didn't think of herself as a celebrity.

"Well, pleased to meet you, 'The'," Dave quipped, and she laughed good-naturedly.

"You'll find Dave has a twisted sense of humor," Rick explained, passing the lasagna. "Don't pay him any mind."

"I was just admiring your art," Chloe said to Dave. "You're really talented.

Have you sold anything recently?"

"Not yet. I'd like to find a dealer. It's not exactly easy to make a name for yourself in New York. Do you know how many struggling artists there are in this town?"

"I can only imagine. So what do you do, Rick?"

"Accountant with Warner & Dunne. *Bor*-ring!" Dave declared, tracing the shape of an invisible square with his fork and knife.

Rick elbowed him. "I know corporate bean-counting is dry and dull, but one of us has to pay the bills!"

"I'm really grateful to Rick, truth be told," Dave said, touching his partner's shoulder. "If it wasn't for him making the big bucks, I couldn't afford to pursue my dream."

"And one of us has to maintain health coverage. Your medications are expens-" Rick stopped mid-sentence, his face contorting as if he'd let an intimate detail slip.

"It's okay, it's no big secret." Dave took his partner's hand, and Chloe noticed they wore matching commitment bands. "I'm HIV-positive."

Chloe stared, not knowing what to say. "I'm so sorry," she said finally.

"Don't be. I'm not ashamed. It's something I've lived with for years. Rick's been tested several times and he's fine. We're very careful." He squeezed Rick's hand. "If it wasn't for this guy working a nine-to-five, I wouldn't be able to afford my medications."

"My firm has an excellent domestic partners insurance program. They're progressive about that issue, even if it is a stodgy old accounting firm." Rick released Dave's hand and ribbed him, as if reminding him about the jab he'd made earlier about his dull profession. "That's why I stay there. One day I'd like to quit and go to work for a nonprofit, so I'd feel like I'm actually making a difference instead of just helping big, dirty corporations count their cash."

"I guess we all have dreams," Chloe said, sipping her wine and reflecting on her as-yet-unrealized acting ambitions.

"You seem like you're living your dreams. I bet your work is really exciting," said Rick, "traveling all over the world and rubbing shoulders with the rich and famous. It sounds so glamorous."

"It is," Chloe said, tracing the base of her wineglass, "but sometimes I think I'm not really doing what I was meant to do."

"Which is?" Dave asked.

"This is probably going to sound really superficial," she said, "but what I really want to do is act." She flipped her hair in an exaggerated gesture, imitating a pretentious movie star. "I know: all models want to act."

"I don't think that sounds superficial at all. I'm the last one to shoot down someone's dreams," Dave said. "When I told my parents I wanted to move to

454

New York and become an artist, they told me I'd never make it."

"Not to mention disowning him when he came out," Rick said through bites of pasta.

"I was eighteen," Dave said. "I had just graduated from high school. Luckily, I had a scholarship to an art college back in Pennsylvania and I moved into the dorms. After college, I came to New York. I haven't been home since."

Chloe shook her head, thinking of her own experience of leaving home at eighteen and her eventual reconciliation with her mother. "What about your parents, Rick?"

"My folks are totally cool. Every time I go home to Chicago, they always insist Dave and I stay with them. They love Dave. They treat him like their own son – better than they treat me, come to think of it."

Chloe laughed. "So how'd you guys meet?"

"At a gallery opening in SoHo. I may be a boring accountant," Rick said, elbowing Dave again, "but I've always been a supporter of the arts. Dave and I clicked right away."

"But we fight sometimes," Dave said, his hand grazing Rick's in an unconscious gesture of affection. "Rick's a neat freak and I'm a slob. I admit it. I hate cleaning up after myself, especially when I'm working on a painting. Sometimes I get so wrapped up in my work, I'd forget to eat and bathe myself if it wasn't for Felix Unger here."

"Well, enough about us," Rick said. "What's your story? When I came upstairs to borrow the sugar, you said you were cooking for your boyfriend?"

"Would that be Sergio Reyes?" Dave said, sounding like one of the entertainment reporters who often accosted her at red-carpet events. "I hate to admit I read that trash, but the tabloids always run paparazzi shots of you two. He's a cutie." Dave punctuated his statement with a lusty tiger's growl.

Chloe looked down at her plate. "I just broke it off with him, actually. He stood me up for dinner."

"I can't believe any guy would stand *you* up," said Rick. "As fine as you are, I'd think men would be falling at your feet."

"Believe it or not, I've had my share of heartache, just like everyone else."

It felt good to open up about the breakup with Sergio, like applying salve to a fresh wound. She sensed she could trust Rick and Dave.

As they talked, a timer went off in the kitchen.

"Don't tell me there's another course. I have a fitting for a magazine cover in the morning and I'm probably going to burst the seams," Chloe said, laughing and placing her hands on her belly like a pregnant lady.

"That's just a reminder that it's time to take my medicine," Dave said, getting up from the table. "Be right back."

"Chloe, can I get you anything else?" Rick said, clearing the table.

"No thanks, I'm stuffed. That was delicious. Please, let me help."

Chloe stacked her dishes and silverware, which Rick took from her. "I'll get these. You're our guest. Plus, I wouldn't want to be responsible for you being on the cover of *Vogue* with dishpan hands."

She chuckled. "You've got a point there."

While Rick and Dave lingered in the kitchen, she sipped her merlot and got up to take a closer look at Dave's paintings.

"These pieces are really amazing," she called to him. "If you're interested, I'd love to auction off one of your works at a big event I'm organizing."

Dave appeared in the doorway of the kitchen, wiping a plate with a dishtowel. "What kind of event?"

"It's a masquerade ball. It's a fundraiser for several charities, including AIDS research. There's going to be a lot of important people there – you guys are invited, of course – and it would be great exposure for your work."

"Sounds like an opportunity you shouldn't pass up," Rick said, pushing past Dave to clear the rest of the dishes.

"It does sound like great exposure, but I'd want to do a new piece," Dave said. "Those paintings are a couple years old."

"I've been telling you, you need to do a portrait," Rick said, gesturing at his partner with a fork. "That's where the big bucks are. Look at how much those Andy Warhol portraits of Elizabeth Taylor and Marilyn Monroe still go for."

"Yeah, but I'd have to get a famous subject who'd be willing to sit for me."

"I just happen to know where you could find one," Chloe said, grinning. "She lives upstairs."

69

The young detective pointed her gun at the suspect as Mardi Gras revelers tossed beads from balconies lining the French Quarter.

Alex Michaud sat at his computer in *Newsline* magazine's offices on the sixty-third floor of the Wellington Tower. With rare downtime between stories, he figured he'd sneak in a little work on *Night Moves*, his novel. Reporters clacked away on keyboards and chattered on phones all around him, but Alex was so absorbed in the fictional world he'd created, he was oblivious to the sounds of the bustling newsroom.

"Yo, Michaud, you deaf or what?"

Alex started at the sight of his sweater-vest-wearing, preppy co-worker Jeff Reardon standing at Alex's cubicle. He had been so lost in the latest caper he'd written his character into, he hadn't heard Reardon calling his name.

"Duff wants to see you in his office," Reardon said.

"What are you, his messenger boy?" Alex shot back, unable to resist getting a dig in at one of the Ivy League-educated white boys who was always playing "teacher's pet" to the managing editor and, thus, got most of the plum assignments.

"No, I applied for the job but didn't get it because I'm not eligible for affirmative action."

Alex dismissed Reardon's predictably insensitive remark with an obscene gesture and reported to the editor's office.

"You wanted to see me?" Alex said, standing in the cluttered office of Thomas "Duff" Duffy, a baby-faced Irish American. When Duff didn't acknowledge his presence, Alex cleared his throat, trying once again to alert his editor of his presence.

Duff looked up from the page he was proofing. With his pudgy face and tousle of thinning, blondish hair, the thirty-something editor was barely more than a decade older than Alex, who'd just celebrated his twenty-fifth birthday. But Duff already had the crusty demeanor of a hard-boiled newsman on the constant verge of burnout, as evidenced by the overturned aspirin bottles and discarded Rolaids wrappers that littered his paper-strewn office.

Every time he entered Duff's office, Alex had to stifle the urge to laugh at *The Godfather* movie poster tacked on the wall next to a cluttered bulletin board behind the editor's desk. It was as if by displaying the iconic tough guy image, Duff was asserting that he was running things in the newsroom – although the ultra-liberal Yale alum was anything but "gangsta."

"I need you to cover a junket this afternoon," Duff said, plopping a press kit on the edge of his messy desk.

Alex picked up the press kit, opened the folder and glanced through the materials inside. "Laurel Cosmetics?"

"They're announcing some big new deal. I need you to put something together for the business section."

Duff went back to proofreading, but Alex continued to stand in front of his desk. Alex had been trying to find a way to broach the subject of the trivial assignments that Duff always seemed to pawn off on him.

"With all due respect, Duff, I haven't worked as hard to get this far so I could sit through press junkets," Alex said, trying to strike the right tone and come across as assertive but not insubordinate. "Couldn't one of the interns handle this?"

"This announcement is a pretty big deal. I don't want to leave it up to some college kid. I need you to be a team player here, Michaud."

"I am a team player, but it's getting kind of hard keeping up the team spirit when I'm never handed the ball. Did you even look at any of the story ideas for investigative pieces I e-mailed you?"

"Do you know how many e-mails I get a day, Michaud?"

"Well, if you have some time right now, I'd be happy to discuss my ideas with you."

"Now's not a good time. I have to finish going over the proofs." He took a swig from his ever-present can of Red Bull. "I don't have time to get into this with you right now, Michaud. I'm going to need you to turn around that story from the junket for this week's edition. Think you can handle that?"

Alex gripped the press kit, trying to restrain himself from telling Duff where he could shove it. "Of course I can handle it."

Alex left Duff's office and returned to his desk. He couldn't help feeling envious when he heard Reardon on the phone in the next cubicle making travel arrangements to cover a story in a war-ravaged Eastern European country. Alex had envisioned himself covering such weighty stories when he started as an intern at *Newsline* fresh out of NYU's "J" school. He had worked his way up through the ranks, but he had yet to find that big story that would establish him as a serious journalist.

For right now, he needed to focus on his current assignment. Upon further inspection of the Laurel Cosmetics press kit, he noticed that the announcement the company was making was about signing Chloe Bareaux as their exclusive spokesmodel. Alex recalled his encounter with her in the elevator a couple of weeks ago – how good she smelled, how preternaturally beautiful she was. At the junket, he would have one-on-one time with her. Maybe this assignment would be worth it after all.

"Get a hold of yourself, Michaud," Alex told himself in an undertone, looking at the framed photo of the beautiful young woman that sat next to his computer monitor. "I've got a girlfriend." Leafing through the press kit and noticing Chloe's stunning photo, he added, "And even if I was single, what chance would I have with Chloe, anyway?"

Chloe sat in a director's chair in a conference room at IDG Media, where Laurel Cosmetics had set up a press junket to announce the new deal. She'd mulled over Laurel's proposal over the past couple of weeks and realized that representing a mainstream cosmetics company as its sole spokesperson was a first for a woman of color, an offer she couldn't in good conscience refuse.

"There you have it, folks," said Vanessa Ramos, the beautiful Hispanic television personality, speaking to one of the cameras stationed around the conference room. "The exclusive on Chloe's breakup with Sergio Reyes. You heard it here first."

The television anchor wrapped the segment for *Entertainment Access*, the syndicated pop-culture news program whose studios were housed in the Wellington Tower.

"The producer and I are going to go right back and edit this piece so it can air on this evening's show," Vanessa informed Chloe as a technician unhooked the tiny wireless mic that was clipped to Chloe's blouse. "Luckily, our studio's just a few flights down."

Chloe flashed the obligatory smile, which she had ample practice rehearsing throughout the day. "Thanks again for your time," she said, happy to finally be freed from the interrogation about her personal life and the glare of the crew's hot lights.

There was a quick break before the next interview, which Chloe used to swig Evian water and nibble fruit, cheese and crackers from a tray in the corner of the room. She was starving, but this quick snack would have to suffice. She had several more interviews to do and she needed to keep up her strength.

She never realized how tedious answering the same intrusive question would be: Were the tabloid reports of her breakup with Sergio true and how was she coping?

She gave her stock reply, that she and Sergio had parted friends and, though not a couple anymore, they continued to support each other personally and professionally. The statement was basically true, although she hadn't spoken to him since leaving her "dear John" voicemail.

Chloe coasted on autopilot as she gave rote responses that were supposed to sound unrehearsed, and kept herself from yawning by pretending she was on a junket promoting her big movie debut.

When the next reporter walked in, she had to sit down to brace herself. She recognized the handsome young black man as the same one she had encountered in the elevator a couple of weeks ago.

"Hi," he said, taking a seat across from her. "I'm Alex."

"I'm Chloe. Thanks for taking the time to speak with me."

"My pleasure," he said in a tone that radiated charm and sex appeal.

A moment passed without either saying anything, their eyes locked.

"I'm sorry for staring," he said finally. "I was just thinking back on the first time we met."

"The elevator," she said. "You dropped your papers and I handed them to you."

"Oh, yes. Thank you for rescuing my manuscript. Like most of the journalists I know, I'm a closet novelist."

She recalled that the passage she'd read had been set in New Orleans and she wanted to ask him what the book was about. She had the urge to turn the tables and interview *him*.

Before she could say anything, Bill Bosworth, Laurel's all-too-efficient PR guru, came to the door and cleared his throat, indicating it was time to get down to business.

"We've allotted fifteen minutes for *Newsline* magazine, just like all the other outlets," Bosworth said pointedly to Alex. "I suggest you use it wisely."

Alex flipped open his steno pad and turned to Chloe. "I guess that was my cue," he said with a good-natured chuckle, "so let's get started."

Throughout the interview, Chloe noticed that Alex had done his homework and was up to speed not only on facts about the company, but her personal background as well. However, instead of prying about the breakup or peppering her with frivolous inquiries about style tips like the other reporters, he asked thought-provoking questions. She liked the fact that he didn't dismiss her as just another airhead model and seemed genuinely interested in her responses.

"So why did you want to represent Laurel in the first place? What makes this deal something more than a big payday for you?" he asked, sounding like one of those *60 Minutes* correspondents grilling a corporate racketeer.

She thought for a moment before responding, appreciating the challenging question. "I have to believe in whatever I attach my name to. They don't do any animal testing and all of their manufacturing plants are environmentally friendly. And I like the fact that they have a whole line designed especially for women of color of all complexions," she said. "Plus, the company has a charitable foundation and they support a lot of causes I really care about, like AIDS research. In fact, Laurel's holding a big fundraiser next month, a masquerade ball. It was my idea. You're invited, of course." Wanting to maintain her professionalism and not sound like she was coming on to him, she quickly added, "The media's invited. We'd love some coverage."

He smiled. "I'd love to come."

Both fell silent again, staring at one another, until Bosworth ducked his head in again.

"I think my time's just about up," Alex said. "Is there anything you'd like to add that I didn't ask about?"

"Thank you for not asking the obvious question," she said.

He gave her a knowing look. "You mean about your recent breakup with Sergio Reyes?"

She nodded, not wanting to reopen the wound.

"I respect your privacy," he said, "but I have to admit, I don't get that Sergio guy. I don't know how any man in his right mind could let a woman

460

like you go."

He looked at her intently and she took a sip of water, not sure if the warmth that overcame her was from the residual heat of the television lights from the previous interview or the chemistry she felt with Alex.

Before either could say anything else, Bosworth signaled that time was up and the next reporter was waiting.

"Thanks so much. I've really enjoyed talking to you," Alex said, closing his notepad.

She smiled. "Me, too."

"Listen," he said, reaching into his pocket, "This is my card. Give me a ring if there's anything you'd like to… Add." His eyes lingered on hers when he handed her the business card.

She examined the card, taking note of his last name. "Michaud? Is it French?"

"French Creole, actually. I'm from New Orleans."

He intrigued her even more, knowing they shared the same cultural heritage. She had the urge once again to ask him a million questions, but before she could say anything further, Bosworth ushered him to the door.

"Be sure to RSVP for the masquerade ball," Bosworth told Alex. "We have a limited number of media passes available."

Upon leaving the room, Alex turned and smiled at Chloe and they locked eyes again for an instant, and then he was gone.

Though her beauty can be intimidating, her girl-next-door charm is disarming. And with her multicultural background, Chloe Bareaux should serve Laurel Cosmetics well as the firm's global emissary.

Alex sat at his desk, putting the finishing touches on his story. He moved the cursor to the top of his computer screen and reread what he had written. Although he initially went into the assignment grudgingly, he ended up taking extra time to give the piece the attention it deserved. Chloe had come across as intelligent and articulate in the interview and her quotes were insightful. She had certainly defied any preconceived notions he had about models.

He thumbed through the Laurel Cosmetics press kit, pausing when he came to her photo. It was crazy, but he couldn't stop thinking about her since the interview.

"Hey, Michaud, you done with that Laurel Cosmetics piece yet?" Duff said, approaching Alex's desk. "I need to finish proofing the business section before we go to press."

Alex shuffled papers on top of Chloe's photo, feeling as though he were engaging in some kind of ethical violation by gazing at a photo of his interview subject. Journalists were supposed to remain detached, as his NYU professors had drilled into him, but doing so was impossible with a subject as fascinating as Chloe.

"Uh, just one more minute. I need to double-check a couple of facts."

Duff launched into his familiar invective about the importance of deadlines.

"Wrap it up and get it to me ASAP, Michaud," Duff concluded, trudging to his office.

Alex turned back to his computer screen. The story was basically finished, but he found himself coming up with an excuse to speak to Chloe again. He hadn't asked her about the new products she would be lending her image to. That was good enough reason to request a phone interview, wasn't it?

When Alex reached Laurel's corporate headquarters, he was greeted by the pushy PR guy from the press junket.

"I'm sorry, Chloe is unavailable for comment right now," Bill Bosworth said. "Is there something I can help you with?"

"No, that's all right. I guess I'll just go with what I've got."

Alex hung up the phone and sunk down in his chair. Not being able to reach Chloe was probably a sign, he reasoned. A gorgeous model with a globe-trotting lifestyle would never be interested in an average guy like him. And besides, he was already involved.

Remembering that his girlfriend would be back in town after a week away on business, he dashed off a text message reminding her about the romantic dinner he had planned. The terse reply he received was typical of the workaholic advertising executive he was dating: *Working late. Have to cancel. – V.*

Faced with the prospect of an unanticipated free evening, Alex hurried to finish up his piece on Chloe. Once he filed the story, he could get in a couple of hours on his novel.

Alex was typing his byline on the story when his smart aleck co-worker swept by and swiped the Laurel Cosmetics press kit.

"Is this your big story for the week, Michaud?" Jeff Reardon said, leafing through the press kit. "Hey, can you get some free lipstick samples for my girlfriend?"

"Sure it's for your girlfriend?" Alex snatched the press kit and the invitation to the masquerade ball, the big corporate fundraiser Chloe had mentioned, fell out. With Reardon on the phone in the next cubicle and finally out of his face, Alex studied the invitation, taking note of the Mardi Gras mask on the cover, and put it back in the folder. If he couldn't even get Chloe on the phone, what good would it do to attend some shindig where he would most likely not get anywhere close to her?

He filed the Laurel Cosmetics piece and opened a file titled "Night Moves." Fiction was his first love, and he was happy to escape into the invented world where he could control what happened.

The young detective pointed her gun at the suspect as Mardi Gras revelers tossed beads from balconies lining the French Quarter.

Alex stared at the computer screen, and the blinking cursor stared back at him. He was stuck on this part, and he couldn't figure out his character's next move.

He glanced down at his desk and saw Chloe's photo peeking out from the press kit. He pulled out the photo and studied it again. He glanced from the photo to the words on the screen, and it occurred to him that she looked just as he had envisioned his character.

He propped Chloe's photo between the keyboard and monitor, then caught a glimpse of the framed photo of his girlfriend that sat next to his computer.

"Sorry, Veronica," Alex muttered, feeling a twinge of guilt as he turned his girlfriend's photo facedown on the desk.

With Chloe's photo as his muse, he began typing and was finally able to bring the climactic scene to a satisfying conclusion.

70

"Hold still so I can zip up the back," Chloe said, helping Gigi into the designer frock she was to wear to the opening of her first exhibition in Paris.

The pair stood before a full-length mirror in the living room of the Right Bank apartment they shared whenever Chloe was in town. Chloe had rented the flat when her modeling career took off and she began traveling back and forth between New York and Paris. Since Gigi was a student at the time and found dorm life at the Sorbonne distracting, Chloe had suggested that she move into the apartment since there was plenty of space. In a roundabout way, Chloe and Gigi had realized their girlhood dream of being college roommates. Chloe often reflected on the irony that it was Gigi who had actually finished college, as if their teenage roles had reversed.

"Okay, got it." Chloe finished zipping up the dress, while Gigi held her breath.

"*Goddamn!* I can barely breathe," Gigi said, turning to the mirror and hugging her midsection. "I dieted for a whole month to fit into this dress. I don't know how you can model these rags day in and day out. It's like they make them for twelve-year-olds with no boobs."

"Remember when we were younger and we used to go shopping and try on clothes together?" Chloe said.

"Yeah, I always admired your height and the fact that you're skinny enough to fit into anything."

"And I always admired your big boobs, child-bearin' hips and *derriere*," Chloe said, slapping Gigi's behind. They both laughed.

"You know," Chloe added, wrapping her arms around Gigi's waist in a familiar, sisterly gesture, "now that we're grown up, I see that we're both beautiful in our own way."

"*You're* beautiful, but I'm not sure about me," Gigi said, fluffing her curls in the mirror. "I feel anything but beautiful right now, with the thought of all those high-society art snobs judging me and my work. My paintings are like my babies, and this opening is like putting them up for adoption."

"You look great, perfect for your opening," Chloe said, stepping away from Gigi to get a better look at her dress. "You're going to be the toast of Paris."

"Thanks for flying back for my opening," Gigi said, studying herself in the mirror, tugging on the shift that was emblazoned with an intricate pattern as colorful as one of her canvasses.

"You know I wouldn't miss it. And remember, I've already booked your ticket for the masquerade ball in a few weeks. It's a fundraiser for AIDS research. I'm planning the whole thing and giving it a New Orleans theme. We're calling it 'Mardi Gras in September.'"

"You know I'll be there," Gigi said, turning to admire her backside. "This dress does do a lot for my curves. Thanks for calling in the favor with that designer. I could never have afforded it – not on a starving artist's income."

"That's all going to change after tonight when the world gets to see your talent."

Gigi put her hands on her hips, striking a pose in the mirror. "And who knows? As good as we both look," she said, eyes flashing the mischievous glint that was uniquely hers, "maybe we'll both score."

At that suggestion, Chloe retreated across the room and began touching up her makeup in a smaller mirror hanging on the wall. The prospect of dating again filled her with anxiety.

"Look, Chlo', I know you're still smarting over the breakup with Sergio," Gigi said in the intuitive way that she and Chloe shared, "but you've got to move on. The best way to get over a broken heart is to meet someone else."

Chloe paused, holding the makeup brush in mid-air, seized by thoughts of the sexy journalist she had been unable to forget since the Laurel Cosmetics press junket a few days ago. "Actually, I've already met someone," she confessed.

Gigi bolted across the room to Chloe's side. "Why didn't you tell me?

Who is he?"

"It's nothing, really," Chloe said, not meeting Gigi's eyes. "It's just this guy, this reporter."

"Yeah? Come on, tell me everything." Gigi began tickling Chloe like when they were kids and would try to torture each other into opening up about a secret crush.

"Stop." Chloe smacked Gigi's hand. "There's nothing to tell. I rode up with him on an elevator one time, then I saw him again when I was doing interviews about the new deal with Laurel."

"And? Did you get his number?"

"He gave me his card, but I haven't had time to call."

"Haven't had time? Girl, you've got to make time." Gigi snatched Chloe's purse and began rifling through it. "Where's that damn card? We're going to call him right now."

Chloe grappled for her purse, but Gigi held it out of reach. "Cut it out, Gi'!" It was like they were back in high school, when Gigi insisted on fixing Chloe up with some boy from St. Thomas.

Chloe reached around Gigi and snatched her purse back. "I can't call up some reporter and ask him out. That would be totally unprofessional."

"Why would the guy give you his card if he didn't expect you to call?"

Chloe reached into her purse to retrieve her mascara wand, stalling. She couldn't immediately think of a logical rebuttal.

"I'm not like you, Gi'," Chloe said finally, putting on mascara in the mirror. "I'm not as bold as you."

Gigi put her hands on her hips again. "If you don't get over this shy routine, you're going to find yourself bitter and alone someday."

Chloe added one last flourish to her lashes and plopped the mascara wand back in her purse. "Thanks, Gi'," she said, snapping her purse shut. "Now you're starting to sound like my mother."

Chloe opened the front door of the Chateau de Chevalier and inhaled the delightful scent of Marie's baking. She hovered in the foyer, savoring the feeling of being back in familiar surroundings. Every time work brought Chloe back to Paris, she always tried to stop in at the chateau, even if just for a quick visit to reorient herself with the place she considered her true home. No matter where she was in the world, it grounded her to know that her old room, the horse she rode as a teenager and Marie's cooking would always be waiting for her return.

Chloe stooped to pet Beeshie, Mother's Bichon Frisé, who ran up and greeted Chloe enthusiastically by licking her face. Scratching the dog behind his ears, Chloe remembered when he was just a puppy, when Jacques first bought the dog for Maxine as a housewarming gift.

"It's so good to be home," Chloe said, greeting Marie with a kiss on the cheek upon entering the kitchen.

"It's good to *have* you home, *chouchou*," Marie said. She pulled a tray of fresh-baked beignets from the oven and handed Chloe one of the piping-hot pastries. "I made these just for you."

Chloe devoured the sample in nearly one bite. "Marie, I've eaten at some of the best restaurants in the world, but there's nothing like your cooking."

Marie began transferring the rest of the beignets to a Tupperware dish. "I'll make a care package for you to take back to New York."

"Speaking of New York, I have an invitation for you." Chloe reached into her purse and produced a postcard-size flyer, which had an artist's rendering of an elaborate Mardi Gras mask lying against a background of crumpled lavender silk and the words *You're Invited to the Inaugural Mardi Gras in September Masquerade Ball* written in fancy script.

"What's this?" Marie said, wiping her hands on her apron and taking the postcard from Chloe.

"It's an invitation to a charity ball I'm planning. I'm inviting everyone who's important to me, and I want you to be there."

"This is in New York?" Marie set the postcard aside. "Oh, Chloe, dear, I appreciate the invitation, but you know how I hate to fly."

Chloe sat on a stool at the island, conversing as Marie went about her kitchen tasks, just like when Chloe was a teenager. "Oh, come on, Marie. You've never been to New York, and the flight will be my treat, of course. First class."

"Flying over the ocean?" Marie looked aghast as she stood at the sink, rinsing dishes. "They'll have to sedate me."

When Marie came over to wipe down the island, Chloe took her hand. "Marie, if it wasn't for you, I never would have been able to survive in New York. I wouldn't be where I am today. This event really means a lot to me, and it wouldn't be the same if you weren't there."

Marie paused, then wiped her hands on her apron again and took Chloe's chin in her hand. "Okay. For you, *chouchou*, I'll do it."

Marie's smile soon faded when Bernard, the groundskeeper, came in the back door and began loading up on beignets.

"Those are for Chloe, you *goinfre*," Marie said, calling him a "pig." She smacked his hand like a frustrated mother scolding her naughty son. "And how many times have I told you not to track mud in my kitchen?"

"Marie, *cher*, I know you only hit me because you love me." Bernard pecked Marie on the cheek and stuffed a couple of pastries in his shirt pocket.

Marie crimsoned. "Get out of here, you!" she called after Bernard, swatting him with her dishtowel as he clomped out the backdoor.

"You know, Marie, that invitation to my charity ball includes a guest," Chloe said, giving Marie a coy look, "and I think you should invite Bernard."

"*What?!* Have you gone mad, young lady?" Marie looked even more shocked than when Chloe suggested she endure a transatlantic flight. "I wouldn't invite that *imbécile* to eat a ham sandwich at my kitchen counter, let alone allow him to accompany me to such a classy affair."

"I've seen the way he's flirted with you all these years. He's a widower, you're a widow. Why not get together?"

"Before you go trying to fix me up with someone," Marie said, fixing the lid tightly on the Tupperware container that held the beignets, as if to protect them from further pilfering from Bernard, "I'd like to see you find a nice young man and settle down. I don't like thinking of you in that big city all by yourself."

"And on that note," Chloe said, rising from the stool, "I think I'll excuse myself. I want to give Mother her invitation. Have you seen her?"

"She's up in her room, I think."

Chloe jogged up the stairs and padded down the hall to the master suite. "Mother?" she said, rapping on the door as she entered the darkened room.

Chloe caught sight of Maxine sitting on the edge of the bed, staring out the window as dusk fell.

"Mother, what's wrong?"

Maxine motioned toward her dresser. "The next disbursement from the trust fund Jacques set up for you came."

Chloe went to the dresser, opened the envelope and studied the check for one hundred thousand dollars. The disbursements had increased each year, and this was by far the largest payout to date.

"You know I don't need the money, Mother," Chloe said, tucking the check back in the envelope. "I want you to make a donation to charity in Jacques' name, like always."

"Whatever you say." Maxine continued staring out the window, not meeting Chloe's gaze.

Sensing her mother's listlessness, Chloe sat down next to her on the bed. "You've been thinking about him, haven't you?" she said, rubbing her mother's back.

"I can't help it," Maxine said, dabbing at her eyes. "Everything in this house reminds me of him. And every year when the trust-fund check arrives, it always makes me think of what a good provider he was, how protective he was of us."

Chloe rested her head on her mother's shoulder. "I miss him, too." After a few silent moments in the dark room, Chloe sprang up, drew the curtains and flicked on the lights. "Look, why don't you give Marie the night off and I'll take you out to dinner? It might help you get your mind off thinking about Jacques."

In the years' since Jacques' death, Maxine hadn't completely moved on. She had dated men on both sides of the Atlantic but never committed, as if she were still playing the role of Jacques Chevalier's long-suffering widow.

"I don't know if I'm up to going out tonight, honey," Maxine said, turning back the covers on the bed. "It was a long day at work and I'm probably going to turn in early."

"Okay, I'll take a rain check on dinner, but mark your calendar for this." Chloe handed Maxine an invitation to the ball.

Maxine examined the invitation. "You know I support everything you do, *ma chérie*, but there's so much going on with work right now I have to check my schedule to make sure."

"Well, just let me know. Since you're my mother, I guess I'll let you slide on the RSVP." Chloe laughed and took Maxine's hand. "You know, planning this event and doing research on Mardi Gras got me thinking a lot about New Orleans. After the ball, when both our schedules clear up a bit, I was thinking we could finally take a trip down there – maybe for the actual Mardi Gras celebration in February. You could show me where you grew up and all the places where Papa Frank and Mama Louise used to perform."

Maxine fluffed her pillows. "I don't know about that, honey. It's not the same place since Katrina hit. I don't know if I could stand seeing my hometown in ruins."

Chloe gave her mother a scrutinizing gaze. It was true that the Big Easy and much of the Gulf Coast were still idling through sluggish recovery efforts. But Chloe was still curious, however, to see the city of her heritage, maybe even assist in the recovery by contributing to tourism. Maxine's insistence that she couldn't bear the pain of going back to a place that no longer bore any resemblance to the vibrant cultural mecca of her youth seemed like just another excuse. When Chloe was younger, the excuse was that Maxine was too busy building her company and making a living. Chloe had a sneaking suspicion that there was some ghost from the past hovering in the muggy bayou air that Mother didn't want to confront, that she was harboring some family secret.

"Why don't you think about the trip and get back to me," Chloe said, knowing not to push when Maxine was in one of her moods. "In the meantime, I have a lot of planning to do for the ball and I might just be calling on your decorating services."

"Sure thing," Maxine said. "And of course I'll make your ball gown."

Chloe smiled. "I'd love that. By the way, I invited Marie and told her she should bring Bernard, since he's always flirting with her. We need to get busy finding you a date for the ball, as well."

Maxine didn't respond. Beeshie, her dog, toddled in and Maxine scooped him up. The dog licked her face, as if instinctively trying to lift his owner's spirits.

"My friend Muriel has a friend your age who's single – divorced, actually," Chloe continued. "He's a handsome black investment banker. I think you'd like him."

"I'll think about it." Maxine set Beeshie down and he scampered out of the room.

"No pressure," Chloe said, getting up from the bed, sensing Maxine wanted to be alone again. She backed toward the door. "You don't have to give me an answer right away. Just let me know when you're ready."

71

"I've never seen you this nervous before, Gi'," Chloe said as they stood in the middle of La Galerie Nouveau, which was filled with friends, Gigi's fellow Sorbonne alums and VIPs of the Parisian art scene.

"I just want everything to be right," Gigi said, straightening one of her paintings' frames. "Oh, *garçon*?" She stopped a waiter, grabbed a glass of wine from his tray and nearly drained it in one gulp.

"Careful, Gi'," Chloe said, taking the empty glass from Gigi and setting it out of her reach. "You don't want to get sloshed, pass out and miss your own opening."

"God, if you get me through this night, I promise I'll start going to church every Sunday," Gigi said to the ceiling, her hands folded in prayer.

Gigi's nervousness seemed to abate somewhat when famed photographer Lucien Girard, celebrated sculptor Hélène d'Orgemont and several other respected well-wishers came up and complimented her on her debut. Gigi grew anxious again, however, when she pointed out a portly man who was standing by one of her paintings and writing on a notepad.

"Oh my god, that's Lyle Pinochet!" Gigi exclaimed.

"So? Who's he?" Chloe said, staring at the man, who had an officious air.

"Only the art critic for *Le Monde*. He has the power to make or break me with his review."

"Don't be so dramatic. I'm the aspiring actress, remember?" Chloe sipped her white wine. "Besides, the fact that he's even here shows there's a lot of interest in your work."

Gigi diverted her attention from the pompous-looking critic when Simone made her entrance, showing off her still-fabulous figure in a clingy blue cocktail dress. On her arm was a handsome man Chloe had never met before. A photographer documenting the occasion for the arts section of *Le Monde* aimed his lens at Simone. Rather than attempting to steal the spotlight from her daughter, however, Simone grabbed Gigi and pulled her into the photo.

"This is your night," Simone said, hugging Gigi. "I'm so proud of you!"

"Thanks, Simone, that really means a lot," Gigi turned to her mother's companion. "And who do we have here?"

"Gigi, Chloe, this is Armand Delicourt. Armand, this is my daughter, Gigi, and my goddaughter, Chloe."

Armand had olive skin and dark, wavy hair, graying at the temples, which gave him a distinguished look. He kissed Gigi's hand and then Chloe's with the gallantry typical of a Frenchman.

"It's rare that a man of my age gets to be in the presence of such beauty," he said in a refined accent.

Chloe flashed Gigi an impressed look as if to say, "This guy seems pretty classy."

"So how did you two meet?" asked Gigi, who seemed to be relieved to have something to focus on other than how her work was being received.

Simone put her hand on Armand's shoulder. "Armand owns Le Excentrique, that hot new restaurant in Montparnasse. When you asked me to oversee the catering for your opening, I knew of no better place. And when I went in to place the order, he asked me out."

"I don't normally hit on my clients," Armand said, cradling Simone's hand, "but I'd like to think I have an eye for beauty." He smiled at Gigi, his dark eyes radiating warmth. "And your paintings, my dear, certainly fit the bill."

"Why thank you," Gigi said, sounding genuinely flattered. "I've worked really hard to get here, and I just hope it's paying off."

"And the food is to your satisfaction?" Armand said.

"Everything's great. *Merci*."

"I tried the escargots earlier," Chloe said. "They were fabulous."

"Great. I think I'll go around and check to make sure my staff is handling everything properly," Armand said. "Simone, *chérie*, can I get you anything?"

"A serving of your wonderful chocolate soufflé. That dish is better than sex!"

Armand bowed and left to fill the order and Chloe and Gigi giggled at Simone's sauciness, which had not mellowed in middle age.

"Let me in on the joke," Maxine said, joining the group.

"We just had the pleasure of meeting Simone's new flame," Chloe said after hugs and kisses had been exchanged. "He seems like a winner."

"Yes," Maxine concurred, "I've had the pleasure of meeting Armand." She gave Simone a pointed look. "A guy your own age for a change. I'm impressed."

Simone folded her arms. "I guess I've finally grown up."

"Haven't we all," Gigi added.

The women shared another laugh, which was interrupted by a man who approached Gigi. Chloe noticed that the color drained from Gigi's face and Simone stiffened at the appearance of a dark-haired, thirty-something man. Chloe looked at Maxine, whose expression said, "I have no idea who he is, either." Upon closer inspection, Chloe recognized the man as Pascal Valotte, the young artist Simone and Gigi had quarreled over years ago. Chloe cringed, recalling the ugly episode.

"Excuse me," Pascal said in his soft-spoken tone, his shoulders stooped as he clutched a crumpled knit hat. "I just wanted to tell you that I admire your work." He glanced at Simone. "Good to see you both again."

Chloe would have laughed at the improbability of Simone and Gigi being rendered speechless were it not for the tension in the air.

"I heard about your opening – you know how word travels around art circles – and I wanted to come by and wish you well," Pascal said to Gigi. "Your talent has really advanced, far beyond my own."

Simone and Gigi continued to glare at Pascal as if he were a furrier at a PETA rally.

"Gigi just completed her degree at the Sorbonne," Chloe said, attempting to break the tension.

"Ah, the Sorbonne," Pascal said wistfully, as if recalling the name of a fond acquaintance. "Back when I was student-teaching there was when I..." He hesitated, looking from Simone to Gigi, seeming to search for the right words. "Knew you both."

"Yes, well, we've both moved on," Simone said, locking arms with Armand, who had returned with a tray of bite-size chocolate soufflé samples.

Pascal nodded. "I'm happy for you both." His expression turned forlorn as Armand set the tray aside and put his arm around Simone. "*Au revoir.*" He put on his hat and left the gallery.

"Who was that young man?" Armand asked.

The innocent question was met with stony silence. When one of the catering staff came up and requested his assistance, Armand excused himself, looking relieved to escape the uncomfortable moment.

The silence continued, until Maxine salvaged the occasion by summoning a waiter and handing a glass of champagne to each woman.

"I propose a toast." Maxine held her glass aloft. "To Gigi."

The smile returned to Simone's face. "To Gigi," she repeated, raising her glass and putting her arm around her daughter.

Chloe held her glass up, hoping to reassure her best friend. "To Gigi."

Gigi finally cracked a smile and clinked glasses with the women. "To Paris."

"Cartier's work shows maturity beyond her age," Chloe read aloud from the paper over a late breakfast the next morning in the flat she and Gigi shared, "and the consistency displayed in last night's opening signals the emergence of a promising new artist."

"Oh my god!" Gigi exclaimed. "Read it again!"

Chloe again recited the glowing review from revered art critic Lyle Pinochet, prompting Gigi to rise from the table and jump up and down in a burst of joy. Chloe laughed at her friend's childlike enthusiasm, until the sound of a crunching bone could be heard and Gigi tumbled to the floor.

A trip to the emergency room followed, with Gigi's yelps of glee about the positive notice in the paper replaced with moans about her sprained ankle.

"What a way to celebrate your success," Chloe said, sitting next to Gigi in the crowded waiting room.

"We've been sitting here forever. I can't wait to get out of here."

The grungy man sitting next to them muttered to himself in French, barely audible over the din of the television set that pumped badly-dubbed American sitcom reruns into the crowded room. The decibel level rose even higher when the automatic doors of the emergency room swooshed open and a frantic mother rushed in carrying a child. The woman shrieked at the nurse manning the registration desk that her son had swallowed some poisonous household cleanser.

The nurse attempted to calm the woman, but the young mother was inconsolable and kept pointing at her sobbing child. The mother looked as though she was about to lose control and turn as blue as her sick child until a tall, good-looking, light-skinned black man in scrubs came out and spoke to her in a soothing tone.

"We'll take him right in and get the insurance information from you later," the young doctor said in French to the woman. "Don't worry. We'll take good care of him."

The doctor placed the boy on a gurney and gave him a stuffed animal, which seemed to placate both mother and child. When the boy had been wheeled away through swinging doors, the doctor picked up the sign-in sheet from the registration desk and called out, "Mademoiselle Cartier?"

Gigi spoke up. "Yes, that's me."

The doctor smiled at her. "*Bonjour*. I'm Philippe. I'll see you now."

As Chloe helped her up, Gigi said under her breath, "Cute doctor. Maybe this isn't such a bad place, after all."

Chloe accompanied Gigi to the examination room, where the doctor took X-rays. Chloe noted the special attention he took when he slipped off Gigi's sock and gently massaged her foot, asking where it hurt.

When the doctor had closed the curtains around the exam table and left to tend to another patient, Chloe couldn't resist the urge to comment.

"That doctor is flirting with you."

"What? He's just doing his job."

"Oh, come on, Gi'. You see how busy this place is, but he took extra time with you. I wish *I* could have gotten that foot massage."

Gigi slapped Chloe's knee. "Hey, I'm the patient here."

The curtains parted and the doctor returned, carrying a chart. "Sorry it took me so long," he said. "This place is a madhouse. I'm just a resident. I'm subbing for the physician who usually runs the ER, and I've had my hands full all day."

"It's okay," Chloe said. "So what's the word on her foot?"

"I just went over the X-rays," he said, flipping through the chart, "and it looks like just a hairline fracture. Just stay off it for a few days and it should be good as new."

With the same sensuous touch he had used before in massaging Gigi's foot, he slipped a brace over the ankle. He then scribbled something on a slip of paper and handed it to Gigi.

"Here's my number," he said. "If you have any complications – any at all – please don't hesitate to give me a ring."

Gigi glanced at Chloe, who gave her a knowing smile.

"*Merci*," Gigi said. "I just might do that."

The ensuing silence was pierced by the wails of the child whose mother had rushed him in, and the doctor excused himself to get back to work.

"I told you he was flirting with you," Chloe said, helping Gigi off the exam table and into a wheelchair. "You should give him a call later on."

"I'll tell you what, I'll call the doctor, if you agree to call that reporter who gave you his number."

"Hey, we're talking about you here," Chloe said, wheeling Gigi through the swinging doors that led to the lobby. "You're the patient, after all."

72

On her first day back in New York, Chloe rolled out of bed at five-thirty a.m., still fighting off jetlag from her most recent trip to Paris, and hailed a cab. She had a busy day ahead of her crammed with the usual flurry of activities, starting with a grueling early-morning workout. She stared sleepy-eyed at the abandoned cars and graffiti-pocked buildings that lined the litter-strewn streets on the way to the gym. Instead of one of those sleek fitness clubs in Manhattan, her trainer, African-American Olympic athlete-turned-fitness guru Marcella Scott Turner, insisted on working out at a gritty Bronx gym where police cadets trained.

Upon arriving at the gym at five past six, Chloe was greeted by Marcella's unsmiling face. "You're lucky my watch is a little slow," Marcella said, tapping the Velcro band on her wrist as Chloe tramped in, lugging her gym bag. "If you got here one minute later, I was going to have you drop and give me twenty before we started your workout."

"You're a drill sergeant, Marcy."

"Yes I am. And I expect my troop to report for basic training promptly at six a.m."

Chloe set her gym bag aside and pulled her hair into a ponytail. "What's it going to be today?" she said, hoping Marcella would be merciful.

"Hop on the treadmill. I'll time you, make sure you're running at a steady pace and keeping your heart rate up. If I have anything to do with it, you'll be marathon material in no time."

Ugh. Chloe pulled off her T-shirt and cutoffs, revealing a sports bra and Spandex shorts, and got to work on the treadmill. Marcella got on the one beside her. The trainer was tough but fair. She said she didn't believe in making any of her clients do anything she wouldn't do herself. She was a winner, a super-achiever who excelled in sports and in life. Chloe admired the fact that Marcella had pulled herself up from a hardscrabble existence in the projects of Detroit. After earning a gold medal for track and field with the help of her husband/coach Bobby Turner, Marcella had parlayed the international fame and recognition she earned at the Olympics into a highly profitable enterprise. Her face adorned cereal boxes and she had made millions hawking track shoes and other athletic gear. She was the creator of her own series of best-selling fitness DVDs, rivaling Donna Richardson as the workout video queen. Marcella's notoriety had helped her become a fitness trainer to the stars, helping countless models and actresses look their best for the camera.

With Marcella's help, Chloe had recently been featured on the cover of *Shape* magazine. And with new television spots for Laurel Cosmetics coming up, Chloe needed to be in tip-top shape.

After warming up on the treadmill, Marcella led Chloe to another machine.

"What is this," Chloe said, still panting from the warm-up, "a medieval torture device?"

Marcella didn't look amused. "A little less talk and a lot more sweat."

Chloe grunted her way through Marcella's patented, killer abdominal workout, which Chloe not so affectionately referred to as "le grind." She never knew the human body could be twisted like a pretzel into so many different painful positions.

The session concluded by doing battle with the Stairmaster. As Marcella programmed the machine, Chloe fiddled with her MP3 player. She felt like hearing the voice of a strong woman as she worked out. Tina? Janet? Beyoncé? Madonna was always good for a jolt of energy. Her music made Chloe want to do a thousand push-ups or go to a hardware store or something.

A dance video by Graciela came on the gym's bank of TV screens. Chloe stepped to the beat, taking heart that at least one of the girls she started out with was truly living her dreams. She clung to the hope that she would one day realize her own dreams of breaking onto the big screen.

Alex strained under the heavily-loaded barbell on the weight bench. "Nine… ten," he grunted, calling out the number of each repetition as he completed the set.

"Not bad." Steve, Alex's friend and workout partner, helped return the weight to the rack above Alex's chest. "But I did twenty reps."

Steve lifted the sleeves of his T-shirt and flexed his biceps, his pale skin tone contrasting with Alex's bronze complexion in the gym's mirrored walls, though they were both African American.

"You've always got to rub it in, don't you?" Alex said, sitting up.

Stephen Spaulding hadn't changed since they were dormmates at NYU – Alex in the journalism school and Steve in the international business program. Steve was as competitive as ever, already a junior partner in his Wall Street brokerage firm with an impressive list of clients, while Alex was still working his way up at the magazine and struggling to finish his novel.

Alex put away the weights as Steve struck bodybuilder poses in the mirror. Male-model handsome like Alex, Steve fit right in with the hip, young professional crowd that frequented Pump, the trendy Manhattan fitness club. For Alex, he cared less about the fact that the gym was the hot new place to pump iron than it was a short cab ride from the office and he and Steve could squeeze in a workout during lunch.

Alex interrupted Steve's self-admiration session by punching him in the arm. "I'm tired of messing around here with you. I'm going to hit the showers and get back to work."

"Don't stay too late. Pam and I are having some people over this evening and she wants you and Veronica to come."

Alex took a swig from his water bottle. "Thanks, but tonight's one of those rare occasions when Veronica's not working late. I was planning to head straight home from the office and cook a big meal."

"Yeah, right. I bet what you'll actually be doing is cooking up some way to get with that model you interviewed. What's her name, Cleo?"

Alex began walking to the locker room as Steve followed. "Chloe. And why would I be thinking about her? I forgot all about her once I filed the story," Alex said, not sounding very convincing, even to himself.

"Come on, man. I saw how your face lit up when you told me about her. Why don't you admit you've got a crush on her?"

"I don't know what you're talking about," Alex said, toweling his forehead as they entered the locker room and turning his face away so as to hide any tell-tale sign that Steve was right.

"The more you deny it, the more I can tell you're lying," Steve persisted. "Admit it. You've got a thing for Chloe."

"Do not." Alex opened his locker, feeling like he was in the hallway at middle school, denying that he "liked" some girl in their class. "And have you forgotten? I have a girlfriend."

"Man, you and Veronica have been phoning it in for months now," Steve said, stripping off his workout clothes. "How many times have you bitched to me that you never see each other because she works so much? Why don't you break it off before she does? It's always better to be the dump-*er*, rather than the dump-*ee*."

"Hey, not all of us can be the perfect couple like you and Pam."

"You know why me and Pam never fight? Because she knows her place. You need to find a woman who doesn't have some big ambition and just wants to get married and have babies, like Pam." Steve closed his locker and wrapped a towel around his waist. "That's why you need to forget about this thing you have for Chloe. If you actually got close to her, it would just be trading in one career-obsessed woman for another." He grinned facetiously, adding, "But of course, there's no chance in hell that a totally hot supermodel is going to get with your broke ass."

Alex pulled his T-shirt over his head and flung it at Steve.

"Keep your sweaty-ass clothes away from me," Steve said, dodging.

"If you don't shut up, the next time it's going to be my jockstrap."

73

Chloe excitedly strode into Q Bar, the popular Manhattan gathering place, for her monthly happy hour with Daniella and Muriel. She smiled at the sight of the always-prompt, super-organized Muriel sipping a margarita at their favorite table.

"It's so good to see you!" Muriel jumped up to hug Chloe.

"You, too. I see we beat Dan here as usual."

Chloe took a seat, ordered a martini and quizzed Muriel about her latest big case. These evenings with the girls had become a much-needed ritual in which the former roommates unwound from the stress of their demanding careers and brought each other up to speed on their personal lives. With Muriel based in D.C. and Daniella in Boston, they would sometimes alternate cities, but New York was usually the destination city since Daniella and Muriel's work often brought them back to the Big Apple.

"I wonder if Ms. Webster's still planning to make an appearance this evening," Muriel said after a half-hour, lifting the cuff of her designer suit and glancing at her watch.

"Court must have run long again," Chloe said, sipping her martini.

They had finished their first round of drinks when Daniella finally arrived, turning heads in her tailored suit and perfectly coiffed blond hair. Rather than an overworked attorney, Daniella looked like she should be strolling the runways with Chloe.

"Sorry I'm late, guys," Daniella said, placing her attaché case under the table and sliding in next to Chloe. "Jury selection just began in the SorCom case and I'm the lead attorney."

"You're representing that huge telecommunications conglomerate? I'm pretty impressed that the big dogs at the firm are letting you handle that one," Muriel said. "That's a pretty high-profile case. They must have a lot of faith in you."

Daniella shrugged. "I guess. I have my reservations about representing this big corporation. It's a class-action suit by several former employees who leaked information that the company was inflating its earnings. But, I figure I'll pay my dues by taking the lead on this case, make partner and start taking on cases that can make a difference – working with people who have actually been wrongly accused and can't afford a lawyer, unlike these fat cats."

"Sounds like you've got it all figured out," Muriel said, sipping her drink.

"That's my strategy," Daniella said.

"What can I get you, ma'am?" a young waiter said to Daniella, approaching the table.

Chloe and Muriel looked at each other and giggled as the waiter eyed Daniella as if she were a delicious new appetizer that had been added to the menu.

"This round's on me, girls. After the long day I've had, I could use a stiff one," Daniella said, her unintentional double-entendre causing the waiter to turn bright red.

Alex stood in his cramped kitchen, stirring a pot. The étouffée was almost ready, and the delectable shellfish-and-rice dish had filled his shoebox of a studio apartment with Cajun spices that reminded him of home.

He heard the front door open and close just as the oven timer went off.

"Right on time," he called out, hearing his girlfriend's Jimmy Choo heels click-click-clacking across the hardwood floor. He ventured out of the kitchen, into the front room, still wearing his "Kiss the Cook" apron. "Are you ready to take a trip to the French Quarter – through your taste buds, at least?"

"I wasn't listening. What did you say?" Veronica, dressed in a black Marc Jacobs suit and carrying her ever-present briefcase, stared at him as if he were an intruder in his own place. Even after a long day at work, she looked beautiful. Not a strand of her dark brown, shoulder-length hair was out of place and her smooth, peach-colored skin was flawless.

"I'm cooking Creole food. Can't you smell?" He scooped up a spoonful of the étouffée for her to sample. "Here, taste."

"Maybe later." She pulled a magazine from her briefcase. "When did you do this?" She held up the magazine, revealing that it was *Newsline*, Alex's employer, and flipped open to the article he'd written on Chloe.

"Earlier this week. Why?" He felt sweat beading on his forehead, not so much from the heat his spicy cooking was generating, but from the abrupt change of subject. He wondered if somehow, through woman's intuition, Veronica sensed his attraction to Chloe.

"I wish you'd told me about it. I've been trying to land the Laurel Cosmetics account for months."

Alex wiped his forehead with a paper towel, relaxing. He should have known Veronica's interest in the piece he'd written on Chloe was business-related. With Veronica lately, the higher she climbed in her advertising career, everything was all business.

"Their new deal with Chloe is a prime opportunity to try to get some of their advertising dollars," Veronica continued as Alex went back to putting the finishing touches on dinner. "Who's your contact at the company?"

"I can put you in touch with their PR and marketing guy. I think I still have his card in my wallet."

"Could you get it for me, please?"

Alex looked at her, baffled. "I'm in the middle of finishing dinner. Can't it wait?"

"Not really. Why don't you get it now so you don't forget?"

Recognizing that "won't-take-no-for-an-answer" tone, he dashed back to the kitchen to turn down the heat on the stove. Retrieving his wallet from the front room, he reflected that their relationship was starting to seem like a business arrangement. She was always pestering him to do stories and generate free publicity for her advertising clients. And in their increasingly rare moments alone, they seemed to spend less and less time talking about non-work-related subjects.

"Here you go," he said, handing her the business card. "Now, enough about work. Dinner's almost ready." He took her hand and began leading her to the dinette he had set up to look like an intimate Bourbon Street bistro.

"Uh, Alex, I didn't come over to eat." She wrested her hand away.

"What are you talking about? We planned this evening three weeks ago. What's the point of us synchronizing our schedules and making dates if you're only going to keep breaking them?"

"I really don't need this grief, okay? You know I have to fly to Atlanta in the morning to pitch the new campaign to our most important client."

Alex put his hands on his hips, knowing he looked like a pouty spouse who'd been slaving over a hot stove for an unappreciative mate. He was tired of coming in second to his girlfriend's ambitions.

Ironically, Veronica's drive is what had attracted him to her when they met at NYU. Even back then, she had shown signs of being a multi-tasking, "Type A" personality. But she'd always made time for him between sorority fundraisers, student council activities and meetings of the Young Marketers of America.

But since landing the job at top Madison Avenue firm F&W after graduation, Veronica's sorority-girl pluck had morphed into ruthless ambition. Maybe she felt she had to overcompensate because she was the only young African-American woman at the firm, but the bigger the accounts she landed, the more she seemed to become obsessed with success at any cost.

"I can't believe this, Ronnie," he said. "I can't believe you're doing this again."

"Doing what again, Alex?" she said, sounding like a flustered teacher who had wearied of a pupil who couldn't grasp a simple concept.

"Bowing out on me again. Bowing out on *us* again."

"Actually, that's why I came over." She slipped the business card in her briefcase, shutting it with an efficient click. "We both need to face the fact that

479

this isn't working anymore."

He stood in place, not knowing how to respond. He was taken off-guard, hearing her verbalize the words he'd anticipated for weeks. Although he'd sensed a split coming on, it hurt that she was so cavalier about it, as if their relationship was something she could simply cast off like a pair of designer heels that were no longer in season.

"So this is it? We're breaking up?" Alex said. "It's not even worth another try? What have we been doing for the past three years?"

"I'll tell you what we've been doing: fooling ourselves," she said. "I'm tired of being made to feel guilty for working hard and trying to get ahead."

"That's not fair, Veronica," Alex said, knowing his face reflected his hurt. "I've always supported your career. I just want to feel that I'm a priority, too."

"Well maybe if you spent more time focusing on your own career, you'd be further ahead," she said, her expression devoid of emotion. "Quite frankly, I'm tired of picking up the check every time we go out because you want to play the struggling writer role."

Alex stared at this woman he no longer recognized as the one he'd fallen in love with. "I'm not playing a role. Writing is my passion. And I've told you, everything's going to change once I establish myself at the magazine and finish my book."

"You've been struggling to finish that book ever since college. Why don't you just give it up? Even if you do finish, do you know what the odds are of getting published? Face it, Alex, it's a pipedream."

"Thanks for believing in me, Ronnie," he said, poking his lip out like a little boy whose mother had snubbed his finger painting.

"I don't know why you insist on working for slave wages at the magazine while you harbor these dreams of being a best-selling author. How many times have I told you that you can make more money writing advertising copy?"

"I have no desire to go into advertising. I don't want to sell my soul." He paused, returning Veronica's cold stare. "But apparently you already have."

She didn't immediately respond, her dark eyes registering shock, and for a second it seemed as though he had pierced her armor.

"Let's not do this, Alex," she said after a moment, her tone businesslike again. "I'm going back to my place to finish packing for my trip. While I'm out of town, I'd appreciate it if you'd gather up all the stuff I've left over here. When I get back, I'll send for my things."

"'I'll send for my things'? You couldn't come up with something more original?" He shook his head, laughing sardonically. "You know, this is just like you. Now that you got what you want from me – that contact at Laurel Cosmetics – you're just going to leave?"

Veronica swiveled on her heels and began walking toward the door, as if answering his question. "Goodbye, Alex."

With that, she whisked into her Lexus and out of his life.

Laughter and distilled spirits flowed as Chloe, Daniella and Muriel caught up.

"My trainer, Marcella, would kill me if she knew I was eating like this," Chloe said, spearing a mozzarella stick from an appetizer platter.

"Oh, live a little," Daniella said, sipping the foam off her second mug of Bud Light. "We deserve to cut loose every now and then, considering how many hours we all work."

"Speaking of which," Muriel said, "I just took on a big domestic violence case here in New York. We're prosecuting this scumbag in Queens who was arrested several times for beating his wife. She later turned up dead. When the police found his wife's body, he fled and became federal fugitive, which is how the Justice Department got involved. I've been working a lot with the office of Representative Ernestine Bates, who sponsored a bill enacting longer jail terms for repeat domestic violence offenders."

"Representative Bates' office, huh?" Daniella said, sounding as though she was interrogating a witness who wasn't being entirely forthcoming. "Isn't that where one Miles Neal is chief of staff?"

"This is the first I've heard of Miles," Chloe said.

"I told you about him," Muriel said, looking down shyly and picking at her quesadilla.

"He's the new guy," Daniella explained. "She kicked the buppie bank executive to the curb."

Muriel elbowed her. "And what about you, missy? You and Darby seem to be getting pretty serious."

"He's the IT director at your firm, right?" Chloe said.

"Yeah. We started talking one day when my computer crashed. He came over to fix it and asked me out. I like the fact that he's not uptight like the other 'suits' at the firm. He wears cargo pants and flip-flops to work." Daniella took a swig of her beer, hiccupped and giggled. "He's a tech geek, but he's cute!"

"And what about you, Chloe?" Muriel said. "You still seeing what's-his-name – Julio, the Latin singer?"

"Sergio. And no, we broke up."

"I'm sorry to hear that," Muriel said, touching Chloe's hand.

"It was for the best. We both work so much that we hardly ever saw each other."

"I know what you mean," Daniella interjected. "If I wasn't dating someone at the office, I'd never have time for a social life."

"It'll pay off when you meet your goal of making partner before you turn thirty," Muriel said.

Daniella twirled her mug, looking down thoughtfully. "I hope you're right. Taking on this big case has me wondering if I'm doing what I'm 'supposed' to be doing with my life."

"I've been feeling the same way," Chloe said. "I just renewed my contract with Laurel and they made me their exclusive spokesmodel."

"That's wonderful, Chloe," said Muriel, raising her margarita glass in salute. "That's a really big accomplishment, especially for a woman of color."

"Thanks. Laurel's a great company and all…"

"I sense a 'but' coming on," Daniella said.

"The 'but' is modeling has afforded me a lot of great opportunities, but I set out to become an *actress* when I came to New York."

"If you want to act, you have to go after it," Muriel said. "My schedule's just as demanding as both of yours, but I *make* the time to do things that make my work more fulfilling, like raising money for the bar association's scholarship fund and tutoring kids at inner-city schools."

"That's not a fair comparison," Daniella said. "You're probably the most organized person on Earth. When we were in school, you always had your papers done weeks ahead of time. I always suspected you're part robot." Daniella pretended to look for an on/off switch on Muriel's back.

"Very funny," Muriel said, swatting Daniella's hand away. "I'm just saying you have to prioritize. I'd never get to know Miles if I didn't *make* time."

"We should probably lay off the relationship stuff," Daniella said, "since Chloe just went through a breakup."

"It's okay," Chloe said. "I'm over it."

"If you're ready to start dating again, Miles has a fraternity brother in New York who's single," Muriel said.

"Thanks for the offer," Chloe said, "but I think I'm going to take some time to be by myself."

"So there's no one else you're interested in?" Daniella asked.

Chloe said nothing, which prompted further questioning from her well-meaning friends.

"There is someone, isn't there?" Daniella pressed. "Come on, out with it. I just got through grilling three dozen potential jurors. I have ways of making you talk."

Chloe swished the olive around in her drink, stalling, not sure if she should tell her friends about the handsome reporter at the press junket. "This is silly, but…"

"Come on," Muriel prodded. "We're your girls. You know whatever you say is going to go no further than the three of us. We practice client confidentiality for a living."

"Well, when I was doing the press junket announcing the new deal with Laurel," Chloe began slowly, "there was this reporter, this really cute guy."

"What's his name?" Daniella said, propping her elbow on the table and looking intrigued.

"Alex, I think. Anyway, when we were talking, I just sort of felt this… I don't know, connection."

Chloe saw Muriel give Daniella a quizzical look as if to say, "What do you make of this?"

"It's silly, I know," Chloe said.

"I don't think it's silly at all," Muriel said. "Both Daniella and I met the guys we're seeing through work. This is no different."

"So what gives?" Daniella said. "Did he ask you out? Or better yet, did you ask *him*?"

"No, we haven't spoken since the interview. He gave me his card, but I never worked up the nerve to call him." She speared the olive and took a bite. "But I can't stop thinking about him."

74

Chloe sat on a stool in her downstairs neighbor Dave's front-room studio while his orange marmalade cat, Oscar Wilde, mewed at her feet. She did her best to ignore the tickling sensation of the cat's tail brushing against her leg and hold still while Dave finished up the painting that would be auctioned off at the masquerade ball.

"I think that should do it," Dave said, adding one last brushstroke. "Sorry to make you sit for so long."

"I have to admit it's a lot different from print modeling where you're constantly moving and striking poses," she said, standing up and stretching to alleviate the stiffness in her neck and back.

"Hopefully the finished product's worth it. Wanna take a look?" He stepped aside, letting her examine the canvas.

Rather than a straightforward replica, Dave had added abstract flourishes to his portrait of Chloe. He used an array of colors and textures on each part of her face, like a mosaic.

"Dave, I love it."

"Really? You're not just saying that 'cause we're friends?"

"No. That's a really different interpretation – not what I expected at all. But I really like it."

"I hope you make a lot of money with it at the auction," he said, setting down his palette.

"I predict it'll be one of the most popular items. I bet you'll have offers pouring in once people see your work."

"I hope so. It'd be nice to finally be getting paid for what I love to do."

The front door swung open and Rick entered, his arms loaded with grocery bags. "Hey, you guys. The painting looks great."

Chloe nodded. "Dave did an awesome job, didn't he?"

"I knew the two of you would make a good team," Rick said, dropping his keys on the end table next to the front door. "You staying for dinner? I'm making my famous lasagna."

"I really shouldn't. I have a shoot in the morning, but what the hell?" she said, taking one of the grocery bags. "I can never say no to your lasagna."

"If you guys don't mind, I'm going to keep working while you two get dinner started," Dave said, unfolding a stepladder.

"What's that for?" Chloe asked.

"Whenever I finish a painting, I always hang it to see what it would look like in a gallery or a client's home. Sometimes I catch little details I need to touch up."

"Don't exert yourself too much, my little perfectionist," Rick said, kissing Dave on the cheek. "You know what the doctor said about overdoing it."

Chloe followed Rick into the kitchen and helped him unpack the bags. "I'm not much of a cook, but what can I do to help out?"

"Actually, I left a couple bags in the hallway outside, if you wouldn't mind getting them."

She retrieved the bags, leaving the door ajar as she headed toward the kitchen.

"I better shut the door before Oscar Wilde gets out," Dave said, stepping down from the ladder. Missing a step, the ladder wobbled and Dave tumbled to the floor.

At the sound of the crash, Rick came in from the kitchen and rushed to Dave's side. "You okay?" he asked, helping Dave sit up.

"Yeah, I'm all right, just hit this big noggin of mine." He rubbed his head. "Luckily, as Rick's always telling me, I'm hardheaded."

They laughed as the cat licked Dave's paint-speckled face. Chloe stopped laughing when she noticed a purplish bruise near his ankle, the cuffs of his coveralls having ridden up in the fall.

"Are you okay?" she said. "That bruise looks pretty nasty."

She watched Dave exchange a glance with Rick.

"It's not a bruise," Dave said, the usual cheerfulness suddenly drained from his voice. "It's a lesion. My T-cell count has been going down lately."

"Oh my god," she said, touching his hand in concern. "Maybe you should be resting."

"I'm okay," Dave said. "It's probably just from stress because I've been working on a couple other projects at the same time."

His insistence that he was all right was proven false when he tried to hoist himself up but fell back to the floor, looking too weak to stand.

"Why don't I get the sneaking suspicion you've been working so hard, you forgot to take your medicine?" Rick said, slinging Dave's arm over his shoulder. "Come on, babe. Chloe's right. You need to rest."

"No, really, I'm okay," Dave insisted. "I need to get back to work."

"That hard head of yours is going to get you in trouble," Rick said, mussing Dave's hair. "Why don't you take a nap before dinner?"

Dave relented and let Rick and Chloe help him down the hallway to the bedroom.

"Is there anything more I can do?" she said to Rick once they'd returned to the kitchen after helping Dave get settled in bed.

"Right now you can chop vegetables for the salad," he said, handing her a bushel of celery. "Dave needs to keep up his strength, and my lasagna is just what the doctor ordered."

Sidney Laveau aimed her pistol at the man. "Don't move or I'll shoot," she said, staring into the suspect's cold, lifeless eyes.

Alex sat at his ancient word processor, straining to tune out the sounds of the busy street filtering into his apartment through an open window. He had once again put his heroine in a bind that he couldn't write her out of. It had been a Sunday afternoon of nothing but literary dead ends.

He reclined in his chair, throwing a small rubber ball against the wall – a nervous habit he resorted to when writer's block set in – until his next-door neighbor banged on the wall.

"Sorry," Alex called out, getting up and pacing in an attempt to work out the plot kink.

Would the suspect run or lunge at Sidney, causing her to shoot him? But if she shot him this early, the suspect wouldn't be around to commit the double murder that Alex planned for Sidney to solve later in the book.

"What should I do, Jack?" Alex said, crouching next to his basset hound. The dog responded by scratching behind his ears and licking himself.

"Thanks for your interest, buddy," Alex said, chuckling and stroking the dog's back.

Alex sat back down at his keyboard, but the harder he strained to find a way to get the action going, the tighter a grip writer's block seemed to have. He couldn't get into Sidney's head, though she was his creation. He stared at the screen, the cursor blinking at him, as if mocking his stifled creativity like a schoolyard bully making fun of a kid who stuttered. Just as he was about to switch off the computer and call it a day, he recalled how Chloe's photo had helped him visualize his character when he was last working on the scene at the office.

He reached into his satchel and retrieved the Laurel Cosmetics press kit. Opening the folder, he again noticed the invitation to the masquerade ball, which was going on tonight and for which he'd never RSVP'd. He set the invitation aside and propped Chloe's glossy against the monitor. With her exotic beauty and Creole background, she was like the living embodiment of his character. With her photo as a visual aid, he began typing away with renewed gusto.

"That's it!" he exclaimed, getting a sudden inspiration. "I'll have Sidney shoot him, but he'll manage to escape, running away licking his wounds like a hunted animal."

He kissed his fingertips, touched Chloe's photo and began clicking away on his keyboard again, thinking out loud. "Of course, the scumbag will leave a trail of blood that Sidney will collect as evidence and later use to nail his hide." He looked over at his dog. "I'm brilliant, aren't I?"

The dog looked uninterested and retreated to his corner, where a dish of his favorite vittles awaited.

"Don't worry," Alex said, "when I get done with this masterpiece, we'll both be eating filet mignon."

The sounds of a couple arguing at full volume on the sidewalk below his window pierced the muggy late-September air, but all Alex could hear was his character shooting at the bad guy. He typed furiously, trying to get the words down as fast as they came. He was finally "in the zone."

Just as he was wrapping up the scene, the blinking cursor suddenly disappeared, along with the words he'd worked so hard to get down. He tapped the monitor lightly, but the screen remained blank. He tapped again, then pounded on the machine.

"Goddamn it!" he shouted, loud enough to temporarily silence the feuding couple outside.

They quickly resumed their shouting match, however. The racket of their raised voices mingled with wailing sirens matched the chaos Alex felt as he furiously plugged and unplugged his computer in a vain attempt to reboot it.

The sound of someone rapping on the door briefly interrupted his frenzied quest to retrieve his lost work.

"*What?*" he barked at the intruder without bothering to go to the door and see who it was.

Alex's buddy, Steve, let himself in. "What's with you?" Steve said as Alex frantically pressed the computer's power button.

"What does it look like, Einstein? My computer just crashed."

"You've had that old clunker since we were in college. I'm surprised it held out this long."

"It *would* wait until I was almost done with the chapter I was working on to zonk out on me." Alex slapped the monitor, as if chastising his unreliable old lab partner from college. "Damn. And I'm so close to being done with my book."

"You mean your 'great American novel'? The one you've been working for years? Man, why don't you just hang it up? This was probably a sign. I'll bet you fifty bucks you never finish it."

Alex threw a paper wad at Steve, who swerved and just missed being hit in the face. "You're on. I'll be glad to collect fifty bucks when I sign my first publishing contract. By the way, did you just drop by to make me feel worse?"

"No, I came by to see if you want to go get a beer. You don't need to be cooped up in here. You've been holing up since the breakup with Veronica. You need to get out and meet some new people."

Alex reached around to the back of the computer and began fiddling with the power chord while he considered what Steve was saying. As much as he hated to admit it, Steve was right. Despite the fact that Steve was totally left-brain-oriented and unable to relate to Alex's creative side, Alex knew his best friend was loyal and had his best interests at heart.

"As much as I'd like to get out," Alex said finally, "I'm having an issue here I need to deal with."

"Oh, I see what the real issue is." Steve spotted Chloe's photo and snatched it from Alex's desk. "You wanna stay here and fantasize about your imaginary supermodel girlfriend." He waved the photo the way Alex dangled treats to get his dog to stand on his hind legs.

"I was not *fantasizing* about her." Alex tried to snatch the photo back, but Steve put it behind his back. "Come on, man, grow up." He reached behind Steve, grabbed the photo and placed it back on his desk. "Chloe reminds me of my main character, so I was just using her photo to help me visualize while I was writing."

"Yeah," Steve said, grinning, "and I read *Playboy* for the articles."

"Look, I got enough shit to deal with right now without you coming in here and pestering me." Alex, his nerves already frazzled, grew more irritated by the second with Steve's intrusion. "Will you kindly get lost? I need to get some work done."

"No, what you *need* to do is stop sitting around here daydreaming about that Chloe chick and actually call her and kick some game."

"And just how am I supposed to that, with a dozen people keeping me from getting to her?"

"You're a smart guy. Figure it out."

Steve let himself out, finally leaving Alex to get back to trying to reboot the computer. Alex alternately banged on it and begged it to spring back to life. When the phone rang, he let the machine pick up, not wanting to deal with any further interruptions. He immediately recognized his father's familiar baritone.

"Hey, son, I know you're probably working on your book. Sorry to disturb you, but I just thought I'd call and check in and let you know we all miss you down here."

As Robert Michaud spoke, Alex could hear the unmistakable sounds of the year-round Bourbon Street festivities in the background.

"I'm about to go onstage at the 317 Club with my band. Don't worry, I won't be out too late. Your mother made me promise I'd be home in time to get up and teach my class at Xavier in the morning, like usual."

Robert Michaud's voice was drowned out by the partiers crowding Bourbon Street. Alex sat back on his haunches, taking in the sounds of laughter and music. He made a mental note to call his father back later on, after the computer was hopefully back up and running.

"Well, I better get back inside the club," Alex's father continued. "The band's taking their places onstage."

Alex heard his father turn to someone in the background and say that he just needed another minute and he'd join the rest of the band.

"They've already started warming up, but they can't start without the trumpet player, right?" Alex's father said. "I better go, but I wanted to leave you with a little piece of home. Can't wait 'til you make it down here again. Love you."

It sounded like Robert Michaud set his cell phone down and began piping out "When the Saints Go Marching In" on his trumpet. Alex stopped messing around with his computer and listened to his father's playing, which combined with the merriment in the background to make Alex feel thoroughly homesick.

With the festive sounds of the French Quarter filling his apartment, Alex picked up the invitation to the Laurel Cosmetics masquerade ball, studied the Mardi Gras mask on the cover, and stepped away from his computer.

75

Chloe, her hair styled in a period pompadour, stood before a full-length mirror in Maxine's plush suite at the Waldorf. Maxine stood behind her, lacing up the corset that Chloe was to wear underneath the elaborate gown that was to be her costume at the masquerade ball later that evening.

"Do me a favor, *ma chérie*, and inhale so I can get the corset a little tighter," Maxine said, tugging on the strings.

"If I inhale any deeper," Chloe said, "I'm going to break a rib."

Maxine kept tugging until she was able to tie the corset strings. "There. Got it."

Chloe slouched. "*Ugh.* I feel like a stuffed sausage." She tugged at the restricting garment. "I can't believe women use to go through this cruel ritual every day. When you made this dress, were you trying to punish me for all the things I did that drove you crazy when I was a kid?"

Maxine, in a lacy dressing gown, laughed. She stood behind Chloe, propping her chin on her daughter's shoulder. "The two of us standing here reminds me of a portrait Mama had when I was growing up. It was of a woman in New Orleans preparing her daughter to go to one of the quadroon balls in the French Quarter."

"I think I remember that portrait. That's the one Mama Louise passed on to you when she died, right?"

Maxine looked wistful. "Yeah," she said, wrapping her arms around Chloe's waist.

Chloe could sense Mother getting emotional and quickly changed the subject. "What went on at those quadroon balls, anyway?"

"Well, parents of beautiful Creole girls would dress their daughters up in their finest so that they would catch the eye of wealthy French landowners."

Chloe shuddered. "I hate to think of parents pimping their daughters out like that."

Maxine laughed. "Hey, while we're on the topic of 'pimping out,' as you put it," she said, letting go of Chloe's waist. "Thanks for setting me up on that date for the ball. I talked to Reginald a couple of times over the phone and he seems nice."

"Good. I'm so glad you decided to come. I think you'll enjoy yourself."

Maxine smiled. "I think so, too. It's about time I stopped moping around and got on with my life." She went to the dresser and unzipped her cosmetics bag. "I better finish getting ready. Reginald's picking me up in an hour."

"Enough of this standing around," Chloe said, making a shooing motion at Maxine. "We've got to make you gorgeous."

"What about you?" Maxine said, applying makeup in the mirror above the dresser. "Who's your date?"

Chloe busied herself fluffing her gown on its hanger, attempting to sound unconcerned. "I don't have a date. I'm going stag."

Maxine put down her makeup brush and looked at Chloe. "What? After all that fuss you made about fixing me up? Simone and Gigi are coming and they're both bringing their boyfriends. You mean to tell me you're going to be the only one at your own event without a date?"

Chloe held her hands up in a gesture of surrender. "The tabloids already have me linked with a variety of actors and musicians I've never even met. So, for the time being, it's probably best that I play it cool and not give the paparazzi any more fodder."

Maxine gave Chloe a disbelieving scowl. "That sounds like a convenient excuse, especially since you were just chastising me about how I need to get out and meet people and stop being such a workaholic."

Chloe took her gown off the rack, attempting to divert Maxine to another, less intrusive subject. "I don't have time to go into this right now, Mother. Would you please help me finish getting dressed? The limo will be here any minute."

"I think this is the first gown I've made for you since your deb ball," Maxine said, helping Chloe pull the gown over her head and smooth the curls of her pompadour.

"It's beautiful," Chloe said, admiring the lavender silk ball gown edged with white lace.

Maxine saw a thread hanging and, being a perpetual perfectionist, couldn't resist retrieving her sewing kit and snipping here and there with miniature scissors.

Chloe topped off the look with her grandmother's wedding ring.

"Maybe you shouldn't wear this," Maxine said, holding up Chloe's bejeweled hand as they stood before the mirror. "Single men at the ball might think you're taken."

"Will you stop trying to marry me off? We've already been down that road," Chloe said, laughing.

"I don't mean to meddle. I know you fixed me up with Reginald because you want me to be happy and you don't want me to spend the rest of my life alone," Maxine said, taking hold of Chloe's shoulders. "I only want the same for you."

Chloe touched Maxine's hand appreciatively. "If there's anything you taught me, Mother, it's how to be independent."

*****

"My knight in shining armor!" Chloe exclaimed when Rick, in a knight's costume, made his entrance to the ball. She stood in the doorway of the Four Seasons Ballroom, playing hostess and greeting guests as they arrived.

"You want to see some card tricks I learned?" said Dave, who was dressed as a court jester.

"Not right now," said Chloe. "Shut up and kiss me, you *fool!*" She chortled at her own pun and gave her friends a big hug.

"Where's your mask?" Rick asked Chloe.

She produced a mask embroidered with lavender and white lace, matching her dress, and held it to her face.

"Ah. Very mysterious. My costume came with its own mask," said Rick, lowering the faceguard. "The fool here needs one," he added, gesturing toward Dave.

"They're passing out masks over at the bar. Help yourselves."

Chloe directed Rick and Dave into the ballroom, which, in keeping with the Mardi Gras theme, was festooned with colorful decorations representing Carnival celebrations around the world. Cirque du Soleil acrobats twirled on silk scarves suspended from the ceiling, jugglers and fire-eaters wowed partygoers with tricks and feats, and mimes drew laughs from even the most serious guests as a DJ spun contemporary dance music.

"I couldn't have planned a better event myself, *ma chérie*," Maxine said when she arrived, looking glamorous as ever in a black lace ball gown.

Chloe hugged her. "Hi, Mother." She was pleased to see Maxine on the arm of Reginald Baker, the African-American investment banker Chloe had fixed her up with.

"I think it's a great way to celebrate Mardi Gras a few months early," said Reginald, dapper in an Armani tux. "I've been to New Orleans on business a few times, but never during the big celebration. I told Maxine I want to visit some time and have her show me around."

Chloe noticed Maxine tense at the mention of her hometown.

"I'm parched," Maxine said to Reginald, abruptly changing the subject. "Would you mind getting me some punch?"

"Sure I can't interest you in something stronger?" he replied in a mischievous tone.

Maxine batted her eyes and fanned herself with a fan made of black feathers and lace. "Why, M'sieu Baker," she cooed, affecting the demeanor of the shy Creole girl she once was, "I do declare you're trying to get me tipsy!"

"Can't blame a guy for trying. Chloe, can I get you anything?"

"A white wine spritzer would be nice."

"Coming right up," he said, retreating to the bar.

Watching Reginald walk away, Chloe surmised that although there seemed to be chemistry between him and Maxine, he would probably soon be history, just like all the other men that her mother insisted couldn't compare to Jacques.

"Thank you for setting me up, *ma chérie*," Maxine said. "I admit, I was reluctant at first, but it feels good to get out."

"Doesn't it, though?" Simone said, making her entrance. She looked every bit the 1920s flapper in a silver beaded gown with spaghetti straps and long strings of pearls dangling almost to her knees. Her flame-red hair was pinned up in the back and styled into slick, lush waves. A Superman curl was plastered to her forehead, underneath a sequined headband adorned with a feather.

Chloe hugged Simone and accepted a kiss on either cheek from Simone's companion, Armand Delicourt, who looked like a Prohibition-era millionaire in a natty tuxedo.

"Don't tell me Marie chickened out and refused to fly?" Chloe said, peering around Simone, but not seeing any sign of Marie.

"I'm right here, *chouchou*."

Chloe nearly fell over when she finally recognized Marie standing behind Simone in a cleavage-baring, black-and-gold ball gown and matching mask. Her usual chignon had been replaced by a sleek wrap.

"My god, Marie! You look amazing!" Chloe declared. "That's some dress."

"I told her the exact same thing," said Bernard, the Chateau de Chevalier's groundskeeper who was dressed like an old-time chimney sweeper. He stared at Marie's décolletage with a mischievous grin.

"Now, Bernard, you behave yourself," Marie said, swatting him with an ornate fan that matched her outfit.

"I'm so glad you came." Chloe embraced Marie and ushered her inside along with Bernard, Simone and Armand.

Chloe returned to the door in time to see Gigi entering with her date, Philippe, the handsome emergency-room doctor.

"Philippe had to get someone to cover his shift at the hospital," Gigi explained, "and he has to fly right back after the party."

"Thanks for coming all this way," Chloe said, glad to see Gigi looking so happy on his arm.

"It's totally worth it," Philippe said. "I work double shifts a lot and I don't get to go to many parties, especially ones as fancy as this."

Gigi motioned toward the bar. "Philippe, why don't you go get us something to drink?"

"*Tres bien*."

When Philippe was out of earshot, Chloe turned to Gigi and said, "He seems really nice."

Gigi nodded. "Yeah. I did pretty good this time." She paused, looking around. "So, where's your date?"

"I don't have one, but I'm doing just fine. Now go get your man before someone else snaps him up and stop worrying about me."

As the night wore on, Chloe circulated and chatted up guests. Sprinkled among the celebrities, New York socialites, Laurel Cosmetics higher-ups and other VIPs from the corporate world were important people from the various stages of Chloe's life. Warren and Barbara Rubinstein showed up looking like a turn-of-the-century couple out for a day at the races, with Warren in a top hat, three-piece suit and long black cape and Barbara carrying a parasol and wearing a ball gown with a bustle and a vintage chapeau with a huge brim covered in artificial flowers.

Chloe's former roommates from Epitome came dressed in costumes that reflected their distinct personalities: Brandi as a Scarlet O'Hara-style Southern belle, accompanied by her rodeo-star hubby in his ten-gallon hat, bolo tie, chaps and cowboy boots; Ayana as Cleopatra, complemented by her reggae-star companion as Antony, and Graciela as a Spanish *contessa* and her Mexican bullfighter boyfriend in his toreador regalia. Arriving "fashionably late," as always, was Roxy as, well, Roxy in a sheer mini-dress, on the arm of her actor beau in casual-chic blazer, T-shirt emblazoned with the Rolling Stones' iconic tongue emblem, jeans and movie-star shades.

"We don't *do* costumes," Roxy explained, and Chloe shared a laugh with the other girls at their former roommate's "I'm-too-cool-for-all-this" attitude. Roxy hadn't changed in all these years.

Daniella and Muriel arrived together, in feathered masks and couture gowns, and introduced Chloe to their respective boyfriends.

"Let me guess, *Animal House*?" Chloe said to Daniella's boyfriend, Darby Payne, who was clad in a toga that showed off his toned upper body and hairy legs.

"Totally," Darby replied, sticking out his tongue and raising his hand in a three-finger salute like a college football fan preening for the camera at a stadium.

"I swear, I'm dating an overgrown frat boy," Daniella said in mock disgust.

"I like your costume, too, Miles," Chloe said to Muriel's boyfriend, who was dressed like a pharaoh.

"I picked it out," Muriel said with a grin.

"I wanted something with an Africentric touch," Miles said, clasping Muriel's hand, "and who better than King Tut?"

"Thanks so much for coming," Chloe said to the group, showing them to their table. "It really means a lot to have you guys here."

Just when Chloe thought she had greeted everyone she knew, she looked up and saw Christy Taylor, her former cohort from her days working at the fashion design school, being escorted in by a rising hip-hop star.

"Christy! It's been ages!" Chloe threw her arms around her friend, whom she hadn't seen in months despite mutual efforts to stay in touch.

"I know," Christy said. "We have to get together for one of our lunch dates."

Chloe twirled Christy around, checking out her costume, which consisted of a navy blue, short-sleeved blouse and red, knee-length wrap skirt. "I bet you made this yourself."

"Of course I did. Can you guess who I am?" Christy said, patting the close-cropped black wig she was wearing.

"Dorothy Dandridge in *Carmen Jones*," Chloe said, immediately recognizing the classic character. "I remember when we went and saw that at that old revival house." She turned to Christy's date and offered her hand. "Pleased to meet you. I'm Chloe."

"I'm sorry. Where are my manners?" Christy spoke up. "Chloe, this is Darius Andrews, aka MC-D. He's a rapper and we met at the BET Awards in L.A. last year. He performed and I styled a couple of the presenters."

"You always were into always into hip-hop," Chloe said to Christy, shaking her date's hand and commenting on the basketball uniform he was wearing.

"So many NBA stars are putting out rap albums, I thought I'd try stepping into their shoes," he said, shooting an imaginary basket.

"Baby, will you get us some Cristal?" Christy said, touching his tattooed forearm.

"Ya know it," he said with a wide grin. "That's the ballers' beverage of choice."

While MC-D reported to the bar to retrieve a bottle of the bubbly he often touted in his rhymes, Chloe caught up with Christy.

"Have you been doing any costume design?" Chloe asked.

"I've done some freelance work for a couple of daytime soaps and sent some sketches to a few production companies, but nothing major yet. My day job at Adriano Ferraro keeps me pretty busy. How about you? You doing any acting?"

"Not yet. I'm still waiting for the right part to come along."

When her date returned with the champagne, Christy raised her glass. "Someday we'll be toasting our first big movie project together, with me as the costume designer and you as the star."

Chloe tipped her glass. "I'll drink to that."

76

"I'm sorry, Mr. Michaud, you're not on the guest list."

"But you were there when I interviewed Chloe. Don't you remember the piece on Laurel Cosmetics I did for the magazine I work for, *Newsline*?"

Alex stood at the entrance of the ballroom, having been intercepted by Bill Bosworth, Laurel's pushy PR guru. Alex remembered him being just as overbearing during the press junket a few weeks ago as he was now.

"You're the one who invited me to this event, remember?" Alex reasoned, tugging at the itchy collar of the costume he'd rented from the all-night costume shop in Times Square. In the black greatcoat, white ruffled shirt, black slacks and riding boots, he resembled one of the nineteenth-century *gens du couleur libre* (free men of color) he'd heard so much about growing up in New Orleans. He lifted the Mardi Gras mask that topped off the outfit, hoping Bosworth would recognize him and let him in.

"If you'd RSVP'd, you'd be on the guest list. The RSVP deadline was clearly printed on the invitation. As a reporter, you're familiar with deadlines, aren't you?"

Alex gnashed his teeth to keep from slugging the guy. "Yes, I'm familiar with deadlines," he said in a measured tone, straining to keep his temper in check. "And, no, I didn't RSVP, but I figured you'd let it slide since I gave your company free publicity."

"I'm sorry. I have strict instructions not to admit anyone who's not on the list," Bosworth said, closing his guestbook with a gesture of finality.

Alex shook his head. These marketing types were all the same. Once you'd served their purposes, they had no more use for you.

"I understand I'm not on the list. But are you sure you can't let me in with a press pass?" Alex said, holding up the laminated ID he used to gain access to events with tight security.

"Like I said, Mr. Michaud, I have strict instructions –"

"What's going on here?"

A beautiful woman appeared in the doorway next to Bosworth. She looked like she could be Creole or mixed-race like Chloe, except that she was fairer, shorter and bustier.

"I'm trying to explain to this reporter than I can't let anyone in who –"

"Alex Michaud?" the woman said, reading the name on Alex's press ID. "Aren't you the one who wrote the story on Chloe for *Newsline*?"

"Yes," Alex said, looking beyond the woman's mask, into her black eyes.

"*Enchanté*. I'm Chloe's friend, Gigi Cartier." She reached out and grabbed Alex's hand, pulling him past Bosworth.

"Ms. Cartier, he's not on the list," Bosworth sputtered. "I can't let you –"

"Chill out," she said, leading Alex through the doorway, into the ballroom. "He's with me."

Chloe stood next to Max Laurel at the podium on the small stage that had been erected next to the dance floor.

"Sorry to interrupt the music," Max said, tapping on the microphone, "but could I have your attention for just a moment?"

The DJ faded out the song that was playing, causing the revelers to stop gyrating and face Max.

"This is a fun evening, but as you all know, the purpose of this event is to raise money for charity," he said into the microphone. "I hope you've all had a chance to bid on the items in the silent auction. And now for the live auction portion of the evening, with all the proceeds going to AIDS research."

Max played the part of auctioneer, needling his moneyed friends and associates to bid high on an assortment of donated items, from jewelry to vacation packages.

"And now for the *pièce de résistance*." Max snapped his finger and an assistant brought out an easel draped with a lavender velvet sheet. "Chloe, would you do the honors?"

Like a game-show model, she pulled the sheet off the canvas with a flourish. The crowd gasped as Dave's abstract portrait of Chloe was revealed. Chloe spotted her neighbor in the crowd and smiled at him, and he beamed with pride.

"We'll start the bidding on this item at twelve thousand," Max said.

The crowd immediately began raising their hands and shouting out bids. Chloe kept the mood light during the feverish bidding by continuing the game-show routine, walking around the painting and gesturing toward it like Vanna White turning letters. When the bidding reached nineteen thousand dollars, she shot Dave a look that said, "Good work." Rick's grin was even broader than Dave's, as if he couldn't be prouder of his partner.

"We have nineteen thousand going once, going twice…" Max said, peering around the crowd.

"Twenty thousand!"

Chloe looked out and saw Rick raising his hand, his arm constricted by the knight's costume. She glanced at Dave and mouthed the words, "What's he doing?" Dave shrugged and tried to pull Rick's arm down, but Rick resisted

496

and kept his hand raised.

"Twenty thousand going once… twice… Sold, to the gentleman in the suit of armor!" Max pounded his gavel and the crowd erupted in applause.

Chloe stepped down from the podium and approached Rick and Dave, eager to find out what prompted Rick's sudden burst of generosity.

"Hey, where'd all the men go?" Gigi asked when she returned to the table that she had staked out along with Simone, Maxine, Marie and their respective escorts.

"They're at the buffet table, where else?" Maxine said.

"And speaking of men," Simone piped up, "who was that handsome young man I just saw you with?"

"He's an acquaintance of Chloe's." Gigi picked up her champagne glass and swirled it, the sparkling bubbly matching the gleam in her eyes. "And if I have anything to do with it, before the evening's over, he'll be more than an acquaintance."

"Uh-oh. I know that look in your eyes, and it always means you're plotting something." Simone snatched Maxine's fan and waved it at herself, as if having a hot flash. "Please don't tell me you've reverted to your old ways. I don't think I can take it."

"Neither can I," Marie chimed in. "That summer you two snuck away to Monaco, I almost had a heart attack." She illustrated her point by pressing her hand to her heaving bosom.

"Relax, ladies," Gigi said, eyeing Alex at the bar, and then averting her gaze to Chloe, who was talking to Rick and Dave on the other side of the room. "This time I have something good in mind. And all of you are part of my plan."

"What gives?" Chloe said, thumping Rick's suit of armor. "The whole point of having the painting in the auction was to get Dave some exposure."

"And with all these important people viewing his work, he got it," Rick said, as if offering a perfectly reasonable explanation.

"And just where are you going to get twenty grand, mister?" Dave said, putting his hands on his hips and sounding like a parent scolding a disobedient teenager for an indulgent purchase.

"I'll exercise some stock options. Plus, I have a big bonus coming at work for an IPO I just prepared for one of the big money-grubbing corporations we work with," Rick said, taking off his knight's helmet. "And I could think of no better way to spend it than on a talented, up-and-coming artist's portrait of a beautiful young woman."

"Keep talking," Chloe said with a laugh, welcoming Rick's compliment.

"I actually would have used the word 'brilliant' in describing the up-and-coming artist," Dave said, affectionately knocking Rick upside the chain-mail coif that was underneath the mask. "The painting *is* a masterpiece, if I do say so myself, but that's a lot of money to plunk down. Why not let one of these Rockefellers buy my painting?"

"The money's going to a good cause." Rick paused, cradling his helmet and looking sheepish. "And I just couldn't bear the thought of some stranger taking possession of a work of art that involved two of the most important people in my life."

Dave pecked Rick on the cheek. "I knew there was a reason I keep you around."

"I say we toast each other," Chloe said, beckoning over a waiter with a tray of champagne glasses. "The three of us make a great team –the artist, the model and the benefactor."

The threesome clinked glasses and when Dave took a sip, he stumbled backward and Rick scurried to hold him up.

"Hey, babe, maybe you've had a little too much to drink tonight," Rick said, helping Dave regain his footing. "Did you remember to take your medicine before we left?"

"Yeah, and maybe that's it. Champagne and protease inhibitors just don't mix," Dave said with a weak laugh, looking pale.

"Why don't we go find a seat, baby?" Rick took his arm. "You've had a lot of excitement for one night."

"I'll catch up with you guys later," Chloe called, watching Rick lead Dave to an empty table.

"Excuse me, ladies and gentleman, may I have your attention again?"

Chloe turned to see Max Laurel standing at the podium. She wrinkled her face in confusion when she saw Gigi at his side, whispering in his ear.

After conferring with Gigi for several moments, his hand cupped over the microphone, Max addressed the crowd again. "We have one more item up for bid. Chloe, would you please join me up here again?"

Chloe looked around, as if Max were speaking to someone else, then lifted her petticoats and made her way to the stage. "What have you gone and done this time, Gi'?" she said under her breath when she reached the stage.

"Just wait and see," Gigi said cryptically, exiting the stage with that all-too-familiar mischievous grin.

Max reached for Chloe's hand and pulled her to his side, and she looked at him quizzically.

"For this next bid, the lucky winner will get to have the first dance with the belle of our ball, Chloe."

An uproar arose from the crowd and Chloe did her best to keep smiling and hide her shock. She looked out over the crowd and spotted Gigi, who had a satisfied expression, confirming that this shenanigan was her handiwork.

"Since this item wasn't listed in your program," Max said, picking up his gavel, "I'll let the bidders set the starting price."

The crowd broke into murmurs, as if deciding on appropriate bids.

"Don't everyone jump in at once," Chloe said into the microphone, laughing in spite of herself.

"One thousand dollars," Gigi said, raising her hand.

Chloe saw Maxine nudge her date, Reginald.

"Fifteen hundred!" he shouted.

Simone prodded Armand, who bellowed, "Eighteen hundred" in his accent.

Apparently not wanting to look like a cad, Philippe sheepishly spoke up. "Eighteen-fifty."

Gigi gave him an annoyed look.

"*Pardonnez-moi!*" Chloe overheard him say to Gigi, shrugging. "You know I'm on a medical resident's salary. I'd have to skip my next student loan payment to make good."

Marie got into the fray, pinching Bernard, who yelled out a bid of two thousand. "I'll have to work a lot of overtime trimming hedges and tending the garden at the chateau to pay for the dance," he said.

"Our Chloe is worth it," Marie replied, adding her own bid of twenty-five hundred.

Before long, fierce bidding had broken out between partygoers of both sexes. Daniella, Muriel and their boyfriends took turns shouting out bids, as did Christy Taylor. MC-D, the hip-hop star who'd accompanied Christy, upped the ante by pushing the bid up to four grand and lifting up the platinum chain around his neck to prove he had the "bling" to back it up.

Warren and Barbara chimed in, as if to prove their top model was a sought-after commodity, and the other Epitome girls each contributed bids. Roxy and Graciela continued their rivalry by engaging in a shrieking contest of increasingly higher bids.

Watching the action from the stage, Chloe felt like one of those Creole girls who was being "pimped out" at the old quadroon balls that she and Maxine had talked about earlier. But it was all in good fun and she was glad the money would be put to good use.

"Looks like we're going to raise a lot of money for charity tonight," Max said in an aside to Chloe.

She had to admit the fierce competition for a spin around the floor with her was a self-esteem boost. "Feels good to be wanted."

When the bidding reached nine thousand, Max readied his gavel. "Nine thousand going once, going twice…" He scanned the crowd for more takers.

"Ten thousand!" someone shouted after several moments of silence. Murmurs again arose from the crowd.

Chloe looked up to see Gigi with her hand raised.

"What are you doing?" Chloe mouthed.

"Trust me," Gigi mouthed back.

Max repeated his auctioneer's mantra. "Ten thousand going once, twice…" After a few seconds passed with whispered mutterings from the crowd but no other offers, he pounded his gavel and declared, "Ten thousand it is!"

The crowd broke out in enthusiastic applause.

"Congratulations, ma-*dam*," Max said to Gigi. "You're the successful bidder. You'll have the pleasure of the first dance with Chloe."

"*Merci*," Gigi said, "but it's not for me, it's for my friend here."

Gigi stepped aside, and a spotlight shone on a tall, handsome black man standing at her side. Chloe squinted, thinking he looked familiar. He was wearing a mask and she couldn't discern his identity, but he looked as taken off-guard by Gigi's little stunt as Chloe was.

With the spotlight still shining on him, the man took a hesitant step toward the dance floor and a party entertainer dressed as a harlequin helped Chloe from the stage. Max signaled the DJ, who cued Prince's romantic ballad, "The Most Beautiful Girl in the World."

The crowd parted as the lights dimmed and the music filled the hall. Chloe, finding herself alone with the man on the dance floor, felt suddenly self-conscious. She considered calling the whole thing off, but the expectant crowd was watching and she felt too much pressure to turn back now. She put on her mask and swallowed, her mouth having gone dry.

The crowd formed a semicircle around the dance floor. To Chloe's relief, her dance partner made the first move. He put his arm around her waist, took her hand and began to slowly lead her around the floor. They seemed to anticipate each other's moves, his body hugging hers. Learning the minuet in Madame de Tornquist's charm school as a teen paid off after all. She imagined the old woman standing on the sidelines nodding approval, as she had done at Chloe's deb ball.

Making eye contact with her dance partner through the slits of their masks, she strained to remember where she knew him from.

"Are you as creeped out by everybody watching us as I am?" he said in an undertone, spinning her.

Hearing his voice jogged her memory and she finally recognized him as Alex Michaud, the reporter who'd been on her mind since their interview a few weeks earlier.

Before she could answer, the music faded and the crowd applauded. They had stopped moving, but Alex continued to look into her eyes. He took a step forward, and she sensed he was going to kiss her in a gentlemanly gesture to complete the dance.

Before he could come any closer, she stuck out her hand, muttered a quick "thanks for the dance," and bolted for the door.

77

The morning after the masquerade ball, Chloe had no time to stew over her act of cowardice with Alex – running out on him before he got close. She had a full day, beginning with an early-morning photo shoot.

Checking her cell phone messages in the cab on the way to the shoot, she found she had several voicemails, all of them from friends and family chiding her for rushing out of the ball.

"What happened, *ma chérie*?" Maxine said in her message. "It was rude to leave that young man standing on the dance floor like that. I taught you better than that. The way you acted last night, you would have thought I never sent you to charm school."

Chloe rolled her eyes at the notion of Maxine thinking she could still chastise her at the age of twenty-five and skipped to the next message. However, Chloe had to concur that Maxine was right that Chloe's etiquette teacher, Madame de Tornquist, would have been aghast that Chloe abandoned her minuet partner on the dance floor.

"Chloe, why'd you run out on that cute guy?" Daniella said. "Call me at the hotel when you can."

Chloe saved Daniella's message and moved on to the next.

"Girl, you ran out of that place last night like a pig at a slaughterhouse," Chloe's former roommate Brandi said in her folksy Southern diction. "What's gotten into you? I'm back at the ranch. Call me."

Before Chloe could check the next message, she saw she had an incoming call from Gigi. She started to let the voicemail pick up, but decided to answer it and get the interrogation over with.

As expected, Gigi started right in on her. "What was up with the Cinderella-at-the-ball routine last night?"

"I should be asking you, what was up with auctioning me off like I'm some hot new item on eBay?"

"They gave Alex a hard time at the door and I knew he probably wouldn't feel comfortable coming up to you and asking you to dance. When I heard his name, I remembered he's that reporter you never worked up the nerve to call, so I decided to intervene."

"*Interfere* is more like it. And where are you going to get the cash to make good on your bid, by the way?"

"I just sold another painting. Plus, I'm splitting it with *Tante* Maxine and Simone."

"Well, at least you're not making Marie clean out her retirement fund." The screen on Chloe's phone indicated that she had another call. "Hold on, Gi'." Chloe clicked over to the other caller, a number she didn't recognize. "Well, hello there."

It took a moment to register, but Chloe recognized Alex's deep, sexy voice. "Uh, hello." She grappled for words, feeling as disoriented as she did the previous night when he moved to kiss her after the dance. His voice was the last one she was expecting, especially after she bailed on him. "Not to be rude, but how did you get this number?"

"A journalist never reveals his sources," he said in a playful tone.

Chloe phone beeped, indicating she still had Gigi on hold. "Can you hold a second, please?" She clicked back over to Gigi. "That's Alex on the other line. You gave him my number, didn't you?"

"I'll neither confirm nor deny that," Gigi said, sounding as coy as Alex. "But the guy at least deserves an explanation as to why you ran out on him in front of all those people."

Chloe's phone beeped again. "I gotta go. Remind me to strangle you the next time I see you." She clicked back over to Alex. "You still there?" She heard typing and murmurs in the background and surmised he was calling from the office.

"Yeah, I'm here. Sorry to call out of the blue like this, but I just wanted to make sure I didn't do something to offend you last night. I was pretty confused when you left in such a rush."

Chloe paused, watching people and buildings whiz by as the cab wended through rush-hour traffic. "I'm sorry to leave you hanging like that. I have a shoot this morning. I had to get home and get some sleep so I could be on time for work."

She bit her lip, hoping her explanation sounded plausible. What she didn't say was that she felt such a palpable attraction to him that she got nervous and didn't know how to act with all those people watching.

"I understand," he said, and she relaxed against her seat. "With all those people gawking at us, I wanted to run away, too." He was quiet for a moment, then added, "Would you like to get together some time? Preferably someplace where there's not hordes of people watching our every move."

She hesitated. She hadn't seen anyone since the breakup with Sergio and she wasn't sure she was ready to jump back into dating, even with someone as attractive and apparently understanding as Alex.

"My schedule's kind of hectic for the next few weeks. I don't have a lot of free time."

"How about tonight?"

"Tonight? Uh, I don't know," she said, stalling. She hadn't expected to see him again after her disappearing act last night, let alone so soon. "I have the shoot this morning, then a meeting with the people at Laurel and IDG Media to go over how much money we raised last night and how the funds will be divvied up among the various AIDS charities. We'll probably be meeting late into the evening."

"IDG Media's office is in the Wellington Tower, right?"

"Yes, actually. That's where my meeting is."

"I'll be working late, too, finishing up a story. There's a really nice restaurant in the building, Hugo's Place. What do you say we meet there for a late dinner?"

Chloe took a moment before responding. She had to admit that she liked his directness, that he took the initiative to call her. "Sure," she said finally. "Hugo's Place, huh?"

"Yes. It's on the ninety-ninth floor, right below the penthouse suite."

She inhaled sharply, an involuntary reaction, suddenly reminded of her fear of heights.

"Is something wrong?" Alex said.

"Um, no, not exactly. It's just that I kind of have a fear of heights."

"It's all right," he said. "I won't let you fall."

Chloe stepped off the elevator, still catching her breath from the dizzying ride to the restaurant on the next-to-the-top floor of the Wellington Tower. She had feared she would be so queasy from the altitude that she wouldn't be able to even think about food, but the atmosphere of Hugo's Place had an immediate calming effect.

A jazz trio in the center of the dining room played standards, which combined with the dim lighting and earth tones to create a relaxed mood. The art deco décor brought to mind an elegant bistro from the golden age of jazz. Fortunately, the few windows around the restaurant were tinted, shielding the startling view.

She spotted Alex at a table in a cozy corner and he waved her over.

"Thanks for meeting me," he said, rising and pulling out a chair for her.

"This is a nice place."

"It's named after the guy whose company built this tower, Hugo Wellington," Alex said. "He was the Donald Trump of his day and built skyscrapers all over the world."

Chloe looked around, taking in the period architecture and furnishings. "I like the atmosphere."

"This place has a lot of history, from what I hear," Alex said.

Alex related that Hugo's Place was a legendary gathering place for Jazz Age musicians, artists, writers and actors who'd drop by after concerts, exhibit openings and theater debuts. Unlike other famed nightspots of the era such as the Cotton Club, Hugo's Place was integrated and would attract artists and art patrons from all walks of life. It was not unusual to see Park Avenue society wives mingling with figures from the Harlem Renaissance and members of the Algonquin Round Table trading ideas with bankers and politicians.

"They say Broadway divas and jazz singers like Billie Holiday would sit on that piano and belt out torch songs," Alex said, motioning to the grand piano in the center of the room.

Chloe listened with interest, imagining the restaurant in its heyday as a center of creativity and progressive thought, fostered by the enigmatic Hugo Wellington. Despite his reputation as an eccentric billionaire, Alex said, Wellington was known as a relentless supporter of the civil rights movement and donated millions to human rights causes around the world.

"Don't they say this building's haunted?" Chloe asked, afraid if the rumors of ghost sightings and weird power surges were true.

"Well, every now and then when I'm working late, the lights flicker and I hear strange thumps," Alex said. "They say it all started when one of Hugo's mistresses, some Hollywood starlet, got drunk and fell down an elevator shaft, dying instantly. As the legend goes, her spirit haunted Wellington until the day he died, and then his spirit joined hers after he died in the penthouse suite, which is right above us."

Chloe shivered at the thought, glancing out one of the tinted windows at the lights twinkling along the Manhattan skyline. "The height's not bothering me as much as I thought. It's a really beautiful view."

"Good, so I won't have to worry about you bailing on me again?"

Chloe looked down, her cheeks growing warm. "Sorry about that again. I guess I just got nervous, with all those people staring."

"I'm glad to know it wasn't my dancing." He laughed, putting her more at ease.

"You were pretty impressive," she said. "My mother sent me to charm school when I was eighteen, and my etiquette instructor would have been pleased with how graceful you were on the dance floor."

"You did the whole coming-out ball? I thought that was just a Southern thing. That's where I learned the minuet. I was a cotillion escort in high school. The ball last night reminded me of some of the dances I used to go to back in New Orleans."

Chloe's eyes widened at his mention of the city. "That's where my mother's side of the family is from, originally. I've been meaning to get down there ever since I moved to the States. I keep trying to plan a trip with my mother, but she's so busy and always has some excuse."

"We'll have to go some time. I'd love to show you around."

"That'd be great. And if you're ever in Paris, I'll do the same."

Chloe and Alex continued talking about their backgrounds over dinner. Maybe it was because he was a journalist, but he was one of the few men she'd been out with who seemed genuinely interested in what she had to say.

The restaurant's jazz trio provided the soundtrack as their conversation drifted to pop culture. They discovered they had similar taste in books and movies.

"Have you ever seen *L'Affaire Scandaleuse*? It's one of my favorites," Alex said, sawing into his porterhouse steak. "It's a French movie I saw in a foreign-film appreciation class in college."

"I saw it when I was in high school. My best friend, Gigi, and I used to sneak into adult movies," Chloe said, sampling her chicken dish. "That's one of my favorite movies; I've always loved Valérie Bourdain. When I saw her magnified larger than life on that screen, that's when I knew I wanted to act."

"I didn't know you're an actress as well," Alex said, "Have you been in anything I might have seen?"

"Not yet." She gazed out at the skyline, reflecting on her as-yet-unrealized ambitions. "I'm still trying to find the right part." She turned back to him. "What about you? Are you happy working at the magazine?"

"Yes and no. It seemed like a great opportunity when I first started out, but all the plum assignments go to the veteran reporters and the Ivy Leaguers who suck up to my editor." He set down his fork and took a sip of wine, as if to gather his thoughts. "Just like you're trying to find the right part, I need to break a big story to establish myself as a journalist." He took another sip of wine, then added, "Then, of course, there's my novel."

"I've written poetry since I was a kid. I have so much respect for writers," she said. "I'd love to read your novel some time."

"That might be a problem."

"Why's that?"

"My computer crashed and I lost the last chapter I was working on." He took a long sip of his wine, looking thoughtful. "My buddy Steve said my computer crashing is probably a sign I should hang it up."

"Some friend." Chloe couldn't imagine Gigi saying something so discouraging.

"Steve's a good guy." Alex paused a beat, then added with a comical expression, "Overall. We razz each other a lot, but sometimes I wonder if he's right that my computer crashing is a sign. Maybe I *should* hang it up." He looked down, his expression indicating he was pondering whether his goal of producing a great work of fiction was unrealistic.

"Don't give up on your dream, Alex," Chloe said, reaching across the table and touching his hand.

He gripped her hand and stared into her eyes for a prolonged moment. It felt good to hold his hand and she allowed her mind to drift to thoughts of more intense physical contact. Her reverie was interrupted when the jazz trio's bass player spoke into the microphone.

"We'd like to thank you all for coming out this evening," he said as his band mates began packing up their instruments. "We'll see you next time."

"I didn't realize it was so late," Alex said when the wait staff began placing chairs on tabletops. "I had a really nice time."

Chloe grabbed her purse and jacket. "Me, too."

They continued talking on the elevator ride down. She was so absorbed in their conversation about books and movies that she didn't notice the terrifying view from the glass elevator.

"I have to admit, I was a bit hesitant when you called," Chloe said after Alex had helped her into the cab, "but I'm really glad we did this."

"Me, too." Alex closed the cab door and stepped back onto the curb. "I'd like to do it again. Why don't I call you some time?"

"I'd like that."

This time, when Alex moved to kiss her, she didn't pull away.

78

Chloe shook off the stress of a hectic day packed with assignments and meetings with a relaxing evening at home, starting with a long, hot shower. She spread lotion over her skin, slipped into comfortable jeans and a camisole and plopped on the living room sofa with a book, flicking on the television. *Breakfast at Tiffany's*, one of her favorite American films, was playing, but all she could do was stare out the window as a late-evening thunderstorm ravaged the Big Apple. She usually loved rainy nights, found them relaxing, but tonight she was restless. She had been out with Alex a few times and now found herself in that awkward, "Should I call him or let him call me?" stage.

She jumped at the sound of the doorbell ringing, pulled on a sweater and got up to answer it. She blinked at the sight of Alex, as if trying to comprehend whether thinking of him had made him materialize.

"Hi. Sorry for just dropping by like this without calling," he said, holding up a takeout bag, "but I just left work and decided to pick up dinner at my favorite Thai place and thought you might be hungry."

She opened the door wider. "I haven't eaten since lunch. I'm famished."

She invited him in, hung up his rain-soaked jacket and satchel and grabbed some plates for the Thai noodles. "I was just settling in to watch *Breakfast at Tiffany's.*"

"One of my favorites," Alex said, taking a seat on the sofa.

Chloe and Alex discussed their chaotic days over dinner, with the movie providing romantic ambiance.

"My editor usually gives me all the fluff assignments nobody else wants, but one of the guys who covers poltics is on vacation and I finally got assigned a story with some meat. There was a press conference with Matt Muldoon."

"That's the congressman from New York who's running for reelection, right?"

"Exactly. I had to shout over a reporter from the *New York Times* to get my question in, but I got to ask Muldoon about allegations that he accepted a bribe from a lobbyist. I could just tell he was lying –"

Alex was interrupted by a loud thunderbolt, followed by the lights flickering.

"I wonder if that was a sign," Chloe said. "God knew that congressman was lying, too."

Alex laughed, just as the lights flickered again and then went out altogether, casting eerie shadows around the apartment. Chloe reflexively slid closer to him.

"You all right?" he said, stroking her back.

"Yeah, I just get a little creeped out when the lights go out."

She started to back away, embarrassed for overreacting to the blackout, but Alex pulled her closer. He kissed her and she allowed herself to lean into him, her loneliness fading.

After several moments of kissing in the dark, she stood up and wordlessly led him to her bedroom. She lit candles and approached him. They lingered at the foot of her bed, reveling in a kiss that foretold the journey that awaited them.

"You're even more beautiful in candlelight," he said, peeling her out of her sweater and jeans. He kissed her softly, embracing her with his strong arms.

She backed away from him, and then, with an adolescent glimmer of adventure in her eyes, she began to undress him, slowly surveying his body. "I want you," she whispered in his ear.

"Patience, my love," he said, slipping her out of her camisole. "We've got all night."

He picked her up, set her on the bed and relished kisses on her back. Flashes of lighting and flickering candles surrounding the bed bathed them in warmth as they made love.

When they were both spent, he got up to extinguish the candles. When he returned to bed, he took her in his arms.

"I want this moment to last forever," she said as they lay there in total darkness.

He enclosed her hand in his. "Don't worry. I'm not going anywhere."

In the morning, Chloe expected Alex to be gone, off to work. But when she opened her eyes, she was elated to find that she was still in his arms.

She turned over, careful not to wake him, and looked at her alarm clock. A busy day awaited – fittings, meetings, a lunch date with a designer. Her schedule was full, but she reached over and turned off the alarm. She'd call Warren and Barbara later and ask them to reschedule her appointments. Right now, she just wanted to block out the world.

She turned over and snuggled against his chest. A couple of hours later, she was drawn out of a pleasant dream by Alex kissing her eyelids. She stretched and yawned. It was nice seeing his face in the morning.

"Good morning, sleepyhead."

"Good morning," she said, sitting up and smiling. Her smile quickly faded when she noticed the time. "Oh, no! It's almost noon. I've got to call the agency. I was supposed to be somewhere this morning. Barbara's going to kill me."

"Relax," he said calmly. "Someone from the agency already called to remind you about your assignments. I hope I wasn't out of line, but I assumed you didn't want to be disturbed. I told them you were feeling under the weather but would be back to work bright and early, first thing tomorrow morning."

Chloe exhaled, reclined against the pillows, and stretched, the satin sheets delicious against her skin. "I could kiss you. In fact, I think I will." She pecked him on his nose. He responded by kissing her in a way that made her never want to get out of bed.

"You stay right where you are. Don't lift a finger, I'll be right back," he said, getting up and leaving the room, dressed only in a sheet wrapped around his waist.

A few minutes later, he came back, carrying a fully stocked breakfast tray: croissants, strawberries, French toast, warm maple syrup, turkey bacon, freshly brewed coffee. Chloe sat up as he placed the tray in her lap.

"You've been busy," she said.

"I ran to the corner market while you were sleeping. If you stick with me, you'll find that I'm a not-half-bad cook."

He picked up a cloth napkin from the tray and fanned it out under her chin. She felt like a spoiled child. This was getting good.

"I'm glad one of us has some expertise in the kitchen. I'd burn water," she said with a laugh.

"Dig in," he said. "*Bon appétit*."

She searched the tray for utensils. "There's no fork or knife."

"Well then, I guess I'll have to feed you," he said, producing a fork he had hidden behind his back.

"There's just one other thing."

"What's that?"

"I want you naked," said Chloe.

"Your wish is my command."

With her foot, she unfastened the sheet from his waist. Being hand-fed breakfast in bed by a gorgeous naked man, it couldn't get any better than this.

She was looking forward to a lazy afternoon, lounging in bed, but they were interrupted by the buzzing of his cell phone from across the room.

"Please tell me that's the sound of the earth moving," she joked.

"Sorry," he said, getting up and wrapping the sheet around his waist. "I called the office to let them know I'd be in late. That's probably my editor."

Alex retrieved the cell phone from his satchel, which he'd slung over a chair, and turned his back while he exchanged words with whoever was on the other end.

"Okay, I'll be right in," he said, hanging up. He turned to Chloe. "I'm sorry. I've got to go file the story about the crooked congressman I interviewed yesterday. The lobbyist who bribed him just 'fessed up in an immunity deal with the special investigator. We go to press tonight."

Chloe affected a mock pout. "I don't want to let you go," she said, tugging on the sheet at his waist.

"I don't want to go either. I'd much rather stay here with you," he said, crouching beside the bed and kissing her.

"Go," she said, resting her hand on his strong shoulder. "I'll be here when you get back and we can pick up where we left off."

"I'll pick up something for dinner on the way back. Do you like duck?"

"You're going to cook for me again? I could get used to this."

Alex kissed her again and got up to jump in the shower. As he rose, she pulled the sheet from his waist and swatted him on the butt.

As he got ready for work, she finished her breakfast and watched him, enjoying being able to take her time instead of wolfing down something quick like she normally did when she was on the way to an assignment.

"I'll see you later, babe," he said with a quick smooch on the cheek, dashing out the door.

She glanced over at the chair next to the bed and realized he'd left his satchel. She threw on a robe and tried to catch him.

"Hey, you forgot your bag!" she yelled out the window. She was drowned out by the street sounds and closed the window. She tried calling his cell, but his voicemail picked up. She placed the satchel back on the chair, figuring he could pick it up when he came back later.

She showered, fixed another cup of coffee and decided to straighten up and get the apartment ready for a romantic dinner with Alex that evening. When she moved the chair in her bedroom to vacuum behind it, Alex's satchel fell to the floor and papers scattered.

She picked them up and stacked them neatly, and a sentence at the top of one of the pages caught her eye: *Sidney Laveau awoke in a haze, her car dangling precariously over the edge of the Lake Pontchartrain Causeway.*

Leafing through the pages, she realized this was Alex's novel. She started to tuck the manuscript back in his satchel, but curiosity got the best of her and she sprawled on her bed to read on, with her cat, Bizou, curled up beside her.

She became enthralled in *Night Moves*, the story of a female's detective's quest to catch a ruthless killer. The New Orleans setting drew her in, igniting her desire to learn more about her family's city of origin.

As she turned the pages, she was impressed by Alex's writing style. In many of the books she read and movies she saw, especially those written and directed by men, female characters were passive and secondary. But Alex had written Sidney Laveau as intelligent, competent and tenacious. She risked her life, put her badge on the line and defied higher-ups at the police department, and would stop at nothing to catch the elusive serial killer.

Chloe could totally relate to this character and, as she read, she envisioned the scenes playing out on the big screen. Alex's story was not only an engaging novel, but she could see it being turned into a movie. She was still reading by the time dusk fell, so caught up in Alex's manuscript that she'd lost track of time.

When the doorbell rang around seven, she sprang up, excited to tell Alex that she had read his book and loved it.

"Hey, babe. I missed you," he said, kissing her when she opened the door. His arms were loaded with grocery bags and she followed him to the kitchen to help him get dinner started.

"It was a long day," he said, setting the bags on the counter and beginning to unpack them. "I had a lot of fact-checking to do on the story about the crooked congressman. And of course, my editor had a million changes to make and questions to ask. I thought I'd never get out of there." He searched for a pot, found one under the sink and began filling it with water. "But enough about me. What'd you do today?"

She smiled and held up the manuscript pages. "I tried to stop you this morning to let you know you left your bag. When I was cleaning this afternoon, your bag tipped over and your manuscript spilled out. I know you're not finished, but I couldn't help myself." She ran her hand over the stack of pages. "Alex, I love it."

He turned off the water, wiped his hands on a paper towel and approached her with an angry expression. "You did what?"

"I read your book – at least what you have so far – and I loved it," she beamed, holding out the pages.

Without a word, he ripped the pages from her hands and bolted out of the kitchen.

"Did I do something wrong?" she called after him, following him into the bedroom.

He remained silent, retrieving his satchel, stuffing the pages inside and striding to the front door.

"Where are you going?" she said. "What's wrong?"

Alex said nothing, slamming the door behind him. She stared at the door, stunned.

79

Chloe stood in Grant Herschel's studio, posing for her latest *Vogue* spread. She did her best to follow Grant's instructions, hoping the emotional turmoil she felt over the abrupt encounter she'd had with Alex last night didn't show on her face.

"What's wrong, Chloe?" Grant said, halting his furious shutter-clicking.

"Is it that obvious?" she said, exhaling for the first time since she'd slipped on the skintight designer jeans she was modeling.

"I can always tell when something's bothering you. Why don't you take five?"

Keiko, Grant's assistant, helped Chloe into a robe, covering the silk blouse that was open to her waist, nearly revealing her bare chest.

She stepped out of the stilettos that were murdering her feet and pulled at the intricate gold necklace wrapped around her neck, which felt like it was cutting off her circulation.

"Is it man trouble?" Grant asked, putting his arm around her shoulder and sounding like a concerned older brother.

"Gosh, you know me so well."

"It's the new guy you're seeing, isn't it?"

"I think I pissed him off."

"Oh, no. What'd you do now?" Grant teased.

Chloe elbowed him, playfully pushing him away. "I read a manuscript of a novel he's working on that he accidentally left at my house, and when I told him how much I loved it, he got mad and stormed out."

Grant nodded, as if he understood the situation. "Artists can be temperamental some time. My girlfriend and I got into a huge argument one time when she came across a file I left open on my computer and snuck a peek at a photo essay I was working on. It was a series of female nudes and she assumed I was having an affair."

"You *are* an international playboy, after all," Chloe said, giving Grant another playful jab. "But seriously, shouldn't we get back to work?"

Grant set his camera aside. "I have everything I need on film. Sounds like you need to go tend to your personal life."

Chloe took Grant up on his offer of an early release, knowing she wouldn't have been her best for the rest of the shoot since her mind was elsewhere. Once she'd changed into her street clothes, she stood on the curb outside Grant's studio, hailing a cab. As she stepped into the taxi that pulled to the curb, something in a store window across the street caught her eye. She waved the cab on and rushed across the street, stopping in front of an electronics store and checking out a shiny new laptop computer that beckoned from the window.

When Chloe got home that night, she checked her messages and was disappointed that Alex hadn't left any. She immediately dialed Gigi.

"What did he say?" Gigi said when Chloe reached her at the Paris apartment.

"Nothing, that's why I'm so confused," Chloe said, stroking her cat as she perched on the sill of one of her loft's enormous bank of windows that overlooked the Village. She could hear the sound of Gigi pulling a brush across a canvass as she spoke. It was early morning in Paris, Gigi's favorite time to work. Chloe was used to Gigi "multi-tasking" when they talked on the phone.

"I don't know if he thought I went through his bag and was upset I violated his privacy," Chloe continued, "or he thought I was patronizing him when I complimented him on his manuscript."

"Well, were you?"

Chloe held the phone away from her ear and stared at it, incredulous. She couldn't believe what Gigi had just said. "Of course not. What kind of question is that? How many times have you asked my opinion about a sketch or a painting and I told you it wasn't up to your usual standards?"

"That's true," Gigi said. "Maybe he was just upset that you read the manuscript since it's not finished and he wasn't ready for anyone to see it. You know I get the same way when I'm just starting a painting; I don't want anyone to see it until I have the concept cemented in my head."

"You creative types," Chloe groaned. "What's a girl to do?"

"Give him time, he'll come around. He probably just needs some time to cool down."

Chloe and Gigi continued to talk, when the conversation was interrupted by the sound of the call-waiting beep.

"Hold on," Chloe said, clicking over to the other line.

"Hi. It's me. You got time to talk?"

Chloe relaxed against the windowpane, relieved to hear Alex's voice.

"Sure," she said. "Just give me a second to let Gigi off the other line." She clicked back over. "It's him. I'm going to let you go."

"Call me back and tell me everything."

"Of course." She clicked back to Alex. "Okay, I'm back."

"I'm sorry for blowing up and walking out," he said. "I had a bad day, and I shouldn't have taken it out on you."

Chloe ran her hand across Bizou's back, the cat purring in appreciation. "I'm sorry, too. I didn't mean to violate your privacy. When your manuscript fell out of your bag, I should have just put it back and waited until you were ready for me to read it."

"After the shit day I had, I was really looking forward to spending the evening with you and having a nice dinner. But when you told me you'd read my book, I kind of snapped. It's not your fault. It just reminded me of something my ex, Veronica, said when we broke up. She told me I was wasting my time on my novel, that it's just a pipedream and I'm never going to amount to anything."

"That's a horrible thing to say," Chloe said, shooing Bizou off her lap and getting up to check on the turkey potpie she'd thrown in the oven. "And it's not true. Alex, your book is amazing. And I'm not saying that to make you feel good. I've always been a big reader, ever since I was a kid, and I loved your book. I could totally see it being turned into a movie and I really relate to your protagonist, Sidney."

"Thanks, I appreciate that, really," he said. "But the book is kind of a sore spot right now. I haven't worked on it since my computer crashed. I try to steal time at work, but there's always so many distractions."

Chloe put on mitts and opened the oven door. "I know it's easy for me to say, but keep at it."

"You really think I should?"

"Yeah. But I have to admit, I have a selfish motivation in saying that."

"Oh, yeah?"

"Yeah. I'm dying to know how Sidney nabs the bad guy."

Alex laughed, and Chloe was glad to hear him finally lighten up.

"Oh, shit!" she exclaimed, examining the potpie with a fork.

"What's wrong?"

"I was cooking a potpie and the crust is all burnt." She laughed at her latest lame attempt in the kitchen. "I told you I could burn water. I couldn't even manage a frozen dinner."

"Look, I owe you a dinner to make up for the one I was going to fix last night. When can I come over and cook for you again?"

"I'm really booked the next couple of days, but how about this weekend? You doing anything Saturday night?"

"Saturday's good. I'll come over and make my succulent duck a l'orange."

Chloe tossed the burnt potpie in the trash. "Sounds divine."

"Mmmm. That was delicious," Chloe said, dragging her fork across the plate and savoring the last bite of the gourmet meal Alex had prepared at her place. "Where'd you learn to cook like that?"

Alex sat back in his chair, beaming. "Growing up in New Orleans with some of the finest restaurants in the world didn't hurt. My mom's amazing in the kitchen, as well, and taught me and my brothers and sisters to cook."

"I'd ask for seconds, but I'm stuffed." She tossed her napkin on the table. "That was *soooo* good."

Alex got up and cleared the plates. "I hope you saved room for dessert. I made chocolate mousse."

Chloe followed him into the kitchen. "Hold on a sec'."

"I know you're in a profession where you have to watch your waistline," Alex said, putting the dishes in the sink, "but live a little." He smiled devilishly. "Besides, I know how we can burn lots of calories later on." He pulled her close and kissed her.

"I have something I want to show you first."

Alex raised his eyebrows suggestively. "Okay, I'm up for a game of show and tell."

Chloe laughed and took his hand. "Come on."

She led him to the bedroom and instructed him to have a seat on the bed.

"With pleasure," he said, taking his shoes off.

She went to the closet and retrieved a gift-wrapped box.

"What's this?" he asked as she handed him the box.

She grinned like a little girl giving the boy she liked a homemade valentine. "Open it."

Alex tore off the wrapping paper and his eyes got big at the sight of a box containing a brand-new laptop computer. "Oh my god, Chloe. This is for me? I don't know what to say."

She crouched by his side. "It took me a long time to find just the right one. This has all the bells and whistles – an Internet browser so you can do research, a Blu-ray drive so you can pop in your favorite movie or CD when you need inspiration."

Alex set the box aside. "This is too much. I can't accept this."

"Why not?" she asked, getting up from the floor and sitting next to him.

"Don't get me wrong, I appreciate the thought, really I do. It's just…" He paused, looking over at the box. "I can't have my woman buying me things I can't afford."

"I want to do this for you," she said, putting her arm around him. "Besides, it didn't set me back much at all."

"That's my point, exactly. This is another relationship where my woman makes more money than me. I don't want to feel like I'm taking advantage of you."

She touched his face. "Alex, I don't care how much money you make. It doesn't matter to me." She took his hands. "It's not about me buying you an expensive gift. I just don't want you to give up on your dream. I want you to keep writing and finish your book." She squeezed his hands for emphasis. "I believe in you."

He looked into her eyes and then kissed her. "Okay."

"Goodie!" she yelped. She clapped her hands, grabbed the box and set it on his lap. "Why don't you fire it up right now? You can probably have another chapter banged out by the time I finish the delicious dessert you made. I can't wait to find out what Sidney Laveau is up to next."

Alex set the box on the floor. "Let's skip dessert," he said, kissing her and pulling her to a reclining position next to him on the bed, "and get right to the main course."

Chloe sat across from Alex in the funky coffeehouse around the corner from her loft, writing in a notebook while he typed on his laptop. Over the last few months, they had developed a routine of coming to this spot that was a gathering place for writers, artists and other Village types. The coffeehouse, which hosted weekly open-mic poetry nights, provided an atmosphere where creativity flourished.

Chloe sipped her fat-free latte while Alex downed cup after cup of black coffee. Sometimes they would go for an hour or more without talking, enjoying each other's company while she read a good book and he pounded away on his novel.

Alex stopped typing and sipped his coffee.

"You look frustrated," she said, looking up from her notebook. "Can I help?"

Sometimes Alex would bounce ideas off her, and she'd give him suggestions to get him through a troublesome scene. She was glad she could give him encouragement.

"I'm at an impasse again," he said, crossing his arms and leaning back in his chair. "Do you think Sidney should shoot the villain at the end, or should I let him rot on death row?"

Chloe set her pen down and thought for a moment. "You know, I hate movies where the bad guy dies at the end. It's like I want to shout at the screen, 'Let him live and pay for everything he's done!'" She took a sip of her latte. "Besides, I've really gotten to know your character since you've been letting me read as you write, and I know she'd want to see the killer brought to justice."

Alex leaned forward and kissed Chloe on the cheek. "Thanks. You just confirmed what I've been thinking all along."

"Glad to be of service. I can't wait to read the last few pages."

Alex went back to typing, and Chloe busied herself making notes for a new product she was going to be launching with Laurel Cosmetics.

"'Inner Beauty?'" Alex said, the next time he took a break, cocking his head and eyeing the phrase she'd scribbled in her notebook.

"I've been brainstorming on names for a new product. The sales of *Unforgettable*, the perfume I endorse for Laurel Cosmetics, have gone so well that they're giving me my own fragrance." She sipped her latte and giggled, licking away her whipped-cream moustache. "It's ironic that I'm going to be hawking my own fragrance, since I used to work behind the cosmetics counter at Bloomingdale's and had to spray perfume samples on people." She placed her pen in the spine of her notebook to mark her place. "But I'm pretty excited. I get to be involved in naming the perfume, formulating the scent, designing the bottle, every little detail."

Alex nodded. "Makes sense, especially if it's going to bear your name. So, what are you doing tomorrow night?"

She plucked her date book from her purse and scanned her schedule. "I have a couple of photo shoots tomorrow and I'm probably going to be pretty beat afterward, but maybe you could come over when I get home and we could order in and watch a movie."

"I don't think that's a good idea."

Chloe gave him a puzzled look. "Why not?"

"Because I think we should go out."

"What's the occasion?"

"To celebrate you getting your own perfume, of course. And," he added casually, clicking off his laptop and closing the screen, "the fact that I just finished my book."

"*What?* Alex, that's great!" She got up and kissed him.

He took her in his arms and twirled her around. "I never could have done it without you."

80

Alex sat at a table in the center of the Gotham Book Mart, autographing copies of his novel for friends and colleagues. Rather than one of the megastore chains, Alex chose to launch *Night Moves* in a small, neighborhood bookstore that reflected the labor of love his novel had been. As he signed copies, he felt an incredible sense of accomplishment seeing his name on the title page.

"I've got to hand it to you, man," Alex's best friend Steve said, approaching the table and slapping Alex on the back. "I didn't think you could do it, but you proved me wrong."

"You owe me fifty bucks," Alex said in mock seriousness. "Don't think I forgot about our bet."

"Ah, I'm sure you won't miss it, what with the big advance you got."

"It's a small publisher, so the advance wasn't that big, otherwise I wouldn't be keeping my day job at the magazine," Alex said. "And stop trying to weasel out of our bet."

"Congratulations, Alex," said Pam, Steve's girlfriend, coming up to the table.

Alex smiled at her. Pamela was an attractive woman, with smooth cocoa skin and big brown eyes, but her beauty was camouflaged by dowdy clothes. With her ruffled pink blouse, conservative mauve suit and hair pulled back in a bun, she brought to mind a mousy Sunday school teacher. As much as Alex knew Steve was a good guy at heart, he also knew his best friend's fragile sense of manhood would be threatened by a more confident woman like Chloe.

"Steve and I are so proud of you," Pam said, shaking Alex's hand.

"Nice ring," he said, noticing the diamond on her finger. He turned to Steve. "Hey, buddy, is there something important you haven't told me?"

Pam took Steve's arm and they beamed at each other.

"I popped the question," Steve said.

"Get out of here!" Alex stood up, reached across the table and hugged them both.

"Sorry. I was going to tell you, but I didn't want to steal your thunder, with your book coming out and all," Steve said. "Of course I want you to be the best man."

"You can count on it." Alex turned to Pam, adding facetiously, "I can't believe you agreed to put up with this guy "til death do you part.""

Pam just continued to grin and cling to Steve's arm as if it were an extension of her own body.

"Sweetheart, why don't you go get me a cup of coffee and some of those cookies?" Steve said, ordering her about in a tone that undoubtedly portended the roles they'd play as a married couple.

"Where's Chloe?" Steve said once Pam had retreated to the refreshment table.

"She had a shoot. She said she'd be here a little later." Alex felt his phone vibrate and reached into the pocket of his blazer to answer it. "This is probably her now."

Alex excused himself and found a quiet corner.

"Hi, hon', it's me," Chloe said, and Alex could hear honking horns and sirens in the background.

"Sounds like you're caught in the rush-hour crunch," he said.

"You got it. I just finished up the shoot and I'm on my way uptown right now. I'll be there shortly." The sound of the cab driver laying on the horn blared through the phone. "I'm tempted to get out and walk, which would probably be quicker at this rate," she said, "but that's probably not a good idea in six-inch Louboutins."

Alex chuckled. "No rush. I'll be here a couple more hours."

"I can't wait to see you, babe. I'm so excited for you. You deserve this success."

"And I have you to thank for it."

Alex's last comment was nearly drowned out by the cab driver honking the horn again.

"I better go. We're going through a tunnel and you're staring to break up," Chloe said. "See you soon."

Alex hung up and went back to signing books.

"Congrats, man," said Duff, Alex's day-job boss, as he approached the autograph table. "Why didn't you tell me you were writing a book?"

"Well, you know, don't all reporters have an unfinished novel in their desk drawer?" Alex said, rising to shake Duff's hand.

"Now that you're a published author, are you going to be leaving us?" Duff asked.

Alex sat down, retrieved a copy of the book from the stack on the table and began signing a personal inscription to Duff. "I'm staying put for now, but who knows what the future holds? My agent's shopping the movie rights."

"Movie rights? You know, I've written a couple of screenplays myself," Duff began. "When I was your age, I went out to L.A. and –"

Before Duff could finish, Alex looked up and saw none other than Veronica, his ex-girlfriend, entering. She looked crisp and corporate as ever in a designer suit and take-the-world-by-the-balls stilettos.

"Sorry to cut you off, Duff," Alex said, handing the book to his editor. "I see someone I used to know. Will you excuse me for a minute?" He got up from the table and strode across the room, intercepting Veronica at the door. "What are you doing here?"

"I heard about you getting your book published and I thought I'd drop by and wish you well."

"You've got some nerve, showing up here. I seem to recall the last time I saw you, you were dumping me and telling me I'd never make it as a writer."

"What do you say we let bygones be bygones? I'm genuinely happy for you," she said, sounding less than convincing. "I never wanted anything but to see you do well. I read the review in the *Times*. That tough book critic loved it."

"Yes, interesting, isn't it, since you said no one would ever take me seriously?"

"You're not still holding a grudge about that, are you?" She ran her lacquered nails down his cheek. "I've missed you."

Alex calmly moved her hand away from his face and placed it at her side. "You never change, you know that, Ronnie? Back when I was some unknown hack, you couldn't get rid of me fast enough, but now that I'm a well-reviewed, published author, all of a sudden you're missing me."

"Can you honestly say you haven't thought about me in the past few months?"

"Yes. I'm in love with someone else."

"You mean your little cover girl? You know, I must admit, I've seen pictures of you two in the papers and you do make a striking couple." She inched closer. "But nothing can ever replace what we had."

Alex shook his head and laughed. "You're horribly predictable, like a bad plot. The minute I get a little success under my belt, you come running back. I'm not interested, okay? I'm not some toy you got tired of playing with that you can just pick back up whenever it suits you. I'm with Chloe now. What you and I had is over."

"Don't kid yourself, Alex. I could have you if I wanted you." She moved closer, leaning in, as if she were going to kiss him. "Because as you know, I always get what I want."

519

Alex remained impassive, not reacting to Veronica's shameless ploy. "Goodbye, Veronica. Thanks for stopping by."

Veronica gave him one last look, turned on her heels and strode out the door, nearly knocking over Chloe as she entered.

"Who was that?" Chloe said, hugging him.

"No one important," he said. "Just an ex."

"Thank you for joining us," Max Laurel said, shaking Chloe's hand as she entered the conference room at IDG Media's Wellington Tower office.

"I'm excited about the new fragrance," Chloe said, seating herself to the right of Max's position at the head of the table. "I can't wait to meet the advertising people IDG is bringing in and hear their ideas for the campaign."

Laurel Cosmetics was shelling out big bucks to promote Chloe's new fragrance. She was set to film several slick print ads with Grant Herschel, and the company had signed French movie director René Lormier to direct her in a series of artsy television commercials. She had requested Lormier, since he had directed her in the music video she'd co-starred in as a teen with Gigi's ex, Montana Blake. Working with Lormier again would be like coming full circle.

"Chloe, this is the team from F&W Advertising," Max said as four Madison Avenue types – three buttoned-down white guys and a young, beautiful African-American woman – entered.

"So nice to meet you," Chloe said, shaking each of their hands.

"Likewise," the woman said. "I'm Veronica. Veronica Harris."

As they shook hands, the woman seemed to hold Chloe's gaze a second too long, and Chloe felt a vague sense of familiarity, as if she had met this woman somewhere before.

Chloe shrugged off the déjà vu and sat back, along with Max and the other Laurel executives, for a Power Point presentation of the ad campaign.

"I like what I see so far," Max said.

"These are the story boards and scripts for the commercials," Veronica said, handing a black leather portfolio to Max to pass around the table.

Max handed Chloe the portfolio and she skimmed through it, making notes about the concepts for print ads and TV spots.

"We'd like to start shooting in Los Angeles as soon as possible," Veronica said, "pending final approval, of course."

Chloe liked how Veronica had taken the lead in the presentation, not allowing her white male counterparts to dominate, as was so often the case. While Chloe admired Veronica's moxie, there was something brusque in her manner. Chloe chalked it up to the hard shell many women in Corporate

America had to develop in order to play in a man's world.

"Pretty impressive," Max said as the team concluded the presentation. "I think this campaign will help us gain market share over Luxe Cosmetics, our biggest competitor."

Chloe noticed that at the mention of Luxe Cosmetics, Veronica's cool demeanor cracked momentarily and she flinched, an odd reaction. Chloe surmised that perhaps Luxe was a former F&W advertising client with whom Veronica had had a bad experience, which would hopefully make her work even harder for Laurel.

Max turned to Chloe. "What do you think?"

"I think these ideas are a great start," Chloe said, "but I have some thoughts of my own."

"Hmmm. Imagine that. A model with a thought," Veronica said flatly.

Nervous laughter erupted around the conference table. Chloe just stared at Veronica, taken aback by her cutting remark.

"That was a joke," Veronica said after an uncomfortable silence. "I always try to lighten things up in long meetings. No offense."

Chloe looked Veronica up and down and decided to give her the benefit of the doubt. "None taken." She slid the portfolio across the table to Veronica. "Anyway, what I was going to say was that while I like the ideas for the TV spots, I have a concept I've been kicking around."

"Please, by all means, fill us in," Max said. "It's *your* signature fragrance, after all."

"Since we're calling the perfume *Inner Beauty*, I have a concept for a series of commercials showing women of different generations. I'd like to film the first spot in Paris, since that's where I grew up. And since we've got René Lormier signed to direct, I'd like to ask Valérie Bourdain to appear in the ad with me."

"The famous French actress?" Max said. "I wouldn't think an award-winning actress like her would agree to be in a commercial."

"Well, I'm hoping she'll say yes for a chance to reunite with René. He directed some of her best films. And," Chloe added with a grin, "I've always admired her and wanted to work with her."

"We'll make it happen," Max said, slapping the table, as if to affirm his statement. "For you, anything."

Chloe smiled in appreciation. "Thank you, Max. It would mean so much to me."

"Sorry to interrupt this love-fest," Veronica said as her team members began gathering their presentation materials, sounding a bit a brusque once again, "but we need to set up another meeting to flesh out the concept."

"Sounds like a plan," Max Laurel said, rising to shake hands with the ad execs.

As the group discussed details, Chloe watched Veronica and tried to figure out where she knew her from.

81

Chloe dug her nails into the armrest of the limousine's passenger compartment as the vehicle wound its way through the Paris streets that were as familiar to her as her name. Though she was surrounded by familiarity, her stomach was tied in knots like the day she first landed on the alien terrain of New York City. Today was the first day of shooting for the commercial for her *Inner Beauty* fragrance, and the prospect of working with her idol, Valérie Bourdain, both exhilarated and frightened her.

When the car pulled up at the outdoor shoot in front of the Eiffel Tower, Chloe considered telling the driver to turn around and take her to the Chateau de Chevalier, where she could hide out in her old room.

"Mademoiselle Bareaux?"

Chloe looked up to see the driver holding the door open and staring down at her with a confused expression, as if wondering why she hadn't gotten out.

"*Merci*," she said after a moment's hesitation, willing herself to get out of the car.

She took tentative steps onto the set, careful to stay out of the way of sound and lighting technicians scurrying about, tending to their various tasks. She took it all in, envisioning the day she would be walking onto a real movie set.

As she maneuvered past towering light stands and stepped over cables snaking along the ground, she saw Veronica Harris, the advertising executive who had been assigned to oversee the shoot. Veronica sat in a director's chair that was monogrammed with Chloe's name.

Donning Chanel sunglasses and talking on a cell phone, Veronica got up from the chair when she looked up and saw Chloe. Rather than the contrite body language of a professional who'd been caught sitting in the star's reserved seat, Veronica's unrepentant expression was that of a teenager who'd been nabbed stealing the car keys but remained defiant.

Chloe gave Veronica a friendly wave, deciding once again to give the young black female executive the benefit of the doubt, but Veronica barely threw up her hand. She continued talking on her cell phone, as if Chloe was a bothersome subordinate rather than the rightful center of attention.

Chloe had no time to ponder Veronica's slight as René Lormier, the director, descended on her like a typhoon, all European kisses and rapid-fire French.

"Chloe, *bonjour*," Lormier said, lapsing into broken English. "I'm so happy to be working weeth you again, and weeth Valérie. You remind me of a young version of her, when we first started working togezzer. Now go get into hair and makeup. Val's already zere."

Lormier aimed her in the direction of the makeup trailer. Chloe opened her mouth to beg him to make the introductions, that she couldn't possibly approach her girlhood idol on her own. But the director's attention was drawn away by a technician seeking his advice on the placement of the lights.

Chloe stood staring at the door of the makeup trailer, anchored to the pavement by an invisible force. Offering up a silent prayer to help her overcome her nerves, she slowly climbed the trailer's steps and swung the door open. A gaggle of makeup artists and stylists crammed the small space, hovered before a bank of mirrors. When Chloe entered, the crowd parted, revealing a well-preserved middle-aged woman sitting in a monogrammed director's chair, her back turned to Chloe.

With her luminous skin, trademark auburn bouffant and those pouty lips that Chloe had seen in action in so many steamy screen kisses, there was no mistaking that this was the one and only Valérie Bourdain. Her blouse was unbuttoned just enough to reveal cleavage that proved that, in her early fifties, she was still voluptuous.

Meeting Chloe's eyes in the mirror, she smiled. "Chloe, come, let's get acquainted," she said, extending a hand that was more rugged-looking, with unpainted nails, than her delicate features and glamorous image portrayed. The unexpected detail made her seem more human, accessible.

"So nice to meet you, Madame Bourdain," Chloe said, shaking her hand with sweaty palms and taking a seat next to her in front of the dressing-room mirrors.

"Please, call me Val, that's what all my friends call me," she said, immediately putting Chloe at ease. The actress' trademark sultry rasp sounded lighter in tone in person. Her Parisian accent was only slightly pronounced, as if she were accustomed to assuming different languages for roles and speaking English to American industry types.

"*S'il vous plait*, forgive the state of my cuticles," Valérie said to a manicurist who began painting her nails with Laurel's Ravishing Rouge polish. "It's an old habit from my modeling days – showing up with no makeup or adornment, like a blank canvas."

"You started out as a model, too?" Chloe said, obediently lifting her chin for the makeup artist, who began attending to her.

"That's how I was discovered. I suppose you already met René?"

Chloe nodded, trying not to stare at Valérie. Seeing her idol in the flesh was more dreamlike than the fantasies she'd entertained since girlhood of meeting her.

"Well, I did a cover shoot for *Vogue* and René saw my photo and thought I was perfect for the film he was casting. I'd been modeling for years, starting as an artist's model. *Vogue* was my first cover, and you can only imagine how excited I was."

"*Vogue* was my first cover, too," Chloe said, trying to keep her voice from rising to a squeak and contain her excitement at discovering she had something in common with her idol.

"Have you thought about what you want to do beyond modeling?" Valérie said, sounding genuinely interested in Chloe's long-term goals. "The fashion world is even more youth-obsessed than the movie business, if that's possible. It pays to have an exit strategy."

"Funny you should mention that." Chloe paused, staring at her own reflection while a stylist began her working on her hair. "I've always wanted to act." She scrunched down in her chair, feeling like an art student showing an amateurish sketch to a master painter.

"Go for it. You have the beauty and, I'm sure, the talent."

Chloe smiled at Valérie in the mirror, drinking in the compliment from the woman she so admired. "Thank you. That's a big endorsement, coming from you."

Valérie waved away Chloe's remark, as if humbly dismissing any suggestion that she was above average. "You don't need an endorsement from me or anyone else to pursue your dreams."

"I suppose you're right," Chloe said, speaking slowly, still adjusting to the fact that she was having an actual conversation with a legend. "But there's one thing standing in my way. Actually, it's a big thing."

Valérie turned away from the makeup artist's brush, directing her full attention at Chloe, her violet-blue eyes sparkling like precious stones in the light from the mirror. "What's that, *cher*?"

"I freeze up at auditions. Every time I'm asked to read for a part, even if it's something I know I can pull off, my nerves get the best of me. I've been like that ever since I was a kid, from my first school play to my audition for the modeling agency when I first moved to New York. Luckily, my career took off after my first *Vogue* cover and I don't have to do go-sees anymore."

Chloe relaxed in her chair. Admitting this character flaw made her feel lighter, like when she was a girl and unburdened herself of some misdeed in confession.

Valérie turned back to the mirror, allowing the makeup artists and hairdressers to finish their work. "Believe it or not, what you're describing is common among performers."

"Really?" Chloe said, hoping she didn't sound too eager for validation.

"*Oui*. We all go through performance anxiety," Valérie said, eyes downcast as the makeup artist applied mascara. "Even after I was discovered by René, I had to fight to be taken seriously. I had to audition for many parts and prove I wasn't just another pretty face. I always got nervous when I had to read for a role."

"What did you do?" Chloe sat forward, mesmerized, feeling as though she were the sole pupil in a master class.

"I studied, for one. When I was first starting out, the studio sent me to elocution lessons with an etiquette tutor."

"Oh my god, Madame de Tornquist!" Chloe suddenly remembered the old woman telling her that she reminded her of a young Valérie Bourdain.

Chloe and Valérie joked about some of the silly phrases that the etiquette tutor made her students repeat endlessly, with Valérie throwing her head back in the throaty laugh that was so familiar to Chloe.

"Everyone has their own secret for overcoming stage fright," Valérie said. She leaned toward Chloe, lowering her voice. "You know what works for me?"

Chloe said nothing and simply stared into her idol's eyes, anxious to become her confidante. She couldn't believe she was receiving guidance from a professional of Valérie's caliber.

Valérie withdrew her hand from the manicurist, reached for her handbag and took out a small, black-and-silver rosary. "I carry this with me everywhere, like a talisman. I've had this since I was very young, since my days at convent school."

Chloe touched her hand to her mouth, overcome with emotion. "I went to an all-girls Catholic school, too." Discovering she had something else in common with her idol was almost overwhelming.

"Well, then, it's only appropriate that I give this to you." Valérie placed the rosary in Chloe's hand.

Chloe stared at the object, temporarily speechless. "Oh, Madame Bourdain, I couldn't –"

"I said to call me Val. And yes you can. That good-luck charm has served me well, and now it's yours."

Chloe dabbed at her eyes, incurring the wrath of the makeup artist, who muttered in French about having to redo her makeup. "Madame Bourd- I mean, Val, I can't thank you enough."

"You know how you can thank me?" Chloe recognized the gleam in Valérie's eyes from when the actress was about to perform some particularly daring feat onscreen. "By acing that next audition. I'd like to think I opened some doors for young women like you, and I want you to do me proud."

Chloe clutched the rosary. "I will."

The intimate moment was interrupted by Lormier flinging open the door of the trailer. "Ladies, don't dawdle in hair and makeup, *s'il vous plait*. I need you on zee set in feef-teen mee-noots."

The director turned his attention to another technician who came up to consult with him and slammed the trailer door.

"René hasn't changed in all these years," Valérie said to Chloe, chuckling. "He always rushes his stars onto the set, and then keeps us waiting for hours while he sets up the shots and argues with the crew to get everything just right." She fluttered her long, dark lashes. "A perfectionist 'til the day he dies."

"I'm just glad to be working with a big director like him," Chloe said, placing the rosary in her purse for safekeeping. "And you. You've been so gracious. Thank you so much for agreeing to do this. It's a real pleasure to finally meet you."

"The pleasure is all mine, my dear."

After Chloe and Valérie had been through hair, makeup and wardrobe, an assistant escorted them onto the set. Just as Valérie predicted, Lormier kept them waiting forever while he barked commands to the cinematographer and crew.

Despite the long wait, Chloe wasn't bored for a moment. She was more than happy to listen intently as Valérie regaled her with show business lore. Periodically, while Valérie was speaking, Chloe's attention was drawn to Veronica Harris. The advertising exec kept her distance and continued to talk on her cell phone in a hushed tone as if she were reporting details while on a covert spy mission, eyes hidden behind Chanel shades. Chloe couldn't shake the sneaking suspicion that Veronica had some other agenda than overseeing the shoot and steering the launch of Chloe's signature fragrance.

Before Chloe could give another thought to Veronica, Lormier summoned her and Valérie to take their places. As the commercial's storyline went, Chloe and Valérie were to stroll arm in arm down the Paris boulevard with the Eiffel Tower as a backdrop. The concept was to depict a friendship between a still-beautiful "woman of a certain age" and an ingénue who had much to learn from her mentor's life experiences.

"Action!" Lormier bellowed.

As the camera careened down a track and followed Chloe as she improvised dialogue with Valérie that was to later be dubbed over by a music score, Chloe felt she had indeed made a new friend.

*****

Chloe sat in an empty office at IDG Media's Wellington Tower headquarters, talking to Alex on her cell phone.

"I'm sorry I can't make the press conference for your perfume launch," he said, nearly drowned out by the sounds of the busy newsroom in the background. "I'm in the middle of finishing up a big story. Those Ivy Leaguers can get away with missing deadlines, but far be it for me to slack off – even with a published novel under my belt."

"It's okay, honey," Chloe said, sensing the frustration in Alex's voice. "I just met your magazine's new health and beauty editor. She's got it covered."

"I just wish I could be there to support you. I know this is a big accomplishment for you. "

Bill Bosworth, Laurel Cosmetics' all-too-efficient PR guru, poked his head in and signaled to Chloe that she had two minutes before the start of the press conference.

"Gotta go," Chloe said. "I'll fill you in on all the details tonight."

She wrapped up the call and followed Bosworth into the next room, where a throng of cameramen and reporters gathered in front of a podium. On her way to join Max Laurel at the podium, Chloe felt a tug at her sleeve. She turned to see Veronica Harris standing before her.

"I guess this is it," Veronica said. "I just wanted to tell you it's been nice working with you and wish you well."

"Oh, thanks," Chloe said, sizing Veronica up, wondering why she was coming to her with what sounded like a farewell speech. "But I'm sure we'll be working together in the future. The product launch today is just the beginning."

Veronica smiled like she knew something Chloe didn't and joined the rest of the F&W team, who huddled together at the back of the room.

"Now that the star of the show is here, we can begin," Max Laurel said when Chloe took her place beside him at the podium.

The assembled media applauded and Chloe fanned her skirt and took a bow in an exaggerated, comedic gesture. She looked forward to the day she would be taking a real bow in front of a paying audience.

Max motioned toward an oversize canvas positioned next to the podium and draped with a velvet cloth. "We brought you all here today to unveil the billboard that will be installed in Times Square to coincide with the debut of the television commercials for Chloe's new fragrance, *Inner Beauty*," he said. "Chloe, would you please do the honors?"

She stepped over to the canvas and, at Max's cue, pulled a rope to reveal a miniature version of the billboard. Instead of the applause she expected, shocked murmurs arose from the press. She was aghast to see that someone had defaced Grant Herschel's latest artful black-and-white photo of her by scrawling devil's horns on her head, a moustache above her lip, and hair under her arms.

"I'm sorry," Max told the crowd. "There must be some mistake…"

Chloe stared in shock at the defaced portrait. Who could have done such a thing? She looked up and saw Veronica slipping out of the room.

"Excuse me for a moment," Chloe said into the microphone. She rushed through the crowd, trailing Veronica into the hallway.

"Why did you do that?" Chloe said, grabbing Veronica's arm when she caught up with her in front of the elevators.

"First of all, I don't know what you're talking about," Veronica said coolly, "and secondly, I suggest you take your hands off me."

Chloe inhaled in an attempt to blunt her rage, released Veronica's arm, and took a step backward. "I think you know precisely what I'm talking about," she said through clenched teeth. "Why did you deface the billboard, Veronica?"

"Why are you accusing me?" Veronica said in the same cool tone, turning her back to Chloe and pressing the elevator call button. "What would I have to gain by pulling such a juvenile prank?"

"To humiliate me, which is what you've been trying to do with your catty comments since the day you started on the account. That billboard was under tight security until it was unveiled. It had to be an inside job, and you're the only one I can think of who would want to embarrass me like that."

Veronica sneered. "You have to admit it was pretty funny, with the hair under your arms and all. Everyone knows French women don't shave their 'pits."

Chloe narrowed her eyes at Veronica, taken aback by the negative energy this woman had barely camouflaged up until now and that had finally bubbled to the surface. "Why, Veronica? Why do you hate me so much?"

"Because you took something that belongs to me." Her voice oozing venom, Veronica glared as if Chloe were a jewel thief.

Chloe shook her head, totally mystified by the accusation. "What the hell are you talking about?"

"I think you know." The elevator doors opened and Veronica stepped in the compartment. "Don't bother trying to get me fired. I've already given my notice. Oh, and tell Alex I said hi. I don't need *him* anymore, either."

Suddenly, it dawned on Chloe why Veronica looked so familiar. Alex's book party. He had told her his ex had attended the event. He had emphasized the word *ex*.

"Good luck salvaging your product launch," Veronica added with a twist-the-knife-in-your-back smirk as the elevator closed.

Chloe stood there, staring into the mirrored doors.

*****

"And when I confronted her, she didn't even apologize," Chloe told Alex. She sat next to him in bed, relating the humiliating events from earlier in the day.

"I'm sorry," Alex said. "I feel guilty. If I had been there instead of at work, I could have stopped her from ruining your big event."

"She didn't ruin the whole event. I'm not going to give her that much credit." Chloe leaned against the pillows and ran her hand through his hair. "And it's not your fault. How could you have known Veronica was assigned to the Laurel account?"

Alex looked contrite. "Actually, right before we broke up, she hounded me for information about the company when she found out I'd done the story on you. I forgot all about it. Knowing how one-track-minded she is, I should have realized she'd follow up and land the account." He shook his head. "I should have known she was up to something when she showed up at my book signing."

"After the whole fiasco this afternoon, I remembered that I'd run into her at the bookstore when I was on my way in. What'd she say to you while she was there?"

"She made a pathetic attempt to get back with me. She's so transparent – of course she'd want me back now that I'm a successful author. But I told her I wasn't interested, that what we had is over and I'm with you now. That probably pissed her off."

"I guess the saying's true: hell hath no fury like a woman scorned." Chloe laughed in spite of the anger that still simmered whenever she thought of the stunt Veronica pulled. "But she had to have some other motive to sabotage my perfume launch other than getting back at me for being with you." She touched Alex's cheek. "Not that you're not irresistible, honey."

"Knowing Veronica," he said, reaching to turn off the bedside lamp, "she always has an ulterior motive."

82

"Hello?" Chloe called out, letting herself in Rick and Dave's apartment.

She went to Dave's studio and marveled at a half-finished mural that took up most of a wall. The mural depicted a neighborhood scene with people of different races going about their daily tasks – an elderly black woman leaning out of her window to water a flowerbox, a Latino shopkeeper sweeping the street outside his bodega, children of various shades playing Double Dutch.

"Dave? You home?" she called, going into the kitchen, where she found the couple's cat, Oscar Wilde, nibbling a tuna sandwich on the counter. It appeared that Dave had fixed himself a snack but abandoned it, half-eaten.

"You hungry, kitty?" she said, taking Oscar Wilde down from the counter and filling his bowls with fresh food and water. The cat lapped ravenously at the food, as if this was his first real meal of the day.

Chloe pressed on with concern; it wasn't like Dave, who was home most of the day working in his studio, to neglect the beloved pet.

"Anybody home?" she said, making her way down the darkened hallway. She stopped at the closed bedroom door. She knocked, and when there was no answer, she gingerly opened the door.

"Hello? Dave?" she said, the door squeaking open.

Despite the late-afternoon sun, the room was pitch-black. She went to the window, opened the curtains and saw Dave lying in bed.

"Chloe, is that you?" he said groggily, rubbing his eyes.

"Sorry," she said, sitting down on the bed. "I was at the front door knocking for a while and let myself in when no one answered."

"I was just taking a nap." He propped himself on his elbows, and the sunlight filtering in through the window illuminated his pale, wan features. He looked haggard, his cheeks sunken and dark circles ringing his eyes.

"How are you feeling?" she said, trying not to sound alarmed at his gaunt appearance.

"Fine, just a little tired. Thanks to the exposure I got from the portrait we auctioned off at the masquerade ball, I've been commissioned to do a mural at a community center in the Bronx."

"I saw it," Chloe said. "It's beautiful."

"Thanks. It's going to be installed at the center in a few weeks and I've been working overtime to finish it. I guess I kind of overdid it today."

"Do you still feel up to going out tonight?"

She'd been looking forward all week to the "double date" she and Alex had planned with Rick and Dave at her favorite French restaurant in New York, Jean Georges. Alex had hit it off with Rick and Dave when Chloe introduced them. The foursome had been trying to schedule a joint outing for weeks, which had been nearly impossible because of their busy schedules. They'd all finally cleared their schedules for tonight, but Dave didn't look well enough to venture out.

"I can't wait to go out to dinner with you guys. I need to get out of the house," Dave said, pushing back the covers. "I'll go get ready. Rick should be home any minute."

Dave struggled to get up, but he lost his footing and fell back on the bed.

"Why don't you rest a while longer?" Chloe said, fluffing his pillows and placing them behind his head. "We have plenty of time."

"I've been in bed all afternoon. I should get up and get going."

He tried to get out of bed again, but his legs seemed to buckle and he fell beside the bed. Chloe was struggling to help Dave up when Rick came in.

"What's going on?" Rick said, setting his briefcase in a chair and rushing over to help.

"I was trying to get up, but I tripped over my own feet," Dave said in his characteristically self-deprecating, joking way, as if downplaying how weak he was. "What a klutz."

Chloe and Rick lifted Dave back in bed.

"I better get up and get ready if we're going to make our dinner reservation," Dave insisted, sitting up.

"No rush," Chloe said. "Alex is meeting us at the restaurant and he can hold our table."

"Maybe we ought to stay in tonight, babe," Rick said, smoothing Dave's hair.

"Don't be silly. I'm fine."

Dave struggled to get up once more, but Rick gently held him down. "Did you remember to take your medicine?"

"Of course. With that chart you posted on the refrigerator door, how could I forget?" Dave snapped.

Rick, unfazed, continued his interrogation. "Did you eat today? You need keep up your strength."

Dave crossed his eyes. "Yes, Mommy Dearest."

Chloe chuckled, glad that Dave's sarcasm hadn't diminished in his weakened state.

Rick touched Dave's forehead. "You're burning up. You best stay in bed and I'll call the doctor."

"Do you want me to call?" Chloe offered.

"No, honey, why don't you go on and meet up with Alex. We probably won't be able to make it out tonight. I'm sorry."

"It's okay. If you need me to stay, I will."

"Go on," Dave said, waving her away. "No need to worry about me. Rick's just making a big fuss."

"Send Alex our regrets," Rick said. "We'll have to do it some other time."

While Rick tended to Dave, retrieving an extra blanket from the closet, Chloe inched out of the room. When she reached the bedroom door, Oscar Wilde ran over her feet and leapt onto the bed. The cat perched on Dave's chest as Rick went to the window and drew the curtains, casting shadows across the room.

*****

"Where's Rick and Dave?" Alex asked when Chloe arrived solo at Jean Georges.

"They couldn't make it," she said, sitting next to Alex at the table. "Dave's not feeling well."

"That's too bad. What's wrong with him?"

Chloe sighed and took a sip from her water glass. "He's HIV-positive and, even though he hasn't come out and said it, I think he's having complications."

Alex put his arm around Chloe. "I'm sorry to hear that. Is Rick okay?"

"Yeah, he's fine. The next time we see them, don't let on that I told you about Dave's condition. It's not a big secret, but they try to be as discreet as possible."

"Of course. I won't say anything."

"I just wish I could do more. This afternoon, seeing Dave lying there like that and looking so weak and fragile, it just made me feel so helpless."

Alex stroked Chloe's back. "I'm sure you've done everything you can."

She opened her menu. "Let's change the subject. I'm depressed enough as it is. How are things going with the book?"

"Great," Alex said, smiling. "I just found out today my novel made the *Times* best-seller list and my agent has gotten a couple of calls from movie producers interested in optioning the rights."

"Oh my god! That's great, honey!" She reached over and hugged him. "See, I told you, you could do it. We'll have to make this a celebration dinner."

Alex poured them both a glass of wine and raised his glass. "To success."

"To success," she said, intertwining her arm with his and clinking glasses.

"And speaking of which," he said, "how'd the promotional tour for the new fragrance go?"

Chloe scowled. "Okay, I guess. But all the media kept asking me about was the fiasco at the product launch, thanks to your girl Veronica."

"Hey, *she's* not my girl," Alex said, kissing Chloe.

"I have a big meeting with Laurel tomorrow to talk about how we can do damage control. I'm kind of dreading it."

"Don't let her spoil your success. That's exactly what she wants."

"I know. The whole incident at the launch isn't really the reason I'm dreading the meeting tomorrow." She took another sip of her wine and stared into space. "It's just that, in addition to going over the initial sales figures for *Inner Beauty*, it's also a review to see how I'm shaping up as the company spokesmodel. I know I'm going to feel like a trained circus animal – did I jump through all the hoops and meet all their expectations."

"If they believed in you enough to give you your own perfume," Alex reasoned, "then they obviously want to keep doing business with you."

"That's true," she said, "but I'm not sure if that's what *I* want."

Chloe and Barbara Rubinstein sat across from the Laurel Cosmetics executives in IDG Media's conference room.

"We can't apologize enough for what happened at the launch," said Max Laurel, sitting in his usual spot at the head of the table. "I handled the matter personally, and I've been assured by the top brass at F&W that Ms. Harris was promptly dismissed."

"Actually, when I confronted her, she told me she quit," Chloe said.

"Well, enough about her," Max said. "We're here to talk about you."

Chloe nodded. She was tired of discussing the whole Veronica episode and simply wanted to put the incident behind her.

"The good news," chimed in Bill Bosworth, the PR guru, "is that all of the publicity generated by the incident at the premiere helped raise consumers' awareness of the new product line and boosted sales."

"Frankly, we couldn't have bought better publicity," Max said, tossing a copy of the *New York Post* with the headline "Defaced Billboard Sullies Chloe's 'Inner Beauty'." "How many perfume launches make the front page of all the papers?"

"As long as they're talking about you, that's all that matters, I always say," Barbara said, holding up the paper and smiling triumphantly.

Chloe remained silent, wishing they would get to the point. These review sessions felt like auditioning, having to prove herself all over again, and she just wanted to get it over with.

"By all indications," said another executive, Susan Foster, pointing to figures on a whiteboard, "*Inner Beauty* is not only going to meet, but exceed our sales projections."

"And therefore," Max said, "we're prepared to not only extend your contract for another year, but offer you a long-term deal and a substantial raise."

"We took the liberty of drawing up the paperwork," said one of Laurel's attorneys, looking the part in a stuffy suit and tie. "All you have to do is review the terms and sign the last page."

The attorney slid a copy of the thick contract across the table. Chloe flipped to the last page, which listed a whopping eight-figure amount. The money was hers, and all she had to do was sign her name. She showed the contract to Barbara, who put on her reading glasses and broke her normally impenetrable veneer by gaping at the astronomical figure Laurel was offering.

"Need a pen?" Max said coyly, reaching into the breast pocket of his custom-made suit and producing a monogrammed, gold-plated pen.

"Actually," Chloe said, clearing her throat and finally speaking up, "what I'd like is some time to think it over."

"Would you excuse us, please?" Barbara said. "We need a moment to discuss your offer."

Barbara took Chloe by the arm and led her into the hallway like a schoolmarm pulling aside a disruptive pupil.

"Have you lost your mind?" Barbara said, speaking under her breath as the executives watched them through the conference room's glass walls. "Normally, I'd say don't sign right away and hold out for as much as you can. But this kind of cash doesn't come along every day."

"It's not about the money," Chloe said. "If I sign, it'll lock me into a long-term, iron-clad contract. Laurel Cosmetics would basically own exclusive rights to my image for the next several years."

Barbara held up her hands, as if giving up trying to figure out an unsolvable equation. "And your problem with that is what, exactly? Laurel Cosmetics is a highly respected, global giant. We have a whole roster of models who would gladly trade places with you."

"I know. I'm just not sure this is what I want right now."

Barbara took off her glasses and peered at Chloe, as if trying to see through her. "I've taught you well, my dear. This little negotiating ploy is risky, but it just might pay off big time. What do you want, for them to throw in a private jet? Shares of the company?"

Chloe shook her head. "I don't know what you're talking about."

"That's it. Play innocent." She turned and looked at the executives, who continued to stare at them through the glass as they whispered among themselves. "Come on," she said, taking Chloe's arm again. "We've got to tell them *something*."

Chloe followed Barbara back into the conference room and sat down.

"This is a most generous offer," Barbara said, "but as always, we'll have to have the contract vetted by our legal team and get back to you."

"The contract will become null and void in thirty days if it hasn't been signed," the attorney spoke up, "so we'll need an answer right away or –"

Max held up his hand, silencing his underling. "We enjoy doing business with you, Chloe, and we understand if you need some time to think it over. If Luxe Cosmetics or Revlon or another competitor is trying to lure you away, I assure you we can match any offer."

Chloe shook her head. "No, it's not that. No one's trying to lure me away."

Chloe felt a nudge from Barbara, scolding Chloe for committing one of the major "no-no's" of negotiation – "showing her cards" and letting the Laurel execs know that no other offers were on the table.

"I see," Max said, reclining in his seat and lacing his fingers. "Well, whatever your cause is for hesitation, we want you to work through it. Take as much time as you need."

Chloe and Barbara thanked Max and the other executives for their time and left the boardroom.

"I'm glad they didn't try to pressure me into signing right away," Chloe said as they stepped onto the elevator.

"Yes, but it's not a good idea to keep a man like Max Laurel waiting," Barbara said as the elevator doors closed. "I just hope you know what you're doing."

Chloe stepped out of the shower, toweled her hair and slipped into Alex's pajama top.

"So how'd the big meeting go today?" said Alex, who was lounging on the bed in the bottom half of the pajamas, as she entered the bedroom.

"Great, I guess," she said, crawling beside him on the bed. "The people at Laurel offered me a boatload of money to sign a long-term contract."

Alex looked at her. "Then why don't you sound happy?"

She shrugged. "Laurel's a great company. I really do believe in their products and I love all the corporate philanthropy they do around the world."

He raised an eyebrow. "But?"

"But I don't know if I should sign or not," she said, petting Bizou as the cat hopped onto the bed. "Sure, the deal looks great on paper, but there's a part of me that feels like signing a long-term product-pitching deal would forever brand me as a model, when I what I really want to do is act."

"Man, that's a tough choice," Alex said, putting his arm around her. "I don't know anything about high-stakes negotiating – the advance for my novel wasn't even six figures – but all I can say is if your gut is telling you to reconsider signing the deal, then you should trust your instincts."

She kissed him and nuzzled his neck. "I knew there was a reason I like having you around."

Alex laughed. "It's funny you should say that," he said, sitting up, "because I've been thinking that we sleep over so much, one of us might as well give up our apartment."

Chloe didn't respond right away. She'd been an independent working girl for so long that she'd never really considered the idea of merging her life with someone else's.

"Both of us have trouble squeezing in the futon at your place as it is," she said with a playful laugh, snuggling under his arm.

"Then maybe I should move in here."

Before Chloe could respond, the phone rang. She reached across him and picked it up.

"Okay, we'll be right down."

"What's wrong?" Alex said as she hung up, reading the look of concern on her face.

"It's Dave."

83

Chloe and Alex sat next to Rick in the waiting room of the hospital's intensive-care unit. They all rose when a tall, gray-haired Indian man in a white lab coat entered.

"How's he doing?" Rick said, his voice shaky.

The doctor looked at Chloe and Alex, and then back at Rick. "Perhaps we should talk in private."

"It's okay," Rick said. "They're friends."

"Why don't you all have a seat," the doctor said, motioning with his clipboard toward a couch.

They all sat down and the doctor pulled up a chair.

"We conducted a series of tests," the doctor said, "and determined that he has acute pneumonia as a result of HIV-related complications."

Chloe put her hand on Rick's back, and Alex clasped her knee.

"How long is he going to have to stay here?" Rick asked.

"I'm not going to lie to you," the doctor said. "His prognosis isn't looking good right now, but we'll do all we can for him."

"Can we see him?" Rick said.

"I'll let you go back, since you admitted him, but the only visitors we can allow right now are immediate family."

"Go on back," Chloe said to Rick. "We'll wait out here."

"No, I want you guys to come with me," Rick said, standing. "Dave and I consider you family."

Chloe and Alex looked at each other and then at the doctor, who eventually nodded and stepped aside, ushering them on with his clipboard.

The walk down the long, sterile corridor that led to Dave's room seemed interminable. When they finally reached his room, Chloe covered her mouth to stop herself from gasping when confronted by the sight of a nearly unrecognizable Dave hooked up to a tangle of tubes, hoses and monitors.

Rick gripped the bed's guardrail and peered down at his lover, stroking his hair.

"Is there anything we can do?" Alex said, putting his arm around Chloe as they warily approached the bed.

"You guys just being here is such a big help, you have no idea," Rick said. "I don't think I could handle this by myself."

Rick, Chloe and Alex kept vigil at Dave's bedside for the next two weeks. They slept in shifts. As Dave drifted in and out of consciousness, someone was always there to hold his hand and tell him they loved him and that everything was going to be all right.

One afternoon when Alex was at work, Chloe told Rick he should go home and try to get some rest.

"I don't want to leave his side," Rick said, the dark circles under his eyes revealing his weariness.

"Honey, you can't go on like this," Chloe said, massaging his shoulders. "You need to go home and get some sleep and eat something other than hospital cafeteria food. You can come back this evening reenergized. You need to keep up your strength for Dave."

Rick wrung his face. "Okay," he sighed. "I'll be back later." He hovered at the bedside and touched his lover's hand. "You'll call me if he wakes up or if he starts to…" He trailed off, and Chloe reassured him that she would call him if there was any change in Dave's condition.

After Rick left, Chloe settled in the reclining chair next to the bed with a book. With the background noise of the television and the steady hum of the respirator, Chloe nodded off. She was awakened by the sound of footsteps and saw a middle-aged couple standing in the doorway. She sat up, realizing they must be Dave's parents. Rick had been leaving messages for them since Dave had been admitted but had gotten no reply, which made their sudden presence all the more jarring.

"Oh, hi," she said tentatively, standing. "I'm Chloe, a friend of Dave's. We're neighbors." She considered extending her hand, but awkwardly clutched her book instead, her index finger still marking the page where she had left off.

"Hi, Chloe," the man said softly, without offering an introduction.

The couple stood at the foot of the bed and stared blankly at their motionless son, who was still unconscious.

"I'll give you some privacy," she said, heading for the door.

"No, please," the woman said, stopping her by gently taking her wrist. "I'm sure he likes having his friends around."

Chloe glanced from the woman to the man, not knowing what to say, and stepped back as the couple moved to the side of the bed.

"If you can hear us, son, we're here," the man said, leaning over the guardrail.

The woman took Dave's hand. "We love you," she whispered.

Chloe noticed Dave clutch his mother's hand. At the response, the woman collapsed into sobs and the man took her in his arms.

Later that evening when Rick returned, he introduced himself to the couple as "Dave's friend."

"Thank you," the woman said to him, touching his arm, seeming to sense the latent meaning in Rick's words. "Thank you for being there for him all these years when we couldn't."

The man pursed his lips into a faint smile, as if also expressing his appreciation to Rick.

Alex soon arrived and they all stood around the bed, not saying anything.

Shortly after the reconciliation with his parents, Dave died peacefully in his sleep, surrounded by friends and family.

Chloe rapped on Rick's apartment door and let herself in. She found him in the front room, which had served as Dave's studio, sorting through his lover's belongings.

"Hi," she said quietly, entering the room. "I thought I'd drop in and see how you're doing."

"I'm hanging in, I guess," he said, folding one of Dave's sweaters.

Chloe reached in a box and lifted out the paint-splattered T-shirt Dave had worn when he'd worked on her portrait. "It must be hard... going through his things."

"That was his favorite shirt. I might keep that one."

She handed him the shirt. "I'm so glad his parents were there for his last few..." She caught herself mid-sentence, not wanting to say anything that would exacerbate Rick's grief. "I'm glad they came around."

"Yeah," Rick said softly. "I'm glad his family could be there for the memorial service."

"I thought you did a great job putting the whole thing together. I thought your friends who spoke were really funny," she said. "Dave had such a great sense of humor and he wouldn't have wanted a formal, somber ceremony."

"You're right about that," Rick said, putting Dave's shirt back in the box.

She looked up at the unfinished mural Dave had been working on before his death.

"It's a shame he never got to finish it," Rick said, coming to stand beside her. "Some people from the community center are coming tomorrow to pick it up. They're going to have student artists finish it up and install it on a wall that faces a peace garden."

"That's nice. He'd like that."

Chloe and Rick were still admiring the mural when Alex came in.

"How're you holding up?" Alex said, putting his hand on Rick's shoulder.

"I'm okay. I'm glad Chloe has you. Now there'll be someone around to look after her when I'm gone."

She looked at Rick, perplexed. "What are you talking about?"

"Some of these boxes are Dave's stuff, which I'm sending to his parents," Rick said. "The rest of them are mine."

"You're leaving?" Alex said, putting his arm around Chloe's waist.

"I'm going home, back to Chicago," Rick said. "I need to be around family right now. Maybe it's all that comfort food my mom made for the reception. It reminded me of home. Most people probably lose weight when they're grieving, but I've probably packed on a few pounds." He patted his stomach, chuckling.

"What about work?" Chloe said.

"I put in my notice at Warner & Dunne." Rick paused, looking down at the boxes that contained Dave's things. "You know, if there's anything good that came out of Dave's passing, it's that it showed me that life is too short to keep doing something that doesn't make you happy. I used to complain about my job all the time and whine that I didn't want to be a corporate bean-counter for the rest of my life, and Dave used to tell me all the time to stop bitching and do something about it. I'm finally doing something."

"I think that's great. It takes a lot of courage to make a change," Alex said. "You have any idea what you want to do?"

"Not really. I've been busting my ass since I was a kid – working my way through college and graduating with honors and then going right into Corporate America. It feels kind of liberating to not have everything figured out for the first time in my life."

"Take your time, man," Alex said.

"Yeah," Chloe said, "you've been through a lot. Maybe you should take some time off to clear your head."

"I might go into career counseling. All I know is, I don't want to work in another stuffy office where I have to wear a tie and take orders. I went in yesterday and cleaned out my office, and it felt good." Rick ran his hand over a box that contained file folders, a desk calendar and other office items, as if reflecting on the stodgy, nine-to-five world he was leaving behind. "This past tax season, I volunteered at a credit counseling agency helping low-income people get their finances together and get out of debt, and I loved it. It made me feel like I was making a difference instead of just collecting a paycheck. I might start my own nonprofit back in Chicago. I want to do something meaningful with my life."

"Dave would be so proud of you," Chloe said, going to Rick and hugging him. "I'm going to miss you so much."

She choked back tears. Losing Dave and now Rick moving away all in the same month was almost too much to bear.

"You take care of yourself, buddy," Alex said, trading places with Chloe and hugging Rick.

"And you take care of our Chloe," Rick said, sniffling and wiping his eyes.

"Be sure to e-mail us your new contact info and let us know how you're doing once you get settled," she said, touching Rick's arm.

"I will. In the meantime, I'll have this to keep me company." He picked up a painting off the floor that was draped with a sheet. He took off the sheet, revealing the portrait Dave had done of Chloe for the masquerade ball. "I'm going to hang this in my new office, wherever that may be. It'll be a reminder of Dave, and of you."

She hugged him again. "I'm in Chicago for work every now and then. I'll come visit."

Rick kissed her on the top of her head. "You better."

84

"Okay, hold still," Gigi said, adding brushstrokes to a canvas as Chloe posed on a stool in the living room of their Paris apartment.

"If I would have known I was going to have to sit this long, I would have charged my usual fee," Chloe joked, squirming.

"Why don't we take a break?" Gigi turned the easel toward Chloe, revealing her half-finished portrait. "What do you think?"

"It's amazing, Gi', of course." Chloe looked away from the portrait and out the window, watching people walking by on the street below.

Gigi set her brushes and palette aside. "You seem really distracted. If you're not into this, it's okay. It's just that after years of doing abstracts and working with still life, I wanted a human subject."

"I'm happy to sit for you, Gi'. It's just..." Chloe gazed out the window again, watching the late evening sun cast shadows. "Posing for you reminds me of when I sat for that portrait with Dave. You remember the one we auctioned off at the masquerade ball?"

"That would be the same ball in which you ran out on Alex after the dance like your hair was on fire?" Gigi said, teasing, her eyes taking on the mischievous gleam that Chloe instantly recognized.

Chloe laughed in spite of her introspective mood, appreciating Gigi's attempt to lighten things up. "Yes, the same masquerade ball in which you and Mother and Simone and Marie teamed up to pimp me out to the highest bidder."

Gigi grinned. "That *was* one of my most brilliant schemes, if I do say so myself. Just think if we hadn't done that, you and Alex wouldn't be together."

Chloe smiled, thinking of Alex waiting for her back in New York. "Yeah, it's pretty great having him around." She slumped, her heavy mood overtaking her model-perfect posture. "It's just that I've been feeling kind of out of sorts lately, ever since Dave died."

Gigi took off her smock and hung it on the easel. "I sense the need for a good, long talk. Why don't you get comfy on the sofa and I'll grab the ice cream from the fridge."

Over a carton of cookie dough ice cream, Chloe opened up to Gigi.

"I feel like Dave passing away and Rick moving back to Chicago has really caused me to reevaluate my priorities," Chloe said, cradling her bowl of ice cream and twirling her spoon thoughtfully.

"How so?" Gigi said, spooning right out of the carton.

"Rick has really inspired me with how he's been able to move on since Dave passed away. It takes a lot of guts to quit your job, especially one that pays really well. It gave me a new perspective on the contract negotiations with Laurel."

"From what you told me, the deal they offered you is pretty sweet."

"Yeah, it is, especially the money. It's just… I think it's time for a change. You know I've always wanted to act, ever since we were kids. Remember how we used to talk about all our big dreams?"

Gigi nodded. "You were going to be the big movie star and I was going to be a world-famous artist."

"You're doing what you set out to do," Chloe said, motioning around the apartment at Gigi's paintings. "I'm so proud of you, Gi', and I feel like maybe now's the time for me to start doing what I've always wanted to do."

"So what's stopping you?"

Chloe sat back, taking a couple of spoonfuls and savoring the sweetness of the chocolate chips. "I guess I've just gotten comfortable where I'm at and feel like I have a home with Epitome and Laurel." She paused, tucking her leg underneath her. "And venturing out is scary."

"That's true, but think about how dull both our lives would be if we *hadn't* ventured out. It took a lot of courage for you to defy *Tante* Maxine and move away to New York. And when I was married to Justin, it really took a lot of strength for me to admit I'd made a mistake and leave him." Gigi grew quiet, staring at the floor. "I had nowhere to go. You were off in New York, and I hadn't spoken to Simone in months. But I knew I had to get out, and I'm doing just fine now." She took Chloe's hand. "And I know you're going to do great as well. Sometimes you just have to make the leap."

Chloe gripped Gigi's hand. "You're right." She paused, glancing out the window again. "I've gotten as far as I have by taking risks."

Chloe was still contemplating her future later that evening when she had dinner with Maxine at the Chateau de Chevalier.

"You've barely touched your food," Maxine said, sitting across from Chloe on the screened-in porch where they used to eat family meals with Jacques.

"What's the matter?" said Marie, refilling Chloe's water glass. "Is the steak *au poivre* too tough?"

"Marie, your steak *au poivre* is just right, as always," Chloe said, taking a large bite to prove her point. "I just have a lot on my mind."

Maxine set her fork down, concern spreading across her face. "Is it something serious?"

"You could say that, I guess." Chloe absentmindedly dragged her fork across her plate, preoccupied with the dilemma of whether to re-sign with Laurel or embark on the uncertain path of trying to launch an acting career. "I just have to make one of the most major decisions of my life."

"Oh my god," Maxine said, her concerned look turning to outright panic. "I know you're probably not equipped to deal with an unplanned pregnancy right now, but please don't get rid of it. There are other options."

"I'm not pregnant, Mother." Chloe scoffed at the notion. "Alex and I are very careful. Why did you immediately jump to *that* conclusion?"

"I'm a mother. I worry. It's my job."

Marie shot Chloe a conspiratorial roll of the eyes, which Chloe interpreted as a sympathetic gesture about Maxine's well-meaning yet overprotective nature.

"I've got some cleaning up to do in the kitchen, so I'll leave you two to talk," Marie said, retreating. "Chloe, why don't you fill me in later?"

As Marie backed her way through the open sliding door that led to the kitchen, Bernard, the groundskeeper who had accompanied her to Chloe's masquerade ball, snuck up and playfully swatted her on the fanny.

"Get out of here, you *canaille!*" Marie shrieked, referring to Bernard by the French term for "scoundrel." "And for the millionenth time, stop tracking mud in my kitchen."

Marie stormed into the kitchen, chasing Bernard out the back door.

"They're so cute together," Chloe said to Maxine once they were alone on the porch. "They've been dating since the masquerade ball, right?"

"I'm not sure 'dating' is the right term. More like Bernard tormenting Marie like a smitten schoolboy." Maxine chuckled, then turned serious, taking Chloe's hand. "What's troubling you, *ma chérie?*"

Chloe wiped her mouth and tossed her napkin on her half-eaten plate. "It's work. Laurel's offering me good money – no, make that *ridiculous* money – to sign a new deal."

Maxine's concerned expression was replaced by a perplexed gaze. "And the problem with that would...?"

"You know I've always wanted to act, Mother. It's why I moved to New York. I just have the feeling that if I lock myself into another multi-year deal, I'll be so busy with promotional activities that I won't have time to pursue my *real* dream."

Instead of responding immediately, Maxine sipped her Cabernet. "None of this was my dream for you, you know," she said after a long pause. "I always saw you graduating from college, going on to medical school and becoming a doctor – a steady career with a stable future. But you chose to do things your way."

Chloe looked into her mother's eyes, but instead of judgment, she saw compassion.

"When you ran off to New York, I was devastated," Maxine continued. "But eventually I came to realize that you had to find your own way, just like I had to find my own way when I left home and came to Paris."

Chloe pressed her mother for clarification, eager for Maxine's endorsement to take such a bold step. "Are you saying I should go ahead and try my luck at acting?"

"I learned my lesson about trying to tell you what to do," Maxine said, getting up and clearing the dishes. "But whatever you decide to do, I'm behind you."

Back in New York a couple of days later, Chloe met up with Daniella and Muriel for their monthly girls' night out. Upon arriving at Q Bar, Chloe was not surprised to find the ever-efficient Muriel had already reserved their usual booth.

"Hi," Chloe said, kissing her on the cheek and scooting in next to her. "I see you've already ordered."

"I'm in the mood to celebrate," Muriel said, stirring her margarita with a tiny umbrella. "Miles proposed." She held up her hand, revealing a shiny new diamond.

"Congratulations!" Chloe pulled her into an embrace. "Have you set a date?"

"We're shooting for a traditional June wedding. The domestic violence case I'm working on should be wrapped up by then."

"How's that going?"

"I think we've built a pretty strong case against the man who killed his wife. If we get a conviction, it'll set a precedent that will put more repeat domestic violence offenders behind bars and save a lot of women's lives." She sipped her margarita, looking satisfied. "It feels good to know I'm making a difference."

"That makes one of us."

"Huh?" Muriel leaned forward, straining to hear in the noisy bar.

"Oh, nothing," Chloe said, trying not to dwell on the professional dilemma she faced and enjoy the girls' night out. "Have you heard from Daniella?"

Muriel held up her Blackberry. "She sent me a text. Court's running long again."

Chloe pointed at the TV screen above the bar. "Hey, that's her!"

"We have breaking news from our studios here in the Wellington Tower in Manhattan. There are new developments in the SorCom case today," the TrialTV anchorman said. "The defense delivered persuasive arguments on behalf of the telecommunications giant."

The TV cut to a shot of Daniella speaking in front of the jury, gesturing toward a complex-looking chart that outlined the details of the defense's case. In her Prada suit and heels, she looked more like the star of a scripted television legal drama than an actual attorney.

"Although SorCom is the centerpiece of this case," the anchorman said in a voice-over, "defense attorney Daniella Webster is making quite a name for herself. Analysts are predicting that she'll become the next Nancy Grace."

Chloe joined Muriel in shrieking their excitement over the anchorman's prediction for their friend.

"That's our girl!" Muriel said, high-fiving Chloe.

"Here she is now." Chloe nodded toward the door, where Daniella was making her entrance, lugging an overstuffed attaché case in one arm and a mountainous stack of legal briefs in the other. As she made her way to the booth, the other patrons applauded.

"*Gawd*, that's so embarrassing," Daneilla said, sliding into the booth and dropping her attaché case and papers next to her. She shrunk down in her seat, as if wilting from the attention.

"Get used to it," Muriel said. "We just saw you on TrialTV and the anchorman predicted you're going to become the next Nancy Grace."

Daniella shrugged out of her suit jacket. "This case is getting so much media attention, I have to wade through a mob of reporters every time I leave the courthouse."

"It'll all be worth it when you win," Chloe said, noticing the sparkle had disappeared from Daniella's blue eyes.

Daniella ran her hand through her blond locks, her disheveled appearance a stark contrast from the polished appearance she had presented earlier on television. "That's a long way off. I've got a ton of depositions to go through tonight, and then I have to be back in court bright and early tomorrow morning. Luckily Darby is really understanding about me spending so much time away from Boston while the case drags on here in New York." She motioned for the waiter. "I need a drink.

"I'm sure your client appreciates your devotion," Chloe said once the waiter brought out the drinks, trying to lift Daniella's unusually serious mood.

"I try not to think about my client. The more research I do into this corporation, the more disturbing information I find out."

"Sounds like you've got yourself a classic ethical dilemma," Muriel said with a knowing look, "like the ones we used to read about in school."

"Yeah, but now I'm in too deep to hand the case off to someone else." Daniella sipped her martini, staring at the opposite wall, lost in thought. "Anyway, that case is the last thing I want to talk about tonight. What's new with you guys?"

"Miles proposed," Muriel said, beaming.

"*Ohmigawd!* That's awesome. I propose a toast." Daniella raised her glass, the sparkle returning to her eyes. "To Muriel and Miles, may you have a long, prosperous life together."

The girls clanked glasses.

"Is everything okay, Chlo'?" Daniella said.

Chloe paused before responding, not wanting to dampen the festive spirit by talking about her indecision over signing the new deal with Laurel. "Sure," she said after a moment. "Why do you ask?"

"You just don't seem entirely yourself," Daniella said in that perceptive way of hers that made her so good at her job.

"Yeah, I noticed you seem a bit distracted, too," Muriel said.

Chloe sighed in resignation, realizing her attorney friends were going to grill her until she 'fessed up. "To be honest, I'm sort of going through a mini career crisis."

"You, too?" Daniella said, looking concerned. "I thought you were about to renew your big, fat endorsement deal with Laurel."

"Well, I was, but I've been having second thoughts."

"Hey, do you want one of us to look over the contract to make sure everything's kosher?" Muriel offered.

"Thanks, but the contract isn't what concerns me, it's the deal itself."

"I'm not following," Daniella said. "I thought Laurel's a great company, especially with all that corporate philanthropy they do. That charity ball is where you and Alex had your first dance, after all."

"Yeah, Alex is great and so is the company." Chloe paused, trying to find the right words to describe the crossroads at which she found herself. "It's just that I don't know if I want to continue modeling. Period. Since my friend Dave passed away, I've been doing a lot of thinking. The reason I came to New York in the first place was to act. And I'm thinking about leaving modeling so that I can concentrate on getting my acting career off the ground."

Chloe saw Daniella and Muriel exchange a look, like they were silently conferring.

"I know, I know," Chloe said, anticipating what her practical-minded girlfriends were going to say. "That sounds really loopy. The contract with Laurel is a sure thing. They're throwing money at me, and it would be really stupid to walk away from that to follow some far-fetched dream."

"Actually, that's not what I was thinking," Muriel said. "Look, we're the ones who tried to dissuade you from signing with Epitome in the first place. If you had taken our advice back then, you wouldn't even have the deal with Laurel to consider."

"Yeah," Daniella piped up, "and doing the sure thing doesn't necessarily offer any guarantees. Look at me, I did the sure thing – went to law school, got on with a prestigious firm, but things aren't working out exactly as I'd planned." She held up the stack of legal briefs. "The reason I went into law was to go after corporate swindlers like this, not defend them."

Chloe took another sip of her drink and contemplated what Daniella and Muriel were saying. "So what do you guys think I should do?" She scanned their faces for some indication of the right direction to take.

Daniella gave Chloe's hand a sympathetic squeeze. "That's a decision only you can make, kiddo."

85

Alex strode into his editor's office and placed a document on his desk.

"What's this?" Duff said, holding up the paper as if it were a foreign object.

"My official request for a leave of absence," Alex said. "It's already been approved by HR."

Duff scanned the document. "What's the occasion, an illness in the family? Did you get a fellowship to work on your master's? Taking a year off to travel abroad?"

"None of the above," Alex said without bothering to elaborate. It was a good feeling to know that for once, he had the financial security not to have to explain himself to his superior.

Duff peered at Alex. "I have to sign off on all extended leave requests. I need to know what I'm signing off on."

Alex stared back at his editor, contemplating what to say. His practical nature had dictated that he keep the possibility open of returning to his day job, but he had worked hard and earned success.

"If you must know," Alex said finally, "the movie rights to my book just sold and I'm taking some time off to work on the adaptation."

Duff reclined in his chair, banishing Alex's leave request to a corner of his perpetually messy desk. "You've gone Hollywood, huh? Sorry to hear that."

Alex didn't flinch, determined not to be discouraged by Duff's cynicism. "Actually, I'm pretty excited about this opportunity."

"Do you know how many reporters are closet novelists or screenwriters? Do you know what the odds are at success, even with a studio deal?" Duff continued in a preachy tone, like an academic advisor lecturing a college student who'd chosen an impractical major. "I'd hate to see you waste your talent."

"With all due respect," Alex said, continuing to look Duff in the eye, "my talent has been going to waste for quite some time."

"Whose fault is that?" Duff replied, sounding superior. "I've been called a lot of things – and probably some of them are deserved – but I'm nothing, if not fair. I'm no harder on you than I am on anyone else around here. Every reporter who's earned a cover has done so by scooping *Time* or *U.S. News* on some big story." He leaned forward. "Maybe if you devoted more time to finding that next big story instead of keeping your head in the clouds, you'd be one of our star reporters. I know you have it in you, Michaud."

Alex motioned toward the unsigned document. "Duff, I've already cleaned out my cubicle," he said, undeterred. "Would you mind signing the form so I can get to JFK? I have a midnight flight to L.A. to meet with the studio brass."

Duff looked at Alex, as if he were considering saying more, then scrawled his name on the form and pushed it to the edge of his desk.

Alex retrieved the form and, without saying anything else, turned to leave.

"Hey, Michaud."

Alex stopped in the doorway. "Yes?"

Duff motioned toward the chair in front of his desk. "Take a seat."

Huffing, Alex grudgingly honored his editor's request. His slumping posture reflected his mood. He wasn't up for another lecture about his foolish decision to leave the security of a regular paycheck to try his luck in Hollywood.

"Sorry if I came off too harsh."

Duff didn't make eye contact when he muttered his apology, and Alex marveled at hearing the word "sorry" come out of the "always-right" editor's mouth.

"It's just that I'm speaking from experience," Duff continued, looking up at Alex. "Failed screenwriter here."

"Really?" Alex sat up, intrigued by Duff's revelation. He had never before given any sign that he had any interests outside of hard news.

"Yeah." Duff motioned to the movie poster of tacked on the wall behind his desk. "When I first saw *The Godfather*, it made me want to get into film, write stories for the big screen."

Alex smiled, thinking of how he'd always assumed that the movie poster meant Duff was trying to compare himself to Marlon Brando's quintessential tough-guy character. Hearing Duff reveal his interest in the movies, Alex saw his editor in a new light.

"I started to tell you this at your book signing before we were interrupted, but when I was your age," Duff continued, "I was full of enthusiasm and big ideas, just like you."

Alex laughed. "When you were my age? You say that like you're a hundred years old."

Duff massaged his forehead in a weary gesture, specks of gray glinting in his sandy brown hair. "Sometimes I feel that old. I'm pushing forty and my youngest started school this year. Time flies." He flipped the top off his ever-present bottle of antacids, downed a couple, then turned back to Alex. "I'm not trying to hold you back, it's just that I've been down that road. I spent a couple of years in L.A., working at the AP bureau by day and hammering out my screenplay at night."

"So what happened?" Alex sat forward, riveted by Duff's confession.

"Nothing, which is exactly my point. I have nothing to show for those years but a stack of rejections, so I ended up coming back to New York. I got married, had kids, and pretty soon my dreams were just a distant memory."

Alex was quiet for a moment, reflecting on what Duff had said. Rather than discourage Alex, the fact that the older, somewhat bitter man had given up on his dreams made Alex all the more determined to not let the same thing happen to him.

"Thanks for sharing that," Alex said, rising, "but I've at least got to give it a shot." He shook Duff's hand and turned for the door.

"Be careful when you're dealing with the studios. It's a totally different world from print journalism," Duff called. "And good luck to you."

Alex acknowledged the editor's words with a nod and left the office.

Chloe entered Epitome's lobby, remembering the first time she met with Warren and Barbara as an unsigned talent when she was eighteen and new to the city. Taking a seat in the reception area to wait for them to call her into their office for the meeting she'd requested, she scanned the walls. Interspersed with headshots of models whose careers Epitome had launched over the past few decades were photos of Chloe and her former roommates, including a framed copy of Chloe's very first *Vogue* cover. She stared at the cover as if it were an ancient artifact. It was hard to believe this chapter of her life would soon draw to a close.

"Warren and Barbara will see you now," said the receptionist, a doppelganger of the fashionable young women the Rubinsteins had employed over the years.

"Thank you," Chloe said, rising. Before entering the office, she took a second to collect herself. She rehearsed the speech in her head, informing Warren and Barbara that she wished to leave the agency that had become like a second home to her in order to start an acting career. After hesitating in the doorway and momentarily reconsidering the decision she'd wrestled with for the past few weeks, she steeled herself and walked through the door.

"What's this about?" Barbara said in typical down-to-business fashion, briefly looking up from her paperwork when Chloe walked in.

"Chloe, you know we're always more than willing to make time for you," said Warren, always the more diplomatic of the two. "Why don't you have a seat?"

Chloe took one of the chairs in front of the Rubinsteins' partners' desk and immediately flashed back to that first day when they summoned her to their office. She had come such a long way since then.

"Can we get you anything? Coffee?" Warren said, refreshing his mug from the pot they kept next to their desk, the percolating java an apt metaphor for the power couple's constantly brewing business activities.

"No, I'm fine. I don't want to take up a lot of your time."

"Good," Barbara said, reading glasses perched on the end of her nose as she made notes on a stack of documents. "I've got to finish going over these contracts and, as usual, I have a ton of phone calls to return, including a message from Max Laurel. He wants to know if you've accepted their terms." Barbara glanced up, her intense gray eyes boring through Chloe. "I assume that's why you're here?"

"Um, not exactly." Chloe squirmed under Barbara's gaze, feeling like she was a boarding-school student again who'd been called to Mother Superior's office. "But I'm glad you brought it up."

Warren sat on the edge of the desk, gripping his coffee mug. "If there's something in the contract you'd like to renegotiate, you name it. We're here to represent *you*."

Looking into Warren's kind face, Chloe was overcome by a sense of sadness. It would break her heart to tell him she was leaving. She clenched her fist at her side, steeling her resolve. She had to go through with this or she'd never get to the next level.

"About the deal with Laurel," she began, the words of her rehearsed speech suddenly vanishing from memory, "I'm going to have to decline."

Barbara finally set her paperwork aside and gave Chloe her undivided attention. "What are you talking about? Is it about the money? They're already offering you a bigger signing bonus than any other deal we've brokered."

"This is not about money. I've been doing a lot of thinking over the past few weeks and I've come to realize it's time to move on."

Warren and Barbara looked at each other, then at Chloe.

"What do you mean, 'move on'?" Warren said. "You mean you're not happy with Laurel's offer and you want us to find you another endorsement deal?"

Chloe groaned inwardly. They weren't making this easy. She was going to have to spell it out. "No, I mean I want to leave modeling. I'm ready to try new things."

Warren and Barbara stared at Chloe and said nothing, with only the sound of the percolating coffeepot breaking up the uneasy silence.

"I've always wanted to act," Chloe continued despite her growing discomfort, "and I figure now's the time to go for it, before I commit myself to another long-term deal as a spokesmodel."

She breathed a sigh of relief, glad to have finally gotten the words out. She ran her fingers along the arm of her chair, waiting for Warren and Barbara's reaction.

Warren looked down at the floor and sipped his coffee.

"Why doesn't this surprise me?" Barbara said after a moment, taking off her reading glasses and tossing them on the desk. "They all want to act. Do you think you're the first? Do you know how many of our girls have gone off to Hollywood, only to have a rude awakening when they find out they'll never be taken seriously?"

Warren looked up. "Now, Barbara, don't be so –"

"Do you know how many girls would kill to be in your position?" Barbara said, ignoring her husband.

Chloe sized Barbara up, wondering if this was some kind of head game. She remembered Barbara saying similar things when Chloe first met with them as a new recruit and asked if she could have time to think over their offer.

"Do you know how many models would love to have this amazing opportunity with Laurel? But if you want to piss it all away to chase some crazy dream, go right ahead," Barbara continued in an increasingly sharp tone. "Just don't come groveling back to us when Hollywood tosses you aside just like every other so-called model-turned-actress."

Warren slammed his coffee mug on the desk. "That's enough, Barbara."

Chloe jumped in her seat, so stunned to hear Warren uncharacteristically raise his voice that she temporarily forgot the sting of Barbara's harsh words.

"Am I interrupting something?"

Chloe turned to see Rachel Rubinstein-Gould, Warren and Barbara's daughter and the company talent scout, standing in the doorway of her adjacent office.

"We're just having a little chat with Chloe," Warren said, his usual calm demeanor returning. "If it's not urgent, could you come back later, dear?"

"Sure thing." Rachel's eyes darted from Chloe to her parents, then she warily backed out of the room, closing the door behind her.

"I don't want to leave on bad terms," Chloe said when she was alone with Barbara and Warren again. "Please understand, it's not that I'm unhappy here, it's just that I feel it's time to take my career to the next level."

"There's just one problem," Barbara said, glaring at Chloe as if she were a disloyal employee who'd raided the company safe.

"What's that?" Chloe said, intrigued to know what Barbara was driving at.

Barbara opened a file cabinet behind the desk and retrieved a manila folder. "Your contract." She placed the folder on the desk with a grand gesture. "You may not wish to renew your contract with Laurel, but you still have a binding contract with us that doesn't expire for more than a year."

Warren sipped his coffee and glanced at the folder, as if deciding to back up his wife in her heavy-handed approach. Chloe had gotten used to this good cop/bad cop routine with the Rubinsteins.

Before responding, she paused. In preparing for her meeting with Warren and Barbara, she'd anticipated what to do in the worst-case scenario – that one or both of them reacted angrily to her decision to leave. As if in a tense poker match, she had a trump card she'd been hesitating to use, but Barbara was forcing her hand.

"Don't you remember the opt-out clause?" Chloe said finally.

Barbara's tough expression morphed into one of confusion. "What are you talking about?"

"When I first signed with the agency, my..." She paused, thinking of how to describe Daniella, who had negotiated on her behalf despite having not yet completed law school at the time. "My representative added a rider to the contract giving me the right to walk away at any time with no penalties."

When Daniella had first proposed the opt-out clause, Chloe had thought it was risky for an unestablished model to make such a demand. But now she was grateful she'd listened to Daniella.

Barbara frantically flipped through the file. "I don't recall that. Show me."

"She's right." Warren set down his mug and closed the file. "We deal with so many contracts, it's easy to forget the details. But I remember that like it was yesterday, since it was so unusual."

Chloe sat back, refraining from making a smug comment. Though she'd won this dispute with the always-has-to-have-the-last-word Barbara and gained her freedom, she felt as though she were losing a key alliance.

"Look, Chloe," Warren said after a long silence, "we've always thought of you like our own daughter. All we want for all our models is to be happy and fulfilled. And as much as we hate to see you go, we understand this might be the time for you to branch out."

Barbara jumped in with another venomous rant. "But if you think we're going to hold your place here while you frolic out there in La La Land, then you're sadly –"

Warren held up his hand, silencing Barbara.

As uncomfortable as the situation was, Chloe had to stifle the urge to laugh at the sight of Barbara in submission. Chloe now saw that even though Warren was reserved in comparison to his iron-fisted wife, the balance of the power in the Rubinsteins' relationship was more equitable than Chloe had initially observed.

"You're always welcome here," Warren said. "And we truly wish you well from here on out."

"Thank you," Chloe said, getting up. "I can't thank you guys enough for giving me my start." She went to shake Warren's hand, but he pulled her into an embrace instead. She moved toward Barbara, who promptly turned her chair in the opposite direction and busied herself with her paperwork.

"I just hope you've thought this through," Barbara said, putting her reading glasses back on and keeping her eyes glued to her desk.

"Oh believe me, I've given this a lot of thought," Chloe said, walking to the door. "This is not a decision I made lightly." She paused. "Thanks again for everything."

On the way out, Rachel cornered Chloe in the lobby.

"Sorry, but I couldn't help overhearing," Rachel said, pulling Chloe aside. "I have to apologize for those horrible things my mother said. You know how she is. All that toughness is just a front. It's too hard for her to say, 'I'll miss you, don't go.' She acted the same way when I decided to go away to college on the West Coast instead of staying in New York. She didn't speak to me my entire freshman year at Stanford. Dad had to be the go-between."

"My mother's the same way." Chloe laughed to herself, thinking about how alike Barbara and Maxine were and how Warren had been a surrogate father of sorts, similar to Jacques, with his gentle nature and generous spirit.

"I'm sorry to hear you're leaving," Rachel said. "One of my greatest accomplishments is that I helped recruit you."

Chloe glanced down, remembering how shocked she'd been when Rachel called and asked her to meet with Warren and Barbara after that humiliating audition at Epitome's annual cattle call.

"Rachel, you have a call on Line One," the receptionist said, peering around the corner where Chloe and Rachel stood.

"I guess I better get back to work. Good luck with everything."

Chloe hugged Rachel. "Thanks. I have a lot of good memories here."

"Listen, if you ever reconsider your modeling career, give us a call," Rachel said, retreating to her office. "You know where to find us."

Once Rachel had disappeared behind her office door and the receptionist turned her focus to another call, Chloe lingered in the lobby. She looked around the room one last time, as if mentally photocopying the surroundings. For all she knew, she would never set foot in Epitome's famous brownstone again.

The front door opened and she turned to see a young black girl approaching the receptionist's desk. The girl was tall and thin with a striking face – all the raw essentials of a top model – but with that shy, hungry look that reminded Chloe of herself when she was first starting out. She smiled at the girl, whose presence was a reminder that although this chapter was closing, it was a new beginning for someone else.

"I'm here to see Mr. and Mrs. Rubinstein," the girl told the receptionist in a barely audible tone, her stooped demeanor a sure sign that she would soon have the timidity drummed out of her by Epitome's rigorous beginner's course, just as Chloe had.

"Good luck," Chloe said, making her way to the door.

The girl's eyes followed Chloe's every step. "Excuse me, aren't you –"

"Yeah. That's me." She stopped, gripping the front door handle with one hand and with the other pointing out her framed *Vogue* cover on the wall. "And I bet that'll be you someday soon."

The girl smiled back at Chloe, but her attention was drawn away by the receptionist.

After letting her eyes meander on her first *Vogue* cover for a few more seconds, Chloe opened the door and left the building without looking back.

PART IV

86

Chloe entered the Polo Lounge and felt a tinge of nervous excitement to be in the midst of the Hollywood movers and shakers gathered at the famous L.A. landmark in the Beverly Hills Hotel. As the maitre d' led her to the table where she was to have lunch with her new agent, she spotted an up-and-coming actor discussing his next project with a well-known director. In another corner, she saw a model she had trolled the runways with on more than one occasion cuddled up in a booth with an Oscar-winning movie star old enough to be her father. Despite the pretentious air that permeated the establishment, Chloe was brimming with enthusiasm to be surrounded by fellow creative types.

Upon nearing a table situated in a prime spot in the center of the dining room, she noticed a middle-aged woman with a Pilates-toned physique swathed in a chocolate-brown Prada pants suit, standing to greet her.

"Chloe, so glad you could join me. I'm Beverly Nolan. Just call me Bev."

The woman extended her hand. Chloe took note of the tasteful gems adorning the woman's French-manicured fingers and dainty wrists. Chloe surmised the well-kept woman probably paid hefty sums to a famous Beverly Hills hairdresser to make her mound of unruly blond curls look windswept.

"Hi, Bev. Thanks for meeting with me."

Chloe shook the hand of the woman who had a commanding presence even though she was substantially shorter. The well-known super-agent had founded the Artists' Talent Agency, or ATA as it was commonly known, after shepherding dozens of hit movies as one of the first female studio heads. Judging from the American Express black card she wielded, it was clear that Beverly Nolan had the power to buy and sell most of the players in the room.

"So, I understand you're interested in transitioning into acting," Bev said as Chloe took a seat across from her.

"Yes. I've been planning this move for quite some time. I've always wanted to act. I sort of fell into modeling and always saw it as a steppingstone to what I really want to do."

"Mmm-hmm," Bev said in a nonchalant tone, giving the menu a cursory glance, as if she had it memorized. "I've helped several former models make the leap."

Chloe listened with interest as Bev detailed the careers of the ex-models she had helped transform into respected actresses. Chloe was distracted, however, by an older man at a corner booth who kept staring in her direction. The man stood out in his brightly patterned Versace shirt, which was open to reveal several thick gold chains and his disgustingly hairy chest. When the waiter approached and Bev began to order, Chloe turned her head, hoping the man was directing his gaze at someone beyond her, but was startled by her own reflection in a mirror on the wall behind her. She turned back around and tried to avoid eye contact with the sleazy man.

After the waiter left the table, a well-built young man in a blazer, a shirt open at the collar and Ray-Bans approached the table.

"You're late, Randy," Bev scolded, tapping her platinum Bulgari watch as the young man took a seat.

"Sorry," he said, tossing his sunglasses on the table. "There was a line at valet parking. You think this place could hire better help."

Bev tsked at the young man's politically incorrect remark and then turned to Chloe. "Chloe, this is Randy Van Patten, my newest recruit."

"So nice to meet you," she said, extending her hand.

"How's it goin'," he said, checking out his reflection in the mirror.

Chloe looked Randy over. With his anchorman-perfect, brownish hair, Randy appeared to be no older than Chloe. Tan and toned, he had the conceited air of some of the self-absorbed male models Chloe used to work with.

"You two have something in common," Bev said. "Randy just joined my agency, and you're my newest client. So I thought you'd be the perfect match."

Chloe looked at Randy, who was still examining himself and running his fingers through his heavily moussed hair.

"But my understanding is that *you're* the expert in helping models, singers and TV people transition into movies," Chloe said, trying not to sound too desperate as she turned to Bev. "I assumed you'd be handling me personally."

"I have every faith in Randy," Beverly said, placing a hand on his shoulder. "He just completed UCLA's business management program."

Chloe sipped her Perrier, regarding Bev's comment. It had been her experience over the years that although education was important, people skills, life experience and common sense were also necessary. Randy, who turned his attention from the mirror to his iPhone, seemed to lack all three.

"If you have any concerns, anything at all, you can always call me," Bev continued. "But I'm confident that I'm leaving you in good hands with Randy."

"I'm looking forward to working with you," Randy said, temporarily putting his phone down and flashing Chloe a toothy grin.

"Oh, no, I'm going to be late for my two o'clock. I'll have to have them box my salad," Bev said, glancing at her watch and motioning for the waiter. "If there's anything you never get used to about this city, Chloe, my dear, it's the smog and the bumper-to-bumper traffic on the expressway."

Bev excused herself, saying that she was going to leave Chloe and Randy to get acquainted, talk about her career goals and strategize. But Bev had no sooner left the table when Randy's electronic gadget went off, chiming with a ringtone that Chloe recognized as the latest hip-hop chart-topper.

"Will you excuse me?" Randy said, rising from the table. "I need to take this."

As Chloe watched him walk out, she once again caught sight of the repulsive man in the corner who continued to stare at her as if she were being served for the main course. Fortunately, the food arrived and she turned her attention to slicing into her endive salad.

Back home in New York, Chloe sprawled on her bed, leafing through the pages of a screenplay and surrounded by other scripts that Randy had FedEx'd her.

Apparently, Chloe was nothing but a brain-dead former model in the eyes of Hollywood. Her new agency sent her piles of scripts on a weekly basis. It was like being surrounded by water, with not a drop to drink. Most of the parts she was offered would require her to do graphic sex scenes. They always wanted her to play the pretty yet dumb, helpless plaything of a testosterone-crazed male action hero. She would get slapped around, scream a lot, and get iced in the first fifteen minutes of the movie.

If the offers she got from mainstream studios were bad, the offers she got from so-called "independent" filmmakers were even worse. The purveyors of these allegedly "gripping urban dramas" always wanted her to play a drug lord's whorish moll who fucked her way to the top of a cocaine cartel. If she wasn't offered the part of the "dopeman's bitch," she was asked to play a murderous prostitute or a beautiful junkie who sold her body for crack.

She was also offered several low-rent, direct-to-DVD movies with lots of nudity and paper-thin plotlines. These cheaply-made vehicles didn't appeal to her at all.

She took a couple of meetings with producers and studio executives, who promised to consider her for projects that never materialized. There was buzz about Chloe being cast as the next "Bond Girl" in the 007 franchise – an exciting prospect that turned out to be nothing but hype.

Chloe's experience with the movie industry thus far left her disillusioned. There were simply no glamour roles anymore. Where were all the parts for strong women that had ignited the screen during Hollywood's golden age? That was a bygone era, and she was beginning to think she was born in the wrong time period.

"Hey, watch it," Chloe said as her cat pounced on the bed and began pawing at the script pages. She sat up and pulled the cat onto her lap. "You're probably right, Bizou," she said, stroking the cat. "I should probably use these awful scripts to line your litter box."

Chloe pushed the scripts aside and carried Bizou into the kitchen. She was filling the cat's milk dish when she heard the familiar sound of Alex letting himself in.

"Hey, babe. You home?"

"In here," she called.

Alex entered the kitchen, carrying a grocery bag in one hand and his laptop case in the other. "I hope you don't mind the interruption, but I've been cooped up in my apartment working on the adaptation and I figured I'd come over and make dinner. I could really use a breather."

"Taking a dinner break is just what I need. I've been reading scripts all day and the stuff my agent is sending me is pure crap." She set Bizou's dish in the corner, prompting the cat to leap from her arms and excitedly lap up the milk. "How's the screenplay coming along?"

"Don't ask." He set his bags on the counter. "I had no idea what I was getting myself into when I insisted on adapting my novel myself. Every time I finish a draft and send it out to L.A., thinking I'm done, the suits at the studio send it back to me with a bunch of red marks and pages of notes. When I wrote the book, it was just me, but working on this screenplay is like writing by committee. They want me to take out this subplot, add this car chase, cut this line of dialogue so that it'll not only pass the ratings board but hold the attention span of some 13-year-old boy at a test screening in Bloomington, Indiana."

Chloe hugged him, happy to have someone to commiserate with. "Who needs Hollywood?"

The phone rang and she recognized one of the now-familiar Los Angeles area codes on the caller ID. "What d'you know," she said, taking the cordless phone off its charger. "This is the West Coast calling now."

She took the call in the bedroom while Alex unloaded the groceries and started dinner.

"Hey, C., it's Randy."

She bristled at the nickname her young agent had bestowed on her without her permission. She resented his informal tone, considering he was so hard to reach. He so rarely returned her calls in a timely fashion, it was as if he'd misplaced his beloved iPhone in the Australian Outback.

"Hi, Randy. How's the weather out there?" she said, addressing him with the same insincere politeness that seemed to be an industry custom.

"Sunny, as always," he said, the unmistakable sounds of L.A.'s rush-hour traffic in the background. He was apparently calling from his drop-top Audi during a commute. "Did anything I sent you grab your interest?"

"Quite honestly," she said, reclining on the bed next to the pile of dreadful scripts, "I'd have rather read the phonebook."

"No worries. I just got a call from a producer who wants to meet with you."

"Oh?" She sat up, intrigued. "What for?"

"The lead in a new movie that's going to be filming in Paris. Sounds like you'd be perfect for the role."

"I'd like to hear more," she said, her mood brightening at the mention of an unexpected opportunity. "Can you set up a meeting with the producer?"

"I already took the liberty of booking you on the red eye out of JFK."

"Red eye? You mean tonight?"

"Yeah. That's not a problem, is it? The actress they originally signed dropped out of the project and they need to recast right away."

She hesitated before answering, restraining herself from going off on Randy. How presumptuous of him to assume she could drop everything and fly out at a moment's notice, especially after not returning any of her calls requesting updates on potential offers.

"I'll have to move some things around," she said finally, "but I'll make it."

"Golden. Listen, I'd love to chat, but I've got another call coming in. Why don't I have my assistant e-mail you the 4-1-1?"

She stifled herself to keep from laughing at his pretentious "L.A.-speak." "Fine."

She wrapped up the call, went to her walk-in closet and pulled out a suitcase. She had only a couple of hours to pack and high-tail it to the airport.

"Going somewhere?"

She looked up to see Alex, stirring a mixing bowl, in the doorway of her bedroom.

"Can I take a rain check on dinner?" she said, tossing clothes in the suitcase, expert at packing for spur-of-the-moment trips after years of modeling. "My agent just called and wants me to fly out to L.A. to meet with a producer about the lead in a new movie. It sounds like an opportunity I can't pass up. Sorry to flake out on you on such short notice."

"Don't be sorry. This is your dream."

"I promise to make it up to you when I get back. Can you freeze dinner? I'll only be gone for a day."

"Sure. In fact, if it's okay with you, I might hang out here and cat-sit while you're gone. I could use a change of scenery to work on my screenplay, and I'm sure my dog'll get along with Bizou just fine."

"That sounds good," she said, reaching for a shoebox on the top shelf of her closet. "It'll be nice to come home to you."

"Speaking of which," he said, stepping further into the room, "have you given any more thought to us moving in together?"

Chloe stood in front of her closet, pretending to look for a misplaced article of clothing. She didn't know how to respond to his suggestion. Part of her loved the idea of sharing her space and always having Alex around, while another part wasn't sure she was ready to give up her independence. This was her first "single girl in the city" apartment, and merging her belongings with a man – even the man she loved dearly – would be an adjustment she wasn't certain she was ready to make.

"Chloe?" he said, coming closer. "Did you hear me? Look, baby, if you're not ready to move in together, just say so."

She spun around, meeting his gaze. "Actually, I was just figuring out where to put all my shoes. We're going to need more closet space."

87

Chloe stepped through the revolving door of the office building in downtown Los Angeles and approached a security desk.

"Excuse me. I'm looking for Titan Productions," she told the guard.

The handsome young black man looked up from something he was reading, and Chloe surmised that he was also an aspiring actor, moonlighting to make ends meet, and had probably been reading a script. "Forty-seventh floor."

She blinked, trying to disguise the panic in her eyes. Another skyscraper. Another mountain to climb.

She straightened her suit jacket in an effort to collect herself. If she was going to succeed at this acting thing, she was going to have to overcome her acrophobia.

She approached a bank of elevators, inhaled and pressed the call button. The doors opened immediately, which she figured was probably because the building was mostly empty at this time. Stepping into the elevator, she glanced at her reflection in the compartment's mirrored walls and pressed the button for her floor. The doors closed and she distracted herself by running lines in her head while the elevator began its ascent.

When the motion stopped and the doors parted, Chloe stepped into an office reception area that looked like it had been frozen in the '70s. Gold-tinted, mirrored squares covered the walls. The floor was covered with deep-pile, orange-brown carpeting – not quite shag, but certainly not contemporary. A gaudy gold-plated lamp and a faux-marble ashtray with a built-in lighter sat atop a black-and-gold end table on one side of the black leather sofa that dominated the room. On the other side of the sofa was an identical end table with a statuette of a man and woman in the act of copulation. Chloe stared at the statuette, unable to believe that a reputable producer would display such tasteless artwork – if it could be called that.

She shrugged it off, figuring the producer to be an eccentric type and glanced into one of the gold-tinted mirror panels to check her appearance before the audition began. She jumped, catching sight of a man standing in the open doorway of an office behind her.

She turned to face the man, and he approached her.

"You must be Chloe." He extended his hand.

Still startled by his unannounced appearance, she looked him up and down. His attire was as dated as the décor of the waiting room – silk Versace shirt unbuttoned to reveal a jumble of gold chains interlaced with chest hair, too-tight cream-colored slacks and shiny white patent leather loafers. She examined his face, taking in the George Hamilton tan and steely blue eyes. His hair, which appeared to be dyed dark brown, was styled in an obvious comb-over. Despite his odd look, she was overcome with the feeling she had seen him before.

"Uh, yes, I'm Chloe Bareaux," she said, clearing her throat and shaking his hand, his oversize pinky ring abrasive against her palm.

"Barry Mangione. Thank you for coming out. Some producers leave this part of the job to the casting director, but I like to see all my girls personally." He smirked, revealing artificially white teeth.

She kept her expression neutral, inwardly bristling at the "girls" comment but trying to remain professional.

"Why don't you come into my office," he said, motioning toward the open doorway. "We'll be more comfortable there."

She hesitated, overcome with the impulse to retreat to the elevator. She had come all this way and, considering her acting's career's sluggish start, she figured she may as well give it her best.

She silently followed him into the office, which was a larger replica of the reception area. A large black-and-gold desk sat at one corner of the gaping room, which was lit only by a view of the sun setting over Ventura Boulevard. Floor-to-ceiling shelves lined an entire wall, with the spines of classic novels that looked like they had never been cracked open mingled with gold-plated statuettes of leopards and photos of Mangione with his arm slung around starlets and celebrities from decades past. His tacky decorating flair extended to animal prints, from an enormous sectional sofa upholstered in faux leopard skin that took up most of a wall to a bearskin rug splayed across the middle of the room.

"Why don't you have a seat?" Mangione extended his arm toward the sofa. "Can I get you something?" He moved to take a book from one of the shelves, pulling on it like a lever, and several of the shelves folded into a mini-bar. He looked at her with a smug expression, as if this little trick was meant to impress her.

"No, I'm fine thanks," Chloe said, sitting on the sofa and demurely crossing her legs. It was as though all of her teenage etiquette training was returning to her in an unconscious effort to counteract this man's crudeness.

He poured bourbon into a glass. "Oh, come on. One drink won't hurt. It might even loosen you up."

She gave him another once-over, unable to believe the unprofessional conduct of this so-called producer. "That's okay, thank you. I never drink when I'm working."

He plopped ice cubes in the glass and sauntered over to the sofa, violating her comfort zone by sitting too close. "I'm hoping this experience will be less like work and more like…" He paused, sipping the bourbon. "Play." He gawked at her like she was a singing telegram sent here for his amusement.

She scooted away from him. "I'm sorry. I don't understand. I came here to audition for the part of Nicolette in *City of Night.*"

"Yes, I'm producing that film. That's just one of my ventures. I made my fortune in the publishing world, you might say."

He set his glass on a coffee table, which was covered with a selection of neatly fanned-out magazines. Chloe noticed that several of the magazines bore the name of the gossip rag *The Weekly Observer*, while the other magazines had scantily clad women on the cover underneath the title *Flesh for Fantasy*. She looked up from the row of magazines and into his cold blue eyes. It suddenly occurred to her that this Barry Mangione was the publisher of Titan Media, which published scurrilous supermarket tabloids and a low-rent *Playboy* knock-off. She recalled reading in the trades that this Hugh Hefner wannabe had recently ventured into film production, sinking some of the dirty money generated from his vast porn and tabloid-media empire into Hollywood film projects in an effort to gain legitimacy.

"I think you'd be perfect for the part of Nicolette. I've been looking for a girl with your exotic looks." He moved closer.

She scooted further down the seemingly miles-long sectional. "I'm sorry, Mr. Mangione. I think my agent made a mistake in sending me here."

Upon mentioning her agent, she suddenly remembered where she had seen this man before. He had been the man staring at her from across the room during her first lunch with Randy and Beverly Nolan at the Polo Lounge.

"Why don't you just relax? Let me pour you that drink after all and then we can get down to that audition." He placed his hand on Chloe's knee, his pinky ring again scratching her skin. "On my bearskin rug."

Outraged, she reflexively reached for his glass and splashed alcohol in his face. "I'll never be desperate enough for a part to degrade myself by sleeping with you, or anyone else for that matter."

"Bitch! You ruined my shirt." He pulled a brightly colored silk handkerchief from his pocket and patted the stains.

Trying to keep what was left of her dignity, she rose from the sofa and walked to the door, taking slow, steady strides to let him know she wasn't afraid of him. Photographers and male models had occasionally come on to her when she was still in the world of high fashion, but this experience was disorienting. She had been naïve enough to believe that the Hollywood casting couch was just a myth, but she had been slapped in the face with cold, hard evidence that it was an unfortunate reality.

"You'll regret this, you know," he called after her. "Everyone has a past. Even self-righteous little sluts like you."

She turned back around, stopping in the doorway. "If you're threatening to dig up dirt on me and publish it in one of your rags, don't bother. I have nothing to hide."

Chloe stormed into the offices of the Artists' Talent Agency and demanded to see Randy.

"He's on a call right now," said the young Asian man sitting at the receptionist desk. "Would you like to have a seat and I'll let him know you're here?"

"No, that won't be necessary." Chloe walked past the reception desk with a determined gait as the young man shouted "*Miss! Miss!*" at her back. She trouped down a maze of corridors, past assistants and a clerk pushing a mail cart, who all gave her bemused looks, until she reached a corner office with the name "Randy Van Patten" emblazoned on a gold star like on a dressing-room door.

"What the hell is going on?" she said, flinging the door open.

Randy, talking on a headset as he stood facing the view of the downtown Burbank skyline, turned to her with a startled expression.

"Let me call you back. A client of mine just showed up," he said to the party on the other end. He took off his headset and motioned toward a leather sofa across from his shiny granite desk. "Chloe, good to see you, as always. Why don't you have a seat?"

"I'm not here to make small talk. I want some answers, and I want them now," she fumed. "What in the hell did you send me to that scumbag Barry Mangione's office for? Those are the types of people you're supposed to protect me from."

Randy approached her and put his hand on her shoulder. "Calm down. No need to raise your voice."

She pushed Randy's hand away. "Don't touch me. And don't you dare patronize me, you little wanker," she said, lapsing into British slang she'd picked up during her boarding-school days in London.

The receptionist appeared in the doorway, panting as if he'd been sprinting down the hall trying to catch up with Chloe. "I'm sorry, Randy. I told her you were on the line and to have a seat, but she just barged in."

"It's okay," Randy said in his smug tone. "Chloe's a client of ours."

"Yes," Chloe said, "but you wouldn't know it for as much work as you've gotten me. I was so humiliated when I found out that audition you sent me on was for some kind of soft-core porn flick."

"Well, you have to start somewhere."

Chloe had to restrain herself from slapping the smarmy expression off Randy's face. "I can see it's a total waste of time, talking to you." She abruptly turned to the receptionist. "I want to see Beverly Nolan. Now."

"I'm sorry, Ms. Nolan is out of town on business," the receptionist replied. "If you'd like to follow me back up front, I can set up an appointment."

Chloe shook her head in disgust. She was tired of being put off. There had been several times over the past six months that she had attempted to call Bev to discuss the fact that she felt her career wasn't going in the direction she'd hoped. Whatever happened to Bev's promise that she'd "always be there" whenever Chloe had a question or concern that Randy couldn't address? In fairness, she couldn't fault Randy for his inexperience, but it was obvious that Chloe's burgeoning acting career wasn't high on the priority list of Beverly Nolan, Super-Agent to the Stars.

"Ms. Nolan will be back in town a week from Friday. I can see if she has an opening then," the receptionist said sheepishly, shrinking as if afraid Chloe was going to slug him.

"That won't be necessary," she said, straightening her jacket to regain her composure. "My business here is done."

"'For personal and professional reasons, I have decided to sever my relationship with the Artists' Talent Agency.'"

Chloe sat across from Alex at the dining room table in her New York apartment, which they now shared, reciting an item in *The Hollywood Reporter* that included a statement she had prepared.

"I look forward to continuing to pursue acting opportunities," she continued, "with different representation.'"

"You were very diplomatic," Alex said, pushing aside his half-eaten bagel and cantaloupe, "especially after the humiliating experience with that slimeball producer. I'm glad I wasn't there, 'cause I'd be in jail right now. I would've kicked that guy's ass, and then went over and wiped up Hollywood Boulevard with that inept, so-called talent agent for putting you in that situation."

Chloe reached over and clasped Alex's hand, appreciating his unwavering support. Despite her initial reticence, she was glad he'd moved his stuff in while she was in L.A. She needed him close-by now more than ever.

"You should hear Beverly Nolan's response," Chloe said, holding up the trade journal. "You'll get a kick out of this: 'We're sorry to lose Chloe as a client, but we wish her well in her future endeavors.' Hah!" She slammed the paper to the table. "If she was so worried about losing me as a client, maybe she should have taken my calls and made herself available when Randy bungled everything."

"I know you're frustrated, but it's going to be okay, babe. You'll show them. Now that everyone knows you're a free agent again, you'll have offers pouring in."

"Oh, yeah? Then why isn't the phone ringing?"

"Patience, babe. Patience."

"I'm afraid that's something I'm running out of pretty quickly." She got up and began helping Alex clear the breakfast dishes. "I know I should get back out there and start knocking on doors again, but I'm sick of the whole dirty business right now. I feel like I need a break."

Alex took the dishes from her and began rinsing them in the kitchen sink. "I bet a trip down South is just what the doctor ordered. How about going home with me, to New Orleans? I'm going there next week with the production team to do some location scouting for the movie version of my book."

Chloe didn't respond, and instead went back to the dining room to finish clearing the table. The prospect of finally getting to visit her mother's native city both excited and terrified her.

"Did you hear me, hon'?" Alex said, following her and propping his elbow on the doorway of the kitchen. "I thought you've always wanted to visit New Orleans and see where you mother's side of the family is from?"

"I do," she said, collecting the *Hollywood Reporter* and the remnants of the morning paper and not looking at him.

Alex approached her and pulled her close. "Honey, if you don't want to go, it's okay. I know you've just gone through a hard time severing ties with that agency, and if you're not up to traveling right now, I understand. There'll always be another time for us to visit New Orleans together."

She set the papers down and looked him in the eye. "If you want to know the truth, I'm afraid of going down there."

Alex looked confused. "Afraid? Why?"

"Because every time the topic of New Orleans comes up with my mother, she starts acting strange and changes the subject. I'm afraid she's hiding some family secret. I'm afraid something horrible happened there."

Alex gave her a reassuring squeeze. "Whatever it is, we'll find out together."

88

"We're here," Alex said, nudging Chloe when the plane touched down at New Orleans' Louis Armstrong airport.

Chloe lifted her head from Alex's shoulder, sat up and rubbed the sleep from her eyes. She felt like she did when she first arrived in New York, like a child taking it all in for the first time.

"Come on," he said, taking her hand. "I can't wait to show you around."

Setting foot on Louisiana soil was an absolutely religious experience. It was as though she were making a pilgrimage to the Holy Land, the place where it all began.

The logical first stop she and Alex made was to the French Quarter, New Orleans' cultural epicenter. Taking a carriage ride through the Vieux Carré, Chloe felt like she was connecting to centuries of history on an intense, cellular level.

She marveled at the bustling Jackson Square, which was teeming with tourists, caricaturists and street performers. It reminded her so much of Trocadéro in Paris – proof positive that the American port city that was her ancestral home and the European metropolis where she grew up were inextricably linked.

"We have to have our fortunes told," Chloe said excitedly, coaxing Alex over to one of the tarot card readers whose stands rimmed the plaza, like a grade-schooler dragging a grudging parent to an amusement-park ride.

"You are a most lovely couple," the older black woman said in Haitian Creole accent when Chloe and Alex sat down at her table. "You look as though you belong together."

Chloe nodded in appreciation, holding Alex's hand. "This is my first time visiting New Orleans. Can you tell me about the future?"

The woman looked thoughtful and began arranging a series of cards emblazoned with mystical images. "Ah, your time here will be fruitful," she said, looking up at Chloe with striking blue eyes that contrasted starkly with her deep ebony complexion. "You will find closure you have long been seeking."

Chloe glanced at Alex, who folded his arms and donned his skeptical journalist's expression. His demeanor indicated that he had grown up with this mumbo jumbo and was *so* not buying it.

"*Merci*," Chloe said, tipping the woman and thanking her for her time. She wanted so much to believe that the tarot card reader really had foretold events that would unfold here.

Chloe clutched Alex's hand as he pulled their rented car into the driveway of a stately plantation house just outside the city. When they reached the house, she rolled down her window to get a better look.

"This is some spread," she said, looking up at the house, which was typical Louisiana style with tall white columns surrounded by sprawling grounds dotted with weeping willows and gardenia bushes.

"This house has been in my family for generations," Alex said, putting the car in park. "As family lore has it, this plantation belonged to a French property baron, and my great-great grandmother on my father's side was his slave mistress. When he died, he caused a scandal by leaving it to her in his will."

"It's beautiful," Chloe said of the house, which reminded her of the comfort and security of the Chateau de Chevalier.

"It's not bad," Alex said, opening his car door. "Well, you ready to meet the family?"

Alex had been able to coordinate the location scout to coincide with a family gathering to celebrate his parents' thirtieth wedding anniversary.

"Is it too late to turn back now?" Chloe said half-jokingly as Alex led her to the front door.

"No need to be nervous," said Alex, taking her hand. "I'm sure everyone's going to welcome you with open arms."

Alex's mother, Lena, did just that when she met them at the door.

"Welcome to New Orleans. We've heard so much about you," Lena Michaud said, greeting Chloe with a warm hug. "It's so nice to finally meet you in person."

"Thank you." She smiled at the well-preserved, fifty-something woman and noticed the resemblance in Alex's facial features, although she had green eyes and was several shades lighter than her son.

A man who looked like a slightly younger version of Alex entered the foyer.

"Man, bro'," the young man said to Alex as he looked Chloe up and down, "you sure went out and found yourself a sexy chick."

"Yeah, and she's all mine, so you better keep your hands to yourself, dawg," Alex said, landing a fake punch to his brother's gut.

"Alexandre and Marcus Michaud, stop the horseplay," Lena said to her sons. "If you knock over my vase, I'm going to tan both of your hides. Neither of you are too big to turn you over my knee."

Chloe smiled at how much Alex's mother reminded her of her own, with her ladylike manner and no-nonsense attitude.

"Mom's right," Alex said to his brother. "Why don't you make yourself useful and help me unload the car?"

"Come on," Lena said, taking Chloe's arm. "I'll show you to your room and help you get settled in."

Lena led Chloe up a winding staircase and down a hallway lined with family photos to a room that overlooked Lake Pontchartrain.

"I hope you'll be comfortable here," Lena said, opening white slatted doors that revealed a balcony with lacy ironwork typical of the region.

Chloe set her carryon bag on the chenille bedspread. "I'm sure I will."

"Everyone else'll be getting in tomorrow. You and Alex are the first to arrive."

"What about Marcus?"

"He still lives here. Typical college student – twenty going on twelve," Lena said, rolling her eyes comically.

"Mom, you know you and Pop love having me around," Marcus said as he and Alex entered with the luggage.

"Come on, help me finish dinner and let Chloe and Alex unpack." Lena ushered her younger son out of the room.

"I hope you don't mind sleeping in the guest room by yourself," Alex said, setting Chloe's luggage next to the bed when they were alone in the room. "I'm staying in my old room. My parents are kind of traditional. They'd flip out if we stayed in the same room since we aren't married."

Chloe laughed. "My mother's the same way."

"I'll introduce you to Pop later on. He's down in the Quarter rehearsing for a club gig."

"I thought he was a professor?" she said as she began putting her things away in the antique chest of drawers next to the bed.

"He is, but he still plays with his band on weekends. When he's not teaching music, he's performing. It's his life."

Chloe grew quiet and retreated to the balcony. She stared out at the lake, which was rippling in the summer breeze. Finally making it to the city that she'd dreamt of visiting since childhood, the place of her family's origins, was disorienting.

"What'cha thinking 'bout?" Alex said, coming to her side and putting his arms around her waist.

She put her hands on his. "Nothing. I'm just glad I'm here with you."

*****

Chloe and Alex rose before dawn the next day to accompany the production crew on the location-scouting mission. Chloe was not only excited to be riding around with a real film crew in the van the studio had chartered, she was awestruck as the city that held so much mystery and clues to her heritage unfolded before her eyes.

As they left the city limits and rolled into nearby Jefferson Parish, Chloe took note of the strange juxtaposition of houses and commercial buildings that had been destroyed in the flood waters of Katrina and perfectly intact structures. They would pass a whole neighborhood that appeared undisturbed, then happen upon some strange sight like a home whose roof had been pried open like a tuna can or a mangled signpost drooping like a weeping willow.

"This is so eerie," Chloe said to Alex, looking out the window next to the spacious van's backseat.

"I know," Alex said, "this is not the area I grew up in. I'm sorry you have to see it like this."

She gripped his hand. "I'm just glad I'm seeing it with you."

The van went over a bump, alerting Chloe that she needed to use the restroom.

"Is it okay if we stop soon?" she said to the driver, raising her hand as if on a school field trip.

"Oh, great," Bryan da Silva, the studio-appointed producer, said in a sarcastic tone from the front passenger seat. "Good thing we didn't all bring our wives and girlfriends, or else we wouldn't get any work done."

Chloe glanced at Alex, who looked like he was about to reach out and throttle da Silva. The self-important man had snubbed her when Alex introduced her at the beginning of the day and made it clear that he wasn't thrilled that the screenwriter had brought his "supermodel girlfriend" along for the ride. She squeezed Alex's hand to keep him from saying something he might regret.

The tense moment lifted when the director, who was seated behind the producer, spoke up.

"We could probably all use a break to stretch our legs," said Hal Forster, one of the most respected black directors in the industry, who seemed to be the buffer between the crew and the abrasive producer.

The driver pulled over to a gas station, where Chloe used the restroom while the all-male crew smoked cigarettes and loaded up on chips and candy bars. The producer hustled everyone back into the van, insisting they had a schedule to keep, and told the driver to get moving.

The next leg of the tour took them across the Lake Pontchartrain Causeway, which consisted of two parallel bridges. The producer instructed the driver to stop along the longer of the two bridges, which at over twenty-three miles, as

Alex informed Chloe, was the longest bridge over water in the world. Everyone piled out of the van, except for Chloe.

"You coming, honey?" Alex said, holding open the sliding door to the van's backseat.

"You go ahead. I'm going to stay here," she said, settling into her seat. "I think the heat's getting to me a bit and I should probably stay out of the sun."

"Okay," Alex said with a slight look of concern, "we'll be back in a bit."

Chloe clutched the armrest and tried not to look out the window. Her fear of heights mingled with visions of Jacques' mangled car on Paris' Alexandre III bridge. She sipped her bottled water and tried to block out the painful memory of the crash that had claimed her beloved stepfather.

She tried to concentrate on the book she'd brought with her, but her hands kept trembling as she turned the pages. She jumped at the sound of someone rapping on the window and looked up to see Alex looking at her with the same concerned expression.

"Yeah?" she said, sliding the door open.

"You okay?"

"Yeah, I was just reading. What's up?"

"The director asked if you'd mind standing in for a shot he's trying to visualize."

Chloe looked out the front window and saw the director and other crew members peering at her as they conferred among themselves. She hesitated, trying to think of what to tell Alex.

"Uh…" she said, stalling, "I'm not sure if I should…"

"If you don't want to do it, it's okay," he said, stroking her shoulder. "I'll just them you're not feeling up to it."

She looked back at the crew, who were still murmuring and gawking at her. She wanted to help Alex and prove that she wasn't just the girlfriend tagging along for the ride, slowing down the process.

"I'll do it," she said finally.

She stepped out of the van, holding onto Alex for support. Following him to the spot at the shoulder of the bridge where the crew was gathered, her legs wobbled and she felt suddenly lightheaded. She held her head high and did her best to get her bearings, determined not to be shackled by the past.

"Thanks for doing this," Hal, the director, said when she came to stand next to him. "We're fortunate to have a professional model as our stand-in."

"Thankfully she doesn't have to read any lines," she heard the annoying producer mutter to one of his flunkies.

Chloe noticed Alex tense with anger and start to say something, but she shot him a look that said, "Don't give him the satisfaction."

Intent on demonstrating her professionalism, she followed the director's instructions and positioned herself at the edge of the bridge. She clutched the guardrail and forced herself not to turn around and gawk at the steep drop to the water below.

"I think this is the perfect location to film the crash scene," Hal said, forming a square with his hands and peeping through it with one eye closed, as if looking through a camera lens.

Chloe could feel sweat beading her forehead as the director discussed the shot with the crew. At least Alex was there, his presence acting like a steel girder propping her up.

"We can film most of the sequence here, then recreate the setup in the studio to shoot the close-ups," Hal said to the cinematographer, who was jotting notes and snapping photos of the site. The director turned to Chloe. "You're shaking. Can you hold still for one more minute? We're just about done."

Chloe tried to relax, but her knuckles were nearly turning white from the clutch she had on the guardrail. After several more torturous moments, Hal finally told her she could go back to the van and thanked her for standing in.

"You take direction very well," he said, shaking her hand.

"That's about the only talent models have," da Silva said to his assistant, loud enough for her to hear.

Alex ignored the snarky comment, coming to her side to help her back to the van.

"You're still shaking," he said, putting his arms around her. "You sure you're all right?"

"Yeah," she said, leaning on him. "I just need to get something in my system."

On the way back into town, the crew stopped at a roadside barbecue stand where Chloe had some of the best ribs she'd ever tasted. "My trainer, Marcella, is going to be so mad at me when she sees all the weight I've gained when we get back," she said, chomping into another scrumptious rib.

"You might as well forget about your diet. Mom's cooking a big dinner tonight for the whole family. It's going to be a down-home, Louisiana feast."

"I can't wait to meet the rest of your family."

89

Chloe nearly lost count of Alex's siblings, their respective mates and their children as they arrived for the big anniversary dinner that evening at the family estate. As it turned out, Alex was the middle child of five. In addition to his younger brother Marcus, there was a younger sister named Denise, an older sister named Monique and the eldest sibling, Robert Jr. Alex's maternal grandmother, whom everyone referred to as Nana Cecile, was also present for her daughter and son-in-law's anniversary celebration.

Before dinner, everyone gathered in the homey living room. Alex's relatives were warm and friendly, and Chloe spent much of the evening answering questions about her background and the glitzy life of a model.

"The name Bareaux sounds familiar," Nana Cecile commented. "Are your people from around here?"

"Yes, but I grew up in Paris," Chloe said, sipping wine to take the edge off the pressure of meeting everyone at once who was important to Alex. "My grandmother died when I was young and I never knew my grandfather."

"Shame," the old woman said, shaking her head of silver curls. "Family's the most important thing."

Chloe was rescued from having to answer any more questions by Lena coming out of the kitchen and announcing, "Dinner's ready!" Everyone scrambled to take their places in the spacious dining room. Before digging in, everyone joined hands for a family prayer, offered up by Alex's father, as tradition dictated.

"Father, we thank you for the food that we are about to receive and for the hands that prepared it, and most of all, for being together," Robert said in his baritone as everyone stood around the table with their eyes downcast. "Now, let's take a moment to reflect on the blessings we have."

As silence enveloped the room, Chloe could feel Alex clutching her hand tightly.

"Okay, let's eat!" Robert finally declared.

Around the dinner table, Chloe struggled to remember the names of Alex's relatives, which didn't seem to matter since everyone referred to each other by terms of endearment and playful nicknames. She liked how goofy and loud everyone was, joking around and cracking on each other. She was a bit taken aback at first, since the irreverence was a stark contrast to the dinner-table manners she'd learned from her mother and etiquette tutor, Madame de Tornquist. But she grew to appreciate the noisiness and affectionate ribbing between Alex and his siblings – something she'd never experienced as an only child.

The Michauds reflected the diversity of many black American families, with every eye color, hair texture and complexion represented. Alex and his four siblings ranged in complexion to the light-skinned, green-eyed beauty of their school-teacher mother to the deep bronze hue and dark brown eyes of their music professor/trumpet player father, who apologized for eating and running but explained that he had to rehearse with his band.

"After dinner, we're going to hear Pop play at this jazz club on Bourbon

Street," Alex said, passing a plate of steaming jambalaya to Chloe.

The Michaud women had prepared a moveable feast of all the traditional Creole foods that Chloe remembered from her grandmother's cooking. Colorful plates of mouth-watering shrimp gumbo, jambalaya and traditional Southern fare such as fried chicken and okra made their way around the table along with family stories and gossip.

"Why don't you have some more of this, baby," Nana Cecile said, piling a second helping of jambalaya onto Chloe's plate. "We're going to have to fatten you up."

Chloe smiled at how much the elderly woman reminded her of her own grandmother, Mama Louise. Chloe loved how she called everyone "baby" and "sweetheart" and was always doting on her children and grandchildren.

"This is delicious," Chloe said, spearing a forkful of the spicy rice, ham and sausage dish.

"Thank you, dear. This recipe was passed down from my mother, and I passed it down to my baby," the old woman said, touching Lena's hand.

"And now I make it for my husband and kids," said Alex's older sister Monique, who was suddenly distracted when her twin boys began fighting over dessert and knocked over a drink.

"How many times have I told you to behave at the dinner table?" Monique exclaimed in exasperation.

Jerry, Alex's brother-in-law, got up to pick up the spilled glass, limping on a cane.

"What happened to your leg, Jer'?" Alex said.

"I fell at the factory a few weeks ago," he said.

"That Dade Chemical is such a corrupt company. They denied his workers' comp claim," Monique fumed, wiping up the spilled juice. "That's how they reward Jerry for giving them ten years of his life."

Lena placed her hand on her son-in-law's shoulder. "You're excused from clean-up duty," she said, lightening the mood as she began clearing the table. "Everybody else pitch in. We don't want to miss your father's band."

Chloe and Alex joined his mother and siblings in a reserved section near the stage at the 317 Club. As Chloe sat snuggled under Alex's arm at their table with a candle flickering to enhance the intimate atmosphere, she observed Lena watching her husband with the admiration of a schoolgirl.

Before taking an extended solo, Robert winked at his wife and then began blowing into his instrument, his eyes closed tightly as if each note were a prayer.

"Dad says he goes into a 'zone' when he plays," Alex whispered to Chloe. "He says he forgets that the audience is here and becomes one with the music."

Chloe found herself getting lost in the music as well. She wondered if her grandparents had once performed on this very stage, Papa Joe seductively playing his horn and Mama Louise crooning the lyrics to a torch song.

The next day after Nana Cecile and Lena whipped up a breakfast of buttermilk biscuits, gravy and sausage, Chloe and Alex set out with the film production crew on a walking tour of the Garden District and other parts of the city to finish up the location scouting.

"What are these strange markings on these tombs?" Chloe asked Alex as a tour guide led their group through one of the historic cemeteries.

"I think that has to do with some kind of voodoo ritual," Alex said. "You know, black magic is a big part of the heritage of Louisiana. You ever heard of Marie Laveau?"

"The famous voodoo priestess?"

"Yeah. As part of the back story for Sidney, the main character in my novel, I wrote her as a descendant of Marie Laveau. Sidney uses her intellect and police training as well as the intuition and other supernatural gifts she inherited to solve crimes."

"Maybe that's why I relate to your character so much. I often use logic *and* gut instinct to make decisions," Chloe said, staring at the markings on the tombstones. "I find the culture of black magic fascinating. My grandmother used to tell me stories about Marie Laveau. She dabbled in voodoo herself. She was a devout Catholic, but if anyone messed with me or my mom, she would put a hex on them."

"Sounds like the women in my family," Alex said, laughing. "Once, when an old boyfriend did my sister wrong, one of my aunts told her to take hair from his brush and bring it to her. I don't know what she did, but no one ever heard from that no-good boyfriend ever again! Pop always says, never mess with a Creole girl."

"That's right, and don't you ever forget it," Chloe said, elbowing him in the ribs.

Chloe was riveted as the tour guide began to describe an outbreak of yellow fever at the turn of the twentieth century in which many of the city's French plantation owners and free men of color were buried in this cemetery. She flashbacked to childhood, sitting on her grandmother's lap. She remembered Mama Louise saying that many of Papa Joe's relatives, the Bareaux clan, had died in a yellow fever outbreak.

With a sudden urgency, Chloe scanned the rows of the ornate mausoleums and tombstones. She felt her heartbeat quicken when her eyes locked on a tombstone, engraved with statues of angels and a large cross, with the letters

"B-A-R" visible, but the rest of the name blocked by another headstone.

"Excuse me a second," Chloe said, letting go of Alex's arm and breaking away from the group.

"Honey, where are you going?" Alex said as she began weaving in between the tombstones.

She stopped in her tracks, standing before side-by-side headstones marked with the names "Joseph Bareaux" and "Louise Dussault Bareaux." She recalled that after Mama Louise's death, her body was shipped back to New Orleans to be buried beside Papa Joe. Chloe began weeping, overcome with emotion.

"Honey, are you okay?" Alex said, catching up with her. "Is something wrong?"

Unable to speak, Chloe simply gestured toward the headstones.

"It's okay," Alex said, taking her in his arms. "I'm here."

Later that evening, Chloe sat on the balcony of her room in the Michaud estate, watching the setting sun casting golden rays on the rippling waters of Lake Pontchartrain. Even in this environment, her ancestral home, she still felt like an outsider. She knew so little about her heritage, as compared to Alex's close-knit family.

She jumped at the sound of a knock on the door.

"It's just me," Alex said, letting himself in and carrying a tray of beignets and lemonade. The smell of freshly baked beignets carried on the evening breeze as he joined her on the balcony.

"Mom just made these," he said, setting the platter on the small table next to her chair. "I thought you might be hungry since you skipped dinner."

She nibbled on a pastry. "These are delicious. They remind me of Marie's cooking." She smiled, thoughts of Paris, of home, overtaking her. "I'm sorry I missed dinner. I hope everyone didn't think I was being antisocial," she said. "Seeing my grandparents' gravesite this afternoon really shook me up. I just needed some time alone."

"I understand." He sat in the chair next to her and munched on a beignet. "I'm sure the whole experience of being down here is kind of overwhelming."

"It's more than that." She stared out at the glistening water. "I still feel like there's some family secret my mother never told me about, and seeing my grandparents' grave makes me wonder even more what it is."

"Why don't we do some research while we're down here? I can arrange to stay a while longer after the rest of the crew leaves. Mom and Pop'll be thrilled we're extending our stay." Chomping into another beignet, he added, "Besides, I've been dying to use my untapped investigative reporting skills."

She hesitated. "I'm not sure if I want to go digging around and opening doors I can't close."

He took her hand. "Honey, you're never going to have closure until you get to the bottom of this, whatever it is."

She stood up, gripping the railing. "You're right. I want to know the truth."

"This is useless," Chloe said, sitting next to Alex in the microfiche room of a local library.

She rubbed her eyes, which were blurry from scrolling through several years' worth of newspaper clippings. She had hoped to come across a review of one of her grandparents' concerts, an engagement announcement, an obituary, anything that would provide some clue as to the family secret Maxine was guarding. But a trip to city hall earlier in the day had proved even more frustrating as an unconcerned clerk informed Chloe and Alex that many birth and death certificates and other official documents had been destroyed in the floodwaters of Katrina. It was as if Joseph and Louise Bareaux never existed.

"I'm ready to call it a day," Chloe said, pushing back from the illuminated screen and turning off the monitor.

Alex continued to stare at the screen next to hers, as if unaware of what she had just said.

"Did you hear me?" she said, peering over his shoulder.

"Yeah, I'm sorry," he said. "This article from the *Times-Picayune* caught my eye."

"'Dade Chemical Fined for Polluting Mississippi River,'" Chloe said, reading the headline. "Isn't that the company your brother-in-law works for?"

"Yeah, and this article said the company has been cited numerous times for illegal disposal of toxic waste, but they always managed to get by with paying a small fine."

"Do you think there's something more to it?" Chloe asked.

"My journalistic instincts are telling me there is. I guess I'll print this article, file it away and look into it some other time. This is not what we came here for." He turned away from the monitor, facing her. "Maybe we didn't find out anything today about your family, but we can't give up. We've got to uncover something if we just keep looking."

"I want to believe that, I really do," Chloe said. "But maybe I should just let the past be the past. I called Mother last night to see if I could wring any details out of her, but she's not talking, as usual. Maybe I just need to make peace with the fact that I'll never really know what happened."

Alex started to say something in reply, but was interrupted when a librarian came to the door and announced that the building was about to close and they needed to wrap things up.

"It's okay," Chloe said, grabbing her purse. "We were just leaving."

Chloe was quiet on the drive back to Alex's family's house. Just as she had assumed, she would have been better off not opening doors that led nowhere. The sound of a car honking jarred her from her thoughts.

"The light's green, honey," she said to Alex.

"Sorry," he said. "My mind wandered."

She craned her neck to look at the object he was staring at from his side of the car: a smokestack emblazoned with the words "Dade Chemical" in big black letters.

Later that evening at dinner, Chloe didn't have much of an appetite. She excused herself while everyone was still eating, saying she was exhausted from the day's activities, and retreated to the den with a glass of chardonnay. She studied the family photographs that lined the oak-paneled walls, with generations of Michauds and Garderes, Alex's mother's side of the family, represented. Some of the relatives were even lighter than Alex's fair-skinned mother and could have easily passed for white, while others had a darker skin tone like Alex's father.

Chloe smiled at photos of Alex and his siblings when they were little, making funny faces at the camera during a family outing at a beach, their parents beaming with pride at graduations and softball tournaments, and embracing each other in candid shots taken at what appeared to be family reunions. She felt a tinge of sadness, wishing she had such experiences to draw on.

She sipped her wine and perused the bookshelves. Alex's parents were apparently history buffs, judging from the thick volumes on everything from ancient African civilizations to music history lining the shelves.

Robert's record collection was even more voluminous. Chloe took great care in handling the vinyl albums, many of which were autographed by the artists. She nearly lost her breath when, at the bottom of a stack of vintage jazz and blues records, she recognized a photo of her grandparents. Chloe ran her hand across the album cover, which read, "The Frank Bareaux Quintet featuring Louise Dussault."

Chloe placed the record on a well-worn turntable and sank to a leather recliner as the song began to play. Tears fell from her eyes as she listened to the voice of her grandmother, backed up by Papa Joe's horn, warbling "*Non jen ne regrette rien.*" Popularized by Josephine Baker during her rein in Paris, the title of the song translated roughly to "No Regrets."

The music was distorted by scratches and pops, but Chloe could almost feel the presence of Papa Joe and Mama Louise in the room as the record played. She sat there long after the needle had moved off the record, crying silent tears as she clutched the album cover to her chest.

"There you are," Alex said, entering the room. "I thought you were up in your room." His smile melted into concern. "What's wrong?" he said, crouching at her side and stroking her tear-streaked face.

"I was browsing through your dad's record collection and found this." She held up the album cover. "It's my grandparents' album."

"I don't know why I didn't think of asking my dad to help us out before," Alex said, standing and smacking his forehead with the palm of his hand. "I'll go see if Pop can ask around and find out if any of his older musician friends knew your grandparents."

Chloe sat up, feeling hopeful for the first time since they'd arrived in the Big Easy. "Do you really think he can help us?"

90

Chloe sat in a silk nightgown at the dressing table in the guest room as dusk fell on the Big Easy, brushing her hair. The scent of gardenias wafting in through the window reminded her of the Chateau de Chevalier's garden.

She looked away from her reflection and gazed at her grandparents' album cover, which she had propped against the mirror. She studied their faces, as if begging them to materialize and tell her their secrets.

At the sound of a knock on the door, she calmly said, "Come in."

Alex cracked the door. "I have good news," he said. "Pop found a man who says he knew your grandparents. He can take us to meet him right away."

Chloe set down her brush and looked at Alex expectantly. "Okay. It'll take me just a minute to get ready."

As Alex closed the door, she returned her attention to the album cover. She stared at the faded black-and-white photograph of her grandparents, wondering if she was finally about to uncover the mystery that had shrouded her family background for so long.

She strained to make polite conversation while riding in the passenger seat of Alex's father's Buick during the trip into town. She had gotten to know Robert well enough to feel comfortable around him, but her thoughts were racing as to what information she was about to discover from his musician friend. She was grateful to Alex for carrying the conversation from his position in the backseat.

Chloe recognized now-familiar landmarks as they drove to the French Quarter. Robert parked near Bourbon Street and, in the manner of a Southern gentleman, opened Chloe's door for her.

"Thanks," Chloe said, getting out of the car and taking Alex's arm.

"We're going to the 317 Club, where my band performed the other night," Robert said. "My friend is gigging there with his band tonight and he said he had about an hour to chat with us before their first set."

Chloe and Alex followed as Robert led them away from the animated street and through a dank alley littered with broken beer bottles and graffiti-stained walls. She wrinkled her nose at the pungent smell of urine and vomit. She gripped Alex's arm tighter and flashed him a look that said, "Where is he taking us?" Alex responded with a shrug.

"This is it," Robert said, stopping at what appeared to be a stage door. "This is the club's back entrance."

Robert rapped on the door three times in what sounded like a special knock, and a bouncer in a T-shirt emblazoned with the club's name soon appeared, swinging the door open. Robert greeted and shook hands with the man and stepped through the doorway.

"Follow me," Robert said, turning back to Chloe and Alex.

Alex took a step forward, but Chloe remained still.

"Are you going to be okay, honey?" Alex said, rubbing the small of her back.

She swallowed. "Yeah. It's too late to turn back now." She took Alex's hand again and followed him through the back entrance, nodding at the bouncer who patiently held the door open.

As Robert led them through the nightclub's kitchen, Chloe's senses were once again assaulted by potent smells, which she recognized as the welcome scent of Cajun spices. Men of different hues who had been raucously joking around, snapping dishtowels and profanity-laced insults at each other, fell silent at the sight of Chloe walking by. She smiled, appreciating that even this ragtag bunch observed the genteel Southern custom of acknowledging the presence of a lady. As she passed, the chef, who looked like a younger version of Aaron Neville, tipped his tall white hat and flashed a toothless grin.

Chloe and Alex followed Robert through a maze of dimly lit corridors that was the nightclub's backstage area. The unfinished walls reminded her of sets where she had filmed commercials for her perfume, the ugly backside camouflaged by the façade where the magic was created.

Robert paused at the entrance of a cramped dressing room, where another group of men of varying ages dressed in silk shirts, suspenders, neatly creased slacks and shiny dress shoes played cards, fiddled with instruments and passed around a joint. They laughed and joked as loudly and raucously as the kitchen crew. Chloe coughed, nearly choking from the thick cloud of smoke emanating from the room.

"Hey, y'all," Robert said, addressing the men in a familiar tone. "Where's

Hank?"

The men looked up from their card game and fell silent, just as the guys in the kitchen had, looking over Robert's shoulder at Chloe.

"We'll tell you where he is," one of the men said between hits on the joint, "if you introduce us to the pretty lady."

The men erupted in uproarious laughter and Chloe was glad Robert and Alex shielded her from the rowdy group.

Robert waved away the man's comment. "I wouldn't introduce y'all rascals to my son's woman if my life depended on it," he said playfully. "Now tell me where Hank is before I call the law and report that funny stuff you all are smoking."

The man who had spoken up passed the joint to one of his bandmates, who quickly snuffed out the contraband.

"He's at the bar; where else would he be?" said another man, gnawing on a toothpick.

"Thank you kindly," Robert said, backing away from the doorway. "Now put those cards down and get back to rehearsing like you're s'posed to."

The men seemed to respond to Robert' professor-like, authoritative tone, abandoning the card game and picking up their instruments. Robert began leading the way down another hallway and Alex followed, taking Chloe's hand. She smiled and waved at the men as Alex pulled her away from the dressing room, and she heard catcalls mingled with the sound of instrument-tuning as she followed Alex and his father down another dark corridor.

"Girl, you so fine, you make a blind man see," one of the men called out, and she laughed, appreciating the momentary release of tension.

Robert led them through another door that led into the club's main room where tables faced a small stage. It was still early evening and the club was just beginning to fill up with patrons.

"There he is," Robert said, motioning toward the figure of a slim, older black man sitting alone at the bar talking to the bartender.

Still clutching Alex's hand, Chloe followed Robert to where the man sat with his back facing them. Her chest tightened and her breath grew shallow. Now that she was actually here, faced with the possibility of uncovering some long-held dark secret, she wasn't sure if she wanted to go through with it.

Robert touched the man's shoulder. "Hey, partner, how you doing?"

The man turned around on the barstool and greeted Robert with an enthusiastic soul handshake, punctuated with a slap on the back. "It's been too long, man. Where you been hiding yourself?"

"Oh, I been around," Robert replied. "I played here a few days ago." He motioned toward Alex. "You remember, my son, Alex, don't you?"

The man slapped Alex's shoulder. "Boy, you done grown! Last time I saw you, you was knee-high to a bullfrog."

Chloe chuckled at the Southern colloquial dialect she was becoming accustomed to.

"It's so good to see you again, Mr. Duchamp," Alex said, pumping the man's hand. "This is my girlfriend, Chloe."

Harold Duchamp turned and regarded Chloe with his piercing light brown eyes. She studied his features, noting how his butterscotch-colored face bore few lines despite the fact that he had to be in his seventies if he had known her grandparents. The musician's dark, wavy hair had only a few traces of gray and he was as sharply dressed as the younger men in the band.

He stared at Chloe. "Girl, if you ain't Louise Dussault reincarnated, I don't know who is. You got that Creole look of the Bareaux women. I ain't seen your mama, Maxine, since she was a girl, but you the spittin' image."

Chloe's breath became more regular and the tightness in her chest loosened. The familiar way in which the man addressed her put her at ease. It was good to finally be face to face with someone who had a connection to her roots, and she saw kindness in his eyes.

"Why don't you all have yourselves a sit-down," Hank said. "I'll buy us a round of drinks."

Chloe, Alex and Robert took seats at the bar next to Hank, who began to talk about performing with her grandparents in his youth.

"I was the baby of the band," Hank said, sipping his bourbon and dragging on a cigarette. "I dropped out of school to go on the road with the Frank Bareaux Quintet. My mama 'bout had a fit, but all I wanted to do was play my sax."

Listening to Hank and Robert discuss the colorful players who had comprised the New Orleans club circuit over the years was like a journey through music history. The men laughed over the good old days. Alex occasionally interjected a question about Chloe's grandparents, trying to steer the conversation back to the task at hand, but the two older men kept drifting back to the nostalgia trip. The club was starting to fill up and the time when Hank would have to join his band onstage was drawing closer, but he seemed in no rush. Chloe had observed that everything down here seemed to move at a more leisurely pace, from the ritual of enjoying large meals with family and friends to making conversation.

A man Chloe recognized from the dressing room approached the bar and interrupted the jaunt down memory lane. "I'm sorry to interrupt," the man said, "but we go on in fifteen minutes."

"I'll be there in a minute," Hank said, picking up his glass and shooing the man away. "Let me finish my drink." He tipped his glass and emptied it, then turned to Chloe, who was sitting closest to him. "Well, little lady, it was sure nice meeting you. Alex here sure is a lucky man."

Chloe smiled appreciatively. Hank took her hand and kissed it again, slammed some bills on the counter, then rose. "I better get backstage and get ready."

Chloe put her hand on his arm. "Wait, before you go, there's something I have to know."

Hank took out an old-fashioned watch suspended on a chain. "I'm running late as it is. Maybe we can talk more after the show?"

"Please, sir, I have the feeling something bad happened to my grandparents, and I really need to know."

Hank's expression turned serious and he sank back to the stool. "You know, I used to perform at this very club with Hank and Louise."

Chloe's gaze drifted to the stage, and she imagined her grandparents fronting the band, her grandfather blowing on his trumpet and her grandmother cooing into a microphone.

"I don't mean no disrespect," Hank continued, "but your granddaddy was a cat back in the day. He had women dark, light and in-between cutting their eyes at him and waiting at the stage door after the show."

Chloe nodded, imagining the handsome man in the family photos, winking back flirtatiously from the stage at his female fans. She remembered overhearing her grandmother and Maxine talking about how Papa Frank would come home with lipstick on his collar. She had surmised that he had tried to be a good husband and father, but occasionally succumbed to the temptations of a musician's life.

"Your grandmamma turned a blind eye and ignored most of it, realizing it was just part of the business," Hank went on, "but there was one time in particular that she caught him with a girl in the back of the tour bus when we was on the road. She got so mad, she threatened to leave the group. Frank promised that he would change his ways and be faithful from then on to get her to stay."

Hank paused, lighting another cigarette. "Frank's sweet talk worked like it always did, and Louise stayed. I think a lot of the reason why she stayed was because your mama, Maxine, was around by then and she was quite the daddy's girl."

Chloe recalled a photo she had seen in a family album of her mother as a child in hair ribbons and kneesocks, sitting on Papa Frank's lap.

"Anyway," Hank said, puffing on his cigarette, "we was all glad that Frank and Louise didn't split up. There was no way we could have gone on if Frank would've had to get another singer. Your grandmamma had some pipes on her, boy. When she raised her voice, she could break glass, strip paint off the walls and turn a sinner into a saint."

Chloe watched a technician plugging in the instruments onstage, and imagined her grandmother standing at the microphone in a beautiful nightgown, a gardenia in her hair like Billie Holiday as she warbled a bluesy ballad.

"This one night when we was playing here, Mary Jane LaSalle was sitting at a table up front. She was the wife of one of the biggest gangsters in town and was always decked out in jewels and furs. She looked like Lana Turner or Jayne Mansfield or one of them drop-dead gorgeous blondes that used to be on TV and in the movies.

"Every time Frank would come to the front of the stage to take a solo, she would lean over so he could look down the front of her dress," Hank continued. "She had a taste for colored musicians, and everybody knew she had her nose wide open for your granddaddy. After the first set, she came backstage and told Frank her husband was out of town and to come over after the show. Louise had her own dressing room and wasn't even in earshot, but Frank turned that Mary Jane down flat. He said he was a married man and she was a married woman and she ought to be ashamed of herself."

Hank paused, taking a drag on his cigarette.

"Old Mary Jane must not have been used to being told no," he said, "because she stormed out of the club. That old devil went back and told her husband that Frank tried to force himself on her."

Chloe's eyes grew wide, riveted to Hank's story. He leaned back, blowing smoke out of his nostrils. It took every bit of restraint she had not to lean over and poke him to get him to finish the story.

"What happened?" she prodded.

"Everybody knew Mary Jane was lying – everybody colored, that is," Hank said. "Frank Bareaux could snap his fingers and have any woman he wanted. He had no need to force himself on anyone. He could have had Mary Jane if he wanted, too, but he had promised Louise he'd straighten up and fly right. When Mary Jane told that low-down, dirty lie, her man showed up at the club later that night, packing a pistol. He met Frank at the stage door. Frank tried to talk sense into him and protest his innocence, but Jimmy LaSalle wasn't hearing it. He shot your granddaddy dead, right there in the alley. Killed him in cold blood."

Chloe shuddered, suddenly cold all over. Tears filled her eyes. The image of her grandfather lying in that filthy alley made her want to vomit. Alex put his hand on her shoulder and pulled her close.

"I'm sorry, I've upset you," Hank said. "I figured you wouldn't take hearing this too well, that's why I didn't want to go into it."

Chloe leaned on Alex for support and wiped her eyes. "No, it's okay. I'm glad to finally hear the truth. Please go on. What happened to the man who murdered my grandfather?"

"Nothing, I'm sorry to say, at least not where the law was concerned,"

Hank said. "He was a powerful mob boss and had higher-ups in the police department as well as powerful people on city council in his pocket. Plus, wasn't no judge this side of the Mason-Dixon Line going to put a white man in jail for shooting a black man, especially not one that a white woman had accused of trying to rape her."

"I wish I could say things have changed," Robert interjected, "but we still have a lot of racism and corruption to deal with down here."

"We gave your granddaddy an old-time jazz funeral. He went on to glory in style, I'm glad to report," Hank said. "That old nasty Jimmy LaSalle got his due, too. A few months after he killed your granddaddy, he was killed during a shootout on a riverboat casino."

"Dirty bastard got what he deserved," Robert said.

Chloe started at the uncharacteristic swearing from Alex's father. Turning her attention back to Hank, she asked, "How'd my grandmother handle everything? What did she do after my grandfather died?"

"That Louise Dussault was a strong woman, I tell you. She went into mourning, but she handled it like a trooper. But she was never the same after she lost Frank. God knows they had their quarrels, but he was the love of her life. After he was killed, she packed up your mama and moved up North, to New York. I guess she wanted to get as far away from this place and the bad memories as she could. From what I heard, she never sang another note." Hank shook his head. "It's a damn shame. They was so talented..." He trailed off, punctuating the statement by snuffing out his cigarette in an ashtray.

"Well, I better get backstage and get ready," he said, rising. "Me and some of the rest of the guys from your grandparents' band have kept playing together over the years. A few of the old-timers like me have passed away, but their sons and one man's grandson is in the band now. They call us 'OGs' – original gangsters – and they keep us young, and our fans keep us going. If we don't get up on that stage soon, they'll have our hides."

"It's good to know you're keeping the legacy alive," Alex said.

Hank exchanged handshakes and manly hugs with Robert and Alex, and kissed Chloe on the forehead, the way she imagined her grandfather would have done.

"We'd like to stay and watch you guys perform," Chloe said to Hank.

"It'll be an honor to have Frank and Louise's granddaughter in the audience," he said. "I hope I've helped you find whatever it is you was looking for, young lady."

She nodded. "You have. Now I know the truth, and you have no idea how much that means to me." She gripped his hand. "Thank you, thank you so much."

91

Chloe took a handful of garments from the antique dresser in the guest room of the Michaud estate and placed them in her suitcase. Before closing her bag, she pulled out her grandparents' record album and ran her hand over the photo on the cover.

"You ready to go?" Alex said, entering the guest room.

She turned and smiled at him. "Yep, just finished packing." She held up the album. "I can't thank your dad enough for letting me keep this and for taking me to see Mr. Duchamp."

Alex came closer and put his arm around her waist. "I hope what he told you wasn't too upsetting."

"I cried myself to sleep last night, thinking of my grandfather dying so brutally and his killer never being brought to justice." She looked down at the album cover. "But at least I have closure, now that I know the truth."

So many things made sense now. Chloe had faint childhood memories of Mama Louise tearing up whenever she spoke of Papa Frank. Chloe had always assumed it was because Mama Louise missed her late husband so much, but now Chloe understood why it was such a painful subject. And it was clear to her now why Maxine was always so reticent to talk about the past and why she did everything in her power to avoid returning to New Orleans, which would have reopened old wounds and reminded her of her father's murder.

"I know finding out what happened to your grandfather was really hard to go through," Alex said, kissing her.

She leaned into him. "I'm just glad you were by my side to help me through it."

Chloe and Alex exchanged goodbyes with the Michauds at the front door.

"Thank you for everything," Chloe said, hugging Robert.

"You take care of yourself and call me if you ever need anything," Robert said, taking her suitcase and carrying it to the car.

"What the hell you got in here, bro', a barbell?" said Alex's younger brother, Marcus, lugging one of the suitcases down the front steps.

"Let me help," Jerry, Alex's brother-in-law, volunteered, limping to the rental car where Marcus was attempting to lift the heavy bag into the trunk.

"Jerry, you know you shouldn't be straining your back," Monique, Alex's sister, chastised. "The doctor said no heavy lifting."

Jerry ignored his wife, taking one side of the suitcase and then dropping it and clutching his back in pain. "Goddamn it!" he exclaimed. "I wish I could sue those dirty dogs for putting me in this condition."

Monique rushed to her husband's aid. "Someone needs to expose Dade Chemical," she said, helping Jerry to the front steps so he could sit down. "Alex, you should do an investigative piece for the magazine. It would make a good story."

"I'd be willing to talk, that's for sure. I got nothing to lose now," Jerry said, sinking to a seated position on the front steps with an agonized expression. "And I know some of my co-workers who'd be willing to talk as long as you didn't use their names."

"I wish I had the time," Alex said, loading the last piece of luggage into the trunk, "but I'm on leave from the magazine and I have a big script rewrite to finish before production on the movie starts. Chloe and I have got to get back to New York, and then I leave for L.A. again to meet with the studio."

"Don't let it be so long between your next visit, you hear?" Lena affectionately scolded.

"Yeah, Mr. Hollywood," Marcus said, punching his brother in the ribs. "Don't forget about your peeps back home."

Alex put his brother in a headlock, then pulled him into a bear hug. Chloe smiled at the undeniable affection that existed between Alex and his brother despite their teasing and horseplay. She thanked everyone for their hospitality again.

"I want you to have this," Lena said, handing Chloe a journal with a floral print cover as Chloe settled into the passenger seat of the rental car.

"Oh, thank you so much, Mrs. Michaud," Chloe said, flipping through the journal, which contained hand-written family recipes.

"You're part of the family now. Call me Mom. And I hope you have fun trying out those recipes. They're Alex's favorites. As they say, a way to a man's heart is through his stomach," she said with a wink. "The Michaud men love food. Cooking for Alex's father is how I got him to put a ring on my finger."

Chloe was quiet and pensive on the drive to the airport. She spent most of the ride looking out at the landmarks, tucking them away in her memory.

"You okay?" Alex said, turning down the radio.

"I'm just trying to savor the experience of being here. You have no idea how much it meant to me, being able to finally connect with my roots. You're so lucky, having such a big family. It's just me and my mom, and we're both so busy that we hardly get to see each other."

"I don't get home as much as I should, either. You heard Mom guilt-tripping me when we were leaving."

"Still, it's so nice that your family gets together for special occasions and everyone gets along."

"Don't be fooled," Alex said. "We fight sometimes and we have our issues. As much as I enjoy seeing them and being home in New Orleans, I'm always glad to get back to my own life in New York."

When the car pulled up at the rental car return, Chloe got an idea. "Would you mind if we took a detour through Paris?"

When Chloe and Alex arrived in Paris, it was her turn to show him around her hometown. Just as Alex had taken her on a tour of his favorite landmarks from his childhood in the Crescent City, she enjoyed doing the same for him in the City of Light. She held hands with him strolling down the Champs-Elysées, snuggled up to him on a romantic boat ride down the Seine, and kissed him in front of the Eiffel Tower.

Marie prepared a homecoming dinner for Chloe and her beau at the Chateau de Chevalier that was on par with the moveable feast Alex's mother had prepared. Gigi and Philippe and Simone and her boyfriend, Armand, came over and Alex hit it off with them all. Whereas Maxine had been coolly polite to the men her daughter had brought home in the past, she was as warm and friendly to Alex as she'd been the few times Chloe had introduced him before.

"He's a doll," Maxine said to Chloe when they were in the kitchen, helping Marie scrape plates.

"I'm so glad you've finally found happiness, *choucou*," said Marie, placing a coffee pot and delectable pastries she had baked for dessert on a serving tray.

"Yes, *ma chérie*, you chose wisely this time," added Maxine. "Alex is a catch. Take your mother's advice. You hold on to that one."

"Yeah, Alex is pretty great," Chloe said, handing Maxine the last plate to load into the dishwasher. "But we're not here just for a social visit."

Maxine closed the dishwasher and wiped her hands on a towel. "What do you mean?"

"When Alex and I were in New Orleans, he introduced me to a musician friend of his father's named Harold Duchamp. Does the name sound familiar?"

Maxine furrowed her brow. "Vaguely. Why?"

"He used to perform with Papa Frank and Mama Louise. He told me something that I think we need to talk about."

Maxine looked stricken and turned her back to Chloe. "Marie, why don't you let me help you carry that tray into the dining room?"

589

"Mother, we need to talk," Chloe said, resolute in her tone despite Maxine's refusal to make eye contact. "It's long overdue that we had this discussion."

Marie picked up the dessert tray. "I think I can manage this, Madame Chevalier. I'll tend to our guests so you two can have a moment to talk." As she backed out of the kitchen, Marie met Chloe's eyes and silently imparted the same steadfast support that had helped the young woman broach sensitive subjects with Maxine in the past.

"It's time we got everything out in the open," Chloe said.

Maxine busied herself wiping an invisible stain on the counter and said nothing.

"Mother, Mr. Duchamp told me everything. I know what happened to Papa Frank," Chloe said, stepping closer to her mother. "I know the truth."

Maxine remained silent, her back still turned to Chloe.

"Why didn't you ever tell me about the circumstances of Papa Frank's death?" Chloe pressed. "It's family history. I had the right to know."

Maxine remained silent, having pressed the dishcloth to her face. Chloe took another step forward and saw that her mother was quietly weeping.

"It's okay, Mother," Chloe said, putting her hand on her Maxine's shoulder.

Maxine turned and embraced Chloe. "I thought I was doing the right thing. I thought I was protecting you," Maxine sniveled. She pulled away, rubbing her eyes. "I didn't want you to be exposed to such ugliness. When Papa was killed, Mama and I never talked about it. I don't think either of us ever really grieved. After Papa died, Mama just packed up everything and said we were moving to New York, like she was closing the book on that part of our lives forever. She was a strong woman, but I don't think she knew how to deal with the pain of losing Papa so suddenly, so brutally. I felt the same way when I lost Jacques." Maxine looked thoughtful. "I guess I took on Mama's way of never talking about painful things. I figured it was best to let the past be the past."

Chloe took Maxine's hand. "But now that I know the truth about the past, we can make peace with it. It was the not knowing that kept us from having closure."

Chloe and Maxine hugged again, clinging to each other for a long moment.

"Well, we shouldn't keep everyone waiting, wondering what happened to us," Maxine said, breaking apart and wiping her eyes. "Is my mascara running?"

Chloe wiped a tear from her mother's face. "You look beautiful, as always. Alex was right when he said we look like sisters."

Maxine smiled appreciatively. "He *is* a doll. You've found a good one this time – a nice young man from New Orleans nonetheless."

"I'd love for us to finally take a trip there together. I'd like for you to meet Alex's family."

"I'd like that." Maxine put her arm around Chloe and began leading her out of the kitchen. "I have a lot to discuss with Alex's parents."

Chloe gave her mother a wary look. "Like what?"

"Like whether we should hold the wedding in New Orleans or Paris."

Chloe laughed, pushing open the swinging door. "Still trying to marry me off, huh?"

Chloe lay awake in bed in her old room, twirling her hair and staring at the ceiling, reflecting on the exchange with her mother earlier in the day. She felt so relieved that the family secret her mother had been harboring was finally out in the open.

She sat up at the sound of a knock on the door. "Come in."

She smiled as Alex padded into the room in his pajamas. Though Maxine said she was smitten by Alex's abundant charm, she was still a traditional-minded Catholic. Like Alex's parents, she wouldn't allow Chloe and Alex to sleep in the same room.

Chloe scooted over, making room for Alex.

"How'd it go with your mother?" he asked, sitting next to Chloe on the bed.

"Really well. We talked about my grandfather's death for the first time ever, and now I understand why she kept it a secret from me for so long." Chloe hugged a pillow to her chest. "She was just trying to protect me."

Alex put his arm around her. "I'm glad we were able to take this trip. I'm glad I got to see where you grew up."

"Me, too. I told my mom I'd like for the three of us to go to New Orleans some time so she can meet your parents. Of course, she immediately turned the subject to marriage."

Alex laughed. "My parents cornered me about the same thing."

Chloe smiled. "I'm sure they mean well, but I don't want to rush into it. I want to wait until we're both established in our careers."

"Speaking of which," Alex said, "I'm going to have to leave earlier than expected and fly directly to L.A. I was hoping we'd have some down time together at home in New York, but the studio called. I have to meet with the production team to go over the script revisions so they can start casting."

"When do you leave?"

"First thing in the morning, unfortunately."

"We've been so busy since we left for New Orleans. I wish we had more time to just hang out." She stuck out her lip in a mock pout, clutching the

591

pillow in her lap like a brooding child. "I'm going to miss you."

Alex lowered his voice. "Let me tell you a bedtime story that will help you remember me when I'm gone," he said, taking the pillow from her and leaning in seductively.

She grinned mischievously, holding him at arm's length. "Okay, but you have to be quiet so we don't wake my mother," she said, feeling like a naughty schoolgirl.

As Alex slipped the strap of her nightgown off her shoulder and began kissing her neck, she felt a surge of excitement, like she was a teenager again sneaking a boy into her room. Making love to her boyfriend in her girlhood bed made her feel very grown-up.

92

Chloe hunched over the stove, poring over a Creole recipe in the book Alex's mother had given her. She added a dash of paprika to the pot of gumbo simmering on the backburner, but somehow the dish didn't resemble the Southern feast Mrs. Michaud had prepared.

"Why doesn't this look right?" Chloe said to her cat, Bizou, and Alex's dog, Jack, who were watching her from their side-by-side beds in a corner of the kitchen. The animals, who had gotten along surprisingly well since Alex moved in, responded with their usual indifferent yawns.

The dog began barking at the sound of Alex's key turning in the door.

"You're home early," Chloe said when Alex entered the kitchen, wrapped his arms around her waist and kissed her.

"I was able to get an earlier flight from L.A." He looked down at the boiling pot. "What's that?"

"Your mother's gumbo recipe. It was supposed to be a surprise." She held up a spoonful of the concoction for him to taste.

Alex obliged, his expression turning sour. "It certainly is a surprise," he said, coughing and spitting the food into a paper towel.

"It's too spicy, isn't it?"

"Just a bit," he said, filling a glass with tap water and guzzling it down.

She picked up the steaming pot and dumped its murky contents in the sink. "I'm starting to feel like I can't do anything right."

"Honey, you know that's not true."

She sighed and began rinsing out the pot. "I feel like I'm going crazy, sitting at home with nothing to do. You know what I did while you were in L.A.? Rearranged my underwear drawer and took Jack for a three-hour walk through Central Park."

"So?"

"Every day."

The dog, who had been lazily lounging on his bed, scurried out of the kitchen, as if worried that Chloe was going to drag him outside for more exercise.

"See, the dog is even sick of me," Chloe said. "How pathetic is that?" She plopped on a stool. "I've got to find something to do with myself or I'm going to go nuts."

Alex stood over her and began massaging her shoulders. "Right now I think you should start packing."

She looked up at him. "Packing? You're not throwing me out, are you? You can't do that. My name's on the lease," she said, laughing.

He crouched before her. "Of course I'm not throwing you out, but I do want to see you go places with your acting career. The studio agrees with me. They're interested in having you play my character."

Chloe stood up, banging her head on the copper pots hanging above the stove. "Are you serious?" she said, rubbing her head.

"Yes," Alex said, standing up. "I talked about casting with the production team while I was out in L.A. They asked me if I had any ideas about who should play Sidney, and I said I couldn't think of anyone who fits the part better than you."

"Gosh, Alex, I'm flattered," she said, taken off-guard. It had never crossed her mind to get involved with his film adaptation. "You know I've loved your story since the day I first read it and I'd be honored to play your character, but I don't want to be handed the part just because I'm your girlfriend."

"That's not an issue. They're looking at several different actresses for the role, and I simply suggested that you be considered as well. You'll have to audition like everyone else. They want to fly you out to do a screen test."

Chloe retreated to the bedroom without saying anything. She didn't know how to tell Alex that if she had to audition, she would surely lose the role. Plus, she was filled with self-doubt that she could compete with the established actresses who were up for the part.

"Chloe, what's going on?" he said, following her into the bedroom. "If you're not interested in the role, just say so."

"Of course I want the role. You created one of the strongest female characters I've ever come across. The problem with most scripts I read is that the women are more like set dressing or cardboard cutouts, but Sidney is complex and three-dimensional – a role any actress would love to play."

Alex came closer, looking baffled. "Then what's the problem?"

Chloe flopped on the bed. "A big reason why my acting career hasn't taken off is I choke up in auditions. It's been that way ever since I tried out for

593

my first school play. And when I auditioned for Epitome when I first moved to New York, I was horrible."

"Well, you must have done something right," he said, sitting next to her on the bed, "'cause Epitome signed you, and look at how successful you were as a model."

"True, but Epitome never would have signed me if they hadn't come across an old music video I did when I was in high school. That was a gig I didn't have to audition for, so that doesn't really count."

"You know what I think? I think you're coming up with excuses not to do this screen test because you're afraid you won't be able to handle it if your dream actually comes true."

Chloe got up and walked to the window, looking out on the traffic going by on the street below. "You're probably right. I just don't want to let you down."

"You could never let me down. If it wasn't for you, I never would have even finished the book."

"Buying you that laptop was something I wanted to do. You don't have to keep thanking me for it."

"I'm not talking about the laptop."

She turned away from the window, facing him. "What *are* you talking about?"

He got up and stood by her side. "I didn't tell you this when we first started dating because I thought it might creep you out, but when I first interviewed you, I thought you looked exactly how I envisioned my character. So I used your photo to help me visualize Sidney Laveau when I was writing."

She stroked his cheek, genuinely touched by his revelation. "Alex, that's so sweet."

"Don't you see? You were my muse," he said, taking her by the arms. "You're smart, you're beautiful, you have Creole heritage. You *are* Sidney Laveau. There's no one else who can play this part."

She looked away, staring out the window again. Now that he'd told her this, she knew she would have to somehow overcome her performance anxiety.

She looked at him, moved by the boyish expectation in his eyes. It occurred to her that if she gave into her fears and didn't go through with the screen test, that would be a bigger letdown – both to herself and Alex – than if she auditioned and didn't get the part.

"Okay," she said finally. "I'll do the screen test."

Chloe pulled her rented car to the iconic gates of Paragon Studios in the

Century City section of Los Angeles and gave her name to the security guard.

"Okay, Ms. Bareaux," he said, waving her through. "You're cleared."

She watched the gates slowly open like the jaws of a whale waiting to swallow her up. She paused, taking a deep breath to gird herself, then finally took her foot off the break and proceeded.

She found the visitors' parking and pulled in a space, releasing the ice-cold grip she had on the steering wheel. This screen test would be her big chance to prove herself, and if she messed this up she may as well forget about any shot at an acting career.

She took out her cell phone and dialed Alex in New York. Hearing his voice would not only bolster her courage, but reinforce her motivation to embody the character he had created.

"I'm here," she said when he answered.

"Good luck, honey. You know I'm rooting for you. I wish you had let me come with you."

"I think it's best that I go it alone. I don't want you to be accused of trying to hook your girlfriend up with the role. I want to earn it on my own."

"I know you'll do fine. I love you."

She paused, savoring his words like the last gulp from a cantina in the desert. "I love you, too." After hanging up, she took one last at herself in the rearview mirror.

Walking across the backlot was like stepping into one of those "film-within-a-film" sequences she'd seen in so many movies about Hollywood. Stagehands lugged scenery from warehouses, and at one point she thought she was facing the Hollywood Sign, only to have the famous landmark revealed as a backdrop when the semi-truck it was attached to drove off. Extras from a gladiator movie brushed by her in togas and Trojan War gear, munching on burgers and fries from the commissary. The experience thus far was totally surreal, and yet she felt right at home. This is where she was supposed to be. Every step she had taken through her entire life, from devouring movies as a girl to searching relentlessly until she found the right part, had prepared her for this moment.

She finally located the soundstage where her screen test was to be held and, upon entering the massive complex, she was intercepted by a well-dressed brunette who appeared to be not much older than she.

"Hi, I'm Sheila Jaffe, the casting director," the woman said, smiling and offering her hand. "You must be Chloe."

The casting director led Chloe through a dark maze to a room that was full of clothing racks, props and scenery in various states of construction. Sheila introduced her to a wardrobe assistant, who took an outfit off the rack and handed it to Chloe.

"Is this what I'm supposed to wear?" Chloe said, examining the drab navy suit and white blouse that looked like the stock "lady detective" garb from every *CSI* knockoff on TV.

"Yes. Is there a problem?" Sheila said, her friendly tone turning sharp, as if cautioning Chloe to remember that she was just another candidate vying for the part.

Chloe slung the suit over her arm. "Uh, no. Not at all." She had probably been in the fashion industry too long, she told herself, and now was not the time to challenge wardrobe choices or any other decision made by the people who had the power to cast her.

She followed a wardrobe assistant to a small dressing room. Once she had changed into the costume, the casting director entered the room, followed by a man carrying a makeup kit.

"This is Kevin Arnett," Sheila said, making the introductions. "He's won several Emmys and an Oscar for makeup and special effects."

Chloe shook Kevin's hand and took a seat next to the table where he was unpacking his kit.

Kevin began applying dark smudges to her face. "I'm going to make you look like you just wrecked your car chasing the bad guy."

She sat back in the makeup chair. "I'm all yours." She closed her eyes and ran lines in her head as Kevin did his job, topping off her car-wreck makeup with a bloody gash across her forehead that looked startlingly real.

"I'll give you a few minutes to go over your lines and let you know when they're ready for you," Sheila said when Kevin was done.

"Thanks," Chloe said as the casting director and makeup artist left the room.

She pulled her copy of the script out of her bag and found the page she'd marked. She had acted out this scene over and over last night in her hotel room and she was fairly confident that she had the lines memorized verbatim. Now all she had to do was convince the director, producer and studio-appointed powers-that-be that she could pull off the demanding role. She had to give Alex props for writing a meaty female role – the one she'd been searching for all these years.

A knock at the door broke her concentration.

"They're ready for you on set," Sheila said, poking her head in the dressing room.

"Thanks. I'll just be a second."

When Sheila closed the door and left her alone, Chloe reached into her bag and retrieved the rosary Valérie Bourdain had given her during their commercial shoot. She clutched the rosary and closed her eyes, said a silent prayer, then opened her eyes and looked at her reflection in the mirror.

"Val, I promise I'll do you proud."

She slipped the rosary in the pocket of her costume's suit jacket and rose to meet Sheila in the hallway. The casting director led her through the dark maze again, past carpenters and electricians who were hammering and drilling away, building the set. A tingle of excitement danced up her spine to think that, if all went well, she would soon be bringing Alex's character to life in this dream factory.

"This is it," Sheila said, stopping at the entrance to a small room.

Chloe followed Sheila inside, relieved to find that the room was set up like the photography studios she was accustomed to working in. A large digital-video camera and several lights were positioned in a semicircle in front of a plain off-white backdrop at the far end of the room, reminding her of the setup for her first *Vogue* shoot. She had also been a novice in that experience, but had managed to overcome her nerves and prove herself. She clung to the hope that she would be able to do the same this time.

Upon approaching the set, she recognized the director, Hal Forster, and Bryan da Silva, the pompous producer, from the New Orleans location-scouting trip. Da Silva gave her a perfunctory handshake, barely acknowledging her, while Hal greeted her warmly.

"Thanks for coming out and meeting with us," Hal said, hugging her. "Are you ready for your close-up?"

"Indeed I am, *Mr. Demille*," she said, catching his reference to the famous line from the classic film *Sunset Boulevard*.

"Let's get started."

Hal coached her through the camera blockings, indicating tape marks on the floor she was to hit while delivering her lines. He introduced her to the cameraman who was to videotape her screen test.

"I'll read the precinct captain's line from off-camera," Sheila said, referring to the character that Chloe was to play off of in the scene. "Just let me know when you're ready."

Sheila, the director and producer took seats in a row of director's chairs behind the camera while Chloe positioned herself on the first tape marking. Calling on her modeling experience, she relaxed her posture so as not to come across stiff on-camera. She inhaled, then nodded at Hal that she was ready to begin.

"Action!" he called.

When she noticed the red light on the camera flick on, she froze up, unable to recall the lines she had so carefully rehearsed. *Damn*, she thought, *not again. I can do this.*

Silence enveloped the room, with the low buzz of the camera as the only sound. She looked past the glow of the lights and caught sight of the cameraman, who was looking at her like she was mentally challenged. She scanned the faces of the casting director, producer and director. She could feel them staring back at her, judging her. She made eye contact with da Silva, who had a smug expression signaling that he was taking delight in her discomfort.

"Chloe, do you need a minute?" Hal said, his voice laced with concern.

She cleared her throat. "No, thanks. I'm ready."

"Okay. We're still rolling." He motioned for the cameraman to keep going.

Chloe took another deep breath and, remembering the good luck charm her idol had given her, she touched the pocket of her suit jacket. Feeling the rosary boosted her confidence and prompted her to finally begin speaking.

"Captain Roubelot, I caught the suspect and we're bringing him in for questioning," Chloe said, reciting her dialogue.

"Laveau, I ought to bring you up on disciplinary charges." Sheila read from the script in a monotone that indicated she had done this dozens of times and was on autopilot. "You overstepped your authority by going after that scumbag. You know the FBI has been tracking him, and tampering with a federal investigation could get us all in a lot of hot water. What do you have to say for yourself?"

Chloe paused before launching into the speech Alex had written for her character. She touched her pocket again, tracing the outline of the rosary for reassurance.

"Captain Roubelot, I know I violated protocol, but sometimes rules and regulations have to be set aside for the sake of justice." She moved to her next mark, feeling more self-assured with each stride. It was as though she were being propelled by some unseen force. "I take full responsibility for my actions and I'm ready to face the consequences. If I'm stripped of my badge, it will be worth it to know that those victims' families can sleep at night and that killer is behind bars, where he belongs."

When she finished her speech, there was silence once again. She remained anchored to her last mark, unsure if she had done something wrong.

"Cut," Hal said after a moment. He stood and came to stand next to Chloe, offering his hand. "That was amazing. You did an excellent job."

She drank in his compliment, feeling the tightness in her shoulders loosening. "Thanks so much. I worked really hard to hit the right emotional beats with Sidney's speech. I didn't want it to sound too preachy."

"That was just what I was looking for."

Chloe cheered inwardly. He hadn't officially offered the part, but she felt an enormous sense of relief that she had apparently aced the screen test and had a decent chance at earning the role.

"Good job," Sheila said, also rising to shake Chloe's hand.

The smug producer remained seated and continued to glare at Chloe, as if her very presence were a personal affront. She didn't allow his seeming lack of approval to faze her; she rested assured in the knowledge that she had done her best.

"We just have one more setup with the stunt coordinator and you can be on your way," Hal said.

Hairs shot up on the back of her neck. "Stunt coordinator?"

"Yes. We've set up the car wreck scene in the soundstage where we'll be filming when we're not on location in New Orleans, and I just want to get a sense of how you and the stunt coordinator would work together."

"I was under the impression this screen test was just going to be a scene run-through in front of the camera," Chloe said, tensing up again. "I didn't know there was any action involved."

"I'm sorry." Hal looked perplexed. "Didn't your agent tell you we wanted you to test for the stunt coordinator as well?"

"Oh, that's right," da Silva chimed in, still perched in his director's chair like a potentate who refused to rise in the presence of a serf. "You don't have representation. Your boyfriend-the-screenwriter got you this audition."

Chloe glared at the producer, but stopped short of saying anything. As much as she'd be justified in telling him where to shove it, she wasn't going to take the bait and give him reason to deny her the job.

"Hey, Bryan, let's keep it civil, okay?" Hal said, sounding as though he were used to serving as mediator between producer and star. "I'm the one who wanted to see Chloe for this part and she deserves a fair shot like everyone else who's tried out." He turned back to Chloe. "We'll use a double for most of the really dangerous stunts, but if you get the part, I'll need you on set for some of the action so I can get your close-ups. Is that something you're willing to do?"

Chloe glanced over at the producer, who looked unconvinced that a former model could handle any kind of acting challenge. "Of course," she said, directing her attention at Hal again. "I'll be happy to try out for the stunt coordinator."

Hal led the way through the maze, with Chloe, the casting director, cameraman and da Silva trailing. Chloe made sure to keep her distance from the producer, lest he say something to cause her to lose the fragile hold she had on her self-control.

The group arrived at a studio that was at least three times the size of the room they'd just left. Chloe looked up and saw a mangled automobile suspended from the rafters of the cavernous soundstage. Her throat constricted, keeping her from screaming, although that was her first impulse.

Hal introduced her to the stunt coordinator, a burly man named Zack who

599

had the light-brown complexion of New Zealand's indigenous Maori people.

"This is the big climax where the character is dangling from the vehicle and jumps down into Lake Pontchartrain to catch the bad guy," Zack told Chloe in a New Zealand accent, confirming her hunch about his ethnicity. "You'll be secured with a wire. It's totally safe."

Chloe said nothing, her eyes still locked on the wrecked car hanging from the ceiling. Her fear of heights kept her from jumping off a curb, let alone leaping from the ceiling of a building that was the size of an airplane hangar, with only a thin wire to keep her from crashing to her death.

"We'll paint in the New Orleans bridge with CGI," Hal explained, pointing out the green screen behind the wreckage, "but we wanted to make the accident look as realistic as possible, so we'll strap you into the wreckage." He motioned to the rafters.

"You look a little shaken up," Sheila said to Chloe, touching her arm.

"What's the matter?" da Silva said. "You scared?"

Chloe locked eyes with the producer. His tone was that of a schoolyard bully daring a timid classmate to recklessly jump off a jungle gym.

"I'm okay," Chloe said, looking away from the producer to Hal and Sheila. "I just need a little time to prepare. Could I have a few minutes to go back to the dressing room and go over the scene again?"

"Sure," Hal said. "That'll give us time to set up the shot."

She somehow managed to find her way back to the dressing room, where she closed the door and burst into tears. She couldn't stop shaking. As hard as she tried, she couldn't shut out the image of Jacques' car twisted around a lamppost on Paris' Alexandre III bridge. The flashback to her stepfather's tragic death, mingled with her fear of heights, filled her with terror, just as it had when Hal had asked her to stand in on the New Orleans Causeway during the location scout. Only this time, Alex wasn't there to hold her hand.

With trembling fingers, she redialed Alex on her cell phone.

"Honey, I'm so sorry they're putting you through all this. I know how you hate heights," Alex said when she told him about the stunt challenge. "If you want to back out, I totally understand."

She didn't say anything right away. The thought of letting Alex down was even more frightening than the death-defying leap that awaited her. She wanted so badly to prove herself. Winning this role was about more than her desire to breathe life into her fledgling acting career. Collaborating with Alex to bring his story to the screen would be like conceiving a lovechild, born of creativity. But it was a cruel irony that she had to face her biggest fear in order to achieve this goal.

"Honey, you still there?" Alex said.

"Yes, I'm still here," Chloe said, sitting up and wiping her tears. "I'm going to go through with it."

"Look, babe, you don't have to prove anything to anybody. Just tell them you can't –"

"No. I can do this," Chloe said, her resolve solidifying now that she'd made up her mind to do the stunt. "I *want* to do this."

"Okay. Call me as soon as it's over."

"Of course I will. But let me tell you something, Alexandre Michaud: Next time you write something with me in mind, make sure all the action takes place on the ground!"

It felt good to share a laugh with Alex and relieve some of the tension. Before hanging up, she promised to call him as soon as she got back to the hotel. She had barely a moment to go over the scene when the casting director knocked on the door.

"Everything's all set up," Sheila said, poking her head in. "We need to get rolling. You ready?"

Chloe nodded.

"Okay. I'll go tell them you're on your way."

Alone in the dressing room again, Chloe reached into her pocket, fingering Valérie's rosary once more. She started to get up, but sat back down and slowly took the rosary out of her pocket and set it on the counter. She reached into her purse and took out the other good luck charm she'd brought with her: Mama Louise's wedding ring, the family heirloom Chloe credited with keeping her safe when she first arrived in New York.

"Mama Louise, I need you to watch over me now more than ever," Chloe said, steepling her hands and looking at the ceiling.

She put the wedding ring in the breast pocket of her costume, placed the rosary in her purse and rose to make her way back to the set. On the long walk back to the soundstage, it occurred to her that her life had been a series of challenges up to this point. Leaving home at eighteen and moving all by herself to a big, scary city like New York took an incredible amount of inner strength. And forging a career in the cutthroat modeling industry required a toughness she had developed along the way. She was stronger than she was giving herself credit for.

She arrived on the set with renewed confidence, where the director and stunt coordinator described the action that was to take place in the scene.

"Got it," Chloe said. "Let's do it."

She tried not to look down as a crane elevated her to the wrecked car suspended from the rafters. With the stunt coordinator's help, she got situated inside the vehicle. As Zack strapped her to a harness attached to the safety wire, she glanced down and saw da Silva observing her discomfort with sadistic pleasure. She tuned him out, going over her lines in her head and telling herself this would soon be over.

"The wire's on nice and tight," Zack said, tugging on the harness. "But just in case, we've put down a mat to break your fall in the unlikely event that anything should go wrong."

Zack's assurance had the opposite effect of making her feel secure, but she steeled herself, determined to prove she was capable of pulling off the stunt.

Zack rode the crane back down to the floor, leaving her alone in the wrecked vehicle. Minutes dragged on like bleak winter days as the technicians adjusted the lighting and Hal conferred with the cameraman.

Finally, Hal took his seat on a camera crane and called, "Action!" He nodded at Sheila, who was seated below along with da Silva, and she began robotically running lines with Chloe again.

"Just hold still, Sidney," Sheila said, in character as Sidney's detective colleague, speaking into a megaphone so that Chloe could hear her from the precarious position above. "The ambulance is on its way. We'll have you out of there any moment."

Chloe paused before delivering her line, her heart racing as she looked down. The mat that was to cushion her fall in the "unlikely event" that the wire malfunctioned seemed a hundred miles away. Maybe going through with this stunt wasn't such a good idea after all.

She was considering telling the director that she'd changed her mind and to get her out of this thing immediately when she caught sight of da Silva smirking at her with an expression that read, "I knew you weren't up to the challenge." She couldn't give him the satisfaction of seeing her quit.

She wet her lips and delivered her line. "No, leave me," she said, in character as Alex's heroine. "Take your men and go to the other side of the bridge. Riker's getting away and I'm going after him."

Following Hal's direction, she moved to the edge of the mangled vehicle. She put her hand to her chest and felt her grandmother's wedding ring. Without another thought, she closed her eyes and jumped.

When she opened her eyes, she was dangling above the mat, the wire having done its job of keeping her from hitting the floor. She heard Hal yell, "Cut!" and the crew broke out in applause.

Chloe ran up to Alex and showered him with kisses when he greeted her at JFK airport upon her triumphant homecoming.

"I take it the screen test went well?" he said.

"I got the part!" she exclaimed. "I got it!"

"Baby, that's great," he said. "I knew you could do it." He produced a dozen red roses from behind his back and gave them to her, like an orchestra maestro presenting an opera star with a bouquet at the conclusion of a well-received performance.

"I couldn't have done this without you," she said, plucking a single rose from the bouquet and handing it to him.

He admired the rose and put his arm around Chloe, leading her out of the terminal. "This is so exciting – making our dreams come true together."

93

Chloe spotted Muriel at their usual booth at Q Bar and joined her.

"Congratulations on the movie role!" Muriel said, kissing Chloe on the cheek.

"Thanks. It was a really nerve-wracking experience, but it's going to be great working on this movie with Alex." She looked around, seeing no sign of Daniella. "Is court running late again?"

"Of course. This case really seems to be taking a toll on her."

"Hey, look. That's her on TV again."

Chloe pointed to the screen above the bar, where Daniella was pictured outside the courthouse speaking to a throng of reporters.

"My clients maintain their innocence," Daniella said, gesturing toward several men standing behind her in dark suits. The men looked twice her age, but she seemed very much in control of the situation. "When everything is said and done, I believe the verdict will bear this out."

The network cut to an anchor in a studio, talking about the case with a photo superimposed over his shoulder of Daniella at work in the courtroom.

"That was defense attorney Daniella Webster commenting on SorCom founder and CEO Barry Sorkin's decision not to take the witness stand," the anchor said. "The controversial decision leaves it up to Webster and the rest of the defense team to convince the jury of the corporation's position. With her stellar performance in the courtroom thus far, legal analysts say she's up to the challenge. Stay with us. You're watching TrialTV."

Not long after the television segment concluded, Daniella rushed in, apologizing for being late yet again for the girls' monthly happy hour.

"You're becoming quite the media sensation," Muriel commented. "We just saw you talking to the press on TV."

Daniella grimaced. "That was a performance – literally. It's so obvious that this company is guilty of lying to investors, but I signed on to defend them, and that's what I'm going to do." She kneaded her forehead, looking exhausted.

"Hey, when'd you get that big diamond?" Chloe said, noticing the ring on Daniella's finger.

"Yeah, is there an important piece of information you're withholding from us, counselor?" Muriel said, leaning across Chloe to examine the ring.

Daniella put her hand on the table, glancing down at the ring. "I'm sorry, guys. I've been so preoccupied with this case, I forgot to mention Darby proposed."

Chloe shrieked in delight, soon joined by Muriel, attracting confused stares from the other people in the bar.

"Sshh!" Daniella chastised. "Do you want to get us kicked out of here for causing a public nuisance?"

"Can you stop talking about the law for five minutes?" Muriel said, reaching for Daniella's hand to get a closer look at the ring. "When's the big day?"

"We're looking at June. Hopefully this case'll be done by then."

"But *my* wedding's in June," Muriel said, sounding more concerned about potential scheduling conflicts than offended that Daniella was "upstaging" her.

"Oh my god. I've been so tied up with this case, I totally forgot." Daniella knocked her palm against her forehead.

"Careful, you don't want to knock yourself out with that big rock," Chloe said, teasing.

"Don't worry," Muriel said. "We'll work it out."

"Yeah," Chloe added, "I've modeled a lot for Vera Wang and I can probably get you a group rate on wedding gowns."

Daniella laughed and shook her head. "Sometimes I think I'm going to go crazy, working on this case *and* planning a wedding at the same time."

"I know what you mean, girl," Muriel said. "The domestic violence case I'm prosecuting isn't nearly as high-profile as yours, but I'm glad my mother's doing most of the wedding planning or I'd be going nuts, too."

"I'd let my mother plan *my* wedding," Daniella shot back, "but since you guys are going to be my bridesmaids, I don't think you want to be wearing chartreuse dresses with '80s shoulder pads!"

Chloe shared a laugh with her friends, glad that good things were happening for them as well.

"Enough about us and our big court cases and our wedding plans. It's all about you tonight," Daniella said, turning to Chloe. "Good job landing that role!"

Chloe couldn't contain her smile. "I'm really excited. I fell in love with Alex's character from the first moment I read his book. Getting through that screen test was an accomplishment in itself."

"You brought the contract from the movie studio, didn't you," Muriel said, "so Daniella and I can look over it?"

"Yeah, but maybe we should do it some other time," Chloe said, observing how drained Daniella looked from another long day in court. "I know you're both really busy. Why don't I make copies and send them to you so you can look over the contract when you have more time?"

"I can only speak for myself, but I know I'll *never* have more time," Daniella said. "Now is as good a time as any."

Chloe reached for her bag and pulled out a thick ream of papers, plunking it down on the table. "Okay. Here it goes. I hired an entertainment attorney, but I do feel a lot more comfortable having you guys go over it."

Daniella fanned through the stack of papers. "We're happy to do it," she said, waving over the waiter. "But the first round is on you."

Several beers and a couple of empty martini glasses later, Daniella and Muriel were still plowing through the dense document.

"Most of this is pretty standard contract language," Daniella said, "but I think I found something you might want to take a look at."

"Oh, yeah?" Chloe said, munching on a handful of mini pretzels. "What is it?"

Daniella pointed out a page toward the end of the contract that contained a large paragraph with barely legible fine print.

Chloe strained to read the section, which was worded in impenetrable legalese. "What does it say in laymen's terms?"

"Basically, it's a morals clause."

Chloe sipped her martini and belched. "What's that?"

"I vaguely remember one of our professors at Columbia talking about morals clauses in that entertainment law class we took," Muriel interjected. "From what I remember, morals clauses go back to the days of the old Hollywood studio system, when the big movie moguls would force rising stars to sign binding contracts."

Chloe nodded. "The stars were called contract players, right?" she said, glad to be able to throw around industry jargon.

"Right," Daniella said, "and to cover their asses, the studios buried these morals clauses in contracts in case one of the actors or actresses they were grooming for stardom got embroiled in some big scandal. That way, the studio could drop them without having to pay off the star for the rest of the contract."

"Corporations sometimes put morals clauses in endorsement deals for professional athletes," Muriel interjected, "just in case the hot young NFL star they hired to push their energy drink turns up in a video on YouTube, doing naughty things in a hotel room with underage groupies."

Chloe took another sip of her drink, taking in, along with the alcohol, what Daniella and Muriel were saying. "What do you guys think I should do?"

"Neither of us specializes in entertainment law, as you know." Daniella put her hand on Chloe's shoulder. "But we do consider ourselves your big sisters and you know we've got your back. If I were you, I'd tell your attorney to have the studio remove the morals clause. I know you and how you put your all into something once you've committed. I'm sure you're going to invest a lot of time and energy into preparing for this role, and you don't want the 'powers that be' finding some excuse to fire you if you get caught running a red light or tearing a tag off a mattress."

Chloe giggled. "Yeah, that's about as daring as I get. But what should I do if the studio execs refuse to remove the clause?"

"That's a tough one," Muriel said. "I understand if you don't want to make too many demands, especially since this is your first real acting gig."

"I wish we could tell you what to do," Daniella said, stacking the contract papers and handing them back to Chloe, "but that's your call."

Chloe and Alex sat across from the studio executives and production team in a booth at the Polo Lounge. As the studio executives, producer and director discussed production deadlines, wardrobe fittings and other shop talk, Chloe looked around the room and observed similar conversations taking place at other tables. Just eight months ago, she had met with her then-agent Beverly Nolan and the bumbling novice Ryan Van Patten in this same room. This was also the place where Chloe had first spotted that sleazy pornographer, Barry Mangione. Back then, Chloe was struggling to jump-start her fledgling acting career and had no idea of the pitfalls that awaited her, but now she was finally a real player.

Chloe redirected her attention to the conversation at her table when she heard mention of the contract she was to sign.

"We can finish up the last stages of preproduction and start rehearsals with Chloe and the rest of the cast as soon as we get the signed copy of her contract," Bryan da Silva, the producer, said in a tone that indicated he wasn't thrilled that the studio had cast her in the lead role. "Did you bring it with you?"

Chloe exchanged a glance with Alex and sipped her water, seeing this as her cue to bring up the morals clause Daniella had flagged.

"There's a small issue with the contract," she said, taking the thick contract from her bag and placing it on the table. "I was going to have my attorney call the studio's legal department, but I figured I may as well bring it up in person at our meeting today."

"What's the problem?" said Preston Hedrick, a bespectacled young studio executive.

She cleared her throat. "I don't know if there's so much of a problem as a minor change I'd like to make," she said, trying to broach the subject as diplomatically as possible. "I'd like to have the morals clause removed before I sign."

The producer and studio exec leaned into each other and conferred in an undertone, like attorneys in a sidebar at a trial.

"The morals clause is standard in all of our contracts with newly discovered talent," Hedrick said finally.

"'Newly discovered' is a nice way of saying 'unproven,' which is what you are," da Silva said to Chloe with his typically smug expression.

Chloe saw a look of anger pass across Alex's face and she squeezed his hand under the table to stop him from lashing out at the abrasive producer.

"That may be," she said, "but I'd feel more comfortable signing if the clause were removed."

"It's just a formality," Hedrick insisted.

"Well, if it's just a formality," Alex spoke up, "then there should be no problem removing it."

Hedrick adjusted his tie and looked uncomfortable. "I'd have to go back and talk to Legal to see if it's possible to have the contract rewritten."

"Oh, for pete's sake," Hal Forster, the director, spoke up, "what's the big deal in having them remove the stupid clause? Hell, I'd take a magic marker and cross it out myself if it would move things along."

"If it were up to me, I'd say it was no problem," Hedrick said, "but the top execs at the studio have to review any kind of change to our contracts. That could take a few days, maybe even a few weeks."

"A few weeks?" da Silva said. "That'll put us behind schedule and over-budget. We've already hired the crew and we'll literally have to pay people to stand around and wait." He directed his gaze at Chloe. "I knew you were going to be high-maintenance."

Chloe felt Alex clench his fist under the table and she nudged him to get up and follow her into the lobby.

"Excuse us," she said, tugging on Alex's sleeve. "We need a minute to talk this over."

Once in the lobby, Alex let loose with a string of profanities. "I don't know who the fuck da Silva thinks he is, talking to you like that," he fumed. "You should have let me punch that motherfucker."

"He's just saying those things to make me quit. He's resented me since I tagged along on the location scout in New Orleans."

"Fuck him. Look, if you want to walk out, I'm right behind you. I'm not going to let them coerce you into signing something you're not comfortable with."

Chloe glanced back at the table, where the producer, director and studio exec conferred while staring at her.

"I've learned to pick my battles, and I don't want to hold up production over something so minor," she said, turning back to Alex. "I don't want to give da Silva an excuse to blame me for the movie going over-budget. I've dealt with his type before. He thinks models-turned-actresses aren't 'legit' and he's looking for any excuse to get rid of me."

Alex shot the producer a dirty look. "I'm just afraid that if we cave into the studio's demands now, what's it going to be like once the cameras start rolling?"

"I guess we'll just have to fight." She took his arm and began leading him back to the table. "Together."

Once Chloe and Alex had returned to the booth, she took out a pen. "Alex and I have talked it over and I'm ready to sign."

"What about the morals clause?" Hedrick inquired.

She hesitated momentarily before signing her name next to the "X" on the last page of the contract. "I'll do whatever it takes to get this movie made."

94

"I've got an in-home session with a client in a half-an-hour," said Marcella, Chloe's trainer, clicking off her stopwatch as Chloe finished calisthenics on the floor of the Bronx gym where they worked out. "It's one of those pampered Park Avenue bitches. She gets pissy if I'm five minutes late, so I better get going. Can I trust you to finish up on the treadmill?"

"Yes, ma'am," Chloe said, sitting up and toweling her sweaty brow. "This role I'm taking on is very physically demanding and I want to be in tip-top shape."

"Congratulations again on getting the part," Marcella said, grabbing her gym bag. "I knew you could do it."

Once Marcella had given detailed instructions for how long and at what pace to run on the treadmill, Chloe refilled her water bottle and got to work. She stepped on a treadmill, programmed it for thirty minutes at the steepest incline and trained her attention on the bank of televisions before her. While watching the "info-tainment" program *Entertainment Access*, her ears perked up when she heard her name.

"A skin mag has acquired nude photos of model-turned-actress Chloe Bareaux," said Vanessa Ramos, the beautiful female anchor who had previously interviewed Chloe. "Hear the shocking details when we return."

As Chloe listened to the report, she felt numb. She stood there, straddling the treadmill as the belt whirred between her feet. *Flesh for Fantasy* magazine, the television anchor said, planned to release nude photos of Chloe in their next edition, which would hit stands in less than a week.

This just wasn't possible, Chloe reasoned. Where had they gotten the photos? She always requested a private change booth when she did outdoor shoots and demanded "kill rights" to any photos that could expose flesh unintentionally when modeling lingerie or swimwear. And with her naturally brown skin, she had no need for sunbathing, especially not in the nude. When the TV flashed a black-and-white photo from the nude spread, with her breasts pixilated, the memory struck her.

"Damn it!" she exclaimed, the other joggers turning to look at her as they huffed and puffed. She felt a sudden urge to cover up the skimpy sports bra and biker shorts she was wearing, certain everyone in the gym recognized her from the TV and were judging her.

The topless photos she took when she was eighteen. She had all but forgotten about them. Why were they resurfacing to haunt her now?

"The aptly titled *Flesh for Fantasy* is a subsidiary of the conglomerate run by porn kingpin Barry Mangione," Vanessa Ramos said.

The show cut to an interview with Mangione in his gaudy gold office, and she recalled the encounter with him. The so-called "audition" in which he threatened to dig up dirt from her past if she didn't take the part in his trashy film. She had been disgusted by him then, and was even more repulsed now.

As Chloe listened to the repugnant man talking about how the latest edition of *Flesh for Fantasy* magazine with her on the cover could be the best-selling edition ever and how much money he was going to make off exploiting her image, she ran to the locker room, sick to her stomach.

"Chloe Drops Seventh Veil, Studio Drops Her," Chloe said, reading aloud the headline from the latest edition of the *New York Post*. She tossed the paper amid the breakfast dishes on the dining room table in the apartment she shared with Alex, who was typing on his laptop. "I'm so sorry I screwed everything up."

"Honey, how many times do I have to tell you it's not your fault?" he said, setting his computer aside and taking her hand.

After the nude pictures had been released, the studio had exercised the dreaded morals clause in Chloe's contract. The studio executives had said the bad publicity would reflect poorly on the movie, but Chloe knew Bryan da Silva, the producer who seemed to resent her presence from that first location-scouting trip in New Orleans, was the force behind her unceremonious firing. He had finally found an excuse to get rid of her, and she was so mad at herself for giving him the noose to slip around her neck.

"I feel like I should be wearing a scarlet letter," she said. "This whole episode has been such a disaster."

"You've got to stop blaming yourself," Alex said. "Look, am I happy that millions of guys have had the chance to ogle you in the buff since that trashy magazine came out? Of course not. But we have to get past this."

Chloe buried her face in her hands in frustration. "I honestly forgot all about those pictures," she said, looking up and being confronted by the newspaper's big, bold headline. "I never thought anybody would see them. When I took those photographs I was eighteen and living on the streets. I had no choice," she said. "It was either pose nude or starve."

"I think we should go after that bastard who publishes that rag, file a multi-million-dollar defamation lawsuit like your friend Daniella suggested. We can't let him get away with this."

Chloe slumped in her chair. "I don't know if I'm up for a big court battle. I just want to forget the whole thing."

"Well, before you do, I think there's something you should see." He turned his laptop toward her. "I was browsing IMDB last night."

She nodded, recognizing the homepage of the Internet database for everything related to film and television.

"Since da Silva gave you such a hard time, I looked up some of his past credits to check out his track record," Alex continued. "It turns out his list of credits includes a series of straight-to-DVD, soft-core porn flicks financed by none other than Barry Mangione."

"The scumbag who dug up those nude photos of me," Chloe said, feeling nauseous at the mention of his name. "I knew he'd been looking for a way to get back at me."

"Right. And when Mangione heard you were cast in the lead of the new movie that his old friend was producing, I think he went to da Silva and struck up one of those dirty little side deals they're always cutting in Hollywood."

"Mangione would publish the nude photos and give da Silva a kickback," Chloe said, following Alex's logic.

"Exactly. For da Silva, it was a win-win situation. He got you kicked off the movie and got a little cash out of the deal."

Chloe stared at the computer screen, her anger mounting as Alex pulled up a shot of da Silva and Mangione slapping each other on the back at a movie premiere. "Those sons-of-bitches set me up."

"We have a lawsuit here. We have plenty of evidence those two were in cahoots to get you thrown off the project."

"I don't know, Alex," she said, running her hands through her bed-head hair, which was as tangled as the mess she found herself in. "I was really naive when I took those pictures and signed a release. That fat-ass photographer who sold me down the river is probably sitting on a beach in Fiji right now, celebrating. Even if I could build a case to sue da Silva and Mangione, I don't want my mistake to jeopardize your career. I want you to go ahead and finish the script revisions after they recast my part and keep working on the movie."

"There is no movie," Alex said. He punctuated his statement by pushing the "off" button on his laptop. "When they fired you, I called my agent and told them I wanted out. There's no way this project is going forward without you, not if I have anything to do with it."

"No, Alex, you can't quit just because they fired me. Can't the studio sue you for breach of contract?"

"Funny thing about contracts," he said, grinning. "Just as the studio saw fit to put that ridiculous morals clause in your contract, I had my agent make sure there was a clause in mine giving me the right to back out if the project wasn't moving forward satisfactorily. And not only can I walk away, but the rights to my novel revert to me."

Chloe kissed him. "I was so looking forward to us working together on this project, but now everything's ruined."

"It's gonna be all right," he said, stroking her face. "I'll go back to work at the magazine while my agent shops the script around to other studios."

"I don't know what I'd do without you. I couldn't go through this alone."

She moved to kiss him again, but was interrupted by the phone, which had been ringing nonstop since the "nude-pictures scandal," as one tabloid dubbed the whole affair.

"I'm not going to answer that," she said. "I don't know how many times I have to say, 'No comment.'" She got up and began gathering the dishes.

"I better get it," Alex said. "Let's hope it's my agent calling with a better offer from another studio."

While Alex answered the phone, Chloe took the dishes into the kitchen and began rinsing them. Shortly thereafter, he came up behind her, turned off the faucet and told her the call was for her.

"Can't you tell whoever it is I'm not available?" she said, eyeing the phone cautiously like it was a bomb that was about to detonate.

"I think you'll want to take this call," he said. "It's good news for a change."

Chloe gave Alex a skeptical look and took the phone, thinking it might be Maxine calling to try and cheer her up. If anything positive had come out of the ordeal, it was that, ironically, it had strengthened Chloe's relationship with her mother. When Maxine found out about the nude photos, she was surprisingly supportive. She told Chloe that she had nothing to be ashamed of, that she simply had done what she had to do when she'd left home.

When Chloe put the phone to her ear, however, it was Gigi on the other end. "*Bonjour, ma amie*," Gigi said, sounding annoyingly cheerful. "Pack your bags."

Chloe sighed into the phone. "Gigi, you know I'm going through a tough time right now. I'm not in the mood for games. What are you talking about?"

"Philippe proposed and I want you to come to Paris to help me plan the wedding."

"I'm pregnant!" Gigi jubilantly announced as she sat next to Chloe on the living room sofa in the Paris apartment they once shared. Since Chloe had quit modeling, she stayed in New York most of the time and Gigi had taken over the lease.

"Oh," Chloe said, passing Gigi the carton of cookie dough ice cream they were spooning from. "Is that why you guys are in such a hurry to plan the wedding?"

"No. That's not it at all. Philippe's going to be finishing up his residency and starting full time at the hospital. We want to get the ceremony out of the way before he has even less time than he does now."

Gigi took a large dip out of the container and shoveled it into her mouth, closing her eyes, as if savoring the sweetness not only of the frozen treat but of the new life she was beginning.

"I'll never be able to replace the baby I miscarried when I was married to Justin," she said, looking down, the corners of her eyes misting. "But now I finally feel like I'm getting a chance to start over."

Chloe reached across the sofa and hugged her. "I'm so happy for you, Gi'. You're going to be the best mother, and Philippe's a great guy and I know he's going to make a great father."

Unlike the flashy, famous, rich guys Gigi had taken up with in the past, Philippe came from a modest background with two working-class parents. And as a medical resident struggling to pay off student loans, he was anything but rich. Even though he stood to make good money as a physician when he became established in his career, he expressed an interest in starting a clinic in one of Paris' less-glamorous areas to assist low-income residents and immigrants. He was generous, socially conscious and, most of all, as Gigi related, he was attuned to her needs.

"Not to mention good in bed!" Gigi cackled, causing Chloe to crack up, too, glad that the old, mischievous Gigi hadn't completely gone away. "But seriously," Gigi added, "I really lucked out this time. He's a good guy, very understanding."

Alex was equally understanding while Chloe commuted back and forth to Paris for several weeks helping Gigi plan the wedding. All the activity helped Chloe push the nude-pictures scandal to the back of her mind. It was nice to have something to focus on other than her public humiliation and stalled acting career.

The night before the wedding, Chloe and Gigi slept over in Chloe's old room at the Chateau de Chevalier, the way they used to when they were teens. They thumbed through old photo albums and put on CDs they listened to in high school.

"This is better than a bachelorette party," Gigi said as they danced around Chloe's old room to the music of their youth. "In my condition," she added, holding her bulging stomach, "I couldn't enjoy a lapdance from one of those Chippendale strippers!"

They laughed and twirled around the room.

"Seriously," Gigi said, taking Chloe's hand and spinning her, "I'll never forget this night."

"Me neither," Chloe said. "I'm glad I get to be a part of your wedding this time around."

Gigi's wedding was a traditional ceremony held at the Sacré-Coeur Basilica. Traditional except for the fact that the bride was very visibly showing her pregnancy. Maxine personally made Gigi's tent-sized maternity gown with yards of silk imported from Japan and enough off-white organdy and ivory lace to curtain all the windows of Louis XIV's grand palace at Versailles. Chloe was overjoyed to be Gigi's maid of honor.

With characteristic abandon for formality, Gigi waddled down the aisle on the arm of her grandfather, tossing her bouquet in the air and catching it just before it hit the floor and sticking her tongue out at Chloe as she neared the altar. Chloe looked at Alex, who'd flown in for the ceremony, and shared a laugh at Gigi's antics.

Chloe's mood turned serious when Gigi and Philippe exchanged vows. She'd promised Gigi she wouldn't cry, but lost her composure. Chloe was moved beyond words seeing her "soul sister" married and settled with a child on the way. Gigi had gone through a lot. She deserved happiness.

The reception, catered by Marie, was held in the ballroom of the Chateau de Chevalier. Before the bride and groom cut the cake, Simone proposed a toast.

"Gigi, my baby," Simone said, standing at her place at the bridal party's table, "I never thought I'd see this day – especially since you eloped the first time you got married!"

Gigi, holding her new husband's hand, laughed along with the intimate gathering of friends and family.

"I just want to say I'm proud of you and I wish you and Philippe all the best," Simone added, her voice cracking. She raised her champagne glass. "Here's to a long and prosperous life together."

Gigi clinked her glass of non-alcoholic sparkling grape juice against her husband's. "And to good friends." She winked at Chloe across the table as everyone clapped.

When Simone took her seat again, Chloe noticed the diamond she was sporting. "Oh my god, Simone," Chloe said, taking her godmother's hand. "Are you going to be next to walk down the aisle?"

Simone looked from Chloe to her longtime boyfriend, Armand, on her other side. "Armand proposed, but I didn't want to say anything until after Gigi's wedding. I didn't want to seem like I was competing with her." She added laughingly, "There was enough of that when you guys were teenagers."

Chloe hugged Simone and shook Armand's hand. "Congratulations." She turned to Alex, who was sitting on her other side. "Doesn't it seem like everyone we know is getting married?"

Alex nodded. "As soon as we get back to New York, I've got to plan Steve's bachelor party."

"I still can't believe Pam agreed to put up with him for the rest of her life," Chloe said, teasing Alex about his obnoxious-but-loyal best friend.

"I guess there's someone out there for everyone," Alex replied with a grin.

"I just wish we could find someone for Maxine," Simone said.

Chloe followed Simone's gaze across the room to where Maxine conferred with Marie about the menu.

"I've given up on that," Chloe said with a sigh. "I think she's pretty much resigned herself to the notion that she's never going to find someone as good as Jacques."

Before they had a chance to recover from their jetlag and all the excitement of Gigi's wedding, Chloe and Alex got swept up in his best friend Steve's wedding. Despite his chauvinistic attitude, Chloe had to admit that the personally-written vows Steve recited sounded sincere and the elaborate ceremony at a Manhattan cathedral was a classy affair.

"You did a great job as best man," Chloe said, running her hands along the lapels of Alex's tux when he came over to her at the end of the ceremony.

"I didn't lose the ring!" he said with a triumphant raise of his fist.

He took Chloe by the waist and they watched from the front pew as Steve and Pam posed for photos at the altar. Chloe had helped the normally mousy Pam get ready for her big day, suggesting that she wear her hair down instead of in her dowdy Sunday-school-teacher bun and helped her apply makeup to bring out her big brown eyes and full lips.

"Pam is a beautiful bride," Chloe said, watching the newly-married couple beam at each other.

"But you'd make an even more gorgeous one," Alex whispered in her ear, taking her by the waist and pulling her close.

Chloe patted his hand to show she appreciated the compliment, but said nothing in response.

The flurry of June weddings continued with first Muriel's nuptials to her fiancé, congressional aide Miles Neal, in Washington, D.C., and then Daniella's wedding to her firm's Webmaster, Darby Payne, in Boston. Daniella and Muriel took turns serving as each other's maids of honor, while Chloe happily took on the role of bridesmaid at both ceremonies on consecutive weekends.

Muriel's wedding was a relatively simple affair for a select number of guests, while Daniella's extravagant parents went all out and flew in all of their California relatives and friends to Boston for the occasion. The ceremony was held at the historic Cathedral Church of St. Paul, with a reception in the backyard of Daniella's boss' mansion in the affluent suburb of Wellesley.

"Now I remember why I moved to the East Coast. My parents have only been in town for two days and they're already driving me batty!" said Daniella, still in her wedding dress and veil, joining Chloe and Muriel as they chatted outside one of the big white tents. "They're already bugging me about writing thank you notes to all the cronies they insisted on inviting. I can't wait to put Dr. and Mrs. Webster on the next flight to LAX!"

Chloe laughed with Daniella about her well-meaning yet overbearing parents and accepted a piece of cake from a waiter.

"I'm so glad I don't have to worry about fitting into my dress anymore," Muriel said, grabbing a piece of the heavenly, butter-cream confection from the waiter's tray as he passed by.

"Darby and Alex and Miles seem like they're hitting it off," Daniella said, looking across the expansive lawn to where the three young men stood by a fountain, conversing.

"That Darby is a character," Chloe said.

Living up to Daniella description of him as an overgrown frat boy, Darby had bucked convention by wearing Nike high tops with his morning suit.

"Yeah, I think I'll keep him," Daniella said, causing Chloe and Muriel to break up laughing.

"You both picked great guys," Chloe said, digging into her cake.

"You didn't do too bad yourself there, missy," Muriel said. "Alex is a great guy. Everything you said about him is true."

Daniella raised an eyebrow. "Any chance we'll get to return the favor and be bridesmaids for you some time soon?"

Daniella and Muriel stared expectantly at Chloe, as if waiting for her to make a big announcement.

"Sorry guys," Chloe said. "I've got nothing to announce."

"Well, we'll have to change that, won't we?" Daniella took Chloe by the hand. "Come on. I'm about to throw the bouquet."

Chloe pulled her hand away and took a step back. "Why don't you start without me? I'm going to stay here and finish my cake."

95

When Chloe entered the apartment after a late-afternoon jog through Central Park, Alex was waiting for her in the bedroom, all dressed up. He had laid out an off-the-shoulder black dress and a string of pearls on the bed.

"Go shower and put that on," he said.

"So I'm not able to dress myself now?" she said playfully.

"I don't want any arguments out of you tonight, woman. You're coming with me. We're going for a ride."

Chloe did what he said. There was something peculiar about the way Alex was acting and she was curious to find out why.

She knew he had something big planned when he blindfolded her before she got in the car. "Where are we going?" she kept asking.

"You'll find out when we get there," is all he would say.

The long ride through rush-hour evening traffic was agonizing; she couldn't stand being kept in suspense. Finally, the car came to a stop and she heard what sounded like the gate to an underground garage creaking open.

"Where are we?" she asked.

"We're not quite there. Be patient."

He parked the car, opened her door and led her to an elevator. Her fear of heights returned as she felt the elevator ascending higher and higher. She leaned on Alex for support.

"Where on Earth are you taking me?" she asked, afraid to let go of his hand.

"Hold on. We're almost there."

She heard the elevator door open with a ding, and he helped her step off and undid the blindfold. Her breath was taken away by the sight that awaited her. He had taken her to Hugo's Place, the elegant restaurant in the Wellington Tower where they had their first date. The restaurant was empty, except for vases of roses and flickering candles adorning every table.

"I rented it out just for us," he said, leading her to a table in the center of the dining room.

"Oh, Alex, this is so beautiful. It's not the anniversary of when we met, is it?"

He grinned. "Nope."

"Then what's the occasion?"

"We'll get to that later," he said, pulling out her chair.

They enjoyed a romantic dinner, just the two of them. The only sound other than their own voices came from a string ensemble that played instrumental versions of their favorite songs. After dinner, Alex snapped his finger and the ensemble started playing a tune on cue.

"This song sounds familiar," Chloe said, straining to remember the melody. "What is it?"

"It's 'The Most Beautiful Girl in the World' by Prince, the song we danced to at the masquerade ball."

She leaned across the table and kissed him. "This has been the best night of my life."

"I wanted to make it special for a reason." He pulled a tiny black box from his jacket pocket and slowly opened it, revealing a large, gleaming yet tasteful diamond ring. He got down on one knee and took her hand. "Every day we're together, my love for you grows deeper and stronger. No other woman has ever made me feel the way you do. I want you to be the mother of my children. I want to be with you the rest of my life. Chloe, will you marry me?"

She was so moved, tears came to her eyes. There was only one thing she could say.

"No. I'm sorry, Alex. I can't marry you."

No one said a word during the drive home.

Chloe quietly got ready for bed, slipping out of her dress and into a silk nightgown. She didn't bother removing her make-up or brushing her teeth; she just wanted to close her eyes and shut out the unspoken hostility between her and Alex. She didn't say anything when she climbed into bed next to him and turned out the light. She turned over on her side, trying to get to sleep, but she was wide awake.

"Why?" he said softly after a long, dark silence. "Why, Chloe? That's all I want to know."

"Alex, let's not get into this right now. I know you're upset. We're both tired. Let's sleep on it. We'll talk about it in the morning."

"No. I want to talk about it now." He sat up and turned on the light. "I want some answers. Start talking."

"It's not that simple," she said, sitting up and rubbing her eyes.

"Why not? You didn't have any trouble turning down my proposal. You should have no trouble giving me an explanation."

She sighed heavily. "Alex, please don't take it personally. I love you with all my heart, I really do. But it's just not the right time."

"Well, when is the right time? A year from now? Five years from now? Ten years from now?"

"I don't know, okay? What's the big rush?"

"There's no rush, it's just that I've come to a place where I feel like I'm ready to start a family."

"I'll be ready, too. Someday. But right now I'm going through a lot. I want to get my acting career off the ground first."

"Haven't I supported you every step of the way in your career? Wasn't I behind you when you decided to leave modeling? Didn't I back you up when the studio fired you from the movie? I thought that's what marriage is about – support. I'm supportive of you now, so what would be the difference if we were married?"

"I just don't know if I'm ready to make that kind of commitment at this point in my life. Marriage is so... Permanent. There's so many things I want to do before I tie myself down."

"'Tie myself down'?" Alex looked wounded. "You make it sound like being married to me would be like having a ball and chain strapped to your ankle."

"I didn't mean it that way. It's just that when I do get married, I want it to be forever. My mother and father split up right after I was born and Jacques died not long after he and Mother got married. I've never had a good marriage modeled for me – at least not one that lasted."

"Oh, so you think being married to me would be a bad experience?"

"That's not what I meant. You're twisting everything I say. This is why I didn't want to discuss it right now. We're both too emotional."

"I'm just trying to figure out where this relationship is going. Tell me that, will you?"

"Alex, please. Can we drop this? Can't we just leave things the way they are? I need time. I'm still trying to find myself."

"I'm tired of waiting around, taking a backseat while you try to 'find yourself.'" He jumped out of bed, threw on some sweats, and stuffed some clothes into a duffle bag.

"Where are you going?"

"Away. Away from here. Away from you. You say you're not ready for a commitment, and it doesn't seem like you ever will be."

"Alex, come on, don't walk out. We can work this out."

"I'm sorry. I just don't think there's anything left to work out."

"Fine. Then go." Chloe picked up vase and threw it at the door as Alex left. She watched it shatter into a million pieces.

Alex sat on the bed in Steve and Pam's guestroom, sorting through a box of his belongings, his basset hound, Jack, curled at his feet. He paused and looked at a photo of him and Chloe holding hands as they sat on the balcony at his parents' house during their trip to New Orleans. He had done such a stupid thing, walking out on her the way he did. He shouldn't have pressured her. But he had too much pride to go crawling back.

He looked up at the sound of a knock on the door.

"Here you go," Steve said, opening the door and tossing Alex a bundle of blankets, sheets and pillows.

"Thanks," Alex said, setting the bedding aside.

"How you holding up, buddy?" Steve said, propping his elbow on the doorjamb.

"Okay, I guess," Alex said, turning his attention back to the box.

"You need anything?"

"No, I'm all right. Tell Pam I said thanks again for letting me stay here. Since you guys are newlyweds, I'm sure you'd like to have your house to yourselves, so I'm going to start looking for a new place as soon as possible." He didn't even want to think about living alone again.

Steve plunked down next to Alex on the bed. "So, what are you going to do now?"

Alex set the box aside. "I don't know. It's like the bottom fell out. Not only did the movie project fall apart, but now Chloe and I aren't together anymore." He exhaled. "I've been thinking about going back to work at the magazine. At least if I did that, there'd be something familiar in my life, something to occupy all this time I've got on my hands now."

"You don't sound too thrilled about the prospect of going back to your old job," Steve said, exhibiting a rare moment of empathy.

"I'm not. I'm sure my editor, Duff, will be thrilled to see me back at my old desk, taking marching orders and being treated like a flunky again. He warned me about the dangers of 'going Hollywood,' and I'm sure he'll be more than happy to say, 'I told you so.'"

Steve slapped Alex on the shoulder. "Hey, keep your head up, bro'. You may have lost your woman and your career's in the crapper, but you've got me."

"I don't know why that's no consolation," Alex said, punching Steve in the shoulder and going back to sorting through his papers.

"I mean, it man," Steve said, getting up and going to the door. "If there's anything else me and Pam can do, let me know. You're welcome to stay here as long as you need."

Alex stopped shuffling the papers when he came across a printout of a news article with the headline "Dade Chemical Fined for Polluting Mississippi River."

"Hey, Steve, man, thanks for the hospitality," Alex said, stuffing the papers in his duffle bag, "but I think I need to go home, back to Louisiana, for a while to sort things out."

Chloe returned to Paris after the breakup to spend some time reevaluating her life. While her relationship with Alex had ended, Gigi's new life with Philippe was just beginning. Chloe spent much of her stay in Paris helping Gigi move out of the apartment they once shared and into a new place with Philippe that would be big enough when the baby came.

"I never realized I had so many brushes and pencils," Gigi said as she and Chloe sat on the living room floor, packing. "Luckily there's a spare room in the new place where I can set up my studio."

"I'm really happy for you, Gi'," Chloe said, taping up yet another box. "But I'd be lying if I said I wasn't going to miss sharing this place with you when I'm in Paris. Especially now that Alex and I have broken up."

Gigi stopped packing. "Have you talked to him since he left?"

Chloe shook her head. "I still can't believe he walked out on me like that. He came and got the rest of his stuff while I was out." She continued taping up the box, keeping her head down to hide fresh tears.

"Why don't you call him?"

"I don't think he'll talk to me." Chloe looked up, dabbing the corners of her eyes. "Do you think I was wrong for turning down his proposal?"

Several moments passed before Gigi responded. She remained silent while she continued packing art supplies. "From past experience of running off and eloping in high school, I don't think you should jump into marriage if you're not ready." She folded the box's flaps and added, "But do you think it's possible you were a bit hasty by flat-out saying 'no'?"

Chloe closed her box and propped her elbows on top. "I don't know. Maybe. I just don't know if I'll be ready to settle down until I'm more established in my career."

"But I thought you and Alex were working to build a future together?"

"*Were*, past tense." Chloe stared out the window at the midday sun. She never imagined that she'd be all alone, with no career and a broken relationship. Her life lay in pieces around her like the discarded items Gigi was leaving behind in the half-vacant apartment.

"I hate seeing you so down." Gigi got up and began lugging the box of art supplies across the room, holding it in front of her very pregnant belly. "I wish there was something I could do."

"You know what you can do? You can stop lifting things you're not supposed to." Chloe took the box from Gigi and placed it next to a stack of other labeled boxes. "And don't worry about me," she said, arranging the boxes so that each pile corresponded with the room they where they were to be placed in Gigi and Philippe's new apartment. "I'm going to find things to keep me busy."

When Gigi remained uncharacteristically quiet, Chloe turned around to face her. "Gigi? Are you okay?"

"Uh, I'm not sure," she said, standing in the middle of the room with a perplexed expression, holding her belly. "I think I'm having contractions."

96

Alex stood in his former editor's office, the sound of clicking keyboards, phone chatter and other once-familiar sounds of the busy newsroom buzzing in through the open door.

"I've got to hand it to you, Michaud," Duff said, looking up from a stack of papers on his desk and peering at Alex through his reading glasses. "This exposé on Dade Chemical's illegal dumping into the Mississippi is brilliant. I always knew you had it in you to produce this kind of work." Duff lifted the papers and fanned them, adding in his condescending tone, "I guess it took a failed stab at Hollywood to pull this kind of copy out of you."

Alex smiled at the backhanded compliment. "I did have a lot of time on my hands after the movie deal fell through, so I went home, back to New Orleans, to research that story. Having the extra time on my hands helped a lot, since it took a lot of digging, talking to dozens of sources and examining reams of documents."

Duff picked up the phone. "I'm going to call the layout department and tell them to hold the piece we were going to run on the cover this week and replace it with yours," he said. "When this story runs, it'll have *Time* and *U.S. News* salivating."

Alex held his hand up to stop Duff from dialing. "Not so fast."

"What's the problem? I can't give the story more prominent placement than the cover."

"Before the story runs, we need to discuss the terms of my employment."

"Oh, yeah, that. I'll call HR and let 'em know you're back from leave. There's a couple of forms to fill out that I'll have to sign off on, the usual red tape, nothing too complex."

Duff began to dial the phone again, but Alex stopped him once more. "I didn't say I was back from leave."

"Oh, so you want a couple more weeks' vacation? Go ahead, Michaud, you deserve it. Just make sure you keep your cell phone on in case we need to fact-check a few details."

Alex stood. "I don't think you understand. I'm not interested in coming back to work for the magazine."

Duff hung up the phone. "I don't understand. If you're not looking to come back to work, why did you send me this piece?"

"Let's just say it's an insurance policy."

"An insurance policy?"

Alex savored the puzzled look on Duff's face. "An insurance policy that I'll be able to do the types of stories I want to do, now that I'm a freelancer."

"Freelancer? What are you talking about? You're still on staff."

"You just said yourself that I can't officially restart my old job until all the paperwork is filled out, so technically I'm not on the payroll anymore."

Duff took off his glasses and tossed them on the desk. "Why don't you level with me, Michaud, and stop playing games. Just tell me what you want."

"I was hoping you'd say that." Alex retrieved another set of papers from his satchel and handed them over.

Duff wrinkled his nose at the papers as if they were written in Sanskrit. "What's this?"

"A freelancer's contract I had my attorney draw up," Alex explained, folding his arms in satisfaction. "It details the severance package I'm to receive once I officially leave the full-time employ of Regency Publications and become an independent contractor. Instead of receiving a miniscule salary and wasting my time covering stories I care nothing about, I'll pick and choose the assignments I want, beginning with the exposé on Dade Chemical."

Duff flipped through the contract. "And what if the higher-ups don't agree to these terms?"

"I'm prepared to tender my resignation and sell the story to the highest bidder."

Duff stared at Alex with contempt. Alex held his gaze with unflinching determination. His days of being ordered around were long gone.

"You know something, Michaud," Duff said finally, scooting away from his desk. "Dealing with Hollywood must have taught you a thing or two about cutting a deal." His glare turned to a welcoming smile and he extended his hand. "I think you've finally learned to play the game."

Alex shook Duff's hand. "My attorney will be in contact," he said, standing and gathering his satchel.

On his way to the elevator, Alex heard someone call his name and turned to see Jeff Reardon, the smarmy Ivy Leaguer who always used to give him grief.

"Hey, Michaud, I heard your big movie deal didn't quite work out," Reardon said with his usual smirk. "I bet you're not looking forward to going back to covering ribbon-cuttings and all my cast-off assignments."

"You're right, I'm not looking forward to any of that," Alex said, stepping onto the elevator. He added, just as the doors closed, "But I am looking forward to writing my own ticket."

Chloe was at Gigi's side when she gave birth to a boy. Since Philippe was in surgery and unable to break away when Gigi went into labor, Chloe stepped in and was there to hold Gigi's hand and coach her through every step of the delivery.

"He's beautiful, absolutely beautiful," Chloe said when a nurse brought Gigi's baby to her after she had time to rest up in her private room. Gigi asked Chloe to be the baby's godmother and she joyously accepted.

"I know just what I'll name you," Gigi said to her newborn son, stroking his little tufts of hair. "Philippe Maurice Toussaint. Philippe, after your father, and Maurice, after *my* father."

Chloe took her turn holding the baby. "He's got your eyes and his father's nose."

As if on cue, Philippe barged through the door, hair disheveled, shirt untucked. "I'm so sorry, *cher*. I just got out of surgery and I rushed over as fast as I could," he panted, sweat running down his brow.

"I got the message," Gigi said calmly. "Come meet your son."

"A boy!" Philippe exclaimed, accepting the bundled infant from Chloe.

"I was just saying he has your nose," Chloe said as the ecstatic new father made gurgling noises at his son.

"And my eyes," Gigi said, stroking the baby's face as Philippe burrowed next to her on the bed. "Hopefully he'll never develop his daddy's big ears," she added playfully, tugging on her husband's ears.

Simone and Maxine burst in, carrying balloons and flowers.

"We got here as soon as we could. I had already sent my driver home for the night and we had to use public transportation," Maxine said in mock horror.

"Armand wanted to be here, but he's out of town on business," Simone said, setting the balloons and flowers next to the bed.

"Say hello to your new grandson," Philippe said, handing the baby over.

"Bonjour, *mon coco*," Simone said softly, kissing the baby's forehead. "I must admit, I wasn't too thrilled at the prospect of being a grandmother. I'm still as vain and youth-obsessed as I ever was, but now that I've looked into these big brown eyes, I've fallen in love."

Chloe watched everyone cooing over the baby. While she was ecstatic for Gigi, she wondered if she would ever experience this kind of happiness. Or if she would be alone the rest of her life.

Alex dribbled the basketball and maneuvered past Steve, jumped high and dunked the ball.

"Two points!" Alex declared, doing a victory dance on the indoor court at Pump, the gym they frequented during their lunchtime workouts.

"Time out," Steve called, hunching over and grabbing his knees.

"Yeah, you would want to take a break now that I'm winning."

"I've got to hand it to you," Steve said, sitting on the floor and unscrewing the cap on his Gatorade bottle. "You've had a lot more energy ever since you signed that contract to freelance for the magazine."

"It's a pretty sweet deal," Alex said, spinning the ball on his index finger. "It's the best of both worlds: I get to do stories I care about, but I'll still have plenty of time to work on fiction and screenwriting."

Steve raised his bottle. "Here's to being back on top."

"Thanks, but it seems kind of empty without Chloe," he said, propping the ball under his arm, his energy suddenly depleted as thoughts of the breakup pushed their way into his head again.

Steve stood and put his sweaty arm around Alex's shoulder. "You're taking this breakup way too hard, man," Steve said. "It's her loss, that's how you have to look at it. The sooner you realize that women are never satisfied, the better off you'll be."

"Oh, so now that you're married, you're a relationship expert all of a sudden?"

"Take it from me, my friend, pretty women are nothing but trouble. Take

Pam, for example. She's not bad, but I don't let her wear too much makeup or tight clothes. I don't want her to get the big head and start thinking she can take me for granted. Chloe got used to big-shot photographers and designers telling her how good she looks twenty-four/seven. It was only a matter of time before she dumped you. She was probably just using you to get ahead."

"Thanks a lot, Steve," said Alex, pushing his friend's arm off his shoulder. "You're making me feel so much better."

"Think about it," Steve said. "As soon as the movie deal fell through, she kicked you to the curb. She's probably in the arms of one of those big Hollywood ballers right now. Why waste your time crying over someone who doesn't care about you?"

Alex dribbled the ball, thinking over Steve's words. Maybe there was some truth to what he was saying. When Chloe turned down his proposal, she had crushed all his dreams of building a life with her. Still, Alex didn't want to believe Steve's assessment that Chloe was cold and calculating like Alex's other ex, Veronica.

"You're full of shit," Alex said, throwing the ball at Steve so hard that it socked him in the gut, causing Steve to double over and cradle his mid-section like a pregnant lady stricken with labor pains. "Chloe isn't Veronica."

"Believe what you want, man, but women are all the same," Steve said, regaining his composure and picking up the ball. "At least with Veronica, you knew what you were dealing with."

Steve dribbled the ball past Alex and moved down the court, scoring a basket. Alex just stood there, pondering what Steve had said.

Chloe was glad Maxine was going to be in New York for a few days, meeting with a new American client about a redecorating project. With Alex gone, she could use the company.

"We're going to have so much fun together," Maxine said as they ate dinner together at Chloe's favorite French restaurant, Jean Georges. "We're two single girls out for a night on the town."

"Don't remind me," Chloe muttered.

"You can't keep dwelling on the breakup," Maxine said, taking Chloe's hand. "You're not the only one in the world who's had a relationship go sour. There are lots of career women out there who have trouble keeping a man."

"Mother, please don't cheer me up, okay?"

Chloe was already feeling bad enough about her newly-single status, and her discomfort was compounded when she looked up and saw Alex entering with some woman on his arm. Upon closer inspection, she saw it was none other than Veronica. Chloe couldn't help but stare. How could Alex betray her like that, getting back together with that bitch who had stabbed Chloe in the back? And he had the nerve to bring his conniving ex to Chloe's favorite restaurant, of all places. Was he doing it just to spite her?

"Oh god. Please hide me," Chloe said, holding the dessert menu in front of her face as Alex and Veronica approached.

"What's wrong?"

"Don't look in an obvious way, but Alex just walked in. He's with his ex, and they're coming this way."

Maxine turned all the way around in her chair and gawked at Alex and Veronica.

"I said not to look in an obvious way," Chloe scolded.

In the most embarrassing, humiliating way that only her mother could, Maxine reached over and tugged on Alex's jacket sleeve as he neared their table. He probably wouldn't even have noticed them if she hadn't taken it upon herself to alert him of their presence.

"Hello, Alex, darling. So nice to see you," Maxine said in a friendly tone.

Chloe gave her mother a swift kick under the table. Why was she being nice to him? She was supposed to be on Chloe's side.

"Hello, Mrs. Chevalier," Alex said, kissing her on the cheek. He turned to Chloe. "Hi," he said coolly.

"Hi," she said in an equally icy tone. She avoided making eye contact with Veronica.

"Aren't you going to introduce me to your lovely lady friend?" Maxine said to Alex, inciting Chloe to reach under the tablecloth and give her a pinch. If Maxine kept it up, Chloe was going to ensure that her meddlesome mother was black and blue by the end of the evening.

"Mrs. Chevalier, this is my, uh, friend, Veronica Harris."

The moment brought a new meaning to the word awkward.

"Nice meeting you, Veronica," Maxine said, extending her hand.

"Nice meeting you, too, Mrs. Chevalier." With a smug glance in Chloe's direction, Veronica added, "Good seeing you again."

Chloe considered impaling Veronica with her salad fork. Instead, she said nothing and stared at her lap.

"Well, it was good seeing you both. Take care," Alex said, leading Veronica away.

"Let's pay the check and get out of here," Chloe said to Maxine. She couldn't stand seeing Alex with Veronica. She tried not to look, but it was as if her eyes were drawn to their table, like a bird flying toward its own reflection in an office-building window and repeatedly thudding against the glass. Every time she caught a glimpse of them together, she wanted to kill Alex and kick

Veronica's ass.

"What did you expect the man to do, dearest, become a monk?" Maxine reasoned.

"Of course not. But he could have at least not taken up with that *mistonne*," Chloe said, referring to Veronica by one of the more common French slang terms for a scandalous woman. She couldn't believe Alex. His side of the bed hadn't even cooled off yet and he was already out with his treacherous ex. "And what's with you being so nice to her? I told you what she did to me at my perfume launch."

Maxine daintily wiped her mouth with her linen napkin and placed it on her half-eaten plate. "If there's anything I've learned, it's that you only hurt yourself by wallowing in bitterness."

Chloe braced herself for a lecture full of unsolicited, motherly advice.

"I want you to be happy," Maxine continued, "and I really think you should move on with your life."

"Funny you should say that, Mother, because I could say the same about you. How many years since has it been since Jacques passed away?"

Maxine looked at Chloe, not responding. Chloe held her mother's gaze without blinking, as if challenging Maxine to admit she was being hypocritical – urging Chloe to shrug off the breakup with Alex, when Maxine herself was stubbornly clinging to her former life with Jacques.

In her unique way of avoiding topics she didn't want to discuss, Maxine failed to acknowledge Chloe's comment and instead summoned the waiter. "Check, please."

97

"Come on, Bareaux, move it," Marcella barked as she sprinted next to Chloe on the row of treadmills at the gym.

"Don't you have any mercy?" Chloe panted, wiping the sweat from her brow. "I've had a rough couple of weeks. I not only lost an acting role that could have made my career, I lost Alex."

"Well, how in the hell do you expect to land another job or find another man if you're sitting around on your rump?"

Chloe lowered the speed on her treadmill. "I can't keep up. I don't have the energy."

"Okay, take a breather, but don't stop moving – which is my motto for life." Marcella brought the speed down on her treadmill and slowed to a fast walk. "I know you probably feel like curling up in a ball right now and pulling the covers over your head, but that's exactly why I came over this morning and dragged your ass out of bed. This is not the time to sit around moping."

Chloe sipped her water and gasped. "Maybe you should be a motivational speaker instead of a trainer."

"Seriously, Bareaux, I know things seem tough right now, but this is the time to dig deep and reach for that inner strength – like when you're running a marathon and you hit a wall and don't think you can go any further."

Chloe pumped her arms as she fast-walked on the treadmill, following Marcella's lead. "I wish I was as strong as you."

"You're stronger than you think, Bareaux. I've been right where you are. I've had injuries that almost ended my career, setbacks I thought I'd never come back from. But I just kept moving and I always ended up coming back stronger than before."

Chloe wiped her face, whimpering from exhaustion. "Excuse me if I'm finding it hard to find reasons to believe in myself right now."

Marcella increased the speed on her treadmill. "Pick up the pace and you'll find your second wind."

The sound of Chloe's phone ringing sent her fumbling inside her armband. "Saved by the bell," she said, retrieving the phone.

Marcella shot her a disapproving look. "You know my rule. Unless it's an emergency, keep it brief."

"Yes, ma'am." Chloe flipped open the phone. "Hello?"

"May I speak to Chloe?" said a vaguely familiar female voice.

"This is she," Chloe said tentatively, trying to place the voice.

"This is Rachel, from Epitome. I know it's been a long time, but my parents asked me to give you a call and set up a meeting with you."

Chloe dropped the phone. She heard Rachel frantically saying "Hello? Hello?" as the phone slid between Chloe's track shoes on the treadmill, like a half-finished product going down an assembly line. Ignoring Marcella's scowl, Chloe hopped off the treadmill, picked up the phone and gathered herself before speaking again.

"Hello? Are you still there?" Rachel asked.

"Yes, I'm here," Chloe said, clearing her throat. "I'm sorry. I dropped the phone. I'm not sure I heard you right. Barbara and Warren want to meet with me?"

"Yes, that's right."

"What do they want?"

"They'd rather discuss it in person. Are you available some time this week?"

Chloe paused before responding, wondering what the Rubinsteins could possibly want with her, especially after the severe tongue-lashing Barbara gave her when Chloe quit the agency. She already felt bad enough over her stalled acting career and ruined love life without Barbara rubbing it in.

"Chloe, you still there?" Rachel said.

Chloe glanced at Marcella, who, with a look of increasing exasperation, was signaling for her to wrap up the call.

"Tell Warren and Barbara I'll meet with them," Chloe said finally. "I have nothing but time."

Chloe sat in Epitome's lobby, jittery with nervous anticipation about meeting with Warren and Barbara like when she had first signed with the agency. She scanned the framed fashion layouts and magazine covers that lined the walls and spotted her first *Vogue* cover. She felt a surge of pride, realizing for the first time how much she had accomplished as a model. She had been so busy rushing from shoot to shoot and flying from one runway show to the next that she had never really taken time to stop and evaluate her career. Her goal had always been to break into acting, but modeling had given her valuable opportunities that she was just now beginning to appreciate now that she was unemployed. She allowed her mind to wander, reviewing the events of the past few months.

"Chloe?"

She looked up at the receptionist, realizing the young woman had been repeatedly calling her name.

"Yes?" Chloe said, straightening her posture.

"Warren and Barbara will see you now."

"Thank you."

Chloe stood, smoothed the business suit she had worn to her last Hollywood meeting, gathered her courage and walked past the receptionist's desk. Upon entering the office, she saw that not much had changed except that the volumes of papers, appointment ledgers and old-fashioned Rolodexes that once cluttered Warren and Barbara's partners' desk had been replaced by gleaming flat-screen computers. Warren was typing away while speaking into a headset while Barbara finished up a call on another line, her back turned.

As Chloe gingerly entered the office, Rachel greeted her.

"Thanks for meeting with us," Rachel said, hugging Chloe.

"Sure, good to see you again." Noticing the bulge in Rachel's waistline, she ventured, "Are you expecting?"

"Yes. I'm four and a half months along – halfway there."

"Congratulations. My best friend Gigi just had a baby boy and I'm the godmother."

"That's great. This is our first child, and Bruce and I can't wait." Rachel gestured toward a seat in front of her parents' desk. "Why don't you make yourself comfortable? Can I get you anything?"

"Some water would be great."

Rachel disappeared to fulfill the request and Chloe settled into the chair. Upon noticing she'd arrived, Warren concluded his call and tapped Barbara on the shoulder, indicating for her to do the same. Chloe stood to greet them.

"Hi, Chloe," Warren said, giving her a warm hug. "I'm so glad you agreed to meet with us."

Chloe smiled, briefly studying Warren's face. He had the same kind eyes and he looked slightly older, his well-groomed hair a bit whiter.

Barbara finally hung up the phone and turned to face Chloe. "Hi, there. Thanks so much for joining us," Barbara said, as if speaking to a potential client she was meeting for the first time. "Won't you have a seat?"

Chloe sat back down, looking Barbara over as she paced behind the desk, as if preparing to make a speech. There was something slightly different about the older woman. She had changed her usual hair helmet into a style that was less severe and her face was a bit more lined. The overall effect gave Barbara a more natural, softer appearance.

Barbara stopped pacing, clasped her hands and turned to Chloe. "How have you been?"

"I'm okay."

Rachel reappeared, handed Chloe a bottle of Evian water and seated herself on the desk near her father.

"Did Rachel tell you she's expecting our first grandchild?" Warren said.

"Yes, congratulations."

"Rachel's husband just got a promotion and they're moving to the West Coast," Barbara said, giving her daughter an accusatory look.

"Oh, Mom, we'll be back for every holiday and special occasion," Rachel said, flipping her hair like an insolent teenager. "You and Dad'll see the baby plenty."

"I still don't see why you can't stay here until the baby's born," Barbara said.

Rachel sighed. "Mom, we've been over this a million times –"

Warren interrupted the exchange, acting as peacemaker between his wife and daughter, a role Chloe had seen him play numerous times before.

"Ladies, we didn't call Chloe here to witness our family drama," he said.

Chloe scooted to the edge of her seat. "Why exactly *did* you call me here?"

Barbara sat down. "Since Rachel and her husband are moving to Los Angeles, she's going to be heading up a new West Coast office for us."

"What's that got to do with me?"

Barbara looked at Warren, who picked up the conversation, as though his wife had lobbed him a tennis ball.

"We've been talking about opening a West Coast division for quite some time," he said.

Chloe looked back and forth between Barbara and Warren as they spoke, feeling as though she were actually at a tennis match. Rachel kept jumping in as well.

"Actually, I've been *telling* them they need to open an office in L.A.," Rachel spoke up. "They've always resisted, and the only reason they're doing it now is because I'm moving there."

"The fashion industry used to be centered in New York," Barbara explained, "but now the industry is much more bicoastal."

"Most of the young girls and guys we sign now are looking to get into acting or use modeling as a way to make money to segue into some kind of entrepreneurial venture," Warren said.

"We need to open a West Coast office to be closer to the entertainment industry and stay competitive," Barbara said.

"Of course, I've been saying this for years," Rachel said. "I'm the one who made them get rid of that outdated paper system and invest in computers and a Web site. I've had to drag them kicking and screaming into the twenty-first century."

Chloe chuckled at Rachel's sassy yet affectionate way with her parents.

"I'm still in the dark about what all this has to do with me," Chloe said, trying to be polite but wishing they would get to the point.

Barbara took a sip from her coffee cup. "It's become harder and harder to attract top talent over the years. We've had several top models stolen away by competitors that could offer them acting representation and other opportunities. Our roster has been dwindling in recent years, which is why I overreacted when you told us you were leaving."

Chloe shifted in her seat. This was probably the closest she would ever get to an apology from Barbara.

"Those of us who have been around for a long time have weathered trends. Fads come and go, and come back again, like bell bottoms. Everything's cyclical," Warren said. "But the era of the supermodel seems to be over, which is why we've been forced to broaden our focus."

"Models have disappeared from magazine covers, replaced by actresses and singers," Barbara said. "This trend seems to be here to stay. It used to be that models were models and actresses were actresses, but the lines have blurred. Models cross over into acting, and actresses pitch products."

"With a lot of prodding from Rachel," Warren said, nodding at his daughter, who beamed in satisfaction, "we've begun to see that Epitome needs to expand from strictly a modeling agency to an international talent management firm that represents not only models, but actors and other artists."

"We're evolving," Barbara said, as if in summation.

"The West Coast office will concentrate primarily on discovering hot new actors," Rachel said. "My husband's an entertainment attorney and he's helping us recruit ambitious young agents."

"This all sounds great," Chloe said, "but did I miss the part where I come in?"

Barbara got up and sat on the front of the desk, just inches away from Chloe. "I realize I shouldn't have been so harsh when you said you wanted to branch off into acting. I'm... I'm..." She paused, as if unable to go through with the apology. She glanced at Warren and Rachel, but they offered no assistance.

Chloe sat back, enjoying watching Barbara squirm.

"I'm sorry," Barbara said finally, her shoulders slumping as if from a great effort.

"What we've been trying to say is we'd like for you to come back," Warren said. "Laurel Cosmetics has been unable to find a permanent replacement since you left, and Max Laurel expressed an interest in re-signing you as their spokesmodel. We'd like to offer you a contract to represent you as a personality – which includes modeling, acting, endorsement deals and whatever else you decide to do."

Chloe sipped her water, trying to take in everything they had said. The offer sounded tempting, but it was too much to digest all at once.

"You don't have to give us an answer right away," Barbara added, as if sensing Chloe's hesitation, "but we'd like for you to come home."

Chloe strolled down Adriano Ferraro's runway in Bryant Park, flanked by her former Epitome roommates. Taking the final strut down the catwalk at the designer's New York Fashion Week show was a fitting way to put an exclamation point on her triumphant return to modeling. It felt good yet a little odd to be making a "comeback" when she was only twenty-six.

Flashbulbs went off excitedly when Chloe and her colleagues reached the end of the runway. In typical fashion, Graciela and Roxy jockeyed for attention, stepping in front of each other and preening for the cameras. Chloe laughed with Brandi and Ayana. Some things never changed.

Before making her grand exit, Chloe caught sight of another old friend, Christy Taylor, smiling at her from the front row. Since Chloe had helped Christy get discovered while a student at the Brooklyn Institute of Fashion, Christy had worked her way up at the Adriano Ferraro label. She had designed many of the pieces Chloe and the other girls wore in the show. Turning to leave the runway, Chloe waved at Christy, who reciprocated by blowing a kiss.

Backstage, Chloe exchanged hugs with the girls. "This was so much fun," she said while they were wriggling out of their couture gowns in the dressing room. "It reminds me of our first runway show when we were all starting out."

Chloe felt as though her life had come full circle. Now that she had re-signed with Epitome, she could take modeling opportunities that came along and continue to pursue her acting ambitions. She had the best of both worlds.

"I'm glad I got to do this with you guys," Brandi said, "because this is probably my last runway show. Brad and I have been talking about starting a family. I'm going to be spending a lot more time in Texas."

"I'm probably going to be cutting back on modeling, too," Graciela said, turning her back so that Chloe could undo the zipper of her skintight dress. "I've been touring and recording so much that I really don't have the time anymore. Plus, Jorge and I have been talking about settling down."

"Same with me and Malik," Ayana said, referring to her reggae-star boyfriend. "We're building a new house in St. Croix. Plus, developing new products for my skincare line takes up most of my time."

Helping Graciela step out of her gown, Chloe reflected on how bittersweet this reunion with her former roommates was turning out to be. While returning to Epitome marked a new beginning for her, the other girls she started out with were all moving on to other phases of their lives.

"What about you, Roxy?" Chloe said. "What are you up to these days?"

"Oh, you know me. A little bit of this and a little bit of that. Nothing too taxing." Roxy sat in front of the makeup mirror, examining her reflection like an art patron admiring a classic Greek sculpture. "I haven't decided if I'm going to stick with the modeling game or not. I never did like getting up early."

"Not to mention you're getting older, just like the rest of us," Graciela, who was attempting to squeeze into a pair of low-rise jeans, said with characteristic disdain for her nemesis.

"Bite me," Roxy shot back. "Maybe if you paid more attention to your own issues, you wouldn't have to struggle to get your fat ass in those jeans."

Graciela, having finally pulled the jeans above her curvaceous hips, flipped Roxy off before setting about the monumental task of trying to button the jeans.

"Anyway," Roxy said, brushing her long, dark hair, "I probably will take some time off from modeling. My boyfriend Shane's going to be shooting a movie in Nepal for a few months and I promised I'd go with him."

"Good," Graciela said, slipping on a camisole. "Maybe you'll discover

Buddhism and finally get some soul."

Roxy sat her brush down and gave Graciela the finger. Chloe chuckled, musing that her former roommates would never change, and sat down in front of the mirror to remove her makeup.

"Speaking of movies," Brandi said, taking a seat next to Chloe at the mirror, "I heard you're going to be playing the lead role in the movie version of your boyfriend's novel."

"The project fell through," Chloe said, her nonchalant tone disguising her hurt and disappointment.

"That's a shame," Graciela said. "I know how much you've always wanted to get into acting, and that would have been a great project for you and Alex to work on together."

"I know what a pain in the ass it is dealing with all the bureaucracy at the studios," Roxy said. "Shane whines about it all the time."

"Alex is a talented guy," Brandi said. "He could write something else for you to star in."

"Alex and I aren't together anymore."

Saying the words out loud made the painful reality all the more jarring. Alex's absence from her life still hadn't sunk in.

"Oh, honey, I'm so sorry to hear that," Brandi said, touching Chloe's shoulder. "Alex seemed like a really nice guy. What happened?"

"We were moving in different directions, that's all. I wish him well, I really do, but I guess we just weren't meant to be together in the long run. I'm okay, though. I've been on my own before, and I'll be fine."

Chloe concentrated on removing her eyeliner, trying not to cry. This talk about the failed movie project was ironic, considering she was drawing on her untapped acting skills. She was putting on a brave front for her friends, but the lines she recited didn't quite ring true.

"Well, at least your modeling career is going gangbusters again," Brandi said, changing the subject, to Chloe's relief. "I heard you renewed your endorsement deal with Laurel Cosmetics."

"*Felicitaciones, mija*," Graciela said, patting Chloe on the back. "What are you going to do with that gi-*normous* signing bonus?"

Chloe shrugged, continuing to remove her makeup. Just as she was about to say, "I don't know," she looked in the mirror and spotted Christy Taylor entering. Recalling her movie-going outings with Christy when they were both starting out, Chloe got an idea.

"Hey, ladies, you all rocked my designs!" declared Christy, who looked runway-ready herself in an asymmetrical, off-the-shoulder blouse, funky jeans and clunky platform heels that exhibited her one-of-a-kind style.

All the girls praised Christy's work and Chloe got up and threw her arms around the rising young designer. "It's so good to see you again! Thanks for putting your personal stamp on all of our gowns for the finale."

"Are you kidding? When you called and asked me to do it, I jumped at the chance," Christy said. "If it wasn't for you, I wouldn't even be designing for Adriano."

"Are you happy there?" Chloe asked as Christy began gathering the girls' discarded gowns and placing them on hangers.

Christy looked thoughtful. "Yes, reasonably so. Since I was promoted to creative director earlier this year, it really gives me a chance to shine."

"Do you still think about designing costumes for the movies?" Chloe asked, lending Christy a hand in hanging the dresses on a rack.

"It's something I still dream about, sure," Christy said, taking extra care in placing a garment bag over the hand-stitched gown she'd made for Chloe. "But I'm always so busy that I never seem to get around to it, especially with my new promotion." She hung up the dress and gave Chloe her full attention. "Why do you ask?"

"I just got an idea," Chloe said. She added with a broad smile, "And I have a business proposal for you."

The runway show with Chloe's former Epitome roommates was the first in a series of bookings around the world. Now that she was back with Epitome, Chloe was more in-demand than ever. Staying busy not only gave her a much-needed outlet for her pent-up creativity, it also kept her mind off Alex's absence and the sting of seeing him with Veronica.

One of the first assignments Chloe agreed to was a new ad campaign to re-launch her fragrance, *Inner Beauty*. Max Laurel and his team had welcomed her back based on the fact that the scent that bore her name had continued to sell well even during her hiatus. The company hired a new ad agency to create a television commercial for *Inner Beauty* to be filmed in Paris. Chloe was more than pleased with the generous signing bonus Max offered for her to renew her exclusive contract with the cosmetics giant, but this time she planned to write in terms that would ensure she was more than just a product pitchwoman.

While in Paris filming the new commercial, Chloe stayed at the Chateau de Chevalier.

"What do you think?" Chloe said to Maxine, holding up a legal pad she'd been jotting ideas on. She was lounging on her mother's bed like she did when she was little. Her hair was pulled back in a girlish ponytail, the way she wore her hair in high school. With all these new opportunities at her fingertips, she felt like a teenager again.

Maxine looked up from her book and scanned the legal pad. "CYB? Yes, I'm well aware of what your initials are. I ought to know. I named you, *n'est-ce pas?*" she said with a giggle.

"CYB is going to be the name of the new production company I'm forming, silly," Chloe said, sweeping her bangs out of her eyes. "CYB Enterprises, Inc. I figure, if I'm going to return to modeling, I should do things my way."

Chloe had been thinking about forming her own company ever since she had re-upped with Epitome. Just a few years shy of thirty, she knew she had a limited amount of time that she could continue to demand top dollar as a model, like an athlete who had reached her peak performance level. While she was basking in the attention that her much-heralded return to modeling had garnered, she knew she wouldn't always be the "It Girl." The modeling industry was notoriously fickle. Girls as young as twelve were coming out of the woodwork every day and would one day replace her and other top models. She needed outside interests, she needed to diversify. The time had come to plan for and invest in her future.

"I've been doing some numbers-crunching," Chloe said. "Corporations make big bucks off me and other models. Now that I've renewed my deal with Laurel, why shouldn't I get a bigger cut of the profits from my perfume and other products that bear my name and image? I mean, after all, I *am* the person behind all those dollars and cents."

Maxine set her book aside and took a closer look at Chloe's notes. "What are you proposing?"

"That I take the reins and gain more control in my career. That's why I've decided to form my own company, to start marketing myself instead of letting others do it for me. I have big plans, Mother." Chloe sat up on her haunches, her excitement cresting. "My first big move is to going to be to strike a merchandising deal with Laurel. Instead of just being a hired hand who's paid to move product, I'll have an ownership stake. I want to be the one making the decisions and earning the lion's share of the profits."

As Chloe told her mother, she realized she was a "brand," a mini-corporation, and should conduct her business affairs accordingly.

Maxine continued flipping through the legal pad, seeming as though she were listening closely, but said nothing.

"I could really use your input, Mother. What do you think?"

"You know what I think, *ma chérie,*" Maxine said, putting her arm around Chloe, "I'm thinking that all that time I spent slaving to build my business when you were growing up was all worth it. I always felt guilty for not spending enough time with you while I was working, but obviously my business sense has rubbed off on you. I must have done something right."

Chloe exhaled, relieved to have her mother's hard-won approval.

"I'm so glad you're getting back to the Chloe I know," Maxine said, handing back the legal pad. "I never stopped believing in you. I always knew you'd have success again. Jacques would be so proud of you."

Chloe reached out and took Maxine's hand. "Mother, I'm sorry for what I said to you when we were at dinner that night we ran into Alex. I was wrong for saying you should move on. I still miss Jacques, and I know you do, too."

"Of course I still miss him. I think about him every day. Sometimes I swear I can feel his presence, as if he's still..." Maxine trailed off, staring at the framed photo of the three of them that sat next to her bed. "He cared about you so much, like you were his," she said, running her hand over the photo. "Which reminds me," she said, turning back to Chloe, "the final disbursement from the trust fund he set up for you is coming up. This is the final payout and will settle Jacques' estate."

"God, it's hard to believe ten years have gone by since he died." Chloe gazed at the photograph on Maxine's nightstand, wishing she could relive that brief moment in time when they were an intact family unit.

"I know. I can't believe he's been gone that long. What do you want me to do with the final payout?"

"Why don't you make a donation to charity in his name like every year?"

"I have a little confession to make," Maxine said, looking uncharacteristically sheepish. "I haven't been sending the money from your trust fund to charity like you told me to."

Chloe sat up, suddenly intrigued. "What have you been doing with it?"

"I set up an investment portfolio in your name and the money's been growing all these years. Please don't be mad, but I just couldn't bring myself to give that money away. It's Jacques' legacy, something he intended to pass on to you. Plus, you never know when you might need it."

"Gosh, Mother, just when I thought there were no more secrets between us, you lay this on me," Chloe said, incredulous. "If I would have known you were squirreling that money away, I could have been contributing to causes I care about – AIDS research, the environment, adopting a Pygmy child."

Chloe laughed at the absurdity of the situation. Rather than angry, she was amused by her mother's revelation. No matter how successful Chloe became, Maxine would never stop worrying about her or nagging her to put money away just in case she went bankrupt, was hit by car and got struck by lightning all in the same week.

"Is there anything else you'd like to tell me?" Chloe ventured, figuring now was as good a time as any to unearth any other secrets her mother might be keeping.

"Actually, there is something else I should tell you."

Chris Bournéa

Chloe grabbed a pillow, bracing herself for another bombshell. "Oh god. What now? Do I have a half-brother or sister you've been hiding somewhere?"

Maxine cracked a smile. "No, nothing that dramatic." Her expression turned serious again. "I've been thinking a lot about what you said that night when we went to dinner in New York, that I should move on. And you're right. So I've decided to sell the house."

Chloe didn't immediately respond, taking a minute to process what her mother had said. Although she was nearly grown when they moved to Jacques' chateau, Chloe thought of it as her family home. It was an anchor in a constantly-changing world.

"I've been thinking about getting a smaller place in the city closer to the office. I love this place, especially since Jacques and I remodeled it together, but it seems foolish for me to be the only one living in this huge house."

"I understand," Chloe said, although she still thought of the Chateau de Chevalier as her refuge, a place she could always return to whenever she felt like getting away and being surrounded by comfort and familiarity.

Chloe started to launch into an argument to selfishly persuade her mother to hold on to the house and offer to pay for the upkeep out of her own pocket, but was interrupted by a knock at the door.

"You two need anything before I turn in?" Marie said, entering the master suite in her robe and nightgown.

"No, Marie, we're fine," Maxine said. "And by the way, I just told her."

"Oh." Marie looked at Chloe with a forlorn expression, as if they now shared knowledge of an unfortunate but unavoidable reality.

"I had to tell Marie first," Maxine explained, "since my decision would affect her employment."

"What are you going to do?" Chloe said to Marie, concerned that her longtime friend and advisor would be displaced.

"I've been planning to retire and move to Avignon to spend more time with my grandchildren."

"What about Bernard?" Chloe said, referring to the chateau's groundskeeper who'd made no effort to conceal his feelings for Marie.

"He's been planning to retire, too," Marie said, looking like a little girl who'd been caught passing notes with an admirer. "He said he's always wanted to see Avignon."

"Oh, I see." Chloe smiled, glad that Marie had finally found companionship after staying single so long after the death of her beloved husband. But Chloe's happiness for Marie was mingled with sadness at the prospect of losing the place she called home. This loss so soon after the breakup with Alex was a lot to process.

"I'll leave you two to talk this over." Marie blew a kiss at Chloe as she backed out of the room. "*Bonne nuit.*"

"I'll wait a while to put the house up for sale to give you time to get used to the idea," Maxine said when she and Chloe were alone again.

"No, it's okay." Chloe decided against trying to talk her mother out of the sale. As much as she hated the idea, she was going to have to face facts. She couldn't force Maxine to keep the chateau any more than Maxine could have forced Chloe to stay in Paris when she was eighteen and decided to move to New York.

Maxine rubbed Chloe's back. "Sorry for defying your wishes about the trust fund. It's your money to do what you want with. If you'd like, I'll write out a big check to the charity of your choice when I meet with the attorneys about settling the estate."

Chloe glanced down at her legal pad and got an idea. "No, don't do that, Mother. I think I know a way to put that money to good use."

98

"These are the last of the invoices," Simone said, entering Maxine's office and setting a stack of papers on her desk. "You going to be getting out of here soon?"

Maxine looked up from her paperwork. "I'll probably stick around a couple more hours and finish everything up."

"You'll be a workaholic 'til your dying day," Simone said, assuming her familiar roost on the edge of Maxine's desk. "You sure you don't want to come to dinner with Armand and I? He has a really cute friend I've been meaning to introduce you to."

"Simone, how many times do I have to tell you I don't need fixing up?" Maxine said, sighing in frustration. "I have plenty of male friends. I'm not hurting for companionship."

"I know. It's just that it's been ten years since Jacques died and you still haven't had a serious relationship. Don't you ever think about remarrying?"

"Oh, look at who's the big marriage advocate now that Armand put a ring on your finger," Maxine said, chuckling. "Aren't you the one who said you didn't want to have to answer to a man? Has it ever occurred to you that maybe that's the reason I haven't remarried?"

"Hey, it's not like I was looking to get married at this point in my life, but when I met Armand I knew he was the one." Simone reached for Maxine's hand. "I just want you to find the same happiness."

Maxine placed her hand on top of Simone's. "I appreciate that, Mo', I really do. But I'm all right. Really. Besides," she added, intentionally changing the subject, "the one we need to focus on right now is Chloe. She misses Alex horribly. I'm glad she has this new business venture to keep her mind off the breakup."

"Chloe's going to be fine. That girl has always had so much initiative. She's definitely your daughter."

"And I know you've got to be relieved that Gigi's finally gotten her life together and has a family of her own now – even if that means you're a *grandmother*," Maxine said, unable to resist the opportunity to razz Simone.

"Excuse me, Madame Chevalier," Henri, Maxine's assistant, said, entering the office. "There's someone here to see you."

"Could you tell whoever it is to schedule an appointment for another time?" Maxine said, not trying to disguise her irritation at the unannounced visitor. "I have a mountain of invoices to go over and I'm already going to be working late as it is."

"*Pardonnez-moi*, Madame. I told him you're busy, but he was very insistent on meeting with you right away."

"Who could this be?" Maxine said, directing a confused look at Simone, who responded with a shrug.

"A M'sieu Renaud Mercier," Henri said.

"Isn't that Jacques' employee who stayed on at the company after you sold it?" Simone said to Maxine.

"Yes. He checks in on Chloe and I every now then." Maxine turned to Henri. "Send him right in," she said in a more patient tone. "I'm never too busy to see one of Jacques' old friends."

Henri promptly ushered in Renaud, and Maxine and Simone rose to greet him with hugs and kisses on either cheek.

"It's been too long, Maxine," Renaud said, taking off his hat in the presence of ladies in his gentlemanly French way. "But I can see that both you and Mademoiselle Cartier haven't aged a day."

"I knew there was a reason I always liked you," Simone said, laughing. "And it's Madame Delicourt now." She held up her hand, displaying the wedding ring that her now-husband, Armand, had given her when they'd eloped in Switzerland shortly after Gigi's wedding.

"Oh, *félicitations*. And you, Maxine?"

"I'm still Madame Chevalier," she said, but quickly added, "but not for long if Simone has anything to do with it."

"Renaud, you've got to convince her that Jacques would want her to move on with her life," Simone said.

"I am moving on with my life," Maxine insisted. "That's why I'm selling the house."

"Actually, that's why I've come to see you today," Renaud said. "Please excuse my dropping in unannounced like this."

"No need to apologize. You're always welcome. Please have a seat." Maxine motioned to the chair before her desk.

"I'm meeting my husband for dinner, so I'm going to say *bonsoir*," Simone said, shaking Renaud's hand. "Always good to see you."

"Likewise."

Maxine pushed the paperwork aside and gave her visitor her full attention. "Renaud, I don't mean to be rude, but if you've come to try to convince me not to sell the house because of the sentimental attachment to Jacques, I've already made up my –"

"*Excusez-moi*, but it's quite the opposite," he said. "I happen to know someone, someone who was very close to Jacques, who's interested in buying the house."

"Oh, really?" Maxine scooted back in her chair, taken off-guard by Renaud's announcement. She was still in the process of getting the house ready to show to potential buyers, and up until now the possibility of selling the Chateau de Chevalier seemed far-off.

"If you have some time later this week, I could set up a meeting," Renaud said.

"Okay," she said tentatively, the prospect of an immediate sale making her wonder if she was truly ready to move on. "But since I don't know this person, I'm not comfortable having them come by the house just yet. I'd like to talk with them first to get a sense of whether or not they're the right buyer."

"I could set up the meeting at my office."

"You mean your office at Jacques' old company?"

"*Oui*."

Maxine fell silent, considering Renaud's offer. She hadn't returned to the offices of Chevalier International Ltd. since she sold the company after Jacques' death. Being in the building where Jacques had spent so many hours might drudge up memories she'd long since locked away.

"Maxine, did you want me to set up the meeting at my office?" Renaud said, repeating himself in a patient tone, as if sensing her hesitation.

"Sure," she said finally. "That would be fine."

"Okay, Chloe, turn your head a little to the right," Grant Herschel said, snapping photos in rapid succession.

Standing against a taupe backdrop in Grant's Manhattan studio, Chloe followed the photographer's instructions. Clad in a Badgley Mischka gown and draped in a million dollars worth of Harry Winston diamonds, she let her imagination run wild, fantasizing that she was being photographed backstage at the Academy Awards after picking up one of those coveted gold statuettes for Best Actress. *Someday*...

"It's great to be collaborating on another cover with you, Grant," she said, pivoting in her Louboutins at his instruction.

Shortly after she announced that she was forming CYB Enterprises to handle her renewed deal with Laurel Cosmetics and other business ventures, *Vanity Fair* called. The editor-in-chief offered her the cover if she would grant an in-depth interview about her "turbulent year," quitting modeling to embark on a "failed foray" into acting and breaking up with Alex. Chloe agreed to the interview on the condition that the magazine printed the full story, emphasizing that she was putting her life back together by returning to modeling and continuing to pursue her acting ambitions with Epitome's trusted representation. She was excited to discuss starting her own company to exert more control in the business aspect of her career. As for the breakup with Alex, she told the interviewer that she was still regrouping and channeling all of her energy at the moment into resuscitating her career.

The only other condition she insisted on in agreeing to the interview was that she get to work with Grant for the cover shoot.

"I still remember our first *Vogue* cover." Grant took the camera off the tripod and moved in closer, shooting handheld. "My 'Parisian discovery' has come quite a long way since then."

Chloe gave Grant a big smile, thinking back on their first collaboration that had launched her career.

"'Scuse me, guys." Keiko, Grant's assistant, entered the studio carrying a bouquet of flowers. "These just came for Chloe." He handed her the bouquet.

"They're probably from the magazine, wishing us well on the shoot," Grant said, crouching to get a shot of Chloe cradling the bouquet like a pageant winner.

Chloe smelled the gardenias, their fragrance bringing back memories of the Chateau de Chevalier. The memories were even more bittersweet now that Maxine was selling the house. She sniffled, trying not to cry and ruin her makeup.

"Why don't you take five?" Grant stopped shooting and returned his camera to the tripod. "You look like you're getting emotional. Are those from Alex?"

"I don't think so," Chloe said, examining the card attached to the bouquet and finding that it contained only the message, "Congratulations on Your Comeback," with no signature. "Somebody out there keeps sending me flowers and gifts whenever anything important happens in my life."

"Ooh, hope you don't have a stalker," Grant said, the faint lines in his well-worn yet still-handsome features becoming more pronounced. "I've worked with girls who had some guy who kept sending them gifts and wouldn't leave them alone. The best way to handle it is to get a restraining order."

"I don't think it's a stalker. I like to think of it as a sign," she said, her eyes misting, "a sign that someone's out there, watching over me."

Maxine looked out the window of her chauffeured car as she rode to the offices of Chevalier International Ltd. A faint smile passed across her face when her driver rode by Alain's, the bistro where she and Jacques had celebrated their anniversary on the last night she'd seen him alive.

She was still reflecting on happy times with her late husband when the car came to a stop.

"Madame Chevalier, we're here," Louis, the driver, said, meeting her eyes in the rearview mirror. She realized she'd been daydreaming about her last night with Jacques and hadn't heard Louis the first time he'd announced their arrival.

"Shall I get your door?"

She gathered her purse, her attention snapping back to the present. "Yes, *merci*. I'm ready."

Walking down the halls of the company that still bore Jacques' name brought back memories once again. Striding to the boardroom, Maxine wiped away tears. She had to collect herself for the meeting with the potential buyer.

"*Bonjour*, Maxine," Renaud said, rising to greet her when she entered the boardroom.

"Thanks again for setting this up. I take it your associate's running late?" she said, noticing he was alone.

"No, he's here." Renaud smiled, as if he knew something Maxine didn't. "He's waiting for you in the office down the hall."

"Jacques' old office?"

"*Oui.*"

She took a step back, unprepared to see her late husband's office again. Being in the building was hard enough. "Why don't you tell him to join us in the boardroom? I think we'd all be more comfortable in here."

"Okay. I'll go get him." He grinned like a little boy holding a handmade gift behind his back. "Why don't you come with me?"

"I'd rather wait here, Renaud, if it's okay with you."

"It'll only take a second. He's really eager to meet with you."

Before she could protest further, he took her hand and began leading her out of the boardroom and down the hallway. At the doorway of Jacques' office, she was greeted by a familiar scent that nearly brought her to her knees. The smell of the Cuban cigars that Jacques had adored wafted into the hallway.

At Renaud's prodding, she inched into the office and saw the outline of a man sitting in Jacques' old chair with his back turned, smoke rings rising above his head as he looked out the window behind the desk. Maxine could only see the top of the man's head, a shock of salt-and-pepper hair that was slightly whiter than she remembered. The man's hands gripped the arms of the chair, those weathered sailor's hands that had caressed her back and held her close.

Maxine told herself that she had to be hallucinating, that she had allowed herself to get carried away with the emotion of returning to his office. She was finally ready to let him go and she couldn't let herself believe that it was possible that by some miracle, he had returned after all this time.

With trembling knees, she took a step forward. The smell of the cigar grew stronger, the distinctive scent of Jacques' favorite brand.

It can't be, she told herself. *It's not possible. I'm daydreaming again.*

She took a closer look at the man's hands and suddenly it all made sense – the mysterious gifts contained in packages with postmarks from secluded, exotic locales; flowers from an anonymous admirer on special occasions; her lingering suspicions that there was something more to the cloudy circumstances surrounding his death. She had always thought it strange that the accident that claimed her husband's life happened not long after the death of that slime, Pierre Rousseau, who had tried to attack Chloe.

Maxine thought back to the last night she had seen Jacques alive and recalled his strange demeanor, his preoccupied state of mind, his insistence that he had put things in place to take care of Maxine and Chloe if something should happen to him.

She examined the outline of the man sitting in the chair. Was it possible that Jacques had staged his death to elude the henchmen who were trying to avenge Rousseau's murder? Had Jacques disappeared until he thought it was safe to resurface?

She took another step forward, and the man turned to face her. She gasped, as if seeing a ghost.

"*Bonjour*," said the man, still puffing on the cigar. His face was obscured by shadows in the dimly lit office, but the voice was unmistakable. "So good to see you again, *amour*."

99

"Congratulations on your new venture, Chloe," Muriel said, raising her martini glass in a toast as they sat next to each other in their favorite booth at their usual gathering place. "It takes a lot of guts to start your own business. I'm proud of you for taking control of your career."

"Thanks, Muriel," Chloe said, clinking glasses with her. "And congratulations on winning your big case."

"Thanks, girl," Muriel said, glowing. "It's a really important victory for domestic violence victims. I'm really proud of our team. All the hard work paid off."

"Speaking of hard workers, have you heard from Daniella?"

"She's going to be late as usual. She gave her closing argument in the SorCom case yesterday and the jury was supposed to give their verdict this afternoon."

Just as Chloe and Muriel were ordering another round of drinks, Daniella arrived in an Armani suit accessorized again by her bulging attaché case and an armful of legal briefs.

"So, what's the word?" Muriel said as Daniella slid into the booth. "Should we order bubbly?"

"Absolutely," Daniella said, shimmying out of her suit jacket, "and this round's on me. The jury found my client not guilty."

Chloe and Muriel applauded Daniella and sent the waiter to retrieve a bottle of the bar's best champagne.

"I guess we have two things to celebrate tonight," Muriel said after the waiter had popped the cork and filled everyone's glasses. "Did you hear about Chloe's new business venture?"

"Of course. How could I miss the big news when her face is staring back at me from every newsstand?" Daniella reached into her attaché case and pulled out a copy of the *Vanity Fair* cover story. "I quote," Daniella said, reading the headline that was superimposed over Grant's gorgeous cover shot, "'Chloe Incorporated: How One of the One of the World's Most Beautiful Women Found Success on Her Own Terms.'"

Chloe sank down in the booth, seeing that other patrons were gawking at the magazine and recognizing her. "Will you put that away?"

"Oh, don't be so modest." Daniella ribbed Chloe. "You know we're proud of you."

Chloe thanked her old friends for their support and told them it felt good to get back to work and take control of her own destiny, rather than waiting around for someone to validate her talent and *give* her a movie role.

"And what about you, Miss Big-Time Corporate Attorney?" Muriel teased. "Now that you've won this big case, I assume making partner is all but guaranteed."

"Yeah. My boss called after the verdict came in and offered me the partnership." Daniella sipped her champagne, looking thoughtful. "But the reason I'm celebrating is that I quit instead."

"*What?!* Are you crazy?" Muriel looked as befuddled as Chloe. "Why would you do that? Do you how many of our classmates from law school would love to be in your shoes?"

"I've been thinking about resigning for a while now; I was just holding out until I finished this case."

"I don't understand," Chloe said. "I thought making partner by age thirty was one of the goals you've been working toward since you and Muriel graduated."

"It was," Daniella said, "but I've had to rethink my goals. Working on this case really showed me how dirty the legal system can be. I realized I've been kidding myself, thinking that if I just made partner, I'd have the power to take on cases that will make a difference. I got into law to go after clients like the one I just got off, not help them get away with their dirty dealings."

"Still, that's a big step, just up and quitting your job like that," said the ever-practical Muriel.

"I felt like I was at a crossroads. When they offered me the partnership, I got a vision of my life five years from now and saw myself turning into my parents." Daniella paused a beat, then added with a grin, "And that scared the hell out of me!"

Chloe and Muriel laughed along with Daniella.

"But seriously," Daniella continued, "I know if I stayed at Westmoreland & McNeil, I'd become career-obsessed and materialistic just like my parents. It's so easy to get caught up in the rat race – the important job title, the money and prestige, the power suits and Prada pumps." She paused, a faraway look in her eyes like she was envisioning her life if she'd accepted the partnership. "I knew it was time to get out of the firm until it sucked me in too deep."

"Now you sound like a John Grisham novel," Chloe said, giggling.

"Turning down the partnership took a lot of courage," Muriel said, "but what are you and Darby going to do now that you're unemployed, especially with the cost of living as high as it is in Boston? I'm sure he can't support the both of you on a Webmaster's salary."

"Funny thing happened," Daniella said. "During the case, a producer with TrialTV approached me when I was leaving the courthouse one day and told me I'm very telegenic and asked me to try out for a new legal affairs show they're launching."

"Really?" Chloe said, excited for Daniella. "Did you follow up on it?"

"I was skeptical at first. It reminded me of when I was a teenager and that talent scout came up to me in the mall. The thought of being on TV and millions of people hanging on my every word scared me to death, but I decided I couldn't go through the rest of my life wondering 'what if,' like I have with that guy who propositioned me in the mall."

"So? What happened?" Muriel said in an impatient tone, as if she couldn't stand the suspense.

"I talked it over with Darby and he told me to go for it. He thinks it would be cool to have a TV star for a wife." Daniella sipped her bubbly, burped and excused herself. "I went in and met with the producers, taped a demo segment, and it turns out I'm pretty comfortable in front of the camera. The gig's right up my alley. I'll be offering commentary on high-profile cases that have drawn media attention. The studio's here in Manhattan, so Darby and I will be moving to New York."

"That's awesome!" Chloe reached across the table and hugged Daniella. "It'll be great to have you back in the city full time."

"Yeah. I'm pretty excited. Since Darby's an IT guy, he can find a job anywhere. Plus, I got an offer to write a book about the case I just won. So with the book advance and the income from the legal-commentating gig, I'll have the freedom to go into practice for myself. I can finally start doing some pro bono work and helping people who really need it."

"If our professors at Columbia could only see you now," Muriel said, slinging her arm around Daniella and pressing their cheeks together.

"When do you your first show? I'll be sure to watch," Chloe said.

"In a couple weeks. I'd love it if you came by the studio for moral support. It's in the Wellington Tower. Hey, if you're looking for office space for your new company, I heard the building's penthouse suite is available."

"The penthouse suite?" Chloe said, her heart racing at the thought of being at such a high altitude on a daily basis.

"Don't you remember Chloe's fear of heights?" Muriel said. "She wouldn't even go to the Empire State building when we were showing her around when she first moved here."

"I thought you conquered that fear when you had to do that screen test," Daniella said.

"I don't know if *conquered* is the right word. *Confronted* is probably more accurate." Chloe took a sip of champagne to calm herself. "And my fear of heights isn't the only reason I wouldn't want to set up my office in the Wellington Tower."

"Is it all those stories about Hugo Wellington's spirit haunting the place?" Daniella said, looking amused. "The TrialTV producers told me all about that. It's nothing but an urban legend."

"I know. That's not the reason," Chloe said. "It's that Alex's magazine is in the same building. The last few meetings I've had with the team at Laurel, I've done by conference call so I don't run into Alex."

"You haven't heard from him since the breakup?" Muriel inquired.

"No. And the last time I saw him, I was having dinner with my mother at Jean Georges and he came in with Veronica. Even though we're not together anymore, I don't know how he could betray me by getting back together with her, especially considering what she did to me."

"Gosh, I'm sorry to hear that. Alex seemed like such a good guy," Daniella said. "But you shouldn't let the breakup keep you from moving forward. Setting up your new office in the Wellington Tower would give you a lot of prestige. You'd be surrounded by all those other high-powered media companies. It's a good environment to be in, especially for a startup like yours." She put her hand on Chloe's shoulder. "Why don't you just call the building's management and set up a time to go check out the space? It can't hurt to just look at it."

Chloe traced the rim of her champagne glass, considering Daniella's suggestion. "I'll think about it."

"And as far as the situation with Alex and Veronica, maybe you should give him the benefit of the doubt. There's probably a good explanation why he was with her," Muriel said. "If there's one thing working in Washington has taught me," she added, "it's that things aren't always what they seem."

100

"Jacques, is that you?" Maxine moved closer to the man sitting at her husband's old desk.

"Yes, *amour*, it's me."

The man moved his chair forward, out of the shadows and into the light. It was Jacques. Except for a few extra lines around his eyes, sun-bleached hair and a deep tan that looked like he'd been in the tropics, he looked the same. Maxine nearly fainted at the sight of him.

"Why don't you sit down, my love?" He got up, helping Maxine into the chair, and pulled up another beside her.

"I'll leave you two alone. I'm sure you have a lot to catch up on," Renaud said upon leaving the room, as if Jacques had simply been away on a business trip.

"What's going on?" Maxine held her fingertips to her temples, trying to get the blood flowing again. "Is this real? How can you be here, talking to me?"

"I owe you an explanation."

"That's an understatement." She stared at him, certain that if she blinked, he would disappear and the daydream would end.

"I don't mean to startle you," he said, snuffing out his cigar. "I've been hiding out all these years, and when I found out you were selling the house, I figured now was the time to come forward and let you know I staged my death."

"I don't understand." Maxine shook her head, still not completely convinced that her husband's reappearance wasn't some kind of hallucination.

"It all has to do with Rousseau."

Maxine looked away, recalling the nightmarish episode.

"I've had a lot of time to think about how wrong I was to take the law into my own hands." Jacques fell silent, the decade that had passed showing in his heavy expression.

"You did it because you were as protective of Chloe as I was," Maxine said, clutching Jacques' hands, afraid to let go. "Maybe even more so."

He smiled, the once-familiar gleam returning to his eyes. "You're right. I felt like she was my own from the first day we met." His smile faded as he continued with his explanation. "I had to pay off the thug I hired who ended up killing Rousseau, not to implicate me. The authorities never found out I was involved, but Rousseau's henchmen kept trying to come after me and even the score." He sighed, his face sagging. "I guess we both should have taken Chloe seriously when she said Rousseau threatened to harm us if she told anyone about what he tried to do to her."

Jacques got up and looked out the window, his face silhouetted by the evening sun. Maxine wanted to get up and stand beside him to reassure herself that he was really here, but she remained anchored to the chair, fearing that if she touched him it would be like bursting a bubble that floated just out of reach.

"Our anniversary," she said, recalling their last night together. "I remember how fatalistic you sounded at dinner. It was as if you knew you were preparing to die."

He nodded, turning to face Maxine again. "I'd already made plans to go away by then. I knew if I stayed around, I'd be putting you and Chloe in danger. I only planned to go away for a little while, lay low for a few months. But then months turned into years, and the longer I was gone, the more I realized it wasn't fair to just pop up again. I had to let you and Chloe get on with your lives."

"It was you, wasn't it? Sending all those anonymous gifts and flowers."

"That was my way of staying connected and sending you a message that I was out there, thinking about you. I thought about trying to contact you, but it was too risky. I didn't even tell my mother I was still alive; Renaud was the only one who knew. He was my eyes and ears. He kept me updated on how you and Chloe were doing. Every time something important happened in your lives, he let me know. He's been running the day-to-day operations of my company, carrying out my directives and keeping things in order for my eventual return."

"But I sold the company..." Maxine trailed off, suddenly realizing what Jacques had done prior to staging his death.

"Yes, you sold it to a fictional investment group headed up by my attorney. I've maintained control of the company all along – from a distance, of course."

"Now I'm starting to understand why I had all those lingering doubts, why I was never able to ID your body." She looked into Jacques' eyes, another realization hitting her. "The coroner who said your body was burned beyond recognition in the car crash and wrote your death certificate based on dental records?"

"An old Navy buddy I begged to help me out and keep my family safe," Jacques said with a sly smile, like a little boy who'd been caught telling a lie to get out of trouble.

Maxine laughed, then wiped away tears. Jacques' sudden reappearance was still too much to comprehend.

"The funeral," she said, struck by a sudden flashback. "You were there, weren't you? I remember seeing a man in the shadows at the cathedral, someone that looked like you. I thought my mind was playing tricks on me, but I felt your presence. I felt it so strongly. I knew it had to be you."

Jacques looked down, then met her eyes again. "I knew there was a chance I'd be recognized, but I had to see you and Chloe and *Maman* one last time before I set sail. The funeral was the only place I could see you all together in one place."

Maxine studied his face, still not fully convinced he wasn't an apparition. "Where have you been all these years?"

"I moved around a lot. I spent a few years in Corsica, a couple of years in the Cayman Islands."

Maxine glanced down at the desk, remembering the nautical maps she'd found under a false bottom in one of the drawers when she was cleaning out Jacques' office after she'd sold the company.

"Have you been alone all this time?" Maxine asked, regretting the question as soon as she'd asked.

"I had *Nathalie.*"

Maxine's heart sank, assuming Jacques had met another woman. "Nathalie?"

"My yacht, remember?" he said with a chuckle, to her relief. "The sea has always been my home." His eyes met Maxine's. "But wherever I went, the hope that I'd see you again is what kept me going."

"God. Do you know how many nights I've dreamed about this?" Maxine stooped over in her seat, the enormity of the reunion she'd longed for hitting her. "No matter how many times people told me I needed to move on, no matter how many times they said I should forget you," she said as Jacques crouched beside her, helping her sit up, "somewhere I always felt your presence. Sometimes I thought I was going insane." She stroked his face. "But now you're here."

He took her hands, kissing them. "*Amour*, I don't expect you to drop everything and accept me back in your life after all this time. That would be selfish. If you still want to sell the house, I understand."

"No, not now. I want you to come home. Having you back, having you with me again is all I've ever wanted." She kissed him, savoring the sweet taste of his lips, at once foreign and familiar.

He embraced her, and with each passing moment in his arms, the pain and loneliness of his long absence seemed to dissipate.

"What about Chloe?" he said. "How do you think she'll react?"

Maxine pulled back. "I think we should wait a while. She's going through a lot right now and I'm not sure she could absorb the shock of seeing you alive again. She just went through a breakup and she's starting a new business, so she's got enough to deal with at the moment."

"I know." Jacques grinned. "Renaud's been keeping me updated, remember?"

Maxine smiled. "For now, I'll just tell her that the next time she comes home to Paris, there's someone important who wants to get reacquainted."

"I can't wait to see her again."

Maxine touched his stubbly cheek. "You'll be so proud of the woman she's become."

EPILOGUE

"Chloe."

She turned to face the person calling her name. She had been mesmerized by the staggering view from the top of the Wellington Tower.

"Hello, Alex," she said as he entered Hugo Wellington's old office in the skyscraper's penthouse suite.

He looked great, better than ever. He approached her, looking fit in a blazer, dress shirt open at the collar and khakis.

"I got the message to meet you here," he said in a businesslike tone. "You look beautiful, as always. I'm glad to see you've been taking care of yourself."

"Thank you. And thanks for agreeing to meet me."

"It was convenient, since I had to stop by the magazine, anyway, to turn in my latest story."

"I read your exposé on Dade Chemical," she said. "It was brilliant."

"Thanks. While I was back in New Orleans researching the story, I convinced Jerry, my brother-in-law, to round up some of his co-workers who'd also been injured on the job and file a class-action suit against the company. When the article came out, the bad publicity forced Dade to settle out of court. Jerry got a nice, fat check, so he'll not only be able to cover his medical expenses, he and Monique and the kids will be set for a while."

"That's great," Chloe said. "And I heard the article's been nominated for a National Magazine Award for environmental coverage."

"Yeah. It's really gratifying after all those years of being overlooked."

"I'm so happy for you, Alex."

"Thanks. I worked out a deal to freelance for the magazine, which'll give me more time to work on fiction and other writing projects," he said. He looked around the suite. "So, what are you doing here?"

"Daniella's got a new gig as a commentator for a legal affairs show that tapes in the building and she told me the penthouse suite was available."

"I read about your plans to start your own company," Alex said. "Is this going to be the future home of CYB?"

"Sure is. I've decided to sign the lease."

"You might want to think twice. This place is supposedly haunted."

Rumors of weird occurrences and ghost sightings of Hugo Wellington in the penthouse didn't faze Chloe. She wasn't at all apprehensive about moving into Hugo's old "haunt." If she were to encounter his spirit, roaming around with a white sheet and rattling chains, she would simply ask him for business advice in running her corporation. She could use all the guidance she could get.

"I don't believe in ghosts," she said, "but it *will* take some time to get used to being up this high."

Alex looked down at the view of the city. "You always were afraid of heights."

"I've finally decided to face my fears. Which is why I asked you to meet me here."

Alex took a step closer. "I'm listening."

"A big part of CYB will be a film and television production company," she said.

As the president and CEO of CYB Enterprises, Inc., Chloe planned to develop scripts and produce motion pictures and TV shows on her own. Why settle for the scraps Hollywood threw to minorities and women? She could employ her own writers and directors, bankroll her own projects, stake her own claim in the entertainment industry. The role of media mogul would fit Chloe nicely, like a pair of designer jeans on the toned physique she worked so hard to maintain. She had plans to build a media empire – and the top floor of the Wellington Tower, with its rich history, was the perfect launching pad.

"I think that's great. I wish you nothing but success," Alex said, adding with a puzzled expression, "but what's that got to do with me?"

"For my first project, I'd like to buy the movie rights to your novel and produce it as an independent film – with your involvement as screenwriter and executive producer, of course."

Alex said nothing, and she couldn't decipher his expression.

"Is that why you called me here," he said finally, "to talk business?"

"Actually, no. In the past several weeks since we've been apart, I've done a lot of thinking." She moved closer. "As confident as I may seem sometimes, I still have a lot of insecurities. I let fear get the best of me sometimes."

"What are you trying to say, Chloe?"

"Look, I know you may be back with Veronica –"

"I'm not back with Veronica. She heard I was writing for the magazine again, invited me to dinner and proposed some crazy scheme where I would write stories about her advertising clients, in exchange for a cut of her commissions."

Chloe narrowed her eyes in confusion. "I thought the agency fired her after she sabotaged the launch of my perfume."

"She's started her own firm, God help us," Alex said, rolling his eyes for comedic effect. "When she came by my book signing when my novel was first released and tried to get me back, I knew she had to have some ulterior motive. She's been planning – or should I say *plotting* – to start her own advertising agency for quite some time and figured she could entice me to assist her in building her clientele with this unethical kickback scheme." Alex shook his head. "Same old Veronica."

"I still don't understand why she sabotaged the *Inner Beauty* launch, other than being jealous that I was with you at the time," Chloe said. "She must have known what she did would eventually come back to haunt her and tarnish her reputation."

"You underestimate Veronica's cunning," Alex said. "When we were at dinner at Jean Georges, she admitted she'd been planning to sabotage the launch of Laurel Cosmetics' new fragrance all along, even before she knew you were the spokesmodel. She was scheming to start her own advertising agency even back then, and guess who she got to sign on as her first client?"

"Luxe Cosmetics, Laurel's biggest competitor?" Chloe said, Veronica's devious plan finally dawning on her. "She must have thought ruining Laurel's product launch would help Luxe gain an edge, and therefore generate more money for her."

"You got it," Alex said.

Looking back, it all made sense to Chloe now: Veronica's chilly attitude from the very first meeting with Laurel, Veronica talking incessantly on her cell phone during the commercial shoot with Valérie Bourdain. She was probably giving details about the shoot to the competition like some kind of Mata Hari-like double agent.

"Of course, I turned her down flat when Veronica pitched me this kickback scheme," Alex continued. "But I wanted to do it in person, to see the look on her face when I told her to go to hell. And I took pleasure in picking up the check, since she always used to rub my nose in the fact that she made more money than me."

"I understand, but did you have to take her to my favorite restaurant?" Chloe said, feeling petty for taking Alex to task over the perceived slight.

"I'm sorry. I had no idea you and Maxine would be there that night," Alex said, looking genuinely contrite. "It's just that I wanted to have a 'home turf advantage' when I confronted Veronica, and with the French cuisine, Jean Georges reminds me of home – Louisiana."

Chloe looked Alex in the eye and saw sincerity. "I just hope Veronica gets her comeuppance," she said.

"She already has," Alex said. "After she tried to talk me into the kickback scheme, I tipped off one of the business reporters at *Newsline*. He wrote a big investigative piece about deceptive business practices among young entrepreneurs who are desperate to make a name for themselves. He cited Veronica as a textbook example of a talented young businessperson with misguided ambition. The story's going to be on the cover of next week's edition." Alex grinned. "I wish I could see Veronica's face when the magazine comes out. She always wanted to be famous, but she's about to become *in*famous."

"I can't think of a more fitting punishment. I'm so glad to know you're not back with her." Chloe paused. "Are you seeing anyone else?"

"Not at the moment."

"Me, neither."

Alex rocked on his heels, as if waiting for Chloe to elaborate. "And?"

"This isn't easy for me. Would you please sit down?"

Alex sat in the chair behind Hugo Wellington's desk.

Chloe got down on one knee. "What I've been trying to say is that I realized I was a fool when I let you go," she said. "I never want to be apart from you again. If you'll still have me, I want to spend the rest of my life with you. I'm asking you to marry me, Alex Michaud."

Alex said nothing, staring at Chloe with a blank expression.

"Damn you, I just poured out my heart and soul to you! Say something, for heaven's sake."

"Yes," he said finally. "Yes to the proposal and yes to working together on the film."

Chloe threw her arms around Alex. "I'm so excited! Oh, there's something I almost forgot."

She reached into her pocket, pulled out her grandmother's wedding ring and slid it onto Alex's pinky finger.

"What's this?" he said, wriggling the shiny diamond on his pinky.

"It's a family heirloom. I thought I should give you a ring, since I'm the one who popped the question this time."

"We'd have to have it resized to fit my ring finger. But I have a better idea." Alex took off the ring and placed it on Chloe's finger. "Why don't you hold onto it? I remember you telling me how it's always brought you good luck." He added jokingly, "And we're going to need it if we're going to be working together."

"Maybe the movie deal falling apart was a blessing in disguise. Now we can do it the right way, without the interference of a studio. I've already talked to Hal Forster, the director, and he said he'd be willing to come on board for a fraction of his usual fee. And an old friend of mine from when I first signed with Epitome, a talented young designer named Christy Taylor, has agreed to do the costumes and give Sidney Laveau a little *flava*."

Chloe had even approached Graciela about recording an original song to play over the closing credits – bringing to fruition the dreams they had shared with each other when they first started out at Epitome.

"You know, I admire your enthusiasm," Alex said, "but producing an independent film is a big undertaking. Are you sure you want to sink every penny you've ever made into a film that may or may not earn back its investment?"

"First of all, I know the movie's going to work because I believe in your story and always have," Chloe said. "Second of all, I won't have to invest every penny I've ever made."

Alex looked intrigued. "You found an investor?"

"More like an angel investor. My stepfather set up a trust fund for me before he died. I got a disbursement every year, which I've been telling my mother to donate to charity in Jacques' name. But God bless her, she invested it instead, and it's been multiplying all these years. With the trust fund and my signing bonus from my new contract with Laurel, we'll have plenty of money to get the cameras rolling. I'm so excited that this is going to be the first big project for my production company – something we can work on together."

"Looks like you have the start of something big here," Alex said, standing and helping Chloe to her feet. "Why don't you show me around your new digs, Mrs. Michaud."

"We're not married yet. You can't order me around," she said playfully, getting up and taking him by the hand.

"Oh, lord. I can already see I'm going to have to domesticate you before the wedding."

"Domesticate *me*? A couple of months of wedded bliss and I'll have you eating out of the palm of my hand."

"Speaking of eating out, is there anywhere around here where a couple can go to consummate their engagement?"

"Alex!"

"I'm serious," he said. "I haven't made love to you in ages and I'm dying to hold you in my arms again."

"Well, there's a bed in the next room, but it's old and rickety and all covered with dust."

"Come on, baby, let's go make some dust fly," Alex said, sweeping Chloe up and heading for the door.

"What are you doing?"

"Carrying you over the threshold."

"Aren't we supposed to wait until our wedding night for this?"

"I think we've both waited long enough."

ACKNOWLEDGEMENTS

I would like to thank all of my family and friends who were so supportive and patient over the course of the many years it's taken to bring this labor of love to fruition.

Readers, I would love to get your insights about this story and these characters that I've lived with for so long and who are so close to my heart.

I'd love to hear your opinions about some of the following points:

• Do you think it's a good idea for Alex and Chloe to collaborate on adapting his novel into a movie, or will working together put a strain on their relationship?

• Is Maxine a good mother, or is she too overbearing?

• Is Gigi a good friend, or a perpetual screw-up?

• Does Veronica, Alex's scheming ex, have any redeeming qualities, or is she a total (rhymes with "witch")?

• Is there any character or storyline you would have liked to have seen more of, such as Chloe's affair with Latin pop star Sergio Reyes?

Please contact me at www.chrisbournea.com and hit me up at Facebook and Twitter. I look forward to hearing from you.

Sincerely,

Chris Bournéa

Chris Bournéa

A preview of *The Chloe Chronicles: French Quarter,* the next installment in the series:

Chloe and Alex began a new year by collaborating on two major projects that had the global media buzzing: a wedding and a movie shoot. It made sense, both logistically and spiritually, to stage both events in New Orleans, where the rising Hollywood power couple had familial and cultural ties.

After filming the exterior scenes for *Night Moves*, the movie adaptation of Alex's best-selling novel that Chloe was producing and starring in, they moved on to their next big production: exchanging vows in front of hundreds of friends and family members.

On her wedding day, Chloe set up camp in the bridal chamber of St. Louis Cathedral, the historic church in the heart of the French Quarter. She sat alone in front of a mirror, her hands shaking as she affixed her veil. She had the same "backstage" jitters as she did just before she was about to go on at a runway show. When trolling the catwalk, she overcame her stage fright by taking on the bold persona of a character she invented. But today she wouldn't have to pretend at all. On the verge of pledging to spend eternity with Alex, she had never been more certain of anything in her life.

Jean-Claude and Christophe St. Evermonde filed into their assigned pew just in time for Chloe to make her entrance.

"*God* she's breathtaking," Christophe sighed as Chloe glided by on the arm of a man whom Jean-Claude recognized as French shipping magnate Jacques Chevalier.

Jean-Claude nodded in agreement with his son, who, at 32, was a freeze frame of his distinguished father in his prime – blond, blue-eyed and boyishly handsome. His gaze drifting from Christophe to Chloe, Jean-Claude reflected on how glad he was that fate had allowed him to be a part of this all-important occasion. Officially, he was here as an invited guest representing SE International, the Paris-based media empire that was distributing Chloe's much-anticipated movie debut. In an unofficial capacity, he was here to claim his rightful place in the ambitious young woman's life.

Jean-Claude spotted Maxine in the front row, beaming at her daughter and looking beautiful as ever. He had intentionally arrived late, so as not to run into Maxine before the ceremony. He anticipated with almost perverse glee, her reaction when she caught sight of him again after all these years.

"What a lucky guy," Christophe said, motioning toward the dashing groom waiting at the altar.

Jean-Claude put his arm around Christophe, a gesture expressing how proud he was of his son for brokering the deal that had brought Chloe's burgeoning production company into SE International's ever-expanding portfolio and, thus, into their lives.

The "Wedding March" faded, prompting Jean-Claude to return his attention to the altar. Witnessing Chloe being handed off to her husband-to-be by Jacques – apparently the man in Maxine's life – Jean-Claude felt a stab of envy. He steeled himself, stifled his emotions and maintained his composure, something he was used to doing in his business dealings. This was Chloe's time to shine. He would continue to wait for an opportune moment to reveal that he was her father.